ASSAULT
ON
GRAVELLY POINT

To Joe with my best
wishes!

Bill Crawford
12-6-97

ASSAULT

ON
GRAVELLY POINT

BILL
CRAWFORD

KILDUCK STATION PUBLICATIONS, LTD.
Williamsburg, Virginia

ASSAULT ON GRAVELLY POINT

A novel published by Kilduck Station Publications, Ltd.,
Williamsburg, Virginia

First Edition 1998

Library of Congress Catalog Card Number 97-93351

Address requests to: KILDUCK STATION PUBLICATIONS, LTD.
SAN 229-3031

ISBN 0-9657463-0-5

10 9 8 7 6 5 4 3 2

PRINTED IN THE UNITED STATES OF AMERICA

PREFACE

I wrote this book out of my love for flying and for the richness it has given my life. It also was written to honor the many aviator friends I have made over my thirty-eight years of flying. Many of their thoughts and deeds have been woven into this story. I trust they will know that I remembered.

Like flying, writing offers me freedom — another chance to move in the vertical plane — to feel the euphoric uplifting of spiritual flight.

July 1st, 1997   B.C.
Williamsburg, Virginia

ACKNOWLEDGMENT

Writing a novel can be likened to taking a long journey to a place you've never been. Excitement builds as you begin the trip with a simple notion, an idea you want to explore and develop, but with no clear picture of the path you will follow. At times, the voyage seems endless and you stop to rest and inquire about the road ahead.

Suddenly, you learn that you are not alone. Family, friends, strangers, and well-wishers hear of your struggle and join your expedition, pointing the way and offering encouragement. Filled with renewed confidence, you eagerly resume your passage, eternally grateful for the help given you along the way.

As I look back at the road I have traveled, special companions come to mind. They deserve my sincere appreciation.

Hope Yelich, a neighbor and research librarian at The College of William & Mary's Swem Library, helped me immensely. Research without her would have been impossible, given the myriad government documents used to substantiate my plot.

James A. Bill, Director of the Wendy and Emery Reeves Center for International Studies at The College of William and Mary, shared his insight of the Middle East mind. A man of enormous compassion and wisdom, Jim articulated a view of the Muslim World and its view of the West that I would not have discovered.

Likewise, I am equally indebted to Christiane Amanpour, Correspondent for CNN International, for her exceptional analysis of the aims and objectives of the various Middle East terrorist organizations and their State sponsors.

To Jean Andrews, Jessica and Michael Crawford, Irene Fitzmorris, Betty and Gene Griffin, Belle and Ryan McBride, Dennis and Vickie Parker, Pamela Smith, Mary Anne and Courtney Whitman — my reading committee — I offer my deepest appreciation for the hours spent on my behalf.

Special thanks to Toni Marsh for editing, Pamela Owens for typesetting, and to Bob Rodriguez for design of the dust cover.

I am obliged to Patricia Delehey for sharing her special lifelong friend, Rosalie Siegel, with me. As my literary agent, Rosalie has given my writing career direction. In Rosalie I found someone who believed in me as a writer and worked diligently to see that I measured up to the role. For that I am profoundly thankful.

Nothing inspires a writer more than the interest peers show in his work. It gives the effort new meaning and compels the author to accept only his best. I owe a debt of gratitude to my fellow pilots and the many flight attendants I have worked with who have shown an interest in my story and in my desire to write. I trust they will find this book a true account of life on the line.

Writing is a lonely undertaking and necessarily deprives loved ones of the writer's frequent presence. For this reason, I could not have undertaken such a task without the complete love, support and understanding of my wife and best friend, Judith. For her, I reserve my greatest love, affection and thanks.

B.C.

To my mother, the late Nancy Crawford Capps

A man who has nothing for which he is willing to fight, nothing he cares about more than his own personal safety, is a miserable creature who has no chance of being free unless made and kept so by the exertions of better men than himself.

John Stuart Mill

PROLOGUE

A MEASURE OF CHARACTER

Wes rolled his F-105D Thunderchief left to counteract wind drift and then paused a second to study his new bomb sight position. Seeing that the pipper, the aiming dot, was tracking straight toward his target — an SA2 surface-to-air-missile site, Wes glanced back inside the cockpit. He checked the rapidly unwinding altimeter and noted his increasing airspeed. Through the bomb sight, he watched as the radar control van — the eyes of the missile battery — rushed up to meet him. As the pipper approached its roof, Wes made a final check of his dive angle. As the altimeter approached his preplanned release height, Wes refocused on the pipper. As it touched the edge of the van's roof, he pressed the pickle (bomb) button and held it down a full second.

Now pulling back on the fighter's control stick, Wes felt the "Thud" shudder as it fought the gravitational force pulling it toward the Earth. Wes waited as the F-105D yielded begrudgingly to the G forces he was applying. Two seconds later, its sink rate arrested and its airspeed starting to decrease, he relaxed the back pressure and selected the afterburner. Wes felt a sudden jolt as the afterburner lit, sending a sixty-foot plume of flame from the fighter's tailpipe. Lowering the nose of the Thud to gain more airspeed, he began a series of "jinking" maneuvers, denying enemy anti-aircraft gunners a decent shot. "CACTUS TWO ONE'S OFF HOT!" he called out as he rolled to the right before pitching back to his left, amid enemy fifty-seven millimeter airbursts.

"TWO'S IN FROM THE RIGHT," chimed Rich Burgess, allowing the nose of the sluggish, bomb-laden F-105D to drop thirty-five degrees below the horizon.

Wes rolled back to the left for a couple of seconds, then pitched back to the right. Looking over his shoulder, Wes spied Rich in his dive, his Thud a thousand or so feet above the release altitude. Then he saw it. Out of nowhere, a triple A shell seemed to burst under Rich's wing.

"I'M HIT, LEAD!" yelled Burgess.

"PICKLE NOW AND BREAK RIGHT!" Wes yelled, seeing the anti-aircraft gun's smoke pattern close on Rich's position.

"WHERE ARE YOU, LEAD?" called Rich as he released twelve cluster bomb units (CBU's) from the Thud's pylons and "broke" right.

"AT YOUR RIGHT, THREE O'CLOCK, SLIGHTLY HIGH," Wes answered, turning toward the coast of North Vietnam. "WHAT'S YOUR STATUS?"

"MY CONTROLS ARE SLUGGISH. I DON'T KNOW HOW MUCH LONGER I'M GONNA BE ABLE TO STAY WITH YOU," Rich grumbled.

Looking east, Wes could see the coast less than two minutes away.

"STAY WITH HER, RICH. THE GULF IS DEAD AHEAD," Wes urged, as he retarded his throttle and allowed Rich to close on him.

"I AIN'T GONNA MAKE IT, LEAD. MY AILERONS ARE FRO-ZEN," growled Rich, frustrated.

"YOU'VE GOT TO, DAMMIT! HOLD HER STRAIGHT WITH THE RUDDERS!" ordered Wes as he caught sight of Rich two thou-sand feet below at his left, eight o'clock.

"SMOKEHOUSE! CACTUS TWO TWO'S BEEN HIT. WE'RE OVER THE COAST, TWENTY SOUTH OF HANOI. TWO TWO WILL BE 'FEET WET' IN ANOTHER TWO MINUTES. ALERT SEA RESCUE!" Wes bellowed

"COPY THAT, CACTUS FLIGHT. WE HAVE HIM ON RA-DAR. WE'RE SCRAMBLING THE CHOPPER," replied the mission controller aboard the KC-135 tanker aircraft.

"I'M LOSING HER, LEAD. SHE'S ROLLING ON ME!" shouted Rich.

Wes glanced down to see the Thud's belly perpendicular to the horizon. In another two or three seconds, Rich would be inverted.

"GET OUT NOW, RICH! GET OUT NOW! EJECT!" Wes hollered.

A second later, Wes saw his wingman propelled out the side and away from the lumbering Thunderchief. His eyes riveted on the tiny speck, Wes waited for Rich's drogue chute to deploy, but saw nothing.

Then farther aft of the descending Thud than he'd suspected, he saw a canopy blossom. "SMOKEHOUSE! TWO TWO'S GOT A GOOD CHUTE, BUT HE'S GONNA LAND CLOSE TO THE SHORE! HE'LL NEED CLOSE AIR SUPPORT, ASAP!"

"ROGER, CACTUS TWO ONE. IT'S ON THE WAY."

Wes rolled his Thud into a tight orbit, capping Rich's descent toward the crystal blue sea. Out of the corner of his eye, he saw the crippled Thunderchief impact the Gulf. The plume was impressive, but unimportant. Glancing down at Rich, Wes judged he would clear the beach by nearly a mile. If only the Vietnamese don't get to him first, Wes thought, as he spiraled closer to the water.

A moment later, Wes saw Rich enter the Gulf of Tonkin. The wind had caused him to drift toward the beach. Not wanting to draw attention to Rich, Wes climbed his Thunderchief and turned southward, still keeping his downed wingman in sight.

"SMOKEHOUSE, CACTUS TWO TWO'S IN THE WATER! WHERE'S THAT CHOPPER?" Wes demanded, pitching back toward Rich's position.

"HE'LL BE THERE IN TEN MINUTES, CACTUS TWO ONE. WHAT'S YOUR FUEL STATE?"

Peering down at his fuel gauge, Wes saw he didn't have enough fuel to make it back to Korat Air Base in Thailand and had barely enough to make it to the closest alternate field.

"ENOUGH FOR A TEN-MINUTE HOLD!" Wes answered, knowing he was already "bingo" fuel minus five hundred pounds. If he stayed with Rich, Smokehouse, the KC-135 tanker, would be his only chance of getting enough fuel to make it to an alternate.

Staring down at the shoreline, Wes saw the wakes of two boats widen as they sped out to sea. They'd spotted Rich.

Lowering the nose of his fighter, Wes rolled in on the lead boat, laying the pipper squarely on its bow. Approaching sixteen hundred feet of slant range, he squeezed the trigger and held it for three seconds. The M61 Gatling gun roared to life, spewing three hundred rounds of twenty millimeter high-explosive incendiary ammunition into the hull of the lead boat, scoring a direct hit. Small pieces of the disintegrating boat raced skyward, chasing his tailpipe as Wes pulled into a four G climb.

Racking the Thud into a hard turn, Wes headed back for the other boat, now within a half-mile of Rich. Lowering the nose of the Thud again, he laid the pipper on the remaining boat's bow and pressed the attack. Approaching firing range, Wes squeezed the trigger, but nothing happened. Had the gun jammed?

Pulling off the target, he quickly recycled the armament switches and squeezed the trigger again, but the gun held its silence. "You sonofabitch!" cried Wes as he bent the Thud around to the left and acquired the advancing enemy boat visually, now less than a quarter-mile from Rich's collapsed parachute. If he didn't stop them on this pass, Rich would spend the rest of the war in the "Hanoi Hilton."

Wes eased the Thud's nose over for a final pass and aimed for the vessel. One hundred feet above the water, he shallowed his dive angle as the F-105D jet reached six hundred knots. Looking ahead, he could barely see the boat as it closed on Rich's position. Wes glanced down at the radar altimeter and began to ease the fighter bomber lower. Passing through fifty feet, he quickened his cross-check. Reaching twenty-five feet above the water, Wes leveled the jet and held his breath. Cross-checking rapidly, he saw the boat grow in size with each glance. Wes had less than twenty seconds to go.

Exhausted, Rich stopped swimming from his collapsed chute. He couldn't go any farther. Suspended by his "water wings," Rich scanned the skies to the east for the rescue chopper, but saw nothing. He'd seen Wes pull off "dry" on his last pass and figured he'd "winchestered" the Vulcan cannon of all its rounds. Knowing he could not escape, Rich pivoted to face his adversaries. As he did, Rich saw a "rooster tail," a plume of water, rising at least seventy feet, trailing Wes's Thud. He'd never seen one that size, let alone one traveling that fast. There wasn't time to imagine the depth of the furrow it was plowing through the water. It seemed to be heading right for the oncoming boat.

Rich watched in astonishment as Wes streaked directly across the front of the boat's path. Suddenly, the boat's stern flipped into the air as its bow dug into the trough of water cut by the Thunderchief's thrust. "Shit hot! You did it!" screamed Rich, as he saw the crewmen, their bodies flailing, crash into the sea. Flinging his thumbs into the air, Rich swore for joy as Wes climbed rapidly while rolling right.

Looking over his shoulder, Wes saw the overturned boat and smiled. "SMOKEHOUSE, FROM CACTUS TWO ONE. WHERE'S

THAT RESCUE CHOPPER? I'M NEARLY OUT OF GAS!"

"THE CHOPPER HAS A VISUAL ON YOUR WINGMAN, CACTUS TWO ONE."

Wes rolled left as his eyes swept the seascape. A second later, he saw the chopper heading toward Rich.

"WHAT'S YOUR FUEL STATE, CACTUS TWO ONE?"

"YOU DON'T WANT TO KNOW, SMOKEHOUSE."

"SAY YOUR FUEL STATE NOW, LIEUTENANT!"

"TWELVE HUNDRED POUNDS," Wes replied, knowing the fuel gauge had a built-in error of three hundred pounds. "GIVE ME A VECTOR TO YOUR POSITION, SMOKEHOUSE. I DON'T HAVE ENOUGH FUEL TO MAKE ANY ALTERNATES!" Wes demanded, annoyed by the mission commander's interruption.

"STANDBY, CACTUS," Smokehouse snapped.

Wes glanced down at the gauge again. It read exactly one thousand pounds. "Shit!" he groaned. "I'm losing my friggin' fuel." Then Wes recalled the muzzle flashes he'd seen coming from the lead boat on his first pass. "Those bastards!" he cursed. "They got lucky."

"CACTUS TWO ONE. COME LEFT TO ZERO SEVEN FIVE DEGREES. YOUR RENDEZVOUS WITH SMOKEHOUSE IS APPROVED. RANGE IS NINE ZERO MILES."

"CONFIRM THE RANGE IS NINETY MILES?" Wes questioned.

"AFFIRMATIVE, CACTUS TWO ONE."

"SMOKEHOUSE, IT'S GONNA BE REAL TIGHT. BETTER ALERT RESCUE. I'M DOWN TO EIGHT HUNDRED POUNDS."

"HE'S STANDING BY, TWO ONE. YOUR RANGE IS NOW FIFTY TWO MILES. SMOKEHOUSE IS FIFTEEN DEGREES TO PORT ON YOUR SCREEN."

Peering into the scope, Wes saw the yellow blip marching down the left side of his radar screen. There was nothing to do but wait.

After taking a few seconds to stow the loose items in the cockpit and cinch his harness straps, Wes keyed his mike. "SMOKEHOUSE, HOLD THE TURN UNTIL EIGHTEEN MILES."

"NEGATIVE, CACTUS. WE'LL USE STANDARD PROCEDURES. SMOKEHOUSE WILL START THE TURN AT TWENTY-ONE MILES."

Looking out to his left just above the horizon, Wes saw the tanker bank left. The radar range showed exactly twenty one miles. "Another cold rejoin," grumbled Wes, staring down at the nearly empty fuel gauge. It read four hundred pounds. Recalling the gauge's reliability, plus or minus three hundred pounds, Wes prayed the gauge would err in his favor.

"WE'RE PUSHING IT UP, CACTUS TWO ONE," called Smokehouse.

"NO! HOLD THE PUSH! I'M DOWN TO FOUR HUNDRED POUNDS!" he shouted. "Anything but a stern chase," Wes pleaded, silently.

"ROGER," replied the tanker.

Halfway through the turn, Wes could see the refueling boom trailing from the KC-135 tanker. Reaching down, he pulled the air refueling handle aft. His closure on the tanker wasn't great, but it was better than he'd expected. "CACTUS TWO ONE'S NOSE IS COLD," he radioed, hoping to expedite the preliminary safety checks.

"ROGER, CACTUS. YOU'RE CLEARED INTO THE PRE-CONTACT POSITION. THE TANKER'S READY."

"RECEIVER'S READY," answered Wes, guiding the nose of the Thunderchief quickly into position as the refueler extended the boom toward the turtle-deck opening behind the cockpit canopy. In another ten seconds he'd be taking on fuel.

Suddenly, Wes felt the sickening deceleration of his jet as the engine turbine began to spool down.

"CACTUS TWO ONE, FORWARD THREE — FORWARD SIX — CACTUS TWO ONE MAINTAIN YOUR POSITION! YOU ARE OUT OF MY ENVELOPE!"

"NO SHIT! Wes said, deploying the Ram Air Turbine, now his only means of power for the hydraulic flight controls. "I JUST FLAMED OUT! LAUNCH THE SEARCH AND RESCUE CHOPPER NOW!" he said with disgust. "AND GIVE ME A VECTOR TOWARD THE CARRIER, SO I WON'T HAVE SO DAMNED FAR TO SWIM!"

"ROGER, CACTUS," replied the mission controller, dejectedly. "TURN LEFT TO A HEADING OF ZERO THREE FIVE DEGREES. THE BOAT WILL BE AT YOUR TWELVE O'CLOCK FOR TWENTY-FIVE MILES."

Shouting expletives to himself as the F-105D dropped lower, Wes banked the crippled jet left and peered out the side of his windscreen.

In the distance, he could see the aircraft carrier. Reviewing his egress procedures, Wes checked to see if he'd remembered to remove the ejection seat pin. "SMOKEHOUSE, I'LL BE GOING FEET WET IN ONE MINUTE!"

"ROGER. THE CHOPPER'S STANDING BY FOR THE RE-COVERY."

Passing through ten thousand feet, Wes pressed the back of his helmet hard against the headrest, raised his chin, and sat up straight in the rocket seat. He would eject at five thousand feet.

Glancing at the unwinding altimeter as though it were counting down the remaining seconds of his life, Wes thought of his wife, Meredith, and his young son, Walker, and Caroline, the daughter he had yet to see. Praying he'd live to see them, he focused on the horizon and squeezed both ejection triggers.

I

EASTBOUND

A waking from his dream, Wes smelled Caroline's gourmet coffee drifting into the bedroom. Wiping the sleep from his eyes, he glanced at the bedside clock. It showed nine thirty a.m. The sun shining through the edges of the lowered blinds confirmed the hour.

Stretching his limbs toward the four corners of the mattress, Wes recalled his ejection twenty-six years ago. It was not the first time he'd relived the event, nor would it be the last. Combat experiences had a way of sneaking back into your life.

Recalling his trip to Saigon and the ass-chewing he'd gotten from General Monroe, Wes grimmaced. "Improper regard for a valuable combat asset," the commander of Seventh Air Force had called it — his F105D Thunderchief. The thought of it still pissed him off. Shocked at later being awarded the Distinguished Flying Cross for defending Rich, Wes had often wondered if Monroe had known of and had approved the nomination. Perhaps he'd misjudged the general. The possibility still bothered him.

The ringing telephone interrupted Wes's thoughts. Dragging the receiver to his ear, he managed a groggy, "Hello."

"Hey, flyboy! Are you going to sleep all day, or what?"

It was Caroline, his oldest daughter.

"Night owls need their rest. Or have you forgotten that I've got to fly back to Paris tonight?"

"Sounds like old age is catching up with you!"

Fond of the fact that her old man was an airline pilot, Caroline loved and admired Wes immensely and never doubted his feelings for her. The two had a special bond. Meredith said it was because they were so much alike. In truth, Wes knew his special love for the Princess was, in a deeper sense, a love of the qualities he liked in himself.

"What are you going to do for lunch?" Caroline asked.

"I don't know. What do you have in mind?"

"Meet me here at the bank and we'll grab a bite at the Reston Town Center. There's a new sandwich shop I want to try."

"That sounds like a winner. How about one o'clock?"

"Perfect."

"Okay, I'll see you then," Wes said as he eased the receiver back on the hook and climbed out of bed. The scent of Caroline's coffee could no longer be denied.

Caroline and her fiancé, Tucker, stared at him from a recent picture as he ambled through the living room toward her kitchen. He paused to study the photo. Where had the time gone? Could she really be twenty-six, he asked of the petite, fair-skinned blonde whose steel-blue eyes seemed to follow his every move.

The thought of her getting married excited him. It was time. Already the highly successful manager of NOVA Bank & Trust in Reston, Caroline had positioned her branch at the top of the "Most Profitable" list in record time. But it was marriage and children she wanted, not the dog-eat-dog, cutthroat business world. That, he knew, she would gladly leave for Tucker as soon as it was financially feasible.

Wes glanced at the picture of the young man who'd unseated him as number one in Caroline's life and knew she'd chosen well. He'd liked Tucker Shaw, the tall, handsome lad with the strong arms and the easy smile—the pitcher for The College of William & Mary — from the day they'd met, four years ago. A successful computer analyst for Defense Financial Consultants, Inc. (DFC), Tucker was the antithesis of his high-spirited daughter. Caroline revolved around Tucker like a planet around the sun. For his part, Tucker enjoyed letting her play the part of the Princess, a role she'd held since childhood.

Wes sipped his coffee and counted himself lucky. Caroline's happiness was all he and Meredith could rightfully hope for. And in Tucker, she had found it.

Dragging the razor around the left side of his face, Wes noticed the beginning crow's feet trailing from the corners of his blue-gray eyes. They led straight to his graying temples. His sandy hair and boyish looks were now increasingly under attack from his eternal parents, Mother Nature and Father Time. His broad shoulders and tapered waist did their best to disguise the growing spare tire he tried to hide. It took more than a little effort to keep the ever-expanding stomach in line with his otherwise trim profile. Ideal, no; acceptable, yes was how Wes saw the sum of his six feet. Not having his glasses on made the self-assessment even easier.

Wes reached the Reston Town Center branch of NOVA Bank in fifteen minutes. Turning into the main entrance of the bank's parking lot, he noticed Caroline's car was not there. Inside, he found Caroline's assistant manager busy at her desk. "Courtney, is Caroline here?"

"Hi, Captain Beacham. No. She was called to an urgent meeting at the main office. She left about ten minutes ago — something to do with a change in equity lending procedures, I think. She asked me to tell you she was sorry she had to leave so suddenly."

* * *

Caroline didn't notice the van that followed her into the underground parking entrance. She pulled into the closest spot she could find. Still mulling over her conversation with Blake Straton's office about the meeting she was racing to, she switched off the engine. Her boss was not one to rush anything. The fact that she had gotten the message from a temp who was filling in for Gloria Alderman also troubled her. Gloria was never absent.

Caroline stepped quickly from her Toyota Camry and reached into the back seat for her attaché case. Suddenly the smell of chloroform penetrated her lungs. Gasping, she struggled against the grip holding her. The fumes were choking her. She tried to cough, but couldn't. Unable to free herself from the gauze pad held tightly over her nose and mouth, she lost consciousness.

A minute later, the van pulled out of the underground garage un-noticed and headed west on the Lee-Jackson Highway. Caroline, blind-folded, handcuffed, and unconscious, lay on the van's floor.

*   *   *

The drive from Reston to Washington's Dulles Airport was quick. Arriving at flight operations earlier than planned, Wes reviewed the computer flight plan and studied the NOTAMS (Notices to Airman) and weather document. The chore required little time. He'd been flying the route to Paris and Geneva continually for the last five months and knew every aspect by heart. Besides, there was another reason for his early report — one he was both excited and uncertain about. Her name was Leigh Simpson. An attractive flight attendant with TIA, Leigh, a single parent, had a young son, Jason.

A radiant beauty, Leigh was frequently taken for a model. Her tall, slender figure and flawless complexion belied her forty years. And yet, it was her sparkling green eyes and loving face that Wes found so enticing. For in them, he saw the elegance, charm, and grace of her character. Like Meredith, Leigh possessed a certain presence that made her special. Her charisma had already shattered his shield of marital honor, humbling him a little more each time they met. Thoughts of her consumed his every free moment, precipitating soul-wrenching ques-tions he tried desperately to avoid answering.

They'd met quite by accident during his first trip last April. The need for Swiss francs had brought them together. The fact that their relationship had grown so rapidly from that innocent afternoon en-counter had amazed and troubled Wes. He hadn't meant for anything like this to happen. Leigh was also concerned about the impact it was beginning to have on her life, yet neither was willing to call it off. On the contrary, Wes sensed they would consummate the affair during this trip. It wasn't planned; he just knew it would happen.

During last week's trip, they'd talked about the affair's implica-tions and the effect it would have on them and their families.

For Wes, the question of deceit was especially difficult to deal with. He loved Meredith deeply, even though he found Leigh sexually attractive. Already feeling guilty, he'd tried more than once, without success, to justify his continuing interest in Leigh. He knew better, and yet her alluring smile and gentleness drew him ever closer. Chemistry pulled them toward one another with a force neither could resist. Wes couldn't bring himself to walk away from Leigh, although he knew their relationship was doomed from the start.

Wes remembered only too well how his father's final liaison had cost him his life. No stranger to the consequences of a discovered affair, Wes knew the pain it had brought upon his family. Vividly recalling the anguish his mother suffered pained Wes, though he found it impossible to stop his own deceit.

Until now, he'd always thought his dad's last affair had been with someone he hadn't cared about, a one-night stand. Had he misunderstood? Had his father actually found himself in love with two women and been unable to deal with it? There was no doubt in Wes's mind that his dad's death had been self-induced. The family doctor had confirmed his suspicion years ago. Was he headed for a similar fate?

Hurting Meredith would be unbearable. She'd given herself to him in every way. She trusted him implicitly. They'd built a life together that was the envy of their children and friends. How could he have allowed such an affair to happen? Even with his feelings for Leigh, Wes could not begin to imagine life without Meredith. She was everything to him. Even contemplating such thoughts made him uneasy.

For the first time in his married life, Wes was sailing in uncharted waters, unsure of the currents and deeply concerned for the changing winds. Though he didn't believe in fate, Wes had a healthy respect for genetics. Were his genes responsible for his weakness? Was he facing the same situation that had brought down his father and destroyed his parents' marriage? More importantly, did he have the will to end it? Wes wondered.

"I was hoping I'd find you here," Leigh said as their eyes met. "I've missed you terribly this past week," she whispered. "I could hardly wait for today. I find myself constantly thinking about you... It's a bit frightening for me."

Wes nodded. He knew what she meant. Gazing into Leigh's alluring eyes, he sensed her expectation. Her sensuous lips excited him. There was no turning back, not for now, anyway.

"I'll see you on board," she said, squeezing his hand gently. "I want to call Jason to make sure he got home safely from school before

Sybil's briefing. The older boys have been giving him a hard time lately."

"Let me know when your crew break is scheduled. I'll take mine with yours."

"We can share a blanket together," she said, playfully.

Wes smiled at the suggestion as Leigh walked down the hall toward the flight attendants' briefing room.

* * *

Tucker Shaw's day had been busy, full of meetings and conferences. An analysis of the proposals for the third phase of auditing the Department of Defense's (DOD) joint services satellite communications package lay on his desk. The report had taken the better part of two weeks to compile, requiring countless visits to the Pentagon. Tucker liked handling defense-related contracts and had made quite a name for himself in the short time he had been with Defense Financial Consultants, Inc. The projects at DOD were all classified and involved programs that most Americans could only dream about. Tucker's natural interest in technology, coupled with his analytical mind, was proving beneficial to the company. His supervisor had persuaded the senior managers to assign him to handle the Satellite Communications (SATCOM) program. Tucker enjoyed his new status and worked hard to enhance his reputation.

Knowing he had ten minutes before his next meeting, Tucker rushed out into the hallway of the Pentagon and phoned Caroline. Disappointed to learn of her emergency meeting with Straton, he asked Courtney to tell her that he would be tied up with clients for the rest of the afternoon and evening but would call tomorrow.

* * *

In pain and frightened, Caroline regained consciousness, opening her eyes to the darkness of a bag tied over her head. At first, Caroline feared she was blind. Then, twisting her head to the side and looking down, she saw a band of light reflecting off the floor of the vehicle.

Her panic subsided. Her left hip and shoulder ached from being tossed about on the floor of the van. Her sinuses burned from the chloroform. Now fully awake, she heard two men speaking Arabic as the van sped along the highway. She guessed they were heading west, judging from the rays of sunlight pouring into the truck. The nonstop hum of the engine told her they were probably on I-66.

Struggling against the handcuffs, Caroline maneuvered her left wrist upward until she could see her tiny gold watch, the one Tucker had given her for her birthday. It was 1:35 p.m. She had been unconscious for five or six minutes.

Questions flashed through her mind as Caroline sought the reason for her kidnapping. Was she going to be raped, or did they seize her to gain access to the bank's vault? Would they kill her? Fear gripped her as she contemplated what they might do. Afraid to utter a sound, Caroline listened for some sign of what they intended, but learned nothing.

It was 2:15 p.m. when suddenly, the van veered off the narrow, winding road and raced up a gravel driveway before coming to an abrupt halt. Lying motionless, Caroline waited for the door to open. Her heart was pounding. She prayed her life would be spared.

A moment later, the door to the van slid open and one of her captors jerked her through the opening. Gripping her left arm, he stood her up as the other captor took her right arm.

"I can walk!" Caroline said, adamantly. "I just can't see!"

The man holding her left arm seemed surprised and let go of her as he spoke in Arabic to his companion. The other didn't reply, but ushered her across a small lawn and up several steps, into a house. From there, Caroline was led down a narrow hallway to a bedroom where she was shoved onto a bed.

Frozen with fear, she lay still as one of her captors removed the handcuff from her left hand and relocked it around one of the iron headboard spokes. Certain she was going to be raped, Caroline began praying out loud. The kidnappers said nothing, but removed the bag from her head and left the room, locking the door behind them.

Safe for the moment, Caroline relaxed her muscles and allowed her eyes to adjust. The room was dark and musty. Using her free hand, she struggled to a sitting position. The cuff holding her to the bed had chaffed her wrist badly. Fighting the urge to cry, she listened to one of the men talking as though he were speaking on the phone. She cursed the fact that they weren't speaking English, knowing that it was her only chance of learning why she had been kidnapped.

Determined to keep her composure, she tried to concentrate on everything she could remember about her capture. Caroline knew she'd been taken to someplace roughly forty-five minutes west of Fairfax, Virginia. Then she remembered the expensive shoes and trousers she'd seen from under the bag as they'd escorted her to the house.

Manure! That was the smell. She was in horse country, probably near Middleburg. But why? What did they want with her? Who did they work for and what would happen to her? What should she do?

Remembering her father's many combat discussions at the dinner table, Caroline knew the best opportunity for escape was as soon as possible after her capture. But how, she wondered, looking dejectedly at the steel cuff around her arm. It was impossible, she told herself, brushing aside the tears that rolled down her cheeks.

Her thoughts turned to Tucker. Would he ever hold her in his arms again? Mom and Dad, Walker and Jacqueline — would she ever see them again? Her tears ran freely. She was alone, and no one even knew she was missing. Anxiety swept over her like an ominous cloud as she faced the full measure of her plight.

Curling into the fetal position, Caroline fought desperately to overcome her uncontrollable trembling. Was she going into shock? She had to regain control of her mind and her emotions. Her thoughts turned again to her father. He dealt with his fear by taking action. He said that action, physical or mental, would dissipate fear and restore self-confidence. The ability to overcome adversity depended on finding the will to fight. That's how he'd put it.

"Whatever it takes." Caroline had heard it time and again from her parents. It was the slogan the Beacham clan lived by. Remembering the airline furloughs with no money, the job changes and forced relocations, and Vietnam, Caroline recalled how her mom and dad had fought to hold the family together.

For the first time, Caroline understood the real meaning of the phrase. It was the essence of their success — and their survival. It would now become hers.

Gradually, calmness replaced anxiety. As her trembling ceased, Caroline gained hope. She knew it was the only way she would survive. She promised herself she would resist, she would fight, and she would find a way to escape.

* * *

Chad Sanderlin bounded through the Ops door, his hands filled with his luggage and his crew kit. "Hi, Wes! I guess we're holding this line together for the month, huh! It was my fifth choice."

"My first," Wes said, looking up at his first officer.

"Looks like a great trip. Twenty-five hours in downtown Geneva. Now that's a pairing I can live with," joked Chad. "Sorry I missed the first two trips. I was off on military, you know."

"I thought that might be where you were. I didn't see your name on the month's vacation roster," Wes said.

"Out training to fight the 'rag heads' these days. Killing commies for Christ is all over. They're on our side now!"

Wes chuckled, remembering his younger fighter pilot days. The lingo was the same, only the buzzwords changed from year to year, depending on who the politicians decided were our enemies.

Wes admired Chad. He was an excellent pilot with a great sense of humor. A former Marine but now a weekend warrior, Chad had spent his early years "trapping" fighters on carrier decks. Never one to take himself too seriously, Chad was always out for a good time. A confirmed bachelor constantly pursued by women, he always seemed to stay one step ahead of the preacher whenever things got too serious. Wes suspected Chad was one of those people who couldn't make a commitment and live with it.

"Which legs are you planning to fly?" Chad asked.

"I'll take the first and last legs. You can have the Paris leg to Geneva. I let 'The Eater' and your replacement have the two long legs last trip."

"Sounds good to me," Chad replied. "I can use the rest."

"The name is Mark Hoffman," said a voice from behind. "I'm your Eater."

Wes and Chad turned around to greet the third member of their cockpit crew, the relief co-pilot and "galley monster".

After several minutes of exchanging bull, Wes said, "Chad, you and Mark take care of plotting the track. I want to take another look at the fuel and review the latest weather."

"Consider it done," Chad said, picking up the chart.

Pulling the current weather from the computer printer, Wes studied the rim (Atlantic) alternate weather, critical to the operation should they lose an engine over the ocean. Gander, Newfoundland, and Lajes Air Base in the Azores looked fine, but Shannon, Ireland's, forecast seemed shaky. The temperature and dew point spread was too close not to have fog there, especially since the winds were expected to be calm. Dublin's forecast was much better. Wes decided to call Flight Dispatch and have them make the change.

The flight would be quick thanks to a strong jet stream they'd be in for most of the way across — only six hours and eighteen minutes en route flying time. Turbulence would be a factor if Gander Center denied them flight level three nine zero (thirty-nine thousand feet) for the crossing. Wes decided to add three thousand pounds of extra fuel to allow for departure delays and deviations around the thunderstorms east of New York.

Finished with the chart plotting ritual, Chad and Mark waited for Wes to approve their handiwork. "If you guys are satisfied with it, I am too," said Wes, motioning for Mark to stow the chart.

"We'll be upstairs at the snack bar," Chad said, as he and Mark headed out the door.

Wes made the short walk down the hall to the cabin team briefing room and greeted the flight attendants. He gave them a quick synopsis of the flight and explained the security precautions and cockpit control entry procedures he wanted. Recognizing Sybil DeVires, the flight service manager, as someone he'd known years ago, Wes lingered after the briefing to chat with her a few minutes.

The years had been kind to her. Sybil, slender and graceful with high cheekbones and chestnut-brown eyes, still looked great. Only the silver tint to her blonde hair suggested her age. Did she recall the night he'd saved her from being raped in their layover hotel in Louisville? If she did, Sybil didn't mention it.

* * *

Chad and Mark took the paperwork and headed out to the aircraft to start the preflight. Cockpit protocol called for Mark to take care of the exterior walk-around inspection while Chad loaded the flight computers. Chad had entered the flight plan in the computer by the time Mark returned from his preflight.

"Have you seen the squall line headed our way?" asked Mark as he stepped into the cockpit and picked up the flight plan.

"You mean out to the northwest of the field? Yeah!"

"It's beginning to look real nasty for our departure."

"I wouldn't worry too much about it, Mark. If I know Wes, he'll take a delay on the ground rather than penetrate that line if it's near the field. I'd bet money on it!" Chad answered.

Wes entered the cockpit and began stowing his luggage and kit bag. The high humidity had already done a job on his nicely starched white shirt. Wiping the sweat from his brow, he picked up the aircraft logbook and started to review the writeups. "Looks like the inbound crew had difficulty with the radar," he remarked.

"Yeah, I noticed that. Maintenance is taking a look at it now. From the looks of the weather to the west of the airport, I'd say we might need it," Chad replied.

"We can't go without it, so I'm sure they'll find a fix. The question is, will it be the usual 'ground checked, okay'?"

"We'll find out when we get airborne," Chad said sarcastically, as he copied the latest airport weather broadcast from Automatic Terminal Information System (ATIS).

"We'll let the storm blow over before we take off," Wes said, checking Chad's computer entries. "These people didn't pay to get the shit kicked out of them," joked Wes. "We can still get them to Paris on schedule, even with a ground delay."

"I can't argue with that," replied Chad, turning to smile at Mark.

2

ENCOUNTERS

The weather radar was covered with red returns as Wes called for gear retraction. The squall line was much larger than he'd anticipated. "TIA 898, TURN RIGHT TO 030 DEGREES AND CLIMB TO NINER THOUSAND FEET."

"Do you see any holes we could get through?" asked Wes.

"It looks like a solid wall to me," Chad said.

"Tell Departure we're unable to turn, but we can accept a climb," snapped Wes. Chad relayed Wes's instructions.

"HOW MUCH LONGER ARE YOU GOING TO NEED YOUR CURRENT HEADING?" asked the controller, annoyed at Chad's response.

"AT LEAST ANOTHER TEN MILES," Chad shot back, not waiting for Wes to respond.

"TIA 898, I'M UNABLE TO APPROVE YOUR REQUEST. YOU'LL BE OUT OF MY AIRSPACE IN SIX MILES. WHAT NORTHERLY HEADING CAN YOU ACCEPT?"

Chad looked at Wes.

"Tell him we can't deviate," said Wes, as he punched on the engine anti-ice switches and set the ignition selectors to the Flight Start position. Wes knew they were going to have to penetrate that line of thunderstorms. Reversing course was out of the question because of following traffic. "What does it look like to the southwest?" he asked.

Chad cycled the radar antenna elevation knob, searching for the tops of the cells. "There appears to be a hole to the right of our course,"

Chad replied, switching the scope's range to forty miles.

Wes didn't like what he saw. "Tell Departure we'll need a heading of about two four zero degrees for the time being. Any other heading will put us into a thunderstorm."

Passing three thousand feet, the heavy 767 began to buffet from vertical downdrafts associated with cells close to the jet's track. Moments later, Saint Elmo's fire began inching a path across the cockpit windscreen. Wes recognized the ever-changing purple arcs of electrically charged particles as a stern warning of what was to come. Within seconds, lightning discharged into a cloud barely a hundred feet from the jet. The thunderbolt was deafening. The flash blurred their vision for several seconds as the autopilot closed on its assigned altitude and began an auto-throttle power reduction to hold two hundred fifty knots.

"Tell Departure we need a higher altitude, now!" Wes demanded, becoming impatient with the controller's slow response. Buffeting, the 767 rolled and porpoised unpredictably as the autopilot fought to maintain straight, and level flight. Chad keyed his mike and complained to the departure controller as Wes checked the status of the APU and reached for his flashlight. The auxiliary power unit (APU), a small turbine in the jet's tail, was normally used for ground operations and engine start, but could provide emergency electrical, hydraulic, and pneumatic power in-flight, if needed.

"Mark, tell the passengers the lightning strike did not hit the aircraft and everything is okay." Wes knew the anxiety his passengers were experiencing. As a commuter, he'd watched their knuckles turn white from their death-grip on the armrests. He'd seen how quickly fear could spread through the cabin as people struggled to deal with their apprehension. He could appreciate their misgivings about flying in bad weather and understood the impact it could have on their future air travel. What troubled them most was the pilot's not telling them the truth.

"TIA 898, YOU ARE CLEARED TO CLIMB TO FLIGHT LEVEL 190. DEVIATIONS LEFT OF COURSE ARE APPROVED FOR WEATHER. CALL WASHINGTON CENTER ON 132.5. SORRY FOR THE DELAY. GOOD LUCK."

"Hot damn," said Chad as he dialed in 19,000 in the altitude alert window and rogered the clearance."

"Nice work, Chad. You do have some clout with the feds after all," Wes said, programming the autopilot for the climb.

Outside, Wes saw the milk bottle haze blackened by ominous dark clouds, extremities of the thunderstorms on either side of the 767's flight path. Suddenly, Saint Elmo's fire — visible static electricity — arced across the windscreen in search of an opposite charge. Then, slowly, an electrically charged spike began to form on the jet's nose as it pushed the positively charged particles ahead of its path. Unless Wes could dissipate the electrical buildup, the jet was certain to sustain a major lightning strike. Engaging the autopilot's Vertical Speed mode, Wes adjusted the thumb wheel controller to increase the 767's rate of climb. Slowly, the aircraft's pitch attitude increased as its airspeed started to slowly bleed off.

He was going to walk the thin flight boundary of trying to avoid an electrical strike while not inadvertently subjecting the aircraft to a stall. As captain, the choice was his. The consequences, however, belonged to everyone on the ship.

Rapidly cross-checking his slowing airspeed, Wes looked for a visible sign that the spike was starting to diminish. He would have to decrease the rate of climb shortly. The aircraft was approaching the flaps-up minimum maneuvering speed. He would not allow the craft to fly slower.

"Aren't you getting a little slow?" Chad asked.

"Yeah, it's intentional, but I won't go below minimum maneuvering airspeed," Wes replied confidently.

Satisfied Wes knew what he was doing, Chad watched and waited. No doubt, Wes had operated around the coffin corner many times during combat, Sanderlin thought.

Chad noticed it first. "The spike's starting to collapse!"

"Yeah, but we aren't quite out of the woods yet!"

Gradually the spike dissipated as the 767 continued its climb. The Saint Elmo's fire and the turbulence subsided, as well.

"Tell Washington we'll stay on this heading for another twenty-five miles before we turn north," said Wes.

The skies started to lighten as the 767 passed through twenty-nine thousand feet. Minutes later, the jet popped out on top. The scene to the right of the aircraft was awesome. Giant thunder cells reached another twenty thousand feet above the 767's flight level. Billowing cumulus clouds stood defiantly against the clear sky as sheets of rain, driven by violent vertical downdrafts, rushed toward the Earth's mantle beneath them. Gazing at the enormous line of thunderstorms in silent respect, Chad and Mark knew Wes had made the right decision.

Mindful of his passengers' comfort, Wes switched on the PA. His announcement was personable, yet delivered with the assurance that such incidents are daily occurrences for the crew. Finishing his remarks, Wes turned off the seat belt sign and offered his passengers a complimentary drink for the delay. Mark, knowing he was scheduled for the first break, fished a paperback novel from his kit bag and headed for the cabin. Assured that the toughest part of the flight was behind them, Wes and Chad slid their chairs aft to a more comfortable position and propped up their feet on the lower portion of the instrument panel. In truth, their workday was just beginning, although both pilots had been awake since seven a.m.

* * *

Meredith Beacham let the phone ring six times before hanging up the receiver, remembering that Caroline had her midterm in Trust Portfolio Management at 7 p.m. Quietly, she wished her oldest daughter success on the test, then lay back on her pillow and rested her eyes.

She adored Caroline. They were so much alike that they'd had a hard time dealing with each other during Caroline's teenage years. Caroline, headstrong, independent, and smart, hadn't been easy to raise. Full of pride and defensive over everything, Caroline was a mirror image of her mother, but didn't realize it; nor did Meredith, for that matter. Now that Caroline was on her own, the two of them were much closer. Meredith beamed with pride over her daughter's happiness and her upcoming marriage to Tucker.

She could almost feel the excitement Caroline and Tucker were experiencing. A chill passed over Meredith as she remembered the happiness she and Wes had shared as young lovers and longed for life to be that way again.

Meredith knew her marriage of thirty years to Wes was secure. More than lovers, they were close friends and companions to each other. There was no doubt in Meredith's mind that Wes loved her dearly. Yet, she regretted their lives being so busy. Everything seemed to take priority over their time together. Even finding the time to exercise required planning.

Relying on her stunning looks and natural beauty, Meredith had succeeded in hiding her fifty years without much effort. Her deep blue, sparkling eyes, dark brown hair and expressive lips still held other women at bay where Wes was concerned. She was able to conceal the extra pounds on her tall frame, but found dieting a constant chore, yet did so without complaining.

She was tired of teaching high school chemistry to kids turned off to learning science and looked forward to retiring and traveling with Wes. It had always been their plan.

Tossing aside the notes for tomorrow's lecture, Meredith thought of him. Was he airborne? Earlier, on TV, she'd seen the massive squall line racing toward Dulles. Tornadoes spawned by thunderstorms had already wreaked havoc in several communities southwest of the airport. He was due to take off about the time the storm was forecast to arrive.

Meredith seldom worried about Wes's flights, having realized years ago that his world was far from hers when he was at work. It all came down to whether Wes walked through the door at the appointed time, allowing for the commute home. She'd disciplined herself not to fret over him until then. Meredith trusted Wes implicitly in every way and he'd never failed her.

*   *   *

Returning to the cockpit several hours later, Mark spelled Chad at the first officer's position. Silence fell over the cockpit as Wes and Mark settled into the familiar routine of cross-checking the flight management computers. Both knew the real enemy of international flying was fatigue, and each had developed his own method for staying vigilant throughout the long night. For Wes, keeping active seemed to work best.

Hearing the HF (high frequency) radio's chimes began to ring, Wes silenced them as Mark acknowledged the call from Paris Dispatch. Both pilots copied the Paris weather and the "Re-release" clearance. Weather at De Gaulle was deteriorating more rapidly than had been forecast. Wes had Mark request alternate weather forecasts for London's Heathrow and Gatwick airports. De Gaulle's weather would necessitate a category III (lowest visibility minimums) approach and autopilot landing.

Before joining Leigh on her break, Wes had Mark check the Ops Specs (operations specifications) to determine if they were legal to shoot the approach. A fully automatic landing would require nearly every support system on board to be operational. They would need at least 175 meters of forward visibility to allow the autopilot to land the craft. That was the equivalent of six seconds of visibility, just enough to control the aircraft as it decelerated on landing.

The coupled approach to the auto landing went well. Wes cleared Runway Zero Nine at De Gaulle and began his taxi to the gate as Chad retracted the flaps and completed the remaining items on the checklist. After a slow taxi through the dense fog to the Uniform Five gate, Wes set the parking brake and secured the engines, while Mark completed the final entries into the logbook. "Seems like the taxi took longer than the flight," joked Chad as he slid his seat aft and tossed his kit bag onto the ACM (additional crew member) seat behind the captain's chair. "It all counts for pay," Wes replied with a grin.

The flight from Paris to Geneva took forty-three minutes. Sybil and the cabin team barely had time to pass out croissants, coffee, and tidy up before Mark extended the landing gear on final approach. Geneva's water geyser at the entrance to the harbor was visible from the left side of the aircraft. Wes called the passengers' attention to it as the 767 descended toward Runway Two Three at Cointrin Airfield.

Following Mark's "greaser," the flight crew, weary from the all-night trip, deplaned the aircraft quietly. Their expressions and glazed eyes told the story of their long, sleepless night. Only an occasional "bon jour" broke the silence as each crew member filed into the waiting van for the short ride to customs and the terminal. The ride to the Hathaway Hotel was equally silent, as most were content to gaze at the beautiful vistas and casually review their late afternoon plans with each other.

Cynthia and Sybil would sleep for a few hours, then shop until dinnertime. Chad had a new young woman to visit. Mark planned to run for a couple of hours in the late afternoon, then join Rachel for a late dinner. No one asked about Frederick and Aaron. Both were gay and kept to themselves on layovers. Austin would be staying with friends in Geneva. Wes and Leigh would rendezvous in her room later that afternoon.

DAY TWO - 22 August   *GENEVA, SWITZERLAND*

Leigh opened the door for Wes, then stepped back into the bathroom to finish dressing. Wes walked into the small hallway, pausing at the bathroom doorway. He watched her slowly pull the bristles of a brush over her long, black hair. A moment later, she laid the brush down and turned to face him, eager to answer his lustful stare. Standing apart, they gazed hungrily into each other's faces without bothering to speak. It wasn't necessary. Their eyes said everything. Touching each other softly at first, their gentle caresses quickly gave way to furious passion as they tore at each other. Clothes tumbled to the floor, marking a path to Leigh's bed as Wes swept her into his arms. Excitement raced through Wes's veins as he lowered her naked body to the bed and settled into her beckoning arms. Suppressing his guilt, he willingly gave in to her passionate embrace as lust overwhelmed reason and physical craving replaced honor. For now, only his insatiable desire for Leigh mattered.

Mark overslept, awaking sometime after four thirty. Dressing quickly for his run, he decided to skip the marathon practice session he'd planned. Instead, he would do the twenty-kilometer course he'd mapped out around the lake. Mark met Sybil and Cynthia in the lobby as he was tying his sneakers.

"Aren't you running a little late, Mark? No pun intended," Sybil asked, admiring his blue and yellow jogging suit.

"Yeah," he replied with a grin. "I forgot to set the alarm."

"You may find it hard running out there now," Cynthia added. "The sidewalks are really crowded."

"Thanks for the tip. I'll keep that in mind," Mark said, heading for the door.

Outside, Mark began threading his way through the crowd, picking up his pace as traffic allowed. Several blocks later, he found clear running room and lengthened his stride. Entering the botanical gardens, he felt the coolness of the luscious foliage that covered the flower-laden islands. The sun's rays splashed between the large sycamore trees, intermittently illuminating the colors in his jogging suit.

Cutting down along the shore, Mark saw that Lake Geneva was inundated with boats of every description. He chuckled at seeing a couple more interested in each other than in the dingy they were attempting to sail. The thought of sailing had always intrigued him. It would be a great contrast to running. Exiting the gardens, he slowed his pace to avoid running into a massive group of Japanese tourists. "Don't they ever get tired of taking pictures?" Mark asked himself, avoiding them.

Constantly dodging boats under tow, cyclists, skateboarders, and anyone else who hadn't found another place to be, Mark realized that choosing a course through the docks had been a mistake. He vowed to use the sidewalks on the return leg.

Reaching the famed nude beach on the far side of the lake, Mark saw that no topless bathers were there. "Too damned late," he muttered as he made a wide, looping turn around the paved parking area. As he did, Mark noticed the attractive young woman jogger he'd passed earlier smiling at him as he jogged by her. Embarrassed by her telling look, he wondered if she'd guessed the reason for his trip to the beach.

Approaching the Rue du Mont Blanc bridge for the second time, Mark frowned at having to stop his running. The sidewalks were covered with people rushing to get home. Picking his way through the swarms of tourists, Mark saw the *Genevee* approaching the harbor entrance. Recalling his first trip around the lake, Mark remembered the view had been awesome. Perhaps he and Rachel would do the boat ride next trip.

Mark reached the crosswalk of the busy Rue du Mont Blanc intersection just as the pedestrian signal turned red. Within seconds, the traffic poured around the congested corner, oblivious to the crowd clustered inches from the roadway. Standing at the edge of the curb, Mark watched impatiently as the traffic accelerated around the corner as if maintaining pole positions at the start of a NASCAR race. Like lemmings, the crowd pushed and nudged each other anxiously, waiting to cross. Suddenly, a force from behind shoved Mark into the path of an oncoming Mercedes.

The car struck him instantly, propelling Mark into the air and over the left side of the vehicle. A trailing BMW in the adjoining lane ran over him a second later, crushing his body under its chassis.

Both cars screeched to a halt as the runner Mark had noticed earlier withdrew from the stunned crowd. No one saw her leave. Only the horror of seeing someone inches away hit by a car and crushed by a second one occupied the minds of those standing at the curb. No one questioned why the runner had jumped into the path of the cars. The young woman jogger, now a block away, slid into a waiting Porsche.

Mark's motionless body lay on the street as police were summoned. Onlookers stared in disbelief as the drivers of the two cars tried to convince each other and the crowd of their innocence. The accident was unavoidable, they said. "The young man should never have stepped into the oncoming traffic," voiced one bystander.

The police arrived first, followed by an ambulance. The older officer examined the victim for signs of life, while his assistant took control of the scene and began rerouting the stalled traffic. Two paramedics joined the officer attending the body. Little could be done for him. Each agreed his death had been instantaneous.

Placing his crushed corpse on a stretcher, the paramedics covered him with a coarse tan sheet bearing the logo of a local hospital and loaded him into the ambulance. The senior officer canvassed the remaining onlookers for eyewitnesses. Several citizens gave their names and addresses and offered firsthand accounts of the tragedy. Each guessed it to have been a careless accident and unavoidable on the part of the drivers of the cars that had struck the victim.

A short while later, satisfied that the death was an accident and having the necessary information from both drivers and the eyewitnesses, the senior officer dispersed the remaining bystanders and accompanied the ambulance to the hospital. En route, the stranger's clothing was searched for identification, but none was found.

*　*　*

"We need to hustle if we're going to make the boat ride," Wes said, taking Leigh's arm gently. She smiled and took his hand as they raced across the Rue de Boulevard Mont Blanc to board the cruise boat

Genevee. Climbing to the top deck, they settled into two seats away from the other tourists. A waiter appeared just as the craft was about to cast off. Knowing Leigh enjoyed Chardonnay, Wes ordered a bottle for their cruise around Lake Geneva. Sharing their drinks in silence, the lovers watched as the vessel slipped from the shore and made its way quietly through the calm waters.

Their time together, though short, had always been spent in the midst of some of the most beautiful landscapes on Earth. Only wealthy people could enjoy such havens, thought Leigh as she sipped the dry wine. Why does life have to be so complicated, she mused, staring at the wake from the boat.

"So what's going on behind those penetrating eyes?"

"Just thinking how lucky we are to have the chance to be together in a place like this," Leigh answered softly.

Looking into her glistening eyes, Wes saw the love Leigh felt for him. She'd made her choice. She was willing to explore the unknown with him. But how could she have arrived at such a decision so quickly? Had her marriage to Grant been a failure from the start, or had his sudden death and her loneliness made it easy for her? Was that it? And how could she make such a commitment, not knowing if he could make the same covenant? The question labored on his mind as his eyes gazed mindlessly at the mansions lining the shoreline.

Inwardly, Wes knew the truth, the same truth his father must have learned too late in his affair. He could never give up Meredith. Even Leigh's entrance into his life could not change his feelings for his wife. His life was their life together. Walking away from Meredith would mean giving up all the two of them had shared for more than thirty-four years. Such a sacrifice would be unbearable, if not impossible. He trusted her with all of his feelings, and she loved him in spite of his weaknesses. How could he live without her love and companionship? How could he face the children? Their love and respect for him would never be the same.

As the sun slipped behind the French Alps, withdrawing its warmth, the lake's breeze quickly turned cold. Leigh broke the silence. "Is something troubling you, Wes?"

Surprised by her perception, Wes recalled Leigh's similarity to Meredith. For the first time, he wondered if he'd fallen in love with

Leigh out of longing to relive his romance with Meredith. He wasn't sure.

"Are you afraid of where our relationship may lead?"

"Not afraid, just uncertain...It's the guilt I'm having to deal with right now," he answered.

"Don't worry, Wes. We don't have to push the affair. Besides, my love for you isn't dependent on your loving me or choosing to live your life with me. Love is a gift, my gift to you. And I'll love you, no matter what you decide."

Smiling, Wes gently brushed his hand against her cheek. His guilt could wait. For now, being with Leigh was enough.

As the *Genevee* neared the entrance to the harbor, Leigh excused herself and went in search of a restroom. Wes watched her descend the companionway, unaware of the man approaching him from the rear. As the stranger walked past, a picture fell from his hand. Without thinking, Wes leaned over and retrieved it. Curious to see the photo, Wes turned it over as he reached up to hand it to the man. Bewilderment filled his eyes as he stared at a snapshot of Caroline.

She was wearing the dress he'd bought for her the night before last. Caroline could only have worn that dress yesterday. "How could this man have such a picture? And why?" Wes asked himself as he stood to face the man.

"Where did you get this picture?" Wes demanded.

"We took this picture fifteen minutes before we seized your daughter yesterday, Captain," the stranger said.

"How do you...." Wes was interrupted.

"Captain Beacham, if you ever wish to see your daughter alive again, you will do exactly as you are instructed," said the Arab. His English was perfect.

Wes weighed the stranger's words while groping for something to say. Suddenly, he felt nauseous. Horror spread across Wes's face as he fought to accept what his mind begged to deny. His hands shook as he fumbled with the picture, unable to take his eyes off the photo of his daughter. Why?

The stranger spoke again, more firmly. "You will be contacted later this evening. Be in your room alone at eight o'clock. Do not speak to anyone of this, if you hope to ever see Caroline alive again!"

"Yes...yes, I'll be there," Wes answered, struggling to make sense of what he'd experienced. Aware that his stomach would wait no longer, he ran to the railing as the stranger disappeared into the crowd that was beginning to disembark.

Leigh made her way through the opposing crowd and up the few steps to the top deck. She didn't notice the Arab who brushed pass her. Her eyes swept over the deck until they came to rest on Wes, who was slumped over the railing at the stern. Leigh saw that something was obviously wrong.

"Wes, are you all right?" she asked with concern. "Are you sick? Is there something I can do?"

"Find a towel or some napkins, Leigh. I'm afraid I've picked up some kind of bug," Wes said, fighting to regain his composure.

"Stay here. I'll go find what I can," she whispered.

Able to stand now, Wes felt the stomach cramps subsiding as the nausea passed. Turning to face the light breeze, he tried to recall the details of the conversation, but his mind kept returning to Caroline's picture.

Who had taken the picture? How did they know she was my daughter? What do they want with me? Why? How did the picture find its way to Geneva? Questions cascaded through his mind. He needed time to think, to sort out what had happened. What did it all mean? Remembering the stranger's instructions, Wes looked at his watch. It was 6:40 p.m.

Leigh returned with napkins, a towel, and a bottle of water. She handed him the napkins and water, but said nothing, sensing his embarrassment. As she watched him, Leigh wondered if she, too, would become sick, but quickly dismissed the notion.

"I'm sorry I messed up our boat ride," Wes finally said.

"Nonsense. I deal with this all the time in-flight," Leigh said, making light of the situation. "How do you feel now?"

"The nausea's passed, but I'd feel better going back to the hotel."

"Do you feel up to the walk, or do you want to take a cab?"

Wes thought for a second about the deadline he'd been given. "Let's walk. The fresh air might do me some good."

Leaving the boat, they climbed the steps to the street in silence. Wes's mind was already an ocean away, praying for Caroline's safety, while Leigh wondered about the mysterious illness that had come on so quickly. The two made the short walk to the hotel in under ten minutes, stopping only once for an ambulance that was responding to an emergency.

After assuring Leigh that he needed only rest and sleep, Wes closed the door to his room and began focusing on the horror of what he'd learned and what he could do.

The room was dark and cool now that the sun had disappeared. The last vestiges of daylight reflected against the glass windows of the office building across the street. He didn't bother to turn on a light, preferring to let the darkness mask his fear.

Caroline's fate lay in his hands. The idea that she had been taken hostage frightened and angered him. What could the stranger possibly want from him? Wes asked himself over and over, knowing he'd have his answer soon enough. He glanced at his watch again as if it held a clue to the terrifying riddle he faced. It was only seven p.m. An hour to wait, he thought, trying to recall the man's face.

Realizing his mind was drawing a blank, Wes thought of the photograph. The photograph! Did he still have it or had the stranger taken it? He couldn't remember. Switching on the wall lamp, Wes plunged his hands into his pant's pockets, frantically searching for it.

Retrieving the snapshot, he noticed the crumpled photograph bore a date and, what looked like initials along the right edge. They were unlike any Wes had seen in the States. He was certain the photo had been developed in Geneva. He scrutinized it for other clues while trying not to look at Caroline. There were no other markings. Whoever had taken the picture must have been on his flight with the film, or must have given it to an accomplice to develop here, Wes thought. TIA 898 was the last scheduled carrier to leave Washington for Paris and Geneva. The courier carrying the film had to have been on his flight.

If he or she had been aboard, there would be a record of his name on the computerized passenger list, "the spill." That would mean checking out all one hundred seventy-one passengers, but it could be done. The photo markings could also be traced. With luck, a positive ID could be made of the courier. But that would take time, lots of time he and Caroline didn't have. Besides, it would require an explanation.

He couldn't risk alerting the authorities. They would have to remove him from the trip, cancel the flight and turn the matter over to the FBI. Federal Air Regulations pertaining to security would not be compromised for any reason. And what about Caroline? She would be found later — dead. He would have to fly to keep Caroline alive and buy time to find her. It was that simple. Her life depended on it.

Wes barely heard the soft knock on his door as he gazed out the window into the dark Geneva skies. Hearing it for certain the second time, he jumped up and rushed to the door. He opened it, but found no one. A folded piece of paper was lying on the carpet. Wes stared up and down the corridor for a moment, then stooped over and picked up the note. He hastily unfolded it and began to read.

* * *

The pizzeria was just opening as Sybil and Cynthia arrived. Sybil asked the Italian waiter for a table outside with a view of the lake. His choice was perfect and soon they were in deep conversation, oblivious to other guests. Only the waiter's request for their orders halted their rambling discussion. Glancing at the menu, both agreed on a mixed salad and a Four Seasons pizza. Cynthia did the honors of choosing a bottle of Ricosole wine before returning to their conversation.

Later, after their pizza was consumed and the bottle was empty, Cynthia abruptly changed the conversation.

"Excuse me, Sybil, but that wine has done a number on my bladder. I must find the toilette now," she said, reaching down beside her chair for her purse.

Surprised, Sybil saw the worried look on Cynthia's face. "My purse is gone!" moaned her best friend.

"Are you sure?" Sybil asked.

"Yes, dammit! Someone's taken it," Cynthia, said angrily. Scanning the faces of nearby guests, she groaned, "I knew I shouldn't have laid it on the floor. It's my own dumb fault. How could I have been so stupid?" she asked, scolding herself.

"It's not over here," Sybil replied, searching the floor.

"Damn, I've lost my ID, passport, driver's license, credit cards, my cash...," Cynthia's anxiety was building. "I don't even have a way to pay for my dinner!"

"Never mind that," Sybil said, pulling out her AMEX card. "I'll take care of the check."

After complaining to the manager, and leaving a forwarding address and phone number, Sybil and Cynthia left the pizzeria in search of the police station. Sybil insisted that Cynthia file a report of the theft to protect herself from illegal credit card charges. Having a copy of the police report to back up her story would make it easier to get through customs, Sybil explained. Cynthia agreed and the two set out to find the police department. Geneva's police headquarters was on Carl Vogt Boulevard, a good fifteen-minute walk from the pizzeria. The station took up most of the block. An off-white concrete building with massive aluminum windows five stories high, its main entrance seemed an afterthought.

Entering the foyer, the two flight attendants passed through double glass doors to the police desk. The officer on duty was very polite, but had trouble understanding Cynthia's English. Sybil, fluent in French, took over and explained the situation, asking if they could speak with an investigator. The desk sergeant finally summoned a detective who invited the women into a small office. His English was impeccable. Cynthia gave a detailed description of the missing purse as Sybil gazed through the glass-walled enclosure at the adjoining office.

Sybil noticed what looked like a blue and yellow jogging suit on top of the desk. It was covered with blood. Continuing to stare at it gave her an uneasy feeling. She wondered why. The suit looked familiar, yet she couldn't place it. Suddenly, she realized Mark had worn an identical jogging suit. Was it his?

A cold sweat formed on her forehead as Sybil turned to face the detective. "Sir! Excuse me!" Glancing over at Sybil, annoyed by her interruption, the detective asked, "Yes? What is it?"

"The jogging suit on that desk in the next office — who does it belong to?" she probed.

"We think it belongs to an American, although we have no positive ID yet. He carried no papers."

Sybil's apprehension heightened. "What happened?"

"He was the victim of a car accident this evening."

Sybil's hands turned to ice as she recalled meeting Mark in the hotel lobby. She knew the clothes were his. They had to be. The emblems on the suit were the same as those she'd admired on his suit at the hotel.

"Officer, I'm afraid I know who those clothes belong to," Sybil said, now painfully certain of her discovery.

Her statement caught him by surprise. "Who?" he asked.

"Mark Hoffman," she replied. "One of our pilots."

Cynthia spun in her seat to face Sybil, stunned by what she'd heard.

"Oh God! What's happened to Mark?"

"If that jogging suit belongs to Mr. Hoffman, I'm afraid I have some unfortunate news for you, mademoiselles," answered the detective sympathetically. "He stepped into the path of a Mercedes and was knocked into the path of another car and killed instantly."

Realizing their shock at his revelation, the officer abruptly stopped his description of Mark's death.

"May I see the clothes, to be sure?" asked Sybil, hoping she was mistaken.

"But of course. It would be a big service if you could help us make the identification," he said. "Please come with me."

Sybil needed only a second to make the connection. Cynthia nodded in agreement after seeing the two emblems sewn on the shirt. The officer, noticing the despair in their faces, knew he had a positive ID.

"You are certain the clothes belong to Mr. Hoffman?"

"Yes," Sybil answered.

"I'm very sorry this tragedy has happened to your friend. Please accept my apologies," he said.

"I appreciate your concern," Sybil said, trying to maintain her composure. Cynthia, numbed by the disclosure, stood silently staring at Mark's jogging suit.

"There is one final matter I regret I must ask of you."

"Yes, I know," Sybil said. "I must identify his body."

Unable to deal with Mark's death, Cynthia excused herself from the unpleasant task and stayed upstairs.

Fighting back her tears, Sybil followed the detective down the corridor. The two stood in silence as the elevator descended to the basement. Looking into the eyes of the officer, a tall, slender, man nearing his forties, Sybil noted the sadness he seemed to feel. His empathy comforted her. She suspected he was a gentle man who found such duty difficult. Not knowing what to expect, she was glad he would be at her side.

The morgue was as Sybil had imagined, cold and sterile. The lighting was harsh. Lifeless, she thought, as the technician responded to the detective's request. Sybil broke into a sweat as the locker holding Mark's remains was opened. Her hands were clammy. Sybil wondered if she would faint. Her legs felt like rubber. As the crushing reality of what she was about to experience consumed her, Sybil felt the strong grip of his hand on her arm. The officer knew her torment and cared for her suffering.

Mark's body was like nothing Sybil could have imagined. Retching uncontrollably as the covering was slowly removed from his body, Sybil struggled to stay conscious. His face was barely discernible. His eyes, deflected in a contorted stare, had no focus. His skull was crushed inward, exposing tissue along the left side of his head. His mouth and jaw were torn from his face just below the sinus cavity.

"It's Mark. Oh God, it's him," she cried out, collapsing into the detective's arms.

Moments later, Sybil awoke to an expression of concern on the detective's face. She saw they were still in the morgue, but Mark's corpse had been removed. The detective's apology was immediate and sincere. The softness of his voice soothed her as she fought to overcome what she had witnessed. It was better she not think about it now, he instructed her. Sybil knew he was right, though she knew instinctively the nightmare of what she'd seen would be with her for a long time.

Upstairs, Cynthia met them as they emerged from the elevator. The two friends embraced as Cynthia sought to comfort her, a task she hadn't had the strength for earlier. Out of respect for the two women and their anguish, the detective left them alone and returned to his office. Cynthia wiped the tears from Sybil's troubled eyes as they followed him.

"Perhaps you would like some coffee," the detective asked.

"No thank you. I'll be okay in a moment or two."

"Mademoiselles, I'm deeply sorry for the loss of your pilot. I thank you for your help. My sergeant will drive you to your hotel," he said. "I shall be in touch with your station manager regarding the necessary arrangements. Please tell your captain that I am at his disposal, should he wish to confer with me."

"I'm certain Captain Beacham will want to talk with you as soon as he learns what has happened," said Sybil, as she and Cynthia followed the detective into the hallway.

The ride back to the Hathaway Hotel was short. Sybil and Cynthia rode in silence. Sybil stared aimlessly into the early evening sky as Cynthia wrestled with her guilt for lacking the courage to support Sybil in her dreadful task. Neither remembered the reason they had gone in search of the police station on Carl Vogt Boulevard.

3

LONG DISTANCE

Wes stopped under a street lamp and reread the note typed on an index card. His hands trembled as he read again the opening phrase, "If you wish to see your daughter, Caroline, alive..."

Fear replaced anger as Wes contemplated the harm that could come to Caroline if he didn't follow the terrorist's instructions. Brushing aside any thoughts of revenge, Wes knew that would have to wait until his daughter was free.

The note directed him to proceed alone to the Pearle du Lac Restaurant in the Jardin Botanique. There, he would find a wrought-iron gate leading to a short wooden pier in front of the restaurant. He was to arrive there at exactly eight thirty and wait on the end of the pier for further contact.

Wes recognized the location immediately. He remembered that the iron gate yielded the only access to the small beach, which was protected by a stone sea wall. The terrorist had chosen well. No one would see him there, nor could anyone see boats come and go. Large trees along the lake's edge formed a natural canopy that hung low over the water, shielding the cove from onlookers. It was a perfect place to rendezvous. The terrorist would come by boat.

Wes grimaced at the thought of the short memo he'd put on his flight clipboard telling of Caroline's kidnapping and his rendezvous with the terrorist. If he, too, were to fall prey to their mischief, a paper trail would at least give his rescuers a place to start.

Stepping from the shadows, Wes casually walked through the iron gate and onto the short pier. The small cove was more secluded than he'd remembered. He waited silently at the end of the pier, uncertain of what to expect. The night air was cool and damp. Wes found the gentle breeze from across the lake chilling as he waited nervously.

Minutes later, he heard the unmistakable sound of a powerboat. Straining, Wes saw two figures standing in the boat as it eased toward the pier. No one spoke as the small boat came alongside the end of the pier. Wes recognized one of the men as the stranger who had confronted him earlier. As Wes stepped into the boat, the stranger handed him an envelope and motioned him to a seat at the stern. Once seated, the terrorist signaled Wes to open the envelope as his accomplice slipped the engine into gear and eased from the cove.

Wasting no time, Wes opened the business envelope. The stranger offered him a small flashlight to see the contents. The envelope contained more pictures of Caroline, recent ones. Seeing her was painful. Wes tried hard not to look at the snapshots, but found himself lingering over each frame.

Reaching the open waters of the lake, the powerboat accelerated rapidly. Wes returned the pictures to the envelope as he tried to make out their route. He noted the luminous hands of his watch and pressed the stopwatch button on the rim of his Seiko. It was eight thirty-five. He wondered where they were taking him. The helmsman seemed to be favoring the northern edge of the lake as they raced along in smooth water. Wes placed the boat's speed at about thirty knots, judging from his own boating experience. He could see the outline of the lake's edge and the clusters of lights surrounding the more populated villages. Wes tried to recall their position in relation to where the cruise boat had traveled that afternoon.

They were approaching the vicinity of the cruise boat's second stop when he heard the engine die and saw they were drifting into a large cove. He guessed they would talk there.

"Captain Beacham, I trust you have had time to decide if you will help us?" asked the terrorist in charge.

"That depends on what assurance you give me that my daughter will be released unharmed."

"Captain, we are aware of the great affection you have for your daughter and we understand your concern for her welfare. Your cooperation is important to us. Your daughter has not been harmed and will remain safe so long as you agree to assist us."

"Really," said Wes, sarcastically.

"Yes. We even have arranged for you to talk with Caroline to satisfy yourself that she is safe and has not been harmed."

"How? We're in the middle of a lake three thousand miles from Washington!"

"Are you interested in talking with your daughter, or not, Captain Beacham?" the stranger asked, annoyed at Wes's outburst.

"Yes. Yes, I want to speak with my daughter."

"It will take but a minute," he said, smugly.

Taking a portable phone from a small locker under the forward deck, the Arab opened the leather pouch, exposing the handset. Rotating the tiny antenna to the upright position, he pressed the power switch to ON. Wes was amazed. The idea of calling from the lake had not occurred to him. Without comment, the stranger selected a preset number from the phone's memory and activated the SEND button. Seconds later, he spoke to someone and then handed the receiver to Wes.

"Daddy, is that you?" Caroline cried. Wes understood immediately why the bastards wanted him to hear her desperate plea for help. It was a cry he wouldn't forget.

Since Caroline's birth, he'd always been there for her. This time would be no different. He would comply, no matter the consequences.

"Are you all right, Caroline?" The question was rhetorical. She wasn't anywhere close to all right, Wes thought as he struggled to sound reassuring.

"I guess so. But I don't know where I'm being held. They've confined me to a dark room and handcuffed me to a bed."

Wes heard the soft sobbing and the sniffles that always accompanied her tears. "Have they harmed or threatened you, honey?"

"No, Dad. They're professionals. I don't think they will do anything to me as long as you do what they want."

Wes thought for a second. If Caroline's assessment was correct, her captors would not let her live, no matter what he did for them. She would be killed once he'd done what they wanted. Her only chance was to try to escape.

"Listen, Caroline, I'll do whatever they ask to gain your release, but you must do your part and be strong through all of this, no matter what it takes. I want you to remember how you used to behave as a child on the beach when I would take you near the ocean. You must find the courage to behave that way again. Do you understand?"

"I guess so," Caroline answered.

"I love you, Princess. Don't worry. I'll do whatever it takes, but think about what I've said. It's extremely important."

"I will, Dad. I love you, too," Wes heard Caroline say, as the stranger reached for the handset.

Tears streamed down his cheeks as the receiver went dead. Caroline was gone, perhaps forever. The anguish of hearing her cry for help would stay with him until she was freed. Brushing the moisture from his face, Wes stared into the terrorist's eyes as he gave up the receiver. The message was clear. They had his help.

Watching the stranger return the phone pack to the locker, Wes silently vowed to kill the sonofabitch and all those he could find who had helped him. For now they had his support. But in time, every one of them would live to regret the day they had taken Caroline from him.

"So now that you've gotten my attention, what do you want me to do?"

"Actually, Captain Beacham, we want you to operate tomorrow's flight normally until beginning your descent into the Washington area. There, you will divert your aircraft and land at Washington National Airport. That is all."

"That's all!" snapped Wes. "For starters, the approach route from Europe doesn't pass anywhere near National Airport. In fact, the profile was especially designed to avoid all conflict with National's traffic. Second, wide body aircraft are not permitted to operate into or out of National Airport."

"Yes, Captain, we know all of that. That is precisely why we need your help. It will be your job to decide how to divert the aircraft and land at National. Need I remind you that your daughter's life will depend on your success?"

Seething at the mention of Caroline's safety, Wes thought about what the terrorist wanted. Getting a 767 on the tarmac at National Airport would be easy enough. The restriction on its being there was only a matter of politics and bureaucracy. Faking a diversion would take some planning, but it could be done successfully.

"Okay, so what happens when I land at National?"

"You will taxi the aircraft to the departure end of Runway Three Six, turn around, and park."

"Is that all? Just park? What about my passengers? The plane? My daughter? When will she be released?"

"Captain, you ask too many questions!"

"Look, you idiot, I'll fly that jet through the gates of hell, but I want some straight answers about what's going to happen when I get there."

"Captain, your anger is understandable, but unnecessary. Once on the ground at National, you and your passengers will be free to leave the aircraft unharmed. Your daughter will also be released at that time."

"What assurances do I have that you'll keep your word?" Wes asked, knowing there were no assurances in a covenant with the devil.

"Captain, we bear you no malice. Our word can be trusted. Do not concern yourself with anything but getting your flight to National Airport tomorrow."

Wes got the message. There was nothing left to say. He would set the 767's parking brake at the National Airport runway intersection tomorrow afternoon, come hell or high water. He had until then to find a way to rescue Caroline.

Motioning to the helmsman, the stranger signaled him to start the engine. Moments later, the boat was underway, making a wide sweep away from the shore as it accelerated to cruise speed. Wes quickly scanned the cove, trying to pinpoint the location where they'd talked, but nothing seemed significant.

"Why are you doing this? What do you hope to accomplish?"

The stranger turned to face him. "You will learn soon enough. For now, you know all you need to."

Wes stepped onto the tiny wooden deck, but didn't bother to look back. Moments later, the small boat eased from the pier and disappeared into the darkness.

The walk back to the hotel was difficult for him. Helpless and alone, Wes thought of Meredith. How could he tell her of Caroline's disappearance and her fate? What would he say? The questions were too painful to contemplate. Wes wished he were with her. He needed Meredith's inner strength, her clear vision, her judgment. Longing for her, Wes walked quickly through the dark, lonely park, afraid of what tomorrow would bring.

Approaching the door to his room, Wes found another note lying on the floor. He recognized Sybil's writing. Her distinctive cursory style, perfected by years of practice, was her trademark. He unfolded and read the note.

> *Dear Wes,*   *8:15 p.m.*
> *I must speak with you at once. Something terrible has happened to Mark. Call me, or come to my room ASAP. I am trying to assemble all the cabin team members now.*
> *Sybil   Room 205*

Wes reread the note. What could have happened to Mark? Dialing Sybil's number, Wes let it ring ten times before hanging up. "Even Sybil could make it out of the shower in that length of time," he growled. Then he noticed the red message light glowing. The hotel operator answered on the second ring.

"This is Captain Beacham. You have a message for me."

"One moment, please," the operator said.

"Captain Beacham, Mr. Roman Leightner, the station manager for TIA, has been trying to reach you for the last hour. There has been an accident involving one of your copilots. He wants you to call him immediately. He left two numbers. Shall I put you through?"

"Roman, Wes Beacham."

"Ah! Captain. I have bad news about First Officer Hoffman."

"What's happened to Mark, Roman?"

"Captain, he was struck and killed by an automobile."

Neither spoke as Wes absorbed the news of Mark's death and Roman silently paid his respects.

"Where's Mark's body, Roman?"

"It's being released to us for preparation and shipment to the States tomorrow."

"Do you have the details of his death, or can you tell me who I should contact to find out exactly how it happened?"

"Your flight service manager, Miss DeVires, has the information, Captain. She identified the body and called me. I called the police and they agreed to release his body. Apparently, he stepped into the path of an oncoming car and was struck. The police said there were plenty of witnesses."

"Have you talked with the company yet?"

"Not yet. I thought it better that I talk with you and get the inspector's report first."

"When do you expect to get the report, Roman?"

"Within the hour."

"Call me when you have it. I'll give Flight Operations in New York a call and tell them to expect a fax of the report. I'm afraid if we wait for the report, the flight will be delayed tomorrow while we wait for his replacement," Wes explained.

"I agree. I'll call you as soon as I have it."

Wes hung up and opened his flight bag to get the number for Leon McGinnis. The vice president of flight operations was a special friend. They'd flown fighter jets together for years in the Air Guard. Leon was used to this sort of thing. As squadron operations officer, he'd been the one to make the visit or write the letter to the next of kin whenever one of the squadron pilots busted his ass.

"Flight Operations, Sandy Howard speaking."

"Sandy, it's Wes Beacham. It's urgent that I speak to Leon. There's been an accident involving one of my copilots."

"Wes, he's meeting with the CEO. I'm not to disturb him."

"Sandy this can't wait. Get Leon now. Tell him one of my crew has been killed in an accident."

Standing by the window, Wes gazed out at the moonlit skies of Geneva. So much had happened in so little time. His future, reduced to a collage of horrible scenarios, haunted his every thought. He longed for the pace of events to ebb. His mind, awash with anxiety over Caroline, was saturated with unanswered questions. Fear lurked in his heart. Age was also making itself heard. Wes was exhausted.

"Wes, Leon. Who was killed?"

Wes briefed Leon.

"You'll need a reserve first officer to take his place on the westbound leg, Wes. I'll have Crew Schedule set up a "deadhead" from Paris. Kifer's been insisting we keep a guy there to protect our European operation during the summer. I guess he knew what he was talking about, huh?"

Wes didn't answer. For once, he was glad about something. Having a reserve on standby in Paris would assure him of getting his flight off on schedule tomorrow. Finally Wes spoke. "I'll call you only if I have any other problems," knowing there would be bigger problems soon enough.

Sybil opened her door and beckoned Wes to enter. "I'm so sorry about Mark," she said, putting her arm on his shoulder as she followed him through the tiny corridor of her room.

Leigh, Cynthia, and Rachel were sitting on Sybil's bed. Austin, Aaron and Frederick were leaning against the windowsill. "I was in the middle of telling the crew about Mark's death, Wes. Would you like to take over?"

"No, Sybil. Continue. I didn't mean to interrupt."

"You're not interrupting. We were waiting for you."

Wes sensed they expected him to say something, to provide them with some sense of how they should respond professionally, if not emotionally. It was his place, his responsibility.

He noticed the tears well in Sybil's eyes and paused out of respect for her suffering.

"I'm at a loss to explain why this has happened. How he could have been involved in such a tragedy will remain a mystery to us all. Until we receive the police report and learn exactly what did happen, I think it best that we refrain from speculating.

"As for tomorrow, we will operate the flight as scheduled, with Mark's body aboard. I've spoken with Leon McGinnis, vice president of flight operations, and he's assured me that Mark's replacement will be here in time for tomorrow's departure. He's also asked me to express his deepest sympathy for the loss you've experienced. I'm sure that certain questions remain. I'll make the inspector's report available to you as soon as I get it. I'm deeply sorry this tragedy has happened...Mark was a fine young man. We'll miss him."

Returning to his room, Wes thought of Caroline as he undressed. Her suffering had to be far worse than his. He'd give anything to trade places with her, anything to take her from harm's way. He'd had a great life, but he would gladly give it up in an instant to free her from the terror she was facing. Wes prayed for his daughter's safety.

Soon, dreams replaced reality as Wes lapsed into a deep sleep, overcome by helplessness.

*   *   *

Renee walked quickly down the dim first-floor corridor toward the side exit of the main building. Leaving the Université, she saw it was a little after ten p.m. Her evening accounting class had been dismissed late. Renee would miss her bus if she didn't hurry. Crossing the Rue de Candolle, she walked the short distance along St. Ours before turning right into the Square de Comendie. From there, Renee had only a three-minute walk to the Round Pointe de Plainpalais and her bus stop.

The young, vivacious wife of Marcel DeMornay, Renee worked as a ticket agent for TIA. Her husband, a much older man, was TIA's lead cargo foreman. Married less than a year, Renee was expecting her first child in five months. Eager to help Marcel support their new family, she had enrolled in several night classes to improve her career opportunities at TIA. Learning came easy for her, and she welcomed the mental challenge but disliked the lonely and, sometimes foreboding, trips home after class.

Renee stepped into the dark square, unaware that she was being followed. Now walking along the edge of the square, she noticed the headlights of a car sweep the walls of the buildings in front of her. Concerned, Renee pushed her long, black hair away from her face and quickened her pace, knowing her bus stop was less than a block away.

Afraid to look at the car that had pulled up beside her, Renee didn't see the man who grabbed her. Unable to scream with his hand over her mouth, she struggled to maintain her balance as he shoved her into the rear seat of the large car and pushed her onto the floor. In pain, she gasped for breath as a scarf was stuffed into her mouth. Her attacker quickly bound her hands and feet and covered her with a dirty wool blanket as his accomplice pulled away from the square. Tears rushed from her eyes as Renee feared for her life and that of her unborn child.

Marcel didn't like Renee using the Transports Publics Genevois bus system to get to and from the university. He worried about her safety and resented not making enough money to afford a car for her. Nevertheless, he admired her desire to help with the family expenses and begrudgingly offered her encouragement in her academic efforts.

Marcel used the time she spent in class to make furniture for their small apartment. The son of a cabinetmaker, Marcel had learned the trade as a boy from his father. Renee loved the few pieces he'd already made, especially the hand-carved headboard for their bed, and had urged him to make a cradle for their child. Ecstatic over her suggestion, Marcel had set about to build a cradle and a matching chest of drawers.

Tonight, like most other school nights, Marcel measured, sawed, and sanded the many pieces needed for the furniture while eagerly awaiting Renee's return. Turning the piece of walnut on its side for more sanding, Marcel glanced at the Swiss clock hanging over the kitchen counter. Had Renee missed her bus or had she stayed to talk to the instructor? Marcel longed for her return. She was his life, the source of his happiness.

Amid concern for Renee's safety, Marcel answered the telephone on the first ring.

"Marcel DeMornay?" asked the caller.

"Yes!" He did not recognize the voice.

"You have a beautiful young wife named Renee, no?"

Marcel's pulse quickened. Why would it matter to this man what his wife's name was, unless...

"Marcel, Renee is with us for now. She is not coming home tonight, but we will let her speak with you."

"What do you mean, you have her?"

"Marcel!" Renee cried out. "I'm afraid. These men...."

"Renee, tell me what has happened! Please!"

"They say I will never see you again if you do not do what they say. Please, Marcel, do as they say ...for me... for our baby, please! I'm so afraid."

Nearly hysterical, Marcel felt the torment in Renee's every word. His voice trembled as he tried to answer her plea, but he was interrupted by the stranger's harsh voice.

"You will think for a while of what your pretty Renee has asked of you. You will give us your answer in one hour. Otherwise, you will never see your wife alive again. If you speak to anyone of this matter, we will kill her immediately. Do you understand?"

"Yes, yes. Please do not harm her. She is ...."

The line went dead.

Collapsing into an overstuffed chair, Marcel felt numb as he stared out the window in disbelief. Nothing made sense. Why Renee? She hadn't done anything. Who? What could they want from me? His mind jumped aimlessly from question to question, never stopping to reason an answer. Why had he let her attend the night school? It was stupid, he thought. Recriminations tore at him as Marcel sought to make sense of Renee's kidnapping. He cursed himself for having given in to her wishes. He should have been stronger, resisted her will. Painfully, he recalled their last moments together. He wept openly, thinking of the terror she was experiencing. Pacing the floor, he prayed they would contact him soon. Marcel DeMornay needed no time to decide. He would do anything they wanted for her freedom — anything.

Exactly one hour later, the phone rang. Marcel grabbed it immediately. He recognized the voice.

"Have you made your decision, Marcel? Will you help us?" His tone seemed less harsh now.

"Yes! Yes! I will do as you say," Marcel answered. "But you must not harm Renee."

"We do not wish to bring harm to your young wife, Marcel, but you must do exactly as you are told if you expect to see her alive. There must be no mistakes. Do you understand?"

"I will make no mistakes. What is it you wish me to do?"

"A certain casket containing the body of a TIA pilot is to be shipped out on tomorrow's TIA flight to Washington. You will make certain the casket is placed in an ALE cargo container and parked between hardstand numbers seventeen and eighteen at precisely 10:45 tomorrow morning. Another cargo driver will approach you pulling an identical cargo container. He will stop and you will exchange containers. You will then take his container and put it aboard the TIA aircraft in the rear of the forward cargo bin. If there is a change of plan, we will contact you. That is all we require."

"Yes, I will do that. There will be no problems."

"It is good for Renee that you will help us, Marcel."

"When will you return her to me?"

"She will come to you as soon as the aircraft takes off for Washington," the caller said. "But remember, Marcel, no mistakes. If you should tell anyone of this or contact the police, Renee will die a slow, painful death. Are you certain of what you must do?" asked the caller.

"I'm certain."

"Then you have nothing to fear."

Marcel hung up and lay back on the bed, his body still trembling. A chill passed over him as he reviewed the terrorist's instructions, knowing Renee's life was at stake. As lead cargo foreman, he could make certain the casket was placed in an ALE container. That was the type of container used to ship caskets anyway. Positioning it between the hardstands wouldn't pose a problem either. No one ever paid any attention to where cargo was positioned for loading. Only the loaders cared about how and where the bins were parked. The switch would go unnoticed as long as the other bin's decals and ID looked similar. But loading might be a problem. The loader conveyor was old and prone to jam. The caller had said a TIA pilot's body was to be shipped back to the States. Who was it? He would ask when he called to confirm tomorrow's schedule. Having the pilot's body as cargo might draw more attention than usual to the loading operation.

Emotionally drained from the pain of Renee's kidnapping, Marcel lifted the receiver and dialed TIA Operations.

"TIA Operations. Kirk."

"Kirk? Marcel. Check the cargo roster for tomorrow and tell me who is scheduled to work the morning shift."

"Yeah, sure. Hold a minute."

"Marcel, Alan and Hans are on with you."

"I thought so," Marcel replied. "What does tomorrow's load to Washington look like?"

"The usual, sixteen to seventeen thousand pounds."

"Oh. There is one bit of news. The relief first officer on this morning's inbound flight was killed in a car accident late this afternoon while jogging. Roman has all the details. He's planning to ship the pilot's body back to Washington on tomorrow's flight," Kirk explained."

"How did it happen?"

"I'm not sure. Roman doesn't want to talk much about it until the company has had a chance to notify the next of kin."

"Makes sense," Marcel said. "Tell Roman I'll be there early to handle the loading."

"Good. He was going to call you. I'll give him the message."

"Ciao," said Marcel.

Suddenly, Marcel understood. The kidnappers could not have known of the pilot's death so quickly unless they'd planned his death themselves. How else could they have known to seize Renee? They were murderers. And if they'd killed once, would killing again matter?

Marcel put away his tools and the unfinished pieces of the cradle. They didn't seem important anymore. Only Renee's release mattered. He dared not go to the police, fearing for her safety. In despair and unable to sleep, Marcel prayed as he wept.

*   *   *

It was nearly midnight when Kyle Anton reached for the phone beside his bed. "Anton."

"Mr. Anton, this is Paris Flight Operations calling. New York Crew Schedule has sent us a message for you. You're to deadhead to Geneva early tomorrow morning to protect Flight 899 leaving for Washington Dulles tomorrow at eleven hundred thirty hours GMT. You're booked on Air France Flight 656 leaving De Gaulle at eight fifteen GMT. Your ticket will be here at Paris Operations."

"Okay the assignment for me... I'll be there at seven."

"I show you okayed, Mr. Anton. I'll advise New York."

Kyle put down the phone and gazed with indifference at the Eiffel Tower standing majestically in the distance before returning to his exercises.

A bachelor with close ties to Europe, Kyle preferred spending his summers in Paris on reserve. TIA crew schedulers loved him. He was their ace in the hole when the search for relief pilots reached the panic stage, as it always seemed to during the summer.

Beads of sweat seeped from the pores of Kyle's muscular frame as he finished the last of fifty push-ups. Exhausted, he brushed the sweat from his mustache and bushy eyebrows, then crawled to his feet in search of a towel. The air-conditioned room felt like a sauna. The air was suddenly thick and musty. Kyle mopped the water from his black hair and wiped down his olive-tanned body before tossing the soaked towel in the direction of the bathroom. Weary from the exercise, he reset the thermostat and dropped into a stuffed chair to rest.

A few minutes later, Kyle placed a call to Geneva and then headed to the bathroom for a hot shower.

4

ALTERNATE PLANS

DAY THREE - 23 August   *GENEVA, SWITZERLAND*

"MID EAST 268 DESCEND TO FLIGHT LEVEL 250 AND TURN LEFT TO A HEADING OF 130 DEGREES." Captain Jabril eased the throttles closed as he banked the cargo-configured Boeing 747.

"Mustufa, call operations and confirm we are to park at our usual hardstand." The first officer switched over to the number two VHF radio. "OPERATIONS, MID EAST 268 ESTIMATING GENEVA AT 0556 ZULU. CONFIRM HARDSTAND ONE EIGHT?"

"AFFIRMATIVE," the ramp controller casually replied. Hearing the reply over his number two radio, Jabril, a silent man, nodded at Mustufa. In another twenty-five minutes they'd be on the ground.

The loadmaster shifted his weight as he stood to make one last check of his cargo before strapping in for the landing. The bay was nearly full this trip with cargo destined for the upcoming trade exhibition at Geneva's newly expanded Palexpo Center next to Cointrin Airport. Mocmoud and his two assistants would be busy for the next hour or so downloading the 747. The load manifest showed a large portion of the night's cargo was machinery. The remainder appeared to be hi-tech equipment except for a casket.

Not one given to a lot of conversation, Mocmoud, a fortyish Arab from Lebanon, had been especially quiet during this flight as if he were apprehensive about something. But he was like that sometimes, and tonight was one of those times. His two loading assistants knew better than to interrupt him with idle chatter, so the two sat silently in their jumpseats, occasionally swallowing to clear their ears as the 747 jet descended toward Geneva.

In the cargo bay, Mocmoud disarmed the main entry door and motioned for the ground handler to position the external stairs against the huge jet. He watched as the stairs closed on the side of the 747's fuselage. Jabril and Mustufa descended the spiral staircase from the upper flight deck. "The aircraft's yours, Mocmoud. We'll see you in four hours," Jabril said. Mocmoud nodded and returned to the cargo bay.

Estimating the downloading would take about two hours, Mocmoud quickly briefed his two assistants on how he wanted it done and then left the aircraft in search of a loader.

All loose cargo would be removed first. Then they were to begin removing the palletized freight. The canisters would be last. Mocmoud would do most of that himself, he told them.

Ten minutes later, his assistants began the task of carefully re-moving the high-value cargo. They stacked it aboard the small carts attached to the battery-powered cargo tractor Mocmoud had pulled alongside the steps. Handling the operation this way would take longer, but it would prolong having to download the casket and use up the extra time he had to kill.

Sipping the lukewarm coffee he'd taken from the galley, Mocmoud watched the pallets roll effortlessly out of the fuselage and onto the carriage of the hydraulically powered loader/conveyor parked next to the large cargo door. The downloading operation was on schedule and progressing smoothly. Soon they would be on their way back to Larnaca.

The morning sun shone brightly as a moist breeze drifted across the sprawling ramp. A cobalt sky highlighted the surrounding moun-tains. But the sky's pristine color was temporary. Soon, the hot haze would settle in the valley, obscuring the sky's royal tint.

A procession of jets arriving and departing from Runway Two Three continued unabated as Mocmoud gazed over the spacious flight ramp. He was anxious. He nervously checked his watch. It was nine thirty. They would begin downloading the canisters at ten. Signaling his assistants for a break, Mocmoud stepped back inside the 747.

Leaning against the fuselage bulkhead, Mocmoud thought again of the family he'd lost and of the pain he'd been forced to endure. He could still hear the sound of the Israeli bombers as they shelled his home in the Bekha valley that early summer morning, instantly killing his wife, daughter and youngest son. Only he and his elder son had been spared. Mocmoud recalled the coolness of Maria's flesh, the agony of holding Arisa's lifeless body against his chest as he prayed to Allah, and the torment of seeing Amail's small body torn into pieces.

Mocmoud noticed his assistants step through the door and walk toward him. He quickly wiped the large tear from his eye and put on his sunglasses. Seldom a day passed that he didn't relive the tragic loss of his family. The pain burned like a torch in the center of his chest, crying out for vengeance. He would not rest until he avenged their deaths. The Israelis... and their American friends...must pay, he promised, crawling to his feet.

It was time to start downloading the canisters from the 747. Without speaking, he and his assistants took their stations. Moments later, the large aluminum cargo containers began to appear from within the jet's belly. Rolling out in sequence, they floated upon a carpet of many tiny casters before being lowered to the carts below. The speed of the downloading was impressive. Only the clicking of the hundreds of rollers and the diesel engine broke the morning stillness.

Returning from his second trip to the cargo dock, Mocmoud noticed that his assistants had stopped the downloading and were huddled over the gearbox of the loader conveyor. The muscles in his neck tightened as he approached the conveyor and set the cargo tractor's hand brake. Nothing must go wrong now, he muttered, as he climbed onto the machine to see what his helpers were looking at. "What's the matter?" he called, stepping between them. "The chain drive to the conveyor is jammed. We cannot free it!" exclaimed the taller assistant.

Bending over, Mocmoud stared at the belt. It was worse than he had imagined. The chain had broken and was lodged against the drive housing. Looking at his watch, Mocmoud cursed as he stood up and debated what to do. There wasn't much time before his rendezvous. "Can it be repaired now?" questioned the shorter helper. "Even Allah will need time to fix this," replied Mocmoud, beginning to worry.

The taller assistant pushed the awaiting canister back into the 747's belly and stood by the control panel. "Back the loader away from the aircraft," Mocmoud commanded. "And drive it back to the cargo area. I'll borrow another," he said, climbing on the electric tractor. Heading for TIA's cargo office, Mocmoud knew someone there would have the same sense of urgency to see that his cargo was downloaded on time.

Marcel hadn't slept. Anxious to fulfill the terrorist's instructions, he'd arrived early at operations.

The company computer showed the inbound flight from Paris on time. Marcel was glad for that. He'd scheduled himself to handle the switch and had already loaded the casket into an ALE container. Marcel looked up as Mocmoud entered the office.

"This is the TIA cargo office, no?"

"Yes," Marcel replied, looking at Mocmoud in surprise.

"I have a problem. My loader has jammed and I still have cargo to download from our 747 at hardstand eighteen. Can you let me use your machine for a short while?"

"No, it is impossible now. We have cargo to unload, too."

"It is very important that I use your loader now. I have certain cargo that must be uploaded by ten forty-five."

Marcel studied the expression on the loadmaster's face. What kind of cargo and why ten forty-five? The inbound flight from Paris was scheduled for hardstand seventeen, next to this man's aircraft. Was this the cargo he was supposed to exchange? He'd received no further instructions from the kidnappers. Had they sent him here? Does he know I'm the one? Fear raced through Marcel's veins as he fretted over whether to help the loadmaster.

"You will help me, no?" Mocmoud spoke again.

"Yes, I'll get the loader."

Nodding his appreciation, Mocmoud walked toward the door. He was certain Marcel was the one with whom he would make the cargo swap. Relieved, he eased into the tractor seat and waited for Marcel.

Driving the loader against the side of the giant 747, Marcel adjusted its cargo platform to match the bottom edge of the cargo belly door. Mocmoud climbed onboard the loader and rode the elevator platform up to the cargo door. Within seconds, the large ALE canisters began to roll onto the loader. Both men coordinated their efforts in an uneasy alliance, downloading the cans of cargo. Marcel strained to see inside the 747 cargo bay for any unusual cargo, but saw none. It was too dark to read any of the markings on the canisters. He would have to wait.

Ten minutes later, TIA flight 898 landed on Runway Two Three. Marcel saw the 767 land and motioned to Mocmoud that this was the flight he was expecting. Marcel and Mocmoud watched from atop the loader as the 767 taxied the last fifty meters.

"I will need the loader now," said Marcel, not wanting to antagonize Mocmoud.

"Yes, I have only one canister to go."

Just inside the 747 cargo bay, Marcel saw a container with TIA markings. Certain it was the cargo he would later load into the TIA 767, Marcel said, "I will go and bring my outbound cargo first. You can finish your unloading."

"That will be good," replied Mocmoud, knowing what Marcel had to do. "I will be back at ten forty-five." Mocmoud nodded. Both men grasped the message implicit in Marcel's last remark.

At precisely ten forty-five, Marcel pulled alongside Mocmoud's tractor parked between hardstands seventeen and eighteen. Sliding off the seat, he decoupled the end canister holding the casket. Out of the corner of his eye, Marcel saw Mocmoud watching him from underneath the 747's wing as he attached the lone Mid East canister to his cargo convoy. Approaching the right wing of the TIA 767, Marcel stopped and disconnected the Mid East canister, pushing it aside.

Walking under the 767's belly, Marcel saw that the canister holding the casket he'd exchanged was already being hoisted aboard the Mid East jumbo jet. He waited, not wanting to interfere. Mocmoud saw Marcel and beckoned him to climb aboard.

"I am finished," Mocmoud said, stepping from the control panel. "You have much to do. I will help."

"We can handle it," Marcel answered, as he stepped to the conveyor's control panel. "I will be under the wing if you have trouble," said Mocmoud, climbing off the loader.

How involved was the loadmaster? Was he an involuntary player like him, or was he part of the terrorist organization? Marcel couldn't decide. His eyes — dark and penetrating — seemed to be filled with rage as if he'd witnessed some horror his mind could not erase. They frightened Marcel.

After removing the last of the canisters from the 767's cargo compartment, Marcel sent one of his helpers in with the arriving cargo and began uploading the aft compartment.

A few minutes later, Marcel closed the aft cargo door and maneuvered the loader around the 767's long wing and up to the forward cargo door entrance. Alan, his younger assistant, stepped into the bay and waited for the first canister. Marcel called down to his older assistant, Hans. "We'll load that one sitting by itself first," he said, pointing to the Mid East canister. Hans nodded and rolled the switched cargo canister into position abeam the loader's elevator. Pushing against the container, he found it would not budge. Marcel's pulse froze as he watched Hans struggle to move the large container. "Wait! Let me give you a hand!" he shouted, climbing off the loader. "You'll have to. I can't get it to move. It's jammed," Hans said, still trying to force the heavy container onto the elevator.

After checking to see that the elevator platform and cargo cart were aligned, Marcel threw his weight against the container and pushed, but the container held its ground until an extra pair of hands joined them. It was Mocmoud. The cargo slid onto the platform rollers without difficulty. Marcel nodded his thanks at the loadmaster as the two of them rode with the canister up the elevator. Moments later, Marcel, his two assistants and Mocmoud rolled the switched canister into the forward cargo compartment and into position for flight.

"Why was that container so damned heavy?" Alan asked.

"It contains the body of a company pilot killed here yesterday," Marcel answered.

"He must have a lot of lead in his ass!" Hans joked.

Mocmoud climbed off the loader without saying a word. Marcel followed, hoping the loadmaster might tell him of Renee, but Mocmoud said nothing as he returned to the Mid East 747. Anxious to see his wife, Marcel headed back to the cargo office to await TIA 899's departure.

* * *

Roland Hildebrand walked down the hall corridor toward the locker room to pick up his bike helmet, not bothering to clock out as he passed. The last several hours had been miserable for him, and he was eager to get on the road. Having to explain how he'd inadvertently backed his fuel truck into the secretary of state's jet had not been a pleasant experience, but a profitable one, he thought. The interrogation had been intense. Voices had been raised and fists pounded on the large table in the conference room in the contract services building at the west end of the airfield. The Swiss official had practically fallen over himself apologizing to the U.S. attaché for the mishap. Roland was amazed at the damage he had caused to the Boeing 707. According to the photos, he'd punctured the number three engine cowling just aft of the engine's compressor section. No doubt a replacement engine would have to be flown in before the jet would fly again. From the gist of the comments, he knew he'd done his job well.

Stepping out into the bright sunshine, Hildebrand scanned the parking lot for a black Mercedes. He spotted the car parked several meters from his BMW bike. He recognized the driver and his companion as the two Arabs he'd met a few days before. They would have the money.

The prospect of returning to Germany in time for the ski season appealed to him. Fifteen thousand Swiss francs was more than he could ever expect to make over the next three months in Geneva. The deal had been easy to accept.

As Roland approached the car, the driver eased a small envelope out the window as he spoke. "You have done your job well, Roland. Here is the remaining ten thousand francs you were promised. You will be leaving for Germany now?"

"Yes. As quickly as I can get on my bike," answered the young German. He took the envelope and thumbed through its contents. It was all there. He tucked the package inside his jacket and nodded to the driver. "Call me again if you need anymore help," he said, pulling the silver and blue helmet over his head. The driver didn't reply, but watched as Roland took a pair of riding gloves from his pockets and slipped them on.

Swinging his long leg over the large bike, he hit the starter. A second later, the engine roared to life and the blonde German shifted the motorcycle into gear.

Anxious to get under way, Roland didn't notice a large panel truck pull out behind him. Turning out of the parking lot and onto the Avenue Louis-Casel, he gunned the bike. Within minutes, he would take the turnoff to Ferney, pass under the east end of the airport and disappear into France, fifteen thousand francs richer.

Roland felt better than he had in a long time. The thing with Nicole had been tough. Getting away now was a blessing he thought, as he opened the throttle a bit further. Moving along the Route de la Vorge at ninety kilometers per hour, Roland noticed a gray truck following him and wondered why it seemed to be closing in on him so quickly. I'll lose him at the turnoff, he thought. With the exit ramp just ahead, Roland downshifted.

Suddenly the panel truck pulled abeam of the biker and began crowding his traffic lane. Realizing he was being forced off the road, Roland accelerated, hoping to avoid a collision, but he was too late. The impact sent his motorbike into the guardrail, crushing his right leg and throwing him into the rising head wall. The blow killed him instantly.

Continuing up the exit ramp and down through the tunnel to the French border, the truck passed into France minutes later. The driver of the Mercedes reached the scene of the accident first and appeared to try to revive the young biker before returning to the car to phone for the police. Approaching traffic slowed to view the smashed motorcycle lying on its side next to the scarred guardrail. Missing from an inventory of Roland Hildebrand's personal effects was the envelope containing fifteen thousand Swiss francs. The driver of the Mercedes was also missing.

*   *   *

Riggs Halston pushed his chair away from the dining table to make room for his protruding belly. The large American breakfast he'd just stuffed down his bottomless pit was crying out for more room. Crumbs tumbled off his paisley tie onto his trousers. His overweight frame was already perspiring from the effects of multiple cups of black coffee. Halston wiped his forehead with his napkin, then crumpled it and dropped it onto his plate.

The secretary of state picked up the newspaper and scanned the headlines for reports on his recent summit conference. Riggs relished seeing his name and picture in the newspaper. He was not to be disappointed this morning. A large photo on the front page showed him expounding on newly adopted policies dealing with the Middle East. Halston admired himself in the picture. The pose looked dynamic. His large head and square jaw presented the image of a tough, forceful negotiator, one not given easily to compromise.

Had he been quoted correctly? Were the salient points he'd hammered out obvious to the reader? Concerned about the public's perception of his accomplishments, Halston considered his post a stepping stone to the White House.

President Mason Tyler McGarth, though not one of Riggs' supporters, had no illusions regarding the secretary's aspirations and hated the fact that he'd been forced to appoint him secretary of state. Political realities notwithstanding, Mason cared little for Halston's antagonistic style and militant views. McGarth, a moderate and highly principled man, felt his commitment as president extended to all Americans, not just to the power brokers who'd paid the freight to get him in office. Riggs was just the sort of secretary of state he didn't want.

Yet Riggs Halston did enjoy a strong base of political power. His hawkish stance on military matters had long ago earned him the support of the armed services and the defense industry. An ardent supporter of Jewish interests and their call for a strong Israeli state, Halston could depend on the Jewish Defense League for considerable financial assistance. Even conservative right wing religious organizations had begun to embrace the hard line philosophy he espoused.

Senior State Department bureaucrats abhorred him and were appalled at the way he bullied allies and lesser nations into backing proposals designed to infuriate the Arabs into retaliation. Relations between the Arab world and the U.S. had deteriorated rapidly following Halston's appointment. Some leaders within the U.S. government suspected that the secretary's ultimate goal was to provoke a second war in the Gulf.

Not one to vacillate, Halston was consistent in his disdain for the Arabs, especially for the PLO. He enjoyed exploiting them economically. He ridiculed them philosophically, and when necessary, would incite them into precipitous action against one another while helping Western oil companies suck every drop of oil from their lands.

Moderate Arab leaders schooled in the practical operation of American government and its political arena knew Halston was a temporary fixture on the American political scene and would pass in time. Radical Arab fundamentalists, however, viewed his presence as a grave threat.

Halston understood well the Arab viewpoint regarding the use of terrorism as a political tool against the West. He believed that unrelenting pressure was the only way to combat this ruthless form of aggression.

The conclusion of yesterday's summit meeting on terrorism had been especially gratifying for Halston. Riggs knew it would mean further support for his political ambitions. Having begun his career in public relations, Halston was anxious to return to Washington and the probing eye of the TV camera he hoped would be waiting.

Ross Straton, his special assistant, entered the hotel dining room and made his way over to Halston's table, apprehensive over having to give his boss the bad news.

"Good morning, Mr. Secretary. Did you sleep well?"

"Sleep was not a priority for me last night, Ross. I spent the better part of the night with the young lady you introduced me to from the embassy. Margaret ... what's her name?"

"Yes, Margaret Habersham. She was quite eager to meet you, sir," replied Ross, knowing nothing was further from the truth.

"She and I are really close friends now," piped Riggs, smiling broadly as he recalled the affair. "See if you can't find a position for that young lady on my staff. I like her style."

Ross made a mental note of the secretary's order.

"How about you, Ross? You get laid, too?" Halston asked.

"No sir, I didn't have time. I spent the evening reviewing the press releases drafted for this afternoon's arrival in Washington... Mr. Secretary, we have a problem with our return flight this morning."

Halston looked up from his paper. "What kind of problem?"

"Sir, the fuel truck servicing your aircraft backed into the side of one of the engines."

"How the hell did that happen?"

"I don't have all the details, sir, but I've been in contact with the aircraft commander, Major Dixon. He's certain that the 707 will need an engine replacement before it can be flown."

"Sonofabitch," muttered Riggs. "Can we get a military transport from Frankfurt? You know I've got to get back to Washington ASAP. McGarth is expecting me for dinner at the White House tonight."

"Sir, I've already made alternate plans for getting you back to Washington on schedule." Halston looked up at Ross, impressed. "You have? How did you do that?"

"I've booked you aboard Trans International Airways leaving for Washington at one o'clock this afternoon. It's scheduled to arrive at Dulles at six p.m."

"What kind of seats did you get?" Halston demanded.

"We blocked the remainder of first and business class seats, sir. But I did have to accept some economy seats for the staff."

"What about the media, Ross?"

"Sir, I've blocked the seat next to you in first class, so that you can selectively give interviews on board as you wish. Once at Dulles, we'll hold a photo op and a short public interview in the terminal. Nothing specific, you know, just a chance to get the cameras on you and mention your urgent dinner meeting with the president this evening."

"You've handled this accident thing nicely, Ross. I like your plan. We can get a lot of mileage out of this fiasco if we manage the press correctly."

"Thank you, sir," answered Ross, relieved.

"Give some consideration to how you want to seat the press. You know who's given us good press. Put them in business class and send the rest of the assholes to coach."

Ross smiled at the secretary's vindictive humor. He knew who he'd put in coach, if the tables were turned. "I've requested a seating chart just for that. Now, if you'll excuse me, sir, I'd like to attend to some remaining details."

Looking at his watch, Halston said, "Go right ahead, Ross. I'll be ready to leave the hotel at eleven forty-five."

"That'll work out just right, sir. I'll have your bags picked up around eleven thirty, if that's acceptable with you."

"Fine! Fine, Ross. I'll be ready."

Walking from the dining room, Ross noticed a well-dressed businessman chatting with an associate at an adjoining table. Had they overheard his conversation with Riggs? The secretary had a bad habit of speaking too loudly. The man's face looked familiar, but Ross couldn't place it. Too many other loose ends to worry about right now, he thought. Stepping into the brass-trimmed elevator, Ross decided the man must be associated with one of the many oil interests Riggs had courted.

*　*　*

Startled by the ring of the bedside phone, Wes fumbled about the night table for the receiver as the deafening noise continued. He tried to recall if the horrible dream he just had was real. Was he too late? Had terrorists already kidnapped Caroline?

Reality set in as he heard the Geneva operations clerk begin his briefing with a personal apology about Mark's death. The inbound aircraft was on schedule. The outbound flight, 899, might be delayed several minutes to accommodate Secretary of State, Riggs Halston, and his entourage. The State Department, in an effort to return him to Washington for an important meeting with the president, had booked all the remaining seats on Flight 899. The secretary of state's aircraft had sustained major damage from a fuel truck and would require an engine change. The computer-generated flight plan called for the use of Track Bravo at flight level 390. The time en route would be eight hours, fifty-five minutes. Concluding his briefing, the clerk added that Mark Hoffman's body had been released for shipment to Washington and would be loaded aboard the aircraft.

Hanging up, Wes lay back on the bed, his head resting on the doubled-up pillow. It was true. He hadn't dreamed the nightmare. It was all real, just as it had seemed in his dreams. Caroline was missing and Mark was dead.

Halston's presence on board was a new twist. Stepping into the shower, Wes wondered who had screwed up the secretary's jet. Was it an accident, or could it have been staged? Rinsing the shampoo from his hair, Wes questioned whether Halston being aboard his flight might have something to do with Caroline's kidnapping. Was he to be the object of a hostage situation? The idea had merit. It might explain why Halston had turned up on his flight. But why the diversion? That part didn't make any sense. If Halston was going to be taken hostage, what difference would landing at National make? Any hostage scenario could be accomplished just as easily at Dulles. Why National Airport?

The crew was in the lobby drinking coffee, munching croissants, and discussing Mark's death as Wes stepped from the tiny elevator, his wheelie and kit bag in tow. Sybil was talking with Cynthia about her missing passport and company ID when Wes walked up.

"Sybil, did operations tell you that the secretary of state will be on our flight today?"

"No, they didn't. You mean to tell me Halston is actually going to humble himself to fly with us?"

"Apparently, he has no choice. A fuel truck ran into one of his jet's engines."

"Serves the bastard right," replied Sybil, with contempt.

"I trust you'll be able to control your strong passion for him and manage the cabin with your usual finesse." Sybil smiled, knowing Wes understood her disdain for the man.

The ride to the airport was unusually quiet, with most of the crew pondering Mark's death. Leigh, beside Wes, was silent, afraid of drawing attention to their affair and concerned about him.

Wes was preoccupied, as well, but not for the same reason. His mind was on Caroline. Looming before him was the question of whether to contact the authorities for help. If he involved them now, he would be yanked off the flight for certain. How could they let him continue the trip? The flight would have to be delayed for hours or canceled. What then? Would Caroline be found before it was too late? Or would the Feds even try? In his heart Wes knew he couldn't trust Caroline's life to the government. He had to go it alone.

5

VIPs

Kyle's flight from Paris had been short, with few distractions. Arriving at operations thirty minutes earlier, he'd completed the navigation plotting chart and was reviewing the weather document when Wes and Chad entered the flight planning office. He looked up from the paperwork.

"Captain Beacham? I'm Kyle Anton, your relief pilot." Wes extended his hand to the young man with dark eyes. "How was your flight down from Paris?", Wes asked. "Rough, but fast," Kyle answered. Chad followed. "Chad Sanderlin." Anton nodded as the two first officers shook hands.

"I've done most of the paperwork. It's on the counter. I got here early," he added.

Wes looked over his work. Then he asked Chad to verify Kyle's plotting of the oceanic waypoints, a ritual no careful captain would leave to chance. Chad read off the coordinates as Wes checked them against the track crossing message and computer flight plan. Wes then checked the route, the rim alternates, and the destination weather before calculating the necessary fuel reserves.

Halston's entourage had increased the payload considerably. Wes chose to top off the fuel tanks. It would give him more flexibility in dealing with the diversion. He'd just finished signing the amended flight release when the station manager walked in.

Roman Leightner had run the Geneva station for years and knew practically everyone holding power in Geneva. The fact that Mark's

body had been released in time for today's flight home was solely because of Roman's influence with the Swiss authorities. A stocky man
given to rich food, Leightner was admired by management and flight
crews alike.

"Captain Beacham, I've just come from a short meeting with the
secretary's special assistant, Ross Straton. I have assured him that we
will make every effort to seat his entire entourage in first and business
class. Claudia, my gate agent, is reworking the flight seating arrangements as we speak."
  "When do you plan to board the secretary?"
  "Mr. Straton will advise me as soon as he is sure of the secretary's
wishes." It figures, thought Wes.
  "Captain, please give Mr. Hoffman's family our most sincere condolences. We are very sad that such a misfortune has occurred here in
Geneva. It is most regrettable."
  "Thank you, Roman. I'll personally express your regrets."

  With bags in tow, Wes, Chad and Kyle passed through crew security and stepped into the waiting flight line van for the short trip down
to hardstand seventeen. As the van approached the 767, Wes saw that
the forward and aft cargo doors were open. He could see the containers
in position. He wondered which one held Mark's body. The whole damn
trip seemed so strange. It was like being over Hanoi again with the
whole world literally coming apart right before your eyes, yet you could
do nothing to stop it. Pausing at the bottom of the boarding steps, Wes
stared at the 767 as if knowing that once he was aboard, Caroline's
destiny would be sealed.
  Stowing his luggage, Wes switched on the three inertial navigation systems and picked up the logbook to check the aircraft status
before settling into his seat. Rachel Meyers stepped into the cockpit
with three crew snacks and set them on the center pedestal and left.
  He was nearly finished with his cockpit preflight when something
outside caught his eye. Looking down from his left side panel window,
Wes saw two men wearing dark suits and glasses walk from the boarding door toward the aircraft. His eyes were riveted on them. He was
certain they were the same Arabs he'd taken the boat ride with last
night. His pulse quickened. He watched them step onto the boarding
stairs together. His eyes focused on a bag hanging from the shorter

man's shoulder. As they drew closer, Wes saw that the pouch was the one the portable phone was carried in last night.

Elated to have the two kidnappers on his turf, Wes imagined the possibilities for securing Caroline's safety. Once they were airborne, he could confront them.

"Captain, look who's coming." Chad spied Riggs Halston strutting up the boarding steps. Wes turned his attention to the entourage. He hardly had time to compose his welcome before Halston appeared in the cockpit doorway.

"Good morning, gentleman. Sorry to have to commandeer your flight on such short notice, but I'm having dinner with the president tonight. He's expecting me to brief him on the results of my Geneva meeting with our Western allies." Wes turned to offer his welcome, but Halston continued. "How long is it going to take to get me to D.C.? Eight to nine hours I suppose, judging by my usual crossings."

"Eight hours and fifty-five minutes," Chad replied.

"Fine. That's fine; just get me there in one piece. Some incompetent fueler drove his truck into the side of one of my engines early this morning and I don't have time to sit here while General Hartwell's boys try to find a new engine. Have a good flight and call if I can do anything for you."

Wes sat back down, shaking his head in disbelief. What an asshole. Sybil was right. Halston was everything she'd said — a braggart, pompous, arrogant, self-centered, the list was endless. You didn't have to be a flaming liberal to find a reason to dislike him.

With Halston's cockpit visit over, Wes quickly returned his attention to the two men he'd recognized boarding the aircraft and the portable phone they had with them. His only chance of finding Caroline depended on deciphering the preset numbers in that phone. Wes tried to decide whether the system required a dial tone to initiate the dial sequence. If so, he would have to copy all of the preset numbers before leaving the coverage area. But could that be done without drawing the kidnappers' attention?

Seconds ticked by as Wes thought through what had to be done. Sybil could retrieve the phone pack from the two men unnoticed. As flight service manager, she had reason enough to be moving about the cabin. And, if detected, she could diffuse the situation without causing much disturbance. But could he really ask her to take on such a task without explaining why? He didn't have a choice. Sooner or later, he was going to have to involve the crew.

Easing the Geneva takeoff data worksheet out from under the stack of flight papers on the center pedestal, Wes shoved it inside his flight kit bag.

"Chad, have you got the takeoff data worksheet? I can't seem to find it here," he said, shuffling through the papers. "No," answered Chad, looking up from the flight computer keypad. He was sure he had put the form in the flight documentation envelope at operations. "Are you sure? They're not in the pile here," said Wes. Thumbing through the pile, Chad said, "I'm sure I put it in the envelope, but I'll be damned if I can find it. What do you want me to do?"

"Ordinarily, it wouldn't matter to me to go without it. The Viking Departure calls for a maximum thrust takeoff anyway. But with Halston on board, there's no telling who will rummage through the flight package. Would you mind going back to operations and getting another one?"

Chad looked irritated. He was convinced the sheet was somewhere right under their noses. "Suppose I give operations a call and ask them to run one out to us?" Chad asked.

"No, you'd better go. They'd likely send the wrong one out and delay us. Then we'd be in a sweat to make our slot time."

"Aye, sir!" snapped Chad. "On the way out, ask Kyle to check with the loaders to see how much more time they will need. Then ask Sybil to come to the cockpit."

"Will do," muttered Chad, climbing out of his seat.

Wes watched Chad go down the boarding stairs with Kyle in tow. The two co-pilots stood at the bottom of the steps talking to the ground service supervisor. A moment later, he saw the supervisor raise the radio and call dispatch. It would take at least ten minutes for Chad to make it to ops and back. Kyle's preflight would take about that long if he did it correctly. Where was Sybil? Had Chad forgotten to give her the message? Wes was anxious. Using the time, he mentally rehearsed what he would say to her.

"You wanted to see me, Wes?" Sybil called.

"Yes, but lock the cockpit door first. I need your help."

Bewildered, Sybil eased the door shut, pressing the cylinder into the handle as it closed. Turning toward Wes, she saw a serious expression blanket his face. Something was wrong. Wes was not one to over-react.

"Sybil, I don't have time to fill you in on the details, but I need your help badly right now."

"Whatever, Wes. You know I'll help," she whispered, wanting to comfort the man who had once saved her life.

"My daughter, Caroline, was kidnapped in D.C. yesterday and is being held hostage."

"Caroline's been kidnapped. Oh my God! Why, Wes? Who would do such a thing? It doesn't make any sense."

"Sybil, a group has taken her to force me to do something for them. That's all I can say right now. Her life depends on my not speaking to anyone about this."

"How can I help?"

"Two members of the group that kidnapped her have just boarded and are probably seated in business or first class. They're both Arabs in dark suits and sunglasses. The shorter one is carrying a portable telephone pack, which...."

Sybil interrupted. "I know the two men you're talking about. They're in first class, row two, seats one and two."

Wes continued, "The portable telephone contains preset memorized numbers. They used one of those to contact my daughter last night. Then they had me speak with Caroline to be sure I knew they had kidnapped her."

"You were with them last night?"

"Yes."

Suddenly Sybil understood the reason for Wes's strange behavior and the dazed look on his face when he finally showed up at the crew briefing in her room.

"Sybil, I need a tape of all of the preset numbers loaded in the phone before takeoff. Will you help me?"

"Yes, but how, Wes? I'm not sure I can get to it."

Wes thought for a second, wanting to choose his words carefully. He told Sybil his plan.

Sybil's pulse quickened as she thought of the task she'd agreed to. She couldn't let Wes down. He'd been there for her when it had counted. How could she say no?

"I'll do it, Wes, but where am I going to get a recorder?"

"Rachel's got a small pocket one. Remember yesterday, she was bitching about always getting hassled by security?"

"Yes, she does have one with her, doesn't she?" Sybil answered, already thinking about where Rachel's handbag was stowed.

A loud knock on the cockpit door signaled the end of their conversation. Sybil stood up and put her hand on his broad shoulder. Wes looked up at her. The anguish in his eyes revealed his pain. "I'm sorry to have to ask you to do this for me, but it's my daughter."

The second knock was louder, the sound of impatience. "I know. Don't worry, I'll find a way." Wes took her hand for a moment. Caroline's life had now become Sybil's burden too. Wes didn't like the thought of it, but there was no other way.

Opening the door, Sybil found Kyle holding a pillow and blanket. Being locked out of the cockpit seemed to have irritated him. He stepped aside as she passed through the narrow doorway.

"Sorry about the door, Kyle. It was rude of us," said Wes, glancing out the window. "We've tried to keep our affair quiet, but sometimes it's hard."

"I'm sorry to have interrupted," Kyle said as he bent over and opened his flight kit bag that was on the cockpit chair behind Wes. "I didn't realize you guys were that close."

"I hope we weren't too obvious," Wes added. "I don't think so," said Kyle, spinning the combination locking cylinders. "I wouldn't have known if you hadn't told me."

Satisfied that Kyle wasn't aware of the real reason for his and Sybil's conversation, Wes picked up the flight plan and began loading the oceanic waypoints. "I'll load those for you," Kyle said. "Thanks. That will help speed things up," Wes said, dropping the three pages of flight data on the center pedestal.

Chad broke the silence as he bounded into the cockpit and tossed the new takeoff data sheet onto the pedestal. "Kyle, swap seats with me. I'll finish loading the computer if you'll copy the ATIS (Automatic Terminal Information System) and take care of this friggin' takeoff sheet," puffed Chad. "You'd think the company would get with the program and use a flip chart for the takeoff settings like everybody else, instead of making us fill out this useless bullshit." Wes shook his head but said nothing. Chad had every reason to be pissed.

*   *   *

Saeed Keshef parked his Mercedes and hurried across the Quai Woodrow Wilson. Stopping briefly at a tobacco shop for cigarettes, he walked the rest of the way to his office. Straightening the knot of his silk tie, he stepped from the elevator. His linen suit hung loosely on his wiry frame. He stopped at the door marked "Fundamentalist Coalition." The letters were stenciled in gold leaf. Opening the door, Saeed walked into the reception room to find Andrea Zahar in the midst of making several computer entries.

"Is Hassan here?" he asked.

"He's in the back office. Shall I tell him you're here?"

"No, I'll go see him," Keshef said, removing his coat.

Andrea stood up and took the coat and hung it in the adjoining closet. Saeed tore open the pack of cigarettes as he admired Andrea's sensuous figure. It was still hard for him to understand why she'd chosen to become a financial analyst and investment broker. A woman of her beauty could easily have enjoyed the unlimited wealth of an Arabian oil minister without having to raise a hand to work.

Trained in economics at Northwestern, Andrea had graduated third in her class before entering Wharton for her MBA. Fluent in French, English, Russian, and Arabic, she'd had no trouble securing a position as an investment portfolio manager with one of Geneva's major banks. Her immediate success at making some shrewd investments for the Iranian government had not gone unnoticed. Upon learning of her hatred of the Israelis, the Iranian Minister of Finance had recommended that Keshef consider her for a position with the FC. Knowing she'd have the chance to avenge the deaths of her two brothers gunned down during an Israeli ambush in the Gaza Strip, Andrea had resigned from the bank immediately and accepted Saeed's offer. Doubling as a receptionist and secretary for the organization had provided excellent cover for her real job.

Keshef was glad Andrea had taken the job. Her sense of financial timing had been incredible. In fewer than six months, she'd posted a 57 percent return on the FC's investments. Her talent had become a vital part of the coalition's mission, since its operations required large funding.

"How is our investment funding operation progressing?"

"Quite well," Andrea explained. "I've loaded the last of the buy orders into the computer. I only need your authorization to execute them."

"We should know by thirteen hundred," Keshef replied. "I only need to know the flight is airborne and on its way to Washington," he added, heading for Hassan's office.

Hassan Khalil was busy checking the video monitor as Saeed satisfied the last of three security access systems before opening the door. Keeping track of the events over the last twenty-four hours had occupied all of the Palestinian's attention. He barely noticed Saeed's intrusion, concentrating instead on the many checklist items still pending. Seeing a shadow reflected on one of the monitors, Hassan looked up at Keshef.

"And is everything going as planned, my brother?"

"Yes, although it appeared for a short while that we were going to have a problem with the loading. But Mocmoud got the TIA cargo foreman, Marcel, to help him complete the transfer."

"It does not surprise me that he would help Mocmoud. He knows we have his wife," Saeed replied. "Speaking of that, how is the beautiful, young Renee doing?"

Hassan leaned back into his chair, stretching his aching back and said, "She spent most of the night crying. I don't think she got much sleep. Our people reported that she will not eat."

"In time, she will appreciate food. Though she doesn't know it, she is lucky her life is being spared. Were it left to me, she would go the way of the others."

Relieved that the young mother's life would be spared, Hassan wondered whether Renee's new life as the wife of a rich and savage sheik was worth the price.

"Yes, she is very lucky," he said. "But Marcel, how will he accept the loss?"

Staring into Hassan's eyes, Keshef answered, "He will probably kill himself once it becomes clear that his Renee will not be returned. He cannot go to the authorities because of what he has done. If he does, he will be arrested once they learn of his assistance to us. He has no choice but to grieve and wait for us to contact him."

"Were there any difficulties with that biker?" Keshef added.

Hassan shook his head. He didn't approve of the killing of these innocent people — the pilot and now the biker. He felt all along that they could have just been detained until the threat of their exposure had passed. It had been Saeed who'd insisted there be no witnesses. It was he who had promised the member countries that as a condition of their support. He'd made an exception of Renee, but Hassan knew Saeed would not consent to another. The rest would be killed.

"Was all the money recovered?" Saeed asked.

"Yes, even the down payment. He had that on him, too."

Saeed smiled at the idea of having recovered the money. Andrea would double it in no time, he thought. "And the truck, did they have any problems at the border?"

"The truck is in Fernay being disposed of. Alonzo said the hit was easy. There were no witnesses, except for our people."

Hassan let the telephone ring twice before answering it. He was expecting the report. Saeed waited as he took the call. Minutes later he hung up. "That was Kamil. Halston's assistant, Ross Straton, has informed the secretary of the damage to his jet and of plans to return him to Washington aboard TIA. He was able to hear most of their conversation. Straton actually convinced Halston the change would enhance his political image."

Keshef nodded. Having Halston on board would make a great difference in how the plan would be executed. He'd worried about whether this part would fall into place as he'd envisioned. Halston's presence would greatly enhance the threat's initial impact. The entire Arab world would rejoice at seeing Riggs inform his president of the coalition's demands. Saeed smiled.

Keshef, the son of an Iranian oil minister, had been educated at Oxford. By all accounts, he was being groomed to take over his father's role in the government, but Saeed had other plans. While a student, he developed an intense desire to change the way the world viewed the Middle East. Filled with resentment over the way his British classmates mocked him and his Arab brothers, Saeed had decided long ago the day would come when he would reckon with those who had slandered his people.

Intrigued with violence as an appropriate political weapon, Keshef joined various terrorist groups as soon as he left school. Serving as a planner and recruiter had afforded him the chance to observe the few successes and the many dismal failures of such plots.

He'd believed from the start that any meaningful terrorist response had to be structured in the same way the Western nations organized their intelligence agencies. An incessant reader, he had subscribed to practically every book, magazine, and journal devoted to power politics and intelligence. Though not in the military, Saeed had studied all of the great treatises on guerilla warfare and incorporated many of their strategies in his earlier campaigns.

Never one to carry out the action himself, Keshef planned and supervised terrorist plots from within the sponsoring country. His ability to manage such operations successfully without being implicated was remarkable.

Articulate, Keshef was recognized in the Western world as a moderate Arab advocating cooperation with the West in cultural and economic matters. Yet, nothing was further from the truth. Saeed Keshef was an experienced master of deceit.

Gazing about the control center room, Saeed reflected on the time and effort it had taken for the FC to reach it's current level of sophistication. The formation had been an uphill battle from the beginning. At times, only intense, undying hatred of Israel and her allies had bound the interested parties.

Iran and Iraq, both mortal enemies, had grave misgivings about the organization from its inception. Neither trusted the other. Both were jealous of the other's power and influence in sponsoring the new terrorist order. Qadhafi, seeking revenge against the United States for bombing his country more than for his hatred of Israel, had agreed to participate first, offering his country as a haven for those planning the attack.

PLO and Lebanese splinter terrorist groups had objected strenuously. They worried most about the erosion of conventional terrorist operations and the loss of funding and support such a change would surely bring about.

Initially, no one had been excited about the coalition. Trusting the FC with the highly secret responsibility of planning and coordinating global terrorist operations for the fundamentalists had required an unusual degree of unity and purpose among the covert leaders of the participants. That the state sponsors had finally agreed to such a coalition had surprised many within the Arab underground, including Saeed.

The fact that most recent terrorist actions had experienced marginal success or even outright failure had no doubt caused the Arab leaders to rethink how best to impose terrorism on the West. Still the most potent form of intimidation of the capitalist countries, it extracted the most anguish for the money invested.

Keshef recalled arguing successfully for transferring sponsorship of terrorism to the coalition. Explaining that the fundamentalists would be free to adopt seemingly fewer confrontational policies, he maintained they could win concessions from the Western powers not otherwise obtainable.

Organizational matters had taken the longest to resolve, Keshef remembered. Structuring the FC's cover to fit that of an Arab cultural league functioning in the open was foreign to the leaders of the earlier terrorist groups. Equally unconvincing was the decision to situate its headquarters in Geneva. Agreeing to rely on Western technology and business know-how had presented other problems to the FC's formation during its early stages.

Persuading fundamentalist leaders to use Western methods to mask their real objectives and immobilize America's ability to support Israel had been the most difficult task for the FC's leadership. Even now, Saeed wondered if the coalition would hold. Since being chosen director of covert operations of the FC more than two years ago, he had spent every moment planning for today's event. His small team of Western-educated strategists and planners had worked tirelessly ensuring that every facet of Operation Shalom would occur exactly as planned. Hours of research and thought had gone into the design of the plan. His multi-objective scenario would bring America to its knees, and with it, all support for Israel.

For once, the fundamentalist demands would be heeded by the West. Previous efforts at trying to deter American aggression into Middle East internal affairs would pale in comparison to the attack about to take place. Nothing had been left to chance, Keshef thought.

Espousing the fundamentalist view, Keshef had engaged scholars and Western businessman, alike. Able to articulate its point of view in a non-threatening manner, he'd developed strong rapport with both Arab and Western leaders. Quietly, but efficiently, he and his small staff had worked hard to gain the confidence and respect of most European governments. As a well-educated moderate cultural organization, the coalition was highly successful at promoting harmony and understanding of the fundamentalist world. The organization's charter had already received recognition within the U.N., although little was actually known of its origin or its funding. Nevertheless, it was accepted as the legitimate voice of moderate fundamentalist thought.

Saeed looked proudly upon what he had helped to create, but more importantly, with an eye to how he would ultimately stand before his

God and his fellow Muslims. He had no fear of dying and demanded the same oath of everyone chosen to serve the FC. On this point, there was no compromise.

Realizing he had been daydreaming, Keshef asked, "How are our brothers in Washington, Hassan?"

"Very good. They say the captain's daughter is no problem and that she sleeps much of the day. They say also that the communications network is in place and that all the mobile units have tested their equipment and are awaiting the flight's arrival," Hassan answered.

"And do they know of the president's exact schedule?"

"Yes. They've confirmed his plans through our intelligence sources there."

Saeed was pleased at the responses. He expected that from his agents-in-the-field, as he called them. He'd personally approved each man for his loyalty to the FC as well as his political or technical prowess. Saeed knew he had chosen well.

"Have they received the declaration you transmitted earlier?" Keshef asked.

"Yes. It's ready for release to the media, if required."

Hassan's knowledge of Washington had been instrumental in establishing safe houses for FC operatives there. With houses in Chevy Chase, Edgewater, Woodbridge, and Chantilly, the operatives could provide total coverage of the district from its periphery if Crystal City control were compromised.

It was Hassan Kahlil who had negotiated and later drafted the FC's Declaration of Demands. Though the exact phraseology had been changed several times, its original content remained essentially intact.

It also had been his idea to form the small courier company, ACE, to provide a front to keep the FBI and CIA from becoming suspicious. ASAP Courier Express, founded as a legitimate Washington courier service, used motorbikes for delivery and was exactly what would be needed to move about the city quickly once chaos set in.

Establishing and coordinating the FC's Washington Council, as it had come to be known, had required much of Hassan's time. Composed of four prosperous Arab business owners, each representing one of the sponsoring factions, the council would collectively decide the direction of the attack. It was to this group that all major decisions would be directed once Operation Shalom reached the United States.

Life for the young Iraqi had not turned out as Hassan had hoped. As a young student at Georgetown, he'd dreamed of becoming a diplomat living in Washington. Since first traveling to the States with his father, a successful Iraqi businessman, he'd wanted to live in America. He liked the country's progressive customs.

War in the Gulf changed all that. His father's profitable rug business, dependent on trade with the West, soured quickly as American sentiment turned against him and his country. With the collapse of Baghdad, he saw his dreams shattered.

He remembered well the day he had been told his enrollment at the prestigious university was in jeopardy, given the turn of world events. In retrospect, he knew the school had done him a favor. With the tide of American opinion hostile toward all Iraqis in the aftermath of his country's attack on Kuwait, he had no choice but to leave.

With his family's fortune in ruins and his educational plans laid to waste, a bitter Hassan gave up his dreams of becoming a diplomat. Taking a position as a reporter and political correspondent in Lebanon, he became a journalist for a Middle East newspaper.

Living in Beirut enabled him to establish his credentials as an authoritative source of news from Lebanon. It also provided him a forum for venting his anger at the West for abandoning his countrymen. His strongly worded protests soon gained him the recognition he so desperately wanted. With access to all Palestinian movements eager to have their story told, he gained the support of their leaders and was encouraged to take an active role in their organizations.

Not long afterward, he quietly accepted the invitation of one such group and began to devote more of his time to its struggle. Within a year, he was a covert leader within the PLO.

"And what about our assault team?" Saeed asked.

"Reza, Mohammed and the others have just boarded."

"And the weapon?"

"Mocmoud passed the automatic minutes ago."

"Excellent!"

"And have we heard from the sponsors?"

"Nothing in the last forty-eight hours," answered Hassan.

Keshef was glad. He had insisted calls be placed only if they were critical to the mission. The fact that none had been received was a good sign. The mission would proceed as planned.

Saeed worried about that more than he cared to admit. He didn't trust Baghdad. Saddam was a loose cannon, even more so than Qadhafi had been in his earlier years. Nor did he care much for the field personnel Iraq had volunteered for the aircraft assault. They were too savage to suit him. Still, they were knowledgeable and highly disciplined for the type of assignment he'd given them.

Anxious to see TIA 899 airborne, Saeed began to pace. Until then, he and Hassan would simply have to wait for reports from the field. "This will be the start of a new day for all Arabs," Saeed said.

Hassan, tired from the hours he'd spent in the command center, nodded his agreement before reviewing, once more, the next phase of Operation Shalom.

6

WESTBOUND

Sybil left the cockpit not knowing how she was going to get the telephone numbers Wes needed. She was also honestly afraid of getting caught. The thought of Caroline's life hanging in the balance made it all the more difficult as she pondered what to do. Getting Rachel's tape recorder would be the easy part.

From the forward galley, Sybil saw that Rachel was in the aisle, handing out magazines and newspapers. Now was her chance. Opening the galley closet door quickly, Sybil grabbed Rachel's handbag and opened it. The recorder was the first thing she saw. Slipping it into her smock pocket, she was careful not to jerk the coiled earphone wire apart from it. After zipping the handbag shut, she eased her head from the closet. Then it happened. Her pocket snagged a passenger's hang-up bag hook, dumping the tape recorder on the cabin floor. Sybil froze as she watched the back of the recorder pop open, releasing the four batteries.

"What's happened, Sybil?" It was Rachel. Horrified, Sybil bent down and grabbed the recorder and the battery cover. She didn't know what to say. Hurriedly, she replaced the battery cover on the recorder, making sure to keep the front of the machine face-down. Rachel would surely recognize her recorder if she saw the tape window.

"Nothing serious," Sybil answered, hoping Rachel wouldn't notice the recorder.

"That's just like the one I have. When did you get one?"

"Several weeks ago. I just hadn't bothered to bring it along until this trip," Sybil said, searching for the batteries.

"They're really great, don't you think? I get so tired of watching CNN on layovers. The music helps me unwind," Rachel said, dropping the remaining newspapers on the bar cart.

"Yes, I feel the same way," Sybil replied, hoping Rachel would leave the area. But it was not to be.

Retrieving two of the batteries, Sybil's heart stopped as she saw Rachel open the closet door and reach for her handbag. Oh shit. How am I going to explain this? thought Sybil, as she anxiously watched Rachel withdraw from the closet.

"Thank goodness they boarded us with extra headsets. That pompous ass, Halston, has already started his shit. He doesn't like the way his earphones fit," Rachel grumbled.

Relieved she'd not been discovered, Sybil broke out laughing as Rachel spun around and stomped back down the aisle, her rosy cheeks aflame with contempt for her VIP passenger. Thank God for small favors, thought Sybil as she looked about the galley floor for the other two batteries. They were nowhere in sight. She would borrow two from Cynthia's small flashlight. It also used AA batteries. She hoped Cynthia still had it with her. If so, it would be about the only thing she hadn't had stolen during the layover.

Walking to the main entrance doorway, Sybil glanced down the left aisle. She could see Cynthia helping a passenger in the middle of business class. Walking down the aisle, Sybil glanced at the two kidnappers. The shorter one next to the window had the telephone pack beside him. Neither paid her any attention. Both seemed more interested in the other passengers. Sybil wondered if they were armed. She hadn't thought to ask Wes.

"Cynthia, can I see you a minute?"

"Sure, just let me get Mrs. Tomlinson a pillow."

Sybil continued to the mid-galley. Frightened at the prospect of having to confront the two men, she found it increasingly difficult to hide her anxiety. Suppose they put up an argument? What if they demand to see Wes, or deplane? Afraid of the task ahead, Sybil clutched her hands as she watched Cynthia ease the pillow behind the young lady's head.

Come on, damn it. I don't have all morning, she said to herself as Cynthia worked her way toward the mid-galley.

"Cynthia, I need to borrow your flashlight."

"Why do you need a flashlight with all the daylight?"

"Just let me use the damn thing, will you!"

"Okay, okay, don't bite my head off. It's in my other purse, unless that's been stolen too," Cynthia said.

Realizing she'd annoyed her flying partner with her rude reply Sybil said, "I'm sorry. I'm just a bit uptight this morning, Cynthia. I've got a lot on my mind."

"Don't we all? I'm still trying to figure out how to handle customs when we get to Washington," Cynthia replied curtly.

Sybil didn't hear Cynthia's comment. She was already entering the left mid-lavatory, eager to find out if the tape recorder would work with Cynthia's two batteries. Locking the door, she quickly unscrewed the bottom of the flashlight and removed the two AA batteries. Taking the small recorder from her pocket, Sybil removed the battery access cover, inserted the batteries, and snapped the cover shut. Then she pressed the PLAY button, but nothing happened.

Were the batteries dead? Oh shit. Now what? Maybe she'd put them in backwards. Near panic, Sybil removed all the batteries from the flashlight and rearranged them in pairs to see that they worked. The batteries were good. This time she loaded them into the recorder carefully, checking their polarity as she snapped each into place.

Again, Sybil pressed the PLAY button. The tape capstan started to turn. Excited, she slipped on the stereo earphones and adjusted the volume. The sound was crystal clear, but the lyrics were strange. Sybil found Rachel's taste in music weird.

Examining the recorder further, Sybil saw it had two speeds. Remembering that memory dial tones occur in rapid succession, Sybil set the recorder on high speed. Wes could play the tape on low speed and have a better chance of figuring out the numbers.

Her confidence returning, Sybil rewound the tape and started to record. She whispered and then talked into the small microphone, trying to produce a variety of sounds to gauge the recorder's quality and sensitivity. Satisfied she had recorded enough, Sybil pressed the STOP button and rewound the tape. The tiny speaker sounded scratchy, but audible. The tapping and clicking sounds were more distinct. It would do.

Pressing the flush handle, Sybil paused for a few seconds, then left the toilet. Claudia Marston, the gate agent, was standing at the cockpit entrance talking to Kyle. Were they waiting to block out? Christ! How long was I in the lav? Rushing up the aisle, Sybil knew she had to get the telephone before pushback. Her pulse quickened as she passed the two Arabs.

Claudia stepped into the cockpit as Wes and Chad finished their responsive readings.

"Captain, we've finished boarding. You have two armed agents traveling with the secretary. Here's their paperwork. They're seated in four dash two and eleven dash three."

Jotting down the seat assignments on the slips, Wes made a mental note of where they were. "Thanks again, Claudia," he said. "Let me know as soon as you're ready to close the door. I'll give you 'schedule.' And I'd like a copy of the spill. With the secretary of state on board, it might come in handy."

"I'll get back to you in a minute," Claudia called out, scurrying out of the cockpit.

"Good morning, ladies and gentlemen. Welcome to Trans International Airways Flight 899. On behalf of ...." Wes plowed through what had become his canned welcome-aboard speech, filling in the specific details of the day's flight, though today his heart wasn't in it. Focused on Sybil, Wes wondered if she'd managed to retrieve the numbers.

"Here's the spill you'd asked for, Captain. We're ready to close you up if it's okay."

"Sure, Claudia. We may sit at the gate for a few more minutes, but you've got schedule," said Wes, struggling to sound cheerful.

"Thank you, Captain," the pretty agent replied. Then remembering Mark's death, she added, "All of us here at Geneva are very sorry about what happened to your co-pilot."

"That's very kind of you. I appreciate your concern. I guess those things just happen," Wes answered.

Waiting to hear the main entrance door close, Wes thought about Mark's accident again. How could he have been so careless? It still didn't make any sense. Wes flipped on the beacon light to signal the ground crew to check in on the ground interphone. It was time to get under way. He'd run out of time. Either Sybil had gotten the telephone numbers or she hadn't. If not, he'd get help from the two State Department agents once in flight.

"Chad, call for pushback. Let's get this show on the road."

For a moment, Sybil thought about walking off the aircraft straight to security and dumping the whole mess into their laps. Wes had no right to involve her in his problem, let alone all the passengers and crew. The idea that he would even ask her to do such a thing now provoked her. Then recalling the desperation in his voice, Sybil knew he would have never asked if there had been another way. Wes wasn't the type of guy to use people. He would have handled the situation himself if he could have, she decided. Besides, hadn't he been there for her in that dark hallway in Louisville twenty-five years ago when she'd needed help? How could she turn her back on him now? Sybil knew she couldn't and still live with herself. Because of Wes, she hadn't been raped.

Glancing through the entrance door viewing lenses, Sybil saw the mobile stairs being eased from the aircraft. She had to go for the phone now. There was no more time.

Beginning her walk down the short first class aisle, Sybil paused at row two and looked directly at the one seated against the window. The portable phone pack was partially covered by a pillow. Sybil was certain he was trying to hide it from her. His dark eyes darted about aimlessly as he tried to avoid direct contact with her. Sybil knew he would resist.

"Sir, may I stow your bag for you?"

He pretended not to hear her. His companion looked up, surprised by her comment. Sybil persisted.

"Sir, I must ask you to let me put your bag in the overhead compartment. Federal air regulations require that all carry-on luggage be stowed for takeoff and landing." Neither gentleman appeared to understand.

Remembering that Wes had said that both spoke fluent English, Sybil leaned over the lap of the taller man and pointed to the bag to make sure the one holding the bag understood what she was after. Their eyes met. Fear gripped Sybil as she fought to maintain her composure while staring into his hate-filled eyes.

"Sir, I must insist. You must give me the bag."

Without warning, he pushed her hand away from his seat and began scolding her in Arabic. None of the words made any sense, but his tone was unmistakable. The bastard was going to put up a scrap.

Rachel, hearing the outburst, joined Sybil. Her appearance concerned the two Arabs as they saw that everyone in the cabin had turned to look at the two flight attendants.

"Are you having a problem, Sybil?"

"Yes. The gentleman by the window is refusing to give me his bag and appears not to understand my request," Sybil replied firmly.

"Would you like me to notify the cockpit?" Rachel asked.

"Yes! I'll call Aaron on the interphone. He speaks Arabic. And tell Captain Beacham I want this gentleman removed from the flight. He's being uncooperative and is refusing to have a small carry-on put in the overhead bin."

Rachel nodded and headed for the cockpit. Sybil reached for the handset and rang the aft cabin as she continued to watch the two men converse in Arabic. Both seemed concerned that she had sent for the captain. It was obvious from their expressions that they understood English.

Rachel knocked at the cockpit door. Kyle opened the door from his bulkhead ACM seat. "Captain, we have a problem in first class," Rachel shouted.

"What's the problem?" Wes asked, worriedly.

"An Arab gentleman in the second row of first class is giving Sybil a hard time over a portable phone he won't let her stow. She's calling Aaron. He speaks Arabic."

Wes winced. He knew only too well what had taken place. Screw this up and Caroline will be dead before sundown.

"Chad, advise Ground we've got a small problem."

"If you want, I'll go back and jerk the phone pack off that turkey" said Chad, reaching for his mike.

"If that were an option, you'd have to fight me first for the chance," Wes replied, as he turned around. "Kyle, would you mind going back there and helping Sybil? Have Aaron explain the situation to the gentleman. If he still refuses, have Aaron tell him the captain will have no other choice but to return to the gate and have him removed from the aircraft."

Kyle nodded and left the cockpit with Rachel. Kyle joined Sybil in the forward galley alcove. Sybil was discussing the situation with Aaron. "Wes asked me to help you. What's the problem?" Kyle asked.

"That jerk in the second row of first class refuses to give me his carry-on to stow in the overhead bin. He's trying to act like he doesn't understand English," Sybil complained. Turning back to Aaron, Sybil continued. "You explain to him that his bag must be stowed in the overhead before we take off?"

"Which one has the bag?" Aaron asked.

"The shorter one seated against the window in row two along the left aisle."

"I'll speak with him."

"I'll go with you. He needs to understand that I'm in charge of the cabin, and if he can't accept that, he can get off this jet right now. I'd just as soon go back to the gate and have security remove him from the flight," Sybil snapped.

"Okay," Aaron said.

Sybil followed Aaron and Kyle down the left aisle to the two men and stood beside them as Aaron spoke. His tone sounded conciliatory as she watched them talk. Sybil was uncomfortable not knowing what was being said, but she was glad Aaron was there. Moments later, Aaron stepped aside and motioned for her to accept the phone bag.

"Mr. Jabarri asks that you accept his apologies for not understanding your instructions."

Sybil took the pack and opened the bin behind the second row. The bin was stuffed with carry-on luggage and several pillows and blankets. Reza looked over his shoulder at her as Sybil put his bag between the pillows and blankets.

"Please inform Mr. Jabarri that he also must stay in his seat until the captain turns off the 'Fasten Seat Belt' sign. You better show him the light, just to be sure he knows what I'm talking about," Sybil said.

Nodding, Aaron pointed out the sign.

"Thanks for the help. I don't have the slightest idea what you said to him, but whatever it was, it worked."

Managing a smile, Aaron said, "Come and get me if he causes any more trouble. It was just a problem of communication."

Kyle, satisfied that the issue had been resolved, quickly returned to the cockpit and reported the outcome. Wes was relieved to learn that Sybil had access to the phone pack. Time had run out. He couldn't delay the flight any longer. He'd have to settle for her making the tape during the climb-out. Even in a worst-case scenario, he could have the phone pack removed discreetly while in-flight and turned over to the FBI in Washington. You can only do what you can do, he reasoned.

"Chad, tell the tower we're ready."

"TOWER, TIA 899 IS READY FOR TAKEOFF."

"TIA 899, CLEARED FOR TAKEOFF."

Chad echoed the tower's command as Wes slowly "walked" the throttles up to full power and started his elapsed time clock.

The 767 quickly roared to life, propelled by the two powerful fan jet engines. Thirty seconds later, Chad called, "VEE ONE." Dropping his hand down behind the two throttles, Wes gripped them at the base of their shafts. They now had enough speed and acceleration to continue the flight on one engine, if necessary. Seconds later, Chad called "ROTATE," as Wes eased the 767's yoke aft while glancing at the attitude indicator. He continued the rotation until the nose reached twenty degrees above the horizon — the Viking Departure they called it. The Swiss countryside quickly disappeared under the nose as the big jet rose into the clear, noonday sky, gaining speed as it climbed. Wes was glad to be in the air again and on his own "turf."

Sybil saw the peaks of the Alps drop below the wing as the 767 started a right climbing turn. The sun's rays slipped toward the plane's rear. Estimating their altitude to be above the tops of the adjoining mountains and clear of most of the turbulence, she rang the other cabin attendant stations to begin work.

Knowing now would be her best chance, Sybil left her jumpseat and casually made her way down the left aisle, pausing at the overhead bin that contained the phone. The whine of the large engines drowned out the sound of the latch releasing as she opened the compartment door. Reaching inside, she slipped a blanket over the phone bag as she fetched a pillow. Removing them both, she closed the bin and walked toward the mid-galley.

Horror swept over her face as she gripped the lav door handle and saw the Occupied sign illuminated. She'd forgotten that Cynthia always used the lav before beginning anything else. She would have to use the right mid-lav. As Sybil turned around, a passenger in the first row of coach spoke.

"Miss, may I have that pillow and blanket you have? It's too cold in here," said the elderly man.

"I'm sorry, sir, but I've promised these to another passenger. I'll be back shortly with one for you," she said.

Sybil carefully held the pillow and blanket above the level of the seat backs to avoid snagging them as she marched through the coach section in search of a vacant lav. Luckily, Aaron and Frederick hadn't bothered making a pit stop before starting their setup. Reaching the left lav, she slipped inside unnoticed.

Latching the door, Sybil put the phone pack on the small counter and set aside the blanket and pillow. She opened the leather bag and removed the phone. It was a battery-powered telephone with memory storage and auto-dial features. Pressing the POWER button, Sybil experimented with the options, deciding how to start the auto-dial.

She recognized the first preset number as being in the Reston/Herndon, Virginia, area. It included area code 703. More surprising, the same number had been preset again, without its area code. Obviously the caller intended to originate calls from within the local area as well, she surmised. Scanning the other preset numbers, it became apparent the phone was programmed for use in the United States and not Europe, as Wes had suspected. Some of the numbers were preceded by D.C. and Maryland area codes. The last seven preset positions seemed to contain international numbers. Sybil recognized their first digits as being the access codes for several European countries.

Confident she understood how to operate the phone, Sybil activated the auto-dial and put the receiver to her ear, but only heard static. Suddenly, she realized why she hadn't heard a dial tone. The phone system was American. It was incompatible with those in Europe. It was hopeless. Frustrated, Sybil cursed at herself and at the phone system. She'd come too damned far to fail now.

Then a thought occurred to her. What if she were to reload the same number into a preset position? Would she hear the dial tone beeps that way? It was worth a try. Taking paper and pen from her pocket, Sybil jotted down the number appearing in the preset window for position 01. Then she touched the STORAGE key and punched in the number she'd copied. Touching the AUTO key, Sybil heard the familiar pitch changes occurring as the phone loaded the digits into memory.

The next several minutes were filled with furious activity as Sybil copied every preset number. Then she took the tape recorder from her pocket and rewound the tape. The hard part would come now, she imagined. Starting the recorder, Sybil held its microphone against the telephone handset speaker and punched in the first number she'd written on the paper.

Worried there might be distortion, she stopped the recorder and rewound the tape. Her heart sank as she strained to hear the tones she'd just recorded. She heard nothing. Had she done something wrong? Why didn't it work? She'd heard the sounds as she punched them into the machine. Maybe the volume control was turned down, she thought. Quickly, she thumbed the tiny wheel to the right and rewound the tape for a third time.

This time as she pressed PLAY, Sybil heard the dialing beeps loud and clear. She'd done it! Again, she placed the recorder microphone against the handset speaker and pressed RECORD. As the tape began to move, she started reloading the numbers into the phone. Five minutes later, she'd finished reloading the last of the thirty preset numbers. Rewinding the tape, she sampled the recording she'd made by alternating the PLAY and FAST-FORWARD keys. It was all there.

Closing the phone bag, Sybil slipped the recorder back into her pocket. Then she draped the blanket over the bag as before and set it on the pillow. Next she pressed the lav flush button, paused a few seconds and exited as the air-driven toilet erupted with the sound of suction. Aaron met her outside the door.

"There you are! Have you been in the lav all this time? Rachel has been looking everywhere for you. Her favorite passenger, the secretary, is already giving her fits."

"Yes, I have, and that's the last time you'll find me drinking that awful hotel coffee! My stomach's been turning flips for the last two hours," she said, trying to appear in pain.

"Hope you feel better soon. We're going to need your help," Aaron added, sarcastically.

Sybil grimaced at his snide remark. "Don't worry, I'll make it!" she snapped, eager to return the phone.

As she approached the mid-galley, the elderly man to whom she'd promised a pillow and blanket hollered at her.

"Miss, where's the pillow and blanket you promised me fifteen minutes ago? I'm about to freeze, and the other stewardess says no more are available!"

At a loss for words, Sybil froze. She couldn't deny him any longer, especially since he knew the truth.

"Miss, I demand that you give me those you have, now!"

The anger in his voice irritated Sybil, as she struggled to find a plausible response. "Sir, I'm certain you wouldn't want these. A fellow passenger just threw up on them!"

Humbled by her reply and embarrassed by his outburst, he sat back down. Sybil flashed a curt look in his direction and continued up the aisle toward first class.

Reaching the first class partition, she noticed that Mr. Jabarri was not in his seat. As she opened the bin, he stepped from the forward galley and walked toward his seat. Numb from her earlier confrontation, Sybil offered him a smile as she shoved the pillow and the covered phone bag back into the compartment. Jabarri glared at her as she closed and latched the bin.

Though she knew nothing of the man, Sybil loathed him. The thought of his being involved in kidnapping Caroline repulsed her. She waited for him to be seated, then continued to the cockpit, eager to give Wes the tape.

* * *

As TIA 899 disappeared into the midday sun, Yuari Shevinsky glanced at his watch before walking to the staircase. A stranger standing at the far corner of the observation deck noted the time of liftoff as well and withdrew a small pocket phone from his jacket. He dialed the FC.

"Our emissaries departed at 1315 hours," the stranger said.
"Thank you for seeing them off," Hassan replied.

Leaving the observation deck, Shevinsky walked briskly down the small staircase and strolled through the busy Swiss terminal toward the short-term parking lot. A warm breeze from the West met his weatherbeaten face as he unlocked the door of a BMW. The drive downtown would take 20 minutes.

Eager to close the transaction, Shevinsky eased the Beamer into a small parking spot across from the Middle East Bank of Commerce and switched off the ignition. With the flight airborne, he needed only to verify the final deposit to their numbered account, effect three electronic funds transfers and make a phone call to his comrade, Andrei.

Quickly making his way across the busy street, he entered the bank shortly after 1345 hours. Following Mr. Eisenstat's explicit instructions, he walked straight to the teller manning the window nearest the bank's entrance.

Yuari informed the young man of his wish to verify a recent deposit and provided him the account number and password. To his relief, Yuari learned the final payment had been made minutes earlier. After receiving a hard copy of the transaction, he made the wire transfers and left the bank, fearful of being discovered by the KGB.

Mr. Eisenstat, the bank manager, expecting Yuari's visit, watched the man he knew as Vladamir disappear through the brass entrance doors before taking the small elevator up to his fourth floor office. There, he accessed the Vladamir Napolovitch account. The computer showed a balance of 144,000,000 Swiss francs with three wire transfers of 48,000,000 francs each pending. Eisenstat erased the three pending transfers and re-entered a new wire transfer of 144,000,000 Swiss francs, returning the funds, electronically to the previous account. Deleting the Napolovitch account from the computer, he noted ENTERED IN ERROR to the empty file. After verifying his entries, he placed a local call.

"Hassan."

"Sir, our audit shows the Athens account is balanced."

"That is good news. We were hopeful you would be successful at finding the error," Hassan said. "Thank you for advising me."

Hassan knew from the message that Eisenstat had returned the funds to the FC's account.

After logging the call, Hassan checked the surveillance notes. Yuari was holding a reservation on the fifteen hundred hour Swissair flight. Using the portable transceiver, he placed a call to a car at Cointrin Airport. "Your flight is approved."

Hassan put the transceiver back into its cradle as he punched the reception desk intercom button. Andrea answered.

"You may enter the remaining buys now," he said.

"I'll transmit them immediately," she replied.

Yuari wasted no time returning to the airport. He parked the leased BMW in long-term parking, wiping clean all surfaces he had touched.

Recalling what Viktor, his other comrade, had said, he put the keys under the floor mat and locked the car before heading for the terminal.

With his coded call to Andrei in Athens complete, Yuari stepped from the phone booth, pleased that the final transaction had gone so smoothly. He began to think of the chess match he would have with his two comrades in Athens. They would battle to a final checkmate before parting for their new lives.

7

LONGFELLOW RADIO

The morning sun shone through the tightly closed blinds as Caroline pulled herself up to a sitting position and began rubbing her blood-shot eyes with her left hand. She was still cuffed to the iron bed. Her wrists ached from the cuffs chaffing her flesh. Every time she moved, they cut deeper. Maneuvering her left wrist into the sun's rays, she struggled to read the time on the small face of her gold watch. Caroline could barely make out the position of the two hands without her glasses. Yet, from their relative position, she saw it was quarter-past seven.

The last forty-two hours of captivity had been a nightmare. Refusing to eat had made her lethargic. Every muscle in her body cried out in pain. Her mouth tasted of yesterday. Her throat was parched. Hearing no sounds, Caroline decided her captors were sleeping. Now fully awake, her mind turned to her father's parting message.

Since talking to him early yesterday afternoon, she'd tried desperately to understand what he had been trying to tell her. None of it made sense. What had she done as a child that he wanted her to recall? Caroline couldn't imagine. Still, knowing her father as she did, Caroline knew he was trying to tell her something important.

Propped up against the headrail, Caroline felt her wrist aching from the lingering pain of the handcuffs. Curiously, the unyielding strain on her arm reminded her of Wes's firm grip on her whenever she was rowdy or tried to pull away. Reflecting on her childhood summers at the Outer Banks, Caroline recalled her father's having to constantly restrain her from running into the ocean. Oblivious to oncoming waves and the treacherous undertow, he'd scolded her numerous times. Was that it? Was it her stubbornness, her strong will?

Suddenly, Caroline understood his message. She was in mortal danger. He was telling her to escape, to run from her kidnappers as she had run toward the sea as a child. Why else would he have said that, if not to warn me to run?

Tears tumbled softly down her cheeks as Caroline felt the strength of her father's love. She didn't mind. They would purge the last feelings of self-pity from her mind. Caroline knew she had to act. She would press her will to the limit. She would find a way to escape.

The plan had to be a simple one that she could easily abandon if the situation changed or she lost the initiative. The advantage of surprise would be hers, but resolve would make the difference. Did she have the guts, even if it meant being harmed or killed? There could be no turning back once she began. A single mistake or just bad luck could end her world. She had to try. Hadn't her father always said that a life worth living for was worth dying for? Caroline knew it was true.

* * *

Tucker's night had been sleepless. Constantly on the phone until nearly midnight, he had called everyone he and Caroline knew in hopes of finding her, but no one had seen or heard from her. Frustrated, he'd driven to her townhouse and let himself in, but found nothing amiss. There were no messages on her answering machine. Worried that she might have rushed home to Williamsburg in an emergency, Tucker had then called Caroline's mother. Mrs. Beacham had no idea where Caroline might have gone, but was concerned that Tucker hadn't talked to her daughter in more than a day. Thinking there had to be a practical explanation for Caroline's disappearance, Tucker finally gave up looking for her and went to bed around two a.m.

Near panic, Tucker poured the coal to his new Ford Explorer, weaving between lanes. Why hadn't he gone to the police last night? Why hadn't he tracked down her boss, Straton, yesterday and insisted he locate her? His anxiety heightened as he raced toward her bank in Reston, afraid she wouldn't be there.

Barely taking time to park, Tucker rushed into the bank. He immediately saw that Caroline was not at her desk.

"Courtney, has Caroline come in yet?"

"No, Tucker, she hasn't and she didn't call in yesterday."

"What? You mean you didn't hear from her at all yesterday?"

"No, I didn't. I thought the two of you had decided to take the day off together and had forgotten to tell me."

Tucker said nothing. His worst fear was true. *Caroline was missing.*

Tucker remembered little about the drive to Tyson's Corner. His mind was consumed with fear for Caroline's life. What could have happened to her? Had she been abducted and raped, or robbed and murdered? All the possibilities frightened him. He had to talk with someone. He had to get help.

Arriving at work, Tucker went straight to Jim Paterson's office. He found his boss laboring over a DOD proposal. He didn't bother to knock. "Jim, I need to talk. I've got a big problem." Paterson looked into Tucker's distraught face and motioned him to sit down. "What's troubling you, Tucker?"

"Caroline is missing. My fiancée has disappeared and no one has a clue where she is!"

Jim listened as Tucker recounted everything he knew about Caroline's disappearance, including his calls and visits to her townhouse and office. "Shouldn't I go to the police now, Jim?" he asked. "I don't know what else to do. I'm certain she's in some kind of trouble."

"The first thing we should do is retrace Caroline's path, beginning with the impromptu meeting she had with her boss over at the main office, day before yesterday," Jim said. "Depending on what we learn from him, we'll know how to proceed."

"Yeah. That makes sense. Why didn't I think of that?"

"Give me several minutes to make a couple of calls, and I'll go with you to find out," Jim offered. Tucker's expression brightened a bit, knowing he'd have Jim's help.

* * *

The flight had been aloft for twenty-seven minutes when Sybil knocked three times on the cockpit door. Chad pressed the cabin door latch release on the overhead panel, allowing her to enter. In a hurry, Sybil leaned over Wes's shoulder and dropped the tape recorder into his lap. Grabbing the tape, Wes laid it on top of his nav kit bag. "It's done. I hope it's what you wanted." Wes turned around and looked up at her. "Thanks, Sybil," he said sincerely. "I really appreciate it."

"It was the least I could do," she answered softly. "I hope it helps."

Kyle interrupted, "Captain, Shanwick radio has our oceanic clearance on the number two radio."

"Chad, you stay with Center. I'll be on the number two radio with Kyle," he commanded. Chad nodded. Seeing the sudden flurry of activity, Sybil excused herself and left the cockpit.

Shanwick Radio cleared TIA 899 to make its ocean crossing on Track Bravo at thirty-seven thousand feet at mach decimal eight zero, or eighty percent of the speed of sound.

Kyle acknowledged the clearance and read back each oceanic waypoint for confirmation. Wes jotted down the clearance on his flight plan.

"Thanks for the help, Kyle. Chad and I can handle things here now. You go ahead and take the first break," Wes said.

Kyle took a minute to slip on a cotton sweater to mask his uniform shirt from the passengers, then left the cockpit.

Wes picked up the tape recorder, adjusted the volume and pressed the PLAY button. Holding the recorder to his left ear, he listened intently for the sounds of the digits being dialed. The changes in pitch of the specific digits were distinct enough, but their sequence was rapid. It would take a lot of concentration to avoid confusing them. He hoped Tucker would be able to figure it out.

Reaching for his Jeppesen manual, Wes flipped it open to the Longfellow Radio frequency page, a section not provided by the company. Though not a part of TIA's communication network and unknown to most of his fellow pilots, Longfellow Radio served a vital need for anyone needing a telephone patch through HF radio to anywhere in the world at any hour.

Using the wave propagation chart, Wes compared the frequencies listed against the current Greenwich Mean Time and picked the closest one meeting his conditions. After setting in the frequency, he keyed his mike.

"LONGFELLOW RADIO! TIA 899 ON FREQUENCY 8975. HOW DO YOU READ?" Wes radioed.

"GOOD MORNING, TIA 899. I READ YOU FIVE BY FIVE. GO AHEAD," the Englishman piped back.

"SIR, I NEED A TELEPHONE PATCH TO THE USA."

"ROGER, 899. WHAT IS YOUR ACCOUNT NUMBER, MATE?" Wes rattled off the alphanumeric code, then waited.

"AND WHAT NUMBER DO YOU WISH TO CALL?" the operator asked, adding, "PLEASE START WITH YOUR AREA CODE."

Wes read back Tucker's office number, hoping he'd answer.

"TIA 899, GO AHEAD WITH YOUR CALL," said the Englishman. "ROGER," answered Wes as he heard the first ring. "I know you're there, Tucker. Answer your phone, dammit," muttered Wes, listening to it ring. Six rings later, Tucker's taped voice answered.

After hearing the beep, Wes keyed his mike and said, "AJAX, THIS IS HOLMES. THE PRINCESS IS IN GRAVE DANGER. STANDBY FOR HER PROBABLE LOCATION AT ONE OF THESE NUMBERS." He placed the microphone against the tiny cassette speaker and pressed the PLAY button. Glancing down, he saw the capstan was turning. There was no way to monitor the playback. Plugging earphones into the recorder would have grounded out the speaker.

Wes had no idea of how long Tucker's answering machine allowed for a message or how many messages were ahead of his. Watching the tape move silently through the tape head, Wes wondered how he could be sure all the numbers were received. Then he had an idea. He could play back the sounds of the tape, rewinding. The sounds would be spaced closer and the digits would have to be deciphered in reverse, but it could be done, Wes imagined.

"SIR, I'M SORRY YOUR PARTY HAS HUNG UP. DO YOU WISH TO PLACE ANOTHER CALL?" queried the Longfellow operator.

"YES," said Wes, "REPLACE THE SAME CALL, SIR."

"RIGHT, STANDBY," the operator replied.

Wes quickly plugged the earphones in to see if the numbers were still being transmitted. Weird music told him they were not. He should have previewed the tape to determine how long it took to transmit all the numbers before he called Tucker.

Wes realized he would have had the same problem trying to determine how much time his recorder allowed for each message. Pressing

REWIND, he heard several seconds of Cynthia's unusual music in reverse, followed by the sound of the rapidly varying tones, the electronic signature of each digit. He pressed PLAY again, moving the tape to the beginning of Cynthia's eclectic rhythms.

"TIA 899, YOUR CALL IS RINGING AGAIN."

"THANKS, LONGFELLOW," Wes answered. Knowing the machine would answer after the sixth ring, he put the mike against the speaker and waited to hear Tucker's recorded announcement. A moment later, he pressed REWIND. The tape reversed, rapidly returning to the start position. The transmission was over in seconds. Wes pulled the mike away from the cassette speaker and held it to his mouth.

"AJAX, HERE'S A SECOND COPY IN REVERSE. USE THESE NUMBERS TO FIND HER, BUT DON'T INVOLVE THE AUTHORITIES UNLESS IT BECOMES ABSOLUTELY NECESSARY. HER SITUATION IS EXTREMELY COMPLICATED. GOOD LUCK." Then pausing for a moment, Wes said, "THANKS, LONGFELLOW. I'M FINISHED."

"What was that all about?" Chad asked, puzzled. He'd monitored the last call to Longfellow and had no earthly idea of what he'd heard or to whom Wes had been talking. Wes gave Chad a quick smile and turned away, hoping he'd drop it. He should have known better.

"Who in the devil is Longfellow Radio?"

"It's a commercial aeronautical radio service operated by the British that provides pilots the ability to communicate via telephone, telex, or fax, while airborne from anyplace on the globe."

Looking down at his FMC, Chad realized they were approaching the oceanic coast-out waypoint. "Oh shit, I damn near missed getting the gross error plot," he said, scrambling for his clipboard. Wes breathed a sigh of relief, knowing he wouldn't have to involve Chad in the crisis yet.

* * *

It was nearly ten a.m. when Tucker and Jim arrived at the main office of NOVA Bank & Trust. The drive to Vienna had taken a little longer than either had expected. Entering the towering, granite building together, they headed for the elevators. Tucker looked for Blake Straton's name posted in the brass case. They were in luck. Mr. B.F. Straton's office was on the twelfth floor, Suite C. Tucker nervously pressed the twelfth-floor button, fearful of what he might learn. Jim understood his anxiety. Caroline hadn't just disappeared into thin air. Something unexpected had happened.

Rising from her tidy desk, Gloria Alderman greeted Jim and Tucker as they entered the large suite. "Good morning, gentleman, I'm Gloria, Mr. Straton's secretary. May I help you?"

Tucker came right to the point. "My fiancée, Caroline Beacham, was called to this office day before yesterday around noon for an urgent meeting with your boss. She hasn't been seen since."

"Sir, there was no meeting between Caroline and Mr. Straton. Mr. Straton and I were both out of the office for the whole day."

Tucker grimaced. "Then could I speak with Mr. Straton? It's extremely important that we find her."

Seeing his distress, Gloria leaned over her desk and pressed the intercom button. "Mr. Straton, Caroline Beacham's fiancé would like to have a word with you. He says it's urgent."

"Certainly, Gloria. Please show him in."

Tucker and Jim followed Gloria into Straton's office. Blake Straton was seated behind a large desk reviewing papers, but rose to greet them. "Please, have a seat, gentlemen." Tucker declined, preferring to stand.

"What can I do for you?" he asked.

Tucker spoke at once, making the introductions before expressing his concern. "Mr. Straton, according to Courtney, Caroline's assistant manager, Caroline received a call day before yesterday around noon advising her that you had called an urgent meeting here for one p.m. Courtney said Caroline left for your office as soon as she got the call. Now, Ms. Alderman tells me that both of you were out of the office that day. Sir, Caroline hasn't been seen since she left for that meeting here!" explained Tucker, in obvious frustration.

"This distresses me, greatly, Mr. Shaw. I called no such meeting, nor did I direct Gloria's temp to call a meeting for me. I will certainly follow up on this right away," he said, reaching for the intercom.

"Gloria, call personnel and tell them I want the name and address of the temp who covered for you day before yesterday."

"Sir, I've got that information right here," Gloria explained. "I'll bring it in to you right now."

Entering the plush office with a steno pad, Gloria said, "Her name is Janice Livermore. Here are her address and phone number. You might want to take a look at my telephone log. It shows every call made from my desk."

Straton glanced at the roster. "Yes, these are the calls I asked her to make before I left. There were no calls to the Reston branch all day," he said, handing the list to Tucker.

It was obvious the temp had done her assignment well. The caller, his number, and his message were neatly logged, with notes in the margins. Convinced the temp hadn't placed the call to Caroline, Tucker asked, "Who could have done it?"

"Unfortunately, Tucker, it could have been almost anyone who knew where Caroline worked and who took the time to learn the name of her boss," Jim said. Straton agreed.

"Have you checked to see if her car is parked here in the underground garage?" Straton asked. "That's the place to start."

"We hadn't thought of trying to find her car," said Jim.

"That does make sense," Tucker added, dejectedly.

"Fine! Then why don't you gentlemen take a look through the garage for her car? Meanwhile, I'll notify bank security of Caroline's disappearance and get in touch with Miss Livermore," he suggested. "I'm anxious to see if she received any unusual calls that morning, and if she gave out any information about Miss Beacham."

"Thanks for your help, Mr. Straton. I appreciate it," Tucker said.

"Son, I'm very sorry about this, for you as well as for Caroline. She's one of the brightest and smartest managers I have. The bank cares a great deal about the safety of all of its employees, especially someone like Caroline. We'll help any way we can," he said. The gravity of his concern was convincing. Tucker knew he was sincere.

"If you will, leave your business and home phone numbers with Gloria. I'll call you as soon as I've talked with my people," Straton said, walking Jim and Tucker to the door. Handing them his business card he added, "My home number is on here, too. Don't hesitate to call me if there's anything further I can do."

Tucker handed Gloria his business card and thanked her for her help. She gave him a reassuring look and said, "Caroline's going to be all right. I just know it," she said, cheerfully. "She's as smart as they come and has a will of steel to go with it!" Tucker grinned. Gloria knew what she was talking about.

He and Jim wasted no time getting to the garage. The concrete superstructure was dimly lit. The large pillars scattered throughout made it difficult to see all the cars from the elevator entrance. Tucker insisted they walk every lane.

As they were about to begin searching the fourth corridor, Tucker saw what he thought was the top half of Caroline's black Camry near the garage entrance. Rushing toward the opening, he realized it was her car. There was no sign of forced entry or damage. Nor was her attaché case in the back seat where she always put it. Caroline had obviously driven to the bank and had parked on her own, stopping to take her briefcase before locking her car.

"Someone was waiting here for her, Jim. They knew she would show up for the meeting," voiced Tucker, staring at her car.

"You're right," Jim replied. "She was set up. You'd better notify the police. This doesn't look good."

Tucker didn't reply. He was still trying to accept the fact that Caroline had been kidnapped. He felt numb, empty. Jim saw the anguish in Tucker's face as he struggled to conceal the tears forming in the crevices of his eyes.

Jim knew the feeling. He'd been there. Two years ago, his daughter had been abducted and raped. He understood the pain his young associate was experiencing. He'd been lucky, if you could call it that. His daughter's life had been spared.

"Suppose we go back to the office, Tucker. I have some friends at the Bureau who could help us. Besides, the forensics people will need to get to work on her car right away."

"Yeah, there's nothing more we can do here," Tucker said, turning away from the car in which he'd shared so many wonderful times.

The drive back to the office was quick. Neither had much to say. Jim was eager to get the police on it. He'd done that as soon as his daughter was missing. He'd learned later that it was his quick response that had saved her life.

"Give Mr. Straton a call, Tucker, and tell him about Caroline's car, while I try and contact my friend at the FBI."

"Okay, but first, I want to call Mrs. Beacham and let her know," Tucker said.

"Good idea," Jim answered, as they separated in the hallway.

Entering his office, Tucker saw that his answering machine light was double-flashing. He had two messages. Disregarding them, he dialed Williamsburg. The line was busy. Pulling Straton's business card from his pocket, he dialed his office. Gloria answered. She said Straton had gone to meet with the bank's security administrator. Tucker told her of finding Caroline's car in the underground garage and that he was going to notify the police. Gloria agreed and said she would tell Mr. Straton. Tucker thanked her, hung up, and re-dialed Williamsburg. The line was still busy. Frustrated at not being able to reach her and annoyed by the flashing message light, Tucker pressed the MESSAGE button.

The voice he heard astonished him. It was Captain Beacham's. The background noise told him Wes had called from the cockpit. Pressing the STOP button, Tucker quickly rewound the tape. Had the light been on that morning? Tucker decided it hadn't. Pressing MESSAGE again, he listened.

Ajax, this is Holmes. The Princess is in grave danger! Stand by for her probable location at one of these numbers!

How could Wes know Caroline was missing? And why was he using their nicknames? It didn't make sense. Wasn't he supposed to be en route from Geneva at that very moment? And numbers. What numbers? Tucker had heard only noise on the tape. Had Wes forgotten them? Puzzled by the message, Tucker tried to imagine what Wes was trying to tell him. More than bizarre, Tucker knew the message was extremely important, but what did it mean?

"My friend, Dave Coleman, will meet with us right away," said Jim, walking into Tucker's office. "Are you ready to go?"

"Wait, Jim! Listen to this!" exclaimed Tucker as he rewound the recording. The tape hit its stop and automatically replayed the strange message. Jim listened intently, frowning as he heard the voice speak of the Princess.

"Who is it, Tucker? Is Caroline the Princess?"

"It's Caroline's father, Captain Beacham."

"But who are Ajax and Holmes?"

"I'm Ajax. Wes is Holmes. And Caroline is the Princess. It refers to an old joke he and I made up about being conned by her into washing and waxing her convertible at the beach several summers ago. Ajax and Holmes were names we gave each other as employees of a fictitious car wash."

Jim began to see the logic. "But why would he go to such an ex- treme to use code names?"

"He's telling me where to find Caroline, and he's afraid someone might discover that he knows something he's not supposed to. Maybe he's worried that if the wrong people learn that he knows of her where- abouts, they'll move her."

"This isn't about Caroline and the bank," Jim snapped. "It must have something to do with her father and his job. How else could he have known that Caroline is in danger?"

"That may be true, Jim. But how are we going to know? The last part of his message is missing. All that's on the tape is some kind of beeping noise," Tucker complained. "Wes stopped recording before he finished the message."

"Play the tape again. Maybe we've missed something."

Tucker rewound the tape again. This time they both listened with- out comment, focusing on the strange noises.

"I've got it!" exclaimed Tucker. "Those beeps are the digits of telephone numbers. He's trying to pass us phone numbers... That's what he means about Caroline's probable location. She's being held at the location of one of those numbers."

Jim looked dumbfounded as Tucker excitedly rewound the mes- sage once more. Jim was amazed at his associate's insight. The tapes still sounded like noise to him.

"Listen carefully this time. Notice the varying pitch of the sounds. They're exactly like the sound you get when you dial a phone number. The differences in pitch distinguish the particular digit."

Listening, Jim said, "You're right. They are dialing sounds. But how are we going to slow the tape speed enough to figure out what the specific digits are?"

"We'll re-record the message at high speed, then play the record- ing at slow speed. The beeps will have a lower pitch and will sound different, but their relative differences will be the same. We can even duplicate the telephone dialing sounds from our phone and match them with the tape's. That should give us a reference point," Tucker explained, elated over solving the noise puzzle.

"I know of a small recording studio near here. They'd be able to do it for us, I think," said Jim. "I'll call my friend at the Bureau and tell him we'll be over a little later." Tucker looked up and nodded as Jim rushed out of his office.

Opening the small answering machine, Tucker removed the tape. What if Wes tried to call again with more information? Quickly, Tucker dug into his desk for a replacement. In luck, he inserted the blank and recorded his usual announcement, then added: "Thanks, Holmes. I figured out your message. We're tracking the Princess's location now." Tucker finished rewinding the tape as Jim returned. "Dave Coleman has agreed to meet with us as soon as we can get there," Jim said. "Hopefully, he'll be able to get the names and addresses to go with those telephone numbers."

"He's got to! It's our only hope of finding Caroline," said Tucker, as they headed for Jim's car.

In the parking lot, Tucker stopped at his car long enough to pick up his pocket recorder. It used the same size tape as his telephone answering system. He inserted the tape into the tiny recorder and pressed PLAY, as Jim started the car. To his surprise, there was a second message from Wes. Tucker realized immediately the second call had been made to ensure that all the numbers were transmitted to the answering machine.

Thirty minutes later, Tucker and Jim had the numbers they needed. Transcribing the pulses into digits had taken less time than they had imagined. Both had recognized the exchange prefixes of most of the numbers. Most were for metro Washington. Pulling out of the parking lot, Jim called Dave Coleman at the FBI Building and confirmed their meeting.

"Do you think he'll agree to help us without alerting his superiors?"

"I really don't know, Tucker. But he's the best chance we've got if you want to get hold of those names and addresses. You'll have to make that decision after you hear what he has to say."

Tucker turned away and stared out the window. If Coleman balked, he would have no choice but to explain the whole situation to Coleman and hope the FBI could find Caroline before her kidnappers found out. But would they get to her in time?

8

FEDERAL AID

Jim and Tucker found Dave Coleman up to his ears in paperwork. Manila folders piled six deep covered the better part of his desk, leaving little work space. Two empty coffee cups filled with cigarette ashes attested to the time he'd devoted to reviewing them and yet, from the looks of things, Dave had barely begun. Whatever the reason, it had to be a thankless job, and one he'd done everything to avoid until now. Meeting Dave, Tucker was sure the paper chase was not what had lured him to the FBI. Even his office had a dated look, as though the real excitement of criminal drama had passed him by long ago. Stagnant aptly described Coleman's current role.

Dave looked to be in his late 40s, judging by his graying hair, bushy eyebrows and weathered face. His physique, once imposing, was now centered on his belly. It was obvious the fitness craze had not fazed him. Pictures on his overcrowded desk announced his family of three, a wife and two daughters. The girls, both blondes, had big teeth, long hair, and favored Dave. His wife wore a friendly smile, giving the impression she was content with her station in life. Tucker wondered if Dave was.

Jim did the talking. He was a master at making presentations, especially when he wanted something. It appeared Dave was willing to help until Jim explained what they wanted.

"No way, Jim! If I were caught, I could lose my whole damn career, not to mention my pension. The Bureau doesn't buy off on shit like this, you know!"

"I know we're asking a lot of you, Dave, but how else are we going to get those addresses? We can't very well walk in and demand them, can we?" Paterson asked. "Besides, how's the FBI going to find out, anyway?"

Dave doodled on his notepad nervously. "I'd really like to help you, Jim. I can see the mess Tucker's in.... but damn, I just can't do it unless you guys come in the front door!"

"Okay, okay, could you at least tell me which telephone office would have the information we need and how we might pick it out of them?"

Tucker could see Jim was laying a guilt trip on his old friend. Squirming in his seat, Dave frowned. "I guess I could get that for you, provided you promise not to say a damn word about this to anyone, okay?" Jim smiled at him approvingly as Coleman picked up his phone and punched in an extension.

Jim and Tucker waited quietly, listening to one side of the conversation. Dave seemed to relax as he spoke to the person on the other end. Apparently, getting the addresses wouldn't be that difficult, from the sound of Dave's voice. Jim winked at Tucker as Dave was finishing his call.

"Paterson, I don't know why I still put up with you. You live right here in the same damn town and hardly ever give me so much as a lousy phone call. Then you come roaring in here like a bat out of hell and want me to put my ass on the line for you with no explanation of what in the hell is going on!"

Paterson grinned sheepishly at Coleman. "We'd like to tell you what we know, Dave, but there's no point going into it, if you're not going to be able to help us."

Dave loosened his tie and gazed down at his notepad once more. "Ah, hell. What's the use of trying to tell you two how to get the info you want? It'd be easier if I just went and got it for you myself," he said. "You two would just screw it up," he grumbled, jerking his coat off the rack. "Besides, I can see you guys aren't going to let me get anything done here until we get those telephone numbers you want, so let's get to work. You can tell me what this is all about on the way," he griped.

"It a good thing you decided to help, Dave. Otherwise, you'd probably be assigned to investigate our screwup," countered Jim. Dave chuckled. He knew he'd been hustled, but it didn't matter. Since hearing their story, he'd known it was a favor he couldn't deny. Anything was better than dealing with those damned files.

"Tell me again, Tucker, how you got those numbers?" asked Dave, stepping from the elevator into the underground garage. "Did Captain Beacham actually call them in as dial tones from somewhere in the middle of the Atlantic?"

"Yes, sir. He transmitted them to my answering machine."

"That's amazing. Technology today is unbelievable. It's impossible to keep up with it anymore."

Exiting the FBI building in deep conversation, the three headed for the phone company office in Dave's agency car. Seated in the rear, Tucker spent the first few minutes giving Dave the details of what he knew. Then he and Jim listened as Dave recounted possible scenarios. None sounded good. Time was the critical factor, Dave explained. They had to find Caroline before Wes landed. He was convinced her kidnapping had something to do with the flight Wes was operating back to Washington, but the reason was speculation.

A news junky at heart, Coleman never went anywhere in his car without having the radio on. This morning was no exception. In the middle of his conversation, Dave abruptly stopped speaking. A news update caught his attention.

"The aircraft of Secretary of State, Riggs Halston, suffered extensive damage while on the ground in Geneva earlier this morning. The secretary was not aboard at the time of the incident, but was forced to make alternative plans for returning to Washington later today. State Department officials said a few minutes ago that the secretary would be arriving at Dulles Airport around six p.m. aboard TIA 899, a civilian carrier."

"That's it. That's the connection we're looking for. It has something to do with the secretary of state being on Beacham's flight," Dave ventured.

Tucker stared out the window of the government vehicle oblivious to the scenery. Was there a connection between Caroline's kidnapping and the secretary of state being forced to make his return flight aboard Wes's aircraft? Had events been staged to get the secretary on his flight? Was he the reason for Caroline's kidnapping? What was it Wes was supposed to do differently? Having the secretary on board would not require him to do anything out of the ordinary — unless the flight was going to be hijacked. But why tell Wes beforehand? Tucker wondered. Nothing made sense except that Caroline had been taken to ensure that her father would do exactly as ordered. Hijacking a member of the president's cabinet was a high-stakes gambit. Any group willing to engage in such an activity wouldn't hesitate to kill anyone they suspected might threaten their operation. Suddenly Tucker realized Caroline was in greater danger than he had imagined. The urgency in Wes's voice made even more sense as he speculated on the impact such a scenario would have on Caroline's life. Sparing her would be the least of their worries.

The midmorning sun's glare flashed across the windshield of the FBI sedan as Dave wheeled around the corner and stopped abruptly. The temperature was already approaching 100 degrees as he switched off the ignition.

"Jim, you and Tucker stay here. This is something I'd rather not have witnesses to, even if they're friendly ones," Dave said, fastening his shirt collar and straightening his tie.

"Whatever you say, Dave. You're the boss," Jim replied.

Releasing his seat belt, Dave grabbed his wrinkled sport coat. It looked as though he'd slept in it for several nights. Reaching inside for a small notepad, Dave said, "It'll probably take me at least fifteen to twenty minutes."

"You've got the numbers with you?" Jim asked.

"How many years do you think I've been doing this sort of shit?" snapped Dave. "Of course I do, you idiot."

Jim smiled back at his former intelligence officer, remembering their days together in the DIA (Defense Intelligence Agency). "While you're at it, get the names," Jim suggested, "They'll come in handy when we make the visits."

"If I get anything, I'll get it all," Dave said, shoving the door closed.

Jim and Tucker watched him disappear through the alcove of the telephone building.

"Will he be able to get the information we need?"

Jim shrugged his shoulders at Tucker. "I'd be stunned if he came out empty-handed. They don't come any smarter than Dave. He'll have those people cranking out everything they know about those numbers in minutes. My guess is they'll even put it all on a computer printout for him. The only question is whether he'll remember to ask for duplicates. It will save us a lot of time running down these leads."

Tucker eased back in his seat as Jim started the car. The heat buildup was already oppressive. "When we get the information, I'll have Dave drive us over to the office to pick up your car. Dividing up the leads will be the fastest way to search. I'll see if Dave has time to help us. We can keep in touch via the car phones," Jim explained.

"What kind of cover story should I use?" Tucker asked. "Something simple — an insurance underwriter or an OSHA field representative, but be vague and get the hell out of there the minute you learn something or think you've been discovered. These guys obviously play rough." Tucker frowned. He'd come to the same conclusion hours ago.

"Jim, I'm going over to the park across the street and use the phone. I've put off calling Mrs. Beacham long enough."

"Sure. Dave will be at least another ten minutes."

Tucker fumbled in his pockets for a quarter and then hurried across the busy street and into the cool shade of the park. It was actually pleasant under the large maple trees. The temperature inside was another matter. The booth felt like a sauna, but smelled of urine and body odor. Tucker quickly dialed the Beachams' phone number, then stepped outside the booth while it rang. Fortunately, the phone had a long cord.

"Beachams' residence." Tucker recognized the voice immediately as Caroline's younger sister, Jacqueline.

"Jackie, this is Tucker. Is your mom there? I need to speak to her. It's urgent." What was Jackie doing at home? She was supposed to be at freshman orientation in Raleigh.

"Mom's not here, Tucker. She's at one of the district's other schools. It's a teacher workday, so she's having to sit through all that central office crap."

"Jackie, I have some bad news for your mom...."

"What's happened, Tucker? Is Caroline okay?" Jackie had her mother's intuition. Tucker groped for the right words.

"Jackie, Caroline's missing."

"Since when, Tucker? How do you know?"

"She's been kidnapped."

"My God! Kidnapped! When did you find out?"

"We got word from your father."

The news stunned Jackie. It was the thing her mom had worried most about Caroline's living in Washington.

"Who's 'we', Tucker?"

"My boss, Jim Paterson, and an FBI agent named Coleman."

"Wait! Start from the beginning, Tucker. This is getting complicated."

Tucker spent the next several minutes relating the events of the last two days, including Wes's strange oceanic call. Brushing her blonde hair aside, Jackie listened as he explained what measures they were taking to find Caroline.

"Tucker, this is horrible. Have you talked to my brother, Walker, about this?"

"No. I'd wanted to talk with your mom first."

Jackie thought for a second. "I'll call Walker and tell him to get up here as quickly as he can. Then I'll come up and join you" said Jackie, talking a mile a minute. "I've recorded our conversation. Mom will get the full story as soon as she returns. With any luck, Walker will be here by then to be with her."

"Jackie, I appreciate your concern, but we can handle it."

"No, Tucker. You need help! she said, jotting a short note to her mother.

"Jackie, it's too dangerous for you to get involved. You stay there and find your mother," Tucker said, seeing Dave return to the car across the street.

"Tucker, you listen to me! I'll be at Tyson's Corner in two hours, thirty minutes. Do you understand? Keep your car phone on. I'll check in with you on the way up I-95."

Tucker knew Jackie was adamant about coming. It was pointless to waste time arguing.

"Do I need to bring anything?"

"Does your father have any firearms?"

"Yes. He has some kind of automatic pistol, a rifle and a double-barreled shotgun. I'll grab everything he's got and bring it."

"Just be careful and watch the speed limit. I'll wait for your calls. If I don't hear from you, I'll meet you at my office in two and a half hours."

"I'll be there shortly."

Tucker dropped the phone back onto the hook and stepped outside the booth. The warm breeze seemed cool as he walked through the park and crossed the street to join Jim and Dave. He decided not to tell them about his conversation with Jackie or that she had insisted on helping him.

Tucker's call was a shock to Jackie. Her older sister meant the world to her. Caroline was like a mother. Learning that her sister had been kidnapped and her father threatened astounded her. Apprehension gripped Jackie as she finished the note to her mom. Wiping the tears from her blurred eyes, she autodialed Walker's bank in Elizabeth City, but got his answering machine. He was either in conference or out playing golf. The two seemed interrelated in the banking business, she decided. Hearing the beep, Jackie said, "Walker, Caroline's been kidnapped! Call mom at home ASAP. I've gone to Washington to meet Tucker. Call me on my car phone." She ended the message with a plea to his secretary to make every effort to find him.

That done, Jackie tore upstairs to find her dad's weapons. She found the shotgun standing in the rear corner of his closest. The Winchester was beside it. The automatic was on the top shelf under some sweaters.

Removing the automatic first, she recalled the chilly autumn afternoon two years ago when she and her father had gone to the farm. Firing the pistol had been the most difficult for her. No matter how hard she'd concentrated on keeping the barrel aimed at the target, it still popped up the instant the round left the chamber. The shotgun had bruised her shoulder, but her first shot had blown away the old jug he'd set on the stump. Her father had bragged about it for days afterward. She liked the double barrel best. It felt like a cannon going off.

Looking down at the firearms lying on the bed, Jackie wondered if there had been some dark purpose for her learning to shoot that afternoon. One at a time, she broke open the guns. Not one was loaded. Even the clip in the forty-five bore no rounds. Opening the tiny access door in the back of the closet, Jackie retrieved the ammo — a half-empty box of twelve-gauge shotgun shells, fifteen rounds of forty-five caliber ammo and an unopened box of high-powered bullets for the Winchester. Satisfied she had it all, Jackie stuffed the ammo and the pistol into one of Meredith's shopping bags. Then, grabbing the other two firearms, she started downstairs. On her way down, Jackie remembered the mace. She still had several canisters in her room.

Seeing the alphanumeric pager on her dressing table, Jackie took it and clipped it to her jeans. She'd used the pager to stay in touch with her mom when she was on modeling assignments. Using canned messages stored on their PC, Meredith had only to fill in the blanks and fire them off through the modem. It took no more than thirty seconds for her to receive the beeper signal and the accompanying eighty space message. Stopping at the telephone desk in the kitchen, Jackie added a "P.S." to her note.

I've called Walker. He should be on his way. Call me on my car phone or use the PC to raise me on the pager! Love, Jackie.

Moments later, Jackie slid her 5-foot, ten-inch frame under the wheel of her Mustang and switched on the ignition. Whipping her long hair into a ponytail, Jackie shoved her Oakleys over her blue eyes and slipped the 5.0 engine into gear. The summer heat was sweltering. Everything she touched burned. She lowered all the windows to allow the heat to escape as her hatchback clawed its way out of the driveway and onto the tarmac. Reaching I-64 West, Jackie lay on the accelerator of the supercharged V8. Nearing eighty miles an hour, she engaged the cruise control and tried to relax, but couldn't. Her mind was on Caroline.

*   *   *

Getting the phone company to surrender the information he wanted proved no contest for Coleman. Eager to help the FBI, the supervisor on duty had insisted on handling the requests and had printed duplicates of everything. Dave had the names, addresses, and limited personal information on all the numbers he'd requested. One was to a location in New York. Two were to unlisted numbers in Geneva and the remaining international number was to an unlisted address in Cyprus.

Tucker pored over the list as Dave raced toward Tyson's Corner. He noted the various locations of the addresses — Alexandria, Chantilly, Crystal City, Middleburg, and Woodbridge, all in Virginia, while Chevy Chase and Edgewater were in Maryland. He noticed most belonged to businesses in outlying Washington.

The Chevy Chase number belonged to North Star Truckers. The number in Edgewater belonged to a company named Eastern Shore Yachts. Southland Realty held the number in Woodbridge, while West Auto Parts was the listing for Chantilly. The Crystal City number was assigned to ASAP Couriers Express (ACE), a motorcycle delivery outfit. One of the Alexandria numbers belonged to the In-Touch Answering Service, the other was to a pay phone in Old Town. The Middleburg number was assigned to a rural address.

The chances of finding any logic to the array of numbers and addresses seemed hopeless to Tucker. It appeared they would have to track down every one of them to locate Caroline, or at least find someone who might know her whereabouts. The task appeared monumental. Wes's flight would be landing around six p.m. Tucker realized they didn't have much time to find Caroline.

"How do you suggest I conduct the search?" Tucker asked.

"While you were on the phone, Jim and I divided the numbers into two groups," said Dave. "We'll work the first list. Jim said you and Conner could take the other."

Tucker looked over the list again, this time noticing the checks and stars beside each. He hadn't thought about getting his associate's help. But if Jim said it was okay, he'd ask him. "Which list do you want me and Conner to work?"

"Dave and I will take the stars. You and Conner take the checks," Jim said.

From the marks beside each address it appeared that Dave and Jim would check out addresses to the east and south and pick up those in Crystal City and Alexandria. Tucker would be responsible for those to the north and west of Washington. "What about the pay phone number? Do you think it's worth stopping to check?" Tucker asked.

"We raised the same question, but I don't think we'll find anything helpful there. It's probably a planned contingency contact. Once we know more about what's going on, we can stake it out or even tap the line, but right now, we need to start tracking down these locations," Dave answered.

Tucker was glad he'd been assigned the western sector. Caroline's kidnapping had occurred in Vienna, west of metro D.C. Hiding Caroline west of town made more sense.

Dave eased the department's sedan into the visitors' parking lot as Jim spoke. "Tucker, give Dave your mobile phone number." Tucker pulled out his business card and handed it to Dave, then hurriedly copied Dave's mobile number on the back of one of his own cards.

"Don't try to go it alone, Tucker. If you detect anything that suggests you may have found her, call us ASAP and keep the situation under surveillance until we get there," Dave instructed. "I don't have any idea who we're dealing with, but from the looks of their network, they're highly organized. My suspicion is they're multinational heavies. They won't take kindly to any intrusions from us. Be careful, son."

The seriousness of Dave's voice had an impact on Tucker as he climbed the granite steps to the entrance of his office building. Dave's assessment had to be taken seriously.

Connor, Tucker's associate, was not in his office. Checking with the receptionist, Tucker learned that Connor had left for the day with a bad case of the flu. Tucker cursed under his breath. He was counting on Connor's help. Dropping into his chair, Tucker put his elbows on the desk, covering his face with his hands. Stress was taking its toll.

"Mr. Shaw, Jackie Beacham is holding for you, sir," announced Liz, the receptionist. Tucker sprang to life as he picked up the phone. The background noise from Jackie's mobile phone was deafening.

"Tucker, I'm on I-95, approaching the Ashland exit. Where do you want us to meet?"

"Are you familiar with Sully Road, the highway that connects Manassas with Dulles?"

"Yes."

"Then meet me in the visitors' parking lot of Sully Plantation. It's about two or three miles south of Dulles."

"Okay. I'll be there in ninety minutes."

Tucker hung up and checked his watch. He had just enough time to make it to Chevy Chase and back before he was due to meet Jackie. Grabbing the list of addresses, Tucker headed for his Explorer.

*   *   *

Free for an hour before her next teacher's meeting, Meredith headed home for a late breakfast and a few minutes' solitude. Beginning another teaching year was always a killer for her. The rest she would get was worth the short drive home.

Walking into the kitchen, she noticed the message light flashing, but she saw no message digit in the window. Dropping her purse on the counter, Meredith pressed the message button.

Tucker's voice surprised her. As Meredith listened to his conversation with Jackie, her lips began to quiver. She felt nauseous. Her hands turned to ice. A cold sweat formed on her forehead as she struggled to comprehend Tucker's message. Caroline missing — for nearly two days — and possibly kidnapped. Wes — sending a coded message to Tucker from somewhere over the Atlantic. Tucker asking for guns and Jackie en route to Washington to join him in the search for Caroline.

Shocked, Meredith pressed the message rewind button and sat on the trestle bench to listen for a second time. When the message ended, she stood up and walked over to the kitchen window and blankly stared out at the bird feeder. Her mind wandered to night before last, when she had tried to call Caroline. Something had told her then to call Tucker just to see how Caroline was doing. Meredith regretted not having made the call. Fighting back tears, she walked to the phone desk and autodialed Jackie's car phone. "Jackie?"

"Mom!"

"Honey, I've heard the tape. It's bad enough that Caroline's missing, but you and Tucker don't have any business going after her with guns. Neither one of you knows what you're doing. Both of you have got to let the police handle this, honey."

"Mom, I know you're right, but Tucker needs my help, and Dad told him not to involve the police. I've got to do this for her. You know how much Caroline is a part of me. Don't worry. We'll be careful. Tucker's boss and a friend of his from the FBI are helping. They'll take care of the dangerous stuff."

Meredith knew there was no persuading Jackie to turn back. She was just as headstrong as the rest of her children. It was the Wes in them. "Okay, Jackie, but don't take any unnecessary chances and keep me posted. I'll try to get in touch with your father and let him know that Tucker got the numbers and addresses. That should ease his mind a little."

"Thanks, Mom. And don't worry. We'll find her."

Hanging up the phone, Meredith thought about Wes. What had he gotten into this time? Living with him for more than thirty years had conditioned her to expect frequent surprises, some good and others not so good, but nothing before had ever been life-threatening to their family. This was different.

At Wes's desk in the loft, Meredith opened the top drawer and removed their lockbox. She recognized the slightly yellowed envelope lying on top of the pile of papers inside. It was a letter she hoped and prayed she'd never have to open. They'd joked about it over the years. Occasionally, she'd ask to see what was in it and he had laughingly told her it was a list of his old girlfriends she didn't need to know about. She knew better. He'd made certain she wouldn't open it out of curiosity by taping the flap of the envelope and writing his name across it.

Digging deeper through the contents, Meredith found the Longfellow Radio sheets. One listed instructions for using the service, along with the costs. The other contained a series of small graphs, each with the name of a city underneath. It was labeled "Wave Propagation Chart." Stapled to it was a page listing the SELCAL identifiers for each aircraft registered to TIA. In the left margin of the sheet, Wes had penciled in the information Longfellow Radio would need to place the call. Meredith studied it for a minute, then booted up his computer and accessed TIA's Pilot Communications Software Program using his password. Pulling up the status of Flight 899, she copied down the aircraft's number. She noticed the flight blocked out on schedule and was estimating Dulles at six p.m.

Lifting the receiver, Meredith dialed the international prefix for the British Isles and then the number for Longfellow Radio. A Brit answered. She explained that the call was an emergency and provided him the details of Wes's flight, including the aircraft number, flight number and SELCAL identifier, departure time and estimated arrival time at Dulles. Sensing her urgency, the operator asked her to stand by while he attempted to reach the aircraft. A minute later he said, "Go ahead with your call, madam. I have TIA 899 on the line." Meredith was ecstatic. To hear Wes's voice would make things so much better.

"WES! IT'S MEREDITH."

"MEREDITH! YOU KNOW?"

"YES! TUCKER GOT THE NUMBERS YOU SENT. HE AND HIS.........."

"Madam, I'm afraid we've lost contact with the flight. Do you wish me to reattempt contact with Flight 899 at this time?"

"Yes, of course. It's urgent," Meredith repeated.

"Right you are, ma'am. I'll have another go at it."

Several minutes later, the Longfellow operator returned. "Madam, I'm terribly sorry, but the flight isn't answering its SELCAL. Perhaps you should try again later?"

Intuition told her further attempts now would be futile. "Thank you, sir. I'll try again later."

9

WHATEVER IT TAKES

Chad looked bewildered as Wes slipped his mike on the small hook next to his instrument panel. "Things must be getting pretty serious on the home front for Meredith to be calling you out here in the middle of the ocean."

"We've got a few complications to deal with right now," Wes explained, trying to appear relaxed.

"Maybe so, but I've been flying with you off and on for more than five years, Wes, and I've never seen you act this strange before. Is something going on that I should know about?"

The question was fair and Chad deserved an answer. He was too perceptive to be kept in the dark. He would have to be told. Knowing Tucker had received the tape and deciphered the sounds into numbers was encouraging, but there was obviously more Meredith was trying to tell him when she lost contact. Wes hoped she'd try again in a few minutes. If not, he'd try to contact her later. Glancing at the time, Wes saw that Kyle's rest period was about over.

"Chad, it's time I level with you about what's happened. I'm going to need your help before this flight is over." Sanderlin looked up from his clipboard. "Shoot. I figured you'd tell me sooner or later."

Wes began the explanation with his and Leigh's boat ride on the lake. Chad listened intently as Wes outlined the chain of events leading up to Meredith's call.

"How are you going to handle it?" Chad asked, curiously.

"I plan to have the secretary's security agents arrest these two guys before we start our approach. I just hope Tucker can get to Caroline before we reach Dulles. I'd rather not have to play my hand until I'm certain she's okay."

"I can understand that. But do you really think these guys are going to take the secretary hostage and hijack the whole flight once we land in Washington?"

Wes didn't speak. The same question had nagged at him since he learned Halston was going to be on board. "I don't know," Wes finally replied. "It's hard to believe they would put all their eggs in one basket." Shrugging, Chad resumed plotting their midpoint position.

Wes gazed down at the choppy waters of the Atlantic, mulling over when to alert the secretary's security agents. If they overreact, he'd have an even bigger problem. Yet, if he left the agents in the dark and the terrorists did make a move, the situation could escalate into an explosive crisis.

"Kyle should be about ready to relieve you in the next few minutes. I'm going to have him cover my seat while I go back and brief the security agents. I'd prefer that no one else know what's going on until later so don't say anything to him, okay?"

"Sure. No problem."

Wes picked up the flight envelope and fished out the weapons authorization slips to see where the two armed agents were seated. A few minutes later, Kyle knocked on the cockpit door. Chad released the electric door latch as Wes unbuckled his lap belt and hung up his headset. The bright glare from the sunny cockpit temporarily blinded the relief pilot. Squinting, Kyle pulled a pair of sunglasses from his shirt pocket.

"Kyle, spell me for about fifteen minutes. I need a short walk to stretch my legs before Chad goes on his break."

Kyle nodded and eased into Wes's chair. Picking up the clipboard, he noted the flight's progress.

On the way aft, Wes checked the authorization slips. Agent Ray Outland was in seat 6-2, the left aisle seat in the first row of the business class. Agent Max Shell was seated farther aft in the last row of the business section in the right aisle seat. Stepping into first class, Wes noticed that Halston was fast asleep, snoring, from the look of his open mouth. That explained why the cabin team hadn't been up front complaining. They'd trashed him on champagne early in the flight.

Agent Outland was engrossed in the movie as Wes approached. He hardly felt the light tap on his shoulder. "Mr. Outland, could I speak with you in the rear galley for a few minutes?" Ray quickly sat up, slipped on his loafers and casually followed Wes down the left aisle.

Reaching the center galley, Wes stopped and waited. "Ray, would you mind asking Agent Shell to join us? I have a problem, and I'm going to need your help."

"Certainly, Captain. I'll get Max right away."

The two separated. Wes continued down the aisle toward the aft galley. Sybil was busy totaling the duty-free sales as he appeared. The other attendants were monitoring the main cabin from their jump seats or were on break, sleeping.

"I'm going to brief the two armed agents now, Sybil. Would you make sure we're not disturbed for a few minutes?"

"I'd be happy to... I was wondering when you would do it."

Moving closer, Wes said, "I got a SELCAL from my wife a little while ago. They got the numbers you recorded for me. They're looking for Caroline right now."

Sybil clutched his arm. "Oh God, Wes, I'm so glad," she whispered. "I was so afraid that I might have messed it up."

Wes saw the relief in her eyes as she let go of his arm. "You did a perfect job, Sybil. Thank you."

Max and Ray appeared thirty seconds later. "What's the problem, Captain?" asked Ray.

"There are two Arabs seated in first class opposite the secretary. I have reason to think they may have some kind of plan that may involve your boss. I need your help to ensure that doesn't happen."

"What, exactly, are you talking about?" Ray asked. "This sounds serious."

From the tone of Outland's voice, Wes knew he was going to have to reveal more than he'd wanted. Reluctantly, he informed them of his earlier encounter with the two men on the boat.

"Why the hell didn't you tell us this before we put the secretary on your plane, Captain?" Ray demanded. "I can't believe you'd put the secretary of state at risk over the life of your daughter! Where's your loyalty to your country, man?"

In no mood to listen to Outland's animosity, Wes exploded. "How I choose to run this operation is between me, TIA and the FAA. When

I made the decision, Halston was not on my flight. If your people had spent more time supervising his aircraft on the ground, he wouldn't have ended up on my flight!"

"So what would you like us to do with your Arab friends?" Max asked, trying to diffuse Ray's frustration and Wes's anger.

"Just keep a close eye on them until about an hour out of D.C., then take them into custody and lock them in the lavs until we land. I'll radio for backup then, if you feel it necessary."

"You're certain they're not armed, Captain?" Max asked.

"As certain as I am that the two of you are," answered Wes. "Security screening at Geneva is as tight as anywhere we fly. If they passed through there, they don't have any weapons on them."

"A piece of thin nylon cord is all that's needed in the hands of a professional," Ray griped. "I think we better take those two into custody right now or, at the very least, move the secretary out of first class."

"I'm not interested in upsetting the entire cabin at this point. If you want to move Halston, be my guest," Wes replied.

"That's easier said than done, Captain," Max interjected. "He isn't the most cooperative official we've ever had to cover." Wes grinned at the comment. For a moment, he was able to get his mind off Caroline and the troubled flight.

"To be frank about it, Captain, he's the most obnoxious prick we've ever had to wet-nurse," Ray growled. "My wife swears he's responsible for my sleepless nights."

"Do you really expect to have difficulty getting him to accept your advice and move?" Wes asked.

"Captain, he's going to raise immortal hell with both of us. He'll insist that we incarcerate those two Arabs, rather than move him out of first class. He's that way. Perhaps that would be the wisest thing to do," Ray said. Max agreed.

"Suppose we let the flight attendants take care of it." Wes suggested. "They'd like nothing more than to have the opportunity to help you guys protect Secretary Halston."

Ray looked at Max and said, "If they want the job, they've got it. We don't care how it gets done. Just move him now."

"Consider it done, but don't complain about their method. I'll let Sybil, our service manager, handle it. She's excellent at dealing with ticklish situations like this."

"We'll take the Arabs during the descent," Max said.

Wes nodded. "I'll brief Sybil now on what you want done. She'll have him out of first class in no time," Wes said, as the three men parted.

Sybil, finished with her duty-free paperwork, was taking a break when Wes slipped into the vacant jump seat beside her and explained what he wanted. "It shouldn't be a problem for us, Wes. Cynthia will jump at the chance," Sybil remarked.

Wes grinned and shook his head. She was right. Cynthia would relish the chance to make Halston's life miserable. "It's in your hands. But get him out of there as quickly as you can."

"I'll get her on it right now," Sybil said with a smile.

Returning to the cockpit, Wes saw Leigh step into the mid-galley. "Minding the store all by yourself, are you?"

"Rachel's on her break," Leigh replied. "How are you feeling to-day? I worried about you all last night. I wanted to call..."

"That's what I wanted to talk to you about. I owe you an apology for what happened yesterday, and we need to ..."

"Nonsense. That could have happened to anyone. I'm just thankful you were well enough to fly us home today. Spending an extra day in Geneva with you would have been wonderful, but it would have caused a real problem for Jason and me."

"I'd like to meet your son one day. Have you ever thought of bringing him with you?"

"Yes, but it's too risky. I'd worry he might get bumped. But I do have some pictures I took of him last week. I'll show them to you on our break."

"Something's happened and I'm going to have to stay in the cock-pit for the rest of flight."

"Is it serious? Is something wrong with the plane?"

"No. That's not it. The plane's fine."

"Then what is it, Wes? I can see you're worried."

"I'm sorry. I just can't talk about it right now. Maybe later, but not now."

Leigh studied the heavy lines on Wes's brow. The stress was there to see, though he was trying desperately to hide it. Reaching for his hand, she held it to her cheek for a moment and then let it go. "Will it be all right if I visit you during my break?"

"Sure," he answered with a smile.

As Wes walked back to the cockpit, he thought about his involvement with Leigh. The affair had been his mistake from the start and he had to end it. He blamed himself for not having the courage to stop it sooner. Leigh deserved better. The truth was he loved Meredith and always would. He could never leave her. Caroline's kidnapping had put that in perspective once and for all.

At the cockpit door, he gave the appropriate number of knocks and pushed on the narrow door as the lock released. "Thanks for covering for me, Kyle. You can relieve Chad now," Wes said, as he hung up his flight cap and loosened his tie. Chad was already unstrapping his seat belt. "What movie are they watching?" Chad asked. "I didn't notice," Wes said, taking control of the 767.

Wes picked up the clipboard to review their progress. The flight was estimating 48 North, 50 West in forty-five minutes. The TIA dispatcher had re-released the flight on to Washington Dulles IFR while he'd been in the cabin. That meant no alternate airport was required. According to the forecast, the weather for their arrival would be VFR (visual flight rules) with no thunderstorms. Wes was glad. He had more than enough to deal with as it was.

*   *   *

Tucker made good time getting to Chevy Chase. Finding North Star Truckers Company was a different story. The address was actually along Highway 191, near Beltway exit 38. Driving past the warehouse and loading docks, Tucker decided to pose as an insurance underwriter. He would explain that he was sent to perform a cursory inspection of the premises by the Maryland Department of Commerce as part of its ongoing program to ensure compliance with recent state-mandated guidelines for worker safety. It was a subject he knew well. He'd audited the program for cost overruns shortly after joining DFC.

Surprised by Tucker's unannounced visit, the manager eagerly gave him access to the entire facility and personally accompanied him on the inspection, providing him details on their operation. Seeing the number of tractor-trailer rigs that passed through North Star Truckers' docks, Tucker realized that, if Caroline had been taken there, she probably would have been shipped out immediately as part of some unsuspecting driver's cargo. The thought of her being boxed and shipped from one of the docks made his stomach turn.

Satisfied that Caroline wasn't hidden in any of the trailers he'd opened or in the warehouse, Tucker thanked the manager for his help and left for his rendezvous with Jackie.

* * *

Caroline heard the van's engine start up outside her window. As the sound of the van's leaving faded, she called to her other captor. He didn't respond immediately, but opened her door a few minutes later. He was the nicer of the two. Caroline was sorry for that, though it wouldn't matter.

"What is it you want?" he asked in perfect English.

"Please, I need to use the toilet."

For a moment, Caroline feared he was going to deny her request. Standing mute, he weighed the situation.

She spoke a second time. "Please, it's urgent."

He said nothing, but walked over to the bed and unlocked the handcuffs from her wrists. Caroline studied his expression as he put the cuffs in his pocket. Did he suspect that she was going to try to escape? Caroline made her way to the bathroom. As she reached for the overhead light switch, he closed and locked the door behind her exactly as he'd done on her three previous trips. Hearing the noisy vent fan automatically start, Caroline eased the tub drain lever to the closed position and suspended a large bath towel from the spout, letting it dangle into the tub. Then she turned on the hot and cold water. Muffled by the towel, the rushing water made very little noise. Caroline estimated it would take four minutes for the tub to fill.

She used the next two minutes to relieve herself. After rinsing and drying her hands, Caroline removed the hair dryer from the wall stand and selected its lowest speed. Then she laid it on the vanity as close to the edge of the tub as she dared, noting its position. Next, she dampened her hair with water from the sink and tossed it over the front of her head so that most of it hung in her face. Peering through the strands of hair, Caroline could see that the tub was nearly full. Quickly turning off the water, she stood up with her hair hanging in her face. For a moment, Caroline feared she would lose her courage.

Her high-pitched screams drowned out the sound of the hair dryer's motor. Now facing the tub with the vanity to her right side, Caroline continued to scream. With each breath, she felt stronger, more willing to fight for her life.

The clicking of the bathroom door told Caroline her cries were being answered. Covering her face with her hands, she continued to scream as her kidnapper entered the bathroom.

"What is the matter? Why are you screaming?" he shouted, struggling to see why her hands were covering her face. Caroline stood her ground and continued to scream.

"Stop it! Stop it! Why do you scream? What is the matter with you?"

Startled by what he was hearing and unable to see what was causing her such anguish, the Arab moved to Caroline's left side and grabbed her. Caroline resisted. Irritated by her screaming, he leaned around to face her.

"My eyes! My eyes! I can't see!" she screamed, flinging her hands at his chest, knocking him off balance and into the tub. Seeing him fall, Caroline swept the hair dryer off the vanity and into the tub behind him.

Jolted by the electrical shock, the young man's body shook violently as he experienced the immense pain of severe muscle contraction. His eyes lost their focus; the sealed lips of his mouth rolled under as his eyelids fluttered uncontrollably under intense electrical pressure. Respiratory function ceased instantly as his diaphragm seized. He couldn't breathe. Seconds later, his heart muscle in spasms, the kidnapper suffered cardiac arrhythmia.

The man's agony was far worse than Caroline could have imagined. Nor did he appear to die quickly. The horror of watching made her wretch. For a moment, she thought of pulling the plug, but decided against it. What was done was done. There was no time to waste. His accomplice would be returning shortly.

Caroline locked the door and fled, taking the key with her. From the hallway, she saw the mobile telephone on the dining room table. She thought of calling for help, but decided against it. Dad's instructions were to run and that meant getting out of the house as fast as she could.

Darting back into the bedroom, Caroline grabbed her heels. Fortunately, they were only about an inch high. As she dashed into the living room, Caroline saw the van turn off the road toward the house. She panicked. It was the other kidnapper. Running into the kitchen, she pulled the heaviest carving knife from the block on the counter before bolting out the back door. Seeing a stand of tall trees beyond the plowed field, she took off running. She was alive and free, but nowhere near safe.

She reached the woods in less than four minutes, breathless and thirsty. Dropping to the ground, Caroline rested. She had stopped only long enough to take off her heels. They made it impossible to run on the freshly plowed ground. She'd dropped the knife somewhere during the run. Having the shoes was more important.

As she watched, the kidnapper appeared on the rear deck and stared straight in her direction. Caroline froze, certain he'd seen her. He would surely see her tracks leading straight to where she was crouching. Caroline could see them herself. Time seemed to stand still as she watched for his next move. Would he pursue her? Fear gripped her as she saw him take out what appeared to be a gun and check to see that it was loaded. He'd seen her tracks. He would come after her. It was only a matter of time, which she couldn't afford to waste.

Carefully, Caroline withdrew into the woods while keeping her eyes on him. Suddenly the kidnapper jumped off the deck and broke into a full run toward her. He'd spotted her. Caroline knew she had to move fast if she wanted to keep her distance.

Choosing a deer path that seemed to meander to the left and down through the woods, Caroline broke into a run. The pace she set was difficult to maintain as she moved deeper into the forest. The underbrush became taller and more dense as Caroline descended into the woods' lower elevation.

As she ran, Caroline tried to picture the position of the ranch house relative to the sun. It would be the only way she could keep her bearings. When possible, she ran toward the sun. She knew looking into the sun's rays would make it more difficult for him to see her and would help her avoid running in circles. Running with the sun also meant she was moving westward, paralleling the highway. At some point, she would turn south and hope to reach the road. From there she could flag down a car. All that mattered was to make it to safety.

Caroline didn't see the log that sent her crashing head-over-heels into a large poplar. Her small frame was no match for the stout tree. In pain from the impact, she dragged herself back to her feet and slowly picked up her stride. Although the pain was severe, Caroline ignored it. She would manage; she had to. Caroline wondered if her assailant was closing on her, but knew she couldn't risk stopping to find out.

A large ravine lay in her path. Stopping short of the edge, Caroline studied it for a moment. A stream ran along the bottom. It looked shallow enough to wade across. Looking at the ridge on the other side, she could make out what appeared to be an open field. Instinctively, she charged down the hill, picking her way around the trees and brush. Reaching the stream, Caroline plunged into the water. It was much deeper than she had imagined. Her heels stuck to the muddy bottom.

Retrieving one shoe, Caroline frantically searched for the other, but it was nowhere to be found. Realizing her chances of finding the other shoe was hopeless, she continued on bare feet. Climbing onto the opposite bank, Caroline looked at the water longingly before remembering it was not fit to drink. Thirst was slowing her pace. Clawing her way up the steep embankment to the top of the ridge took at least five minutes and used most of her remaining strength.

Knowing she would have to rest for a few minutes, Caroline dropped onto a thick cover of decaying leaves. She searched the ravine for signs of her assailant, but saw nothing. Listening intently, she heard only her heavy breathing. Perhaps he was having a tougher time in the woods than she. Were there any forests where he came from? Resting with her arms on her knees, Caroline began to ache from hitting the tree and falling. She had to get under way before the pain got worse. Rolling over on her side, Caroline struggled to her feet.

A bullet tore the bark off the side of the tree next to where she'd been sitting seconds ago. Hearing the slug ricochet off the tree, Caroline dived to the ground and crawled behind a large oak. Peering across the gorge, she saw her stalker running down the ravine. She had no more than five minutes lead on him.

Leaping from her crouched position, Caroline began running toward the open field. Open land meant tended grounds and roads. Caroline knew she could not continue her pace much longer. She had to get help soon before her attacker closed the gap enough to kill her. Thinking of Tucker, Caroline realized her life with him had just begun. It wasn't fair that this asshole could end it for her now. Swearing she would not let that happen, Caroline forced herself onward, quickening her pace.

* * *

The rendezvous at Sully Plantation worked perfectly, but the visit to West Auto Parts Shop in Chantilly was a disappointment for Tucker and Jackie. Posing as an inspector for the Virginia Department of Commerce, Tucker had introduced Jackie as a rookie to the inspection process which explained her ignorance of most everything he talked about. She'd simply nodded her head and smiled eagerly at what was said.

Irritated by their impromptu visit, the owner, a man of Middle Eastern descent, seemed to run a legitimate business. The inspection had lasted less than fifteen minutes. A quick walk-through of the premises had convinced Tucker that Caroline was not there and probably never had been.

Returning to his Explorer, Jackie sensed his frustration. "We'll find her," she said. "Caroline will be okay."

Tucker lowered his sun visor and adjusted the temperature lever to get colder air from the Explorer. "Maybe and maybe not. Have you stopped to consider that trying to find her using these phone numbers might turn out to be a complete waste of time?"

"You can't think about it that way, Tucker. We'll find her. It's just taking more time than you'd hoped. It could be that your boss and his FBI friend have already found her."

"No. They would have called me if they'd learned anything."

"Why don't you call them and see if they've had any luck?"

"I've thought about it, but I'd feel worse if they said no. What are we going to do if we don't find her using these numbers? We don't have anything else to go on, Jackie."

"Tucker, if Dad said he talked to Caroline on one of those numbers, then she is at one of them or she was there when he talked to her. Otherwise, why did he go to the trouble of transmitting them to you in-flight?"

Tucker didn't have an answer. Losing Caroline and the fear of not finding her was taking its toll as he raced toward Middleburg. If he didn't find her shortly, he'd go directly to the FBI and ask for their help. Something told him he should have done that to begin with. Tucker wondered if he had enough information to justify the FBI's intervention or whether they would remand his case to the Virginia State Police or some other enforcement agency. That could take forever.

A stop at the post office in Middleburg helped pin down the location to a ranch house three miles southwest of the town. The postal clerk seemed surprised that the place was being used. She said that the owners had tried unsuccessfully to sell it for years.

Tucker and Jackie spied the rusted mailbox with no number sitting on the weathered post. It was just as the postal clerk had described it. Looking up the gravel driveway they saw a van parked in front of the house.

"That's got to be it, Tucker. The description of the mailbox checks," argued Jackie as he wheeled into the driveway and stopped. "Okay, but I want you to stay in the Explorer until I check things out. If you see anything funny, get the hell out of here fast and call 911. Understand?"

Jackie didn't answer. She was too interested in the house and the van several hundred yards ahead.

Easing the Explorer into first, Tucker started up the long drive. The vehicle made little noise running on the hard ground except for striking an occasional pothole made by the summer rainstorms. Stopping just short of the van, Tucker switched off the ignition. They waited, as if half-expecting someone to come out of the house and welcome them in.

"It doesn't look like anyone's around," Tucker observed.

"But there's a van here, Tucker. Somebody must be here."

Reaching over the back of his seat, Tucker picked up the forty-five automatic. He hadn't taken time to check it out. The gun filled the palm of his hand. Keeping the barrel pointed toward the windshield, Tucker gave it a quick inspection. After several attempts, he figured out how to eject the clip before loading it with eight rounds. Shoving the clip back into the handle, he made sure the safety was off. Jackie watched Tucker handle the weapon, certain he would use it if he had too. Realizing there could be trouble, she decided to load the double-barreled shotgun.

"I'll check out the van first, then the house. If someone comes, blow the horn," Tucker said, slipping the forty-five into his pants. Jackie nodded at him through the window and watched as he walked cautiously toward the van. Then, reaching over the seat, she pulled the twelve-gauge shotgun into her lap and opened the glove compartment to get the shells.

The van's hood was hot. Tucker couldn't decide if it was because of the hot afternoon temperature or whether the van had been driven recently. A sample of the other surfaces confirmed his suspicions. The intensity was due to residual engine heat. Peering through the window into the van's front seat, he saw nothing unusual. Tucker debated opening the doors and having a good look inside, but decided against it, concerned that someone in the ranch might see or hear him.

Stepping onto the porch, Tucker noticed the front door had been left open. After rehearsing his speech once more, he knocked on the door and called out. "Is anyone at home?" After waiting a couple of seconds, he knocked again. "Hello! Is anyone here?" There was no reply. Tucker leaned in toward the half-opened door and listened intently, but heard nothing.

Looking back at Jackie, Tucker entered the house. The place obviously had not been lived in for some time. Dust and cobwebs were everywhere. A bag of fast food sat on the dining table next to a mobile phone. Standing in the living room, he called again, but no one answered. Satisfied there was no one in the house, Tucker relaxed and began canvassing the rooms for evidence of Caroline's presence.

Entering the master bedroom, Tucker smelled the faint scent of Caroline's perfume. Looking across the room, he noticed the bathroom door was broken and hanging by one hinge. Frightened by the suggestion of foul play, Tucker withdrew the automatic from his pants and crept toward the opened door.

Seeing the dead man lying in the tub, his eyes still open, stunned Tucker. Looking closer, he saw what looked like a hair dryer. It was submerged, lying on the bottom of the tub. His experiences with death had always been in the movies. This is for real, he thought, continuing to stare at the lifeless Arab in his final death pose. Had Caroline done this? Had she escaped? Questions raced through Tucker's mind as he tried to imagine what had happened.

Caroline was alive, and perhaps nearby. Tucker felt it. He had to find her, quickly. Walking back through the bedroom, he was sure she'd been held in the room. The smell — it was the same perfume Wes had brought her from Paris on one of his many trips. Glancing into the dining room, Tucker looked again at the unopened fast food bag on the table. Noticing two cups beside the bag, he surmised there were at least two kidnappers. Had the other one caught up with her? Was Caroline alive?

Running from the house, Tucker leaped off the porch and flung open the rear doors to the van. Caroline's attaché case lay on the floor. He found an earring of hers that must have come off in the struggle.

"What is it, Tucker? Have you found her?"

"No, but she's been here. There's a dead Arab in the tub. Caroline electrocuted him."

"No way!" cried Jackie in disbelief. "Where is she?"

Tucker turned the ignition key and punched Dave's preset number on his mobile phone. "Tucker, where is she?"

"I'm not sure, but she's close by, maybe hiding in those woods. Another kidnapper's involved, Jackie. My guess is he's either got her with him, or he's chasing her right now."

"Then why don't we go back to the highway? We can blow the horn and make enough noise so she'll know we're nearby. We'll never find her in the woods, Tucker."

"Okay, we'll do it after I check out the back of the house."

"Coleman."

"Dave, it's Tucker. Caroline has escaped. She was being held near Middleburg at a ranch house about three miles southwest of the town. We need help now!" Tucker was talking a mile a minute.

"Who's got her, Tucker? Are they armed?"

"There are at least two of them, Dave. One is dead — electrocuted. The other one has Caroline, or is chasing her through the woods. Please get help here fast. Jackie will give you the details. I've got to go check the back of the house!"

"We'll do it, Tucker but stay near the phone. I'll call you back in a minute."

Tucker handed the phone to Jackie. "Give him the directions and then start up the Explorer. I'll be right back!" Eyeing the shotgun resting beside her leg, he said, "Use it if you need to, Jackie. This guy could be anywhere."

Exiting the Explorer with the forty-five in his hand, Tucker rushed around the edge of the house.

* * *

Caroline reached the edge of the clearing and paused a minute to catch her breath while debating which direction to take. The land immediately in front of her was partially cleared. Large piles of uprooted stumps had left gaping holes in the earth. Beyond the scarred land appeared to be a fenced pasture. She would travel along the edge of the forest, bypassing the rough terrain. Attempting travel across the newly broken ground would be too risky. It would be safer to stay on hard ground until she reached the pasture. Then she would turn south toward the highway.

Leaning against a large oak, Caroline rubbed the bottom of her right foot. It was bleeding, cut along the inner edge from her toe. Her arms and legs were covered with scratches from the briars she'd brushed against. The painful knot on her arm had swollen even more.

Suddenly, Caroline heard the unmistakable sound of her captor struggling up the embankment to the left of where she stood. He couldn't be more than a hundred yards behind her. Leaping to her feet, Caroline broke into a full stride, running along the edge of the forest. She tried to stay just inside the tree line, hoping he would think she had gone for the cleared land. Unable to sustain the fast pace for very long, Caroline slowed down, but kept a close eye to her rear. Several minutes later, she stopped and looked behind, but the guman was nowhere in sight. He's got to be as exhausted as I am, she thought.

The afternoon heat was oppressive. Thirst was now a serious problem. Her body, drenched in sweat, was covered with small bits of dirt and leaves. Salt from her perspiration burned her eyes, forcing her to continually wipe them with her dirty hands.

Reaching the meadow exhausted and out of breath, Caroline collapsed onto the warm earth, secure beneath the tall grass. She couldn't go any farther without rest. No part of her body was free from pain. Her throat was parched from the lack of water. Hiding among the tall grasses would have to suffice. She would not risk raising her head. Instead, she would keep her ear to the earth and listen. It would be safer that way.

Lying on her side and dazed from exhaustion, Caroline thought at first she was dreaming. Someone seemed to be calling her. "Caroline! Caroline! Where are you?" It couldn't be. I'm hallucinating, she thought. Then she heard the familiar voice, again. "Caroline! Caroline! We're here on the road!" Certain she heard her sister, Caroline carefully raised her head slightly, peering over the grasses in the direction of Jackie's voice. She could barely make out the top of a vehicle about a hundred yards away. For a second, she wanted to stand up and shout back at them, but she knew it would reveal her position. She had to make her way through the grass quietly until she got nearer to them. A quick glance about told her the gunman was nowhere in sight.

Scrambling to her feet, Caroline began moving through the grass cautiously, at first. Then, gaining some of her energy, Caroline ran as hard as she dared, scanning the field for the gunman as she ran.

Running toward the vehicle, Caroline could see it was an Explorer — midnight blue like Tucker's. Drawing closer, she could make out the outline of a man sitting behind the wheel. It had to be him. The Explorer was moving. There were no more calls. "Oh God, they're leaving!" she cried out. "Don't leave me!" Stopping, Caroline screamed, "Tucker, don't leave me!"

Then she screamed it again, knowing it would surely alert her assailant and signal the end of her life.

Tucker heard Caroline's second scream. Slamming on the brakes, he threw the truck into reverse. "It's Caroline! I heard her!" he shouted. Jackie turned her head to see her sister running toward them, still more than fifty yards away.

Racing back in reverse, Tucker stopped his Explorer abeam Caroline's path as a shot ricocheted off the hood of his truck.

Horrified, Jackie, saw the gunman running from the edge of the woods toward Caroline. "He's going to kill her, Tucker!"

Grabbing the forty-five automatic off the front seat, Tucker leaped from the truck and ran toward Caroline, firing wildly at the man running toward her. Less than thirty yards from her attacker, Tucker stopped and aimed. He got off two rounds, forcing the gunman to the ground, before the automatic jammed. Caroline reached his side as the gunman stood up from the grass and cautiously moved closer. Seeing the look of fear in Tucker's face, the killer slowly closed the distance between them.

"Get behind me, Caroline!" commanded Tucker as the gunman's first shot hit him midway down his left thigh, causing him to collapse in pain.

"No! No! Don't shoot him! Don't shoot him!" cried Caroline as the gunman closed for the kill.

Pulling Caroline to the ground, Tucker crawled over her as the killer moved within twenty feet, taking aim with his nine-millimeter Beretta.

The blast from Jackie's shotgun struck the attacker squarely across the knees, knocking him to the ground in excruciating pain. Jackie screamed, "Get up and run, now!" as she held her bead on the downed gunman.

Caroline got to her feet, but saw that Tucker couldn't move, and refused to leave him.

Seeing Tucker immobile, Jackie stepped from behind the truck while keeping her aim on the assailant. Her hands trembled as she slowly moved into the grass, making her way toward them. Her right shoulder was numb with pain. The smell of gunpowder burned her nose.

Suddenly, Jackie saw the flash of the killer's gun as he pointed it at her. She squeezed the second trigger. The other barrel's blast tore the gunman's chest open, sending his weapon flying through the grass. Standing a short distance away, Jackie watched in shock as blood gushed from the dying man's mouth. Satisfied that he no longer was a threat, she rushed over to Tucker and Caroline and knelt beside them.

Tears streamed from Jackie's eyes as she cried for joy and for sorrow. Her voice quivered as she tried to speak, but couldn't. Caroline knew her pain and held her younger sister tightly as Jackie broke into deep, uncontrollable sobs. Tucker put his arms around both of them, trying to console them. No one spoke as they held each other in silence, content to let their hearts speak. The warmth of their love was enough.

Minutes later, they heard the distant, but unmistakable, siren of a police car. Using the shotgun for a crutch, Tucker struggled to his feet. Caroline stood up and placed his arm over her small shoulder. Jackie took the shotgun from Tucker and offered him her shoulder as the three made their way slowly through the grass toward the Explorer.

Trooper Amos Harper's State Police cruiser came into view just as they were approaching the Explorer. Seeing the three of them, he slowed the silver and gray sedan, while reaching for his mike. Radio-ing his position, Harper brought his Chevy Caprice to a stop in front of the Explorer. Tucker threw up his hand as Jackie rifled through his golf bag, looking for something to use for a bandage.

"Are you Agent Coleman?" the trooper asked.

"No, sir. I'm Tucker Shaw. This is my fiancée, Caroline Beacham, and her sister, Jackie."

The trooper looked at the young women and tipped his hat as he spoke, "Afternoon ladies. Are you all right?"

"Except for my cuts, bruises and thirst, I'm okay, Officer," an-swered Caroline, rubbing the big knot on the back of her arm. "Tucker needs medical attention. He's been shot in the leg."

The officer nodded and squatted in front of Tucker's leg to exam-ine the wound. "It's just a flesh wound. You'll be all right," he said, giving Tucker a reassuring smile.

"What happened here? Who shot you?" asked Harper, eyeing the shotgun and rifle lying on the back seat of Tucker's truck.

"Officer, I don't know where to begin," Tucker said.

"That can wait. Let's get some medical support on the way first, then we'll discuss the details."

Jackie interrupted. "Sir, I think you should know there's a man lying over there in the grass. I'm sure I killed him."

Amos glanced in the direction Jackie was pointing, but saw no one. Drawing his weapon and clutching it with two hands, Harper moved cautiously into the grass as Jackie continued to point.

"Over to your right, a little more," she said. "That's it."

Walking a few more feet, Harper stopped. "Damn! You did shoot him!" mouthed Harper staring at the gaping hole blown in his chest. He studied the mangled body for a minute more before walking back toward the Explorer.

Realizing he hadn't seen the gunman's weapon, Harper walked back over to the dead Arab. After considering the position of the body, he walked into the grass about eight or nine feet. He found the Beretta lying in the dirt. Fishing it off the ground with his ball-point pen, he carried it to his cruiser. There, he withdrew a plastic bag from the car and slipped the gun into the bag. Returning to the Explorer, he handed Jackie a small first aid kit. "This might help you, ma'am."

"Thanks," said Jackie as she opened the kit on the hood of the truck. Removing the tube of antiseptic and all of the largest gauze pads and some adhesive tape, she handed them to her sister. Caroline dressed the wound and then held the gauze pads against Tucker's thigh as Jackie wrapped the tape around his leg. Harper took the small scissors from the kit and cut the excess tape.

"Which of you want to give me the details of what happened? I know it isn't very pleasant to have to go over this right now, seeing what you've been through, and I'm sorry, but I need the information now," Amos said.

"I can explain it to you, Officer."

"You know about the other one?" Caroline asked Tucker.

"Yes, I've seen him, too."

Harper looked at Caroline. "There's another dead Arab?"

"Yes, sir. He's lying in a bathtub at the ...."

"Is it open season on Arabs today, or what? Where is the other one?"

"...at the last house you passed coming here," added Tucker.

"I see. And how did he die?" Harper asked.

"He was electrocuted," answered Caroline.

"Electrocuted?"

"Yes, sir," Caroline said.

Harper shook his head and muttered something to himself as he walked back to his cruiser to get his clipboard. The dispatcher was on the horn calling for him. "Fifty-seven here."

"Fifty-seven, has FBI Agent Coleman made contact with you?"

"Negative."

"He should be arriving there momentarily to take charge of the investigation. The Feds have a strong interest in this one. It has inter-national implications."

"You could say that," Harper growled. "I know of two dead Arabs for starters."

Coleman's FBI sedan appeared from around the curve as the trooper signed off with his dispatcher. He parked behind the officer's cruiser.

"Officer, Dave Coleman. I'm with the FBI. This is Jim Paterson. He's with DFC." Harper nodded as Coleman displayed his ID. Jim rushed over to see Tucker. "Amos Harper, Virginia State Police. I was expecting you. My dispatcher just called to advise me that you boys will be handling this one. And, from what I've already seen, you're welcome to it."

"What happened?" Dave asked, glancing at Tucker.

"You've got two dead Arabs and a young man over there with a superficial gunshot wound. One of the young women, the smaller one, looks like she's spent the better part of the day running through briars. She's skinned up pretty bad. The younger girl says she shot the dead man lying over there in the grass. She gave him the ugly end of her double-barreled shotgun. It's over by the Explorer. His Beretta is in my car. The shorter blonde, the one who's scratched up, says there's another dead one lying in a tub of water in a house up the road. Seems he was electrocuted," Harper added. "You've got one hell of a mess to straighten out, Coleman."

"Yeah, it does get messy at times. Thanks for your help. We'll send your people a copy of our report," Coleman said.

"By the way. There should be a rescue squad here within the next several minutes. It's a volunteer outfit, I think. They're good, but it sometimes takes them a little longer to get it together," said Harper, as he fetched the Beretta. "Anything else I can do for you guys?"

"Yeah, we're going to need to move these two bodies to a morgue. Can you help us?" Dave asked, not certain how he was going to explain his involvement to his boss.

"Sure. I'll radio the county to expect them. The rescue squad can handle the transportation for you," Harper said.

"Any chance you could block the traffic along this road until we can get things cleaned up here? I'd rather not have these guys' friends knowing they've fallen on hard times."

"No problem. I'll handle it," called Harper.

Tossing the Beretta onto the front seat of his car, Dave watched the trooper speed away as he walked over to the Explorer. Jim was listening to Tucker and Caroline's description of what had happened.

Hearing their bizarre tale, Coleman sensed there was far more to the story than any of them knew. He needed to talk with his boss ASAP, but first he needed to get Tucker and the young women to a safe place.

"I've got to level with you all. I haven't the slightest idea what these guys were up to, but it's obvious they were professionals, willing to do whatever was necessary for their cause. Until we know for certain who and what we're dealing with, I want the three of you to stay out of reach," explained Dave, "After we get your leg taken care of, Tucker, I want Jim to drive you three to Williamsburg. You'll be safer there."

"What about my work at the bank?" Caroline asked.

"I'll contact Straton and explain the situation. He's been extremely supportive. He'll understand," Jim interjected.

"Once you get home, write down everything you can remember, Caroline. It could be very important," Dave said. "Jackie, I'll need the same kind of report from you concerning your activities here, okay?"

Jackie nodded. The discussion was interrupted by the wailing siren of the rescue squad ambulance.

With Tucker's wound bandaged and Caroline's cuts and abrasions cleaned up, Tucker insisted they could make it to Williamsburg on their own. Jackie agreed and offered to drive.

They were barely under way when Jackie saw Harper's cruiser parked diagonally across the road up ahead. Slowing the Explorer to a stop beside the trooper's patrol car, Harper shouted, "Coleman's asked us to escort you down to Williamsburg. Another patrolman will join you about three miles down the road and follow you."

Nodding her thanks, Jackie eased around the roadblock as Caroline used the mobile phone to dial her mother.

"Mom. It's Caroline — I'm okay — Jackie and Tucker are with me — We're on our way home now — We'll be there in three hours."

"Caroline!" cried Meredith, unable to talk for tears of joy at hearing her older daughter's voice.

"Are you all right? Are all of you okay?"

Caroline spent the rest of her call talking to her mother in riddles to avoid being understood.

Jackie stared out the window, still in shock over the shooting. She'd had no choice, she kept telling herself. If she hadn't killed the gunman, both Caroline and Tucker would be dead, and so would she. The killing was justified. And yet, Jackie knew in her heart that taking a life was against everything she had been taught to believe in. The contradiction troubled her. It would take a long time to forget. No longer innocent, she would never be the same again.

Caroline looked at Jackie. Her lips quivered as she imagined the courage it had taken Jackie to act as she had. She'd always been special to Caroline — more than a sister, like a daughter. Fighting back the tears, Caroline leaned over the seat and took her sister's hand. Jackie squeezed her hand back and smiled. Jackie knew she had done the right thing.

IO

IN HARM'S WAY

Cynthia was ecstatic over the chance to help Halston's security agents remove him to the business section of the cabin. "Are you sure it's O.K. for me to do this, Sybil? I don't want to lose my job," said Cynthia, topping off the serving pot with fresh coffee.

"Look, you've always wanted to get even with that jerk for the way he's treated you on previous flights. Now is your chance," said Sybil. "I'll help, if you like."

"How's that?"

"Get into position and I'll come by and bump into you at just the right time."

"You're serious, aren't you?"

Sybil's attitude surprised her. Normally, Sybil would have raised hell if an attendant had done anything to harass a passenger on her flight, no matter how rude and abusive they had become. "Okay. Here goes," announced Cynthia, setting the hot coffeepot on the tray.

Halston was deep in conversation with Chad as Cynthia approached him. Chad's expression told her he was miserable being stuck next to the pompous windbag. Pausing at the secretary's row, Cynthia looked over her shoulder at Sybil before she spoke.

"Mr. Secretary, would you like a fresh cup of coffee, sir? I brewed it especially for you."

Riggs looked up at Cynthia, annoyed by her interruption until his eye caught her flaming red hair and buxom figure. Smiling, he beckoned her closer. "Why yes, my dear, I'd like that with a brandy," he said, lustfully.

Seeing she had aroused his sexual interest, Cynthia rewarded his admiration with a sensuous smile as she took a china cup and saucer from the tray and handed it to him. Halston eagerly seized the cup and saucer and waited.

"Oh I'm so glad, sir. I'll pour your coffee now and then run to get a brandy for you right away."

Out of the corner of her eye, Cynthia saw Sybil start down the aisle toward her as she lifted the full pot of coffee from the tray. Chad leaned aft to allow her clear access to Halston's suspended cup.

"Dammit, girl! What in the hell are you doing to me?" Halston screamed, as hot coffee streamed into his lap. Frightened by his outburst, Cynthia froze. A look of horror covered her face. Sybil's impact was much harder than Cynthia could possibly have anticipated. Whipping about in his seat trying to avoid the burning hot coffee, Halston shoved the empty pot from his scalded crotch.

"Oh, my Lord! Oh, Mr. Secretary, how stupid of me! I'm so sorry, sir! Please, let me get something to wipe it up with!"

"Just get the hell away from me!" shouted Riggs, thrashing. "You damned near burned me to death, you idiot!"

Chad hopped out of his seat, brushing the coffee from his trousers and making way for Halston's exit. Sybil rushed up and offered her own apology, admitting that she had caused the accident and absolving her flying partner of any blame.

"Then you're both a bunch of incompetent fools!" bellowed Halston, now standing in the aisle, brushing his pants.

Coffee stains covered the entire upper part of his trousers and extended down the inseams to the bends in his knees. Sybil fetched a towel. Riggs snatched it from her, nearly running over her on his way to the lavatory.

Smiles and snickers erupted into full-blown laughter as he slammed the lav door, illuminating the Occupied sign. Cynthia and Sybil made one last apology to those passengers seated nearby, hoping to solicit their sympathy. Smiling, Chad gave them a subtle thumbs-up as he waited in the alcove.

It took several minutes for Ray and Max to regain their composure enough to go forward and check on their boss. "Ma'am, what happened to the secretary?" Max asked, fighting the grin on his face. Turning around, Sybil said succinctly, "The secretary has had a slight accident with a coffeepot!"

"Is he okay?" Ray asked.

"Well yes and no, if you know what I mean," she replied with a devious look in her eye. Ray didn't press the issue any further, fearing Sybil might say something to implicate them.

Returning to the coffee-soaked seat, Cynthia tried to clean it. Realizing it was hopeless, she removed the cushion and took it to the galley.

Remaining in the lav for quite a spell, Halston finally came out. Ray was waiting in the small alcove. "Sir, I'm sorry about your accident. I'd like you to have my seat." Halston thought about Ray's offer. He'd heard the chuckles from the passengers who had seen his outburst. Having to sit among them would be humiliating, he decided. "I appreciate your offer, Ray. I accept."

Moments later, Halston eased into Ray's seat in business class and tried to forget the incident, thinking he'd handled the situation poorly. He'd have Ross make the apologies to the attendants. Heaven forbid, if the media learned of it and chose to play it up.

Noting the secretary had accepted Ray's offer and had taken his seat in business class, Sybil returned with the cushion and a handful of linen napkins. Pushing the cushion back into the seat, she covered it with a brown plastic trash bag and spread several napkins over the seat. "There, gentlemen, I trust you'll find the seat acceptable. Would either of you care for coffee?"

"No, ma'am!" replied Max, smiling at her humor. Ray leaned over and whispered, "Thanks for your help. I only wished we could have filmed the incident." Sybil smiled. She was glad the charade was over. She still had an uneasy feeling about the flight and the two Arab businessmen. Their presence troubled her.

Wes had waited long enough. He had to know what else Meredith knew about Caroline's kidnapping.

"LONGFELLOW RADIO, TIA 899 ON 6634, REQUESTING A PHONE PATCH TO THE U.S." The background noise that had interrupted Meredith's earlier call seemed to have dissipated somewhat.

"GOOD AFTERNOON AGAIN, TIA 899, LONGFELLOW RADIO. YOUR ACCOUNT NUMBER, PLEASE." Wes read back his number then glanced down at Kyle's communications selector panel to see if he was monitoring the number two HF radio. He was not.

"TIA 899, WHAT IS THE NUMBER YOU WISH TO DIAL?" After reeling off his home phone number, Wes paused again.

"MEREDITH, IT'S WES. TELL ME WHAT YOU KNOW ABOUT CAROLINE."

"OH WES, THANK GOD YOU CALLED. CAROLINE'S ALIVE AND SAFE. SHE'S ON HER WAY HERE NOW WITH TUCKER AND JACKIE........."

Suddenly Meredith's voice was interrupted by the sound of the HF radio re-channelizing. "What the ...," groaned Wes, seeing Kyle remove his hand from the HF frequency knob. "What do you think you're doing?" snapped Wes, retuning the HF radio back to Longfellow's frequency. Kyle glared at him, but said nothing.

Furious with Kyle, Wes tried to control his temper as he tried to re-establish contact with Longfellow Radio.

"TIA 899, LONGFELLOW. I SAY, OLE CHAP, YOU SEEM TO BE HAVING A DIFFICULT TIME OF IT TODAY. DO YOU WANT ME TO GIVE IT ANOTHER TRY?" In no mood for the Englishman's frivolity, Wes answered, "YES. TRY IT AGAIN, LONGFELLOW."

"THE SAME NUMBER?"

"AFFIRMATIVE."

"STAND BY. I'LL HAVE ANOTHER GO AT IT, 899."

The muzzle of the nine-millimeter Beretta felt cold against Wes's right temple. Holding the gun on him, Kyle reached up and switched off both HF radios as he spoke. "Don't touch any of the radios, Captain Beacham."

"Are you out of your friggin' mind, Kyle? Put that gun away!"

"No, Captain! You listen! If you don't do exactly as I say, I'll kill you. We've already eliminated one of your crew and I will not hesitate to shoot you, if need be. Do you understand?"

Wes gazed into Kyle's black, narrow-set eyes. A silent rage glared back at him. His tone was dead serious. Kyle's metamorphosis unnerved him. How could this be happening, Wes asked himself? A chilling uneasiness moved over him as he thought of Mark's mysterious death. Was Kyle involved?

Nudging him with the Beretta, Kyle demanded, "Your answer, Captain. I won't ask you again. It makes no difference to me whether you or I fly us to Washington National Airport."

"All right! All right! You have my word, but you'll live to regret it!" mouthed Wes, his anger growing by the second. "It's you who will live to regret the day you ever boarded this flight, Captain."

"Who are you? And what are you after?"

"My real name is Ahmed, Kahlid Ahmed. You will learn of our objectives soon enough. For now, it is only important that you do exactly as you are told. You've already made a very serious mistake by contacting the authorities. Your daughter, Caroline, may be free, but your entire family will suffer the consequences of your stupidity."

Wes realized that responding to Ahmed's threat would serve no purpose. The fact that Caroline was free was proof enough he'd won the first round with these bastards.

"So what is it you want from me?"

"You will continue to act as pilot-in-command of the flight. I will give you instructions as needed."

Wes watched as Ahmed pressed the cabin call button and told Sybil that Chad was needed up front for a few minutes. Unsnapping his seat belt, Ahmed climbed out of the F/O seat and stood against the aft bulkhead.

Chad knocked twice and then pushed on the cockpit door.

"What's the problem, boss? Did I oversleep my rest period?"

Ahmed jammed the gun into Chad's right ear as he spoke. "Shut up and do as I say, if you want to stay alive, Chad."

"What in the........"

The blow to Chad's head knocked the ex-Marine unconscious.

"You didn't have to do that!" Wes snapped. "He would have done what you wanted without that."

Not responding, Ahmed quickly tied Chad's hands using a headset cord. Chad began to stir as Ahmed finished lashing the co-pilot's hands together. Wes watched as Chad gradually came to.

"Wha..t happened? My head."

"Get to your feet, Chad," ordered Ahmed. Still groggy from the blow, Chad pulled himself up using the back of Wes's cockpit chair. "Get into the bulkhead seat, now," Ahmed commanded. Chad didn't resist.

Ahmed fastened another cord around the one that bound Chad's hands and routed the loose end over the small coat rack above the bulkhead seat. Then he pulled the cord tight, stretching Chad's tied hands up against the pole. Finished, Ahmed strapped Chad into the seat and stuffed a linen napkin into his mouth. "Captain, I'm going to leave the cockpit for a minute. Do I need to remind you of your commitment?" Wes shook his head. "Do not open the door unless you receive four knocks. Understood?"

"Yes. Yes, I understand," Wes answered. Ahmed glanced at Chad as he shoved the Beretta into his pleated-trouser pocket, opened the door and disappeared into the cabin.

Ahmed went straight to where Reza and Mohammed were seated. Reza was reading a newspaper as his companion dozed. Seeing Ahmed, Jabarri sat up and put down his paper. Something has gone wrong, thought Reza, remembering that they had agreed not to speak until it was time to act. The expression on his accomplice's face showed his concern.

With the second service not due for another thirty minutes, Leigh knew this would be her only chance to visit with Wes before they landed. Gathering the photographs of Jason from her purse, Leigh made her way up the left aisle toward the cockpit.

Ahmed spoke hurriedly to Jabarri. Leigh noticed them talking and stepped around Kyle, continuing toward the cockpit. Ahmed stopped talking and watched her. Suddenly, he realized she was going to the cockpit. Concerned that Wes might unlatch the door, he straightened up and quickly moved toward her. Jumping to his feet, Reza stepped into the aisle.

Ray and Max both saw the silhouette of a gun in Ahmed's pocket as he stood up. There was no mistaking its shape. Both agents also knew federal air regulations precluded crew members from carrying firearms.

Scrambling from their seats while drawing their weapons, Ray leaped across the couple sleeping in the middle seats as Max darted into the business section to cover the secretary. Landing in the left aisle, Ray saw Ahmed brandish the gun as he jerked Leigh away from the cockpit door.

"Drop the gun, now!" Ray shouted at Ahmed, crouching into the firing position. "Put it down!" he added, bringing his thirty-eight special into his field of vision.

Unarmed, Reza ducked into the small alcove connecting the right forward galley and the left main entrance door as Ahmed hid behind Leigh and opened fire on Ray.

Outland saw the muzzle flash of Ahmed's first round and felt the bullet tear open his left side. Ray squeezed off his first shot. Missing, his bullet struck Leigh as Ahmed fired again. Ahmed's second bullet found its mark, hitting Outland in the chest. Ray slumped to the floor.

Pushing Leigh off him, Ahmed kicked the fragile cockpit door open and stuck the nose of his Beretta into the side of Wes's head. Reza, seeing Ray hit the floor, rushed into the cockpit behind Ahmed. "I should kill you now!" shouted Ahmed as he ripped the PA handset off the rear of the center pedestal and thrust it into Wes's lap. "How many more security people are onboard, Captain?" demanded Reza in perfect English.

Alarmed by the sound of gunfire and shocked by what had happened, Wes was slow to respond to Jabarri's question. Chad watched in anger as Reza struck Wes violently on the head with the heel of his palm. "I asked you a question, Captain. I expect a quick reply. Do you understand?" Struggling to recover his vision, Wes nodded. "One more," he said. "And what is his name?" demanded Reza. "Max."

"Captain Beacham, you will make an announcement informing all passengers to return to their seats immediately. You will tell them that the aircraft is now under the control of the Fundamentalist Coalition and any attempt to intervene in our operation will be met with instant death. Do I make myself clear?"

"Yes... I understand."

"You will then direct your flight service manager to retrieve Max's weapon and the weapon of the other agent and bring them to the cockpit. Should he choose not to obey my instructions, I will begin by shooting your first officer and will continue killing crew members until he decides to comply."

Wes knew Reza meant every word and would accept no compromise. Picking up the mike, he pressed the PA button.

"Ladies and gentlemen! This is your Captain speaking. Return to your assigned seats immediately! It is my unpleasant duty to inform you that our flight is now under the control of an organization calling itself the Fundamentalist Coalition. Their leader is with me in the cockpit. He has directed me to tell you that any — I repeat, any — intervention by anyone on board will be met with instant death. Please remain in your seats. Max, you are to surrender your weapon to the flight service manager immediately. If you do not comply, their leader will begin shooting crew members. Sybil, you are to retrieve Agent Outland's weapon, as well, and bring them both to the cockpit ASAP."

"You are a wise man, Captain," said Reza, pleased with Wes's announcement. "Now we will wait and see if it is necessary for me to shoot the large one Ahmed has tied up. Wes turned in his seat to look at Chad. A silent rage answered his glance. Wes looked away, praying Max would see the futility of trying anything.

A few seconds later, the cockpit chimes rang twice. Wes looked at Reza for instructions. Ahmed stepped over into the co-pilot chair. Increasing the volume on his cockpit speaker, he pressed the interphone transmit button. "Cockpit. Go ahead." Wes recognized Sybil's voice. "I have the agents' guns. What do you want me to do with them?"

Wes breathed a sigh of relief as Ahmed told Sybil to bring them to the cockpit. Seconds later, Sybil appeared in the doorway. Tears were streaming down over her high cheekbones as she stood holding the weapons by their barrels. Seizing them, Reza jerked her into the cockpit. He wanted to know where the secretary and his security agent were seated. She told him they had moved to the rear of the plane. Reza asked about the condition of the other agent. "Agent Outland is dead," Sybil said. "Leigh has also been shot, Wes. I think she may be dying."

Sybil's words crushed Wes. Feelings of guilt rushed through his mind as he blamed himself for her being caught in harm's way. If only I hadn't allowed her to come to the cockpit, he thought, sliding his seat aft.

"Sit down, Captain!" Reza demanded. "You get the hell out of my way! I've got a crew member down and she's going to get all the attention she needs to stay alive... I don't give a damn what you want!"

Stunned by Wes's response, Reza debated whether to shoot him or let him pass. Knowing their mission was more important, Reza stepped aside. "You may do what you can for her," he said.

Rushing from the cockpit, Wes knelt beside Leigh. A large pattern of blood covered her right side as he lifted her limp body from the carpeted floor and lowered her onto the vacant center aisle seat. She was unconscious and barely breathing.

Sybil pleaded for a doctor over the PA, but no one volunteered. She took the sealed medical kit from the overhead bin and broke it open, hoping to find something to help restore Leigh's consciousness, but saw it was futile.

Wes held Leigh's head in his hands. Gazing into her face, he saw her open her eyes. "Where... am I..., Wes? Wha..t happened?"

"There's been an accident, Leigh." Unable to tell her more, he looked into her gentle eyes.

"I feel so cold. Am I going to die?"

Wes couldn't answer. He didn't know how. Tears seeped from the crevices of his eyes as he saw that she was losing her strength.

"I am dying, aren't I?"

"Yes," he whispered.

"Promise me you'll see Jason and tell him that I love him and that I'm sorry ..., please."

"Yes...I will," Wes answered, sorrowfully.

Suddenly it was over as the veil of death moved across her face and life fled her crippled body. Wes pulled the flight blanket over her face. Feeling numb, he wasn't aware of Sybil's hand on his shoulder. "Leave her be... I'll take care of her," Sybil said. "There's nothing you can do for her now."

*   *   *

Finding the portable telephone on the dining room table of the ranch house, Dave Coleman suspected he'd uncovered a terrorist plot to seize the secretary of state. Nothing else made sense. Hadn't the radio said Halston was aboard TIA 899? And didn't Caroline say her father was flying that flight? Dave realized that what had started as a simple information-gathering exercise for Paterson had quickly mushroomed into a double homicide with international implications involving a member of the president's cabinet. It was the very thing he'd feared would happen. No doubt, Beamer would have his ass for violating FBI policy, thought Dave, as he dialed Emerson's office at the Bureau. The fact that he'd successfully interceded in the kidnapping and found enough evidence to legitimately justify the Bureau's intervention wouldn't matter to Beamer. A verbal reprimand would be the least he could expect. Something worse was more probable, Dave imagined, as he heard Beamer.

"Chief, Dave Coleman."

"What in the hell have you been up to, Coleman? You were supposed to have had those Middle East files back on my desk three hours ago."

"It's a long story, Chief."

"Hell, Dave, I just love long stories. Get your ass back to my office and tell me all about it!" he growled.

"Yes, sir. I'll be there as soon as I get these two dead Arabs on their way to the morgue."

"What dead Arabs?" shouted Beamer, his curiosity piqued.

"They were involved in a kidnapping, Chief. The victim, a young woman, managed to free herself with help from her sister and fiancé. Apparently, there was no ransom demand. It appears she was held hostage to induce her father to take some kind of action, but I'm uncertain what that might be. Both gunmen were professionals, Chief. Maybe terrorists, I ....."

Beamer interrupted. "What does her father do?"

"He's a pilot with Trans International Airways. He's the captain on TIA 899 coming from Geneva right now. According to his daughters, he's due to land around six p.m."

Emerson didn't reply right away.

"Chief, are you still with me?"

"Yes! I'm trying to recall if that's the flight the radio said Secretary Halston was returning on this afternoon."

"Yes, sir, it is. I heard the same broadcast earlier."

"That's what I thought. Finish up there as quickly as you can and meet me in my office, Dave. I'll give Security at the State Department a call and see if they've heard anything. You may have stumbled onto something serious."

Anxious to justify his intervention, Dave explained to his boss the details of what he'd found before hanging up. Surprised by Coleman's command of the facts, Emerson never asked how he'd become involved.

*   *   *

Trying to calm her passengers following the outbreak of gunfire had been a monumental task for Sybil and her team. Seeing two people shot and killed had sent the entire forward cabin into chaos. Grown men cried openly as mothers thrust their small children to the cabin floor under their seats, trying to protect them from further violence. Others had bolted, seeking a safer haven in the rear of the plane. Vulgar exchanges broke out between passengers as each tried to make his case for deserving the safer seats. More caring travelers did what they could to help those caught in the clutches of despair. Some offered their seats, while others took infants into their laps to protect them from the pushing and shoving panic-stricken adults.

Ross Straton, the secretary's special assistant, had slept through the initial outburst. Awakened by the passenger seated next to him stepping on his legs, Ross tried to escape from his window seat. Realizing there was no place to run, Straton had cowered behind the seat in front of him. Only the sight of Sybil's movement up the aisle brought him back up into his seat. "Miss. Where is the secretary?"

"He's in the rear of the aircraft with Agent Shell. I'll tell the secretary you asked about him." Ross started to get up, but thought better of it. The secretary was on his own now.

II

CHECKMATE

Forest Lindsey, a middle-aged man with bushy hair and a penchant for fastidious dress, walked into the Oval Office just as Gaylord Elliot was concluding an impromptu briefing with the president. Seeing Elliot huddled with President McGarth surprised him. He wasn't aware of their meeting, nor did he remember having seen it on the president's appointment list. Not one to be left in the dark, Forest barged in, hoping to learn the reason for their unscheduled meeting.

"Oh! Excuse me, sir. I wasn't aware you were in conference. I'm sorry to have interrupted," said Lindsey, retreating for the door. Aware of his chief of staff's propensity for wanting to know everything that happened in his office, Mason McGarth waved him over as he spoke. "Never mind that, Forest. We were just discussing the implications of Halston's latest talks in Geneva."

Reversing his course, Forest walked over to greet the president's national security adviser. "Good afternoon, Gaylord. Nice to see you again."

Elliot, a discerning man of impeccable character and the president's best friend, stood as the two men shook hands. A senior partner of the prestigious, highly successful Washington law firm of Cantwell, Elliot, & Delehy, Gaylord had reluctantly agreed to leave his practice at McGarth's insistence. Prevailing on their friendship, the president had sought Gaylord's advice on those issues that mattered most to his administration — the nation's security. A slender but towering gentleman with formidable insight, Elliot enjoyed the president's confidence and knew Lindsey envied their relationship.

"Was there something urgent I should know about, Forest?" asked the president. Forest felt a bit foolish as he spoke.

"No, I just wanted to inform you that Secretary Halston's scheduled return from Geneva has been delayed several hours because of damage to his aircraft on the ground earlier this morning. He is aboard Trans International Airways Flight 899 due to land at Dulles around six p.m."

"Does that mean we don't have to dine together?"

Knowing how the president felt about Halston, Elliot said, "It's your lucky day, Mr. President." McGarth laughed. Lindsey laughed too because the president had, but wished he'd been quick enough to have made the remark himself.

"Actually, I guess I shouldn't be so rough on Halston. In spite of our philosophical differences, he's done a hell of a good job bringing our European partners around to our point of view over this Middle East situation."

Both men knew only too well what McGarth was referring to. Since taking the leadership in trying to settle the question of Palestinian sovereignty, the White House had found itself increasingly on the defensive from both congressional conservatives and liberals alike. Each claimed U.S. support for an independent Palestinian state would severely undermine Israeli national interests and polarize America's trading partners in Europe. McGarth didn't think so, nor did most moderates on Capitol Hill.

U.S. policy-makers favored maintaining intense pressure on terrorist groups, including the use of covert operations, when feasible, to disrupt and neutralize their organizations. The Europeans were more vulnerable to terrorist attacks and advocated proceeding with greater caution. The president had sent Halston to Geneva for top-level meetings on the terrorist issue. Today's meeting with McGarth concerned a particularly disturbing piece of information. Elliot had debated long and hard over whether he had enough details to request today's meeting with the president.

"That's all I have to report at this time, Mr. President."

"You will keep me informed of this development, Gaylord? I share your concern, but let's hope your suspicions are unfounded."

*   *   *

"TIA 899, CONTACT MONCTON CENTER NOW ON 132.6." Wes listened as Ahmed read back the new frequency before re-channelizing the number one VHF radio. They would be in U.S. airspace in ten minutes.

With barely more than an hour to go, Wes tried to think of some way to regain the initiative. Still in the dark over who had hijacked his flight, he recalled the suggested methods he'd been taught for dealing with terrorists.

The truth was, most of the training he'd received had been centered on weapons and explosives recognition, political and psychological profiles of terrorist organizations, and video debriefings of crews fortunate enough to have gained their freedom. Little attention had been given to seizing the advantage, except when on the ground, where fleeing the aircraft could be employed to render the aircraft unflyable. Cooperation with the demands of the hijacker had proven to be the best course of action. After reviewing his options, Wes reluctantly came to the same conclusion. He had no other choice. Too many lives were at stake to do otherwise.

"Captain Beacham, what is your plan for diverting the flight to National Airport?" Reza asked.

The question surprised Wes. He'd given up considering any such plan since learning Caroline was free. Until the shootings, he'd expected to turn Reza and his traveling companion over to the FBI on arrival at Dulles. In retrospect, Wes knew he'd handled the situation poorly. Leigh and Ray's deaths could attest to that. He had no plan.

"Captain, you will tell me of your plan now!" Reza demanded.

"I think we should fly the profile we've filed right to Dulles Airport. Then, while being vectored on the downwind leg for a right visual approach to Runway One Right at Dulles, we should feign radio failure. Changing the transponder to the code for radio failure, we should then fly directly toward the Wilson bridge, just south of National Airport. Crossing over Springfield and the I-495 Beltway interchange with I-95 South, we'll begin to descend and configure for the landing. At that time, we'll switch to the emergency code, giving air traffic control and tower the impression that we have an in-flight emergency. Turning onto the final approach, we will insert the hijacking code into the transponder and monitor 'Guard' and National Tower. At the last minute, we will advise them that we intend to land on Runway Three Six."

Reza looked at Ahmed for his assessment of Beacham's plan. Ahmed smiled. "The plan is a good one," he said. "It will give the authorities no chance to react. It would be impossible for them to barricade the runways on such short notice."

Reza, satisfied that the plan would work, nodded his approval to Ahmed and left the cockpit to discuss their arrival with Mohammed.

"How did you get messed up in something like this, Ahmed?" Wes asked. "You had a great future here at TIA. Why would..."

"Do not concern yourself with what I choose to do with my life. I am a Palestinian freedom fighter first and foremost. To be a pilot for TIA means nothing to me."

Wes reviewed Ahmed's comments and wondered how he'd made it this far in his career without being detected. His success obviously represented a failure in TIA's ability to focus on all aspects of an applicant's resumé. He knew from experience that all too often the aviation community placed too much emphasis on flying time and ratings. Seldom was much attention devoted to assessing the candidate's character and judgment. Only major carriers addressed such concerns and their decisions were often overruled whenever the issue of minority quotas came up. No doubt, TIA had dismissed such questions regarding Ahmed's background, offering him the job just to satisfy a congressional mandate. Wes hoped they wouldn't all live to regret it.

Staring out the cockpit window, Ahmed reflected on his past. The son of a prosperous Jordanian businessman, Kyle, known to the Muslim world as Kahlid, had enjoyed the wealth of his father's position. Fiercely loyal to the crown, his family had always supported Hussein's Western-oriented policies. It had surprised no one that he received the king's appointment to become a pilot in the Jordanian Air Force some years earlier.

Kahlid still resented his father's belief in capitalism. He'd never accepted its views and preferred instead the Muslim fundamentalist philosophy prevalent among his many Palestinian friends. His attendance at Cambridge had done nothing to dissuade him from hating the West. Interested in Middle East politics, Ahmed earnestly studied the issues affecting his homeland.

At Cambridge, he'd met Mohammed Al-Farsi, the son of a Palestinian merchant from Lebanon. Mohammed despised Western intervention in what he said were the Middle East's internal affairs. He resented America's support for Israel and had silently vowed to help his countrymen resist its influence. Kahlid admired Mohammed's determination and the two became inseparable.

Ahmed and Mohammed believed that only through a strong and unified organization could fundamentalist groups expect to achieve the impact needed to drive Western influence from their lands forever. Despite their vision, neither had much success convincing the group's leadership of the value of using Western methods to achieve greater success. Only Reza Jabarri, then a guest lecturer and professor from Tehran and Saeed Keshef, a political strategist with ties to Iran and Libya, had shown interest in their radical ideas. Flattered and still very impressionable young men, Kahlid and Mohammed sought their counsel.

Turning from the window, Ahmed thought of tomorrow. He tried to imagine the impact his actions would have on the world. Elated over the prospect of becoming a leader of the fundamentalist movement, he recalled his days as a student military pilot in Arizona and the humiliation he'd endured at the hands of the American fighter pilots.

Undergraduate pilot training at Williams AFB in Chandler, Arizona, had been a grueling experience. Flunked check rides, repeated training, and marginally qualified rechecks were vivid reminders of his misery. A mediocre pilot by USAF standards, Kyle had known better than anyone that he would never have been seriously considered for advancement to F-16 air combat training had he not been part of a foreign military training contract. His move to Luke AFB for F-16 training had been a mistake. Only he had failed to acknowledge what everyone else took for granted. Driven by fierce Arab pride, he'd continued in the program until the day he collided with his wingman.

The crash had killed his instructor instantly and destroyed two F-16's. Only by ejecting from his disabled jet had he survived his mistake. The accident investigation board later concluded that he'd become disoriented at the top of a tactical pop-up maneuver and had inadvertently flown into his wingman instructor. Details of the accident and the board's decision barely received notice. With his self-esteem in ruins, Ahmed had resigned from the Jordanian Air Force and, with help from his father, left the United States for South America.

Angry over his failure as a fighter pilot, Ahmed sought employment as a transport pilot, flying cargo in Colombia until he joined a small air carrier in Mexico. Two years later, as a veteran transport pilot with legal alien status, Ahmed returned to the United States and applied for a job with Trans International Airways. Conspicuously absent from his resumé was mention of his midair collision at Luke or even of his military training.

* * *

The flight to Athens took nearly three hours. Yuari could recall very little of it, having drifted off to sleep shortly after takeoff. He had slept until awakened by a flight attendant and told to prepare for descent. That was the way he preferred it. Not one who enjoyed flying for its own sake, or for the vistas, Shevinsky flew only because it was efficient.

The late afternoon breeze drifting across the airfield felt invigorating. Stepping onto the platform stairs, Yuari made his way down the steps to the waiting ramp shuttle bus. The trip through customs and passport control was uneventful. With only a single piece of carry-on luggage, he bypassed the crowd waiting for their bags and left the terminal quickly.

A familiar voice called out to him from a waiting taxi. For a moment Yuari didn't respond. Then remembering his alias, he turned to his right and walked the ten meters to the taxi's opened door. Andrei took his old friend's bag as Yuari stepped into the back seat. Andrei motioned to the driver to begin their short trip to the hotel. Neither man spoke as they rode through the crowded streets of Athens toward their majestic hotel overlooking the Mediterranean. They'd planned it that way. Only when they were alone would they speak.

Entering his suite, Yuari locked the door and walked to the glass doors leading to the balcony. The curtains fluttered as he stepped out to take a long look at the sunset making its way over the Western horizon. He pulled a chair from under the glass-top table and sat down.

Glad today had finally arrived, Yuari was eager to begin his new life. Yet, he felt a certain sadness. So much had happened to change his life. Things would never be the same again. Destiny for him and his two companions would be permanently altered by the events about to unfold.

He'd known for some time the day would come when he would have to give up his identity and vanish. The idea had never been pleasant for him and his two friends, but they'd agreed it was the only solution that made any sense, given the crumbling Soviet empire.

A dedicated soldier, highly decorated for heroism in World War II, he had advanced quickly within the Soviet Army, attaining the rank of colonel well ahead of his contemporaries. The eldest son of a Soviet physicist, Yuari had excelled in mathematics and science, benefiting from his respected father's influence. Recognized for his strong sense of duty and allegiance to the motherland, Yuari was soon appointed manager of the USSR's nuclear arsenal.

As deputy commander of the USSR Rocket Forces, he attained honor and stature in the eyes of his peers and countrymen. Privy to the best that life in the Soviet Union could offer a man of his distinction, Yuari became accustomed to owning fine cars, living in spacious flats and vacationing at Black Sea resorts.

Focused on the consequences of the SALT I and II treaties, he'd barely noticed the subtle changes occurring in the streets of Moscow. A proud man not easily dissuaded from his beliefs, he had found it increasingly difficult to deny the underlying changes.

Not until Sarah, his beloved wife of forty-five years, suffered a massive stroke and died, had Yuari paused to take inventory of his life. Her loss brought him to his knees. Suddenly he knew only emptiness and sorrow.

Alone, Yuari struggled to regain his sense of purpose as his homeland was setting its course on a path of destruction. Troubled by what he saw, Yuari began to ponder the meaning of the new Russian order. Once-humorous comments made in jest by Andrei and Viktor, his two closest comrades, began to take on new meaning as he searched for answers.

Yuari recalled first broaching the subject two years ago while the three of them had played chess in the park. To his surprise, they both had expressed reservations over the changes. Their revelations had disturbed him, given their equally important roles in the motherland. He was especially appalled by what Viktor had had to say.

As a KGB officer, Viktor Khasnichev was the assistant deputy for Military Security, responsible for preserving the security and integrity

of Soviet weapons, specifically strategic ones. Hearing him, a leader
of the KGB and member of the Communist Party, so bluntly voice his
concerns over the political direction his country was taking had unnerved Yuari.

Viktor, more than most, was in a position to know of the
proletariat's internal workings. The fact that he would risk expressing
such a notion convinced Yuari that the dissolution of the USSR was
inevitable.

Andrei Karpolov, his childhood friend from Kiev, now a renowned
Soviet weapons expert and superb chess theorist, had held equally strong
reservations about the future of the Soviet Union. Yuari knew his friend's
fear was the result of considerable observation and insight and not due
to subversive impressions from political leftists.

Honored nationally for his innovations in nuclear technology,
Andrei had devoted his life to perfecting the Soviet Union's nuclear
capability. To see it all dismantled overnight was more than he could
endure. It meant that everything he had accomplished was to be wasted.

The intensity of his convictions had startled even Viktor, though
both men had openly professed what amounted to insurrection in Yuari's
mind. Chess for them would never be the same, nor would their minds
be on the game when they met next. Each had exposed his feelings to
the other two in ways that forced them to remain loyal to each other.
Each had bid the other a warm farewell and vowed to continue their
discussions soon. Leaving the park that warm April afternoon, Yuari
realized life's trauma had invaded their recreation permanently.

The next meeting several weeks later had been even more bizarre
than the first. Yuari recalled having spoken first.

"Your thoughts on the state of our motherland have troubled me
greatly. I find that I cannot disagree with you on the points you have
raised, nor do I doubt the outcome you've both predicted. Yet, the question I keep asking myself is where and how do we fit into the changes
taking place?"

"I'm not certain we have a place," Andrei had said. "My work is
finished. A life of teaching is all that remains for me, though I suppose
there are worse things."

"You are fortunate, Andrei. You will not have to contend with the
political purges that will inevitably happen," Viktor interjected. "Yuari

and I could both face a fate worse than death. You've only to recall Russian history to know what happens to military and political leaders whenever there is a purge. We will be lucky if we are not tossed into prison by the revolutionaries. And who knows if we will be able to hold on to our pensions."

Yuari knew Viktor's assertion had merit. It was one thing to suffer the humiliation of surrendering one's rank and privilege. But it was quite another to be imprisoned or even shot for doing one's duty to his country.

"Your point is well-made, Viktor. I, for one, am not prepared to endure such a fate at my age. I am too old and set in my ways to give in to such tyranny without a fight."

Andrei and Viktor had agreed. Yuari had spoken vehemently about the betrayal he was experiencing. The dismantling of Soviet nuclear missiles was but the start of things to come, he'd said. The SALT talks have paved the way for an irreversible reduction in nuclear weapons, and with it, the erosion of military influence, Yuari had gone on to say. Both men had listened intently as he outlined the events that were sure to follow. The warm Moscow afternoon turned cold as he'd proposed a way out for the three of them.

The plan — leaving the USSR, relocating to another country under an assumed name, and severing all ties with family, friends and associates — weighed heavily on each man's mind as the three sat around the chess table thinking. No one wanted to go, but each, in his own way, saw no other alternative, save suicide.

"Is there another choice for us but to go?" Victor voiced. "I think not," Andrei replied. "Our world is changing for the worst. Within six months to a year, our country will be divided into a series of nation states, each vying for what little food and resources are available. We're not likely to find the new order as generous to us as the old one has been."

"Andrei is right," Viktor said. "Soon we will have no place in the new society. My concern is not that we should leave, but of how we shall exist if we stay. If capitalism takes hold, my ruble pension will not be enough to buy Siberian salt."

"I have a way," offered Yuari, studying his comrade's reactions carefully. "Imagine for a moment that we could obtain control of a tactical nuclear weapon and could smuggle it out of the country without its being missed or our being implicated."

"Is it possible to do this?" Andrei asked.

"Yes," said Yuari, "If we work together."

"And you, Viktor. How do you see it?" Andrei questioned.

"I think it's risky and will mean certain death if we are found out, but entirely possible," he said. "But certainly no worse than trying to exist in a country gone mad with anarchy."

"Then we all agree?" asked Yuari.

"Yes," his two comrades answered.

Recalling his plan, Western Harvest, as they'd named it, Yuari still found it difficult to believe that he and his comrades had succeeded in stealing the weapon. Access to the nuclear arsenal had always been highly controlled, except for those having a need to know. Having been responsible for the control and management of these weapons had enabled him to misplace one during its scheduled maintenance and reassignment to the field.

The SALT agreements had simplified its acquisition. The scheduled reduction of nuclear weapons spelled out in the treaty had created a nightmare for commanders trying to maintain accountability for weapons removed from the field. With field commanders rotating the weapons from site to site in a never-ending shell game to confuse Western intelligence, Yuari found his chance.

As a ranking member of the KGB, Viktor had ensured that all necessary security requirements were satisfied each step of the way. Establishing false ID and supporting histories for the three had been a part of his responsibility, too.

With the weapon secure in Cyprus, Yuari, with Viktor's help, had handled marketing the device. From the start, negotiations had been touchy. Security matters had proved to be the most complicated part of the transaction, given the number of groups and Third World nations bidding for it.

Legitimate Soviet Aid programs had provided the path for moving the device and the necessary cover for negotiations. The fact that several nations were attempting to acquire such weapons directly from the USSR, while at the same time participating in clandestine discussions with Shevinsky, made bargaining dangerous. Of paramount concern had been the question of what use the successful bidder intended for the device.

Taking a weapon from the homeland that would, in all probability, be destroyed as called for in succeeding SALT talks was seen from the outset as an acceptable compromise. Having it turned against the motherland was, however, a different matter.

The decision to sell the weapon to the coalition had been a difficult one for Yuari and his accomplices. Experience had taught them to distrust Arabs. Andrei had found it ironic that a Soviet nuclear weapon might at last reach the shores of America, the world's remaining superpower.

Financial considerations had never been an obstacle in discussions with the FC. Only the question of from whom the coalition would get its funding had ever been an issue. Satisfied with the organization's motives, Yuari had settled on a price of 144,000,000 Swiss francs (roughly $96 million dollars). Paid in two installments of forty-eight and ninety-six million Swiss francs, the first installment had been credited to Yuari's account upon inspection of the device and the start of modifications to permit easy detonation by unskilled technicians. It had been agreed that the final installment would be made once the device was en route to its objective.

With negotiations complete, Yuari and his associates had requested retirement and had resigned, while discreetly making plans to leave the country.

The first to leave, Andrei had taken a circuitous route to Cyprus to perfect the detonation options and install the support harnesses and other equipment necessary to modify the weapon for shipment. Viktor had joined him a short while later to handle their security.

Yuari, the last to leave, had made his way to Switzerland and into the hills surrounding Geneva to coordinate matters with the coalition. Though dubious at first of their ability to integrate such a weapon into a coordinated terrorist campaign, Yuari had found himself increasingly impressed with each succeeding phase of their plan. It had a high probability of being effective, though Yuari shuddered to think of how America would respond.

Lost in his thoughts, Yuari didn't notice the sun disappear. A chill settled over the balcony as he stepped inside and pulled the glass doors together. An unopened bottle of vodka sat beside glasses and a bucket of ice. He surveyed the bar before deciding to have his vodka straight up.

A short while later, Yuari heard a light tap on the door. Downing what remained of his third vodka, he opened the door. There stood Viktor. He hadn't seen him in more than two months. Grabbing his comrade by both of his forearms, Yuari pulled him through the doorway. "It is good to see you, my friend," he said. "Where is Andrei?"

"He will join us shortly."

"Ah! And is he ready for the final match?"

"That is all he has spoken of since arriving in Athens," replied Viktor, with a broad smile. "We are both eager to celebrate our success and be on our way, Yuari."

Shevinsky grinned at seeing his companion so pleased. "Ah, yes! And it was a monumental success, but one which I fear may come back to haunt us in the end."

Frowning, Viktor laughed at Yuari's cautiousness.

Minutes later, there was another tap on Shevinsky's door. "That will be Andrei," said Viktor, putting down his drink to open the door. "He has the chess set with him."

"Come in, comrade," Viktor said. "We must begin before the vodka destroys us all."

Andrei smiled as he entered. Seeing Yuari, he asked, "Is the suite to your liking?"

"Excellent, Andrei! You have done well, my great friend; the view is without equal."

"And did you rest?"

"For a short while."

"Then you are ready for the final match?" asked Andrei, opening the familiar wooden box containing the chess set they had played with for years.

"Yes, yes!" Yuari answered. "Comrades, I have already grown weary of learning how to live in this new Western world. There is so much to know," he added.

"This is true," Viktor observed. "But with our new wealth, it will be a pleasant experience."

"And much better than trying to live on our pensions in Moscow," Andrei added. "I hear the ruble is worth nothing."

"Then let us toast our friendship and good fortune tonight and leave our future parting for tomorrow," Yuari said. Lifting his glass, he saluted his loyal comrades.

As they downed their drinks, Yuari poured them more vodka. Andrei and Viktor set up the chess pieces. Yuari would play Andrei in the first match, with Viktor playing the winner. Each would have sixty seconds in which to move. Viktor would serve as judge for the first match. Another toss of the coin decided the issue of color — who was black and who was white. Andrei won the toss and made his initial move quickly. Yuari had anticipated his opening and countered as Viktor looked on.

The first two games moved quickly, as did the vodka. Yuari managed a checkmate of Andrei before being caught in the second game by Viktor. Rising from his seat, Yuari said, "It's time we eat, comrades. I'll have the kitchen send up the food I ordered."

"Tell them to bring more vodka," said Andrei, tossing down the last of his drink.

"As you wish," Yuari said, dialing room service.

Midway into the third match, play was interrupted by a loud knock at the door. Yuari allowed Andrei to complete his move before carefully removing the board from both men's field of vision. Viktor rose and answered the door, stepping aside as the pretty waitress rolled a large, linen-covered cart into the suite. No one spoke until she removed the covers from the dishes, exposing the chef's best efforts. "Splendid!" exclaimed Viktor as the scent of caviar reached his nose. "We shall dine like kings!" added Andrei, viewing the sumptuous assortment of seafood delicacies.

"You are pleased with my selections?" Yuari asked.

"But of course!" uttered Viktor as he sampled the sturgeon's eggs on a piece of toast.

Working quickly, the young woman removed two bottles of vodka from the lower shelf and put them on the bar. Viktor, full of lust and fascinated by her beauty, said, "You must stay and drink with us. We will pay you well."

Shaking her head, the petite waitress retreated toward the door as Viktor scoffed at her refusal.

"Have you no shame, Viktor?" Andrei laughed. "Can you not see you have frightened the young peasant to death?"

"Perhaps, but it would do her purse well if she would stay with me. I would pay her more than a month's wages to have her warm the sheets of my bed tonight!"

"Please, comrades, she is but a child," lectured Yuari, following her to the door.

Suddenly, the waitress pulled a small automatic from under her full skirt and fired two shots into Yuari's chest, killing him instantly.

Andrei and Viktor, hovering over the dinner cart, heard the muffled gunshots and looked up as Yuari collapsed, clutching his heart. Horrified, both dashed for cover as the assassin stepped over Yuari's body and continued the slaughter. "No! No!" Andrei shouted, cowering behind the sofa, pleading for his life. Continuing to fire, she unloaded two shots into his head and then turned on Viktor.

"The KGB sent you?" he asked, wild-eyed, knowing his life was about to end. Showing no mercy, the young woman raised her weapon a third time, clustering three shots into the Russian officer's forehead.

After detaching the suppressor from the nine-millimeter automatic, she removed the stolen uniform and left the room. Taking the elevator to the mezzanine, she walked down the remaining flight of stairs to the crowded lobby, entered a phone booth and placed a long distance call. A familiar voice answered.

She spoke quickly. "It is done. There were no complications. I will leave tonight as planned."

"I will advise them to expect you at dawn," came the reply.

"Ciao."

12

IN-FLIGHT EMERGENCIES

"TIA 899, REPORT ROBERT INTERSECTION AT 10,000 AND 250 KNOTS. CONTACT DULLES APPROACH ON 132.55."

Ahmed repeated Washington Center's clearance and reset the altitude alert window to read ten thousand. Wes dialed in 250 in the airspeed window and pressed the flight level change button on the auto flight panel. Both throttles began to move aft as the 767 started its descent out of seventeen thousand feet. ROBERT intersection lay twenty-six nautical miles ahead.

"DULLES APPROACH, TIA 899 IS DEPARTING 17,000 FEET TO CROSS ROBERT AT TEN AND TWO FIFTY WITH ATIS YANKEE," announced Ahmed, expecting a reply.

"GOOD AFTERNOON, TIA 899! WELCOME BACK," the controller replied. "DEPART ROBERT HEADING 190 DEGREES, THEN DESCEND TO 7,000 FEET. KEEP YOUR SPEED AT 250 KNOTS FOR NOW. YOU CAN EXPECT A RIGHT BASE FOR A VISUAL APPROACH TO RUNWAY ONE RIGHT AT DULLES."

Ahmed read back the instructions as Wes reset the altitude window and started to alert the cabin. Reza leaned forward from his seat directly behind Wes. "The escape slides are to be disarmed for the landing," he said. "I will direct Sybil to do it. Mohammed will observe her," Jabarri explained.

Having considered activating the EVAC alarm as soon as he could stop the aircraft, Wes was afraid the terrorists would retaliate by shooting crew members and passengers. Instead, he would wait and look for a safer opportunity to escape.

Ahmed made the usual pre-landing announcement and requested that the flight service manager report to the cockpit. Wes grimaced as he heard him order Sybil to the cockpit. The next twenty-five minutes would seem like a lifetime, he thought, mentally reviewing the diversion plan. He wondered what would happen to his crew and passengers after that.

Sybil's knock reflected the immense fear she felt for the safety of her passengers and crew. Pressing Ray's thirty-eight special against her right temple, Reza directed her to disarm the escape slides. "You will then go and tell Secretary Halston and his security agent to return to their seats in first class. Then you will handcuff them together using the cuffs from the medical kit. Do you understand my instructions?" he asked.

Sybil looked at Wes for direction before answering, but saw none. "Yes. I understand."

"I must warn you that there is a bomb onboard this aircraft that can be detonated by any one of us. Should you or your crew make any attempt to alert the authorities or begin an evacuation once we have landed, we will not hesitate to explode it. You are to tell your crew that the cabin doors must not be opened by anyone, unless instructed by Ahmed, Mohammed, or me. We do not wish to harm anyone, but we will not tolerate disobedience. Two people are already dead because of the stupidity of your captain. He has enough blood on his hands as it is. You will include my warning to your passengers when you make your cabin announcement. Is that understood?" Reza questioned. Sybil nodded yes as he removed the gun from her head.

"TIA 899 CONTINUE YOUR DESCENT TO 3,000 FEET AND CALL THE AIRPORT IN SIGHT."

"ROGER," Ahmed answered.

Wes glanced out in front of him. The Reston Town Center lay just to the left of his flight path. Looking out the left quarter panel, he could see Caroline's townhouse. He wondered how she had managed to escape. Passing over the town center complex, he stared at the tall office building that housed the bank she managed. He thought of his conversation with Courtney, Caroline's assistant, the day before yesterday. It seemed so long ago.

"TIA 899, DO YOU HAVE THE FIELD IN SIGHT NOW?"

"AFFIRMATIVE," Ahmed replied.

"YOU'RE CLEARED FOR A VISUAL APPROACH TO RUN-WAY ONE RIGHT. CALL TURNING A RIGHT BASE."

"ROGER," Ahmed answered.

Wes looked southeast to the point where the Wilson bridge crossed the Potomac River while he rotated the autopilot heading selector to the left. The 767 responded immediately, rolling into a thirty degree left bank. Ahmed dialed in the radio failure code as Wes rolled the Boeing out of its turn, aligning its flight path with the distant point spanning the Potomac — the Wilson Bridge.

"TIA 899, WHAT IS YOUR HEADING?"

Ignoring the request, Ahmed monitored Dulles Approach.

"TIA 899, HOW DO YOU READ DULLES APPROACH?"

"TIA 899, IF YOU READ DULLES APPROACH, SQUAWK IDENT, NOW!" the controller said, excitedly.

"TIA 899, I SHOW YOU SQUAWKING 7600. UNDERSTAND YOU ARE EXPERIENCING TRANSMITTER FAILURE."

Disregarding approach control's frantic radio calls, Ahmed dialed in National Airport's tower frequency as Wes disengaged the autopilot and lowered the jet's nose to allow the aircraft to accelerate.

Minutes later in a shallow descent to fifteen hundred feet, the 767 crossed Springfield. Now at 290 knots, Ahmed switched the transponder to seventy-seven hundred, the emergency code.

Scanning the sky for other traffic, Wes had a clear view of the Potomac and the Wilson Bridge. ATC, busy clearing traffic away from the 767, continued calling the flight. Multiple transmissions were made to the flight to confirm the nature of the emergency, but Ahmed refused to reply.

Nearing the final approach course, Wes pulled the throttles to idle and extended the spoilers, quickly slowing the big jet. The bleed-off of airspeed was immediate. Ninety seconds later, he saw the Instrument Landing System (ILS) localizer course needle move off its stop. They were closing with the final approach course of Runway Three Six at an angle of approximately forty-five degrees.

As the speed slowed below 240 knots, Wes called for the flaps, extending each notch as soon as its limit speed was reached. Now converging rapidly with the localizer center line, he rolled the 767 into a thirty degree bank and called for the gear and remaining flaps to be extended. Ahmed extended the landing gear and selected full flaps as the tower transmitted, "EXPRESS JET 275, GO AROUND. I HAVE AN EMERGENCY AIRCRAFT BEHIND YOU ON SHORT FINAL! I SAY AGAIN GO AROUND! ACKNOWLEDGE!"

Wes watched as the light twin jet abruptly aborted his approach and initiated a go-around. They were now a mile and half from the end of the runway.

Descending through four hundred feet, Ahmed dialed in the hijack code and keyed his mike: "NATIONAL TOWER THIS IS TIA 899. WE HAVE BEEN HIJACKED AND MUST MAKE AN EMERGENCY LANDING ON RUNWAY THREE SIX. DO YOU COPY?"

"TIA 899, YOU ARE CLEARED TO LAND ON RUNWAY THREE SIX. CONFIRM YOUR SQUAWK PLEASE. UNDERSTAND YOU HAVE BEEN HIJACKED!"

Crossing the threshold of the overrun at thirty-five feet, Wes closed both throttles and smoothly rotated the nose of the 767 upward as he waited for the *trucks* to kiss the tarmac. Two seconds later, the automatic spoilers deployed as he lowered the nose wheel to the pavement and selected full reverse. Instantly, the wide-bodied jet began to slow as automatic braking occurred. "Let it roll to the end, then do a one eighty on the runway and set the brakes, Captain," Ahmed ordered. Approaching sixty knots, Wes moved the thrust reversers to idle as the auto brakes continued to slow the jet.

Approaching the end of Runway Three Six, Wes braked the jet to a near standstill then cranked the steering lever hard left, and added a short burst of thrust from his right engine. As the nose of the jet completed its one hundred-eighty degree turn, he saw many vehicles racing toward the big jet.

Reacting angrily, Ahmed commanded, "TOWER! THIS IS TIA 899. WE ARE UNDER SEVERE DURESS. WITHDRAW ALL MEN AND EQUIPMENT FROM THE VICINITY OF THE AIRCRAFT IMMEDIATELY, OR THE HIJACKERS WILL BEGIN KILLING PASSENGERS! I REPEAT! WITHDRAW ALL YOUR MEN AND EQUIPMENT ASAP! DO YOU UNDERSTAND?"

"ROGER, TIA 899. THE TOWER WILL COMPLY WITH YOUR INSTRUCTIONS. . . ATTENTION, ALL RESPONDING VEHICLES. WITHDRAW FROM THE AIRCRAFT IMMEDIATELY! I SAY AGAIN. WITHDRAW FROM THE AIRCRAFT!"

"Shut down the engines now, Captain," Reza said. Nodding, Wes switched off both fuel cutoff switches, causing the engines to begin spooling down as the jet's auxiliary power unit (APU) picked up the electrical and air-conditioning chores. Glancing at the fuel indicator, Wes saw that ten thousand pounds remained.

"Captain, you will come with me to the cabin. There is something I wish you to see." Wes slid back his chair and crawled out of his seat, bewildered by Reza's demand. "What about Chad? Can he see it?"

"No. He must remain here with Ahmed, should the authorities attempt to board the aircraft." Wes didn't want to think about the implications of Jabarri's comment.

Walking back into the first class section, Wes found the secretary of state seated in his original seat, cuffed to Max. The cabin was quiet. Looking about, he saw the horror on his passengers' faces. "Take a seat, Captain," commanded Reza, handing a video cassette to the flight service manager. "Play this tape for us, Ms. DeVires," he said, removing the PA handset from the main entrance door console.

"Ladies and gentlemen: You will direct your attention to the film about to be shown!"

Moments later, Wes, his crew, and the passengers learned, for the first time, the real reason he had been made to fly the aircraft to Washington National Airport. After seeing the initial frame, Wes knew what would follow. Burying his face in his hands, he cursed himself for his stupidity.

A voice explained the explosive potential of the nuclear weapon aboard the aircraft. Continuing, the narrator spelled out the havoc it could wreak on the lives and property of those within twenty miles of the jet.

From the rear of the cabin, Wes heard the sorrowful crying of mothers and fathers alike, as they moaned among themselves, each trying to explain to the other what they were seeing and what it meant. Raising his head, Wes forced himself to watch the film, disgusting as it was. Life for him, his passengers, and the citizens of Washington, D.C., had suddenly become a living hell — one he had unknowingly helped create.

"TIA 899, CAN YOU CONFIRM THAT YOU ARE BEING HELD UNDER DURESS?"

Ahmed answered, "THAT IS AFFIRMATIVE."

"ARE YOU ABLE TO TELL US WHO HAS CONTROL OF
THE AIRCRAFT?"

"WE ARE UNDER STRICT ORDERS NOT TO GIVE OUT
THAT INFORMATION AS YET," Ahmed radioed. "WE WILL AD-
VISE YOU OF THIS INFORMATION, WHEN INSTRUCTED."

"CAN YOU TELL US OF THE CONDITION OF THE PAS-
SENGERS AND CREW?" the tower controller asked.

"THE PASSENGERS ARE UNHARMED AS OF THIS MO-
MENT. YOUR FULL COOPERATION WILL DETERMINE
WHETHER THEY REMAIN THAT WAY!" Ahmed replied. "DO
NOT ASK ANY MORE QUESTIONS. WE WILL CONTACT YOU
WITHIN FIFTEEN MINUTES WITH INSTRUCTIONS," he added,
annoyed by the controller's questions.

* * *

Returning from a cross-country flight to Richmond, Bud Waterman
had been monitoring the Dulles Approach Control frequency when TIA
899 strayed off its assigned course. Skirting south of Washington to
stay clear of commercial traffic inbound to National, Bud had seen the
Boeing 767 heading east moments after hearing the ATC controller's
call. Knowing that wide-bodied aircraft were prohibited from flying
into National, Waterman had questioned why the 767 would be flying
directly toward the inbound path of traffic approaching National.
Switching to the tower frequency at National, he learned the flight had
an emergency and planned to land at National. Moments later, Bud
had heard the pilot advise the tower that the flight had been hijacked.

Grabbing the small pocket phone from his flight kit, Waterman
called the *Examiner* news desk and asked for Jill Simmons, his assistant. "Jill, it's Bud. We've got a big story unfolding right now. TIA
Flight 899 was hijacked in flight and has just landed at National. That's
the flight Secretary of State Riggs Halston is on. I know, because it
came over the wire as I was leaving the office this morning. File the
story and head over to the White House. Take your pocket phone. I'll
feed you and the news desk updates from the airport."

"Great, Bud. I'll get right on it now! But aren't you supposed to be
flying back from Richmond?"

"I am. That's the reason I know about the story. Go file now before the story gets away from us. I'll stay in touch."

Waterman had waited a long time for a good story, especially one involving his first love, aviation. This was too good to pass up. Tower's reaction convinced him the situation was serious. His instincts told him to go for it.

Turning toward the Wilson Bridge, Bud lowered the nose of his Cessna Skylane and switched his transponder to code 7700. Having heard the tower controller close National to inbound traffic, he knew the approaches to the runways would be clear of other aircraft. He would wait until the last minute to call the tower.

A mile from the approach end of Runway Three Six, Bud keyed his mike. "MAYDAY, MAYDAY, NATIONAL TOWER, THIS IS CESSNA 622 GOLF FOXTROT, ONE MILE SOUTH, SQUAWKING 7700! I'VE GOT A FIRE IN THE COCKPIT! I'M DECLARING AN EMERGENCY! I'M GOING TO LAND ON RUNWAY THREE SIX NOW!"

Hearing the Cessna's mayday call, Harry spun around to see the Cessna less than a mile from the end of Runway Three Six. "NEGATIVE! NEGATIVE! CESSNA 622 GOLF FOXTROT! DO NOT LAND ON RUNWAY THREE SIX. AN AIRCRAFT IS ON THE RUNWAY. USE RUNWAY THREE THREE. ACKNOWLEDGE!" cried Harry.

"Sonofabitch! Where in the hell did he come from?" shouted the ground controller, activating the crash-rescue alarm for a second time in ten minutes.

"ROGER, TOWER. I'VE GOT THE BIG JET IN SIGHT AT THE FAR END OF THREE SIX. I'LL LAND ON THREE THREE!"

Breaking off his approach to Runway Three Six, Bud pulled up and banked his Cessna sharply to the right to intercept the glide path to Runway Three Three. Glancing out his window, he saw the Boeing sitting on the north end of Runway Three Six. Banking again sharply to the left, Waterman joined the new glide path.

"CESSNA 622, YOU'RE TOO HIGH FOR THE APPROACH!"

"I'LL MAKE IT!" said Bud, extending the rest of his flaps. Wanting to land close to where the 767 was parked, Bud planned the touchdown for the last third of the runway.

"TIA 899. BE ADVISED, I HAVE A SMALL CESSNA WITH AN EMERGENCY LANDING ON RUNWAY THREE THREE.

EXPECT HIM TO CROSS WELL IN FRONT OF YOUR POSITION, MOMENTARILY."

Touching down too late to make the main turn off at taxiway November, Bud grinned as he continued down the runway to intersection Juliette. There, he swung the nose to the right and taxied off to the side of the taxiway and into the grass.

Jumping out of his Cessna, Bud aimed a small extinguisher onto the front seat beside him, putting out the fire he'd just started with a cigarette.

Harry set the binoculars back on the console as he spoke.
"That bastard doesn't look like he's got much of a fire. Tell the trucks to hold their position until we clear it with the hijackers!"

Reaching into the cockpit, Waterman grabbed his mike. "TOWER, THIS IS CESSNA 622 GOLF FOXTROT. I'VE EXTINGUISHED THE FIRE IN MY COCKPIT. NO FURTHER ASSISTANCE IS NEEDED."

"CESSNA 622, REMAIN WHERE YOU ARE. STAY WITH YOUR AIRCRAFT. WE HAVE A HIJACKING IN PROGRESS. I REPEAT, STAY WITH YOUR AIRCRAFT UNTIL FURTHER ADVISED."

"ROGER TOWER. I'LL STAY HERE," radioed Waterman, smiling at his good fortune. Parked off to the right of the hijacked jet, Bud was less than a hundred yards away, a perfect position from which to monitor the unfolding events.

Using his cell phone, Bud called Simmons again. "Jill, it's Bud! I'm beside my aircraft within a hundred yards of the hijacked aircraft. Take your pocket tape recorder with you to the press room. I'll feed you information for as long as I can."

Jill could feel the excitement in the air, knowing the TV cameras would pan on her as soon as she announced that her partner, Bud Waterman, was on the ground at National Airport, beside the hijacked aircraft. This was the break she'd been waiting for. Reaching into her pocket, Jill whipped out her press pass as she approached the White House gate.

Bud's career as an investigative reporter for the *Washington Examiner* had been less than stellar for the last several years. A flying buff, passed over by the Air Force and Navy years earlier because of poor eyesight, he still managed to devote a significant portion of his free time to flying, much to the chagrin of his managing editor. Bud's strength lay in his strong instinct for a story. According to his editor, Bud's love of flying kept him from realizing his true potential as a journalist. He wasn't around when most sensational stories broke.

Clearing the call on his portable phone, he pulled his wide-angled telescopic lens camera off the back seat of the Cessna and raised it to his right eye. Sighting his first shot, Bud snapped the picture he hoped all of Washington would see tomorrow morning splashed across the *Examiner's* front page.

Harry Mann, the tower shift supervisor, had already advised the FAA and notified the FBI of the situation when Ed Shaffer of the State Department called. Assigned to meet Secretary Halston at Dulles, he'd been in the control tower monitoring the flight when the diversion occurred.

"Tower, Mann here! Make it brief!" Harry said.

"Mann, this is Ed Shaffer with the State Department. Can you confirm that TIA Flight 899 has been hijacked?"

"Shaffer, I'm sorry, but I'm unable to give out any information regarding that flight."

"Are you aware that the secretary of state is on board that aircraft?"

Harry's silence answered Shaffer's question.

"Who did you say you are?"

"Ed Shaffer. I was assigned to meet the secretary on his arrival at Dulles. I'm in the control tower at Dulles."

Harry thought for a second. "The aircraft's here, parked at the departure end of Runway Three Six. The hijackers have ordered us to remain clear. They've told us that the passengers have not been harmed. We don't know who is in control of the aircraft at this time."

"Thanks, Harry. I was afraid it was true."

Hurriedly, Shaffer dialed the White House chief of staff's special number. His secretary answered.

"Ed Shaffer, State Department, Chief of Security. It's urgent that I speak to Mr. Lindsey!"

"Mr. Lindsey is in conference with the president and has asked not to be disturbed, Mr. Shaffer."

"Miss, the secretary of state is being held hostage on an aircraft parked on the runway at National Airport. Interrupt them, if you have to, but get him on the line. I'll stand by."

Thirty seconds later, Lindsey, shocked by the news, answered. Ed briefed him.

Putting down the receiver, Forest stood in silence for a second, trying to decide how to break the news to his boss. Finally he said, "Mr. President, Halston's flight has just been hijacked. It's parked on a runway at National, sir. No one knows who has seized the aircraft or what they want."

"What did you say?" the president asked. Forest repeated the information as McGarth listened, stunned.

"Who told you the flight has been hijacked?"

"Ed Shaffer, Halston's chief of security over at State just called. He's confirmed it with the tower supervisor at National."

"How long ago did it happen?"

"Within the last twenty minutes, or so, sir."

The president sat back in his chair and said nothing for a moment. He preferred to think situations through before deciding anything. Understanding his boss, Lindsey folded back the top sheet of his note pad and started jotting down the names of key personnel the president would want to consult with immediately. He was listing the fifth name when McGarth spoke.

"Alert the Crisis Response Center. Then call Elliot, Sinclair, and Williamson. Advise them of what we have learned — have them get over here right away. Then send one of our security people to the tower and make sure the direct line to the control tower stays open. Have the crisis manager contact me immediately."

"What about the media, sir?"

"Have Frances join us. Until we know for sure who we are dealing with and what they want, I don't want any press releases." Pausing, McGarth added, "I was afraid something like this might happen. Halston has pissed off too many people for too long."

"I'm surprised it hasn't happened to him sooner," echoed Forest, summoning the key personnel.

* * *

Sybil switched off the video machine and returned the cassette to Reza. He took the film, but said nothing, content to study the look on Halston's face. It was an expression he had worked hard for the last two years to see. Riggs's face was pale and drawn. Sweat formed on his forehead as he fought to hide his fear, but it was impossible. Shaken, Halston sat quietly, trying to imagine what would happen next and where it would lead.

"Tell me, Mr. Secretary, what do you think of our little surprise? Did you ever expect this might happen to you Americans one day? Or did you think Arabs were too stupid and disorganized to plan and execute such an operation?"

Riggs sat in quiet defiance of Reza's taunting question. He would not dignify the question with an answer. Reza smiled broadly at the secretary's misery. Satisfied that he'd made his point, Jabarri said, "It's time we discuss our intentions with your president and find out if he is amenable to serious negotiations. I think it will be in Washington's best interest if he does. Don't you agree, Mr. Secretary?"

Riggs stared back at the meanness in Jabarri's eyes, but didn't answer, certain the president would never honor his demands.

"Mr. Secretary, it will be your duty to inform your president of what you have just seen. You must convince him that it is imperative to the life and welfare of this city that he meet with me immediately at the White House. You will personally escort Captain Beacham and me there. Insist on an armed escort. You will inform him that we are deadly serious about the meeting. Tell the president that I will begin shooting civilians should he choose to procrastinate in making his decision. Need I tell you of the ultimate consequences for the people of Washington, if he does not?"

Riggs knew he had no choice, nor would the president. How could he afford to risk the life of every man, woman, and child in Washington? A nuclear detonation at National Airport would kill everyone and destroy everything within a ten-mile radius. The death toll would run into the millions. The seat of power of America — its historical and cultural heritage — would be instantly annihilated, and with it, the function of the U.S. government. Man's most noble accomplishment, American democracy, would lie mortally wounded for all the world to see. Washington, more than any other place in the world, stood as a beacon to all freedom-loving people on Earth. To see it destroyed in a single act of vengeance would be intolerable to the American people. The institution of democracy would be reduced to rubble within a second.

"Your silence surprises me, Mr. Secretary. I have never known you to be a man to hold his tongue. Perhaps these revelations have humbled you somewhat, no?" An answer would solve nothing, Riggs thought. Let the bastard wonder what I'm really thinking.

"We will adjourn to the cockpit. It is time you had a talk with your president, Mr. Secretary! I am certain he will want to know your assessment of the situation." Riggs wasn't so sure. He and McGarth had never seen eye-to-eye on anything.

Ahmed was speaking to the tower as Reza, Riggs and Wes returned to the cockpit. Mohammed remained in the cabin and took control of the passengers, now assisted by seven fellow terrorists who had covertly boarded as passengers.

"We are making progress," Ahmed reported to Reza. "A direct line has been established for us from the White House to the control tower." Reza seemed pleased at the importance the White House had accorded the situation. "Have you informed them of our identity yet?" Ahmed shook his head. "It's time the president receive his secretary of state's report of the situation," Reza said coldly, motioning to Halston. "Mr. Secretary, please sit in Captain Beacham's chair. Ahmed will give you a microphone with which to talk to the White House."

Halston squeezed around the side of the seat back and settled into the captain's chair. Ahmed set up the number one radio to transmit and turned up the volume on both cockpit speakers.

"Please, Mr. Secretary. Call your president and arrange the meeting for us!"

Riggs glared at Reza as he keyed the mike. "THIS IS SECRETARY OF STATE HALSTON. WHO AM I TALKING TO?"

"YOU'RE TALKING TO HARRY MANN, THE TOWER SUPERVISOR, MR. SECRETARY."

Lowering his voice, Riggs continued, "I UNDERSTAND YOU HAVE A DIRECT LINE TO THE WHITE HOUSE. IS THAT CORRECT?"

Again, there was no quick response. Riggs was certain the shift supervisor was taking his orders from a third party, probably Forest Lindsey.

"YES, MR. SECRETARY, WE DO HAVE A PHONE LINE TO THE WHITE HOUSE. I CAN RELAY A MESSAGE FOR YOU."

Riggs cleared his throat, then said tersely, "HARRY, WHAT I HAVE TO TELL THE PRESIDENT IS FAR TOO IMPORTANT TO TRUST TO SUCH A RELAY. PLEASE CONVEY TO PRESIDENT MCGARTH THAT MY MESSAGE HAS EXTREMELY GRAVE IMPLICATIONS FOR OUR GOVERNMENT, AND ESPECIALLY FOR THOSE OF US HERE IN WASHINGTON. I STRONGLY SUGGEST THAT HE SEND AN ARMED ESCORT TO THE AIRCRAFT TO ACCOMPANY ME, CAPTAIN BEACHAM, AND THE HIJACKER'S DIPLOMATIC NEGOTIATOR TO THE OVAL OFFICE FOR A MEETING WITH HIM AT ONCE."

"I WILL PASS THE MESSAGE, MR. SECRETARY," Harry replied.

A full minute passed before Mann answered. "MR. SECRETARY, THE WHITE HOUSE HAS YOUR MESSAGE. I EXPECT A RESPONSE WITHIN THE NEXT FEW MINUTES. PLEASE STAND BY."

Unsure of whether he'd made his case sufficiently strong, Halston said, "TOWER, IF YOU'LL BRING A PHONE TO THE AIRCRAFT, I'LL EXPLAIN THE SITUATION TO THE PRESIDENT PERSONALLY."

Surprised by Riggs's suggestion, Reza remembered the mobile telephone. It was programmed for metro Washington. Returning to the cabin, Jabarri removed the phone pack from the overhead bin and took it into the cockpit.

"You have a number for the White House, Mr. Secretary?" Halston gave the piece of equipment a discerning glance before pressing the power button and dialing an unlisted number. Reza, Ahmed, and Wes watched as Halston waited for an answer.

"The Oval Office, Lindsey speaking!"

13

JIHAD

"Forest, Halston here. I must speak with the president immediately! I'm being detained by a group of hijackers on the plane over here at National Airport."

"Yes, we've heard, Mr. Secretary. Just a moment."

"Riggs, this is Mason. What's the situation?"

"Mr. President, the passengers and I are being held hostage by an unnamed group that insists I set up a meeting with you at the White House immediately."

"Riggs, that's impossible."

"I know that, Mr. President. But after seeing the video they have made, I urge you to accept the meeting they've requested, sir. To do otherwise, Mr. President, is to invite a disaster of unparalleled proportions."

"What are you talking about, Riggs?" Forest interrupted.

"Mr. President, the issue has extremely grave consequences for our country and Washington in particular. It's simply too sensitive to be discussed over the phone. Please, Mr. President. Accept the meeting they are demanding!"

McGarth paused.

"Must you have an answer now, Riggs, or can I have some time to think this over?"

"Sir, there is no time. I suggest you have Forest send a staff car to the airport immediately to pick up their negotiator, the captain, and me. The negotiator will be unarmed and has agreed to a body search by the Secret Service."

"Just a minute, Riggs."

McGarth knew Halston would not have used the phase *extremely grave consequences* unless he meant to convey a very serious threat to the country. Such a phrase was rarely used otherwise. The fact that he wasn't speaking in his usual condescending tone was disturbing, too.

"Riggs, I'll have Forest make the arrangements you have requested. Inform their negotiator that my consenting to hear their concerns in no way implies that our government will enter into a dialogue with their group."

"Thank you, Mr. President. We will await the escort."

Hanging up, McGarth turned to stare out the window for a moment. Raking his fingers through his silvering hair, Mason contemplated the situation. He hated having to make snap decisions. Already feeling a touch of remorse for agreeing to meet with the hijacker, he turned to Forest. "What do you make of Halston's request, Forest?"

"Sir, I got the distinct impression he was desperately trying to convince you of the gravity of the situation. He's much too articulate to mince words in a crisis like this."

Turning back toward the window, Mason wondered if the crisis would be as foreboding as Halston had made it sound. His words had been deliberate and explained his formal tone. But what did he mean by *extremely grave consequences*? Such terms were reserved for only the most provocative confrontations.

* * *

Jill rushed into the White House press office, mentally arranging the sequence of questions for which she wanted answers. Evelyn, one of Frances Buckner's White House media assistants, was elaborating on the administration's interpretation of several pieces of legislation pending on the Hill. Not a regular member of the White House press corps, Jill wasn't sure how to begin, nor was she the least bit certain of the response she'd get.

"Excuse me, Evelyn. I'm Jill Simmons with the *Examiner*. I've just received a report that a Trans International Airways jet, returning from Geneva with Secretary of State Riggs Halston aboard, has been hijacked and was forced to land at Washington National Airport about twenty-five minutes ago. Is the White House aware of this development, and do they have any idea who the hijackers are and who they represent?"

Silence filled the briefing room as everyone turned to face Jill, stunned. From the looks on their faces, it was obvious no one knew what she was talking about. Evelyn was speechless. Sean Abbot, a reporter for the *Richmond Courier* spoke up. "Please Ms. Simmons, continue."

Hesitating, Jill said, "My associate, Bud Waterman, is within a hundred yards of the aircraft and has confirmed the hijacking from monitoring radio communications between the tower and the Boeing 767. He..."

"Ms. Simmons, I have no knowledge of a hijacking, but I'll try to get the details as quickly as possible and get right back to you," Evelyn said. "Do you plan to stay here in the press room?"

"Yes," replied Jill, seeing every reporter in the room scurrying for the desk phones.

* * *

Bud stood beside his silver Cessna, peering through the lens of his camcorder as a black limousine followed the mobile stairs truck down Runway 36 toward the parked 767. The truck disappeared behind the left side of the wide-bodied jet before maneuvering into position adjacent to the left main entrance door. The limo pulled alongside the bottom of the stairs and waited.

Seconds later, he saw three men descend to the tarmac. The first he recognized as Riggs Halston. The second he concluded was the captain, judging by the four gold stripes on his jacket. Both entered the limo as the third person, a smaller man, stopped, spread his legs and raised his hands. Zooming closer, Bud taped the body search as he pondered the man's identity, certain he was one of the hijackers. Then he laid the video camera on the seat of his plane and picked up his pocket phone.

The first call went to the news desk, the second to Jill. Simmons jotted down the additional information and gave him an update on her progress as Frances Buckner walked into the press conference briefing room. "I've got to go now, Bud. The White House is about to make a public statement," Jill whispered. "Hang in there, girl. Give'em hell! The news desk already has the update," Bud shouted as Jill pressed the END button.

Looking up, Jill was amazed at how quickly the media had assembled in the small room. She felt conspicuous as TV cameras panned the corps, stopping on her several times before returning to Ms. Buckner. Jill wondered if they knew she was the one who had broken the story. She felt important. Bud's latest observations would be even more valuable once the questioning began. Knowing the importance of real-time information, Jill decided not to wait to be recognized once the floor was opened for questions, though she knew she would catch hell later.

Buckner's speech was short and to the point. They didn't really know anything, although she went to great lengths to make it appear otherwise, using her persona to the maximum. Jill sat on the edge of her seat waiting to make her move. Suddenly, Buckner was finished. The surge of questions was deafening. Jill realized she'd waited too long to make her move.

Without speaking, she stood up. A hush fell over the room as fellow reporters whispered among themselves. Several recognized her as the one who'd broken the story earlier and suspected she might have more to offer. Seeing the deference accorded her, Frances addressed her directly.

"You are with the.....?" asked Buckner, not knowing the name or the credentials of the young woman about to pose her question.

"The *Examiner*. Jill Simmons with the *Washington Examiner*."

"Yes, Ms. Simmons. Your question?"

"Ms. Buckner, approximately five minutes ago, three men deplaned from the Boeing 767 parked on the north end of Runway Three Six at National Airport. One was Secretary of State Riggs Halston. The second was the captain, and the third appeared to be one of the hijackers, as he was searched by two security officials before joining the other two in a black limousine. First, would you tell us if the White House has had a role in arranging for the secretary's release, and, if so, what's his destination? Secondly, will you tell us who the third person was and whether he is one of the hijackers?"

Frances stared at Jill in disbelief, wondering how she could have known what arrangements had been made in the Oval Office fewer than twenty minutes ago. Aware of the silence permeating the conference room and feeling the glare of the network video cameras on her,

Frances fumbled for the right phrase to field the reporter's blunt questions.

"Ms. Simmons, I am unable to comment at this time. I trust you understand the critical nature of such a crisis and will bear with us for a little while longer."

Jill countered instantly. "Then are you acknowledging that the White House did have a role in the secretary's release and does know where the party is headed?"

"I didn't say that, Ms. Simmons," Frances replied heatedly.

"No, you did not, Ms. Buckner. But for what other reason would you have chosen not to answer my question?"

Seeing she had failed miserably at managing the initial round with the media, Frances frantically tried to extricate herself from the conference. "Ladies and gentleman of the press, this concludes our preliminary briefing of the hijack situation at National Airport. I hope to be able provide you with more specific answers shortly. Thank you for your patience."

Suddenly, Jill was the center of attention. Senior White House correspondents congratulated her for her factual knowledge and penetrating questions as network reporters pursued her for spontaneous interviews. Some wanted to know her sources, while others were content to hear her speculation on the meaning of the secretary of state's release. Jill rose to the occasion. Her replies were smart and short, as though she had more to divulge at the right moment.

"Dammit, Forest, where did she come from?" asked the president, as Lindsey switched off the press room monitor.

"I was afraid something like this would happen, sir."

McGarth rubbed the back of his neck before dropping both hands to his hips. His chestnut-brown eyes narrowed. "Judging from the opening press release, we're going to be fighting an uphill battle with the press on this one. Their sources are better than ours!"

Just as Lindsey was about to reply, Betty interrupted. "They're here, Mr. President. Shall I show them in?"

"No. Give me another minute or two, Betty."

"Yes, sir," she replied, returning to the outer office.

"Have you activated the surveillance system yet, Forest?"

"It's on now, sir." McGarth glanced about the Oval Office, trying to recall the location of the hidden cameras and microphones before speaking again.

"How long before we'll be able to convene the National Security Council?"

"Betty completed the notification process just before Frances's press briefing. I expect most members will be here within the hour, except for Maggie. She's at a UN Security Council meeting in New York."

"Then we'd better show them in now, Forest. We can't do much more about the situation until we learn from Riggs who and what we're dealing with," said McGarth, gazing out at the White House lawn, parched from the summer heat.

* * *

It was nearly one a.m. in Geneva when Hassan Khalil placed a call to Saeed Keshef, director of the Fundamentialist Coalition. Hassan had spent the better part of the evening closing down the FC's nerve center and transferring its addresses, codes and files to their alternate control center elsewhere in Geneva. Andrea Zahar had downloaded all of the FC's financial records from her mainframe onto diskettes before deleting the hard drive. Only the FC's cultural records and files remained in the office. He and Andrea had carefully canvassed every desk drawer and file cabinet to ensure that there was no evidence of their covert activity before locking the office. They would not return.

"It is done. The office is clean," Hassan said.

"Very good. I was expecting your call. Reza is en route to the White House. I will await your final report," Keshef replied. Hassan hung up and walked over to the corner of the reception room and activated the timer as Andrea made a final check of the explosive shroud strung around the walls of the office complex. Minutes later, the two locked the office of the FC and disappeared down the stairway, unnoticed. Satisfied that no one had seen them, they walked two blocks along the Quai du Mont-Blanc before climbing into a black Mercedes.

Twenty minutes later, a violent explosion ripped apart the FC's office, setting the building on fire. Hearing the explosion from two blocks away, Hassan pulled onto the roadway for the fifteen-minute

drive to the new operations center. Andrea, seeing the building engulfed in flames, reported the explosion to Keshef over the car phone.

* * *

"Mr. President, allow me to present myself and my credentials,"
Jabarri offered.

McGarth stood behind his desk, silent and angry at the terrorist's
audacity. Deciding to ignore him, the president directed his initial statement to Wes. "My compliments to you, Captain Beacham, for getting
your flight safely on the ground. You have my gratitude."

"Thank you, sir, but I'm not certain I handled the situation that
well."

Turning toward Halston, McGarth was about to speak when Reza
interrupted, annoyed at having been intentionally slighted by him.

"Mr. President, I did not come here to exercise social protocol
with you. We have more serious matters to discuss."

Mason looked at the expression on Halston's face and knew the
Arab was dead serious. "Then suppose you start by telling me who you
are and what you and your group want!" the president said bluntly.

"Sir, I am Reza Jabarri, a representative of the Fundamentalist
Coalition, otherwise known as the FC." McGarth saw the anguish in
Halston's face. "Continue, Mr. Jabarri."

"Mr. President, the coalition has prepared a list of demands that it
hopes you and your government will comply with."

McGarth said nothing, but watched as Reza removed a file folder
from his briefcase and presented it to him. The president didn't bother
to open it. Instead, he dropped the folder on his desk, never taking his
eyes off Jabarri.

Reza, infuriated by the president's seeming arrogance, continued.
"The coalition, concerned that you and your government would not
take our demands seriously, has prepared a video that accurately states
our intentions should you choose not to honor all of our terms. I strongly
urge you to review its contents immediately. I suggest you consult
with Secretary of State Halston and Captain Beacham, if you doubt the
seriousness of our intentions. They will enlighten you, sir."

Mason glanced at Halston, then at Beacham. The sadness in their
eyes corroborated Reza's assertion. Looking back at Jabarri, the presi-

dent said, "I will review the tape in due time."

Reza exploded.

"You will look at it this minute, sir. The life of every citizen in Washington dictates that you comply with our demands immediately! You will see the tape, now! Do you understand?"

McGarth fought to maintain his composure as Riggs interceded.

"Mr. President, it is in the interest of the country that you do as he wishes. Sir, we have no alternative."

"Thank you for your assistance, Mr. Secretary. I trust the president will accept your intelligent advice," said Jabarri, more calmly.

"Very well. Forest will arrange for us to view the tape."

Forest stepped forward and took the tape from Reza, examining it to see if it would fit the Oval Office VCR.

"It will fit your system," Reza snapped. "We have prepared many copies for use on a variety of machines, as you will soon learn."

Satisfied that he had the president's cooperation, Reza resumed his diplomatic role, but McGarth wasn't buying it. Wes saw the contempt in the president's eye as he moved from behind his desk to watch the film. Tension filled the room as Forest switched on the video.

The president learned immediately that a Soviet nuclear weapon - an ALCM (air launched cruise missile) - had undergone extensive modification so it could be detonated by remote control. Several frames later, he discovered that the warhead had been taken from an AS-15A cruise missile, decommissioned and stored at Uzin Air Base in the USSR while awaiting shipment for recycling. The tape revealed the changes made to adapt the weapon to its new container, a sealed coffin. Andrei Karpolov, a noted USSR special weapons technician, was shown making the alterations to the nuclear device. His narration included a detailed explanation of the modifications, the available detonation options, and a warning that the weapon would explode immediately if any attempt was made to disarm it. The final frames showed the weapon being installed in a coffin and placed inside a TIA cargo container for loading aboard a 747 Mid East Cargo jet bound for Geneva.

No one said anything as the horizontal lines rolled across the screen, signaling the end of the eight-minute video. The last several frames had caught Wes's attention. Something about the location looked familiar, but he couldn't place where. Looking over at the president, Wes saw McGarth was speechless, stunned by the revelation he had just witnessed. Only Reza seemed pleased by the presentation.

"I see from the look on your face, Mr. President, that you have a better understanding of our determination! Within the hour, sir, an updated video will arrive, showing the TIA cargo container being loaded aboard Captain Beacham's aircraft," Jabarri said. "In the film you will see that an identical container bearing the body of a TIA pilot is switched with the one containing the bomb. That bomb is now in place at National Airport."

"Mr. Jabarri, I gather you will provide me enough time to give serious attention to the coalition's proposals?" asked the president, rising from his seat.

Smiling at McGarth, Reza said, "Mr. President, you have until nine p.m. Eastern Daylight Time to deliver a televised address to the American people outlining the current situation facing their government. You will ensure that your presentation includes the list of demands I have given you. You will also inform them of our organization, the Fundamentalist Coalition. I have included the necessary background information on the FC to aid in your preparation. Should you choose not to address our demands on television by nine tonight, we will shoot one American passenger for each minute you delay until they are all dead. Then, if you still have not met our demands, we will detonate the device via remote control.

"I should also point out that we have prepositioned identical information regarding our purpose and list of demands in key cities throughout the world, ready to be delivered to the media, should it be required. We will, of course, make copies of the video available to them, as well."

The president showed no emotion as he listened to the terrorist. Staring into Reza's narrow-set eyes, McGarth said, "It appears that I have much to accomplish. Do you have further concerns to discuss before we conclude our meeting?"

Pleased at McGarth's response, Reza said, "Yes, there are several minor matters that need to be addressed. But in view of the time constraint facing you, Mr. President, I will agree to let Secretary Halston handle those for you."

"Very well, he has my authorization."

"Excellent! replied Jabarri, satisfied with the meeting.

"And how shall I reach you?" asked the president.

"I will make my whereabouts known to your chief of staff."

Reza motioned for Halston to lead him from the Oval Office. Wes stood up and was about to join Riggs when the president spoke. "Mr. Jabarri, do you still require the services of Captain Beacham?"

"Captain Beacham has served us well. You may do with him as you like."

"Mr. President, begging your pardon, sir, but I should return to the aircraft," Wes said.

"Captain Beacham, you've done quite enough," the president snapped. "You will stay here until the attorney general decides if charges are warranted. Is that clear?"

"Yes, sir," answered Wes, stunned by the president's anger.

Reza smiled at McGarth's decision, pleased at the discord Wes had caused. At the door, he paused and said, "I look forward to your address this evening, Mr. President. But, I wish to remind you that every point in that folder must be addressed. Omitting even one will bring about the total destruction of the 'Seat of Democracy' as you Americans like to call it." McGarth stood in silence, glaring at the terrorist as he disappeared through the doorway of the Oval Office.

Wes was numb. The president's words were still ringing in his ears. Until now, the thought of being arrested hadn't entered his mind. He'd expected to return to the aircraft and take charge of his crew and passengers.

"Captain Beacham, I'm sorry to have humiliated you that way, but I had to be certain Jabarri, or whatever his name is, would not insist that you return to the aircraft. Your knowledge and expertise is far more important to us right now. I trust you can understand my position?"

"Of course, Mr. President," replied Wes, relieved that he had misread McGarth's intentions.

Forest was already scanning the contents of the folder. His sober expression reflected his frustration as he digested the list of demands.

"Bear with us for a while, Captain. As you've heard, that bastard has just screwed us all royally. I'm certain we're going to need your help."

"I'm sorry, Mr. President, I had no ...."

"Save it, Wes. I've already reviewed your service record. You don't owe me an explanation. I assume you acted in your crew and passengers' best interests."

Wes wanted desperately to own up to his mistaken judgment, but it wasn't the time. Washington's survival was at stake.

"What do they want, Forest?" McGarth asked.

"Everything! Every damn thing in the Middle East!"

"It figures," the president said. "I would probably do the same if I were in their position. It's just hard to believe they got their hands on a nuke without our finding out. Until now, I would've bet it was impossible."

Forest didn't answer. He was already ticking off the facts that had to be included in the president's speech. "How much time have we got, Forest?" Lindsey glanced at his watch. "An hour and forty five minutes, sir."

McGarth paced the carpet, contemplating his next move. "Get Frances in here to help you put the address together, and tell Betty to send for my speech writers. They can clean it up after I've looked it over. While you're at it, have her run off copies of the file for the NSC members and send them in as soon as they arrive."

Lindsey nodded as he pressed the intercom on the president's desk and relayed his instructions. "Better have her get Sloan over here right away. I want the Federal Emergency Management Administration (FEMA) involved. And give the mayor and the Metro Police chief a call. Tell them to join us. The chief will have his hands full once the news gets out."

"What about the governors, sir?"

"I'll hold off talking with them until I've had a chance to meet with the secretary of defense and the chairman of the joint chiefs. I want Chris and General Griffith's input before I activate the National Guards."

Turning to Wes, McGarth said, "Captain, I'd like you to attend the meeting. Call your family and let them know you're okay. Tell them you're helping me for now. You may want to consider sending them somewhere else until this thing blows over. You're not going to be very popular once the media starts to analyze the situation."

"Yes sir, Mr. President," Wes said. "I'll take care of it."

"Use one of the phones in the outer office, then join us," McGarth motioned. "The switchboard will put you through."

* * *

Jackie pulled into the Beacham driveway a little after seven p.m. Caroline and Tucker had fallen asleep during the last fifty miles to Williamsburg and were still out as she set the parking brake and shut off the Explorer's V6. She was glad they had decided to leave her car in Washington. Meredith and Walker had seen the flash of the headlights coming down the drive and rushed out to greet them. Tucker came to first. His leg really hurt. Caroline, still exhausted from her ordeal, hardly knew where she was. Seeing her mom, Jackie began to cry, softly at first, then collapsing into deep, uncontrollable sobs. Meredith pulled her from the truck and into her arms. Walker lifted Caroline from her seat and carried her into the house as Tucker hobbled behind. Meredith and Jackie stood in the driveway holding one another for several minutes before Meredith led her younger daughter into the house.

After examining Tucker's gunshot wound, Walker decided he needed to see a doctor right away. Not wanting to call attention to what had happened, Walker leafed through the physician's section of the phone book until he found the number of his former college roommate, Jeremy Shipman. Jay, a resident at Williamsburg Memorial, answered the phone on the third ring. "Jay, this is Walker. I need a favor. Can you help me?"

"Well sure, Walker. Where are you?"

"I'm here at home in Williamsburg."

"What do you need?"

"It will take too long to explain. Just bring what you need to take care of a gunshot wound," Walker said. "Caroline's fiancé has been hit in the leg. I'll give you the details when you get here. The FBI is handling the investigation."

"I'll be there in twenty minutes."

Walker hung up and walked into the sunroom. Tucker was stretched out on the chaise lounge with a throw pillow under his leg. The bandaged wound was swollen and blood was seeping through the gauze. Meredith, returning from the kitchen, handed Tucker a towel packed with ice cubes for his leg.

Meredith knew her children well enough to know they would talk when they were ready.

Suddenly the phone rang. Meredith imagined it was Wes calling to check on the kids and to say he was on his way home. That was the way it had always been.

Walker answered. It was Claire Adams, his fiancée.

"Walker? Have you seen the evening news?"

"No."

"Your father's flight was hijacked to National Airport earlier this evening. It's the only thing they're talking about on the major networks."

"Are you serious?"

"Of course I am. I wouldn't joke about a thing like that." answered Claire, annoyed at his response. "There's more. The jet's on the ground at National. The secretary of state was on the flight. It's rumored that your dad and one of the hijackers has gone with him to the White House to meet with the president. Nothing's been confirmed, but that's what they're reporting."

"Claire, I'll call you back in a few minutes."

Walker rushed into the den and switched on the TV. A news commentator was in the middle of a live interview with Jill Simmons, a reporter from the *Washington Examiner*, speaking from the White House. Easing into his father's leather wingback chair, Walker listened intently as the reporter summarized the events. Wes was in the White House, talking with the president.

"Mom, you better come in here right away," shouted Walker. "Dad's at the White House talking with the president."

"What!" cried Meredith, dashing into the den, followed by Jackie, Caroline and Tucker. The room fell silent as the commentator recounted the events of the last hour. No one wanted to break away from the TV to answer the phone, until finally Meredith, unable to tolerate the ringing, went into the kitchen to answer.

"Wes, it's you! Are you really at the White House?" Hearing Meredith call their father's name, Jackie and Caroline left the den and headed to the loft for another phone.

"Yes, I'm at the White House with the president but I can't discuss the situation. You'll know later on tonight when he makes a special address to the country at nine."

"Can't you tell me anything more? Are you all right?"

"Physically, yes, I'm fine. Emotionally, I'm wasted. Two of my crew and a Secret Service agent are dead, killed by the terrorists who hijacked my flight. Is Caroline okay?"

Hearing her father's voice, Caroline broke into tears. "Yes, Dad, I'm right here with Tucker, Jackie and Walker. We're all safe," she said, brushing her tears aside.

"Thank God, you're safe, honey. The last twenty-four hours have been hell on Earth for me worrying over you. Who found you?"

Meredith waited patiently on her end, knowing how much the girls needed to talk to their father, especially tonight. It had always been that way. She would start the conversation and they would join in. Listening to Wes offer the girls his encouragement, she knew their inner strength came from him. It wasn't surprising that the two had acted so bravely and with such tenacity. She envied the bond they had with their father. Meredith, hearing them share their experiences with him, understood it was the start of their healing. The thought of their being exposed to such a harrowing experience made her shiver. She heard both of them describe, in minute detail, their confrontation with the two terrorists.

"Meredith, are you still on?"

"Yes, I'm just waiting my turn," she responded. "What you had to say to the girls was just what they needed to hear, Wes."

"As frightening as all of this has been for you and the girls, it's nothing compared to what we will have to face."

"What are you talking about, Wes?"

"Remember my mission as a fighter pilot in England?"

"Of course." Then it hit her. "Oh no, Wes! Oh no!" Suddenly, Meredith knew why he had gone to the White House.

Talking around classified information on a White House telephone was dangerous and Wes knew it, but Meredith had to know. He owed her that. "I can't say any more except that it will be common knowledge around nine p.m. Once we hang up, get the family together and leave for Duck, immediately. Take as many vehicles as you can drive, fill them up with fuel, and withdraw as much cash from the ATM as possible before leaving. You'll be able to hear his speech on the radio. I'll join you when I can. The important thing is to get started right away. I'll give Walker and Tucker the same information. You better go, honey. I love you."

"I love you too, Wes."

There was nothing more to say. It was as if his trip had been delayed an extra day, thought Meredith, as she handed the phone to her son. She knew what had to be done. They'd talked about such a scenario many years ago. Now with so much about to take place in their children's lives, the nuclear issue had to raise its ugly mantle once more. Meredith was afraid.

For thirty years, her life with Wes and the children had been too perfect. She recalled having to make small sacrifices and having to do without at times, but never anything major like dealing with a nuclear threat.

Resentment set in as Meredith fought the temptation to lash out at the disruptions her family would have to endure. Meredith understood herself perfectly. She would let her resilience take over. Within minutes, she and the girls were packing the few things they'd need. Most of their summer clothes were still at Kilduck Station, their beach house. The drive to Duck on the Outer Banks would take a little more than two hours, Meredith thought, as she tossed the last of her clothes into a large canvas bag. They would manage.

Wes's conversation with Walker lasted less than five minutes. Their talk was all business. Wes said nothing of his plan to return to the aircraft. Although he would have given anything to be with his family, Wes knew his duty still lay with his passengers and crew. Walker would understand. He always had. Blessed with exceptional wisdom and insight, Walker usually knew the message before it was sent.

Wes put down the phone and paused before returning to the Oval Office. It seemed strange being able to simply walk back into the president's office. A chill passed through him as he thought of the decisions that would be made in that office within the next hour. His responsibility as captain of his flight paled in comparison to the burden the president faced, a burden he'd foisted on him without warning. Wes admired McGarth. He was a far greater man than the press had made him out to be, a man of stature and character. Wes had tremendous empathy for the president.

Walking into the Oval Office, Wes saw numerous familiar faces, men whose faces had appeared on *Time, Newsweek,* and *US News & World Report*, deeply involved in discussion over the threat as they viewed the terrorist's video. The president beckoned him.

Wes had the uncomfortable feeling he was going to have to explain the role he'd played in bringing the nuclear threat to America's doorstep.

"Gentlemen, I think a quick overview of what led to the situation we face is critical to our understanding of where we stand and what we're dealing with. Captain Beacham will give you a concise account of what he knows... Captain."

Suddenly, Wes's years of giving military briefings came together. Within five minutes, he'd covered nearly every detail of the flight, including Caroline's kidnapping, his meeting with the terrorists on Lake Geneva, and most importantly, his retrieval of their list of telephone numbers and addresses.

Gaylord Elliot, the president's national security adviser and Bert Williamson, director of the CIA were impressed by his resourcefulness under pressure and complimented him. FBI Director John Sinclair, pleased with the outcome of agent Dave Coleman's initiative in helping effect the rescue of Beacham's daughter, seemed equally satisfied with his performance.

The issue of blame never surfaced. Surprised, Wes took a seat against the wall and listened to the council members discuss the terrorist demands and the president's response. He noticed that McGarth rarely spoke except to redirect the focus of the discussions. Content to listen, the president allowed the debate to go on for at least fifteen minutes before interceding.

"Gentlemen, in less than an hour I must make a statement to the nation and to the world. There is little time to do otherwise. It's obvious to me, and I presume to you, that for the moment, these terrorists have the upper hand. Each of you needs time that we haven't got. It is unfair, and more importantly, unwise for us to try and formulate a plan of attack with such little information. As yet, we don't know the true identity of the threat we face, let alone enough to design a plan to defeat its objectives.

"Therefore, I must appear willing to give serious consideration to their demands until we can figure out a way to get our hostages back and that nuke out of our backyard. Repercussions from what I must appear to agree to will be monumental, but must be managed effectively by each of you within your areas of responsibility if we are to have any chance of defeating these lunatics without bringing ruin to our people and their capital.

"Gaylord, I want you to chair a committee to analyze the threat and formulate possible courses of action. As a minimum include the secretary of defense, the joint chiefs of staff, the FBI, CIA, and the secretary of state. Feel free to augment the committee as you see fit. I've already asked Forest to activate NEST, the Nuclear Emergency Search Team. They should be on their way from Albuquerque shortly.

"Specifically, I want confirmation that what they have shown us in that damn video is real. I hate like hell having to go before the American people with this revelation, having only a cassette for justification. I also want to know who we're dealing with and who are their sponsors. The amount of financial backing needed to acquire that nuclear weapon almost assures us that we are dealing with some form of state-sponsored terrorism. Halston's people at the State Department have some preliminary information concerning the FC. You may want to start there.

"I want your committee to come up with a set of comprehensive responses that will enable us to rescue the passengers aboard that aircraft, while preserving the lives of our citizens and our institutions of government. I urge each of you to cooperate fully with one another. Are there any questions?"

"Mr. President, in view of the threat to our government, do you plan to leave Washington for the Alternate Command Center?" General Griffith asked.

"That's a fair question, Clayton. It cuts directly to the issue of how I exercise my duties as commander in chief. I've decided to send the vice president to the Alternate National Command Center in Raven Mountain and will recommend that the Speaker of the House accompany him.

"I think it's extremely important that those of us charged with the obligation of defending the country do so in a visible way. The American people will look directly at my leadership to decide how they should respond. If I leave, what kind of argument can I make for asking the rest of Washington to stay in place and see this through? Edward is more than qualified to become the next president, if things don't go as we hope.

"Each of you review your department's contingency plans in light of our Emergency Action Plans(EAPs) and ensure that your input to the Key Personnel Locator file is up-to-date. Seriously consider manning a remote center of operations and designate a second to represent you. Sloan Kilgore will brief us later this evening on FEMA's EAP for this contingency. Now if you'll excuse me, gentlemen, I must attend to the details of my Armageddon Address."

No one laughed at the president's effort to minimize the danger he and the country faced. The truth was, no one in the room knew for certain that the terrorists wouldn't detonate the device in spite of what the president agreed to.

One by one the National Security Council members filed out of the Oval Office. Wes stayed in his chair, unsure of where to go. He was about to ask Forest Lindsey when a voice called to him from the door.

"Captain?" Gaylord Elliot, the national security adviser, waved at him. As Wes stood up, the president saw that he was still in the room. "Captain, I want you to assist my national security adviser. Your information will be invaluable to us in trying to find a solution."

"Yes sir, Mr. President."

"Fine. Gaylord's waiting for you."

Wes nodded and walked quickly to the door. Elliot handed him a temporary White House ID and the pair left hurriedly for the Situation Room in the White House basement.

14

NO RECOURSE

The last hour had been one of fear for the passengers. Ahmed and Mohammed had insisted on keeping the female passengers on the floor in front of their seats. The males were forced to stay in their seats with their belts fastened and their heads covered with blankets. They were told they would be shot if they removed them. Flight attendants were confined to their jump seats. Only Sybil was allowed to move about the cabin and then only when directed by the terrorists.

Positioning himself at the doorway to the cockpit, Ahmed monitored the activity in the forward cabin. Mohammed stationed himself near the mid cabin galley and took responsibility for the aft cabin area. Their seven accomplices patrolled the aisles, harassing those who complained.

With the onset of darkness, the cabin lights were turned on and the window shades lowered. The escape slides remained disarmed, preventing passengers from trying to rush the doors. Use of the lavatories was prohibited initially. Only after Sybil protested to Ahmed did he agree to allow women and children to use them, escorted by one of the terrorists. Some women chose to forgo the need to avoid drawing attention to themselves and their offspring. Mothers tried to control their children's crying, and husbands sought to comfort their distraught wives.

Sybil heard the moans of despair. It pained her to see the agony passengers were forced to endure with no sense of when or how it might end. Ahmed's inhumane treatment of the hostages was unnecessary, yet he seemed to delight in their suffering. Sybil's contempt for him escalated with each passing minute. Only years of professional discipline enabled her to keep from lashing out at him. He was there for his pound of flesh and nothing she could say would dissuade him.

The sound of the cockpit radio speakers startled Sybil as Ahmed hurried past her to respond.

"TIA 899, WE HAVE A MESSAGE FROM MR. JABARRI."

"TOWER! YOU WILL ADDRESS THIS AIRCRAFT AS THE 'FC.' THE FUNDAMENTALIST COALITION IS IN COMMAND OF THIS JET."

"ROGER, FC. ARE YOU READY TO COPY YOUR MESSAGE?"

"GO AHEAD," snapped Ahmed, satisfied he'd made his point.

"MR. JABARRI ADVISES THAT HIS VISIT WITH THE PRESIDENT WAS A SUCCESS. HE WILL RETURN TO THE AIRCRAFT WITHIN THE HOUR. YOU ARE TO EXPECT THE ARRIVAL OF AN ARMED SECURITY FORCE THAT WILL ENCIRCLE THE AIRCRAFT AT 100 METERS. THEY WILL PROVIDE PROTECTION AGAINST UNAUTHORIZED INTRUDERS. A VEHICLE BRINGING ASSAULT WEAPONS AND AMMUNITION WILL APPROACH THE AIRCRAFT. RETRIEVE THE WEAPONS AND INSPECT EACH ONE ALONG WITH THE AMMO."

A faint smile formed at Ahmed's mouth as he acknowledged the message and walked from the cockpit. After shouting something to Mohammed in Arabic, he turned to Sybil and Cynthia. "We will soon see how strong you Americans are when your president tells you of our demands and the nuclear bomb we have planted at your doorstep. It will help you to know the fear that Arabs live with each day. Sybil, set the system up for TV."

Cynthia moved the picture screens into position as Sybil programmed the system for local TV. News of the hijacking and the impending mystery flooded the major networks as each attempted to portray its on-the-scene reporter as having the latest information. Selecting local affiliate WBSU, Sybil adjusted the volume and was about to close the access panel when she heard the local reporter mention Bud Waterman, a journalist for the *Washington Examiner*. He was said to be reporting from his Cessna parked within a hundred yards of the hijacked plane. The reporter went on to say that Waterman had been the first to report the departure of Secretary of State Halston, Captain Wes Beacham and an unidentified man from the jet.

Sybil wondered if any of the passengers had pocket phones. If so, she could try to establish contact with someone outside. As the only one allowed to move about the aircraft, she could provide authorities a firsthand account of what was taking place inside the plane. She would hide the phone in the lav, behind the towel dispenser. It was risky, but worth a try. Closing the entertainment compartment door, Sybil decided she would try to find out if there was a pocket phone aboard.

Ahmed was standing in the doorway peering out at the movement at the terminal when Sybil spoke. "Kyle?"

Spinning on his heels, he snarled at her in Arabic before realizing she hadn't understood a word. "I am Ahmed. I have always been Ahmed. Only you foolish Americans thought of me as Kyle," he shouted in perfect English.

Sybil ignored his outburst. "Ahmed, in the name of Allah, will you please allow the bodies of Leigh and the security officer to be removed from the aircraft? It serves no purpose for them to remain on board. Certainly your God is one of compassion, as well as power."

Ahmed looked into the cabin at the two blanket-covered corpses.

"Perhaps they can serve a purpose. Their deaths will emphasize the seriousness of our demands. Yes, I will allow their bodies to be removed when the weapons are brought to the aircraft."

"Thank you, Ahmed." Sybil said in disgust.

Waterman also heard the tower relay Jabarri's instructions to Ahmed aboard the 767. He realized that explained the flurry of activity near the terminal. Knowing the movement was not in preparation for an assault on the aircraft, he dialed the news desk number again.

Waiting for an answer, Bud imagined the accolades he and Jill would receive from the front office and the news editor. The recognition had been long in coming, but from now on he would be taken seriously by the *Examiner's* leadership. He and Jill would enjoy getting the inside sources that usually led to the front page stories. Even White House and congressional staffers would leak tips to them.

The news desk staffer took Bud's latest information and read it back to him before hanging up. Bud smiled as he rang Jill's preset number. "Jill, it's Bud with an update."

"Just a minute. Let me move away and get a pen. You caught me in the middle of an interview," she said, digging into her overstuffed purse. "All right, I'm ready to copy. Go."

He fed her the details of the tower conversation.

"Bud, what's going on here? There's something very unusual about this whole hijacking. Why is the president going to address the nation? The secretary of state doesn't appear to be in any immediate danger. And no former president has taken it upon himself to become involved in a hijacking."

"I don't have a good answer, Jill, but it's compelling enough to make McGarth think he has to respond."

"That's what bothers me, Bud. I think it's real serious."

"Well, we'll know about it within the next forty-five minutes. Just stay with it. I'll be in touch."

Jill needed Bud's encouragement. The pace of events was alarming to her. Real-time news reporting was far more demanding than she had ever imagined. Staying focused was becoming increasingly difficult. Everyone was now looking to her for the next news flash and wanting to know her views on its meaning. She was quickly moving from her role as a reporter to that of a news maker and it troubled her. It was not what she wanted, but what instant fame, in the eyes of her peers, demanded.

* * *

Chief of Staff Lindsey and Press Secretary Buckner were close to completing the rough draft when Betty rang for them to come back to the Oval Office. The president was at his desk reviewing the list of demands for a third time. "Forest, there isn't a damn thing here I consider negotiable."

"I know, sir. There's really little point in trying. Congress and the American people will never stand for it, not to mention Israel and our Allies."

McGarth shook his head as Lindsey laid the rough draft on his desk. "Forest, isn't there anything short of total capitulation we can do to somehow save face?"

"I'm afraid not, sir. They really have us over a barrel."

"Do you think these terrorists will actually detonate that nuke if I stonewall them and refuse to accept their demands?"

Lindsey looked into McGarth's weathered face, trying to decide how to answer. He knew the president respected his opinion and would consider it. "Sir, I know you want me to recommend a hard line with these terrorists. But I don't think you can afford to call their bluff. The consequences of being wrong are too great."

"I hate to admit it, but that's the way I see it, too. It's so damned hard to imagine how they pulled it off, given our commitment to national security. What in the hell has the CIA been doing all this time? Aren't they supposed to be on top of this sort of thing?"

"My guess is that their initial assessment of this organization was based on incomplete information."

"That's for damned sure," McGarth said, angrily.

"Excuse me, sir, but it's eight-fifteen. We need to get a final draft into the TelePrompter and proof it," Lindsey said. "Do you plan to speak with the Israeli prime minister before the address?"

"Yes, I'll talk with him now. He's got to understand that we don't intend to comply with any of these demands over the long haul. Give me five minutes to look over the draft and then get him on the line for me, Forest."

Somberly, Mason McGarth focused on the five pages lying on his desk. It was Armageddon for his administration. No one in America would forgive him for having allowed such a breach in national security.

*   *   *

Wes found the *crisis center* pretty much as he'd expected, similar to the major military command centers he'd frequented as an officer in the Air Force, but more complex. The level of activity impressed him. Myriad checklists were being run as staffers sought to notify and prepare governmental agencies to deal with the situation the president was about to announce. Classified intelligence flowed across the computer monitors as specialists pieced together unrelated fragments of information from around the globe into meaningful facts. Few telephones remained on their hooks as other team members issued instructions and coordinated civil and military agencies.

Huddled in the glass-encased conference room above and behind the command center were Gaylord Elliot, the president's National Security Adviser; Burt Williamson, director of the CIA; John Sinclair, director of the FBI; Chris Jacobson, Secretary of Defense; General Clayton Griffith, chairman of the Joint Chiefs of Staff; and Edgar Wilson, assistant to the secretary of state for Middle East affairs. Invited by Elliot, Wes sat at the far end of a long, mahogany table and listened.

The speculative discussions focused on the probable sponsors and funding of the FC. Council members unanimously agreed that the cost of acquiring a nuke dictated state sponsorship, but were divided over which states might be involved. Fundamentalist ideology was explored, particularly its exportation of terrorism to achieve its objectives. Skepticism abounded. Members found it difficult to imagine how such a coalition could exist. Several questioned its use of Western methods of organization to orchestrate the terrorist attack, while others argued over whether the coalition's motives were politcal or religious. Issues were raised about the FC's ability to plan and coordinate such a complex operation while maintaining a cohesive relationship among members.

Elliot used the latter part of the meeting to summarize the points of consensus and to prioritize the council's activities. He appointed a joint investigative task force comprised of elements from the DOD, CIA, and FBI. Analyzing the videotape, locating Andrei Karpolov and determining the modifications to the weapon were made top priority. Gaylord intimated that McGarth would intervene to secure Yeltsin's cooperation.

After announcing an increase in the DEFCON (Defense Condition) status, Elliot told members to expect implementation of those emergency action procedures (EAPs) deemed appropriate by the president, including numerous changes to the Continuity of Government checklist.

Aware that it was nine p.m., Elliot directed the NSC's attention to the TV monitor in the conference room. As the screen came to life, a voice said, "...Speaking from the Oval Office in the White House, the President of the United States."

15

ARMAGEDDON ADDRESS

Good evening, my fellow Americans. At approximately six thirty this evening Trans International Airways Flight 899, returning from Geneva, was hijacked and forced to land at National Airport. Secretary of State Riggs Halston was among the passengers aboard the Boeing 767.

An organization calling itself the Fundamentalist Coalition, or FC, has claimed responsibility for the hijacking and is in control of the aircraft on the ground at National Airport, several miles from the White House.

Their leader, Reza Jabarri, a passenger aboard the jet, was granted an invitation to meet with me in the Oval Office. At that meeting, he, as the representative of the coalition, provided our government a video revealing the existence of a nuclear weapon aboard the jet. In addition, he presented me a list of demands from the coalition. After considering the evidence, I have concluded that the threat to the citizens of Washington and to our government is real.

The FC's demands and the threat it has made against our government is the reason I must speak with each of you tonight.

The list of demands made on our country is onerous, but one that I, as your president, must honor, if we are to avoid having the weapon detonated here in Washington. Let me assure each one of you that I have no intention of allowing that to happen.

For this reason, I have agreed to take the following actions:

The United States will immediately and unilaterally cease providing economic, financial, and military assistance to the following Middle East nations: Israel, Jordan, Egypt, Saudi Arabia, and Kuwait.

The United States will begin a withdrawal of all its military units from the Middle East region, including those stationed in the Mediterranean.

The United States will use its influence to ensure that all Arabs being detained or held captive in Western prisons are released and provided safe passage to their homeland.

Finally, the United States will immediately release all funds being held in U.S. owned and/or controlled banks belonging to nations of the Middle East and will use its auspices to insist that all other Western powers do the same.

I have been advised that the failure to carry out any one of these demands will result in the detonation of the nuclear device aboard the jet.

At this time, I have no assurances of when the weapon will be removed from National Airport, even though I have consented to meet all of the demands on their list.

As your president, I resent having to accept these terms and I sincerely regret the impact that my actions will undoubtedly have on our Middle East allies. But the lives of a great number of Americans lie in harm's way and must receive my primary consideration. I trust that each of you will understand the reasons for my decision.

As Americans, we are sometimes called upon to make sacrifices for the benefit of our countrymen. It is the way we have chosen to live with one another. This is such a time. We must, as a nation of free men and women, work through this crisis together, if we are to neutralize the threat upon us. We can be sure that the entire world will be watching to see if we measure up to the challenge. I am certain that we can and will prevail.

As your commander in chief, I must do everything possible to preserve our democratic government. To this end, I have taken certain actions to ensure the survivability of the government and its major departments and agencies. Having made those provisions, I have decided to stay here at the White House through this crisis and will expect all government department heads to do the same. I have requested

that both houses of Congress consider reconvening outside the threat-
ened area. I intend to make the same request of the judicial branch.

In the interim, I intend to use the full power of this office to find an
acceptable solution to this crisis and will not rest until I have achieved
that goal. I will ask Congress to assist me in this endeavor.

Finally, I must call upon you, the American people, to do your
part, to accept responsibility for the care of those citizens who will
choose to leave their homes and jobs, to support your government's
effort to make these necessary adjustments with dignity and order and
to stand tall in the face of this adversity as Americans before you have
done.

For those who are residents of Greater Washington and who are,
therefore, directly threatened by this crisis, I caution each of you to
resist the temptation to flee your home or business without giving civil
defense and police authorities the chance to mobilize and take control
of the roadways from the city. To do otherwise will place you and your
family's life and property at much greater risk and will hinder your
government's ability to ensure your safety.

In conclusion, let me state emphatically that neither I, nor my
administration, will rest until we have resolved this conflict in a man-
ner acceptable to you, the American people. I shall ensure that you are
kept abreast of my progress toward that end through future addresses
and press interviews.

God bless you and God bless America. Thank you and good night.

Lindsey watched silently as the president arose from his desk and
walked toward him, his eyes dilating as he passed from the glare of the
floodlights. "Was I convincing enough, Forest?"

"Sir, no one could have stated the situation more eloquently or
honestly. But I suspect for many Americans, especially those living
here, learning that they are threatened with a nuclear bomb controlled
by militant terrorists will prove to be more than they can handle. My
guess is that we're apt to see sheer panic as they struggle to deal with
the crisis."

"I'm afraid you're right, Forest. But you really can't blame them.
Asking them to stay calm and avoid fleeing their homes after telling
them their government has failed them is unrealistic."

McGarth walked over and sat down in front of the TV as the technicians finished removing the camera and lights from his office. Know-

ing he wanted to get the media's reaction to his address, Forest switched on the TV. The commentator had just finished summing up the major points of the president's speech and was about to throw it open for discussion with his panelists. McGarth watched the debate for several minutes before flipping to another network. Journalists were unanimous in their opinion that the citizens of Washington would panic. Their focus turned to a discussion of the size of the area directly threatened by the nuclear weapon. Switching channels again, McGarth paused to hear reporter, Charlene Richards of WBSU, discuss the ring of possible lethality with a retired Air Force general who had written extensively on terrorism and its potential for precipitating a nuclear crisis.

The president studied the concentric circles overlaid on a map of the District and the bi-state area as the general discussed the probable outcome of such a nuclear detonation centered on National Airport. His analysis was chilling to McGarth, contemplating massive casualties if the coalition decided to explode the device. Listening further, the president realized that even if the bomb were set to the smallest kilo-tonnage yield, the loss of lives and property would be unfathomable. His stomach churned as the general went on to explain the long-term implications of such a catastrophe and how it would render Washington and the surrounding area uninhabitable for years.

Was it a coincidence or an omen — Elliot's troubling message delivered only hours before? Mason wondered. He'd said an undercover CIA operative had discovered an investigation by the KGB regarding a missing tactical nuclear weapon. While vague, the report had raised the question of accountability for a special weapon (nuclear) believed to have been misplaced in the field.

A discrepancy found during an internal security audit by the KGB of recycled nuclear material had caused the file to be reopened nearly two years after the event occurred. The document, acknowledging the discrepancy — missing nuclear weapons material — had attributed the error to improper accounting and not to clandestine activity.

Most troubling to the CIA operative was that the undercover KGB agent had solicited his interest, arranged the meeting, and practically forced him to read the report. The CIA agent was certain the document was being leaked to Langley as a warning. Someone in a position to know within the KGB did not believe the report's conclusions, nor had he succeeded in learning the truth, the CIA operative had said.

What a cruel act of fate — to be forewarned with no time to act, thought Mason as he shifted his attention to the unfolding crisis covered with frightening clarity by the networks. How was it they could marshal so many experts on such short notice? Had they known such a disaster was inevitable and planned for it? "Dammit! How could I have been so stupid, so naive," moaned Mason, furious at himself.

Forest interrupted, "Mr. President, the press corps room is in chaos. Frances says they're bombarding her with impossible questions. She wants to know if you could come down and make a statement, or at least field some of their questions? Also, Betty says security is holding the second video Jabarri mentioned we would receive. Do you want to preview it?"

"Tell Frances I'll be down to meet the press in fifteen minutes, but first I'd like to review that tape. Maybe there's some additional information I can use when I talk to the media. From what the networks are saying, I need anything I can find!"

McGarth leaned back in his chair and closed his eyes for a moment, hoping to find relief for his anguish. All at once everything was a priority. The scope of the crisis was widening by the minute, driven by the fear of knowing the government was unable to protect its citizens from the horror of the nuclear weapon poised at National Airport. Inwardly, he had no idea of how he was going to dispose of the weapon or the terrorists who had put it there.

Until now, he'd never given much thought to his role as the commander in chief. Comfortable at negotiating with Congress and jawboning special interest groups into backing his programs, he'd considered himself an articulate political leader, capable of successfully pushing legislation through even the toughest of adversaries.

Now, all of that seemed trivial. His skill as the commander in chief would determine whether the nation would survive the ordeal in one piece. Aware that he was alone, Mason began to feel the solitude of command. Few men had ever learned to command from the top and yet that was precisely what lay before him. He would have to master the skills as he exercised command. He had no choice. There wasn't time. Success would depend on his choosing the most capable talent available and making sound judgments on the basis of their opinions. Reviewing the list of appointments he'd made to the key positions in his administration, McGarth knew he'd chosen wisely.

Hearing Forest switch on the VCR broke his train of thought. Both men recognized Geneva's Cointrin Airport. As a former member of the Congressional Banking Committee, McGarth had attended several international banking conferences in Geneva. Lindsey, then his special assistant, had gone with him.

The video began with pictures of a casket being placed into a TIA container by Marcel, the lead TIA cargo foreman. The narrator explained that the casket contained the body of Mark Hoffman, the relief pilot of TIA Flight 899. The tape went on to say that although his death had been ruled accidental, it was staged by the FC to provide a way to get the nuclear weapon aboard the flight. It also enabled the coalition to have its pilot become one of the cockpit crew.

The next several frames showed the Mid East Airlines 747 cargo jet taxiing to hardstand number 18. An Arab identified only as Mocmoud was shown with two assistants downloading cargo containers identical to the container shown holding the casket. Shortly, the camera, equipped with a telescopic lens, focused on Marcel as he drove TIA's cargo tractor with the container holding the casket toward the 747. TIA's 767 was then shown parked at hardstand 17 with its cargo bay doors open.

McGarth and Lindsey saw Marcel stop adjacent to the lone container just downloaded from the 747 and switch the two carts. The markings on the switched container were the same as those previously seen on the container used to load the nuclear weapon for Geneva. The narrator called attention to this point. Moments later, they were treated to the final scene as Marcel and his assistants struggled to load the heavy ALE container into the 767's belly. Mocmoud was seen giving Marcel and his assistants a hand with the loading. The narrator explained that the coalition had received Marcel's full cooperation in loading the nuclear weapon aboard TIA's 767 after learning that his pregnant wife, Renee, had been kidnapped and held hostage to ensure his participation. The last frames showed Mocmoud loading the container carrying the casket aboard the Mid East Airlines 747 and meeting with the TIA copilot identified as Ahmed.

Lindsey stood up and pressed the VCR STOP button. The president sat in silence as if his mind were a thousand miles away. Forest didn't interrupt him. He could tell the president was laboring to find a way to gain control of the situation. He wasn't one to give in. Having to agree to the FC's demands had been particularly hard on him. He'd done the only thing he could, but the decision was killing him.

* * *

The mood in the crisis center conference room had been subdued as the president concluded his speech. No one ventured an opinion on his address. Their attention rested on the many and varied tasks each faced and the little time they had to accomplish them. Rising from his seat at the conference table, CIA Director Williamson said what the others were thinking. "I hope to hell those terrorists aren't really bent on detonating that nuke any time soon!" The others nodded in agreement as they followed Burt out the door.

Wes stayed in his chair. He was physically exhausted and needed sleep, but his mind was on his passengers and crew. Gaylord walked over to him and sat down. "The coalition has really caught us with our pants down."

"I feel awful. It's my fault that weapon's here."

"I don't agree with you, Wes. You had no way of knowing that damned thing was on board."

Wes thought about what the national security adviser had said. "I suppose, but it was my poor judgment that cost the life of one of my flight attendants and a dedicated security agent."

"Don't be too hard on yourself, Wes. Not one of us is ever completely in control of anything. Besides, you're not the only one to get caught with his pants down over this thing."

"How's that?"

"I've known for the last three weeks that a Russian nuclear weapon might be missing, yet I waited till today to brief the president."

"I don't think it would have made any difference, sir."

"Perhaps you're right, Captain, but it might have if I'd told him earlier."

"Are you suggesting the missing nuke is aboard my flight?"

"I don't know, but we had been warned."

Wes said nothing, surprised by Gaylord's revelation.

The duty officer broke in. "Sir, the president's secretary just sent this video for you to review. She said you'd know what it was about."

Gaylord examined the cassette, then handed it back to the officer and asked him to set it up. Minutes later, Wes learned that Mark Hoffman's death had not been accidental. Zooming closer, the camera filmed the loadmaster passing Kyle a gun as he inspected the 767's landing gear. Wes cringed, knowing the presence of that weapon had caused Leigh's death. Filled with anger, he stared in amazement as the cargo containers were switched on the ramp at Geneva, demonstrating a breach of security.

Gaylord absorbed the information in silence. When it was over, he remarked, "The thing that troubles me most about this threat is that the FC is so well-organized. It's not at all what we're used to dealing with. Their organization mimics Western technology. It's as if they have adopted our methods and are using them against us."

"I suspect their leaders were educated in the West. Every one of the terrorists speaks fluent English. The intell guys should spend some time looking into where these Arabs were schooled."

Taking a pipe cleaner from his pocket, Elliot began scaling out the bowl of his cherry pipe. Wes's suggestion made a lot of sense. He'd cover it during their six a.m. meeting.

"Wes, I'll have the duty officer set you up with a place to rest here for the night. Judging from the length of time you've been without sleep, I'd say that you're way overdue."

"I won't argue about that."

"Then I'll see you at six. Perhaps we'll have learned more about the identities of these terrorists by then."

"I hope so," Wes answered.

*   *   *

A hush fell over the crowd of reporters as the president entered the press room. Focusing on him, some hoped to learn more about the crisis, while others were more interested in seeing how he was holding up. He went straight to the podium and stood silently for a moment before speaking.

"Ladies and gentlemen, Frances has asked me to come and talk with you for a few minutes and to try to answer some of your questions about the crisis we are facing. As you can imagine, we only learned of the threat a couple of hours ago and have not had sufficient time to fully evaluate the situation. I trust you will understand that some of my answers may be vague. As we learn more, I shall make every effort to elaborate on those issues. I would also like to point out that the threat we are dealing with involves our national security and as such will most certainly involve classified information. Where this is an issue, I shall say so and hope that you will accept whatever answer I am able to give. Thank you. And now I would like to start the questioning."

Hands flew into the air as the president scanned the familiar faces of the veteran press corps. His eyes rested on the intense blue eyes of a young woman he'd never seen before. "Yes, Ms. ... I apologize, but I don't know your name. Your question, please."

Jill felt the blood rush to her face as she stood face-to-face with the president. "I'm Jill Simmons with the *Examiner*, Mr. President."

"Ah yes, Ms. Simmons, I do know your name, but I haven't had the pleasure of meeting you. I would like to add that my staff is indebted to you for your timely revelations pertaining to this crisis. Perhaps you would consider coming to work for me?"

Jill beamed as veteran reporters scoffed at McGarth's remark. They knew of the long-standing animosity between the fiercely independent *Examiner* and his administration.

"Thank you, Mr. President, for your kind offer. It would be an honor to serve on your staff."

The president continued. "I suppose it would be prudent of me to ask first if you have any additional news to share with us before I try to field your question."

Jill blushed at the president's compliment as she searched for the right response. McGarth smiled approvingly and waited for her question.

"Mr. President, can you tell us if you know the origin of the Fundamentalist Coalition and if their organization is sponsored by one or more of the Middle East nations?"

It was a smart question, but one he didn't have an answer for. "I must be honest with you, Ms. Simmons. We have very limited information on the FC. What we do know is that it has recently established an office in Geneva and has, until now, concerned itself with trying to foster a better understanding of the fundamentalist point of view among Europeans."

Pulling a crumpled note from his pocket, McGarth continued. "We do know that their titular leader is Saeed Keshef. Whether he is also its political or spiritual leader we don't know. But we are doing everything imaginable to learn what we can about this group. I hope to have more information once we've had more time to conduct an investigation."

Satisfied with his answer, McGarth turned his attention to another questioner. Standing her ground, Jill waited for the opportunity at a follow-up question. She'd seen the veteran correspondents do it.

"Then, Mr. President, could you tell us whether you suspect one or more of the Middle East nations to be a sponsor of this group, and if so, sir, what might that nation be?"

Shuffling his feet, Mason debated how to respond. There was no question in his mind that the act had to be the result of one or more of the Middle Eastern countries. The money needed to acquire a nuclear weapon dictated that at least one Arab nation had a role in funding the operation. But admitting his beliefs at this point would do nothing except ignite speculation and create a bigger problem.

"Ms. Simmons, at this time I have no evidence to cause me to believe that any Arab nation is involved in this threat against our country. I would also suggest that any speculation at this time would be premature, given our lack of fact. I would, however, like to reserve the right to change my answer to your question, should we learn otherwise."

Jill smiled and took her seat, pleased with the outcome of her first presidential performance. Still flushed from the excitement of questioning the president, Jill glanced down at the notes she'd jotted to herself. Flipping the page, she tried to write down his comments, but drew a blank.

The mood became more serious as McGarth fielded numerous technical questions.

"Yes, the exact ring of lethality is unknown because we are not certain of the yield of the weapon."

"Yes, we have been told of the weapon's arming options, but I hesitate to accept them at face value in view of the fact that we have only the coalition's word on that."

"Yes, I have already convened the National Security Council. They are meeting right now."

"No, we have no plans for our military forces beyond attempting to comply with their demands. As commander in chief, I have instructed the secretary of defense to take those measures necessary to recall our forces from the area in question."

"Yes, I have spoken with the Israeli prime minister and informed him of my decision to meet the demands of the FC."

"Yes, I will federalize certain National Guard organizations if it becomes necessary. Yes, they will be armed and authorized to use lethal force to keep the peace."

"No. I'm not certain when I will meet again with the coalition's negotiator. That should be addressed to Mr. Jabarri. He's in a better position to know the answer to that question."

"Yes. I am extremely concerned for the welfare of the passengers held hostage on TIA Flight 899 and I will take no action that might further endanger their lives."

"No. Our meeting was not a heated debate. Having a gun to your head is not a good time to challenge the gunman to a debate about the use of firearms. Even if you win, you lose!"

The president's straight answers were having a positive effect on the press. Used to having their questions answered evasively, even the most seasoned veterans warmed to his candid responses. An air of confidence replaced uncertainty as the press saw that he was still very much in control and didn't appear intimidated by the nuclear threat foisted on him. McGarth noticed the difference in their attitude.

"Mr. President, would you please elaborate on what you see as the FC's ultimate goal in threatening our country in such a humiliating manner? Is it revenge or what, sir?"

"Martha, your question is a difficult one. I've been asking myself the same thing since learning of the threat. While I'm certain you would appreciate a concise answer, I feel the answer is much more complex. To begin with, I suspect that there are any number of motives for wanting to challenge us in this manner. I am certain there are some who have been intimidated by our government and its policies. For others, hate, humiliation, and revenge serve as motive enough for such an act. Still other factions see in this operation a chance to bring about a change in the balance of power in the Middle East. I suspect their agenda is as varied as the individuals making up the coalition. Suffice it to say they are seriously misguided in believing that they can change the world order in that region with this act of terrorism. The world cannot and will not allow this to happen. For now, our nation is held hostage by people who are extremely frustrated at being disenfranchised from life as they would have it. My hope is that, through negotiation, we can explore those areas of concern and can find some common ground on which to work out a solution. Nothing can or will be done in this regard as long as the threat to our country exists."

"Mr. President?" voices erupted.

"Ladies and gentlemen, there is much I have left to do tonight. While I welcome the opportunity to provide you with as much information as I can, I must conclude this conference. I trust you will understand. Before going, I would like to make this comment.

"It is directed at those of you here. I am extremely proud to be associated with each one of you in this conference room, and I want to congratulate you on the professional manner with which you view your responsibility to the public. I, for one, am well aware of the jeopardy you have placed yourselves in by staying at your posts. Having the courage to continue working under these circumstances is very admirable to say the least. Your presence here epitomizes what I meant in my address about Americans standing tall. And, although we may have our differences from time to time, I want each of you to know that I have the utmost respect for you and the part of America you represent. God bless you!"

As he stepped from the podium, the press corps rose from their seats en masse and applauded. It was a response Mason hadn't anticipated. Nodding his appreciation, he left the room. Few reporters had anything but favorable comments for McGarth as they filed out of the conference room. Most were impressed by his candor. Others seemed to find in his comments a deeper wisdom than they had observed before.

Reading the group's reaction with relief, Frances Buckner, the White House press secretary, was pleased that the adversarial atmosphere had subsided. It was as though the president and the press corps were on the same team for once, though she knew that it wouldn't last.

Lindsey accompanied McGarth to the Oval Office. Neither had much to say. Each was reflecting on the outcome of the press conference. Finally breaking the silence, Forest said, "It was a splendid meeting, sir. I think you made a lot of progress at pulling the country together."

"Let's hope you're right, Forest. It's going to take everything we've got to find a solution to this mess... we don't have a hell of a lot of time," said McGarth, switching on the TV.

Sadness returned to the president's face as a WBSU mobile TV camera panned down I-395 South at the scene of a violent, sixteen-car pileup. The carnage was just beginning.

16

CHAOS

Swooping down over the jammed lanes of I-395, his camera and searchlights scanning the stalled cars below, Buzz Gorski rattled off instructions to his pilot in between TV broadcasts to anchorwoman Charlene Richards and her *News at Ten* audience.

"It's difficult to adequately describe the chaos here on 395 South, Charlene. Traffic is at a virtual standstill! The HOV lanes are barely moving. Even the shoulders are clogged with vehicles trying to escape from the city. There appears to be a major accident ahead, near the Seminary Street overpass! Yeah! Oh yeah! There's a terrible pileup just south of the Seminary Street intersection. Oh God! It looks like an eighteen-wheeler has jackknifed across the highway and is blocking the three inside lanes. The cab and trailer are lying on its side. People are running in all directions," Buzz shouted over the pounding chopper blades.

"Buzz, it looks like a tanker truck to me," Charlene said. "Can you verify that?"

Gorski pointed his forefinger downward at the pilot as he zoomed his camera on the overturned truck. As the chopper descended, Buzz could see the truck's markings more clearly. "Yes! It's a gasoline tanker truck! No wonder people are fleeing their cars!"

"You guys watch what you're doing, Buzz. The shots we're getting are great, but don't put yourselves in danger."

"Oh no! Oh shit! Get out of here now! Take it up! screamed Buzz to his pilot, unaware he was still broadcasting live.

Seeing the fiery explosion of a car ahead, the chopper pilot raced for altitude as the flames chased the fuel spill back up the roadway toward the tanker. Charlene and her viewers saw it, too. Flames, racing back up the hill toward the overpass and the ruptured fuel truck, were setting fire to every vehicle within its path. Some exploded instantly, while others were engulfed in fire. Stunned by the growing inferno, viewers watched in disbelief as families frantically struggled to get out of their burning vehicles. Focusing his mobile TV camera, Gorski filmed a woman running from her car carrying a small child. The woman's clothes were ablaze. She collapsed with the child in her arms. Shocked by what he was seeing through the lens, Buzz was speechless. As he panned on an older couple trapped in their car, viewers saw them disappear in flames as a man fought to free them from their metal hell. At least sixty vehicles were on fire as the flames raced toward the crippled truck.

Suddenly, debris from the explosion streaked into the air, chasing the chopper's flight path as Buzz's camera continued recording the unfolding tragedy. Looking down again, he scanned the area around the tanker. The scene was devastating. His camera counted at least twenty people caught in the fireburst. They perished instantly. Another thirty or more vehicles lurched fore and aft in a vain attempt to flee the disaster.

"Charlene, the situation here is just awful! There must be at least forty or fifty fatalities and there's no sign of any assistance. Call for help, will you?" Buzz screamed. "And tell the viewers to stay put. The roadways are treacherous. Nothing is moving!"

"What about the police, Buzz? Are they able to control the traffic?"

"It's hard to say, Charlene. Their flashing red lights are everywhere, but there's no evidence they're able to manage this chaos. We understand the police have been overwhelmed responding to robberies and assaults... mostly at ATM machines and service stations. We do know that all Virginia State Police have been told to report for duty immediately, but their impact won't be felt for some time."

"What else can you tell us from your vantage point, Buzz?"

"Charlene, we're starting to see a growing number of fires as we look northeast toward the District. Some appear to involve gas stations, judging from their size and intensity. The situation is beginning to look like the fires that blanketed much of south-central L.A. in 1992."

"Are any other avenues open to exit the city?"

"We'll check on that and get right back to you!" Buzz answered.

Glancing at the monitor, Charlene saw that Larry Bledsoe was standing by with a live report.

"Our viewers are with you, Larry. Tell us the latest!"

"Charlene, we're about six blocks northwest of the Capitol with the Metro police. The scene is ugly. Two officers have been gunned down in what appears to be a driveby shooting. Details are sketchy, but we do know the two were responding to a call for help from a disabled couple living in the house across the street. From what the officer in charge has told us, the two patrolmen had just stepped from their cruiser when four men in a dark green Lexus turned the corner and opened fire. Witnesses said there were at least three men firing automatics. One officer was killed immediately. The other was able to make it back to the car and radio for help before collapsing. His status is unknown."

Bright floodlights from atop the mobile camera van cast an eerie glow over the neighborhood as a rescue team hustled to place the bodies of the two slain officers on litters. Larry's cameraman panned the crowd behind him for a closer look at their expressions. Bledsoe took the occasion to collar the officer in charge for a quick interview.

"I'm speaking with Sergeant Jack Thompson of the Washington Metropolitan Police. Sergeant, tell us what happened."

"They both were assassinated! No doubt about it. It was a setup by one of the gangs operating within this community."

"How would you characterize the violence here?"

Thompson glanced over at the two bodies being loaded into the rescue van, then looked back at Bledsoe. "Violence? You want to know about violence? There's a war going on here, man! Driveby shootings like this are happening all over town. It's suddenly open season on every law enforcement officer in the District. In the last hour, we've had more reports of shootings, car-jackings, rapes and looting than we usually have in a month. This nuke threat has every criminal element in Washington active. With people in a panic to evacuate, the hoods are having a field day!"

"Are you saying the police department is unable to handle the situation?"

Thompson stared into the lights of the camera as he tried to suppress his rage. "That's a question you'd better put to the chief. He's in a better position to make that call."

Moving closer to the patrol car, Larry and his cameraman listened as Officer Thompson ducked his head into the cruiser to answer a call from the dispatcher. The news was not good. There was another car-jacking at the intersection of First Street and Massachusetts Avenue, near the government printing office. A family of four had been stopped and dragged from their Cherokee. The driver had resisted and was shot twice in the head. His wife and teenage daughter were forced back into the car and kidnapped by the gunmen. The dispatcher said that the son had made the call for help and was waiting for assistance.

Larry backed off a bit, his camera still live, as Officer Thompson shouted to another patrolman. "Banks, take Lorenzo and get over to First and Mass now. We've got another car-jacking and homicide!"

Viewers watched as the officers slid into their police cruiser and sped off in the direction of the scene.

"Charlene, the situation here is very tense. Violence is rampant. There's a real question of whether the police can handle the siege with-out some backup. Caution your viewers not to venture out unless abso-lutely necessary, especially if they live here in the District. Now back to you."

"Thanks for your report, Larry! Take care of yourself."

As the studio camera sprang alive and moved in on her for a closeup, Charlene saw the message flashing on the TelePrompter. Cheryl Larson, with the Mobile Two News Team, was in position for an on-scene report.

"Cheryl! Where are you?"

As Cheryl spoke, viewers could already sense the disaster unfold-ing as they saw flames leaping into the hot summer sky, illuminating many of the buildings in Alexandria.

"Charlene, we're reporting to you from Old Town. A major fire has broken out in the large hotel across the street. We're unable to give you many of the details, but we do know that the fire erupted in the vicinity of the hotel's kitchen as workers panicked and abandoned their jobs when they learned of the nuclear threat. Authorities don't know how many people are in the building. Firefighters responding to the blaze were hampered by the heavy outbound traffic and were unable to combat the fire for least forty-five minutes.

"A few moments ago, I talked with a young man who had spent the last thirty minutes rescuing people before he was overcome by the dense smoke. He said many had been watching the president's address and were not aware of the fire until seconds before the smoke filled their hallways. He expects there will be significant fatalities because of no advance warning. Apparently, there was no one to sound the alarm."

"Cheryl, can you tell our viewers if authorities think the fire can be brought under control before more lives are lost?"

"That's a difficult question to answer, Charlene. The fire marshal is on the scene trying to coordinate the firefighters and the rescue teams and is unable to comment. Several helicopters have been sighted trying to approach the building, presumably to rescue those who made it to the roof and are trapped now. So far, the choppers have been unable to hover close enough for a rescue. My sense is the fire and smoke is just too intense to permit a rescue at this time."

Charlene and her viewers watched in awe as the camera's vivid pictures told the whole story. The fire was out of control. Screams could be heard from people stranded in their rooms, left to face the blaze's unrelenting onslaught. Firefighters, their extension ladders stretched to their limit, rushed to pull those they could reach from the burning building as pumper trucks shot steady streams of water into the hot flames.

"Cheryl, we're going to leave you and your crew for now, but keep us informed!"

Unable to reply as tears streamed down her cheeks, the rookie reporter nodded as cries for help grew louder.

Reza Jabarri switched off the TV in the high-rise penthouse suite overlooking National Airport and smiled approvingly at what he'd just witnessed. Charlene Richards' *News at Ten* program had confirmed his expectations. Seeing the core of American democracy and its capitalistic empire shudder under his nuclear threat delighted him. The chaos he'd hoped for was far greater than he or his fundamentalists could have imagined. It was their revenge for the havoc America and its Jewish puppet, Israel, had visited on his people for the last thirty years, he told himself. He would see that the threat lingered long enough to bring America to her knees. Only then would he and the coalition consent to any meaningful negotiations with President McGarth to remove the weapon.

Scoffing at the president's plea for Americans to stand tall, he picked up the phone and dialed the Oval Office. Betty answered. "This is Reza Jabarri. You will tell Mr. Lindsey that I wish to visit the aircraft immediately. He is to arrange to have me picked up from my quarters here in Crystal City. Secretary Halston has given him the necessary information on how to reach me. I will expect to be picked up in thirty minutes."

"Yes, Mr. Jabarri. I will inform Mr. Lindsey of your request," she replied.

Reza hung up and sat back on the leather sofa. Thus far the plan had worked perfectly, except for the escape of Beacham's daughter, Caroline. It was a minor problem, but one he would have to investigate. How could such a petite young woman as the captain's daughter have managed to free herself? Had his men been apprehended by the police? The questions troubled him. Tomorrow he would contact the coalition council members to confirm they were in position to detonate the bomb, should anything happen to Mohammed, Ahmed, or him. The possibility seemed real that he might have to explode the device if the Americans took a belligerent stand. If it were necessary, he would do it.

17

INSIGHT

Bud was tired and hungry. He'd listened to the president's address and heard the reports of chaos over his Cessna's audio directional finding (ADF) radio. Nothing had happened around the jet for the last hour and a half. Even the troops assigned to guard the flight ramp's perimeter had settled down. Bud was surprised no one had bothered to investigate his being there. He wondered if he was being purposely left alone because of the information he was providing.

The monotonous squeal of the 767's auxiliary power unit (APU) was beginning to sound like a dentist's drill. His left ear ached from having his earphones on for the last couple of hours. The ground, getting harder by the minute, punished his lanky, fiftyish frame. Bud lifted the baseball cap from his head and mopped the beads of sweat from his balding scalp. His sport shirt, drenched with perspiration, clung to his flesh as he lay sprawled on the burned grass beside his plane.

He didn't pay much attention to the lone pair of headlights that swept the ramp area before appearing to lock on to the 767. It was probably a galley wagon. He could almost taste the hot coffee as his stomach growled for a doughnut. Bud wondered how long he could hold out without food.

The headlights paused briefly at the perimeter before continuing toward the aircraft. As it drew closer, Bud could see it was an Army jeep with a dolly attached to its hitch. The mobile stairs truck, withdrawn from the aircraft earlier, followed. Recalling the tower's message to Ahmed more than an hour and a half ago, Bud decided it must be the cache of weapons Jabarri had said would arrive later.

Reaching for his camera, Bud focused on the vehicles as they pulled to within twenty yards of the jet's nose. The mobile stairs truck eased toward the plane's left forward door as its stairs telescoped upward to the wide body's floor.

Peering through the lens of his video camera, Waterman saw several men deplane and walk to the rear of the dolly. Seconds later, Bud saw them remove weapons from the trailer and examine them before carrying them up the mobile stairs. Bud watched as each made four trips up the stairs carrying weapons and boxes into the jet. The guns were short and stubby with long clips extending beneath the weapon's stock — submachine guns. Bud suspected they were Uzis from the FBI's arsenal.

Some minutes later, the terrorists reappeared, carrying a body. Judging from the difficulty they were having lowering it to the ramp, Bud figured it to be that of a rather large man. Reaching the bottom of the stairs, the terrorists dropped him on the pavement and returned to the jet.

Seeing the body dumped on the ground angered Bud as he continued filming the event. As he was about to release the camera's trigger, the terrorists made a second trip down the stairs carrying another body. Were they shooting passengers? He'd heard no shots. Would he have heard it over the squeal of the APU? The second body was smaller, probably a woman or child. His pulse racing, Bud considered calling the tower for help. If the terrorists were killing passengers, someone had to intercede, even if they did have a nuclear weapon on board.

They put the smaller body on the dolly and walked back up the stairs. Two men in uniform crawled out of the jeep, lifted the larger body and walked it to the rear of the dolly and placed it beside the smaller one. Wasting no time, they climbed back into the vehicle and drove toward the terminal.

Surprised by a second pair of bright headlights racing toward him, Bud stepped from his Cessna as the car stopped twenty feet away. Afraid to speak, he waited for some sign from the car. Suddenly the back door of the car swung open and a short figure stepped out. Bud recognized the man immediately. It was the same one he'd seen deplane from the 767 nearly three hours ago. The man, he now knew, was Reza Jabarri.

"And who might you be? Jabarri asked.

"Bud Waterman. I'm a newspaper reporter for the *Washington Examiner*," he answered, unsure of how Reza might react.

"A reporter for the *Examiner*?" Reza repeated curiously.

"Yes, and you are Reza Jabarri, I presume?"

"And how would you know that, Mr. Waterman?"

"I've been here monitoring the tower's frequency and the local radio stations since shortly after you landed."

"Then tell me, Mr. Waterman, how was it you managed to get a clearance to land behind us?"

"I didn't. I declared an inflight emergency and diverted here to cover the event."

"You knew of our hijacking?" Reza asked, clearly interested.

"Yes. That's why I had to land. Secretary Halston was aboard and that made for a good news story."

"So you landed here by feigning an emergency to report the story of our hijacking to your *Examiner*?"

Bud nodded yes.

"And how are you able to report your story from your plane?" Reza asked, stepping around Bud to look into the cockpit.

Pointing to the small portable telephone lying on the seat, Bud said, "I used that mobile phone."

Withdrawing from under the wing, Reza said, "Would you like to come aboard and see what our passengers are having to contend with?"

The idea had already occurred to Bud, but he'd dismissed it as strategically unwise. Now that the Arab had made the offer, he felt obligated to accept. Something told him Reza would compel him to go, either way. "Yes, it would help. Eyewitness reports do make the most credible stories," Bud answered, trying to sound detached.

"Very well. You will come with me."

Deciding that the best way to deal with Jabarri would be to humor him, Bud mustered an enthusiastic response. Then, remembering his camera gear, he asked, "Will you permit me to film the passengers and perhaps get an interview or two?"

"Bring the equipment. I will decide what you can film."

Bud almost wished he hadn't asked. Reza's answer made him uncomfortable. Slinging his camcorder over his shoulder, Bud hurried over to the car as Reza waited. Jabarri opened the rear door and motioned for him to enter first.

Getting out of the car, Bud looked up at the eerie 767 with its dimly lit cabin. He felt the urge to run. Unsure of what he would find, Bud followed Jabarri up the steps to the entrance. "Wait here, Mr. Waterman."

Bud peered into the cabin, but saw no one. Glancing through the cabin windows, he saw figures draped with blankets. The sight made him nauseous. Most were Americans just like him — ordinary people wanting to get on with their lives — but caught in the midst of this horror because they happened to be in the wrong place at the wrong time. How many times had it happened that way? Bud asked himself.

Reappearing at the entrance, Reza motioned for him to enter. Walking into the 767's small foyer, Bud immediately sensed the tension. The cabin smelled of human sweat. His nose caught a whiff of urine. The silence was broken only by an occasional murmur or sigh of helplessness. The cabin had a foreboding glow, one that reminded him of death. It was difficult for Bud to imagine how more than one hundred seventy human beings could be so quiet.

He felt the passengers' fear, their hopelessness, their unanswered whys, and their doubts about whether they would survive. In an instant, Bud experienced the real meaning of freedom and what it meant to lose it.

"Mr. Waterman, you will come to the cockpit with me." Bud turned to his left and followed Jabarri. Another terrorist was seated to the right in the first officer's chair. Remembering the outburst he'd heard over the tower frequency, Bud surmised the man was Ahmed — the traitor pilot.

Reza spoke to him in Arabic as Bud set his video camera down on the seat behind the captain's chair. The sound of a groan startled him. Spinning around, Bud saw another pilot. His wrists were cuffed over the coat rack adjacent to his seat, forcing his torso upward in an awkward, twisted position. His swollen hands told of poor circulation. His agony was understandable. Bud saw his three stripes and assumed he was the first officer. How long had he been forced to endure such pain? As he stared into the man's face for a sign of life, the copilot opened his bloodshot eyes and mustered a smile. "The name's Chad Sanderlin. Sorry, I can't shake your hand. As you can see, I'm tied up at the moment."

Bud grinned at Chad's humor. Admiring the young man's courage, Bud liked him immediately. Although Chad was shackled, the terrorists were nowhere near subduing his will to live. It was difficult for Bud to turn his back on Chad, but he knew instinctively that he must.

"Mr. Waterman, you will please, as you say, interview me."

Bud was astounded. The idea of interviewing the terrorist hadn't entered his mind until Reza made the comment. He'd assumed the primary purpose for his being invited to the aircraft was to report on the condition and treatment of the passengers, or more aptly, the hostages. The fact that Jabarri was serious about being interviewed troubled Bud. What if he asked the wrong questions?

There were important differences in the way the coalition perceived the event and the impact that its outcome would have on the world. Waterman wasn't sure he wanted to be held responsible for what his interview might precipitate. Controlling his intense dislike for Reza and his Fundamentalist Coalition would not be a problem, but directing the questioning so as not to antagonize Jabarri could be. Yet, if he could earn the terrorist's confidence and trust, perhaps he could do some good. At least he could learn more about Jabarri and his cause. Besides, did he really have a choice?

"Mr. Waterman, we will sit in the first class cabin for the interview." From the excitement in his voice, Bud realized the interview was what Reza had had in mind since learning that Bud was a reporter. It would provide him one more avenue from which to make the FC's case to America and the world. The fact that it would fall on angry eyes and inflamed hearts never occurred to him.

Understanding the *Stockholm Syndrome*, Bud decided to assume a sympathetic point of view regarding the coalition's concerns. He would avoid antagonizing Jabarri by asking open-ended questions; hopefully yielding some measure of the man.

Dropping his gear into his seat, Bud spread the spindly legs of his tripod apart. He attached the video camera to its apex as Reza watched. "We'll need more lighting, Mr. Jabarri. Perhaps the cabin lights could be turned up."

"Ahmed, we need the lights turned up in the cabin."

Ahmed appeared in the doorway, turning up all the cabin lighting from the flight attendant's control panel as Bud loaded a fresh cassette into the camera's magazine. Attaching the remote lanyard, Bud said to Jabarri, "I'm ready."

Reza nodded, motioning Bud to take the seat adjacent to him. Settling into his seat, Bud prayed. Not a prayerful person by nature, he suddenly felt the need for spiritual guidance.

"This is Bud Waterman, speaking to you live aboard hijacked Flight 899 at National Airport. "Mr. Reza Jabarri of the Fundamentalist Coalition is with me. Mr. Jabarri..."

"Please call me Reza," Jabarri said.

"Yes, of course, Reza," he answered. "Could you explain why the coalition feels it necessary to take such drastic action against the people of America without first attempting to reconcile the differences through negotiations?"

"The Fundamentalist Coalition does not consider this act as aggression aimed at the American people, but rather at its government and the imperialistic policies it employs throughout the Middle East. We bear no malice toward your people, only your government."

"But surely you understand that our government is one of the people. So when you attack our government, you attack our people."

Reza looked puzzled as he searched for his rebuttal. "You Americans only think you control your government. Your newspapers and televisions are filled with accounts of the corruption of your chosen leaders who have bought their positions of power with the financial support of big business and special interest groups. They do not respond to the needs of the common people. They serve the masters of money and greed."

Knowing he would not convince Jabarri of the distinction, Bud pressed Reza for a more definitive answer to his initial question. "What U.S. policies does the FC take issue with?"

"Mr. Waterman, the Arab world resents being manipulated by your country for its own gain. The United States, at one time or another, has armed nearly every state within the Middle East and has constantly meddled in the internal affairs of our region. To its credit, it has succeeded in pitting Arab against Arab while picking both sides' pockets mercilessly. America installed the shah in Iran in an effort to control that region and give it easy access to the Soviet Union. It provided Saudi Arabia and Kuwait with military weapons in exchange for cheap oil. It armed Iraq and set it against its neighbor, Iran, ultimately exhausting the resources of both nations and causing the slaughter of millions of people. It formed an alliance with Egypt to establish a base of operations to replace the one lost to Qadahfi in Libya. I could go on, Mr. Waterman, but we both know you are a journalist, and therefore are no stranger to the actions your country has taken to thwart our growth.

"Our land has a history of being dictated to by foreign powers. Before America, it was the British and the French and before them, the Turks. The coalition is a direct outgrowth of the Muslims' contempt for such intervention and it is our overall aim to see that it never happens again. America must broker such an agreement, if it is to survive its current predicament."

Jabarri had said a mouthful without once mentioning the Jews, thought Bud, as he parlayed the next question. "And so where does Israel stand in view of the FC's aims?"

Responding immediately, Reza said, "Everyone knows Israel is a puppet of American Jewish influence and as such belongs in America. It is not possible for the Arabs and the Jews to live in harmony, given the fact that we have fought for more than two thousand years. It is a foolish notion to believe that peace can come to a region so vehemently opposed to Judaism and its teachings. They must leave as they have in the past. Only then will peace come to the Middle East."

"From your answer, I would assume that the coalition is committed to the destruction of Israel?"

"Yes, if the Jews persist in trying to establish a nation in this region. America and Europe are the bastions of Christianity as is Asia for Buddhism and Hinduism. Is it not right that our faith should also have a region of the world in which to practice its beliefs? That region is the Middle East."

"Reza, I am intrigued by the very name of the organization you represent — the Fundamentalist Coalition. Will you enlighten me as to who the coalition is and who its members are?"

Jabarri paused. Bud sensed Reza was caught between wanting to make a full disclosure and avoiding compromising the real sponsors of the FC.

"Are you a Christian, Mr. Waterman?"

The question shocked Bud. "Of course."

"Then you understand that even though the vast majority of Americans are Christians, America is not the only country practicing the Christian faith. And so it is with the Islamic faith. Our faith also crosses national boundaries, embracing all those who worship Allah and follow the teachings of Mohammed, which includes those of the fundamentalist persuasion.

The FC is essentially a coalition of fundamentalists — people of like mind — who view your country's intervention into our world as an assassination of our faith and an affront to Allah. Thus we must defend our faith if we are to become worthy of Allah's blessing."

Bud wondered if Reza really believed what he'd just said. His tone was one of conviction. His message made a certain sense, except that Bud found it hard to comprehend a religion endorsing such violence as the price for acceptance into the faith. What kind of religion fosters killing infidels, non-believers? Perhaps one of more primitive times? It was a possibility if one were to assume that religions, like people, evolve with time.

"Can I assume then that the coalition includes groups from all the Arab nations?"

"Yes. That is precisely the situation," Reza added, outwardly pleased at Bud's conclusion.

"Then you would have us believe that this conflict is one of religious persecution and not of politics?"

"Yes and no," Reza answered. "You Americans prefer to see it in either-or terms, but, in fact, we in the Muslim world do not separate our religion from our daily lives. The practice of our faith necessarily encompasses our political beliefs. That is why you Americans have a difficult time understanding the impact the IRA is able to have on the British government. You cannot accept the fact that people of religious conviction involve the practice of their faith in carrying out their political views."

Although his views were contrary to Western beliefs and his arguments, at times convoluted, Jabarri's sincerity was impressive. "Under what conditions will the coalition agree to remove the nuclear device from this aircraft, Reza?"

Jabarri winced at the question. It deserved a careful answer, if not a specific reply. "The FC must first be assured that the United States has fully and unconditionally complied with all the specific demands given to your president. And further, that it will pledge not to meddle in the affairs of the Middle East once the device is removed."

Bud couldn't imagine how the United States could agree to such nuclear blackmail, but let it pass. "Could we discuss your immediate intentions for the hostages aboard this aircraft? I presume you can appreciate the goodwill and sympathy that releasing the passengers would generate for the FC's cause."

Reza's facial expression turned dead serious. "Their fate must go the way of the country's. They will be set free in due time as it suits our purpose."

"But surely, Reza, you can recognize the political advantage to be gained by making a small humanitarian effort toward relieving the suffering of these people. At least, free the women and children and elderly. They serve no purpose. You have the city under the threat of a nuclear holocaust. What more is to be gained by holding these passengers? They complicate matters for your men."

"Your points are valid, Mr. Waterman. I will give the issue thought, but for now, they stay." Pausing, Reza said, "It is late and there are things I must do before I sleep, Mr. Waterman. We will conclude the interview now. You are free to go."

Bud stood up instinctively. Jabarri did too. For a moment, he thought Reza was about to extend his hand. The notion was repulsive.

"You will publish this interview in your newspaper and give the tape to one of your TV stations," Reza directed.

"Yes. It will receive the widest dissemination possible," said Bud, hurriedly dismantling his equipment.

"That is good. I will look forward to seeing it on TV tomorrow," Reza said, escorting Bud into the humid night. "It is unpleasant to have strangers from a distant land dominating your every move, no?" called out Reza as Bud reached the bottom of the stairs.

Waterman nodded without thinking. His thoughts were of Chad and the faceless figures covered with blankets. It was a sight he would never forget. Bud wondered if the U.S. would find a way to rid itself of the terrorists and their nuclear hammer, or if it would be forced to endure days of humiliation and then be destroyed anyway?

Bud walked in darkness back to his Cessna. The air chilled his bare arms. Dropping the camera on the seat, he picked up the mobile phone. Jill would be overwhelmed by his latest news and the work she'd have to do for it to make the morning run.

As the phone started to ring, Bud debated how to get the videotape to WBSU. Then he remembered their weather chopper reporter, Buzz Gorski. He could fly in and pick up the film.

Jill finally answered on the fourth ring. Still at the White House Press Room putting the finishing touches on tomorrow's story, she'd been promised the front page. Hearing her voice, Bud launched into his explanation of the last hour's events, explaining the interview.

"Bud, slow down. We've got a bigger problem."

"Problem? What kind of problem?"

"We've lost the presses, Bud."

"What do you mean, 'we've lost the presses?' What's wrong with them?" he demanded.

"Nothing's wrong with the presses, but there's no one to operate them. The printing department has a massive no-show because of the terrorist threat."

"Is the paper going to be printed tomorrow, Jill? Standing out here beside this friggin' nuclear bomb is not my idea of a fun night on the Potomac!" Bud growled.

"The front office is trying to arrange to have it printed outside the city. We should know something definite in another thirty minutes."

"Ah, shit! Wouldn't you know something like this would happen just when I've landed the story of our careers. It figures."

Jill didn't respond. She felt the same way, but didn't want him to know it.

"So what does the news desk think? Are they optimistic?"

"I think so. They're set to fax all the input as soon as they have an address."

"Maybe there's still hope, huh?"

"Bud, we've got to assume it's going to print and let the front office worry about how to do it. Give me what you have. I'll try to put it together before they call me back."

"I just got back from interviewing Reza Jabarri."

"An interview! You had an interview with Jabarri? I can't believe it, Bud. How?" Jill shrieked.

"It's a long story. I'll tell you about it when we have more time. Alert the White House. They might find it helpful."

"I'm sure they will. I'll tell Frances Buckner. She's still here in the press room practicing damage control."

"The interview's on videotape. I'll get it to you and the White House as quickly as I can."

"Keep me posted, Bud. I'll be here for another hour."

"CESSNA 622 GOLF FOXTROT, CALLING THE FC!"

"THIS IS AHMED. GO AHEAD."

"AHMED, BUD WATERMAN HERE. REQUEST APPROVAL FOR THE WBSU TRAFFIC HELICOPTER TO LAND HERE BRIEFLY TO PICK UP THE INTERVIEW TAPE I DID WITH MR. JABARRI."

"STAND BY, I WILL CALL YOU BACK."

The minutes seemed like hours as Bud waited.

"MR. WATERMAN, THE CHOPPER MAY LAND AT THE IN-
TERSECTION OF RUNWAYS THREE THREE AND THREE SIX.
YOU WILL ADVISE THE PILOT TO CALL ME BEFORE MAK-
ING HIS APPROACH TO LAND. NO ONE MAY DEPLANE. YOU
WILL WALK THE TAPE TO HIM. OUR ORDERS ARE TO BE
FOLLOWED PRECISELY. DO YOU UNDERSTAND?"

"ROGER," Bud answered.

Getting the coalition's approval for Gorski's chopper to land proved
easier than Bud had expected. Rooting through his flight kit, Bud found
the control tower's unlisted number. As a reporter, he'd learned long
ago the advantage of collecting such information.

"Tower, Mann here. This is a recorded line. Go ahead."

"Tower, this is Bud Waterman, the Cessna driver."

"Yeah, Waterman, so we heard. We copied your call to the FC."
Harry was pissed. There was no mistaking his tone, but he was too
professional to let it interfere. "Have the chopper pilot give us a call on
a land line. We'll give him the okay without disturbing that asshole,
Ahmed, and his terrorists. By the way, Waterman, what's your mobile
number? Some agents would like to huddle with you."

"Two five two, six three seven eight. Copy?"

"Yeah, we got it. Have your chopper friend bring you a new battery when he comes, so you can stay in touch with us."

"Will do," Bud replied.

Bud didn't waste any time dialing WBSU and after several attempts he got through. It took another three or four minutes to convince the station he was legitimate. Gorski was airborne, but within
seconds the station effected a phone patch.

"Buzz, Bud Waterman of the *Examiner*. I need your help."

"Doesn't everybody? What can I do for you?"

Outlining his plan, Bud passed along the tower's approval and
number along with his request for food, water, film, and a fresh battery. "Just make sure you call the coalition for your clearance to land
before you begin the approach."

"Roger that," said Gorski. "I'll see you in thirty minutes."

Bud then called Jill and briefed her on the video delivery plan.
"Are we going to press tonight?"

"Yes, it's a go. The front office has worked out a deal with an out-of-state newspaper. The paper's going to be printed in Jersey and flown here by helicopter before dawn."

"Thank God for small favors," Bud said, imagining the impact he and Jill would have on tomorrow's news.

18

ORDERS

Wes tossed about on the single cot. The covers were dangling at the foot of the small bed. He couldn't sleep, though his eyes ached from a lack of rest. Even dozing was a problem. He couldn't erase the sight of those people on fire, fleeing their burning cars and the explosion. He could not escape thinking it was all his fault. He searched frantically for some reason to justify his decisions, but found none. Knowing sleep was hopeless, Wes switched on the TV mounted on the wall and scanned the channels, stopping again on WBSU.

Gorski was back in the air, heading north of the District, his camera panning the northwestern metro area. The story was the same, mammoth traffic jams caused by anxious citizens fleeing for their lives, numerous fires, primarily from gas stations overrun by careless drivers needing fuel, and a steady stream of violence by criminals intent on capitalizing on the masses' fears.

As he stared blankly at the screen, Charlene Richards, WBSU anchorwoman, interrupted Gorski's report and switched her viewer's attention to Mobile Team One's Larry Bledsoe at the mayor's office for an announcement. Wes refocused his eyes on the TV screen as the mayor of Washington tried to answer Bledsoe's question.

"Larry, after consulting with the chief of police, I decided the situation was deteriorating too rapidly to wait for the mobilization of the National Guard, so I called the White House and asked that federal troops be sent here ASAP. The president has ordered units of the Eighty Second Airborne Division, stationed at Fort Bragg, to be flown into

Washington immediately to help restore order to the District and its outlying areas. He has assured me that the first troops will be landing here within the next several hours."

"Does this mean you are declaring a state of martial law here in the District, Mayor Evans?"

"Yes, Larry. I urge all citizens of the District to return to their homes immediately and to stay there for the duration of the evening. All major roadways from the city are blocked and are expected to stay that way for the rest of the night. A state of martial law is in effect and will remain in effect until civil order is restored. Those who disobey the law will be taken into custody and may be fired upon. Again, I urge all citizens: Stay in your homes."

"Mayor Evans, could you tell our audience where the troops are expected to land?"

"My understanding is that the initial force will deplane from helicopters on the Washington Mall somewhere between the Hill and the Washington Monument."

"Could you tell us if the president has plans to inform the terrorists of his decision to bring troops into the city?"

"Yes. It's my understanding that he has notified the FC."

"Thank you, Mayor Evans. Now back to you, Charlene."

Wes saw the crisis was growing by the minute. He dressed and went to the Situation Room.

"Good morning, Colonel Beacham," the duty officer said.

"Do I know you from somewhere?" Wes asked, shielding his eyes from the glare of the dozen or so video screens.

"No, sir. At least I don't think so."

"Then how did you know I was a colonel? I've been retired since eighty six."

"It's all in the envelope I just handed you, sir. I couldn't help but notice your rank when I was downloading the orders DOD sent over."

"Orders! What orders?" Wes asked, puzzled.

Was he asleep? The duty officer seemed serious, but what he'd said made no sense. Smelling the aroma of fresh coffee that permeated the room, Wes had the uneasy feeling he wasn't dreaming. "Could I bum a cup of coffee off you guys?" he asked, tearing open the envelope.

"How do you take it, sir?"

"Black," he replied. "What the...? I'll be damned!" Wes muttered, scanning the freshly printed orders.

It had been eight years since he'd looked at his last set, the ones that had retired him from the 192nd Tac Fighter Group at Byrd Field in Richmond. They hadn't changed much, he noted. If memory served him correctly, he could only be reactivated if war were declared or by the secretary of defense. Looking closer, Wes saw Christopher Jacobson's name and signature in the "By Order Of" block. They were real. This was no dream. He was back on active duty.

The hot coffee was strong, with a bite to it. Wes guessed it had been on the warmer for more than an hour, judging from its bitterness. Staring at the orders, he wondered whose idea it was to put him on active duty and more to the point, why? What possible need could they have for him on active duty other than for a court martial?

"They told me you'd stopped in for coffee. Having trouble sleeping?" Wes looked up as the president's national security adviser walked into the conference room and pulled up a chair.

"Yeah, it's rough," Wes answered. "I can't shake the fact that this whole thing wouldn't have happened if I'd handled it right to begin with. Seeing those innocent people on fire, running from their cars, hurts like hell."

"I saw the same news," Gaylord said. "I can imagine the misery you're going through, but it will pass. Don't beat yourself. Anyone of us would have reacted the same way. Besides, it doesn't matter. These fundamentalists were determined to plant that bomb in Washington one way or another."

Picking up the orders, Wes looked directly at Elliot. "Did you have anything to do with these?"

"Yes, along with several others, including the president."

"The president? Why would he want me on active duty?"

Gaylord could see he owed Wes an explanation. "Wes, the president, the secretary of defense and I, along with General Griffith are all of the opinion that you can be a great deal of help to us in handling this terrorist situation. For one thing, you're the only one who was aboard the jet and has a feel for the situation.

"According to your file, you were previously involved in the planning and rescue of another airliner hijacked in the Middle East in July of '86. There were some very interesting, but vaguely worded, letters of commendation in it. We feel that your experience in mounting such an assault could be very beneficial."

"What do you and the president have in mind?"

"To be truthful, we're not sure right now. The situation is too fluid at the moment to be sure of anything. We haven't gotten enough information on the scope of the problem to even begin to decide how we want to approach it. But at some point, there's a likelihood that we'll want to take back the jet. That's where you come in. The president wants you to help plan a SEAL assault. You've worked with them before, haven't you?"

"Yes, sir."

"And what was your impression?"

"They're the best. I don't think you can beat them."

"I'm glad you admire their work because I'm sending you down to Little Creek Amphibious Base in Norfolk after the NSC meeting in the morning to meet with them. We want them ready in the event we can find a way to negate that bomb."

"That may be easier said than done, given the arming options Jabarri alluded to."

"That is the most critical part of this problem, isn't it?"

"It would certainly help to know how they've programmed the weapon. I'd hate to take their word for it," Wes added.

"Hopefully, DOD will be able to shed some light on the matter, assuming we can pin down where the device came from."

"Without knowing, I'd bet it's Russian," Wes offered.

"Why do you say that?" queried Gaylord. "I suspect China."

"Well, if you consider the START Treaty implications and the fact that the Soviet Union is undergoing a tremendous internal upheaval, I think there's a strong chance someone in the right place might have succeeded in pilfering a bomb. The other aspect is getting the expertise to make the modifications to the weapon. That implies that more than one person was involved and suggests an inside job."

Gaylord was silent. Could it be that with the breakup of the USSR, someone in power could have managed to get hold of a special weapon? Was that what the KGB field agent was trying to tell the CIA by leaking the USSR's audit report of their nuclear recycling program? Had the Russians discovered that a nuclear bomb was missing? Elliot wondered.

Wes looked up as the duty officer interrupted. "Sir, we've just received this report from Athens via satellite. It's from the CIA station chief there." Gaylord took the classified document and read it before tossing it on the table for Wes. The details were sketchy.

"It looks like you may be right," Elliot said. "Finding three retired Russians shot to death in a luxury hotel in Athens is certainly worth investigating, wouldn't you say?"

"Luxury hotels are expensive, especially for Russians trying to make it on a ruble-based pension," Wes added.

"Maybe we've stumbled onto something, Colonel. It'll be interesting to see what they turn up from their investigation," suggested Elliot, as he stood up. Wes glanced at his watch. It was a little after midnight.

"I'll see you in the morning, Colonel. I'm going to try to get some sleep. You'd do well to give it another try yourself." Wes nodded and yawned deeply, following Elliot out the door.

The next hour passed slowly for Wes. Lying on the bed, staring up at the ceiling, he recounted the day's events, one at a time, as though they were set in a slide tray carousel for him to preview. Each brought him more anguish. He remembered the fear-stricken faces of the passengers and his crew as he left the 767 with Halston and Jabarri. He worried over Chad, his arms hanging from the coat rack in senseless misery. A deeper sadness fell over him as he remembered Leigh's last words to him about Jason. Who would care for her son? How could he have let it happen? He'd caused Leigh's death as sure as if he'd done the job himself. Was Caroline's life worth the suffering he'd forced on so many others? Wes wasn't sure.

* * *

The drive to Duck seemed endless to Meredith. Traffic was unusually heavy. Was it because of the nuclear threat hanging over Washington? Caroline, Jacqueline, and Tucker had lapsed into restless sleep, waking only seconds at a time to find a more comfortable position.

Left to her own thoughts, Meredith pondered the outcome of what lay before her and the family. Would Wes survive the ordeal? Would the government find a way to defeat the threat or would the country's worst fears be realized? What kind of life would they have to endure once their friends and neighbors learned that it was Wes who'd brought the bomb to American soil? Would they ever understand, or would their friends turn their backs on years of friendship out of fear of being associated with the man responsible for bringing such horror to Washington? And what about their livelihood? Would he be fired or forced to retire early, or imprisoned? They were not financially prepared to make it without his job, especially with Jacqueline entering college. Who would give Wes a job? How would it affect the children? Would they have to move and start all over again just to find peace?

The questions seemed as endless as the night. Wes had done his best. He always had. How could something like this have happened to him? Life was so unfair, she decided. Hadn't they put up with enough misery — Vietnam, multiple airline furloughs, and the attendant job changes that inevitably followed. Or were they destined to live their entire life together, struggling to keep their heads above water? Where was the elusive airline lifestyle that she'd heard so much about? Was it an illusion, like so many other things in the world?

As she reached the Currituck Sound bridge, Meredith's thoughts were interrupted by the midnight news broadcast from WOOB. She turned the volume up slightly.

"Word from Washington this hour is that civil unrest is escalating. Authorities continue to plead with citizens to stay in their homes to give law enforcement agencies time to restore order and open the roadways. Reports indicate people are ignoring the plea and are fleeing the city by any means possible. All major arteries leading from the city are jammed. Auto accidents and fatalities are too numerous to count, say traffic officials.

"Mayor Robert Evans, in an unprecedented move, has requested that federal troops be rushed to the District immediately to help quell the violence that has erupted in the face of this catastrophe. Police are overwhelmed with reports of driveby shootings, robberies and assaults. Units of the Eighty Second Airborne Division, stationed at Fort Bragg, North Carolina, are en route to Washington and should reach the capital in the next several hours.

"On another note, it has been learned that after a late-night emergency meeting with President McGarth, congressional leaders from both houses have unanimously agreed to reconvene the Congress in

an alternate location. Unnamed sources close to the discussions are certain that Charlottesville will be chosen, although consideration is being given to the quasi-government facilities at White Sulphur Springs, West Virginia. Rumors continue to surface, suggesting that plans are under way to have the Judicial Branch moved, as well.

The fate of the passengers still aboard TIA Flight 899 is unknown. So far, only Secretary of State Riggs Halston, Captain Weston Beacham, and Reza Jabarri, the terrorist leader, have left the ill-fated aircraft. However, the Washington Examiner is reporting that two unidentified bodies were taken off the jet several hours ago. Those close to the situation think the two were crew members or government employees. Some discussions have taken place with the terrorists, but details are sketchy. Washington TV station WBSU is reporting that Washington Examiner journalist, Bud Waterman, remains within sight of the Boeing 767 and has held an impromptu interview aboard the aircraft with the terrorist leader. Arrangements are under way to get the taped interview from Mr. Waterman at National Airport. And that's the latest we have on the crisis in Washington. Please stay tuned throughout the night to WOOB, voice of the Outer Banks, for the latest information on terror on the Potomac."

Caroline awoke as Meredith switched off the radio and slowed the Explorer. The traffic lights in Kitty Hawk, N.C. were all flashing caution as she passed them one by one before turning north toward Duck. With less than five miles to go to Kilduck Station, their beach home, Meredith turned her attention to what she might expect from her neighbors. Would they understand and support her? Or would they pretend they were too busy and shun her? With Wes gone and the children recovering from their frightening ordeal, she'd need them.

*   *   *

Watching in silence from an upstairs window in the White House, Mason McGarth saw the first contingent of helicopters sweep in from across the Potomac in their descent to the grounds of the Washington Mall. The sight of federal troops racing to respond to massive civil unrest was disconcerting, yet he knew they were necessary.

Nothing could have been further from his mind a year ago, when he was sworn in on the same grounds in front of the Capitol. The oath he'd proudly acknowledged seemed to take on a new and very personal meaning as Mason contemplated the threat he and the people of Washington now faced.

"Sir, may I speak with you?"

McGarth turned from the window. "Yes, Forest?"

"Sir, Director Sinclair phoned to say the FBI has recovered the bodies of the two people shot in-flight yesterday. During a preliminary examination of the body of the flight attendant, they found a computer printout list — something the airline calls a *spill*—stuffed into her underwear. A brief note was scratched on the form identifying seven passengers as terrorists. Their seat numbers were circled. The note was signed Sybil."

Mason reflected on what Lindsey had told him. "Can you imagine the courage it must have taken for her to do that?"

"It was remarkable," Lindsey echoed. "Sinclair has the entire Counter-Terrorist Division working to identify the terrorists right now. He also said the CIA has given the FBI full access to their files."

"It's about time those two agencies start cooperating with each other. Any more word on the Russians murdered in Athens?"

"Yes, sir. A joint investigative team of the CIA, DIA and FBI are en route to Athens. The French lent us one of their Concordes for the flight. A portion of the team will be dropped off in Geneva to start examining the explosion of the FC's headquarters there."

"Let's hope they learn something quick. Thank you, Forest."

"Good night, Mr. President."

19

INSTANT REPLAY

Emerson Beamer had sensed from the start that Agent Coleman's revelation was germane to the crisis at hand and had seen to it that FBI Director John Sinclair was kept abreast of the situation. With Coleman's report now an open file, counter- terrorism technicians pored over it, examining every minute detail for some shred of evidence of who was behind the threat.

Communications specialists had already deciphered every telephone number in the mobile phone found at the ranch house in Middleburg. Tucker's list of phone numbers, together with the corresponding addresses Dave Coleman had obtained earlier from the phone company, had been compared with the preset numbers loaded in the phone. The numbers were identical. Composites had been made of the dead terrorists and were in the hands of every law enforcement agency friendly to the United States. Photographs of Reza Jabarri, taken by security agents during his visit to the White House, and a personnel photo of Kyle Anton, the Arab relief officer of TIA, were also being circulated in the hopes of learning more about the origin and base of operations of the Fundamentalist Coalition.

The Nuclear Emergency Search Team (NEST) from New Mexico and special (nuclear) munitions teams from DOD were busy assessing the video given to the president by Jabarri. Neither group doubted the validity of the threat nor found any reason to question the weapon's authenticity.

Burt Williamson, director of the CIA, accustomed to keeping late hours, read carefully for a second time, a file containing the memorandum of a recent meeting between a field agent of the CIA and an officer of the former KGB. The report, viewed in the context of the current crisis, seemed to suggest the possible origin of the weapon now poised at Washington's doorstep.

"Sir, John Sinclair is here to see you."

"Show him in, Janet," Burt said as he stepped from behind his desk to greet his counterpart from the FBI.

"Come in, John. We need to talk."

"Like two survivors clinging to a single life vest, wouldn't you say?" Sinclair suggested, offering his hand.

The two exchanged greetings and then settled in the chairs surrounding the large glass coffee table in front of Burt's walnut desk. Sinclair glanced around the room before his eyes came to focus directly on Burt.

"Look at this report and tell me what you think."

John looked up. "You're thinking this might be the source of the weapon the coalition's pointing at us?"

"I don't think there's much doubt about it, do you?"

John gazed at the large portrait of Dulles hanging behind Burt's desk. "Considering the few sources for obtaining a nuclear weapon, it makes sense. I've thought that from the start," John explained. "I can't see any Third World country parting with its nuclear capability, regardless of the price. Besides, would they risk a confrontation with us?"

"Then you agree the weapon was stolen from the Russians?"

"I think so," Sinclair answered. "The question is, by whom?"

"Knowing Russia's internal security procedures, we're reasonably certain it had to be an inside job."

"I wouldn't argue that. I'm anxious to learn what the joint task force finds out about those three Russians found murdered in Athens. I've a hunch they were involved. Your station chief's report said the three were found shot to death without a struggle, presumably by a professional."

"Who do you think made the hit?" asked Burt.

"Based on this memorandum, I suspect the KGB may be trying to clean up its mess quickly. The last thing they need to have happen is for the American public to learn that one of their weapons has ended up on our shore. Considering Russia's need for our financial support, repercussions from such an event could destroy any chance of future U.S. support and risk the collapse of Yeltsin's government," John concluded.

"Is there a chance the terrorists may have decided to cover their trail by taking them out?"

Sinclair looked startled. "Frankly, I hadn't considered that angle. But if the FC fears we could get to the Russians and learn how to defuse the device, they might."

Recalling the video and the weapons technician who was shown modifying the weapon, Burt was certain one of those three Russians was the same person. Knowing for sure would require a meeting with the KGB. The Russians could make the ID, if they wanted to. But would they see it in their own best interest to do so, especially if it meant admitting the weapon was theirs? Given the nature of the crisis, Burt knew the president would have to approve such a move.

"Have you talked with Chris Jacobson since the NSC meeting last night?" Sinclair asked.

"Yeah, briefly. General Griffith has already begun to make contingency plans for taking out the jet with, or without, the passengers," Burt explained.

"Do you think McGarth will buy off on it if, he can't find a way to remove the passengers?"

"He'll have to, but I'd hate to have to make that call."

"Is Chris satisfied the jet can be hit without causing the bomb to detonate?"

"No. But for now, he feels he's got to put something together for the president. He'll have a tough time convincing McGarth to let him bomb that jet with passengers on board unless there is no alternative. I hope the president decides to play for time until we can get a better handle on the weapon. We don't have much to go on, let alone enough to warrant taking a chance on having that thing go off. Besides, suppose the bombs or artillery miss. Would Jabarri explode the device in retaliation? I don't know," Burt added.

"I agree. McGarth can't afford to authorize anything like that as long as there's hope he can find another way out. Count on me to back you up when the question surfaces," John said.

"It will come to that," Burt said. "General Griffith raised almighty hell at having to order the Navy out of the Gulf last night. I understand that Clayton is trying to put up a show of withdrawal while dragging his feet. I don't think he's going to want to put off indefinitely taking some kind of action."

"I can see the general's position, but bombing that aircraft would be a real gamble," Sinclair argued.

"John, you and I both know the president will have only so much time to find an alternative solution to the crisis before political pressure from all quarters will demand some kind of decisive action. Americans aren't known for their patience in situations like this."

"Where does Elliot stand on this issue?" Sinclair pressed.

"Gaylord has a great deal of respect for the think tanks and their assessment of the situation. I believe he'll want to move very cautiously. I don't think he shares the general's confidence in the DOD's ability to achieve the results DOD boasts are possible. But once he's had his say, Elliot will agree with the president."

Nodding, John glanced at his watch. It was 2:15 a.m.

"Thanks for the coffee, Burt. I'll see you at six."

*　*　*

"WBSU CHOPPER ONE CALLING THE F C."

Ahmed sat upright in the first officer's seat and picked up the mike. "CHOPPER ONE, YOU'RE CLEARED TO LAND AT THE INTERSECTION OF RUNWAYS THREE THREE AND THREE SIX. DO NOT SHUT DOWN YOUR ENGINE. WATERMAN WILL COME TO YOU."

"ROGER," answered the chopper pilot as he eased the helicopter downward, approaching National Airport.

Reza Jabarri, dozing in the captain's chair, heard the call and motioned for the terrorist guarding the main entrance door to step into the cockpit. The rugged gunman said nothing, but nodded as Reza spoke to him in Arabic. He was to take three men and stand guard outside the aircraft until the helicopter left. If anyone deplaned, he was to shoot them.

"Have you decided when you will set the women and children free?" Ahmed asked Reza as they watched the lights of the helicopter descending toward its landing site.

"Perhaps tomorrow morning. I want to see how our operation is received around the world first," he replied. "The hostages are very important to the Americans. Their release must be a big event if we are to benefit by allowing them freedom. I will have Mr. Waterman report the event and interview us again. It is important for the American people to understand that Muslims value life, too. The difference is, we are not afraid to die following Allah's will. They're weak and have no stomach for such suffering. They can never be true believers."

Moments later, the jet chopper settled onto the runway as the figure of a man made his way toward the aircraft. The exchange took less than a minute. Reza watched as Bud withdrew from under the blades. Lifting itself effortlessly off the ground, the chopper accelerated south and away from the 767.

"Ahmed, tell the tower to send the limo for me," Reza said. "You will go to the hotel and sleep tomorrow. Mohammed will remain here with you tonight. I do not expect the Americans to give us any problems. They are powerless."

Ahmed noticed the headlights of a lone vehicle turn toward the 767. "Your limousine is approaching."

"I must go and speak with our brothers," Reza said.

Mohammed joined Reza and walked him down the mobile stairs to the car that was waiting at the foot of the stairs. Ahmed watched from his seat as Reza disappeared into the balmy night.

Moments later, Mohammed joined Ahmed in the cockpit. They would keep the vigil together for the remainder of the night. Both knew their duties and believed in their cause. If the Americans were stupid enough to try and seize the jet, they would destroy Washington in an instant. They had no fear for their own lives. They were Allah's soldiers. To die for him would be an honor.

Sybil was numb, too tired to be frightened. Her passengers, forced to watch TV reports of Washington dealing with the crisis, were in shock. Fear for their families caught in the midst of the chaos gave them a new cause for worry. For some, the vivid examples of the civil unrest in a town already besieged by crime was too much. Collapsing into a stupor, they were unable to cope with even their basic needs.

It was to them that Sybil and her attendants felt the greatest need. Though confined to their jump seats, the flight attendants did what they could, offering what water and food was left and providing spiritual encouragement.

More than once, Cynthia disregarded her captor's instructions and left her seat to comfort a mother needing help with her child. On her third trip down the aisle to the mother's side, Cynthia was struck unconscious by one of the terrorists. Austin Seibert, seeing her fall, left his seat, picked Cynthia up and carried her back to her jump seat while Rachel, her flying partner, went to care for the ailing mother. The terrorist stood in the aisle, but did not interfere after an Arab passenger spoke out against what he had done in a tongue the terrorist could understand.

Sybil, angry over the abuse of her passengers and crew, stepped into the cockpit. Her voice startled Ahmed and Mohammed.

"Ahmed, I must talk with you, please."

"Why are you not in your seat, Sybil? You must do as you were told or you will be beaten," he snapped.

Sybil felt her blood boil at the suggestion. "You listen to me, Ahmed. Is that the best you can do — beat me?... I'm here to tell you to think about the passengers' needs as well as those of your own men. The plane is out of water, food and toilet paper. The lavs need dumping, and sooner or later you're going to run out of fuel to run the air conditioning so you need to start thinking about that. And, if your friend, Mr. Jabarri, keeps his word and does decide to let the women and children leave, how they appear to have been treated is going to have a lot to do with how the world is going to receive your cause. You better think about that too. I don't imagine there are a lot of commissary people standing around just waiting for you guys to call up and ..." Sybil shrieked as Ahmed lashed out at her, striking her across the face. "Get back to your seat, now!"

When she was gone, Ahmed thought of what Sybil had said. It made sense. The world's impression of their cause would be influenced by how the passengers were treated. He knew from years of living in the States that perceptions have a great effect on people's impressions. Harassing passengers would be considered petty when viewed against the major threat they'd imposed on the U.S. Increasing their misery by withholding food and water would not bring any change in the outcome of the confrontation, but could cause the government to feel it had to respond more quickly out of concern for the passengers.

Ahmed spoke to Mohammed in Arabic. "There is some truth in what the wench said. Perhaps we should order the tower to prepare for our needs."

Not a man of many words, Mohammed nodded. "Our brothers will need feeding. Speak to the tower."

* * *

General Clayton Griffith, chairman of the Joint Chiefs of Staff, crushed his cigar as he listened to the hot debate among the Joint Chiefs. There was no consensus about how to respond to the threat or even as to its scope. For the last two and one-half hours, he and the Chiefs had been briefed by a bevy of technicians from each of the services on topics ranging from Russian variable yield detonation options to PK (kill) probabilities of hitting the jet using laser-guided bombs. Used to analyzing technical information, they were not intimidated by the material, but were concerned with the interpretation assigned to much of it. The JCS was well aware that most of the data they were considering was based on tests conducted under optimum conditions, or data provided by contractors eager to sell their wares to the U.S. government.

Defense Intelligence Agency analysts and special weapons experts, armed with reams of information on every known weapon system employed by any country having nuclear weapons, discussed those weapons' capabilities and limitations. White papers previously presented by think tanks employed by the government were reviewed to focus on the likely repercussions of a terrorist-initiated nuclear attack against the United States, including ways of dealing with it.

Clayton waited silently as the last briefer collected his notes and excused himself from the conference room. "Vic, how do you see the situation from the Air's point of view?"

Lt.Gen. Victor C. Bruchessky, chief of staff of the Air Force and a highly decorated combat veteran of Vietnam, stroked his thick eyebrows as he looked up from his notes. "Frankly, I have serious reservations about whether we can safely bomb the aircraft and destroy the weapon without its being detonated. I don't question the experts' credibility, but I'm concerned about the data on which they've based their conclusions. I didn't detect a feeling of consensus among the briefers on the question of spontaneous detonation. We have to be extremely candid with the president on this matter. He must be made to understand the danger and consequences involved in exercising the air strike option. There are no guarantees. On the basis of the evidence so far, I don't think anyone can assure us that a secondary detonation won't occur.

"The PK tables assure us the nuke can be effectively knocked out on the first attempt, provided we adhere to the recommended ordnance mix. But, things don't always go as predicted."

"Then you think bombing the jet should be held as a last resort, Vic?" Clayton asked.

"Yes. Given the situation and allowing for the possibility of an error, there's no question."

Surprised by Bruchessky's position, Griffith didn't comment immediately. Instead, he glanced around the room to gauge the others' expressions. Admiral Thompson, the short, stocky chief of Naval Operations, appeared to sympathize with Vic.

"Mack, do you agree with Vic?"

Thompson, a graduate of the Naval Academy, had been close to the nuclear arena for most of his Navy career.

"Yes, sir. Bombing the jet should be the president's final option. It's just too damned risky unless he has no recourse."

"Gentlemen, it's obvious we must take a serious look at other options. Because of the complex nature of the problem we are facing, the final course of action chosen by the president is likely to involve a joint effort, including operations with the CIA and FBI. It's incumbent on us to coordinate our plans with these organizations. From what Elliot said last night, we can anticipate a joint task force of elements from a variety of agencies. The solution to terrorists' threats rarely tends to fall in line with our government's organizational structure."

"Clayton, are you saying that what is in essence a military operation, might be run by the FBI?" Admiral Thompson asked.

"Possibly, Mack. This operation will have its own structure, drawing assets from whichever organizations can meet its needs. Does that make sense?"

Mack knew it did. He just didn't like it.

"Clayton, are you suggesting military assets may be put under the command of someone other than a uniformed commander?" asked General Robin Curshner, the fiery, hard-nosed commandant of the Marine Corps, his jaws tightly clinching a stub of a cigar.

"Robin, It wouldn't surprise me to see that happen. This threat doesn't lend itself easily to any one agency's domain. We have to expect to share the major decisions with our counterparts at the CIA and FBI. The final plan will be decided by a consensus of the security council and presented to the president for his approval.

Robin shook his head. He'd already experienced one colossal screw-up using a similar approach in the Desert One operation in Iran. In theory it had sounded great. In reality it had been a farce, he remembered. The stakes were high then, too, but nowhere near what they were now. Robin knew joint ventures had a nasty habit of failing more because of false assumptions than from poor planning. Units accustomed to doing things a certain way expect other units to operate the same way.

"Clayton, I don't like what I'm hearing. If the DOD is given the responsibility for taking out that nuke, then the operation should be directed by a uniformed commander."

"Dammit, Robin, don't you think we all feel the same way? It's just not going to happen that way. Elliot told me what to expect and he has the president's ear. It's as simple as that!"

"All right, Clayton. We've had our say. Now what do you want from us?" Vic asked.

"Give me a ground assault contingency plan using the air strike option as a backup. I want us to be ready to take that blasted nuke out anytime the president gives us the go-ahead. Also make certain you're satisfied that the briefers we heard from weren't overstating their case. They can expect to be called on to brief the NSC sometime tomorrow," Clayton directed. "Anybody have anything else they want to say?" His question was answered with silence. "Then let's adjourn."

*   *   *

Jabarri peered down at the street from his high-rise hotel suite above Crystal City as he pressed the SEND button of his portable telephone. He was certain the Americans had bugged the phone in his room. Standing out on the balcony, he was convinced they could not monitor the calls he would make from his mobile telephone.

"Rashid speaking. Reza?" he asked in Arabic. "I expected your call earlier. Is there a problem?"

"No. Everything is progressing according to plan. And you?"

"I have nothing to report, except that I've not heard from Tariq or Jared. Neither has called to confirm that the girl has been disposed of."

"They may have had a problem. We think she escaped."

"That would explain them not calling. They were to call only after they had killed her," Rashid said.

"Have you spoken with the others?" Reza asked.

"Not since the jet landed. We agreed not to talk unless it becomes necessary to transmit the code. It appears the U.S. is preparing to comply with our ultimatum," Rashid explained.

"They would be fools not to, given the threat they face."

"But they have done foolish things before, Reza. I'll check on Tariq and Jared tomorrow," Rashid said.

"Jack, did you get a positive plot on the location of that call?" asked the FBI technician's supervisor.

"Yeah. We got it with no sweat. He's our little puppy now."

"And the tape?"

"Quality material. I'll have the address in two minutes."

"Great. Rush it over to the Counter-Terrorist Division. They've got an Arab interpreter waiting to translate. I'll notify the director and then go there myself."

"Consider it done," Jack said, wondering what the two Arabs had said. Would it be enough to break the case?

20

RECALL

A petite lady wearing leather pumps stood by the curb and waited as the chauffeur tossed her two bags into the back seat of the limousine. The sun was barely visible as she slid into the rear seat and removed her black raincoat. The driver handed her a business envelope as he pulled away from the curb at the JFK International Terminal. Opening the envelope, she removed a single sheet of paper containing names and addresses.

Inside the list were photos. She checked the names against the pictures. They were all there. Next, she examined the map that was enclosed. It was marked. Satisfied that she had what she needed, she returned the contents to the envelope and stuffed it in her tote bag. Looking at the driver, she said in a sharp tone, "You are missing something!"

"Here," said the driver, handing her a flat, zippered case and two smaller square boxes.

She took the packages, but said nothing. Opening the case, she removed the weapons, one at a time, examining each carefully. Then she checked the contents of the two smaller boxes. The ammunition was all there. Stuffing the weapons into her tote bag, she settled into a more comfortable position for the ride to Jersey. The night flight from Athens had been long and tiring for Isabel Yessad, mostly spent in moderate turbulence.

She hated flying as a passenger, preferring instead to be her own pilot. Minutes later, Isabel was asleep. Sunglasses still covered her closed eyes as the driver sped along the Southern Parkway toward the Verrazano Bridge.

* * *

Gaylord Elliot was already in the Situation Room drinking coffee and studying the latest intelligence summaries when Wes walked in. Looking up, he asked, "Did you manage to get any sleep last night, Colonel?"

Wes grinned a bit. "Not so you could tell, but the hot shower really felt good."

"Sit down and take a look at these reports, Wes. I think there's some stuff here you might find interesting."

Wes surveyed the long table. Nameplates identified the major players of the National Security Council meeting. He saw that a leather-bound notebook and folder had been placed in front of each seat. He took a seat in one of the chairs along the wall. They, too, had notebooks and folders on them.

He opened the folder and glanced through the pages. Someone had obviously spent the entire night putting it together. A concise summary of the situation was followed by a chronological events log referenced to a specific document included in the appendix. Scanning the log, Wes stopped at the item, entitled, "Interview with Reza Jabarri."

"What's this?" he asked under his breath. Elliot heard him and replied, "The *Examiner* reporter, Bud Waterman, the guy who landed his Cessna right behind you yesterday was able to get an interview with Jabarri last night at the terrorist's request. We'll run it as soon as we begin the meeting."

"Most of it propaganda?" Wes asked.

"For the most part, yes, I'd say so," Gaylord answered. Then he changed the subject.

"Take a look at item thirty-eight, Colonel. That Sybil DeVires is one smart flight attendant."

Wes glanced at the heading and went straight to the reference document and began reading. The synopsis was short.

Most of the NSC members filed in and took their assigned seats as Wes was finishing the article. Closing the folder, he thought of his crew and of what Sybil had done. She'd put herself at great risk. He was proud of her, but was concerned for her and the crew's safety. He hated not being able to return to his crew and was sure they thought he had abandoned them.

"Gentlemen, the President!" Wes jumped to his feet as everyone came to attention. McGarth entered and took his seat.

"Good morning. Please, ...take your seats. I trust you were able to sleep in spite of the nuke down the street?" Nervous laughter broke out as those present sensed the president was trying to keep the situation in perspective.

"As you know, I've asked my national security adviser to chair these meetings and to coordinate the preparation of my response to this crisis. Gaylord, proceed."

"Thank you, Mr. President, and good morning, gentlemen. We have much to cover, so I'll get to the point. You'll notice a folder my staff has prepared for you. I call your attention to those items that have been added most recently.

"We are certain that the nuclear weapon pointed at us is of Russian origin, having been stolen by Yuari Shervinsky, the former deputy commander of the USSR's Rocket Forces; Andrei Karpolov, a senior special weapons technician; and Viktor Khasnichev, a former KGB assistant deputy for Military Security. We have learned that these same three men were assassinated by an unidentified assailant last night in a hotel in Athens. We have not been able to determine who the assassin was or who he was working for. We suspect it may be the work of Russian security, but we are not certain. It may also have been done by those responsible for the threat we now face, although we don't have any evidence to support that contention.

"Based on confirmation received from Mr. Yeltsin's government and on CIA field intelligence, we are virtually certain the weapon aboard the 767 is a variation of the Soviet ALCM AS-15A cruise missile and poses a serious threat to Washington and the immediate area. We are uncertain how the weapon was taken or where it was modified, but we are following several leads and hope to have a better grip on it shortly.

"It's extremely important that we learn where the missile was modified. It could provide us a clue as to where and from whom the terrorist obtained the timers and arming devices. Suffice it to say, we have little chance of learning more from Andrei Karpolov, the man assassinated in Athens early last night.

"We've also learned that seven terrorists accompanied Reza, Mohammed, and Ahmed on the flight here. The flight service manager aboard the aircraft sent us her passenger list marked with the seat location of each of the terrorists. The names are being screened for any relationship to known terrorist organizations.

"Several hours ago, the FBI monitored a phone call between Mr. Jabarri and a Mr. Rashid, one of the four terrorists living outside Washington. We have not determined the role these people play, but expect to learn more from subsequent conversations.

"In a related development, we've obtained a copy of a taped interview given by Mr. Jabarri to Bud Waterman, a reporter from the *Examiner*. It may shed some light on the threat and on Mr. Jabarri, the terrorist we're being forced to deal with."

As the lights were dimmed, quiet discussions broke out among members of the NSC. The president said nothing, preferring to study the reactions to Elliot's briefing. Wes kept his eyes on the commander in chief. He well knew the pressure McGarth was under.

The interview with Jabarri was informative, but didn't reveal much useful information, thought Wes, as his mind drifted off to the video he'd seen in the Oval Office yesterday. Something was familiar about the background of that tape, but he couldn't place it from the few frames that had caught his eye. Remembering the importance the president's security adviser had placed on identifying the location, Wes decided to ask Elliot if he could review the tape.

"Gentlemen, this concludes a synopsis of the latest information we have on the situation, with the exception of a CIA follow-up report on the assassination of the three Russians in Athens. Burt will you bring us up-to-date on that?"

"Yes, sir," answered the CIA director, removing a classified message from his valise.

"In the course of examining the personal effects of the three Russians assassinated in Athens, we have uncovered a very disconcerting piece of information. Our agents found a half-written letter from Andrei Karpolov to his older sister in Western Siberia. He expresses his guilt for having participated in the theft of the nuclear weapon belonging to his country. He goes on to say that he's very concerned over the use the group intends to make of the weapon and the videotape. He is especially upset that the explanation of the arming and detonation options was purposely changed to deceive those who would view the tape. The

remaining paragraphs give a specific description of the actual modifications and urges her to hold on to the information in the event that he
is killed. The letter was incomplete and there was no signature. However, we were able to compare his writing against the sign-in card for
his hotel registration and they matched.

"The arming conditions and detonation options in Karpolov's letter indicate that the weapon would have been armed and a timer activated during the aircraft's deceleration on landing at National. He made
no reference as to how long the timer was preset for, or what type of
timer was used. He says that the timer could be overridden by either a
four digit alphanumeric code or by a digital code programmed as a
phone number. Without saying so, he implied a telephone transceiver
had been included in the options package, presumably to allow the
terrorists to detonate the weapon by simply placing a phone call."

"Are you telling me that it's possible for Jabarri or any of his terrorist friends to detonate that bomb using the telephone?" Everyone
focused on the president.

"Yes, Mr. President, I'm afraid that's exactly what it means," answered the CIA director.

"And you say that in all probability, the bomb is already armed
and a timer has been activated and is now counting down to an unknown zero hour?" Burt's expression foretold his reply.

"Yes sir, Mr. President. That's our understanding."

"Well that's a helluva lot different from what Jabarri said, isn't it?"

No one ventured a response, but each nodded his agreement. Unaccustomed to being misled by anyone, let alone by the FC and its
band of terrorists masquerading as negotiators, McGarth was visibly
angered by the CIA's latest intelligence.

"Perhaps I will have another meeting with Mr. Jabarri," McGarth
muttered, motioning at Gaylord to continue.

"At this point, I'd like to focus on possible alternatives we have in
dealing with the crisis. Clayton, would you outline what DOD sees as
our military options?"

Wes watched as the general removed several documents from his
briefcase and put them on the table. At the same time, copies were
distributed to the president and the NSC members.

"Mr. President,... and gentlemen, the secretary of defense, the joint
chiefs, and I have examined in detail what we know about the weapon
or bomb poised to go off. In the document before you, we have out-

lined the options we think are most likely to enable us to negate the threat. They have been prioritized according to the probability of success and not on the risk to the population. We believe the danger to civilians will remain constant, no matter which option is exercised — with the notable exception of those passengers aboard the aircraft.

"Several options call for an assault on the jet and the rescue of the passengers as a prelude to destroying the weapon. As you might expect, such an operation could provide the terrorists sufficient time to successfully detonate the device, in spite of our efforts. So, these options are considered among the riskiest and least likely to avoid the destruction of the city."

Wes felt a cold sweat come from nowhere as Griffith probed deeper into the issue of rescuing his passengers. He'd known from the beginning their fate would be that of pawns with no say in their destinies. Their lives hung in the balance of what would be expedient. As a former military commander, Wes understood that life must sometimes be treated as expendable if a greater purpose is to be served. He could see the general's briefing was pointed in that direction. The Pentagon would ultimately recommend sacrificing the passengers and crew to have the greatest chance of saving Washington and its citizens. Wes couldn't argue with their logic. It was the only approach to take, given the gravity of the problem, and he knew it. And although he was certain McGarth was a compassionate man, not given to taking life from anyone, Wes realized that eventually the situation would force him to choose that course, unless a better solution could be found.

Wes knew he would have to find a way to rescue his passengers and crew or return to the jet to be with them in their final hour. The president couldn't deny him that. He could not live with their deaths on his conscience. It would be more than he could endure, thought Wes, as he tried desperately to refocus on Griffith's presentation.

"....and in conclusion, the JCS recommends the aerial bombing option as the one mostly likely to save the city and result in the fewest loss of lives, even though we have very serious reservations regarding the validity on which we were forced to make our judgment. We feel that we must be very candid with you, sir, on this point. The JCS wants you to know that, after listening to all the testimony, we do not honestly know for certain whether we can strike the device without detonating it. For this reason, we suggest you employ all other means at your disposal before directing such a strike. Thank you, Mr. President."

"Gentlemen, let's take a short break."

Wes stood up and walked over to Elliot. "May I have a word with you, sir?"

"Sure, Colonel. What's on your mind?"

"Sir. I'd like to view the tape the terrorists gave the president yesterday. I think I may have recognized the location of the facility where the bomb was modified."

"You do? Where?" Elliot asked in amazement.

"I think it's Larnaca Airport in Cyprus."

Elliot dialed the Oval Office and talked with Lindsey. Hanging up he said, "Colonel, the tape is on its way. Tell the duty officer to set it up for you as soon as it arrives and to buzz me when it's ready."

Returning to the conference room, Wes noticed the president deep in thought over the proposals before him. Wes watched him deliberating the options, believing he was near a decision. He'd heard that McGarth was decisive. Perhaps he'd already decided what to do.

"Gentlemen!" It was the president. Conversation died immediately as every man took his seat. "First, I'd like to thank each of you for your steadfast loyalty to your duty and to your country during this most trying time. I'm most appreciative of the sacrifices each of you have had to make, and I trust that together we can successfully extricate the country from this nightmare.

"Foremost in my mind is the preservation of the citizens of Washington and the surrounding area. We can build another seat of government if we have to, but I will not take any action that will further endanger the lives of our people until and unless I am forced to do so.

"I will not approve any plan that calls for the outright slaughter of the passengers until I am convinced that I have no other choice or the terrorists force my hand. I concur wholeheartedly with DOD's position of exhausting all other remedies before any consideration is given to bombing the jet. I appreciate their candor and I share their reservations.

"It concerns me greatly to learn that these terrorists may be planning to humiliate us first, then detonate the device regardless of whether we keep our part of the bargain. I find that reprehensible. Yet, we shouldn't expect any more from such a cowardly band of degenerates seeking vengeance.

"I would therefore ask that you each continue to explore every avenue leading to a solution to this problem. I remind you that our nation has a reputation for solving problems through ingenuity and technology. Encourage those you supervise to be creative in their approaches to looking for solutions.

"Meanwhile, I shall do everything in my power to extricate us from this threat through negotiation. But I must warn you that I will not allow our country to suffer such humiliation at the hands of these thugs indefinitely without taking some kind of action. Nor can I afford to sit by and let them detonate this device without doing something about it. The amount of time I have before I must act is apt to change. I urge you all to make every minute count."

As the president left the room, Wes saw the duty officer beckon him. "Colonel, if you'll follow me. I have the film set up in one of our briefing rooms." As Wes was about to enter the smaller room, a voice called out to him, "Captain Beacham." Turning around, Wes saw the president standing in the corridor. "Mr. President?" Wes said, walking toward McGarth.

"Colonel, has Gaylord explained why we felt it necessary to recall you to active duty?"

"Yes, sir, he did," replied Wes, trying not to appear dejected by the decision.

"I can understand your wanting to return to your flight, Colonel, but right now your expertise is needed here. I presume Elliot has explained that we want you to meet with the SEALS immediately and develop an assault plan. If it becomes necessary to implement the plan, you will get your chance to rejoin your passengers and crew," the president said. Wes smiled at the possibility.

"I understand you'll be leaving for Norfolk shortly?"

"Yes, sir. I think that's the plan."

"Well, good luck. What you men come up with is apt to make a great deal of difference in the outcome of this situation. I don't relish having to bomb your plane, Colonel. Give it your best shot."

"I will."

McGarth extended his hand. The two clasped hands for a moment. Then Wes watched as the president disappeared down the corridor. He'd never met a man with more control and conviction. McGarth was forceful but gracious, quick to comprehend but patient with others.

Dimming the lights, Wes waited for the tape to fast forward. He was fairly certain the frames he wanted to look at were near the end. He was right. On the first attempt, he overshot them and had to rewind the tape. His second effort was better. Recalling that there were, at the most, only one or two seconds of the building and background, Wes focused on the overall setting. Suddenly, the scenes he wanted appeared, but were quickly gone. He rewound the tape again. This time, as the frames came into view, Wes knew what to look for.

"There. It is the odd-shaped hangar at Larnaca," he said under his breath as he summoned the duty officer through the glass. "Can photos be made from the frames of this film?"

"I think so, Colonel," the major said. "Mark the frames you need and I'll take care of it for you." Wes reversed the tape and stopped at the beginning of the frames he needed. Removing the cartridge, he handed it to the major. "Begin here and go forward for the next eight to ten frames," Wes said, heading back to the conference room to find Elliot.

John Sinclair, in the midst of speculating on the reasons for the other terrorists scattered about the periphery of Washington, paused and looked up as Wes entered.

Interrupting, Gaylord asked, "Colonel, what did you learn?"

"It's the airport at Larnaca on Cyprus, sir."

"You're certain?" Elliot quizzed.

"Yes, I am."

"Nice work," Elliot said. "At least we know now where to begin looking. Burt, you and John need to huddle with Colonel Beacham briefly before we continue. Gentlemen, let's take a ten minute recess."

"So they modified the weapon on Cyprus, Colonel?" asked Sinclair.

"Yes, in a warehouse hangar at Larnaca Airport. Photos of the building are being made from the video. There should be enough detail to identify the facility."

"I hope your information is accurate, Colonel. We desperately need a place to start," Williamson added.

Two minutes later, Wes had told the two directors all they needed to know. As he was about to take his seat, Elliot motioned for him. "The helicopter set up to fly you to Norfolk will land on the White House lawn in ten minutes. You'd better get moving, Colonel. See the duty officer on your way out. He has your orders and your itinerary. He'll also check you out on the use of the KL-43 encryption device."

"A KL-43? What's that?"

Gaylord smiled. "It will allow us to talk over unsecured phone lines. Stay in touch with me and good luck."

"Thanks," said Wes, as Elliot walked him to the door.

21

A THIRD ECHELON

Isabel awoke to the limousine's weaving motion. Rubbing the sleep from her eyes, she imagined they were nearing the Jersey foothills. Her back ached from the cramped position she'd been lying in for the last hour. The sun was much higher in the hazy sky than when she had drifted off to sleep. The glare was blinding. Her sunglasses had fallen from her face. Looking about the car, Isabel found them on the floor and put them on.

"How much longer?" she asked.

"Less than ten minutes," said the driver.

"What time is the chopper due to land?"

The driver glanced at the car's clock. "Fifteen minutes."

"Then slow it down a bit if we've got five minutes to burn."

"Yeah, okay."

Isabel lowered the window. The morning air was heavy, but refreshing. The smell of honeysuckle was in the air.

Opening her soft luggage bag, she took out a pair of jeans, a red and white cotton blouse, bra and panties, and her sneakers. Removing her pantyhose first, she changed her underwear and then unbuttoned her black linen dress. Noticing the driver had shifted the majority of his attention to the rearview mirror, she let the dress fall open, exposing her breasts. Isabel saw the lust in his eyes and smiled. She enjoyed his interest. Men amused her. She did not find him appealing, but suspected he had a high opinion of himself. She was about to pull the dress over her head when she felt the car leave the road for a second.

"Look where you're going, you idiot!" she shouted as the driver swerved, narrowly missing a guardrail.

"Haven't you ever seen a woman undress before?" she asked angrily.

Muttering, the driver returned his eyes to the road as Isabel finished dressing.

Pulling her long, black hair tight against the sides of her head, she fashioned it into a simple ponytail. It made her look even younger. Then Isabel wiped her face with a towelette and applied her makeup.

Isabel stuffed the last of her street clothes into the bag as the car stopped at the edge of a clearing surrounded by large gum trees. The grass had been freshly mowed, its tips burned by the summer sun. A windsock devoid of wind, dangled against the side of its mast.

Massaging her sore muscles, Isabel stepped from the car and began her stretching exercises. Minutes later, she began jogging around the edge of the cleared space. Her driver waited in the car, guarding her passage.

On the third lap, Isabel heard the unmistakable sound of a helicopter making its way to the grassy landing pad, its large blades pounding the humid air. She saw its shadow first as it pulled up into a hover position before descending carefully through the tall foliage. The touchdown was gentle. The lone pilot feathered the blades and waited as Isabel retrieved her bags from the car and ran toward the front of the chopper and climbed aboard.

The pilot handed her a headset with a boom mike and pointed to the communications control box. Nodding, she slipped the headset on and pressed the intercom selector.

"Leesburg, right?" he asked.

"Yes, the private field southeast of town."

"I know the place well," he replied, raising the collector.

Isabel felt the helicopter lift off the ground. She watched as the trees around her fell back. Now, barely above their tops, she felt the full warmth of the summer sun as the chopper began to move forward.

"You want to fly?" Isabel nodded and took the controls. The pilot handed her the chart showing the course to Leesburg.

It had been four months since she'd flown a chopper. Civilian choppers were much nicer, she thought, as she took up a southwesterly heading. The military ones she trained in were never as well-maintained.

Reaching seven hundred feet, Isabel leveled the rotary-winged jet and let its speed build. The run to Leesburg figured to be a little over an hour, she noted from the chart. Looking down, she saw the chopper's shadow racing over the Jersey countryside as it sped along. It was nice being able to fly in the open and not have to fear anti-aircraft fire or missile attacks.

Things were so different in America, thought Isabel. Its towns and villages were tidy, unblemished by the eternal wars that had lain siege to the people and property of her country. Americans could not begin to comprehend the impact of war and suffering that she and her people had endured for years. It would be a frightening experience for them, she decided. Her mission would see to it. America would finally know the pain it had foisted on her country. It would never be the same here again. Washington would soon become a horrible memory, a nightmare of unparalleled proportions. Isabel wondered if the smug TV analysts would still report the devastation in their usual detached manner, or if they would be shocked into speaking of the annihilation as though it were personal.

She didn't care as long as America got the message. It would not bring back her children and husband. Only her parents and sisters had survived. One of America's cruise missiles had seen to that. How many times had she seen the instant replay of the Tomahawks streaking low over the flaming skies of Baghdad while the announcer applauded the technical superiority of Yankee know-how and scoffed at the poor marksmanship of her country's gunners?

Isabel thought it ironic a Russian cruise missile, delivered to America by one of its own fighter pilots, would be the instrument that would destroy their security and bring down the center of their power structure. Isabel hated America and what it had taken from her.

*   *   *

Walking across the lawn of the White House to board the waiting helicopter felt peculiar to Wes. It humbled him to walk the short path that McGarth and presidents before him had taken on the first leg of their many journeys. As he approached the aircraft, Wes could see the faces of the two pilots at the controls. They seemed to be staring at him. He wondered if they knew he was the fool responsible for bringing the nuke to America. It was an awful feeling he'd have to learn to accept.

"Morning, Colonel! Welcome to Special Ops, sir." Wes nodded his thanks and managed a smile at the lieutenant. "Right this way," he said.

Wes followed the junior officer forward through the tight companionway and into the cockpit. The two pilots extended their hands as Wes entered. Wes shook each one. Both of their grips were firm. Did they know?

"Glad to have you with us, Colonel Beacham. I'm Hal Thornton and this is Sam Schofield, my copilot," the commander said. "How does it feel to be back in uniform?"

"To tell you the truth, Hal, I'm really not sure."

"Yeah, I can imagine, but hell, the way I heard it, you guys had no idea you had that thing aboard until it was too late."

Wes wished it had been that simple. "Well, I hope they remember it that way at my court martial."

"I wouldn't spend any time worrying about it, Colonel. We'll just run down to Little Creek and put together a plan and come back up here and take that sonofabitch away from those rag heads before they hurt themselves with it."

Wes grinned at Thornton's air of confidence. It gave him hope. It helped being with these guys. They were his kind of people — they understood.

"Do you want to ride up here with us or take a seat in the back? It's okay with us, either way."

Wes glanced down at the classified packet Elliot had given him as he'd left the Situation Room. "I'd enjoy the ride up here, but I'd better read through this classified first. I'm supposed to meet with the SEALS at eleven o'clock," Wes explained.

"Didn't they tell you? That meeting has been rescheduled for later this evening, Colonel. Commander Marino isn't due back from the West Coast until five this afternoon. I guess Ops didn't get the word out quick enough. I'd say you've got time to burn."

Wes thought for a moment. There was little he could do until his meeting with Marino. The idea of sitting around Little Creek for most of the day seemed senseless.

"Hal, what's the chance of your dropping me off on the Outer Banks, near Duck? I can drive back to Little Creek in plenty of time for the meeting with Marino."

"I'd say it's damned good if you can show me where I can set this crate down when we get there. Forget about the driving. We'll come back and pick you up around six. How's that?"

"Thanks. I'd appreciate it."

"Your family down there now, are they?" asked Thornton.

"Yeah, how'd you know?"

"Just a guess."

The thought of seeing Caroline alive again had all but become a dream to Wes. Suddenly all that could change. Wes imagined the thrill of seeing his family together one more time before whatever.

Dropping into one of the uncomfortable webbed seats along the wall of the large Marine helicopter, Wes opened the manila envelope. He'd just started to peruse the material when he felt the pull of gravity. Peering through the oval window, he watched as the chopper rose into the air. The view of the White House was beautiful. Wes could see the famed Rose Garden and the spot where the Christmas tree was put up each year. For a moment, he forgot the agony that was tormenting his soul.

The jet swung its nose southward and continued to climb. His perspective suddenly changed, and with it, his mood. He could see the outline of the Potomac and its bend to the south, and National Airport — Gravelly Point. His stomach turned as he thought of his passengers and crew. Were they coping? He hated not knowing and not being there.

As the helicopter climbed higher, he could see the 767 sitting on the black tarmac. Now abeam the Pentagon, he saw the small Cessna parked nearby, as well. Off to the side, he saw the immobile freeways, littered with countless vehicles inching out of harm's way. He felt undeserving of the chopper ride. He should be made to suffer their misery. Wes saw the scorched roadway and knew it was all that remained of the fiery tanker-truck disaster last night. How many had died? His mind wouldn't let him remember.

* * *

Reza Jabarri switched off the TV and walked out on the balcony overlooking the Potomac. The news program pleased him. The chaos was even greater than he could have anticipated. Continuous live coverage rehashed every detail of the unfolding catastrophe. Experts from every conceivable area of concern heightened the fears of viewers as they predicted with certainty the horror and devastation inherent in detonation of the bomb. Political analysts suggested the possibility that the world order would likely change, regardless of whether the weapon was ultimately exploded. Others said the United States had already suffered irreparable damage to its image as a superpower. Republicans pointed their fingers at the Democrats for having slashed the defense budget to near post-World War II levels to pay for health care and other social programs at the expense of national security. Hawks chided doves for naively believing the threat to America had lessened with the collapse of the Soviet Union and blamed them for the crisis. Foreign leaders, eager to support the United States, hammered away with their rhetoric, but promised nothing tangible. The prime minister of Israel was reported to have placed his country's entire military on maximum alert in preparation for an assault from elements of the Arab world. Journalists aboard U.S. warships exiting the Persian Gulf filed their stories, reporting the withdrawal of fleets spanning the Middle East as commanders grimaced at their new orders.

Financial analysts in New York were aghast at the run being made on the dollar at the British, German, and French exchanges. There seemed to be no floor, despite assurances offered by the secretary of the treasury and the chairman of the Federal Reserve Board. Everyone wondered what the opening bell on Wall Street would mean for millions of nervous investors. Would they hang tight or would the bottom fall out as they opted to dump their stock positions in favor of gold or other more stable currencies? That seemed to be the pivotal financial question of the hour. Most were afraid to speculate for fear of exacerbating the situation. No one spoke with much confidence about when the markets could expect to return to normalcy.

Reza put his cup aside, lifted the receiver of the hotel telephone and dialed a special White House number.

"Mr. Lindsey's office. Betty speaking."

"Yes, this is Mr. Jabarri. I must speak with the president."

"One moment, Mr. Jabarri. I'll see if he is available."

Reza smiled at the civility in her voice. He was certain she de-spised him. He recalled her glaring eyes as he insisted on being heard by the president. He could imagine the chagrin on her face at having to announce his call.

"Good morning, Mr. Jabarri, this is Forest Lindsey. The president is unable to come to the phone at the moment. Could I be of service?"

"Ah.... Mr. Lindsey, good morning to you, as well. It is most un-fortunate that your president is unable or unwilling to speak with me. I called to discuss with him the possibility of my releasing the women and children from the aircraft this morning. I suppose it will have to wait for now. Good day."

Reza set the phone back on the hook and waited. He would give the president exactly five minutes to return his call. For every minute he was late, the women and children would remain on board another day.

Reza tried to imagine what the level of despair in America might be like in six days when he and his brothers would depart. The thought of leaving behind the un-detonated bomb as a warning to the world of the power of the coalition and its Arab brothers intrigued him. He thought of the humiliation America would have to endure before nego-tiating its removal. The phone rang.

"Mr. Jabarri, this is President McGarth. I apologize for not being able to answer your call."

"Yes, Mr. President. I commend you for your quick reply. Had you waited another fifteen seconds, I would have let the women and children remain on board an additional day."

McGarth fought to contain his anger, choosing not to respond. Reza noted his silence and changed the subject.

"Mr. President, I am a man of my word, as I believe you to be also. Yesterday, I indicated to you that I would not harm the passen-gers if you complied with my instructions. It would appear from the countless reports I have observed on the TV over the last twelve hours that you have made a sincere effort to meet each of our directives. As I also said, we do not wish to harm your people or to cause them exces-sive hardship. For this reason, I have decided to release all of the women and children at noon today, provided you agree to accompany me to the aircraft and to assist me in welcoming their release. What do you say to that?"

"Thank you, Mr. Jabarri. I accept your offer."

"Very well. I will give Mr.Lindsey the necessary instructions, Mr. President."

"That will be fine. He will call you immediately. Good day."

"And a pleasant one to you, as well, Mr. President."

* * *

Now barely above the trees, its transponder off to avoid detection by Dulles surveillance radar, Isabel's helicopter crossed the Potomac just east of White's Ferry. Lansdowne lay just ahead. Isabel, relinquishing the controls to the pilot, prepared for the final part of her journey. Removing the weapons from the nylon partitioned case, she attached the telescopic sights and suppressors and set their safeties. Then she loaded the six clips. When she had finished, she put the two semi-automatic weapons and the clips into a padded, canvas bag.

Glancing through the Plexiglas bubble, Isabel saw the town of Leesburg off to her right. Both lanes of all the roads were still clogged with traffic. It would not present much of a problem, she thought, as she removed a nylon jacket from the tote bag. Its vivid gold and royal blue colors sparkled in the bright sunlight. The logo on the left breast pocket featured the letters ASAP. ACE COURIER was written across the back of the jacket in script. She checked again to see that the map, list of names and addresses, and photos were in the large left pocket.

Isabel read through the list of names and addresses and looked at the photos once more as the chopper abruptly slowed to maneuvering speed for the final phase of the descent. She had them memorized. Satisfied her preparation was complete, she stuffed the materials back in the pocket and zipped it shut.

She surveyed her surroundings as the pilot maneuvered the craft for a landing. The small airstrip, abandoned long ago, was now mostly covered with parched grass. Overgrown trees encircled the single runway. A building that she guessed had once been the operations shack, was boarded up. Otherwise, there was little else to see.

The touchdown was firm. She wasn't surprised. The sun-baked clay soil, devoid of moisture, had the hardness of brick.

"I will expect you here at twenty-one hundred hours tomorrow night unless I call. I will flash my light twice in quick succession. You answer by turning your rotating beacon off for ten seconds. Any questions?" she asked. The pilot shook his head. Removing her headset, Isabel unlatched her seat belt and climbed out of the chopper, carrying her jacket and the canvas bag. Once clear of the blades, she turned and gave the pilot a thumbs-up. Within seconds, the chopper lifted off and began its climb. Isabel didn't bother to watch. By the time she reached the ops shack, the helicopter had disappeared.

Isabel saw that the double doors in the rear of the maintenance shed were secured with a combination lock. She expected they would be. Tilting the lock upward, she rolled the four barrels to match the day and month, and gave a tug on the lock. It opened easily.

Two large trail bikes occupied most of the shed. Helmets rested on the seats. Jerry cans, cases of oil, and a workbench covered with tools took up the rest of the space. Isabel checked out both bikes carefully, then rolled one out of the shed. She hid the key to the second bike before relocking the shed.

Outside, Isabel strapped the canvas bag and her tote bag on the rear of her bike. She donned the helmet and turned the ignition key. The engine roared to life immediately. She paused to check the idle, then slapped the bike into gear and took the path leading from the shack to a break in the tree line.

There, she joined a dirt road for the two-mile ride to US 15. Reaching the highway, Isabel stopped to check the time. She estimated the ride to the West Auto Parts Store in Chantilly would take thirty minutes. Turning south, she realized why Hassan had insisted she use the motorbike. The traffic was horrendous.

*   *   *

Reza had nearly finished reading Waterman's interview with him when he heard the phone. He let it ring several times before he answered. Jabarri knew it would be Forest Lindsey, the president's chief of staff.

"Mr. Jabarri. The president asked that I call you to receive instructions for conducting the release of the women and children."

"Yes, of course," replied Reza. "Tell the president to meet me at the aircraft at noon. He must come alone. Make sure that Mr. Waterman, the reporter for the *Examiner,* is present with his video camera. The president and I will greet each passenger as they deplane. You will arrange for a bus to pick them up at the aircraft. Only Mr. Waterman will be allowed to cover the event. He will make his tape available to all other media organizations after I have previewed his work. Is that understood?"

"Yes, Mr. Jabarri. I will inform the president. I will also arrange to have your limo in position at your hotel at eleven thirty, if that is acceptable to you."

"Excellent, Mr. Lindsey. Good day."

* * *

Wes could see from his window the ribbon of sand stretching southeast. It was the Outer Banks. He would be home in less than ten minutes. Looking west, he saw the Intracoastal Waterway winding southwest through the village of Coinjock.

"Colonel, the skipper needs you up front," called the chief. "I'm on my way," Wes shouted back.

They were tracking down the center of the Currituck Sound, in sight of Duck, as Wes entered the cockpit. The skipper saw Wes was on deck and motioned him to take the seat behind him. "I'll need your help from here on in."

Wes leaned forward over Thornton's left shoulder. "See the high ridge a half-mile south of the village and west of the paved road?"

"Yeah. I got it."

"It's the third cul-de-sac west of the road leading south from Duck."

"Talley-ho!" hollered Thornton, swinging the giant chopper left as he dumped altitude.

Wes watched as Hal made a pass over the spot to check for obstructions. He could see Walker's Explorer parked in the driveway. Neighbors poured out of their homes as the huge jet returned and squeezed itself onto the circular roadway. Wes's face broke into a wide grin at the sight of Meredith on the balcony. Then he saw Caroline and Jacqueline standing with her.

"Okay, Colonel. This is where you get off," Hal said. "I'll be back at eighteen hundred hours," he shouted as he touched down and feathered the blades.

"See you then," Wes said, scrambling back toward the exit. Sand was swirling everywhere as he ran from the jet toward Kilduck Station and his waiting family.

Meredith met Wes in the street as the chopper was lifting off. Neither tried to speak over the pounding air as they locked arms in an embrace. Caroline, Jacqueline, and Walker rushed down the driveway to welcome their dad home as neighbors kept their distance out of respect. Tucker waited on the porch, his gunshot wound still too painful for him to do much moving about.

Holding on to Meredith, Wes opened his right arm as Caroline ran to him. Then Jacqueline and Walker closed the loop as they wrapped their arms around him, Meredith and Caroline. No one said anything as they held one another silently in the radiant morning sunlight.

Wes felt the softness of Meredith's tears as they brushed his suntanned face. He sensed the fear that had tortured Caroline as she nuzzled against his chest. Wes knew her pain. It was his. Jackie fought back her tears as she reached out for her father's caress. The touch of Walker's hand on his shoulder consoled Wes as he struggled to maintain his composure, wanting to be the pillar of strength his family needed. They needed his love and support more than ever.

For the first time in days, Wes felt the inner peace of being with his family. Their love gave him strength. It renewed his confidence. It restored his self-respect. No longer would guilt ravage his mind and heart, robbing him of the will to overcome the horror he'd brought to his country.

He gazed into their eyes and smiled. They felt his pride and approval, and he, theirs. Then Jackie noticed something different about him.

"Dad! What are you doing in that uniform?"

"It's a long story, honey. Let's go up on porch and I'll tell you all about it."

Meredith stepped back and admired him as she always had when he'd returned from a trip. She could see the stress in his eyes. She knew he needed rest. But that could wait, she thought.

"I haven't seen you in that uniform in eight or nine years, Wes," she said affectionately. "How did that happen?"

"The president did it," he answered seriously. "He and several members of the National Security Council thought I might be able to help train a team to rescue the passengers and take back the jet, so they ordered me to active duty."

Meredith understood. She recalled Wes had done that once before, ten years ago. The children didn't.

"Does that mean you'll have to leave again soon, Dad?" asked Caroline.

"Yes, Princess. The chopper will be back for me at six."

"How long will you be gone this time?" asked Jackie.

"It's hard to say. I guess until this mess is over." Meredith saw the serious expression on Wes's face. He was doing his best to minimize what was in store for them for the sake of the girls. She changed the subject.

Reaching the porch, Wes and his family walked around to the southwest end of the house out of sight of their neighbors and settled into their usual seats, eager to exchange stories and make use of the little time Wes had.

22

STRANGE PROTOCOL

Forest, I don't see that I have any choice. Either I meet Jabarri at noon and get the women and children off that jet, or I stay here and wait for him to threaten to shoot them if I don't," McGarth argued.

"I understand that, sir, and I'm not saying don't go. I'm simply suggesting that we try to negotiate having a security team accompany you. God knows what would happen if one of his terrorists were to shoot you, Mr. President."

"If they did, having the Secret Service with me wouldn't make a damn bit of difference. If anything, the terrorists might find them intimidating and do something irrational. We've already had two casualties because of Halston's security guys overreacting."

Answering the phone, Lindsey frowned at McGarth's decision.

"It's for you. Millicent Longsworth says it's urgent."

"Yes, Millicent. What is it?"

"Mr. President, I'm sorry to have to interrupt, sir, but we've got another crisis. The dollar is dropping like a rock on all of the exchanges. And the Federal Reserve doesn't see any floor to it anytime soon, with the terrorist situation."

"Where is it now, Millicent?"

"Its down over sixteen percent against the major currencies and still heading south, sir."

"What do you recommend?"

"I'd like to push for a suspension of trading immediately. The Fed needs time to try to establish support for the dollar, and that's going to take coordination with the European and Japanese banks.

"Do what you have to, Millicent, and keep me posted. If necessary, I'll lean on Blair and Schmidt for help."

"Thank you, Mr. President."

"Damn! That's all we need now is a run on the treasury," snapped McGarth, as Forest switched off the intercom.

Mason looked away as his thoughts returned to the passengers aboard the 767. Was he being set up? Perhaps Forest was right.

"What's the security situation here in the District now?"

"Sir, Mayor Evans advised me earlier that the troops you ordered have the District under control."

"Good. At least we're making progress in some area," McGarth said. "Have you talked with Halston in the last hour? I'm interested in what the Israelis have decided."

"No sir, but his special assistant called to tell me that their Parliament is still in session. He confirmed that DOD's information was correct. The Israelis have put their entire military on maximum alert and have begun a general mobilization of all personnel," Forest said.

"Well," the president said, "you can't blame them. That speech I was forced to make left them high and dry when it comes to support. I imagine they're trying to assess the short-term impact. I hope they decide to hold off on any drastic action."

"The Pentagon is certain they've already taken a defensive nuclear posture," Lindsey replied.

"I'm sure they have, Forest. Netenyahu said they would be forced to do that once we began our withdrawal."

Slipping on his coat, McGarth remarked, "It's time for my appointment. Let's hope Jabarri sticks to his part of the bargain."

Lindsey looked up with a worried expression. "Good luck, Mr. President."

*   *   *

Seeing the West Auto Parts sign in the distance, Isabel slowed her bike and used the remaining distance to survey the area around the shop. Several cars were parked in front of the convenience store next door, but none was occupied. Two men sat in a gray sedan across the road at a gas station, but didn't seem to be paying any attention as she pulled up in front of the small store. She saw they were engrossed in reading the newspaper. She thought it odd, given the crisis.

Deciding to keep her helmet on to avoid being recognized, Isabel parked the bike and casually removed a piece of flexible tubing from the luggage box. She stretched the tubing and examined it in the sunlight, as if trying to find the puncture. Satisfied she had established the legitimacy of her visit, Isabel opened the shop door and went inside, removing her helmet. She kept her gloves on.

Isabel immediately recognized Rashid Sedki from the picture she'd been given. He was at a desk reading. He appeared to be alone, though she couldn't be certain. Hearing her enter, he came to his feet. "Can I help you?" he asked, as Isabel set her helmet on the parts counter. He saw the logo, but pretended not to notice.

"Yes. I must replace this piece of fuel line. You see, it has a pinhole leak here."

Rashid took the line and found the hole. Rolling the tubing between his fingers, he said, "Yes, I have this type of tubing. Please wait and I will check."

Isabel watched as Rashid disappeared down one of the parts corridors, then stepping around the end of the service counter, she followed him. He was busy pulling a like amount of tubing off a large wooden spool when she found him.

"I wanted to tell you that I need two pieces of the tubing."

"That will be no problem," he said, pulling a second piece from the spool. "Do you wish them cut equally?"

"Yes."

Picking up the razor knife attached to a chain, Rashid cut the lines from the spool. Isabel watched as he coiled the two pieces and taped each to keep it from uncoiling.

She wondered if he planned to ask her about the FC. He had to be wondering if she was going to say anything that would allow him to acknowledge her association with the coalition.

"Is there something else I can help you with?"

Isabel glanced about the stockroom again, but saw no one. "No. This will be all," she answered.

"Praise Allah for you!" he said, retracing his steps through the parts aisle. "No one else has come here today to buy. They all run from the bomb!" he moaned, throwing up his arms.

"They are foolish," she said, following him closely.

Suddenly, withdrawing a dagger from her jacket, Isabel plunged it into Rashid's back, puncturing his lung before it entered his heart.

The aging Arab collapsed immediately. Isabel stood over him for several moments before withdrawing the weapon and wiping his blood from it. Rashid lay on his side, his eyes opened wide, barely alive, as blood rushed from the corner of his mouth. He would be dead in minutes from internal hemorrhaging. Satisfied that his death was certain, Isabel dropped the bloody rag she'd taken from his workbench, stepped around his body and made her way to the front of the store. Grasping her helmet, she pulled it over her head and left the building.

Outside, Isabel paused at her bike and put the small package Rashid had given her in the luggage bag. She noticed the two men in the car across the street watching her. Did they suspect her? Was Rashid under surveillance? Had he known?

Knowing she was being watched, Isabel took her time starting the bike before casually putting it in gear. She chose an exit that kept her behind other cars and hidden from view of the car across the street for most of the way. Reaching the exit, she glanced over at the sedan. The two men had gone back to reading their newspapers. Relieved that she'd not been detected, Isabel engaged the clutch and merged her bike into the heavy traffic.

Agent Johnson crushed out his cigarette in the ashtray and stared across the street at the auto parts store. His partner still had his head buried in the morning paper.

"Joe, who do you suppose that biker was who just left?"

"Damned if I know, but we both agreed he didn't look suspicious, right?"

"Yeah, but you know what bothers me about that guy?"

"No, what?" Joe answered, irritated by the interruption.

"He never took off his helmet or gloves," Johnson said.

"So?"

"Well, it's got to be hot as hell under that helmet."

Joe dropped the paper on the seat between them. "What's your point, Al? Do you want to check on Rashid or what?"

"Well, I just think it's kind of strange that the biker didn't take off his helmet and leave it on the bike like every other biker does. That's all."

                                    *   *   *

McGarth peered through the protective smoke-colored glass of the presidential limousine as it made its way down Fourteenth Street sandwiched between an armed convoy of troops. Forest had insisted upon the security. Mason couldn't help but notice the empty streets and sidewalks. Policemen and troops outnumbered visitors. Traffic seemed light, despite his convoy's slow pace.

Mason wondered if Lindsey was right. Suppose Jabarri and his terrorists did mean to take him hostage in exchange for removing the bomb. The thought made sense. The choice would not be his. Either way, the outcome would be terribly humiliating to the government — having to give up its president to save its people and its Capital. The idea bothered him.

Security around National Airport was extremely heavy and visible as his limousine pulled to a halt at the military perimeter surrounding the Boeing 767. Reza Jabarri stood beside his own limo just inside the ring waiting for the president.

"Sir, Security wants to know if you intend to comply with Mr. Jabarri's demand that you travel the remainder of the way with him?" the president's chauffeur asked.

"Yes. I see no difficulty in doing that," McGarth answered.

A moment later, the president emerged from the car. Every soldier instinctively snapped to attention as he walked the last hundred feet unescorted and without protection.

"It is good to meet with you again, Mr. President," Reza said. McGarth nodded, allowing Jabarri to assume the best.

"We will ride together to the aircraft, yes?" Again, the president nodded as he opened the car door for himself. Reza was amused by the president's silence, and took it as a sign of acquiescence.

Neither man spoke during the short ride out to the Boeing 767. McGarth used the time to mentally prepare himself for the unexpected.

Jabarri seemed content to bask in his heightened role of importance. As they approached the wide-bodied jet, McGarth noticed a lone figure standing to the left of the limousine's path. He wondered if that was Bud Waterman, the *Examiner* reporter. He tried to recall if he'd ever met him, but decided he hadn't. It would be left to the exclusive domain of this relatively unknown reporter to interpret the actions of the president of the United States in dealing with what was to become the most famous hostage negotiation ever recorded. McGarth thought it ironic that none of his PR staff had ever had any direct dealing with Waterman, except to review his taped interview with Jabarri. He thought Bud had handled the situation well, considering the circumstances. McGarth hoped he would do as well now.

"Mr. President, you will please wait here. I will send the women and children down to you, shortly," Reza ordered. McGarth answered with a nod as he watched Jabarri climb the stairs to the jumbo jet and disappear into the cabin. Being left alone at the bottom of the stairs felt awkward. Then he noticed Waterman walking toward him, his video camera recording light flashing. Drawing closer, Waterman switched off the camera.

"Sorry, Mr. President. I had to run the camera in order to get up to you, sir. His orders, you understand."

"Yes, perfectly. He's had my undivided attention since he landed," McGarth replied sarcastically.

"Sir, my associate, Jill Simmons, will take this tape to the White House for editing before I release it to the media."

"That would be very helpful, Mr. Waterman. Thank you for the consideration."

"Mr. President?" called a voice. The president and Waterman looked up to see Jabarri in the doorway beside a young woman and her baby. Bud switched on his camera as McGarth answered. "Yes, Mr. Jabarri."

"Sir, the Fundamentalist Coalition return the women and children of Flight 899 to you as a show of good faith and of our willingness to resolve our differences in a peaceful manner."

McGarth fought back the rage building inside him and managed a conciliatory reply. "The people of the United States appreciate the FC's gesture of goodwill. Thank you."

Seeing the young woman falter as Jabarri released her arm, Mason climbed the steps and took her child. "Take my arm," he whispered, as they started down the stairs. Waterman stayed at the bottom and recorded the release. He smiled at the president's eloquence. Tears rolled down the cheeks of the young mother as she clung to McGarth's arm, happy to be alive.

An airport shuttle waited near the mobile steps as the trio reached the ground. The president escorted her to the bus. He waited for her to enter, then followed with her child. As he laid the infant in her arms, he said, "I'm sorry you and your child have had to endure this horror. God bless you both." Cradling her child, the young woman gave him a grateful smile, "Thank you, Mr. President." Waterman stepped aside as McGarth emerged from the bus and walked back toward the stairs.

Jabarri was standing at the top of the steps with another young woman and her toddler. McGarth didn't wait for Jabarri to speak, but called out thank you again and climbed the stairs for a second time. Jabarri seemed pleased with his message and motioned him to take the second hostage.

Waterman continued to film the release as the terrorist brought women and children to the jet's doorway and the president escorted them to the bus. Bud found the whole scene bizarre. What message was Reza trying to convey? Bud asked himself. Didn't he understand this kind of PR enhanced the president's image in the eyes of his people? Did he actually believe that freeing these woman and children would excuse the terrorists' actions against America?

"Mr. President, I give you your final hostage," Jabarri called out.

Tired from the exercise and out of breath from climbing the steps, the president nodded as he reached the top. "Our nation thanks you," he uttered, taking the arm of the elderly lady and gently helping her down the steep stairs. The old woman was quite feeble and seemed unsure of her footing.

"Don't you worry about me, Mr. President," she said. "You go see about getting the others released. I'll be all right." Mason smiled, but held onto her as they made their way across the ramp to the bus.

"You may leave now. She is the last they plan to let go."

The driver nodded as McGarth stepped back. Knowing the hard part of the president's ordeal was still ahead, the driver gave him a thumbs-up and whispered, "Good luck, Mr. President."

"Thanks. We can all use a bit of luck right now!" called McGarth as the bus pulled away.

23

BEACH PLANS

The warm, moist breeze blowing off Currituck Sound felt refreshing to Wes. The wind chimes fluttered at the end of the porch. Their gentle, unending sound gave rhythm to the sun's rays that danced on the ever-changing prism of water. A small flotilla of racing-class sailboats, their white sheets aligned, dotted the horizon. They seemed to move in unison. Looking up, Wes saw purple martins patrolling the skies in pairs searching for insects, while an osprey repeated the circuitous trip to the ocean for fish to feed its young.

By outward appearances, life in Duck seemed untouched by the crisis to the north. Even vacationers, here for their one-week retreat from life's troubles, moved about as though they were not affected by the trauma in Washington.

Recalling his mother's wisdom about appearances being deceiving, Wes decided her observation was particularly appropriate now. Things were not as they seemed. Only nature moved in her preordained manner, unfettered by the terrorist attack. Wes knew without being told that people here, as in every other part of the nation, were beset with anxiety, fear, and confusion. Wes gazed at the bright, noonday sky from behind his sunglasses, still pondering the course that the terrorist situation would take. It was never completely out of his mind.

"Want to go for a walk on the beach, Dad?" Walker asked.

Wes smiled. "Yeah, give me a minute, and I'll be right with you."

Rolling out of the hammock, Wes thought about his son and their special relationship. Walker was there for him now.

Climbing the stairs to the main living quarters, Wes felt much stronger. The short nap had done him good.

"Walker and I are going down to the beach, honey."

"It will do you both good," Meredith said.

The two, father and son, struck out for the beach. Neither had any interest in sunbathing or swimming. Both understood that the reason for their trip to the beach was to be alone — to talk out the substantive issues confronting Wes.

"So how bad is the threat?" Walker asked.

"I can't imagine its being much worse."

"How's that?"

"Well, in addition to what you've heard from the media, the weapon was apparently armed during the deceleration phase of the landing and is programmed to detonate after a predetermined amount of time, unless the terrorists disarm it beforehand."

"That's clever, don't you think?"

"Yeah. But there's more to it. They also have the capability to override the timer and detonate the bomb by remote control."

"Damn! They've really got their act together."

"I'm afraid so," Wes said, "And the worst part is we don't even know how much time we've got before that bomb goes off. Nor can we trust them to disarm it before it does, even if the president complies with all of their demands."

"They've thought of nearly everything, haven't they?"

"Yes, thanks to me."

"Don't lay all the blame on yourself. Anyone in your situation would have done the same thing, especially when the guys tell you they've got your daughter."

Wes knew Walker was right. But trying to forget the mistake he'd made was easier said than done.

"How can they disarm the weapon?" Walker asked.

"We're not sure. We think they can do it by remote control, probably by using a code transmitter of some sort — like a car or garage-door opener."

"That makes sense. With the bomb sealed in the cargo bay, I wouldn't think it would be too easy to get at otherwise."

Reaching the top of the embankment, both men stopped to gaze at the ocean. No matter how many times Wes saw it, he still felt a certain excitement at seeing the Atlantic, as if it were his first time. Today was no exception. The ocean was timeless, the origin of life, the largest entity on the face of the Earth, exhibiting all the forces known to man. It was more than worthy of his awe.

Glancing at Walker, Wes recalled the many hours they'd spent together sailing the Laser. He longed for those days. But like the weather, Walker's interests had changed. Now it was golf, tennis and swimming.

"Tide's out," Walker said, dropping the cooler on the sand.

"Yeah. And that sand bar is larger than I realized," added Wes, digging his feet into the sand. The space around them was vacant. It was a good place to talk.

"So what does the president have in mind for you?"

"Do you remember the Beirut hijacking I told you about that happened nearly ten years ago? The one I was involved in?"

"You mean the one where you helped plan and train the SEAL team to rescue the hostages?"

"Yes. The president's national security adviser, Gaylord Elliot, seems to think that somewhere down the line the president will have to order an assault on the jet. He and the president want me to help plan the attack."

"And that's what tonight's meeting in Norfolk is about?"

"Yes. I'm to meet with the commander of a SEAL team and some of their special operations planners. Hopefully, we'll be able to come up with a way of seizing that nuke."

Walker stared out to sea as Wes burrowed his feet deeper into the wet sand. A chilly breeze blew off the ocean, absorbing the sun's intense heat. Wes lifted his baseball cap and wiped the sweat from his forehead. Walker glanced up as a string of pelicans flew low over the beach. He watched them pass.

"As I see the problem, you need a way to block the radio signal from their remote transmitter," Walker said. "If you could do that for a short while, the SEALS could overpower the terrorists and free the hostages. Then the 767 could be ditched in the Atlantic."

"That's the crux of the problem isn't it, blocking that radio signal?"

"I think so," Walker said.

Wes was silent. Walker was right. If the signal were blocked, he could easily fly the nuke into the ocean.

"Jammers do exist. British Vulcan bombers used frequency jammers against our Phantoms during practice intercepts over the North Sea. The Soviet's war strategy placed heavy emphasis on barrage jammers. Electronic counter measures, ECM as it's called now, has been a major player in all our tactical and strategic planning for a long time. But I'm not certain the Air Force or Navy have any equipment capable of jamming that part of the frequency spectrum. And then there's the critical problem of getting it close enough to the jet for an extended period without being discovered," Wes explained.

Walker looked back toward the sea, but didn't say anything. He was watching the pelicans again as they skimmed the waters just off-shore. Wes joined the silence, content to think.

"I may know a way," Walker said.

"A way to do what?"

"To block the radio signal."

"How? We don't have a hell of a lot of time."

"I know, but the technology already exists."

Wes gave his son a puzzled look. Had Walker stumbled onto something? It'd happened before. Although Walker had no obvious interest in becoming an engineer, Wes had noticed long ago his aptitude for science. He'd often wondered why his son had not pursued a career in physics. Walker was a natural.

"With what?" Wes asked.

"Remember five years ago when the Navy tried to conduct tests of its fleet communications security in the event of a nuclear strike?"

"Vaguely. Why?"

"You should. You were president of the homeowner's association then. Don't you recall writing a letter to protest conducting those tests here?"

"Yeah, the Navy had a large generator on a barge. They wanted to use it to transmit electrical energy into the atmosphere near ships to simulate the phenomenon of EMP."

"That's it! EMP," Walker cried.

"Electro-magnetic pulsing," Wes added.

Neither spoke as they sat in the sand, pondering Walker's revelation.

"Isn't that what you're facing now?" Walker asked.

"Perhaps. But there's the question of frequency. Military units rely primarily on UHF. I wouldn't have the slightest idea if that EMP generator would cover the entire frequency spectrum or whether it could be modified to do so. Besides, if memory serves me correctly, that generator sends out pulses, rather than continuous energy. Then there's the question of determining the frequency band of the remote control device. I don't know," Wes, said, skeptically.

"If it were designed to simulate energy patterns associated with an atomic blast, I would think it might cover a fairly large part of the spectrum, wouldn't you?" Walker probed.

"I guess it would. Yes....it would have to, to do any good."

"Then the Pentagon should look into whether that barge is still around and whether it could do the situation any good."

Wes stirred his feet in the sand as he thought about Walker's idea. It might work if the remote transmitter's frequency could be determined. Perhaps the generator could be modified to work as a barrage jammer, blanketing all the frequencies. The idea was intriguing. But more importantly, it offered an approach that didn't require bombing the jet.

"Your suggestion makes a hell of lot of sense, son. I'll give Elliot a call as soon as we get back to the house. He may want to have DOD consider your suggestion."

"Then let's go, so you can make that call," Walker said, as he watched the pelicans in close trail skim the water once more.

Hiking back to the cottage, Wes and Walker discussed how to neutralize the terrorist's remote control transmitter. Wes wasn't sure the EMP generator could be modified. Walker was positive it could be done.

"With all the electronic gear available at the Norfolk Navy bases and the Newport News Ship Building docks, that generator could be modified to jam any frequency," Walker said.

"You're probably right, but do they have the necessary manpower to get it done in time?"

"They'd have the time if they made the modifications while the barge was under way, don't you think?"

"Perhaps."

Walker nodded and continued thinking out loud. "The way I see it, the generator would have to jam the entire remote control spectrum to be absolutely certain of jamming their transmitter.

A frown crossed Wes's face as he spoke. "How can you be so certain that the remote control device was designed to conform to the FCC requirements?"

"Think about it, Dad. You told me both of those terrorists passed through security at Geneva, right?"

"Yes. Why?"

"Well, don't you see? They had to have had the remote transmitters with them during the flight. You told me that at one stage, Ahmed threatened to detonate the bomb if you didn't comply with his instructions."

"Yes, but he could have been bluffing."

"That would have meant he would have been bluffing the president, too. And my guess is that would have been too much of a gamble to risk that early in the game."

Wes thought for a minute. "So if they had the transmitter on board, how did they get it through security?"

"Actually, I think it might have been fairly simple, if you assume they appeared to be well-dressed businessmen."

"Why do you say that?"

"There arc at least two remote control devices I can think of that could meet their needs and at the same time wouldn't raise any suspicion with security — a garage door opener and a car door opener. Both of those could be legitimately carried in their attaché cases without drawing attention, as long as they hadn't been tampered with."

"You have a point," Wes said. "And each usually uses a digital code that can easily be programmed to whatever code is required once that has been determined."

"Exactly!"

"That scenario makes a lot of sense," Wes said.

Walker continued. "Suppose airport security had been concerned about the transmitters. They would have asked you to carry the device in the cockpit, right?"

"Yes."

"And you would have done it too, correct?"

"Of course," Wes said. "We do that sort of thing a lot."

"And then Ahmed would have had access to it, as well."

"Yeah. He would have!"

"Another reason for assuming the terrorists are using U.S.-made equipment is that it can be easily replaced here if theirs becomes damaged or is misplaced," Walker suggested.

"Your hypothesis is awfully convincing. Its genius lies in its simplicity. I wonder if the security people would recall seeing such a device on either of those two Arabs."

"Photos of remote control units might trigger their memories," Walker added, as they climbed the cottage stairs.

Meredith was waiting for them on the porch. "I wondered if you two had decided to spend the rest of the day on the beach. Can we talk?"

"Sure, but first let me find my old homeowner's file."

"What on Earth do you want with that old folder?"

"Walker's come up with an idea for neutralizing the terrorist's control of that nuke. A description of the equipment he suggested using is in there."

Meredith looked confused "Try the bottom drawer of your nightstand."

The homeowner's file was where Meredith said it was. The large, brown envelope Wes was looking for lay on the bottom. Leafing through the contents, he found a historical account of the EMPRESS project and began to read:

EMP or electromagnetic energy given off as part of a nuclear blast has long concerned the Department of Defense. Known by scientists as the "Compton electron effect," EMP poses a serious threat to the survivability of critical electronic equipment necessary to continue a nuclear war.

Depending on the distance, size, and height of burst of a nuclear weapon, EMP can cripple all but the most hardened communications systems and electrical grids. Radios, TVs, faxes, telephones, satellites, missile guidance computers, and major power distribution centers are all extremely vulnerable to the electron pulse effect. EMP literally has the potential to render much of the U.S.'s communications, command and control (C3) useless in time of war. Noted physicists have determined that a nuclear detonation in the vicinity of Kansas above the Earth's atmosphere could affect every contiguous state within the United States.

Military strategists have long known of the phenomenon of EMP, but didn't really address the problem until much later. Finally, in the late sixties and early seventies DOD began to seriously examine the possible effects of EMP on their ships, planes, missiles, and support equipment.

As part of this research, the Navy commissioned a ship, the EMPRESS I, to test the ability of its ships and electronics equipment to withstand the effects of EMP. The EMPRESS I, stationed near Patuxent Naval Air Station, provided the initial simulation of EMP. Naval ships were brought in close proximity to the EMPRESS and bombarded with massive pulses of electron volts to test their hardness against the effects of EMP.

The EMPRESS I, by all reports, seemed to do a good job. However, because of the presence of a small bridge blocking critical access, the Navy's larger cruisers and carriers were precluded from reaching it.

Its sister ship, the EMPRESS II, was not really a ship, but a barge on which two powerful diesel electron generators and a gigantic antenna array were mounted. Capable of emitting pulses up to seven million volts for a billionth of a second, the EMPRESS II experienced the wrath of a multitude of interest groups from its inception.

Fisherman fretted over its possible impact on fishing, while conservationists and environmentalist groups fought its development at every stage, mostly in the courts and newspapers. Unsubstantiated claims were made by each group seeking to drive the testing from their areas of interest. Congressmen, pressured by their constituents' fears, championed their causes and sought legislative remedies, often using their considerable influence with DOD.

The EMPRESS II was driven first from the Chesapeake Bay, then from the shores of the Outer Banks and even from the Gulf of Mexico. The courts finally settled the issue and allowed the Navy to resume testing in the Atlantic offshore from the Outer Banks of North Carolina.

Extensive offshore testing proved that the Navy's fighting ships were capable of withstanding the effects of EMP on their communications and fire control systems. At the conclusion of the tests, the EMPRESS II was berthed in the York River. Some years later, while under the tow of two commercial tugs, the ill-fated EMPRESS II managed to incur the wrath of its citizentry a final time by inadvertently striking the Coleman Bridge at Yorktown, Virginia, stopping all traffic. As a result, motorists were forced to take an extensive detour in order to cross the York.

No doubt, Walker had remembered the EMPRESS colliding with the Coleman Bridge, Wes thought, as he stared out at the Currituck Sound from atop a bar stool in his kitchen. The KL-43 device lay on the counter.

"Colonel? This is Gaylord Elliot. What's on your mind?"

"Sir, my son, Walker, and I have come up with a plan that would allow us to neutralize Jabarri's use of his remote control device and take control of the plane."

"Let's hear it."

"We suggest modifying the Navy's EMP test barge, the EMPRESS II, so it can jam the remote control frequency spectrum assigned to remote control devices the terrorists have said they have. Walker thinks the terrorists are relying on fairly common remote control systems, like an automatic garage opener or car door opener to provide them the option of instantly detonating the weapon."

"What makes him think that's the case, Wes? Not that he's wrong, but that's a big assumption, don't you think?"

"I thought so too, at first. But, the more I thought about it, the more I had to agree with him. He says they needed something that wouldn't draw attention from airport security, as well as a device they could replace here easily, if it were taken from them. Something that simple would allow them to get as many remote control (RC) units as needed without arousing suspicion."

"I don't know too much about those things, Wes. Are remote control units programmable?"

"Yes. Most units have a numerical code that can be programmed into the receiver and transmitter."

"So the terrorists could have installed a remote control receiver on the bomb and set a code that would initiate the detonation process if the matching code were received from one of these remote control transmitters?"

"Exactly."

"It makes sense, Colonel. I'll alert the joint task force en route to Cyprus to pay particular attention to anything that might suggest the use of a remote control device. Now tell me more about the EMPRESS II and how we would use it."

"Walker thinks we should modify the EMP generator to emit electronic barrage jamming over the entire RC frequency band, which he says is usually between seventy-two to seventy-six megahertz. We found the frequencies by checking several of our own RC units. They were all in that range.

"Modifications to the generator would be made while under tow to a point in the Potomac just south of National Airport. Jamming the RC band would coincide with an assault launched from the river by the SEALS. All nearby microwave transmitters would be shut down temporarily to preclude the possibility of their being able to detonate the device by telephone. A pre-dawn attack would give the terrorists little time to react and would minimize casualties. As the hostages deplaned, an aircraft ground servicing truck would pump enough fuel into the tanks to allow the jet to be flown to a predetermined point in the Atlantic before crashing."

Gaylord was silent. Did Elliot doubt the plan would work? Or was it too far-fetched to even consider?

"And you would fly the 767 out of National?"

"Yes, sir. I am the most qualified to do it. Besides, isn't that what you and the president had in mind when you told the secretary of defense to activate me, sir?"

"It has crossed our minds that, at some point, the bomb might have to be flown out," he answered. "And, the president did suggest that you might want the chance to do it."

"He's correct, sir."

"You're willing to make the flight, knowing you'll die?"

"Actually, I hadn't planned on staying with the jet unless it became absolutely necessary."

"I don't understand, Colonel," Gaylord replied.

"Sir, I'd make use of the 767's three autopilots and program its two flight management computers to automatically fly the final stage of the profile. If the mission went as designed, I would bail out of the jet about fifty miles short of its impact point and would hopefully be rescued by the Navy within the remaining twelve to fifteen minutes before the weapon detonates."

"And you're certain this can be done with the 767?"

"Yes, sir. By using the lateral and vertical navigation modes together, the jet can be made to automatically fly to a pre-determined descent point and land or, in this case, crash. My backup scenario would call for F-14 Tomcats to escort the jet into the ocean and, from a stand-off position, shoot down the aircraft, if that became necessary."

"Do you think the bomb will explode on impact, Wes?"

"I think the chances are fifty-fifty, depending on whether it's programmed for impact detonation as well. DOD's special weapons people would have a better handle on that question. I think we have to honor that option until we find out otherwise."

"I think the plan has possibilities, Wes. But first, I want to speak with the secretary of defense and General Griffith about it. I'll be in touch with you shortly."

24

PAWNS

Yes, I do understand what you're trying to say and I'm doing my best to gain your release, but you must realize this is a very tenuous situation we're in.... I just can't promise you anything at the moment," the president said.

Sybil, the flight service manager, watched as McGarth tried desperately to console the elderly man with the trembling voice. She knew firsthand the helplessness he was experiencing. Seeing the president being forced to meet with each passenger and acknowledge his inability to free them angered Sybil. More than once, Sybil had told herself that, had she the means, she would gladly kill Jabarri. Yet such feelings would only make matters worst. She was amazed that the president could handle the enormous pressure of the crisis and not buckle. She prayed for him. It was all Sybil could do.

"Mr. President, please,... please give them whatever they want to let us go. I can't stand this much longer... the blanket over my head is smothering me. This is the only time they have allowed me to remove it. I can't sleep. Please get me out of here...I beg you!" the middle-aged sales rep cried out.

Knowing there was little he could say that would alleviate the man's fear, Mason gripped the man's hand firmly. "You and I will make it through this. Bear with me." As McGarth withdrew his hand, the sales rep nodded and slumped back in his seat, convinced of the president's pledge.

Approaching the business class from the rear with the president,

Sybil worried that the passenger in 8-8 might become violent again. Turning around, she leaned toward the president and whispered, "Mr. Luchinno, the gentleman in row eight, seat eight is very excitable, Mr. President. He's apt to become physical, sir." McGarth nodded and made a mental note of the situation before pausing to speak with a gentleman whimpering in seat 9-8. Then it happened. Luchinno bolted from his seat.

"It's all your goddamned fault that we're going to die here in this flying coffin! You and your Jewish friends are responsible for this! You don't give a damn about the rest of us! You ought to be made to die here with us!" he shouted wildly. Mason ducked as the man swung at him and then collapsed on the floor, struck on the back of the head by one of Jabarri's men. "You didn't have to do that," the president complained, angered by the terrorist's viciousness. "He wouldn't have hurt me."

"He did so on my orders, Mr. President," said Reza. "Your own Secret Service would have done the same. Do not be offended by our desire to assure your safety, Mr. President."

McGarth paid no attention to Reza's comment. He was concerned for Luchinno, who was still unconscious. "Miss DeVires, will you give me a hand?" McGarth asked. "Let's get him back to his seat." Sybil nodded and took the man's arms as the president lifted him into his seat.

Out of the corner of her eye, Sybil had seen Waterman film the scene from over Reza's shoulder. She hoped he'd captured the assault. If so, Jabarri's little PR act would be a colossal failure.

As McGarth ended his visit with the hostages, Jabarri said, "Mr. President, I'm certain your countrymen appreciate your taking time out from your busy schedule to come and visit them here. I trust you have a clearer understanding of their plight. I hope you will keep their welfare in mind as you seek to meet our demands."

Still seething from the assault on Mr. Luchinno, McGarth labored to maintain his self-control. "I can assure you that I will."

"Good, then let me escort you to my limousine, Mr. President. We both have much to do."

Jabarri stopped as he reached the limo. McGarth saw the fire in Reza's calculating eyes and knew he had more to say. "Mr. President, do not be deceived by my cordial manner or by the protocol I observe in my relationship with you and your government. We are very much at war with one another, albeit a *jihad* or holy war as you would say. Were it my decision alone, your government and all of Washington would already lie in ruins. But that is not the case. It is left to others to decide your fate. The terms I outlined to you yesterday still stand. Thus far, it would appear from the media reports that you have wisely chosen to abide by them. Should you continue on that course, in due time, you and your government will have the weapon removed from your shores. Until then, may I remind you that any delay in carrying out our demands will be judged accordingly, and you should expect that the FC will carry out its edict — the total destruction of Washington. Have a pleasant day, Mr. President."

* * *

Agent Johnson turned on the ignition of the Bureau's sedan and drove out of the parking lot. He was tired of wondering about the status of their suspect, Rashid. It was time to find out.

"Al, I don't know why you're so concerned about this guy. He hasn't had but one customer since we arrived."

"Yeah, I know, Joe, but I'd feel a hell of a lot better knowing he's in there and okay. Besides, we've been sitting in this old bucket too long. I've got to get out and stretch my legs," Al argued. Joe shook his head. "Have it your way."

Al wheeled the four-door cruiser through the burger joint and out onto the highway. Joe kept his eyes on the auto parts store as Al eased into a parking spot next door.

"It won't take but a minute."

"And who are you going to be this time?" Joe asked in jest.

"I don't know. I'll tell you when I come back."

"Whatever," Joe moaned, annoyed by his partner's paranoia.

Joe watched as Al got out of the car and walked over to the auto parts store. A moment later, he saw him disappear into the small shop. Bored, he turned on the radio to get the latest news on the terrorist threat. He didn't have to move the dial far. There was nothing else to listen to.

"Joe. We got a real problem. Come here!" Al hollered from the doorway. Rolling out of the sedan on the run, Joe burst through the store's doorway.

"Take your time," Al said. "Our man, Rashid, isn't going anywhere. He's out to lunch for good."

"Damn! It was that biker," Joe snapped, staring at the man lying in a pool of blood. This guy is obviously a professional."

"Terrorists usually are, you asshole!" Al replied, pissed that he'd let Joe talk him out of following his hunches.

* * *

"Gaylord, Sinclair's on the phone for you," Forest said. "He says it's urgent."

Picking up the receiver, Elliot switched on the speaker as the FBI director began his explanation of Rashid's murder.

"... I don't know what to make of the hit unless there's a third echelon at work here. I don't have a clue who that might be, do either of you?" Sinclair asked.

"No, John. We'll have to kick that one around awhile. Have you talked to Burt about this yet?"

"Yes. He's as much in the dark as we are. He suspects it might have something to do with a disagreement among the coalition members, whoever they are."

"That would be my thought," Forest interjected.

"How close are we to nailing down the identity of the coalition members, John?" Elliot asked.

"We're nowhere near finding hard evidence. We're hopeful the task force can find something tangible amid the rubble of the FC headquarters building in Geneva. The team's been working non-stop since it arrived. Burt and I expect a preliminary report by five this afternoon. We should have something for you by the time you convene the NSC meeting. It's still on for seven, isn't it?"

"Yes, we're still shooting for it then, unless the president changes his mind," Elliot said.

"Good, then I'll see you at seven. I want to stay on top of this assassination thing. Reza's still expecting a call from Rashid to bring him up-to-date on the status of the two Middleburg terrorists. I don't know how long it will take him to figure out they're not around any longer. When that happens, he'll think we're responsible. You best discuss that contingency with the president, in case he gets blind-sided by Jabarri." I'll be in my office if you need me."

"See you at seven, John."

* * *

Emerson Beamer's nose burned from the smell of water-soaked charred wood. For the last forty-five minutes he and the joint task force had been sifting through the rubble that had been the coalition's main headquarters in Geneva. Nothing of consequence had been found, although damage to some areas of the office was less extensive than others.

"Mr. Beamer, can you come here for a minute? I think I may have found something!" called the FBI's most seasoned forensics technician. "Yeah, but you'll have to wait until I can climb through this mess in front of me," Beamer replied, plowing through the debris with his beer belly and powerful arms working in tandem. Eli Cochran watched as the FBI inspector charged through fallen beams and ceiling tiles. "Look out for those wires in front of you!" he called out.

"Thanks. I damn near got myself tied up in them," Emerson puffed, as he joined Cochran.

"What have you got?"

"Look right here," Eli said. "Do you see that thin red edge barely protruding from under that drawer?"

Brushing his mane of graying hair from his horn-rimmed glasses, Emerson leaned over, straining to see what the specialist was talking about. "Yeah, you mean the red thing about three inches long?" he asked.

"That's it! If I'm right, it's a diskette," Eli said.

Beamer was excited. "Can you get it?"

"I think so, if you'll give me a hand and hold the drawer while I ease it out."

Emerson held the large, wooden drawer as Cochran fished a piece of wire he'd found on the floor around the back of the plastic diskette. Then he took both ends of the wire and tugged. The diskette broke free.

"I got it and it looks undamaged," Eli said. Beamer tossed the heavy drawer over to the side. "Let me see what you've found," he said, eager to see it for himself.

Cochran examined the diskette carefully for markings, but found none. "Better take a closer look at that desk," Beamer said. "We may be able to figure out who might've used it or what it might've been used for." Nodding, Eli pried open the other drawer. "This desk must have been used by a woman," he said. "There's a tube of lipstick here. With any luck there will be prints," he added.

Beamer still had his mind on the diskette. "I need to get this diskette over to the embassy and have Casales decipher it," Beamer said.

"Here, I've lifted the prints," Eli said. "My guess is they'll match those on the lipstick." Beamer took the diskette and the lipstick and slipped each into a plastic bag and put them in his pocket. "I'll meet you at the hotel, Eli." Nodding, Cochran said, "I'll finish up here."

Working his way back through the rubble, Beamer thought about what Cochran had said. He recalled that the preliminary report from the Geneva police had indicated the coalition had a female receptionist.

At the U.S. Embassy, Emerson took the diskette to the senior computer technician and asked her to decipher it while he phoned Washington. Twenty minutes later, Ginger Casales had its files on the screen. She was surprised to find that it was a backup disk for a financial spreadsheet.

At first, the numbers made little sense. But scanning the data, Ginger realized she was looking at bank accounts or investment account entries. The headings of each of the four vertical columns appeared to contain a specific account number, while the horizontal rows along the screen's left side seemed to correlate with specific transactions. The dates were all recent. On the second page, she found that the four account balances had been merged into one. The amounts were numerically staggering, but the absence of a currency denomination precluded her determining their actual values. She suspected Swiss francs. Looking at the initial page once more, Ginger noticed the account numbers were entirely different, as though they were unrelated. On the last screen page, she learned why.

The four accounts corresponded to four separate Arab banks in Geneva. The name of each was listed adjacent to its assigned number, along with a name.

After copying the data to her hard drive, Ginger made copies of the diskette. She knew from what she'd seen, that Beamer's task force had found a record of the FC's funding. With luck, they could track its origin. Emerson was talking on the secure phone to Washington when Ginger found him.

"What's on the disk?" Emerson asked, cupping the phone.

"Plenty!" Ginger answered. "We've found their sources of funding, I think, though there are some accounts that don't quite make sense. They appear to be records of investment transactions. Each account is referenced to an Arab bank here in Geneva."

A giant smile blanketed Emerson's face as he resumed talking with Director Sinclair, relaying Ginger's discovery before hanging up.

"Sinclair wants the contents of that diskette transmitted via satellite to him and the CIA director immediately. He'll brief the NSC staff on the situation within the hour. He's virtually certain the treasury department will have no trouble deciphering the data further."

"I'll get it to them right away, Mr. Beamer," Ginger said.

*   *   *

Isabel mopped the sweat from her face with her sleeve. Her clothes were like a sponge, soaking up whatever moisture her body didn't slough off. The humid air was stifling, made worse by the absence of a breeze. She leaned against a maple tree and waited. A privet hedge between her and the building she was watching provided her cover, shielding her while leaving an opening sufficient for her to monitor the activity. Her motorbike was parked amid a clump of forsythia in preparation for a rapid departure. An Ingram M-11 submachine gun fitted with a suppressor and a thirty-two round loaded clip rested against the tree.

Isabel didn't relish the idea of killing another Arab brother, but those were her orders — orders she would not and could not refuse to obey, no matter how onerous. She was a professional assassin. The decision of who was to be killed was never hers to decide — only the method. She left the reasons to others.

Sitting on the ground beneath the maple's green canopy, Isabel remembered her first trip to the States. As a young, impressionable exchange student about to enter college at Georgetown, she had admired everything she saw in Washington — wealth, money, power, and prestige. Schooled in Baghdad and then in Paris, Isabel had grown accustomed to moving in affluent circles. Her father, an arms broker, was wealthy and had spared no expense in providing her the finest education. His wide and varied contacts with the elite of America's military-industrial complex made her admission to one of the U.S.'s finest universities easy, though hardly necessary. Her propensity for learning was legendary even among her competitors.

America was Iraq's most steadfast ally then. Her father's American friends frequently dined with her in D.C.'s fashionable restaurants, eager to remain in his good graces. It was a time of joy for Isabel. Life seemed to open its doors a little more each day as she pursued her bachelor's degree in physics. American men found her exciting. Strong-willed, yet vivacious, Isabel enjoyed her role in America and dreamed of becoming a U.S. citizen and the wife of a prosperous businessman. She saw the customs of her homeland as an obstacle to her happiness. The Muslim faith seemed too primitive. She resented the subservient way women were treated, though she gave lip service to the mullahs' wishes.

Then came the Gulf War and with it America's hatred of Iraq. It had happened almost overnight. Suddenly, Iraq was the enemy and Iraqis everywhere in America were shunned. The impact on her had been devastating.

Isabel's daydreaming came to a halt as she saw a dark sedan turn the corner and stop in front of the Southland Realty building. She immediately recognized the driver. He was her victim.

Scanning both sides of the street, Isabel checked to see that no one had followed Abdulla El Laben. Having noticed several unmarked patrol cars pass by earlier, she wondered if they were shadowing him, perhaps alerted by Rashid's death. It was a possibility she had to consider.

The street appeared deserted. Raising the submachine gun to her shoulder, Isabel cradled it against a branch of the maple. As Abdulla opened the car door, she aligned the sights on his chest. Tracking his movement, Isabel pivoted the stubby weapon slightly to keep the thoracic portion of his body dead center in her sights.

The burst of shots barely made a sound as they rifled through the suppressor, striking Abdulla in the sternum before exiting his back and carrying with them massive amounts of blood and tissue. A second burst penetrated the back part of his neck, severing his spinal cord as he collapsed. Wanting to make absolutely certain he would die, she fired a final burst into his skull as he lay on the ground. It was a mistake.

Without warning, the hedgerow in front of her whipped violently about as a hail of automatic weapons' fire ripped through the spindly branches. Instinctively, Isabel dived to the ground and rolled toward the clump of forsythia and her motorbike as volley after volley hit closer. Then the firing ceased.

Seconds away from death, Isabel leaped to her feet, switched on the ignition and hopped on the bike. The engine roared to life instantly as gunfire erupted once more. Slamming the bike into first, Isabel spun the throttle wide open as bullets ricocheted off the rocks and trees around her. Crouching in the seat, she clung to the bike as it leaped forward and tore down the grassy knoll toward the street ninety yards below.

Midway down the hill, Isabel felt the unmistakable sting of a bullet as it grazed her left forearm. She was hit. The blow left her arm numb. Screaming at the pain, Isabel jumped the curb and swung the bike to the left. The pattern of gunfire was now less than six feet behind and closing.

With less than fifty feet to go for cover, she glanced ahead. Fear gripped Isabel as she recognized the gray FBI sedan turning into the roadway a hundred yards ahead.

Wrenching down on the hand brakes, Isabel shifted her weight to the inside of the turn and slid the bike into a one hundred eighty degree reversal before accelerating again to full throttle. A dead-end sign caught her eye as she raced back down the street. Bullets from the trailing car whizzed close to her head as Isabel broke left and jerked the bike upward from the pavement into the rear yard of a row house. A narrow entrance gate separated her from the main driveway. Slowing the bike, she struck the gate with the front tire, ripping the latch from its post. The gate flew open, allowing her passage as Isabel gunned the motorbike down the concrete driveway toward freedom.

25

FAREWELL

Lindsey noticed the drawn expression on the president's face as he entered the Oval Office. He knew from the look that his trip to the jet had been painful. He waited for McGarth to speak.

"Well, Forest, Jabarri kept his word. The women and children are free," said the president, tossing his coat aside.

"At least we've got that to be thankful for," Lindsey added.

Reflecting on those still held by the terrorists, McGarth promised himself once more that he would not rest until they were also freed. He understood the cruel game Reza was playing and loathed him for it.

"Sir, Frances has worked out a press release, but needs your okay. She thinks it would help the situation if you were to hold a short press conference soon. The media is clamoring for it."

"What do you think?" Mason asked, wincing from the bursitis in his shoulder.

"I agree, providing you confine the address to a discussion of the hostage release and the steps we've taken to comply with the FC's demands. You might want to direct some attention to the fact that law and order has been restored to the District....and perhaps compliment the units of the Eighty Second Airborne that responded to the crisis..."

"....and maybe tell them we managed it without having to resort to the Continuity of Government provisions of NSDD55," McGarth said sarcastically. Glancing at the time, the president closed his eyes and tried to relax for a few minutes.

Lindsey flinched, recalling NSDD 55 — National Security Decision Directive Five Five — the document granting omnipotent powers to the president and his administration in a national crisis. He knew how onerous McGarth thought those top secret plans were. "Unconstitutional," he'd called them, "the single most dangerous directive ever enacted by the White House — the work of zealots attracted to power and intimidated by the limits of the Constitution — a body of law enacted behind the backs of the electorate without their knowledge or consent."

"Tell Frances I'll do the press conference at five o'clock," McGarth said. "Are we any closer to learning who's backing the coalition?"

"No, but there's a disturbing new development."

"Now what?"

Forest told the president of Rashid Sedki's death.

"And we still don't know what the connection is between these four associates and the terrorists, do we?" McGarth snapped.

"No, we don't, sir."

"I can see why Sinclair is worried. We all have to be if Reza learns of Rashid's death. He's sure to blame us for it."

Forest could see that the news had angered his boss.

"Haven't we been able to get anything positive on these guys from the Israelis? The prime minister promised me we'd have the full cooperation of the Mossad on this."

"I spoke to Burt at Langley an hour ago. He assured me that the Mossad is close to having a positive ID on the two Arabs Captain Beacham's daughters killed. Sinclair had already discussed the matter with him before we talked. I would assume the Mossad has Rashid's name by now, sir."

"Who do Sinclair and Williamson think killed the Arab?"

"Neither is certain, but both suspect a disagreement among the coalition. They hope to have more information at the NSC meeting at seven tonight."

McGarth rose and walked over to the windows behind his desk. He had an uneasy feeling about the implications surrounding Sedki's death. Things were difficult enough without the terrorists fighting among themselves.

"Forest, have Elliot, Sinclair, and Williamson meet me here thirty minutes before the NSC meeting. I want to review, in detail, what they've learned about Sedki's murder.

"Anything else I need to deal with right now, Forest?"

"Sir, Gaylord called a few minutes before you returned from National Airport and wanted to discuss an assault plan. He suggested meeting at six tonight."

"That's fine. I should be finished with the press conference before then," Mason said, yawning as he loosened his tie. Stretching out on the sofa, McGarth shoved a pillow under his head. "Forest, I've got to have a thirty-minute nap. Otherwise, the press will notice the bags under my eyes and swear that I'm buckling under the pressure of this crisis."

"I understand, Mr. President. I'll wake you in plenty of time," Lindsey replied, as he walked to the door.

* * *

Meredith turned away from Wes as she brushed aside a small tear. She didn't want him to see her cry. He needed her strength, not her weakness. She would cry later. "When must you leave?"

"The helicopter is picking me up at six."

"And where will you go from here?"

"To Little Creek. I'm supposed to meet with a Navy SEAL team to plan an assault."

"Do they expect you to participate in the assault?"

Wes hesitated. Meredith's question caught him by surprise. He'd hoped she wouldn't press for details, but he should've known better. Meredith was like that. She had to know everything about everything. It was her way of coping.

"Well, not exactly."

"What do you mean, 'not exactly'?"

"I won't be directly involved in the rescue, but I am expected to fly the jet out once the terrorists are subdued and the hostages are freed."

The expression on Meredith's face changed as she realized what he was trying to say. "The president is depending on me to fly the jet from National into the Atlantic."

Fear replaced her curiosity. "And then?"

"I'll parachute from the 767 before it crashes into the Atlantic. A Navy chopper will be standing by to pick me up, and..."

Meredith looked away again. She couldn't control the tears. He pulled her close as she buried her face into his chest. Wes felt her body quiver. He hated telling her, but there was no other way. She deserved to hear it from him.

Wes watched as the wind blew gently across the sound and up the dune toward Meredith and him. Her dark brown hair, lifted by the breeze, brushed his face. It was a time of silence as they both clung to each other, knowing it might well be their last.

For more than thirty years he and Meredith had kept a watchful eye over their children, mindful of the many ways tragedy visits the young. It was years ago, he recalled, that they both had vowed to do whatever was necessary to keep them from harm and he'd kept that vow even now. Caroline was free. And yet a debt remained for that freedom, one that could tear them apart forever. Wes was no longer sorry for the way he had handled the situation. He'd answered a higher calling the only way he knew how, and for that he would not feel ashamed. His daughter was alive. He had seen her with his own eyes.

"It just isn't fair, Wes. Why does it always have to be you?" Meredith cried. "Haven't we been through enough already?"

He couldn't answer her. There was no answer she would accept. He kissed her forehead gently as she withdrew from his embrace. Her eyes glistened in the sunlight, their sparkle heightened by her tears. Wes saw that she was finished crying. He knew that from her sadness would come her strength. She understood what lay ahead for both of them. Meredith would cope, no matter the pain or the outcome. Pride in herself and for her family demanded it.

Pushing her hair from her face, she smiled. "What can I do to help you get ready for your trip?"

"How about a beer and a sandwich?" he said, with a smile.

"I can manage that."

Meredith sensed he was trying to cheer her up. She knew nothing could be done to change things. Wes would do what he had to do and she would wait and pray that he survived. Fate would dictate their future, as it had so often.

* * *

FBI Director John Sinclair laid the preliminary report of Abdulla's assassination on his desk. The death of a second Arab associate of the FC within the last four hours was obviously the work of a third echelon bent on sabotaging the coalition's plans. Unanswered were the questions of what role the dead Arabs were to have played in the terrorists' scheme and who it was that didn't want them to perform their duties. Sinclair was worried. He was certain Jabarri would suspect the U.S. of the assassinations, no matter how strenuously the president denied it. It had occurred to him that this might be what the third echelon hoped to achieve. More important was the question of what Reza's response would be once he learned of the deaths.

Using the captured mobile telephone to monitor the coalition's calls was still the best chance the FBI had of learning their roles. But unless he could capture the assassin quickly and stop the killings, Jabarri might feel compelled to accelerate the FC's schedule of terrorism, or worse, detonate the bomb.

Sinclair didn't relish having to make a second call to the White House, especially since his men had failed again to catch the assassin.

"Sir, Agent Coleman is here."

"Send him in," the FBI director said.

Sinclair looked up from his desk as Dave Coleman entered. Coleman appeared intimidated.

"I suppose you're wondering why I sent for you, Dave?"

Coleman shifted his weight, trying to hide his nervousness. "I expect you want to talk to me about the Middleburg affair. I was way out of line doing what I did, sir."

Sinclair smiled. That explained his apprehension. "Dave, what I want to discuss with you is related to the Middleburg affair, as you call it, but you're not here to be reprimanded. Emerson Beamer and I have already discussed the matter. Although what you did was not in keeping with the Bureau's policy or the law, it has provided us the best source of information on the coalition's activities."

"You mean the mobile telephone, sir?" Coleman asked.

Sinclair nodded and explained: "Yes, and the list of names, addresses, and telephone numbers too. No, the reason I asked you here is to assign you to head the team monitoring the two remaining FC associates. We think they, too, are being stalked by the assassin and are next on his list. You're familiar with their locations. I want you to keep them under surveillance while denying this assassin the opportunity to murder them, if that's possible."

"Do we know why these people are being murdered?"

"No, I wish like hell we did. We have several theories, but nothing concrete. That's why we desperately need to capture this assassin. Questioning him could provide us the information we need. We don't know who is behind the killings, nor do we have any evidence suggesting the nature of their agenda. Our primary concern is the impact the murders will have on Jabarri and the FC's plans. We're doing everything we can to keep the homicides quiet, but that won't last. Too many people are already aware of what has happened to conceal it from them much longer."

"So when do I start?" Dave asked.

"Immediately," Sinclair answered, handing him a large multi-sectioned folder. "Here's the complete file on what we know about the FC. Familiarize yourself with it. The Counter Terrorism Division will give you an update on the current situation. Good luck."

* * *

The bright sunlight moving across the hot afternoon sky found its way into the Crystal City hotel bedroom, waking Ahmed. Checking his watch, he realized he'd been asleep for three hours. Accustomed to hotel living, Ahmed grabbed the TV remote and switched on the news.

Charlene Richards of WBSU was conducting a live interview with Mobile Team Two's Cheryl Larson in Chantilly. News of the unsubstantiated death of the owner of West Auto Parts Shop in Chantilly startled Ahmed. It had to be Rashid, he thought. Seeing the mobile camera zoom in on the small auto parts shop confirmed his worst fears. It was Rashid's place of business.

Larson went on to say that authorities would not release the name of the deceased, pending notification of next of kin, but that witnesses at the scene reported the victim to be of Middle Eastern descent.

Bounding out of the bed, Ahmed took the portable phone out to the balcony and called Jabarri at the aircraft. Hearing Reza's voice, Ahmed shouted in Arabic, "Rashid is dead. He's been killed!"

"Killed? Where did you hear of this?" Jabarri demanded.

"It is on TV, Reza. A reporter is at Rashid's store now. People said the owner was from the Middle East. There is no doubt. Someone wants the bomb to go off, and they know our plan."

Jabarri interrupted. "Impossible! It can not happen that way, Ahmed. We have code backup. We can still stop the detonator. His death changes nothing."

"But, Reza, suppose Jared and Tariq have also been killed. We have not heard from Middleburg. Rashid was to have made contact with them, and now he is dead."

"I suspect the Americans, Ahmed. I'm afraid our brothers may have died because of their mistakes. The American captain's daughter, Caroline, must have led the police to Middleburg, and if they found Jared and Tariq, they may have located Rashid."

"But Reza, if they captured Jared and Tariq, why would they kill Rashid? It does not make sense," Ahmed argued.

"Perhaps Rashid resisted. He would have done it. Rashid would not allow himself to be taken alive. He took the same vow we did."

"What would you have me do, Reza?" Ahmed asked.

"Make certain that our other brothers do not fall into a similar trap. We will have to forgo security precautions for the moment. Call the others and tell them of Rashid's death and of the possibility of Jared's and Tariq's capture. I will talk with Mohammed about alternative measures we must take. Call me when you have spoken to the other three. Do not worry, Ahmed. The plan will survive, even if we perish. I must remind the president that, only through us will Washington be spared."

Minutes after Ahmed's call to Reza ended, FBI technicians, monitoring the captured phone, translated the conversation and faxed a classified transcript to every member of the NSC.

Elliot, Jacobson, and General Griffith were in the White House Situation Room concluding their discussion of Beacham's EMPRESS II proposal when Elliot's secretary interrupted.

"Excuse me, sir, but I thought you should see this report immediately. It's a transcript of a recent phone conversation between Jabarri and Ahmed."

Elliot scanned the memo and handed it to Jacobson.

"Gaylord, this is very disturbing," Jacobson said. "It implies that these Arab associates somehow have control over the code needed to disarm the detonator."

"That's the way I read it," Gaylord said. "What's your assessment, Clayton?"

General Griffith glanced up from rereading the transcript. "I don't think there's much doubt. This conversation pretty much confirms what we learned from the Russian, Andrei's, letter. I think we can assume the bomb was armed on arrival or before landing. It's quite likely that a mechanical timer of some sort was activated upon landing. And from Karpolov's letter, we know an alphanumeric code option exists. I suspect the code option has two functions. I think it gives them the option to bypass the timer and detonate the bomb instantly, or stop the countdown of the timer."

"Assuming your conjecture is accurate, Clayton, what do you see as the roles of the Arab associates?" Jacobson asked.

"My guess is they're involved with handling the code material and providing backup for the coalition in case Jabarri and his terrorists are seized."

"But why would they be involved with the code material, Clayton? Reza claims he can detonate the weapon instantly, if necessary," Elliot questioned. "I don't see where needing them would matter if he has the code."

"I agree. But let's suppose the issue isn't one of concern over exploding the nuke, but one of controlling the decision not to detonate it," the general explained. "Suppose the FC's plan all along has been to threaten the United States, forcing us to accede to their dictates and, in the process, suffer humiliation in the eyes of the world. Then, at the last possible moment, they announce their decision to terminate the timer countdown and remove the weapon, presumably in recognition of our compliance with their edicts. Their political objective would have been achieved without disrupting the world order. And they would still have the weapon, which they could use again."

"I follow your logic, Clayton, but where do the other Arabs fit in? What is their role?"

"They either hold the code material to stop the timer or they decide which course to follow."

"Clayton may be right," Jacobson said. "It could be they constitute a committee with authority to approve such a decision. But we still don't have enough information to really know what their ultimate intent is, Gaylord."

"Of course, you're correct, Chris. But for the sake of argument, suppose these Arabs do make up a committee that decides whether to allow the bomb to explode. Then we assume that one of the coalition members insists on having the bomb detonated, regardless of U.S. compliance. Wouldn't that explain the reason for Rashid's murder?" Elliot suggested.

"It's possible, but he might have been killed by an irate citizen," Jacobson said. "We're only dealing with the death of one of these guys. Even Jabarri said, 'Nothing has changed.'"

"Clayton, I .... Yes, Franklin?" Elliot said, seeing his secretary appear for a second time. The look on his face suggested more bad news.

"Sir, Director Sinclair just called. Abdulla El Laben, one of the other Arabs under surveillance, has also been murdered. He was gunned down as he was getting out of his car."

"By the same gunman?"

"Yes, sir. And, he eluded capture again, but one of our agents is certain he wounded him."

Elliot paused. "Thank you, Franklin."

Secretary Jacobson and General Griffith said nothing until Franklin had left. Elliot's expression was pensive. Each man knew the second death could not be written off as unrelated. There was a connection. A third echelon was definitely at work.

"It looks like my skepticism was unwarranted," Jacobson said. "This second murder doesn't leave much doubt about its being premeditated."

"The question is, who's behind them and why?" Elliot interjected. "If what Clayton suggests is true, we've got very little time to act before the coalition's options run out."

"I hate to imagine what Jabarri's response will be when he finds out about Abdulla's death," Jacobson added. "It's possible he might decide it constitutes enough provocation to justify exploding the device immediately."

Clayton shook his head. "I doubt it. Except for taking the action in anger, there's nothing to be gained by doing it now. The timer will eventually take care of that, anyway. Besides, doing it right away would deprive them of the opportunity to further humiliate us. I don't think he'll believe we have anything to do with it, even though he may accuse us of it. He has to know better."

"Who's most likely behind these attacks?" Elliot asked.

"That's hard to say. There are quite a few who come to mind. I think we have to look real hard at Qadahfi, Saddam Hussein, and the Iranians," Clayton answered. "I could make a strong case for suspecting any one of them, given their hate for the United States," the general explained.

"Then you think we ought to focus on these three?" Elliot asked.

"Yes, and I'd start with Saddam. He has the bigger ax to grind," Clayton suggested.

Elliot frowned. "I suppose we could spend the next hour debating his motives, but unfortunately we don't have the luxury. I promised the president we'd have a preliminary proposal for his review by six. If I'm going to meet that deadline, we better press on, gentlemen.

"Can I tell the president that the two of you support the EMPRESS II option as our best choice?" he asked.

Jacobson glanced at Griffith. The JCS chairman nodded his agreement. "Yes, we'll go with it," Jacobson replied. "Colonel Beacham's plan tracks closely with what our operations people have proposed. Modifying the EMPRESS II to jam the RC band made a lot of sense to them. They'd encountered the same remote control problem and had decided to modify a Lockheed Electronic Counter Measures (ECM/C-130) aircraft to handle the task. But operations is still concerned about being able to get close enough to the 767 to ensure complete band saturation without being detected. Presumably, the EMPRESS II, once in position, will solve that problem."

"Clayton, what is the earliest time you'll be in a position to launch the assault? McGarth will want to know," Elliot probed.

"I can't pin down a time right now, Gaylord. There are still too many details to be worked out. Fortunately for us, the EMPRESS II is moored off Bloodsworth Island in the Chesapeake Bay, but we're still rounding up the necessary equipment and technical support for the modifications. How quickly the changes can be made is uncertain at this point."

"I understand that, but can you make some kind of an educated guess or give me a window?" Elliot pressed. Looking away for a moment, Clayton said, "Tell the president we would *like*, and I emphasize the word *like*, to begin the assault before dawn, day after tomorrow, between four and five, providing we can get the EMPRESS II modified and into position."

Jacobson intervened. "Gaylord, the president also has to be told that we're taking one hell of a chance assuming we know for certain the frequency band of their remote control transmitters. If we're wrong on that one thing,...."

"I'll tell him, Chris. And let's hope the Athens task force can find some evidence to verify our assumptions. They're supposed to be going over that warehouse where the modifications were made with a fine-tooth comb right now. If there's anything to be found, they'll find it."

"I hope to God you're right. We sure as hell won't get another chance," muttered General Griffith as he and Jacobson moved toward the door. "I'll see you at seven," he added.

Returning to the conference room, Elliot picked up the phone. He had to talk with Sinclair about the remote control issue. Clayton's parting remark troubled him. The success of the mission depended on it.

* * *

The extra-strength aspirin had done little to ease the throbbing pain Isabel felt in her wounded forearm. The makeshift tourniquet she'd fashioned from a piece of bungee cord had stopped the bleeding, but was sending out its own brand of pain. Her throat begged for water. Her eyes pleaded for rest as she hid behind the disposal bin of the convenience store, waiting. Her motorbike lay on its side, seeping hot motor oil from a crack in the crankcase. The bike was shot. Isabel was now on foot.

Eyeing the store, she saw an unmarked van pull into the parking space nearest the entrance. A man in his early twenties, wearing khaki shorts, got out and walked inside. Isabel had shed her biker's suit. Clad in jeans, her white blouse, and sneakers, she stood up and walked casually across the parking lot to the waiting van. As Isabel approached the vehicle, she could see the owner inside the store talking with the sales-clerk. He seemed to be receiving directions as he poured coffee into a paper cup. Isabel stopped beside the passenger door long enough to see keys dangling from the steering column. Glancing into the van's rear, she noticed camping gear and provisions.

Looking toward the store, Isabel decided no one inside had seen her. Making her way around to the driver's side of the van, she jerked the door open, jumped into the seat and switched on the ignition.

The engine came to life effortlessly. A second later, she shoved the gear into reverse and floored the accelerator pedal. The van leaped backward thirty feet, then sprang forward as it rolled hard right out of the parking lot and onto the roadway.

It was then that Isabel realized she had left her biker's jacket behind and with it, the address list, map, and photos. For a moment, she considered going back, but decided it was too risky. Yaqoob Shah and his Eastern Shore Yacht Company wouldn't be that hard to find. Edgewater couldn't be that big a town, Isabel told herself. She still had a small pistol and two ammo clips in the baggy pockets of her jeans.

Approaching the intersection, Isabel saw a sign pointing to US 1 South. The thought of having to drive thirty-five miles south to Fredericksburg, then twenty-five miles farther to Dahlgren just to cross the Potomac irritated her. Yet she knew it was the safer route to Edgewater, Maryland, and the South River. Months ago she had determined that crossing the Wilson Bridge would be far too risky.

Tired, she gunned the van through the intersection and into the right-turn lane without noticing the Virginia State Police cruiser following her. Then she saw it — the swirling blue light through the side door mirror! Isabel panicked as the trooper switched on his siren. Instinctively, she pulled the pistol from her pocket as he surged past, accelerating away from the van. Relieved, she laid the gun on the seat and tried to relax. It was hopeless. Isabel was exhausted and in pain. She remembered that the map showed a nature area several miles short of the Dahlgren toll bridge. She would stop there for rest.

As she brought the van to a stop for traffic, Isabel noticed a small cooler on the floor in front of the passenger's seat. Reaching down, she pulled the insulated box onto the seat beside her and opened it. Inside, she found a small bottle of water, two cans of soda, and a sandwich. Isabel took the water and put it to her parched lips. Swallowing was hard, at first, but she managed to down the bottle's contents. Seeing a handkerchief on the center console, she scooped up a handful of ice and placed it on the cloth. Hurriedly, she folded the cloth over the ice cubes and pressed them against the burning wound. The ice pack stung her flesh for a few seconds until the coldness began to penetrate the wound.

The traffic in front of her was moving again. Gripping the steering wheel with her left hand, she continued to hold the ice pack against her left forearm as she accelerated the van toward Fredericksburg. The water had quenched her. She began to feel better. Numbness was replacing the pain in her arm. The ice was working, but the wound would have to be cleaned and dressed sooner or later. It could wait. Her rendezvous in Edgewater couldn't.

* * *

John Sinclair read the Athens Task Force's preliminary report, then thumbed through its appendices and attachments. Seeing the page marked Appendix Two, Attachment One - Tangible Evidence, he stopped. Remembering Elliot's urgent call, he scanned the list for anything pertaining to remote control equipment. There seemed to be nothing. Looking through the list again, item fourteen on page two caught his attention.

* found - one crumpled 2 3/4" x 5 3/8" end flap of retail shipping box - Aladdin Automatic Garage Door Control Unit Model 6123 - quantity "4", manufactured, Baltimore, Md., wedged between two cushions of a sofa in office adjacent to warehouse used to modify subject device.

"That has to be it," John muttered, reading it a second time to be certain. Picking up the phone, he dialed the White House Situation Room. "Sinclair here. Get Elliot to the phone now."
"What's up, John?"
"Gaylord, the Athens team has found the evidence we're looking for. Check page two of Appendix Two to Attachment One of their preliminary report."
"Just a second... Let me see if we've gotten it."
Waiting for Elliot, Sinclair scratched in a bold red box around item fourteen.
"John, this has to be what we're looking for," Elliot shouted. Sinclair grinned at Gaylord's unbridled excitement.
"It would appear four of those units were included in the box, but the report doesn't mention finding any of them," Sinclair continued. "I'm sending a team of investigators over to Baltimore now. I should hear something pretty quick."
"Let me know the minute you've got confirmation," Elliot said. "It will make the president's decision a lot easier."
Hanging up, Sinclair summoned Burke Ramsey, chief of the Counter Terrorism Division to his office. Minutes later, a team of spe-

cial agents was dispatched to Baltimore to investigate the Aladdin Automatic Door Company, specifically the design and operation of remote control model 6123.

* * *

"How long will you be gone, Dad?"

"I don't know, honey. It depends..."

A sadness fell across Jacqueline's face as her intuition filled in the details. The thought that her father might not return frightened her. Gone was the confident promise she'd come to depend on since child-hood — replaced by the solemn truth. Looking into her father's steel-blue eyes, she saw the torment troubling him. She nestled against him as they communicated silently.

Meredith's call to dinner a few minutes later found Caroline, Tucker, and Walker already seated. Wes took his usual seat at the head of the table as Jacqueline settled into her place to his right. Meredith scooped up the last few crab cakes and slipped them onto the serving dish before seating herself at the other end.

"Heavenly Father....." Jacqueline said. Meredith gave Wes a surprised look and bowed her head. "Bless this family and especially our father in this time of crisis. Give him the strength and courage to do what is right. Guide and protect him. Help us to understand. And, if it be your will, spare all those lying in harm's way. Bless also this food and us to thy service in Christ's name, we pray. Amen."

"Amen!" the family replied in unison.

Twenty minutes later, the Beachams heard the familiar pounding of the approaching helicopter as it closed on Kilduck Station. Everyone looked at Wes. He gazed first at Meredith, and then at each of his children. The pounding became louder as the giant chopper approached the cul-de-sac.

Outside, the Beachams' neighbors stood in front of their houses to witness the scene as Wes, Meredith and their family walked down the driveway toward the chopper. Thumbs went up from hopeful friends as they wished him well. Meredith clutched his arm, carrying a small bag in her other hand.

Pausing at the edge of the cul-de-sac, Wes knew it was time to part. One by one, Jacqueline, Caroline, Walker, and Tucker stepped forward and took their turn saying farewell as Meredith waited patiently, determined to be brave.

Then it was her turn. She stuck out the shopping bag. "Here. You'll need this," she said. Wes opened the sack. A broad grin spread across his face as he pulled out the flight suit and held it up. "Where did you find this, honey?" he shouted. "I got it out of the attic before I left home last night," she replied over the pounding noise. "There's a letter for you in one of the pockets."

Reaching out, Wes pulled her into his arms. "I love you, Meredith, and I always will," he said as their lips touched. And then he let her go. Though inches apart, they were separated again, perhaps forever this time.

Meredith watched with her children as Wes walked the rest of the way to the chopper's doorway. Their hands went up spontaneously as he turned to catch one last glimpse of them.

Within seconds, the whirl of the blades intensified as the jet broke free of gravity's hold and began its ascent. Watching silently, they saw the helicopter clear the rooftops and make its way back toward Currituck Sound.

Meredith knew they would talk again before the assault, but it would not be the same. It couldn't be. Now the wait would begin in earnest. As she walked back toward the cottage, her thoughts turned to Jacqueline's prayer. Meredith felt a chill, despite the hot August sun. A familiar loneliness settled over her as she and the family ambled up their driveway. Looking about, she saw that her neighbors had returned to their homes. She knew the terrorists' threat weighed heavily on everyone's mind. Meredith wondered if she would ever see Wes again.

26

THE CHOICE

Jabarri glanced at the clock on the captain's instrument panel. It was five fifty-five p.m. Looking over at Mohammed, he said, "The news will begin in five minutes. Tell Sybil I wish to see the news from station WBSU."

Mohammed climbed out of his seat and left the cockpit. Reza's thoughts turned to the plan. Rashid's murder was disturbing. What had gone wrong? Why had he been killed? Had an enraged citizen done it, or was it, as he suspected, the work of the Americans? The real reason would remain a mystery. And why hadn't he heard from Middleburg, from Jared and Tariq? What had gone wrong there? How had the young girl gotten free? Recalling the sound of her helpless voice over the phone two nights ago in Geneva, Reza knew it was impossible that she could have escaped on her own. She had to have had help, but how could the Americans have known where to find her? He and Hassan had chosen the place very carefully during their visit to Washington more than three months ago. How did they .....

"Reza?" interrupted Mohammed, standing in the doorway to the cockpit. "The news program is beginning." Jabarri slid from the captain's chair and made his way to the cabin in time to hear Charlene Richards of WBSU-TV.

"Good evening, viewers. Washington, D.C. still remains under the shadow of the Fundamentalist Coalition's nuclear threat, some twenty-four hours after Trans International Airways Flight 899 from Geneva was seized in-flight by hijackers and forced to divert to National Airport carrying with it a nuclear bomb..."

Reza smiled as the anchorwoman referred to him and went on to announce details of the hostage release and his second meeting with President McGarth at the airport. He liked her comments about his willingness to free the women and children, but became angry as one after another hostage stepped forward in front of the camera and answered reporters' questions about their experiences on board the aircraft. Listening to their statements, Reza felt betrayed. Had McGarth not promised there would be no interviews with those he agreed to release? Could the president not control these few women, or had he decided to break his commitment with the FC, allowing those freed to discredit the coalition's humanitarian act? Reza struggled to contain his anger.

"In a related matter, authorities in Chantilly and Woodbridge are at a loss to explain the murders of two Arabs today in their respective communities. First a report from Mobile Team One's Larry Bledsoe, live from Chantilly...Larry?"

"Hello, Charlene. Police here are still trying to determine the motive for the slaying of Rashid Sedki, owner of the West Auto Parts Store here in Chantilly. In what was considered an unusual move, the FBI took responsibility for the investigation and thus far has been very tight-lipped about what actually took place here this morning. We've learned from police that the murderer fled on a motorbike shortly after leaving the store, although police here tell us they are not at liberty to disclose further information."

"Larry, do authorities there think the murder is related to the current terrorist threat?"

"Charlene, about the only thing FBI investigators have told us up to this point is that they do suspect robbery as the motive, but they've been unable or unwilling to confirm those suspicions. Larry Bledsoe, reporting live for WBSU."

"Thank you, Larry, for that report."

"And now we go live to Cheryl Larson and the Mobile Team Two crew in Woodbridge for an up-to-the-minute report on the second murder. Cheryl, tell us what the situation is there...And is it related to the earlier slaying of Sedki in Chantilly?"

"Charlene, the two blocks surrounding the Southland Realty Building have been sealed off as authorities try to learn what took place here early this afternoon. Eyewitnesses to the homicide tell us the slaying took place as an Arab man stepped from his car. They described the shooting as an obvious assassination similar to a gangland killing. And what was even more frightening to observers was that hidden plainclothes detectives fired automatic weapons in the direction of the assailant immediately after seeing the Arab collapse, as though they were expecting the hit."

"Cheryl? Were any of the witnesses able to get a description of the assailant?"

"Authorities here aren't saying, citing the fact that the FBI is handling the investigation, but two witnesses told us they saw a person they described as the killer, race away on a motorbike under a hail of gunfire. They said it appeared the assassin may have been wounded while escaping."

"Have authorities there identified the victim yet, Cheryl?"

"No, Charlene, but we've learned from the tow truck operator that the car driven by the victim belonged to a Mr. Abdulla El Laben, owner and broker of Southland Realty."

Leaping to his feet, Jabarri shouted in Arabic. Sybil froze as she watched him rip the PA from its cradle and yell into the phone. Suddenly, more Arabic shouting was heard from the terrorists as Reza continued to vent his frustration into the handset. Without warning, Jabarri turned to face Sybil. "Lies! All lies! Your president has broken his word to the FC! He is not to be trusted," he screamed. Sybil stood speechless, frightened as he lashed out at her. "The president must be taught a lesson! He will learn not to lie to me!"

Shouting in Arabic, Jabarri bellowed his plans to his confederates. The terrorists took up his chant and began assaulting the hostages.

Sybil saw blood pour from the side of an elderly man's ear as one terrorist smashed the side of his head with the butt of his machine gun.

"Please!" she screamed. "Stop it! Stop it! These people have done nothing!" Hearing her cry, Reza turned on her. Sybil saw the contempt that filled his dark, menacing eyes. He was going to kill her, Sybil thought, as he shrieked for silence and slowly walked toward her. "You would dare tell me what to do," he said. "I should have you beaten!"

The fire in his eyes told her he meant it. Suddenly, Sybil realized the civility she had come to believe him capable of was a myth. Reza was no different from the others, an animal with no respect for life. If he were to kill her now, she was ready. Better to suffer now than endure his punishment for days and be blown apart anyway. Deep inside, she'd known all along it would end like this. Who was she kidding? The president, the military, the FBI, the police, Wes — they were all powerless against these crazed terrorists.

Suddenly Sybil felt the steel grip of Reza's angry hand around her arm as he began dragging her down the aisle toward the coach section. His accomplices cheered as he jerked her about. Stopping abruptly, he shouted, "You will choose!"

Sybil stared at him, confused. "What do you mean, 'choose'?"

Releasing her arm, Jabarri smiled. "You will decide who is to die for your president's mistakes," he replied, fiendishly.

His words made no sense. Surely he couldn't mean...her mind went blank.

"Yes, you will choose who is going to die. You will pick four! NOW!" he yelled, pointing at the men with their heads covered with blankets. Sybil was alert now. He really did mean for her to choose who would be put to death. "I can't do this!" she pleaded. "It's inhuman!"

"Perhaps you would rather I kill them all? It matters little to me!" he said. "An eye for an eye! That is the law!" He continued, "Your president has taken four of my men. I shall do likewise! Is it not fair?" Reza asked tauntingly, his white teeth appearing between the lips of his sadistic grin.

Sybil paused. He was mad. No, worse, much worse. How could she let him kill them all? "God? Why me?" she silently pleaded.

"Ma'am?"

Stunned by the sound of a compassionate voice, Sybil turned away from Jabarri. There, standing with a blanket still over his head, stood a man. "Choose me, ma'am. I volunteer!" he said. It was the voice of a young man, one of the three servicemen returning to the States on leave. She had talked with him before the hijacking. Sybil recognized his distinctive accent as the kind young man from North Carolina. For an instant, she recalled his handsome looks and boyish charm. The thought of his offering to die crushed her.

"Miss, I'll volunteer too," said another, much older voice from under another blanket. "Choose me," he called out.

Turning, Sybil saw the feeble figure struggle to his feet. From where he was standing, Sybil knew the voice belonged to the elderly man returning from his visit to Switzerland to see his first granddaughter. Remembering the small photograph he'd shown her, Sybil recalled the pride she'd seen in his eyes as he spoke of the child and his love for her and her mother. Recalling his need for supplemental oxygen during the flight, Sybil knew the ordeal was slowly destroying what little stamina he had left. Had he decided it was time to end it all? Was he affirming what he'd said earlier — that he had no one left to live for but his grandchild?

"Count me in, too!" came a third voice, as a fourth man also stood up to be chosen.

Shocked by what he'd seen, the smile vanished from Reza's face as he stared at the four figures wondering in darkness about their fate. The choice had been made.

Hurriedly, the four were led to the front of the cabin. Their blankets were replaced with blindfolds. Their hands were tied behind their backs, and they were led to the main doorway.

Sybil and her crew were made to go forward to witness the execution. Assembled inside the main cabin doorway, they stared in horror as two of Reza's terrorists raised their weapons. Instinctively, the crew joined in prayer as four deafening shots rang out in succession. They continued to pray. Tears fell, but not one wavered as together they finished the prayer each had learned as a child.

The sound of gunfire startled Bud as he sat in the grass near his Cessna. Suspecting an assault was under way, Waterman grabbed his camcorder to film whatever he could. Then, seeing no movement in or around the jumbo jet, he watched and waited for some clue as to what might have taken place. He was certain the sounds he'd heard were of gunfire.

Several minutes later, through his camera lens, Bud saw a body dumped on the tarmac from the mobile steps. Before he could dial the control tower, a second body followed.

"Tower. Harry Mann."

"Harry. It's Waterman. Put your glasses on the ground near the bottom of the mobile stairs and tell me what you see."

"Just a minute!" Bud waited. "Oh shit! Are you telling me they're what I think they are, Waterman?"

"Yes. I saw them toss two bodies to the ground before I called and just now I saw them toss out two more!"

"Damn, I've got to have help. Stay on the line, Waterman! I'm going to put you on hold, but stay with me."

Pressing line two, Harry hollered for the Crisis Team's on-scene commander. The two men talked for no more than ten seconds. Then Harry picked up the hot line.

"The Oval Office. Forest Lindsey speaking."

"Mr. Lindsey, Harry Mann, tower chief. Sir, the terrorists are shooting hostages. We've seen at least two bodies dumped on the ramp and Waterman, the reporter, is certain at least one or two more have been tossed out!"

"Where is the on-scene commander?"

"He's on his way up here to the tower now."

"Have him call me before he takes any action, Chief. I'll advise the president immediately."

"Yes, sir," Harry replied, hanging up. Picking up the binoculars, Mann could clearly see the other two bodies.

McGarth was in the midst of listening to Gaylord's briefing when Forest interrupted. "Sir, we've got a serious problem. That was the tower chief. Jabarri has started killing hostages. At least two have been killed, possibly more."

McGarth jumped to his feet. "For Christ's sake! What did you tell him to do?" the president snapped.

"I told him to have the on-scene commander take no action until he had talked with us."

"That sonofabitch!....Gaylord, what do I tell him to do?"

"I'd have him confront Jabarri over the aircraft radio ASAP and demand an explanation. Something has inflamed Reza and whatever it is, we'd better address it."

"Forest, call the tower chief and give him those instructions. Tell him to have that idiot Jabarri call me here. We know he has the number!"

"Yes sir," Forest answered, rushing for the tower hot line.

"Gaylord, we've got to bring this damn thing to a close pretty quick or else that idiot is going to detonate that nuke right under our nose...and there won't be a damn thing we can do to make him stop it!"

"We're doing everything we can, Mason."

"I'm sorry, Gaylord. I know you're all doing your best. It's just that killing innocent people is so senseless."

Elliot nodded, realizing the enormous pressure the president was under. Of greater concern to him was the cause of Jabarri's irate behavior. There had to be a very serious reason for him to start shooting hostages without provocation.

"Reza's learned of the Arabs' deaths. That has to be it."

Running his fingers through his graying hair, Mason said, "I hadn't thought of that...but, if that's the case, we're going to have one hell of a time convincing him that we had nothing to do with it." Elliot agreed.

Forest returned to the Oval Office and recounted the details of his conversations to the president and Elliot. He'd also learned that Harry Mann had received confirmation from Waterman that two more bodies had been dumped on the ramp. The news distressed McGarth even more.

For the next five minutes the three men debated the reason for Reza's reprehensible action. Then the white phone on the president's desk rang. Forest instinctively moved toward it.

"I've got it, Forest," the president said, grabbing the receiver. "McGarth!"

"Mr. President...You have lied to the FC and you have lied to me... Your word is not to be trusted. You..."

"You shut up and listen to me, Jabarri! I haven't lied to you one damn bit! Suppose you stop killing innocent people and tell me what in the hell you are talking about. I frankly don't know," McGarth said.

Forest and Elliot were dumbfounded by the president's words. For a moment, both men thought the conversation had ended, and with it, any chance to halt the madman's vengeance.

"Mr. President, did you not have two of our Arab brothers killed today by one of your people on a motorbike?"

"The answer is an emphatic, 'No'! As a matter of fact, my people have been working around-the-clock trying to catch the person who murdered your Arab friends. Think about it. What on Earth would we have to gain by doing something that stupid? It doesn't make a damn bit of sense, wouldn't you agree?"

"Yes, but your men were seen at both places and were there at the time of the second shooting. How do you explain that?" Jabarri demanded.

"Of course they were there," McGarth said. "It's extremely important that we catch the person responsible. We see these two assassinations as a direct threat to us and our security."

"And how did you know where to find Abdulla El Laben?"

"Mr. Jabarri, the FBI has many sources of information. Some of those from whom your organization has drawn support may have unknowingly compromised parts of your plan. Suffice it to say, that we were able to piece together enough details to know where the assassin would likely strike next, but we didn't anticipate the killer would strike in broad daylight."

Reza was silent. McGarth waited. Finally, Jabarri spoke. "You wish me to believe that you and your government did not order these murders, Mr. President?"

"That's exactly what I wish you to understand. We are a nation of laws. We do not order executions. It is simply not the way we do business," McGarth explained.

"Then if the FBI has such contacts, they should know who is responsible for the murders."

"I wish it were that simple," the president said. "The fact is we suspect the killer is from within your organization, though we can't prove it. Perhaps you should look closely at those in your own camp. We have absolutely no reason to undertake any action which would further endanger our situation."

"It is possible, Mr. President, though I doubt it."

McGarth could tell from Reza's tone that he'd diffused the situation enough to inquire about the hostages Jabarri had executed.

"What can you tell me about the bodies of those killed?"

"You may send a truck to pick them up. We are a people of laws as well, Mr. President. You are familiar with the Arab's law that demands an eye for an eye?"

"Yes, I've heard of it."

"That is good! Then we have nothing more to talk of for the moment. Good evening, Mr. President."

McGarth hung up and walked to the window. He watched the sun's late afternoon rays cut through the trees before striking the White House lawn. He wondered how the four had been chosen. Did they have families, loved ones? Were they young or old? One question begged another as Mason stood in quiet solitude weighing the sacrifices each had made. He would see to it that their lives had not been taken in vain. He would not rest until the Fundamentalist Coalition and its bomb was driven from American soil.

27

SEAL TALK

Wes entered the Special Operations building and made his way down the corridor to the ops desk. The duty officer saw him coming and stood up.

"Colonel Beacham?" Wes glanced about the room. It was still hard to get used to being called colonel again.

"Yes?" he answered.

"Sir, Commander Marino is expecting you. One moment and I'll get him for you."

Wes nodded as he walked over to admire the unit's trophy case. The awards and decorations officer had been a busy man. The SEALS' accolades were extensive. Numerous Presidential Citations adorned the walls over the case. In the corner, among a long list of previous activities, there was mention of an action involving the hijacking of an American jetliner — a 727 to Beirut. Wes recognized the date. It was the one he'd played a covert role in.

"Colonel Beacham. Doug Marino."

Wes turned around and stuck out his hand. "Wes Beacham."

The two men spent a split second sizing one another up before Doug spoke. "How about some coffee before we get started? It's going to be a long night from the looks of things."

"Sounds good to me," Wes answered, following Marino to a small lounge. Wes studied the SEAL commander as Doug poured the java.

Of average height, Marino had the body of a professional running back. His movement suggested lightning speed. Yet, it was not his awesome strength that stood out, but the intensity of his presence — his powerful sense of focus — that commanded attention. His penetrating, dark eyes seemed in constant communication with everything around him as his mind sprinted ahead of the present, assessing the future. A deadly serious man, Wes imagined Marino was a loner, finding few men able to compete with his physical and intellectual prowess.

"Tell me, Colonel. How did you come to know about the EMPRESS II?" The question surprised Wes. He hadn't any idea his suggestion had made it that far.

"Actually, I found out about its mission through a citizens' action committee in Duck, N.C., where my wife and I live in the summer. The locals were pretty hot under the collar over what they thought it might do to the environment.

Doug chuckled. "Yeah, it's a different world out there, isn't it?"

Wes nodded in agreement.

"Well, I must hand it to you, Colonel, your idea sure got the attention of the JCS and the national security adviser's ears fast. They've already sent us a preliminary plan, with instructions to amend or add to it as necessary," he said. "The plan calls for us to make the assault at O four hundred local, day after tomorrow."

"I'm surprised they're waiting that long," Wes said.

"Apparently, they don't think they can get the EMPRESS II modified and into position any faster."

"What does that do to your assault?"

"It shouldn't make much difference, provided we don't have to slip it much. It's still fairly dark at that time of day."

Wes followed Marino down another corridor to the intelligence office. Doug signed them in after Wes provided his ID. Inside the intelligence briefing room Marino handed him a folder stamped "TOP SECRET."

Doug watched as Wes opened the folder and scanned the contents of the multi-page operations order. The document's thoroughness amazed Wes. Every task organization was named and had been assigned. Thumbing through the appendices, he noted the units chosen to support the plan.

"You'll notice the approving official's signature is missing," said Marino. "You and I are set to brief the president on the details of the plan at Camp Peary in Williamsburg tomorrow night. If he's satisfied we can pull it off successfully, he'll sign off on it. Otherwise, I don't know."

Wes nodded. They both knew the plan had to work.

"It's your operation, Doug. What can I do to help?"

"My biggest concern initially is getting my people onto the aircraft quickly. We've worked a couple of jobs on smaller jets, but nothing with these jumbos. What's involved and what are we going to need in the way of support?" Doug asked.

Wes looked up from the folder. "First off, there's the question of the door slides and whether they will be armed. Without knowing for sure, I'd bet Ahmed, the traitor TIA hired as a copilot, had Sybil, the service manager, disarm the doors," Wes explained.

"How fast could her crew rearm them if she knew in advance?"

"Within five seconds," Wes answered. "Why?"

"I'm thinking that if the assault is initiated from the front of the aircraft, it would give the cabin crew time to arm the doors and get the hostages on the way out before the terrorists have time to respond. Our major problem is finding that remote control device. Not that I don't think the EMPRESS jamming idea will work — it's just that I'll feel a lot better when that thing is totally under our control."

"I couldn't agree more," Wes replied.

Doug looked at the fuselage diagram reprinted from TIA's Flight Handbook. "How difficult would it be to climb up the slides, assuming they were automatically deployed?"

"Not hard. It would take less than six seconds, providing the terrorists aren't shooting at you, but having scaling ladders cut to fit the height of the door would work better."

"What kind of height are we talking about?" Marino asked.

Wes tried to visualize the height of the emergency door sills. "Maybe fourteen or fifteen feet, I suppose, but I couldn't be sure without seeing the doors, Doug. You'd think as much as I'm around the jet I'd know shit like that but..."

"I know what you mean. I have the same problem," Doug said. "That's something we can measure later tonight."

"What do you mean?" Doug smiled. "Your chief pilot, Spence Riker, is flying one of your 767's into Oceana later tonight. We're going to use it to practice on."

"I should have known," said Wes. "We did the same thing back in nineteen eighty six."

"You've been through this kind of thing before?"

"Not exactly like this, but yes, I did fly a 727 in here to be used the same way nearly ten years ago."

"Then you understand what we've got ahead of us."

"Yes," Wes replied, knowing it would be a long night.

"Tell me about your cabin team. What kind of people have we got there to depend on?"

Wes took time to answer. "Sybil, the flight service manager, is a highly disciplined leader. She's level-headed and cool under fire, even when she's frightened. More important is the fact that her cabin team has a tremendous amount of respect for her and will do whatever she tells them."

"Are there any other leaders within the crew?"

"Well, there's Cynthia Roseman. She's Irish and has the temper to go with it. She can be tough as nails when she has to."

"Where's her station in the cabin?" Doug asked, looking down at the cabin diagram.

"Right here at the 'R 2' position."

"Where does she go in an evacuation?"

"She's responsible for the right over-wing exit," Wes said.

"Would she be the one you'd turn to if Sybil were taken out?"

"Yes. She'd assume the role if it came to that."

"Who's in the rear of the aircraft?" Marino asked.

Wes glanced at the list of names adjacent to the pictures. "They all do an excellent job in-flight, but I don't know much about any of them except that Aaron and Frederick are gay."

"Real 'butt buddies,' huh?" Doug said. Wes grinned at the remark. He hadn't heard the phrase in a while.

"Are they wimps or jocks?"

It was obvious Marino didn't give a flip one way or the other about their sexual preference. He just wanted to find out how they might react.

"Jocks, I suppose. Both are young and quite strong, they'll handle themselves okay."

"From the looks of their resumés, we've got a fairly skilled group to work with," Marino said. "The question is, can we get word to them before the assault? It will make our job easier and can make a big difference in limiting the casualties."

Wes didn't reply. He was thinking of Leigh.

"Any thoughts on how we might get word to Sybil, Wes?"

"What's that again? I was thinking about something else."

Doug gave him an irritated look. "I said, 'Have you got any idea how we can get word to Sybil or Cynthia before the assault?'"

Wes thought for a minute. He recalled Sybil's sending out terrorist information pinned to Leigh's underwear. Then he thought of the pilot reporter. "Bud Waterman. We'd have the best chance of getting word to them through him," Wes answered.

"You mean the newspaper man camped out by his Cessna?"

"Yes. Waterman's already been inside the aircraft once to do an interview. If he could persuade Jabarri to give him another interview, he might be able to pass them the message."

Doug reflected on Wes's idea. "Maybe we could get the word to them that way," he said. "But what could we come up with to entice Jabarri into giving Waterman another interview?"

"Why not let Gaylord Elliot worry about how to pull that off? He's clever enough to come up with something."

"Good point. We've got too many other things to work out," Marino said, reading through the last of his notes. "You mind giving him a call? There's a secure line in the other office. We'll take the chopper over to Oceana when you're done."

Wes found his way into the next room and dialed the now-familiar private number to the White House.

* * *

Alone in the cockpit, Reza's thoughts returned to McGarth's comments. They troubled him. Was he telling the truth? Was someone trying to scuttle the operation? And if so, who? With Rashid and Abdulla dead, only Yaqoob and Nsar had the means to stop the detonation timer. If either of them were killed.... Reza dismissed the thought as he reached for the mobile phone and dialed the White House.

"Forest Lindsey."

"Mr. Lindsey, this is Mr. Jabarri. I must speak with the president. It is most urgent that I do so immediately."

"Just a moment, Mr. Jabarri. I will get the president."

Wiping the sweat from his neck, Reza waited in the captain's chair. The late afternoon sunlight penetrating the windscreen stifled what little cool air emerged from the tiny vents.

"McGarth."

"Mr. President. I've given great thought to your suggestion that someone from within our organization may be attempting to alter the outcome of our operation by murdering certain of our members..." Reza hesitated. Was he certain?

"And?" McGarth asked.

"I have therefore told our two remaining council members to join me at my hotel in Crystal City to ensure their safety for the duration of our stay in Washington."

"And what is it you want from me in regard to this matter?" Reza was quiet. Mason read his silence as indecision.

"I want your guarantee they will not be harmed while en route," he said. "You must understand their welfare has a direct bearing on that of your government — it is to your advantage to see that no harm comes to either of these people," he added.

"Mr. Jabarri, I think I understand what you are trying to say, but I cannot provide you with any assurances until I know who these two people are and where I can find them."

"Do I have your word they will be protected if I give you the necessary information?" Reza asked.

"Of course. I'm well aware of your position. Please understand, Mr. Jabarri, I intend to do nothing that would provoke you into exploding that weapon."

"That is very wise, Mr. President. I will leave the names and addresses of the two men you will escort here with Mr. Lindsey. I will advise them to remain where they are until your authorities arrive."

"As you wish, Mr. Jabarri. Please wait one moment for Mr. Lindsey," McGarth said.

After giving Lindsey the information needed to locate the remaining council members, Jabarri hung up and dialed Ajmani. Reza felt an immediate sense of relief as he heard his friend answer. Speaking in Arabic, he said, "Nsar, it is Reza. We have a problem."

"The deaths of Rashid and Abdulla?"

"Yes!" said Reza. "You know about them?"

"Their deaths were reported on the news thirty minutes ago," Ajmani said. "Do you know the reason?"

"That is why I have called," Reza explained. "Someone is trying to interfere with our plan. I fear you and Yaqoob are also in danger."

"Is it the Americans?" Ajmani asked.

"No. They have no cause to do so."

"What would you have us do, Reza?"

"Remain where you are for now. The president has agreed to have you escorted to our hotel in Crystal City. The FBI should be arriving within the next hour. You and Yaqoob will stay here until it is time to activate the code to stop the timer."

"You are certain the Americans can be trusted?"

"Yes, Nsar. I have the president's word. You will be safe," assured Reza as he hung up.

Cursing under his breath, Reza listened to Yaqoob Shah's phone announcement as he waited for the beep. As he was about to finish dictating his message, Yaqoob answered.

"Yaqoob?" Reza asked in Arabic.

"Reza. I got your message. I saw the same thing on the TV. Do you think the Americans have done this?"

"No. It is not the work of the Americans. That is why you must do exactly as I say. Someone else is trying to sabotage our plan," Reza explained.

"Who?"

"I do not know for certain, but I suspect someone from within the coalition," Reza replied. "Remain where you are for now, Yaqoob. The FBI will come and escort you to our hotel. The president has given his word. They will not harm you."

"Reza, You are certain the Americans have not done this?"

"Yes, Yaqoob. They need you and Nsar alive for the code material. Without it they are doomed."

"You are right," Yaqoob answered. "It will take me about forty-five minutes to get back to the docks. Tell them I will be on board my yacht when they come."

As Reza was about to place the call to Lindsey to tell him that Yaqoob was aboard his sailboat, he saw their limousine pull to a halt at the bottom of the mobile stairs. As the door opened, Reza recognized Ahmed. He looked different. As he emerged from the vehicle, a cheer went up for him from the Arab guards below. Reza quickly saw why.

Ahmed now wore the black garments of his homeland. Around his neck hung the black and white checked revolutionary scarf of the PLO. Seeing him dressed that way angered Reza. It was just the kind of radical display that would harm the coalition's credibility.

Reza waited impatiently as Ahmed climbed the stairs and greeted Mohammed amid cheers of victory from his Arab brothers. Seeing

Mohammed board the limo for his trip to the hotel, Reza decided to talk with Ahmed of his foolishness. It could not wait.

Jabarri said nothing as Ahmed entered the cockpit. Their eyes met as Reza spoke in Arabic. Ahmed saw immediately that Reza was displeased with his dress. He did not mince words. Ahmed listened as Reza expressed his concern. Minutes later, Ahmed removed the inflammatory scarf from his neck and stuffed it into his crew kit. He knew Reza was right. It was a foolish thing to have done.

Reza slid from the captain's chair and went back into the first class cabin. He would give Ahmed time to think about what he had said.

*   *   *

"Go on, John. You were about to explain what you've found out about the remote control devices," the president said.

"Mr. President, the investigators I sent to Baltimore this afternoon have confirmed that four automatic garage door units were shipped to a commercial construction company under contract to refurbish a warehouse at the Larnaca Airport on Cyprus. The people at Aladdin Automatic Door Company provided us an exact model of the equipment they sold to the company, together with copies of the shipping invoices. The models shipped match the model number on the box flap we recovered in the adjacent warehouse office. We've already faxed photos of the remote control box to our team there to assist them in the final verification."

"Are you and Burt satisfied that the remote control device used in this garage door is identical to the one carried by Jabarri to detonate the weapon?"

"Yes, we are, although we're trying to get further confirmation of the device from Geneva Airport security."

"How's that?" McGarth asked.

"We've also faxed pictures of the remote control device along with photos of Reza Jabarri and Mohammed Al-Farsi to Emerson Beamer in Geneva. He's heading up our joint effort there. We're hopeful the security people on duty at the time TIA Flight 899 was boarded will recognize the Arabs and perhaps remember seeing the remote controllers."

The president stood up and paced his Oval Office for several moments, as he did so often when facing a difficult decision. Shoving his hand into his right rear pants pocket, he turned to Elliot. "Gaylord, do you think we have enough information about this remote control device to safely initiate the EMPRESS assault plan without Jabarri's blowing us up in the process?"

Elliot stood up and walked over to McGarth. "Mr. President, I think it represents our best course of action, given the situation. Of course, we'd all like to be one hundred per cent sure of what we're proposing, but that's a luxury we don't have. Furthermore, the longer this thing lingers, the greater the chances are they might, out of fear or frustration, elect to detonate the bomb regardless of what we do."

McGarth said nothing, but walked to his desk and paused long enough to gaze out the large, paned window once more. "How much time do I have before I have to give final approval to the plan?"

"I'd planned to have the SEAL team commander and Colonel Beacham brief you at Camp Peary tomorrow night."

The president nodded as he paced in front of the window. "And at what time will you begin the assault?"

"At four a.m., day after tomorrow. It's the earliest we can be sure of having the EMPRESS II in position."

"I see," the president said.

Sinclair, still seated at the small conference table on the far side of the room, could sense the tremendous pressure McGarth was facing. "Mr. President, with your approval, Burt and I will go on down to the meeting now."

McGarth looked over at the two directors and waved. "I'll be there shortly."

Gaylord watched, but said nothing as Sinclair and Williamson left. He didn't envy his friend's position, though he was glad Mason would be the one to decide.

"We won't be able to initiate an evacuation of the aircraft before the assault will we, Gaylord?"

Elliot shook his head. "No." He could tell from McGarth's question the president had the hostages at the forefront of his deliberations. Elliot knew it was the president's compassion for those he served that made his choice so tough. He also knew Mason would not back down. It would be out of character for him. Elliot waited. His president needed time.

"You know, Gaylord. I've wanted this job all my political life so that I could, for once, be in a position to make what I feel is the right choice for the situation at hand. And yet, until now, I haven't been called upon to decide much of anything. Other people I've appointed seem to delight in doing it for me."

Elliot smiled at his boss. "It's true, Mason. In many ways, the job is not what we had imagined. It took getting here to find out the truth about the office."

McGarth grinned at his old friend's insight — the man he most trusted for advice. Their eyes met. Both knew the decision had been made. Elliot noticed Mason's confident smile return.

"Order the EMPRESS ASSAULT, Gaylord. I'll sign it."

28

DANGEROUS WATERS

Isabel eased the stolen van into the left lane of Route 214 and turned onto Soloman's Island Road. A road sign pointed the way to Edgewater, Maryland, less than three miles ahead. She knew the Eastern Shore Yacht Brokerage wouldn't be difficult to find.

Approaching the South River bridge, Isabel was startled by the flash of a dark gray sedan as it darted around her and slid into her lane, just missing her van's fender. Without thinking, she slammed on the brakes and grabbed the pistol as the car raced on ahead, oblivious to the accident it nearly caused. Cursing in Arabic, Isabel checked the rear mirror as she regained speed. The car's movements hadn't frightened her nearly as much as the look of the car. She'd recognized it immediately as a government car, those used by the FBI. She'd seen the ugly gray vehicles, devoid of chrome, moving about on black-walled tires all over Washington during previous visits. Were they headed for Edgewater? Did they know about Yaqoob Shah? Or was it only a coincidence that their paths had crossed? The thought troubled her. She could not afford to be caught any more than she could allow Yaqoob to live.

A gas station lay just ahead. Isabel slowed the van, flashed her right signal and drove pass the pumps toward the pay phone stand. Parking in a secluded area, she opened the door and stepped into the phone booth.

The directory hung beneath the phone. Isabel noticed pages were missing as she thumbed through the weathered print. In the Yellow

Pages under Boats & Brokerages, she saw the name she was looking for. Tearing the page from the book, she folded it twice and stuffed it into her jeans hip pocket. Then she walked the short distance to the store and went inside.

Isabel saw a map rack in front of the cash register. She leafed through the spindly wire frame until she spied the one she needed. Removing it, she partially unfolded it to expose the town of Edgewater. In the lower right corner, she noted the street address she'd seen in the Yellow Pages. Isabel guessed the location was close to the water, judging from the single-digit building number. Taking it around to the cashier, she asked, "How much?" The old man glanced at the map and said, "Three twelve with tax."

Isabel shoved her hands into her pockets as though she would pay, but withdrew them as she swore. The old man grinned. "I left my billfold in the van. I'll be back in a minute," she said, taking the map with her. He didn't notice. His eyes were focused on the tight white bandage around her arm.

Reaching the van, Isabel swung open the door, tossed the map on the front seat, and fired up the engine. As the van's V-8 roared to life, she slapped the gearshift into drive and threw the gas pedal hard against the floor. The van lurched forward, its tires squealing on the pavement. She was under way in seconds.

The cashier, hearing the screaming tires, shrugged his shoulders. "Shit, if I had known she needed it that bad, I would have given her the damn map!" he said in disgust to a customer.

Certain that she was not being followed, Isabel turned down the winding roadway and drove carefully past each shop in search of the Eastern Shore Yachts office. According to the building numbers, it would be near the end of the next block on the right. That made sense, for the South River ran behind those stores on the right.

Suddenly, Isabel stopped. Ahead, parked off to the side of another small marine shop, she saw the same ugly gray sedan. The two men inside were talking. Slowly, she eased the van backward while keeping her eye on them. After backing the van into a small driveway, Isabel drove quickly back up the street.

They knew and they were waiting, she thought. They were FBI

agents, but why were they sent there — to arrest Yaqoob? Or, are they waiting for me? Isabel asked herself.

Taking a different route to avoid the gas station where she'd stolen the map, Isabel made her way back across the South River bridge just as the sun slipped out of sight. She had thirty minutes of daylight left. It was enough. From the bridge, she saw powerboats tied to the private docks of homes to the south.

Minutes later, Isabel pulled into the empty driveway of a large, secluded waterfront home and drove up under the double car port before switching off the ignition. The entire neighborhood was deserted. She was certain no one was at home. The bomb must have sent them all packing. Casually stepping from the van, Isabel walked through the open breezeway and across the rear yard to the dock.

Floating quietly beside the dock rested an eighteen foot runabout. A sixty-five horse outboard was clamped to its stern. Isabel stepped into the boat, examined the battery, and checked the gas tanks. They were both full. It was then she noticed the ignition system required a key. She could jump the connections if she had to.

Returning to the van, she picked up the map she'd swiped and then walked to the side door entrance. Pressing her small fingers against the edges of the wooden door, she measured its strength, then stepped back.

Her second karate kick severed the door lock assembly. Pushing the door open, Isabel walked through a small hallway into a large kitchen. She opened the map and studied it for a minute before removing the phone from the wall cradle. She punched in a long distance number and waited.

Her eyes darted about the room as she listened to the rings. On the side of the telephone desk, she saw a red and white plastic miniature buoy. Two keys were fastened to it. Isabel smiled as she lifted the keys from the small brass hook.

"Aero Special Services, Tony speaking."

"Tony, my plans have changed. Pick me up in two hours."

"Where?"

Looking down at the map, she said, "At Lee Airport, south of Edgewater, Maryland, just west of the South River Bridge adjacent to Beard Creek. I'll use a flashlight. Look for the signal before you land," she ordered.

"I show it's seven forty-six," Tony said.

Isabel checked her digital watch. "Be there at nine forty-five."

Returning to the dock, Isabel quickly untied the mooring lines and stepped into the powerboat. She slipped the key into the ignition. It fit. Turning the key, she heard the engine sputter to life, idle roughly for thirty seconds and die. Cursing her stupidity, Isabel opened the bleed valve on the gas tank and squeezed the hand pump. Again, she turned the ignition key. This time the engine spun up effortlessly. Looking about, she shoved the gear lever forward and opened the throttle. A minute later, Isabel was in the open waters of South River en route to her final assignment.

Yaqoob Shah eased the *Eastern Sun* around the last buoy and cut the forty-four foot sailing yawl's iron sail, a 185 horsepower diesel engine. He let the boat drift under its own momentum toward the pier as he went forward to set the fenders. Consumed with worry over Reza's call, he wondered what would happen when the Americans arrived. Something was seriously wrong for Reza to have insisted on American protection. Yaqoob thought of the two numbers he'd memorized. It was still hard for him to imagine their importance.

Now fewer than ten feet from the pier, he spun the destroyer wheel hard to the right. Expending the last of its kinetic energy following the rudder's command around the turn, the yawl came to rest alongside the catwalk. Yaqoob stepped over the stanchion lines and onto the narrow boards. Walking to the end of the tiny pier, he grabbed the stern's starboard mooring line he'd tossed during the turn and looped it around the heavy brass cleat. Then he went forward and tied off the bow's starboard mooring line.

After securing the vessel topside, Yaqoob went below to close off the petcocks, drain the bilge and shut off the fuel line. There would be no time to do it once the Americans came. He'd sailed the *Eastern Sun* for the last time on the Chesapeake. Climbing down the companionway into the cabin, he walked to the TV cabinet, pulled open the two doors, and switched on the television. News of the crisis filled the small screen. Not anxious to leave, he settled into a club chair and listened.

In a related matter, Upper Marlboro police are still trying to determine if the young woman who commandeered an Emergency Medical Services ambulance and forced two paramedics to bandage her gunshot wound is the same person who earlier this afternoon shot and killed Abdulla El-Laben in Woodbridge. The assailant reportedly flagged down the returning EMS vehicle and pleaded for help, saying she had been shot by her fiancé. After dressing the wound, the two paramedics were held at gunpoint while their hands and legs were taped. A Maryland State trooper found the two young men unharmed an hour later. Until now, authorities had suspected the assailant was male. The FBI has refused comment.

Yaqoob didn't hear the powerboat approaching. His mind was on the Americans and his uncertain fate. The assassinations troubled him.

Isabel peeked at the NOAA nautical chart she'd found tucked away in the powerboat's side pocket. According to the chart, the lead-in markers were dead ahead. Seeing the NO WAKE sign, she eased the throttle back. The boat's speed suddenly dropped as its bow began to settle gently on the water. Ahead, she saw the last of the sun's rays reflecting off the Eastern Yachts waterfront marquee. The engine idled smoothly as she glided past several rows of slips toward the main dock. To the right, she saw the name *Eastern Sun* on the stern of a large yawl. Its companionway was open. The vessel's name seemed vaguely familiar, but she couldn't place the connection.

Approaching the wharf, Isabel noticed the Eastern Yachts office looked abandoned. Yaqoob was not there. No one was. Had he been picked up by the FBI or had he fled after learning of Rashid's and Abdulla's deaths? She feared it was a distinct possibility. She knew Abdulla's hit would make the news quickly.

Still crouched behind the boat's steering wheel, Isabel raised her head enough to see the full length of the boardwalk. She saw no one, except at the far end. A hundred yards away, two men stood facing one another. They didn't seem to notice her. Were they the same men she'd seen thirty minutes ago in the parked gray sedan? She couldn't decide. If so, they were waiting for Yaqoob.

Lowering her head, Isabel thought through her next move. Then she remembered the open companionway. Perhaps someone there would know of Yaqoob, a local yachtsman. It was worth a try.

Isabel slipped the engine back into gear, but left the throttle in idle. The boat stirred in the water, then gradually began to move away from the wharf. Looking back over her shoulder, Isabel checked to see if the two men had noticed her. Deciding they hadn't, she cracked the throttle open a little wider. Responding to the prop, the small boat quickly moved away from the docks and toward the larger sailing slips. Two minutes later, she cut the throttle and allowed the boat to drift toward the *Eastern Sun's* stern.

Drawing closer, she saw the sailboat had a stainless steel ladder permanently mounted to the right side of its quarter board. She was in luck. Six feet away, she switched off the ignition and went forward to fend off her bow. Seconds later, she scrambled up the boarding ladder and slipped the boat's line around the yawl's cleat. Then she crept toward the open companionway. As she did, she heard the sound of a TV below. The sounds seemed to be those of an announcer or newscaster. She wasn't sure as she peered into the dimly lit cabin. Inside, Isabel saw part of a man's head extending above the top of a stuffed club chair.

Debating what to do, she stepped back and called out, "Excuse me, sir."

Startled, the man leaped to his feet and spun around to face her with a gun in his hand. Isabel saw instantly that the man was Yaqoob. She remembered his unusual, broad, dark face and dark eyes, and the heavy black beard. Instinctively, she moved to the side and shouted, "I'm sorry! I didn't mean to frighten you!"

The man looked confused as he lowered the gun and asked, "Who are you? What are you doing here?"

"I'm ... I was sent here to warn you, Yaqoob."

"Who sent you?" he demanded. She didn't answer immediately, but watched as he lowered the gun to his side.

"Reza sent me."

"That is a lie! Reza is sending an FBI escort for me."

"NO! It is a trick! That is why Reza has sent me!" she said. "We are surrounded by FBI agents this very minute. There are two at the end of the boardwalk now. We must hurry. There is no time!"

Yaqoob stared into the young woman's beautiful dark eyes for an answer. She smiled at him. He wanted desperately to believe her. Anything would be better than accepting the Americans' protective custody.

"Hurry. We must go now to join Nsar. Please!"

Yaqoob switched off the TV and climbed silently up the steps to the cockpit. She pointed to the two figures on the boardwalk, then motioned him to the stern as she removed the line securing the powerboat. Yaqoob looked in their direction and nodded. Then he obediently followed the young woman into the powerboat.

Pretending to ignore him, Isabel started the engine and shoved the gear lever into RUN. Not wanting to alert the agents on the boardwalk, she carefully eased the throttle open as she cranked the wheel around. Slowly, the boat pivoted toward the channel markers.

Suddenly Isabel felt a sharp pain in the middle of her back. Her head snapped back violently as Yaqoob jerked her hair and pressed the gun deeper between her shoulders. "You are the woman who killed Rashid and Abdulla! Your left arm; it's the bandaged wound they spoke of on the TV!" he said. "You are the assassin who has murdered our brothers! I will kill you myself!"

Reacting instantly, Isabel rammed the throttle full forward as she spun the small steering wheel full starboard. The jolt threw Yaqoob to the floor as he fired. The bullet barely grazed her neck as she spun the wheel back to hard port, throwing him across the cockpit, striking his head against the rail. The gun flew from Yaqoob's hands overboard. He struggled to regain his senses. Isabel released the wheel and struck him on the nose with the heel of her palm, knocking him unconscious.

Grabbing a coiled nylon rope from the stern, Isabel fashioned a loop, slipped it over his head, and pulled the line taut. She lifted his body and shoved it over the side before returning to the wheel.

Certain the agents had heard the gunshot, Isabel looked over her shoulder as she gunned the throttle once more. Her suspicions were confirmed. The wharf was a flurry of activity as agents swarmed about in search of a boat. The boat's engine strained under the dead weight of Yaqoob's body as she debated what to do. She'd have to release his body to get any speed out of the boat.

Approaching open water, Isabel closed the throttle abruptly and slipped the gear lever to neutral. At the stern, she released the pelican quick-disconnect clasp and tossed it into the water. As she was about to return to the wheel, she saw Yaqoob's lifeless body rise to the surface. Wanting to be certain he was dead, she swung the boat around and pulled alongside his semi-submerged corpse. There was no pulse. She allowed herself a second to contemplate the exact cause, though it mattered little. Then she turned the boat again toward the South River and gave the engine full throttle. She calculated it would take ten minutes to reach Lee Airport.

A minute later, Isabel eased the wheel to starboard and took dead aim for the center of the South River Bridge. Glancing up, she saw flashing lights on the bridge. It had to be the police or worse, FBI agents. Her blood ran cold as several shots hit the water close to her. Immediately rolling the boat into a hard turn, she held the heading for a few seconds and reversed course again. Her only chance was to keep up the jinking turns. It would make their aiming more difficult.

Now fewer than a hundred yards from the bridge, Isabel wished she'd turned back as the rounds struck closer to her. It was too late to change course. Passing under the bridge, she stopped the S turns to gain speed. As she reappeared from beneath the bridge, a hail of gunfire slashed the water around her. Quickly rolling into a hard left turn, Isabel righted the craft for a split second before breaking hard left again. Bullets spit water as they inched toward the boat's stern. Then she heard one hit metal. Afraid to look aft, Isabel continued jinking as violently as she dared. She needed only another hundred feet and she would be out of their range.

Sheets of fire flashed into the sky as the small fuel tank exploded, spewing flames forward. Seeing the fire spread, Isabel banked the boat on its side and dived overboard into the black waters of the South River.

29

ELUSIVE PREY

Agent Dave Coleman paced the operations floor as he downed his fifth cup of coffee. Director Sinclair's call was explicit. The president had directed that he take the two remaining Arabs into protective custody immediately. Dave looked at his watch. It had been ninety minutes since he'd passed the order to bring in Nsar Ajmani and Yaqoob Shah. Only Yaqoob remained at large.

"Dave, it's for you. Agent Baxter — he says it's urgent."

Coleman grabbed the phone off the console. "Yeah, Bernie. Have you picked up Yaqoob yet?"

"Yeah, we've got him," Baxter growled. "But not soon enough, Dave. The girl got to him first and broke his neck. We've got every boat we can get our hands on looking for her now!"

"The girl? What girl, Bernie?"

"Dave, the assassin we're after is a female. A convenience store clerk here in Edgewater tipped us off after she stopped there and stole a local map."

"Bernie, how in the hell did the clerk find out that this girl is the assassin?"

Baxter, frequently interrupted by Coleman's questions, spent the next several minutes recounting his investigation into the Arab's murder and his assassin's escape.

"So where is she now, Bernie?" Dave asked, disgustedly.

"Somewhere in the middle of the South River just north of the bridge I'm standing on. We managed to get a round into the gas tank of her powerboat and set the boat afire. One of our agents was sure he saw her dive overboard just before it blew up," he added. "Dave, this lady is a real mean bitch."

"She's a professional, Bernie. Tell your men not to take any chances with her."

"That's not likely at this point. She's got their undivided attention," said Bernie. Thoroughly pissed, Dave didn't reply.

"Are you still there, Dave?"

"Yeah, Bernie. I'm just trying to decide what to do next. Sinclair is going to explode when he finds out Yaqoob is dead. His death is more serious than you can imagine."

"Yeah, well that may be so, Dave, but we gave it our best shot. The guy just never showed up, and no one ever told us he lived on a fucking boat!"

"I know, Bernie, I know. So you think she's in the river?"

"Yeah. She's probably trying to make it to the nearest shore. We've got every avenue out of here covered and we're going door-to-door checking every residence near the water. She's bound to turn up, and we'll nail her for good."

"Bernie, do everything you can to take her alive. She may hold the only key to who is behind this terrorist plot. And, try to find the van she drove there and lift any fingerprints you find. Do what you can to keep the media out of there. Seal off the entire area and don't, under any circumstances, reveal that Yaqoob has been killed. It's extremely important that this information be withheld from the media. If you have to tell them anything, say an agent was shot. I'll get there as soon as I give Sinclair the news."

"Right, Dave. I'll keep you posted," Bernie said.

Dave put the phone down and stared out at the Washington landsape. How was he going to break the news to Sinclair? What would the director say — that he'd really screwed up a simple task — that he'd embarrassed the agency — that maybe the terrorists would decide to detonate the nuclear weapon. The possibilities seemed endless. Dave was worried. It was Baxter who'd fouled up. If only he'd thought to check out the boatyard more carefully. But it didn't matter now. Yaqoob was dead, killed by a female assassin, by one of his own.

She had to be taken alive, thought Dave. Only then could she be interrogated and turned over to the terrorists. They would get her to talk in ways the Bureau couldn't fathom. That would surely convince the coalition of the president's sincerity.

*   *   *

Isabel lay in the saw grass exhausted from the long swim to shore. Her body ached. The bandage on her arm was soggy and needed changing. Twice, she'd come close to being discovered by the numerous police patrol boats cruising the river with their lights scanning the water. Struggling to sit up, she felt her wrist. Her watch was gone. What time was it? How long had she been there? Groggy, she tried to recall what time the chopper was due to pick her up.

Suddenly, a strong beam of light flooded the area around her. She slithered back into the water as the beam swept over her. Lying motionless just beneath the water's surface, Isabel held her breath until the light was gone. Crawling out of the water, she moved away from the sounds of the voices stalking her. The razor-sharp grass cut into the soles of her feet as she made her way along the shoreline. She would stop only long enough to hide from the ever-present searchlights. From what she could remember of the map, Beard's Creek lay just to the northwest of the airport. She would travel along the creek bank until it was safe to move toward the airport. She knew Tony would not land if he saw the searchlights. She would have to find another way out if the search for her continued much longer.

Isabel didn't see the lone figure moving toward her until his flashlight flashed in her face from fifty feet away. Momentarily blinded, she dropped to her knees and hugged the earth. The crushing sound of the tall grass in front of her confirmed her worst fear. She'd been spotted. Preparing for the attack, Isabel waited.

Not ten feet from where she was crouched, the stalker paused and swept the grass again with his searchlight as though he'd lost sight of his prey. Not wanting to even breathe, she debated whether to confront him or stay hidden and hope he retreated. Her weapon would be helpful; being discovered would not. Isabel held her breath.

It seemed an eternity before the stalker made his move. Sweat poured from her swollen face as she listened to the sounds fade. She was certain he'd seen her. Why hadn't he pursued her? It didn't matter. She was safe for the moment, but she would have to keep moving. She knew the dogs would be arriving soon. They wouldn't lose her scent once they found the trail of blood from her cut feet.

Easing her body slowly upward, Isabel peered through the taller blades of grass. The stalker was gone. Stooping, she began threading her way through the grasses again. She'd gone about sixty feet when an intense beam of light hit her squarely in the face, blinding her.

"Halt or I'll shoot! You're under arrest!"

Stunned, Isabel stood motionless. She knew resisting would be futile. Her work was done. She had only to keep quiet for a while longer. She could do that. Perhaps there would be a chance to escape. Otherwise, she would die the death of a martyr, the same as so many before her.

Her captor seemed surprised that she didn't resist. He made her put her hands on top of her head. He warned her he would shoot if she removed them. She believed him. He was smart and kept his distance as the two of them walked toward the car lights. He kept his gun on her even while he spoke into the small FM radio.

"Why didn't you come after me when you saw me the first time?" she asked.

"Keep walking."

"You lost sight of me as you got closer, didn't you?"

"No. I knew you were there in the grass maybe ten feet in front of me when I turned back. But, I don't hunt that way, ma'am."

"How do you mean?"

"It's better to flush the bird first. You get a cleaner shot that way. Besides, my orders were to take you alive. If I pursued you in that grass, I would have had to shoot you to keep you from getting me."

She smiled. He was right.

Suddenly, Isabel collapsed, grabbing her ankle. "My ankle! I've sprained it," she said. "Help me."

Stepping clear of her reach, he said, "No way. You'll have to crawl. Get moving. A lot of people in Washington are real interested in having a long talk with you."

It wasn't going to work. He was too smart to let her get close enough to use her martial arts.

Crawling to her feet, Isabel thought of running anyway. Taking a bullet now might be easier than what lay ahead. It was the quickest way out, but also the most final. Deciding to stay in the game, she hobbled ahead of him toward the lights. There would be other opportunities.

A voice called out as they approached the edge of the runway. "Carson! Is that you?"

"Yeah! It's me!"

"Who's that with you, man?" the caller asked.

"It's the girl, the one the Feds have been looking for!"

"No shit! How did you find her out there in all that grass?"

Approaching the sheriff's cruiser, Carson answered, "I guess you could say I got lucky, Buck. Fetch me a set of those cuffs. Then get on the horn and call the Feds."

Buck swung open the Chevy door and grabbed a set of cuffs off the front seat. "Take your gun out and lay it on the seat, Buck." The deputy gave Carson an annoyed look, but removed his gun as he was told. "She's that dangerous?" he asked. "She's put the lights out in three of her own kind today alone. I'd say that makes her pretty dangerous in anybody's book."

"I guess you're right," said Buck, sizing her up.

"Okay, ma'am, I want you to turn around and lower your hands, but keep them behind your back."

Isabel did as she was told. Buck started toward her with the cuffs.

"Stand clear, Buck! Not yet," Carson commanded. Buck stopped in his tracks.

"Now, ma'am, I want you to spread your legs." Isabel moved them a bit. "Wider," Carson shouted, "Or I'll shoot you in the ass right here and now." Isabel knew he meant it. She stretched her legs farther apart. "That's better," he said. "Now cuff her, Buck."

Seconds later, Isabel felt the cold steel bracelets close tightly around her wrists. An instant later, the deputy gave her a shove. Isabel hit the ground hard as her feet flew out from under her. She hadn't expected to be cuffed at the ankles. Jerking her legs together, Buck snapped the cuffs around her small ankles and jumped to his feet as though he'd roped a steer in record time.

"Open the trunk and toss her in," Carson ordered. "The Feds up on the bridge are waiting." Buck popped the trunk lid and stuffed her inside. Only then did Tom Carson, the county sheriff, lower his three fifty-seven Magnum.

The short ride to the bridge was miserable for Isabel. Her side ached from lying on top of a shovel. Her feet were numb. The gunshot wound was raw from the chaffing bandage and was bleeding again. Isabel wished she had chosen the bullet.

30

DEJA VU

Wes watched as Spence Riker taxied the 767 off the end of the runway and onto the secluded concrete apron. It was dark, with just enough light to make out the tops of the tall pines surrounding the hidden ramp. He and Marino got out of the jeep and walked to the mobile stairs as Spence cut the last engine.

A minute later, the main cabin door popped open and Riker and Fritz Hamilton stepped onto the platform. Neither wore a uniform. Wes waited at the bottom of the stairs. He wondered what Spence would have to say to him. He didn't have any idea what to expect. What was the feeling among his fellow pilots? Had he been fired? One question after another raced through his mind as the company's chief pilot descended the stairs.

Commander Marino looked on impatiently, wanting to get on with the task at hand. Wes felt the same way, but first he'd have to deal with Riker.

"Hello, Wes," Spence said as he stuck out his right hand. "I see you've changed uniforms since I saw you in New York." Wes managed a smile as he shook hands with TIA's chief pilot.

"Yes, I've been recalled to active duty."

Riker seemed cordial enough. Did he not know the whole story? Wes debated whether he should give him the details. There would be time enough for that once the inquiry began.

Spence looked over at Marino. "Spence Riker."

"Doug Marino." The two shook hands.

"Commander, the aircraft is yours." The look on Doug's face turned dead-serious as he spoke. "Let's hope we can make your trip down here worthwhile, Captain Riker. Now, if you'll excuse me, I've got work to do."

Wes, Spence, and Fritz stepped back as Marino bounded up the stairs and disappeared through the cabin entrance. "Is he always that serious, Wes?" Riker asked. "Only when he's working, I guess," Wes answered. Spence frowned.

"What's going on here, Wes? I can't get anyone to tell me a damn thing," Riker said. "What have you heard, Spence?" Wes asked. "Just that the White House needs this 767 and will accept full responsibility for it. Otherwise, not a blessed thing," he said. Wes could see Spence was pissed.

It was obvious the NSC didn't want anyone to know any more than was absolutely necessary about the operation. Still, he was going to need Spence's help with some of the more technical details of his plan, and Spence could be trusted. Fritz was another matter. He'd never learned to keep his mouth shut.

"Who did you talk to at the White House?" Wes asked.

"The president's national security adviser."

"You mean Gaylord Elliot."

Riker looked surprised. "Yeah, he's the one. He seems to have a high regard for you. Matter of fact, he said the president did too. Do you know the president, Wes?"

"Not really. I only met him when I went to the White House yesterday. I sat in on several security council meetings he attended."

"Elliot says you're a key player in the solution to this thing, Wes. What in the hell have they talked you into doing?"

Wes weighed his question before he answered. "Fritz, I need to talk with Spence alone for a few minutes. Would you mind?"

Fritz gave Wes an annoyed look and walked off toward the waiting Navy staff car. Wes and Spence turned around to face the 767.

"Spence, the SEALS are going to take over the jet in a pre-dawn assault day after tomorrow and I'm going to fly it into the Atlantic as quickly as we can get it launched."

"And after you get it out there, what then?" Spence asked.

"Then I take a flying leap into the deep blue sea and hope the U.S. Navy can haul my ass out before that sucker goes off." Riker's expression changed. "How do you feel about that? There's a hell of a lot of water out there."

Wes gave his boss a serious look. "Spence, there's more to it than you know. Besides, who else is in a better position than I?" Riker stared into Wes's weathered face. "What can I do to help?"

"First off, make certain Fritz doesn't speak a word of the flight down here or anything he might have heard along the way. The guy's got a big mouth. I know from experience," Wes said. "More importantly, I'll need your help in making sure we have the necessary ground support when we take control of the aircraft. I'll need at least ten thousand pounds of fuel in the trucks ready to be driven out to the aircraft and at least two pneumatic starter carts and an external power cart ready to be pulled into position as soon as the SEALS seize the jet."

"I can handle all that. Should I work through Elliot?" Spence asked.

Wes thought for a second, then reached for his billfold. "Have you got something to write with?" Riker pulled a pen and a business card from his pocket. "Shoot." Wes read him the number. Spence copied it down, then read it back. "It's a private number to the White House. It rings the chief of staff's office. Tell whoever answers that you're part of the EMPRESS operation and need to speak with either Gaylord Elliot or Forest Lindsey, the president's chief of staff. Either man will ensure that all the necessary arrangements are made to put you in control of the support effort at National," Wes said. "Oh, and keep the name EMPRESS to yourself. Don't let another soul even hear the word. Its classification exceeds TOP SECRET."

Spence took a hard look at Wes. Glancing back at the jumbo jet, Riker shook his head in disbelief. "I'll handle it for you, Wes. If you need anything else, call. I guess the White House will know where to find me," he said. Wes offered his hand. Spence gripped it solidly. "I thought you were coming with us."

"No, I'll be up most of the night with the SEALS. We've got to put the assault plan together."

"I'll drink a cold one for you. Good luck."

Riker gave Wes a parting look and headed for the waiting staff car. Suddenly he turned around and asked, "What about your family, Wes? Anything I can do for them?"

Wes smiled. Knowing Spence had them in his thoughts made him feel good. "They're okay for now, but they may need everything you can do for them later."

"Don't you worry about a thing, buddy. They'll get the best TIA can offer as long as I have anything to do with it."

"Thanks, Spence. I appreciate it."

Alone, Wes stood on the dark ramp underneath the August night's canopy. Only the drone of the 767's auxiliary power unit disturbed an otherwise beautiful night. He missed Meredith already. Wes thought of her and of what he would have to endure before they could be together.

"Tell me about the slides on these doors, Wes? How are they armed?" Doug asked. Wes bent over and pointed to the two small yellow tabs. "When the yellow tabs are in view, the slides are armed," he answered.

"And to disarm them?"

Wes pointed to the lever and moved it to the DETENT position. The tabs disappeared. Marino nodded his understanding. "We'll want to pop one of these slides just to get a feel for what we may have to deal with," he said. Doug saw Wes smile. "What's the grin for?" he asked. Wes answered, "Deja vu!"

"What's that suppose to mean?"

"Nothing really," Wes replied, "except that ten years ago at this exact spot on a 727 another SEAL commander told me the same thing."

"And what happened then?" Marino asked. "His men popped a door to see for themselves."

"Was it a problem for them?"

"No, they ripped the bladders open with their knives before the CO_2 cartridges could even begin to inflate them."

"Let's hope it works that way here, too," Doug said.

"Colonel Beacham, could you come here a minute?" Wes turned around and walked down the left aisle. Several SEALS were checking out the over-wing exits. One spoke. "Sir, how do you operate these over-wing chutes?"

Wes completed his briefing and went forward to find Marino. He found the SEAL commander seated in first class, engrossed in his notes. Doug looked up at Wes. "I want to know exactly what you think we can expect once we gain access to the cabin. I need to know where you think the terrorists will be stationed and where the cabin team might be."

"That's a tough one. The cabin team could be anywhere in the cabin, depending on what Reza has told them. The same is true for his men," Wes replied. "Yeah, I know that, but give me your best guess."

"From what we learned from the president's visit, all of the hostages were dispersed in the aft cabin and they all had blankets over their heads. All but two flight attendants were positioned there, as well. My guess is that at least three of the terrorists will be in the aft cabin. The rest are probably stationed in the mid-cabin business section and outside, beneath the jet. There may be a single guard at the main entrance. Only Ahmed, Mohammed, or Reza will be in the cockpit," Wes said.

"Where would the terrorists rest?" Marino asked.

"Near the front section of business class, I would imagine."

Marino looked at the cabin seating chart in his lap. "Suppose the aircraft burst into flames while waiting to take off and you decided to evacuate the aircraft. How would you start a ground evacuation?"

"From the overhead panel in the cockpit, I would lift a red guarded switch to activate the EVAC alarm. The same could be done from the flight attendants' control panel at the left main entrance door — the L1 position."

"How can it be silenced?"

"It can only be silenced from the station from which it was activated. The reasoning is that once an evacuation has begun, it should not be stopped until the person who initiated it has determined the need no longer exists."

"Suppose you lose electrical power to the EVAC system?"

"First, that's highly unlikely because the EVAC alarm is considered essential equipment and is wired directly to the battery bus and..."

Marino interrupted. "Yeah, but what if it malfunctioned?"

"I'd use the PA and give the command EARLY VACATION. The flight attendants would know from that phrase to start the evacuation without further direction."

Wes watched as Doug jotted down the information. "Do you want to hear what the alarm sounds like?" Wes offered. The SEAL commander shook his head.

"No, not now. We'll hold off on that until the plan is ready for a dry run."

"Now tell me about cabin lighting. What kind of problems are my men going to have once they penetrate the cabin?"

"You mean how they're apt to be set and where the controls to change it are?"

"Yes, that, plus the cabin emergency lighting system."

"The master emergency lighting switch is on the overhead panel in the cockpit and has three positions. When passengers are on board it is normally set in the ARMED position. This enables the emergency lights in the cabin, including the escape path lighting system in the aisles, to come on automatically the instant it senses a power failure. It can also be switched on by putting the switch to the ON position."

Wes paused as Doug continued to write. He used the time to reflect on the role he had yet to play. He would need a couple of parachutes equipped with water wings, a helmet, an inflatable dinghy, signaling and survival gear, and a pair of flight boots. A trip to the life support shop here should take care of that, he thought.

"Take a look at this and tell me what you think," Doug said.

Wes took the steno pad and studied the sequence of events carefully. Marino had done a thorough job of planning. "I've marked the probable terrorists and initial SEAL team positions," he added. Wes flipped the page and studied the diagram. The symbols reminded him of the football plays Coach Cranford would draw on the blackboard. Somehow it hadn't seemed to matter. Most of the backs, including him, could never seem to find the hole they were supposed to run through. Wes prayed the SEALS were better at carrying out their coach's plays.

"Deciding to use the over-wing exits to get your men aboard the aircraft makes a lot of sense because the slides are disabled when the exits are opened from the outside," Wes said. "But you're going to need specially constructed boarding ladders to get them in there quickly without damaging the aircraft."

Taking another look out the cabin window, Doug agreed.

"The fabrication shop at the hanger did it for us the last time," Wes said. "Do you want me to handle the coordination while you work with your men?"

"It would be a big help," Doug answered, gratefully.

Wes got up and went to the cockpit. He gave tower a call, then went outside to wait for the welders.

The SEALS were getting their first hard look at the 767. Wes studied the young men as they moved about the aircraft. He didn't recognize any familiar faces, but the spirit and intensity of commitment was the same. Nothing will stop these men, he thought.

31

OPLAN EMPRESS

M cGarth and the National Security Council listened intently as Gaylord Elliot summarized the major features of what was now the EMPRESS plan. No one bothered to interrupt as he walked them through the scenario, pausing briefly where applicable to explain pertinent aspects of the plan's chronology.

"Gaylord, what happens if the jet is damaged during the assault and isn't flyable? What then?" Burt Williamson asked.

"I'll let General Griffith answer that one," Elliot replied. "Once we've secured control of the aircraft, a specially shaped charge will be placed in the vicinity of the cargo compartment, and we'll detonate it."

"How certain are you that it won't inadvertently set off a chain reaction?" questioned Secretary of State Halston.

McGarth noticed the reticence in Clayton's voice as he answered, "We're reasonably certain."

A hush fell over the Situation Room.

"It's our only other alternative, gentlemen," said the president, "unless you would prefer to wait for the timer to do it for us."

"Why so much delay before we initiate the attack, Clayton?" Sinclair asked. "I'd think we'd be better off getting this thing over with as soon as possible, wouldn't you?"

"John, we're going to need every minute of that time to modify the EMPRESS II. Not only do we have to essentially redesign the electronics on board to cover a different frequency spectrum, but we also have to re-engineer the antenna array so we can get it through the Wilson Bridge. We'll be lucky to get it all assembled by O four hundred day after tomorrow. Much of the work will have to be done while it is under tow."

"What about public notification plans, Gaylord? Is FEMA (Federal Emergency Management Administration) going to warn coastal residents of the possibility of a tidal wave?" Lindsey asked.

"Yes. It's included in our sequence of events," replied the FEMA director. "Once the jet is airborne, we'll activate the Emergency Broadcast network system. Alert advisories will be transmitted continuously until we receive confirmation of the weapon's status from DOD."

Mason hated the fact that FEMA would not be able to use tomorrow for an evacuation of the District. It had been a tough call, but under the circumstances, he had no choice. McGarth knew it was a decision that would be debated for months afterward.

"Gaylord, what's the situation with the murders of these two Arabs, Rashid and Abdulla? Do we know how they fit into the terrorists' plans?" asked the treasury secretary.

Elliot looked at Sinclair. "John, why don't you go ahead and start your briefing now? You can cover Millicent's question while you're at it."

The FBI director nodded and flipped open a single classified red folder. "Millicent, we're nearly one hundred per cent sure these four Arabs hold code material that can be used to disarm the weapon's mechanical timer should the coalition's sponsors decide not to detonate the device. We're less certain of the specifics of the code, and we don't have any feel for what criteria the FC has established to rule out exploding the bomb.

"We've learned that Aladdin Automatic Door Company did ship four automatic garage door remote receivers to a construction company in Cyprus. We suspect that system has been employed to give the FC a form of two-man control over the decision to stop the timer. Middle East specialists seem to feel the arrangement was set up more as a way to give each sponsor a final say in the decision. They suspect that each sponsor may hold a single digit to the code that he would have to authorize the use of, much like a vote. Presumably, all the sponsors would have to agree to stop the timer before the code would be known.

"Aladdin's automatic garage door opening system uses a four-digit code. The operator is given three chances to input the correct code before the system locks out further attempts.

"We think one or more of the FC's sponsors is determined to see that the bomb is detonated and has sent this assassin to kill those with the digits. We suspect Rashid and Abdulla were killed because they held parts of the code. However, we are at a loss to explain why it is necessary to kill both men unless each sponsor holds two of the code's four necessary digits. In that case, three of the four Arabs would have to be eliminated to ensure that the timer could not be stopped."

"John, do we know for certain who is backing the coalition?" asked the secretary of state. "We've drawn a complete blank from our contacts at the State Department," Halston complained.

Sinclair looked across the table at the treasury secretary. "Millicent, how much progress has Treasury made in deciphering those accounts on that diskette discovered in Geneva?"

Longsworth directed her reply to the president. "So far, we've been able to trace the accounts to four Middle East banks with strong ties to Iran, Iraq, Lebanon, and Libya, although we've found nothing concrete to prove any one of them is behind the attack. All accounts are governed by Swiss banking regulations. This is proving difficult for us to breach. But we have made some progress with the banks involved. We can expect more information once the accounts receive activity again. Major withdrawals in the form of electronic transfers appear to have been made for investment purposes. We are reasonably certain the coalition has been 'shorting' the dollar with significant purchases of yen, Deutsche marks, francs, and pounds for the last several days. If that proves to be the case, we can expect them to start buying back the dollars at the height of the crisis."

John glanced at McGarth before he spoke. "To follow up on the status of our continuing investigation in Geneva, we received less than an hour ago a positive ID from the two airport security people who screened Jabarri and Mohammed Al-Farsi. Both recognized Jabarri from his photograph and recalled examining his mobile phone and a remote control unit that he carried in his briefcase. The RC unit appeared to be the same as the one pictured in an Aladdin brochure. They were less certain about his associate, Mohammed.

"The Mossad has also furnished us with extensive background information on the seven terrorists. All have, at one time, been associated with well-known terrorists organizations.

"Fingerprints on the diskette matched those found on a tube of lipstick belonging to Andrea Zahar, the receptionist. The prints also matched those the FBI has on file. Our records indicate that Zahar was arrested at a political protest demonstration five years ago while a student here in Washington. It might interest you to know that she holds an MBA from Wharton, where she majored in investment portfolio management. A State Department diplomat from Germany confirmed her identification. He remembered her from several visits to the FC office in Geneva. The Mossad has managed to tie her recent activities to several fundamentalist movements."

The president interrupted. "Do we suspect Andrea's responsible for the financial operation of the coalition?"

"From what we know now, yes, sir," replied Sinclair.

"Then shouldn't there also be a record of the purchase of the automatic door equipment on that disk?" McGarth asked.

John looked at Millicent for support. "Sir, it may well be that there is a record of those transactions on that diskette. I will have the Treasury re-examine it immediately," Longsworth answered.

"Millicent, I realize your major concern has been the currency issue and it must remain that way until we can find solid support for the dollar. The point I want to make is that we need to look at every piece of evidence with an eye toward building an infallible case against the sponsors of this act. Once we've gotten this nuke off National Airport, I intend to send Maggie back to the U.N. with enough ammunition to get maximum economic and, depending on whose involved, military sanctions against each of the sponsors," the president explained. "Please continue, John."

"Could we go back to the four Arabs, John?" interjected the secretary of defense. "What do we know about their backgrounds?"

"Their detailed biographical histories are listed in the folders in front of you. What we suspect is that each of these men represents one of the members of the coalition. Rashid Sedki was Iranian. Abdulla El Laben, though an Egyptian by birth, spent the majority of his time in Lebanon and was connected with the PLO. Yaqoob Shah was born in Libya and had ties to the Qadafhi regime. And, as we only learned recently, Nsar Ajmani, an Iraqi, has maintained a long association with the government of Saddam Hussein."

"Is it the consensus that these four men are acting as proxies for these governments, John?" Jacobson asked.

"Yes," Sinclair replied.

Gaylord glanced at the other members and then the president before he spoke. McGarth appeared to have nothing he wanted to say.

"Before we adjourn, I've asked Sloan Kilgore to cover FEMA's Covert Actions plan. He'll brief you on the specific details of the inter-agency lateral dispersal plan. The most important aspect of this plan is to ensure that it is implemented in such a way so as not to draw the media's attention. I can't overemphasize that while we must preserve the continuity and integrity of every governmental agency, we cannot afford to compromise the EMPRESS plan and tip off these terrorists. Therefore, each of you must use the utmost discretion in its application. Sloan."

As Sloan Kilgore, the director of FEMA was about to speak, John Sinclair, holding a note just handed to him by a staff aide, interrupted. "Please excuse me, sir, but there is an urgent matter that has just been brought to my attention. Yaqoob Shah has just been found dead. His neck has been broken. With your permission, Mr. President, I'd like to follow this up personally."

McGarth frowned. "Dammit, John! That's three in one day! And I gave my word to Reza the other two would be given safe passage if we were allowed to bring them in. There's no telling what kind of response he'll have to this news!"

Sinclair stood silent and waited for the president's answer.

"Yes, by all means, John. Go and find out what's happened. And, while you're about it, find out if we've actually got the fourth one in protective custody...and get back to me right away," McGarth said. "I'll have to come up with one hell of a story to keep Jabarri from blowing us all up right now!"

*   *   *

The chopper flight back to D.C. from Edgewater took less than thirty minutes. Coleman spent the time debriefing Baxter. He needed to know every single detail of what had transpired prior to seeing Director Sinclair. He dreaded the meeting.

The young assassin had not spoken a word since being turned over to him. Shackled at the wrists and ankles, she pretended to sleep. No one knew her name, let alone where she had come from or for whom she worked. Dave wondered what Sinclair would do with her.

FBI personnel greeted the flight as it landed and took charge of the prisoner. Coleman and Baxter were told to go straight to the director's office. Sinclair was waiting for them. "What happened, Dave? How did we lose Yaqoob Shah?"

Coleman explained the best he knew how, stopping to allow Baxter to fill in the details. Sinclair listened intently, interrupting occasionally for clarification.

"So, in essence, we never received any information suggesting Yaqoob Shah was likely to be on the company's boat or that he often stayed on the boat for long periods? Is that correct?" Sinclair asked.

"Yes, sir," Dave answered. The director looked down at the notes on his desk. "I just talked with the president's chief of staff, Forest Lindsey. He said Jabarri didn't mention anything to him about Yaqoob spending any time on the boat either. My guess is Jabarri either didn't know it or forgot to tell us." Glancing over at Baxter, Sinclair said, "It's just too bad for us you didn't think to check out that possibility, Bernie, although I doubt it would have made that much difference. From what you've told me, Yaqoob had just arrived at the marina shortly before the assassin."

"Yes, sir," Bernie replied.

Sinclair didn't say anything for a few seconds. Then he stood up and walked from behind his desk. "I don't have any more questions, gentlemen. I'm satisfied you did the best you could with the information you had. Dave, I want you to stay on the case. See what you can get out of her and keep me posted."

Sinclair waited until the two agents had left his office, then he called the interrogations section. Agent Stafford answered. He recognized the director's voice. "Stafford, have your people been able to get anything out of the girl?"

"No sir. She's a tough one — won't speak. I talked with the sheriff from Edgewater who captured her. He said she spoke to him in perfect English. He got the impression she may have been educated here in the States."

"Has her in-processing work been completed?"

"Yes sir, the data, prints, and photos have been sent out by wire. I've requested priority handling. Whatever is on file should be in here within the next several hours."

"Let me know the instant you learn anything, Stafford."

Sinclair had barely gotten the receiver back on the hook when his phone rang. He recognized the resonant voice. It was Forest Lindsey at the White House.

"John. It's Forest. Have you gotten the girl to talk yet?"

"No. She's being interrogated now, but we're not having much success. She's not talking."

"We've got another problem, John. Jabarri just called. He wants to talk to Ajmani and Yaqoob. The president wants your thoughts on the matter before he gives Reza an answer."

"How much time do we have?"

"I told Jabarri we'd get back to him by midnight. He sounded impatient, but said he'd wait for us to set it up."

"I'd better come over there. Give me ten minutes."

"I'll tell the president you're on the way."

Sinclair put the phone down. There was no way they could deny Jabarri's request. One way or the other, Reza would have to be told the truth. The question was, how would he react? Sinclair wondered, heading for the door.

Shortly before midnight Sinclair walked into the Oval Office. President McGarth, Forest Lindsey, Gaylord Elliot and Burt Williamson were huddled deep in conversation over Jabarri's latest request. Forest and Burt were doing most of the talking; McGarth and Elliot, the listening. John took a seat next to his protegé from the CIA. There was a noticeable difference of opinion over what to do. Burt wanted to hold off telling Reza until the last minute in the hopes of getting a positive ID on the assassin. Forest favored giving Reza the truth immediately.

"Forest, you don't have any assurances that Jabarri is going to take a rational approach to the news. Hell, he shot four innocent people before he learned the president hadn't lied to him! What makes you think he's going to behave any differently when he finds out a third Arab associate has been murdered?" Burt argued.

Forest countered. "That's just the point, Burt. The man reacts violently whenever he senses he's been misled. That's precisely why we can't afford to lie to him over this. Besides, if he chooses to challenge us to produce Yaqoob Shab in the flesh, we will all be dead in the water!"

"What do you think, Gaylord?" asked the president. "I tend to agree with Forest. I think we have to be candid with Jabarri, but Burt's got a point. He's unpredictable and prone to react irrationally when left to reason out the details."

McGarth leaned forward in his seat. "What do you suggest?"

Gaylord continued. "I think we have to set up the meeting he's requested and give him the assassin in place of Yaqoob. I would tell him that we don't think his Crystal City hotel is secure enough, given the situation, and we prefer to hold them at FBI headquarters. I would then stage a meeting at the Hoover Building and present him with all the evidence we have supporting our claim that we had nothing to do with the murders."

McGarth looked at the other three men. "What about Elliot's proposal?" he asked. "Giving Reza the girl makes a lot of sense to me," John said. "It's going to be hard for him to deny she did it, if we've got the evidence to prove it."

The president glanced at Burt. The CIA director put up his hands as he spoke. "I have to admit that's one way of maybe dampening his reaction. Of course we'll have to accept whatever he chooses to do with her and that in itself could be awfully gruesome."

"I don't think we have any choice if it comes to that," Forest argued. "Human rights isn't an issue at the moment," he said, sarcastically.

McGarth checked his watch. It was midnight. A few seconds later, his private phone rang. Forest rose from his chair and walked over to the chief executive's desk. "What shall I tell him?" McGarth paused a last second to decide.

"We'll go with Gaylord's plan," answered the president.

Lindsey picked up the receiver. "Forest Lindsey speaking."

"Yes, Mr. Jabarri. The president wishes me to tell you that he is very concerned over Mr. Ajmani's and Mr. Shah's safety and would like to have them held at FBI headquarters until morning. He assures you they will be given the best of care and protection. For security reasons, he would also like to suggest that the meeting take place at the Hoover Building at eight hundred hours, if that is agreeable."

Reza did not respond immediately. Forest held his breathe. Would McGarth's proposal evoke his rage?

"Eight hundred hours at the Hoover Building? That will be fine," Reza finally replied. "Have the limo pick me up at the aircraft fifteen minutes beforehand."

"Yes, of course. Good evening, Mr. Jabarri."

Forest hung up quickly, hoping Reza wouldn't think to ask to speak to his two associates. There was no contingency plan for that.

32

BETRAYAL

The morning sun's rays poured through the open window of Hassan's small fourth story flat on Rue de Candolle. Khalil enjoyed living near the Université in Geneva. It served as a safe haven for his coalition activities while providing him the chance to cultivate relationships with students of his same persuasion. Work on his doctorate had consumed much of his time during the initial stage of his program, but was now quite manageable. Hassan savored his clandestine duties. He relished not being openly linked to the fundamentalist movement, yet holding a key position in its hierarchy. He coveted the intrigue associated with his position.

Today, Hassan awoke troubled. He paid no attention to the beautiful sunshine nor would he bother to pause at the window before getting dressed as he usually did. Preoccupied, he had a strange feeling something had gone wrong.

Rolling over in his bed, Hassan stared at the clock on the nightstand. It was seven hundred hours. The six hour difference meant it was one a.m. in the United States, he reasoned. Lying back on the bed, he gazed at the ornate ceiling. Why had he not heard from Isabel? He'd expected her call more than four hours ago. It was unlike her not to keep him posted. Had she been captured or killed? What should he do now? Saeed was expecting him at nine hundred hours.

Not bothering to shower, he dressed quickly and made his way down the long, winding staircase and into the busy streets of Geneva. Students moved hurriedly from one building to another as he stood debating his route. Concern over being followed required that he take a circuitous course to the FC's covert headquarters each day. This morning he would make an exception. He needed to arrive before Saeed and Andrea.

The short walk to the Porte de Plainpalais bus stop took less than five minutes. Boarding the bus, he found an abandoned Swiss newspaper. The headlines told of America's ongoing nightmare over the terrorists' attack and of their hopes for an early end to the siege. Hassan smugly recalled the role he'd had in planning it. He longed to be recognized for his role in humbling the Great Satan. Farther down the column, he found the sketchy details of Rashid's and Abdulla's deaths. There was no mention of Yaqoob Shah. That explained why Isabel hadn't made contact. Yaqoob must still be alive.

Stepping off the bus at Pl. du Rondeau, Hassan walked around the corner to a building near the intersection of Rue Ancienne and Rue Jacques Dalphin. Seeing no one, he stepped inside the alcove and unlocked the wooden door. Reaching the third floor, he slipped the key in the lock and opened the door. To his dismay, Andrea was already there.

"Andrea! Why are you here so early?"

"I had several trades to enter before the financial exchanges open this morning."

"Have you seen the paper?" Hassan asked.

"No. I was here before they hit the streets."

Hassan handed Andrea the newspaper he'd found on the bus and pointed to the feature. "Read this," he said. "What is it?" she asked. "More discussion of our campaign?"

"Yes, but that's not the important part," he replied.

Andrea focused on the paragraph just above Kahlil's finger. "Rashid and Abdulla are dead? How?" she exclaimed.

"Both were shot by an assassin, according to the paper."

"But who, Hassan? Who would do such a thing? Certainly not the Americans — they have too much to lose."

"Perhaps the Mossad. They would like nothing better than to drag the United States into a confrontation with the Middle East."

"I find it hard to believe that even the Mossad would risk such a venture. The consequences would be too great if they were discovered," Andrea replied, reading farther. She had an uneasy feeling about their associates' deaths.

Hassan walked over to the small console and sat down in front of the bank of portable telephones. He was worried. Yaqoob's name was missing from the list. Baghdad would have already read the same paper. They would want to know what had happened. Sweat broke out across his forehead as Hassan recalled Baghdad's instructions and the consequences, should he and Isabel fail. His stomach turned as he fought the urge to wretch. He debated leaving, on the pretense of being sick. He could then call Tony, the chopper pilot. He would know the score. But if she were safe and the job done, Isabel would be angry. He would wait. There was enough work to keep him busy. *Operation Chunnel* was still in the early-planning stages.

As Hassan was about to open his valise, Saeed entered the office. Hassan could tell from his expression that he had seen the article. He paused in front of Andrea's computer. "You've read the newspaper?" he asked.

"Yes," she answered.

"Who has done this? The Americans?" Saeed questioned.

Andrea glanced at Hassan before she replied. "No. There is no reason to suspect them. The Americans are as much in the dark over their deaths as we. Besides, would you try it with a gun to your head?"

Hassan saw the puzzled look on Saeed's face as he reflected on Andrea's reply. Did she know? Her glances unnerved him.

"Then who? And why?" Saeed asked.

As Andrea was about to respond, one of the portable telephones rang. Saeed glanced over at the small console desk and saw Hassan pick up the receiver. It was Reza. Beckoning for Saeed, Hassan laid the phone on the desk. He knew the call was unplanned. It had to be about Rashid's and Abdulla's deaths. As Saeed walked across the room, Hassan offered his seat, but Saeed shook his head and motioned for him to stay seated. Placing the receiver into the amplifier/speaker cradle, Saeed adjusted the volume. Hassan watched as a small tape recorder switched on automatically to tape the conversation.

"Yes? Please go ahead," Saeed replied.

"We have a serious problem here. Someone is trying to sabotage our operation." Hassan recognized Reza's voice. He was angry.

"Yes, we've just seen the newspaper," Saeed said.

"Then you know of the deaths of two of our council members?"

"Yes, it is very unfortunate. What is the status of the other two?" asked Saeed.

"They are safe for now, in protective custody."

Saeed's eyes narrowed as he asked, "What do you mean, 'protective custody'?"

"It was the only way I could be sure that the other two members would not also be killed. I had no choice. We need them both for the code."

Saeed nodded. One was no good without the other.

"Where are they now?" he asked.

"The FBI is holding them, on the president's orders. I will meet with both of them at eight hundred hours this morning."

"Does the president know of their roles?"

"No. I haven't told him. The president knows only that America's welfare depends on their safety."

"And you are confident the authorities will not try to interrogate them?" Saeed asked.

"Yes. They will not try anything. Our threat has them completely subdued, but I'm very concerned over these deaths. We have an internal problem," Reza answered. "You must find the infidel immediately. Our plan must not be compromised."

Saeed's face turned serious as he promised Reza, "I will learn the truth behind this disgrace before the day is done, my brother. Call when you have seen the members. I will know by then who has jeopardized our mission."

"I will call at sixteen hundred hours," Reza said. "That is good," replied Saeed, as he took the phone from the tape machine cradle and hung it up.

The lightning blow to his jaw knocked Hassan to the floor. Afraid to cry out, the young Arab lay where he had fallen as Saeed stood over him. "It is you who have betrayed us! It could only be you, Hassan!" he shouted. Kahlil covered his head as he cried out. "It was not me! I did not want this.... I had no choice! I only followed orders!"

"Whose orders, Hassan? Saddam Hussein's?" shouted Saeed, striking Hassan again. Hassan cried out in pain as Saeed jerked his head back, exposing the frightened young man's unshaven face. "You will answer my question now, or die by the knife, Hassan! I will not tolerate infidels!"

Kahlil felt blood — his blood — trickle down the side of his neck as Keshef pressed the blade deeper into his flesh. Would he not die the death of a martyr? Saddam had promised he would. Blood was rushing down the side of his neck now. He had no time. "Yes, yes....It was

Saddam. Those were his orders.....It was the only way he would agree to join the coalition!" Hassan cried out.

Easing the knife from Kahlil's throat, Saeed spoke. "And you betrayed us by not telling me of his terms?"

"Yes! Yes! He made me swear an oath of allegiance that I would tell no one. He vowed to kill all my family if I revealed his plans!"

Saeed withdrew the knife from Hassan's neck. "Tell me of his plan," Saeed demanded. "Hussein has no respect for our cause."

Quietly intervening, Andrea wrapped a towel she'd taken from the adjoining bathroom around Hassan's bleeding neck. Saeed waited as she helped him back into his chair. Hassan pressed the cloth hard against his neck as he spoke.

"Saddam demanded the names and addresses of the other three coalition representatives in return for his participation. I gave him the information on the condition he agree to join. But once Saddam had the names, he threatened to expose me if I did not cooperate with him."

Saeed's expression softened as he listened to his comrade. Hassan continued, "He told me a girl named Isabel would contact me and that I should report her every move via telephone to a number in Baghdad. He said that if I failed to do as I was told or if she failed in her assignment, we would both be killed along with our families."

Keshef stared at Hassan and then at Andrea. "Go on."

"Her first contact with me was two days before the flight left Geneva. She wanted information on the Russians."

"What information?" snapped Saeed.

"Where they were going once they received their money." Saeed looked puzzled. "How did you know where to tell her to find them? Only Andrea knew that."

"I knew. I used her computer to find out where their money was being wired. I was sure they would go there first. Don't you remember that I had Shevinsky followed from the airport after he saw that the bomb was airborne aboard the TIA flight? I told you it was to make certain he was not discovered by the KGB. After he left the bank, I had him followed back to the airport to verify his destination was Athens."

Hassan saw anger flare in Saeed's eyes as he learned of the betrayal, but continued. "Isabel was already in Athens, watching Andrei. Isabel killed the three of them in Athens two nights ago."

"And why was this not in the newspaper?" Saeed asked.

"It was, but I took that page from the paper before you arrived yesterday. Had you seen it, I was to have suggested robbery as the motive," he added, mopping the blood from his neck.

Saeed took a chair from the conference table and pulled it up to Hassan's desk. The story was more complex than he'd thought. Andrea put a fresh towel around Hassan's neck. Noticing his bleeding had subsided, Andrea saw the cut wasn't as severe as she'd imagined, though Hassan had lost a lot of blood.

"And killing the Russians was to make certain they would not reveal the code?" questioned Saeed.

"Yes. Baghdad was uncertain whether Andrei might have given the numbers to Shevinsky and Kashnichev in the event something happened to him," he explained.

Saeed thought for a second and then asked, "Before or after the council members made the trip to meet with Andrei to get their code digits?"

"They decided after. Baghdad used their visit to collect information and pictures for Isabel," Hassan replied. "You recall that was when Andrei showed the members how to transmit their input to disarm the bomb and verify the timer stopping."

Impatient to know the whole truth, Keshef recapped the plan's next step. "Then Isabel flew to the U.S. armed with names, addresses, maps and photographs and began to systematically assassinate the council members, knowing their deaths would effectively block any chance of our defusing the weapon and avoiding Washington's destruction."

Hassan said nothing, hanging his head in shame.

Saeed looked over at Andrea as he spoke. "I should kill him now," he said with disgust. "He is a disgrace to us all. Were it not for Reza having Yaqoob and Nsar in protective custody, our plans for retaining the bomb would be useless."

"We knew from the start Saddam could not be trusted. He was always our weakest link. He only cares about revenge," Andrea said. "He would do anything to provoke a holy war within the Middle East. It's the only way he has of staying in power."

Looking at Hassan, Andrea said, "Spare him. His testimony to others is worth his life. The others must learn who they can trust before we attack the channel tunnel. Besides, we've lost only our backup for the code. Yaqoob and Nsar are still alive."

* * *

Sinclair answered on the fourth ring. The voice on the other end was apologetic. The FBI director was used to it. "Yes, never mind the hour. What's happened?" he asked.

"Sir, we've intercepted a call from Jabarri to Geneva. It was to the other international preset number on the mobile phone we confiscated from Middleburg. It's to a mobile number there."

John sat up in bed. "Yes."

"We believe he spoke to Saeed Keshef, the coalition's covert leader, although the voice at the other end never identified himself."

Now wide awake, John felt a surge of adrenalin as he listened without interruption to a taped account of the conversation. When it was over, he had the Bureau communications specialist replay it.

"Have you notified the CIA, yet?" John asked. "No, sir."

"Call Director Williamson and play the tape for him, then send the CIA a copy. Prepare two copies for the White House and have them delivered to Forest Lindsey and Gaylord Elliot, immediately."

Sinclair put down the phone, already digesting the meaning of the conversation. Jabarri was worried. He knew the U.S. was not to blame for the assassinations. But an even greater threat now loomed. There was no way left to defuse the bomb. Only Reza could stop the bomb from destroying Washington and everything in its path. The chances of that happening were slim to none. To do so would subvert the purpose of the terrorist attack and represent an enormous embarrassment to the Fundamentalist Coalition. Jabarri would not let that happen, no matter what the consequences. He couldn't. Operation EMPRESS had to succeed, if Washington was to be spared.

With barely two hours sleep, Sinclair called for his driver, then dressed. He knew Gaylord would want his opinion as soon as he heard the tape. Predicting Reza's response to the news of Yaqoob's death would be easier now that they knew he didn't hold the United States accountable for the Arab's death. Checking the time, John saw it was three a.m., five hours before Reza's visit and seven hours before he would call Geneva again. Rubbing the sleep from his eyes, he slid into the back seat of the limousine for the short ride to the White House.

The town had an eerie look about it — still — devoid of action and people. Sinclair tried to visualize how Washington would appear after the bomb had exploded. Deciding it was impossible to imagine such an apocalyptic event, he tried to dismiss the thought. A shiver passed through him as he wondered how a catastrophe of that magnitude would alter the nation's future. He drew a blank. Too much of what Americans had come to take for granted would be permanently changed to make any sense out of what such a future would hold.

As the car sped past the Washington monument, John's thoughts turned to Dave Coleman and the plan he'd proposed several hours ago. For a second, he regretted having given it even his tentative approval. Parts of it were clearly unlawful and lay well beyond his power to authorize. Yet, with the veil of terrorism surrounding Washington, would Americans really care whether what he had approved was lawful? Sinclair asked himself. Was it ethical, or rational, to send thousands of soldiers to death to ferret out the likes of a tyrant such as Hussein, when equally effective covert options could have been applied at much less cost in human lives? Did the means justify the end? Perhaps.

Turning into the White House driveway, Sinclair reversed his feelings on the matter. He was satisfied with his earlier decision. If Coleman were successful, he would propose the plan to the president.

33

THE PROPOSAL

Cynthia Roseman dozed as she lay in the fetal position across the two right corner seats to the rear of the business class section. The center pedestal separating the seats had been pulled out and discarded long ago to make sleeping possible. Two cabin pillows cushioned her head against the wall seat's armrest. Though Sybil had insisted on them using a buddy system to enhance their personal security, Cynthia had paid it little mind. Tossing caution to the wind, she chose to sleep alone, unsupervised. It was enough that Reza had agreed to allow them to sleep at all.

From her jump seat at the main entrance to the cabin, Sybil had noticed that the terrorist patrolling the aisles seemed to pause each time he passed Cynthia's seat, but she thought nothing of it and soon fell asleep herself. Rachel, her back to the rear of the cabin, watched Sybil nap. Neither had seen the terrorist slide the partition curtain closed.

At first, Cynthia thought the pressure she felt against her body was caused by the position she had been lying in. Still asleep, she tried to move, but couldn't. A second later, her eyes flew open wide as she stared into the faceless shadow of a man fondling her breasts. Cynthia recognized the putrid smell of his unwashed body. It was one of the terrorist guards—the one she'd seen with the lust-filled eyes—the Ugly One.

She lashed out at him, clawing the left side of his face with her fingernails. As she tried to scream, the palm of his hand clamped over her mouth like a vise, crushing her jaw into the side of her face. Then she saw the flash of his knife blade as he brought it first to her eyes, then lowered it to rest against her throat. A fiendish smile spread across his unshaved face as he spoke with his eyes. Cynthia understood immediately what he wanted. He would not be denied his desire for her flesh.

Cynthia felt him casually strip away the clothes from her body, pausing frequently to admire and kiss her supple white flesh. He seemed in no hurry to have his moment of satisfaction, content to paw her body as though she were the fallen prey of a conquering predator. She prayed for unconsciousness, but it was not to be. The stench of his breath made her wretch. He mistook her involuntary abdominal movement as arousal and tore off the rest of her clothes while shedding those of his own that would impede his act.

Griping the calves of her long legs, he made his way up her naked body. Cursing herself for being so defiant of Sybil's warning, Cynthia struggled to focus on anything but what was taking place. Cringing as she felt his penetration, every nerve in her body begged for relief from his savage attack.

Imagining herself divorced from her body as he heaved his body against hers, Cynthia told herself what was happening was only a nightmare. Rage supplanted fear as she gradually came to accept her rape.

Releasing her as he withdrew, Cynthia silently swore she would kill him before the siege was over. Staring directly into his dark eyes, she sensed he understood her scorn. He scoffed at her as he stepped into his trousers. Lying motionless and afraid to move, another wave of fear swept over Cynthia as she thought of him returning. It would not happen again, she vowed. Kill or be killed. That is the way it must be. It was the only law they understood — an eye for an eye. The next would be his.

* * *

Isabel sat quietly in front of a small table in the interrogation room. Her head lay on her folded arms. By her calculations, she'd spent the last four hours listening to myriad questions without uttering a sound. Though tired, hungry, and in pain, she never faltered. Isabel understood what Baghdad expected — demanded — from her. If necessary, she was prepared to die in order to succeed.

Isabel didn't bother to look up when Dave Coleman entered the room. She saw only his shadow as he paced around the table in silence. Was he debating what to ask next? Surely he'd observed her through the one way mirror to know what had been asked.

"Alexandra?" the voice called.

Instinctively, Isabel raised her head before she realized what she had done. "That is your real name isn't it?" Dave asked. Isabel struggled to mask her mistake, but it was too late.

"Alexandra Jamel! That is your real name. You are Iraqi by birth, attended school in Baghdad, Paris, and later at Georgetown, where you studied physics and wined and dined with your father's arms merchants," continued Coleman.

"So? You know my name. What does that prove?" she said, mockingly.

"I think it tells us a lot about you, Alexandra. But more importantly, it gives us the information we need to force you to speak openly about who sent you to kill your Arab brothers."

"Never!" she blurted. "You will never bring me to tell you that. I would rather die first!"

His silence unnerved her. "Now that you know my name, what is yours?" she demanded. "Dave," he said. "Agent Dave Coleman."

She tried to read his face, but found little to go on except that he appeared to be smarter than he looked. She worried that he seemed content to simply stare at her. "Who told you my name?"

"In a way, you did." Alexandra looked puzzled.

"And how is that?" she demanded.

"We found the van you stole parked in the driveway of the home you took the boat from. Your fingerprints were all over the phone you used to call Tony at...."

"How did you find out about him?" Her dark eyes narrowed as she silently cursed herself for having been so careless.

"The telephone you used to call Tony had a redial feature. We simply pressed the button and got Aero Services of New Jersey. We have your pilot, Tony, in custody. I spoke with the agent handling his interrogation in Newark before I came to see you. It seems Tony is being very cooperative."

"He knows nothing!"

"True, but the Bureau has had your prints on file since you were first arrested as a student activist at Georgetown."

"You think you know so much! What you know is worthless!"

"Alexandra, we know you were sent here by Saddam to block defusing the nuclear weapon at the last available moment. That, we are certain, is fact. We also know you have succeeded in your assignment. Yaqoob Shah is dead."

Pausing, Dave saw the smirk on Alexandra's face grow larger as he mentioned the Arab yacht broker's death. "We also understand that there is no way the safety code can be retrieved and that detonation will occur once the timer's countdown is complete."

"And with it, will come the fall of America and its puppet, Israel," Alexandra added, proudly.

Dave made no effort to counter her assumption. "Miss Jamel, the fact is, you are of no real use to us now that you've been apprehended. Our other sources have already confirmed what I have revealed to you. For this reason, you will be handed over to Reza Jabarri and his fellow terrorists at eight hundred hours tomorrow morning. Mr. Jabarri's visit here has been scheduled by him for the express purpose of speaking with Mr. Ajmani and Mr. Shah. As you can imagine, the shock of learning that Mr. Shah is dead, and with it any chance of obtaining the necessary code material, is apt to come as a major surprise to him. From what we've come to know of Mr. Jabarri, I wouldn't expect him to be in the best of moods."

Unable to restrain her tears, Alexandra lowered her head to avoid having to listen to Coleman's analysis. The thought of suffering at the hands of Jabarri and his thugs was too painful for Alexandra to imagine. Her hands trembled as she placed them over her head. Death would be preferable to being handed over to that barbarian. She felt nauseous. She would have to try to escape. The worst would be a bullet through the head.

"Another point worth mentioning is that, although you've been successful at accomplishing your mission, Saddam doesn't know it, and with luck on our part, he will never discover it unless we so choose. That aspect of your predicament could be quite harmful for your large family, especially your young, innocent sisters."

Alexandra leaped at Coleman from behind the table. "You animal, you filthy swine! How dare you speak of my family!"

Dave sidestepped her as the two agents monitoring the interrogation rushed into the tiny room and subdued her with restraining cuffs around her arms and legs, Dave watched as Alexandra wept openly for her life. When he was certain her will was broken, he said, "Alexandra, life is full of alternatives, with death there is only emptiness. It is also true that few of us are strong enough to imagine life continuing for others while we lie abandoned in our own grave. Perhaps there is a way for you to avoid falling into Jabarri's hand."

Gradually, sadness replaced the fear in her eyes as she listened to Coleman. "How?" she asked softly. Dave lowered his voice. "By giving us Saddam — not now, but later."

Wrestling with the idea for a few seconds Alexandra sighed, "Impossible. It can't be done, even if I were to agree to it."

"Most people would have said the same thing about what you have already accomplished. Not trying would seem to be worse."

Though she said nothing at first, Dave sensed he'd piqued her interest. He waited patiently for her to speak. A minute later, Alexandra asked, "How would you protect me and my family from Saddam if I were able to do this for you?"

Knowing it was a pivotal question, Coleman took his time answering. "You and your family would be brought to America and, after sufficient schooling, would be given new identities and relocated to a state of your choosing. With careful planning, a good portion of your father's wealth could be salvaged and made available to your family to ensure that they could maintain their lifestyle. Their security, and yours, would be assured for the remainder of their lives. None of you would have to fear Saddam any longer."

"And how will you avoid handing me over to Jabarri?"

"On that point, we are less confident," Dave answered.

"But you said ....."

Dave interrupted. "Yes, I said there is a way, but it's not without risk."

"Then how? What will you do?" she asked.

Dave hesitated. "You will be shot, in a coma, and near death when he arrives. He will be told you tried to escape and were shot." Alexandra winced at the notion of being shot again. "Your being left for dead by Reza will depend on how convincing we can be," he added.

"What about Saddam? Why would he welcome me back?"

"Word would be passed that you were paralyzed and near death and that you were being held in a prison hospital. At the appropriate time, we would stage your escape. A local TV station would broadcast that Yaqoob Shah had been killed by the same assassin who murdered the other two Arabs, in spite of denials by our government. Eventually, proof of that would be leaked to the same source and it, too, would be made public. By the time of your escape, Saddam would have every reason to welcome your return."

"What if I were to double-cross you?" she probed.

"Saddam will receive proof, through indirect channels, that you had agreed to work for us. If necessary, we can manufacture proof using sound bites and film clips from this very conversation. It's being filmed and recorded, you know."

Alexandra glanced about the room for some indication of a camera or a microphone, but saw nothing. Dave continued. "And, of course, there's always your family, though we would hate to have things go in that direction."

"Your government would never allow it."

"True enough, Alexandra, but there are others who would gladly do our bidding for a price. You should know that."

"How long do I have to decide?"

"Take as long as you need. It's your life and the lives of your family that are at stake. The guards will come and get me when you have chosen."

"I will give you my answer within the hour."

34

CHARADE

Director Sinclair and Agent Coleman watched as the president and Forest Lindsey stepped from the White House limousine and passed through the service entrance of the Hoover Building.

Greeting McGarth as he walked into the foyer, Sinclair noticed his pensive look. The president was clearly worried about Jabarri's visit.

"Well, John, are we all set for this charade?"

"Yes, Mr. President. It's all taken care of."

Looking at Dave, McGarth said, "You must be Agent Coleman?"

"Yes, Mr. President."

Dave could tell from McGarth's eyes that the president was sizing him up. He wondered what kind of impression he was making.

"Dave, John and I are going to have to rely on you to carry the ball on this one."

"Yes, sir. I'll do my best."

"The thing you're going to have to be ready for is Jabarri's sudden mood swings. He's apt to do most anything. He's very excitable, especially when he misinterprets the situation. I'll try to delay giving him the news of Yaqoob's death until after he's visited Ajmani and we're near where you're holding the young girl. I'll expect you to take over from there. Take it slowly and show Jabarri as much as you can. He responds better to tangible facts. Beyond that, you'll have to wing it."

Burt Williamson, the CIA director, walked into the foyer and joined the president just as Jabarri's limousine pulled up to the service entrance. A hush fell over the room as the president and his staff watched the terrorist emerge from the car and walk into the foyer. McGarth waited for Reza to speak.

"Mr. President!" Jabarri called out as he strode over to McGarth. "It is good that we meet again!"

Trying to mask his disdain for Reza, McGarth stepped forward to greet him. "Yes, Mr. Jabarri, likewise."

Glancing at the men surrounding the president, Reza asked, "Shall we begin?"

"John, will you lead the way?" McGarth asked.

Nodding, Sinclair led the president's party to the open elevator and waited until everyone entered before he stepped in and pressed the floor button. Walking from the elevator, Sinclair led the entourage down a corridor before pausing in front of two uniformed officers. They were expecting him and opened the door, then stood at attention as the party entered the suite. Nsar Ajmani was seated in an overstuffed chair, but jumped to his feet when he saw Jabarri. They greeted one another in Arabic.

McGarth and his party waited for the conversation to subside before he spoke. "Mr. Jabarri, perhaps you and Mr. Ajmani would prefer to talk in private?"

Reza looked surprised. "That will not be necessary, Mr. President. We have nothing to hide."

Turning toward Ajmani, Reza said, "Nsar, you will join us now. You and Yaqoob will return to the jet with me." His compatriot grinned slightly as he responded in Arabic.

"Now, I wish to see Yaqoob, Mr. President."

McGarth glanced at Dave. "Agent Coleman, will you take us to the assassin's room first?"

"You have the murderer here?" Reza asked, surprised.

"Yes," McGarth answered, "but she's in critical condition and isn't expected to live."

Jabarri was stunned. "A woman! The assassin... a woman?"

"Yes," said the president. "And a very dangerous one at that." Pointing at Dave, he said, "From what Director Sinclair has told me, Agent Coleman came close to being killed by her late last night during an escape attempt."

Reza's curiosity heightened. Jabarri looked at Coleman, then back at the president.

"He was forced to shoot her. Unfortunately for us, the bullet struck her spinal cord before piercing her lung and grazing the wall of her heart. The doctors have told me she is paralyzed and in a coma. They don't expect her to live," the president explained.

Reza looked puzzled. "Is that why you do not have her in a hospital now?" he asked.

"She was taken to a hospital for treatment, but I insisted she be returned here for you to see and to avoid having her identity discovered by the media. Her medical team has assured me nothing else can be done for her."

McGarth's explanation seemed to amuse the terrorist. "I will see the assassin, now!" Jabarri insisted.

"Very well. Agent Coleman, take us to the assassin's room."

"Yes, sir," Dave replied, moving for the door.

As Coleman entered Alexandra's room, two uniformed nurses and a doctor withdrew from her bedside and stood against the sterile wall opposite her bed. Dave walked to the foot of her bed and stood, so as not to obstruct Jabarri's view.

Reza leaned over and stared into Alexandra's face. Her eyes were closed. A small, nasal oxygen mask held by two elastic bands, hugged her swollen face. A suction tube dangled from the side of her lips, making an occasional gurgling sound as it vacuumed saliva from her mouth. Plastic pouches suspended from a mobile pedestal at the head of the bed dripped blood and IV fluid into the two clear plastic tubes fastened to her arm with adhesive. Wires tailed out from under the white sheet draped over her torso, feeding information into a computer attached to the headboard. Other small electrical boxes beside the computer had their own wires and seemed to be monitoring different life-support functions.

Raising the sheet, Reza peered at the massive bandage covering a large portion of her bare chest. He saw traces of blood around the edges of the bandage and saw the catheter tube strapped to her right leg. Dropping the sheet, Jabarri turned to McGarth. "Her death is regrettable," he said. "I would liked to have questioned her concerning the deaths of my colleagues."

"We had hoped she would survive," said the president. "Her confession could have proved that my government had nothing to do with the killings."

Reza grinned sadistically. "I've seen enough. It is as you say. She is close to death. You have saved me the trouble of killing her. I will see my brother, Yaqoob, now."

The president turned toward the door without answering. Dave caught his eye and knew it was time to intercede.

"Mr. President?" Dave called out from the doorway.

"Yes, Mr. Coleman, what is it?" asked McGarth, as he and Reza approached the hallway.

"Sir, the man you and Mr. Jabarri are here to see is dead."

"Dead? What do you mean dead?" the president bellowed.

"Yes, sir. His neck was broken in a struggle with the woman. She killed ..."

"Yaqoob is dead? This cannot be!" Jabarri shouted. "Where is he? I must see him!"

McGarth's disposition changed as he snapped at Sinclair. "How long have you known of his death, John?"

"Since shortly after midnight, sir, but we weren't able to get a positive ID on him until just before you arrived. I thought..."

"And you waited until now to tell me?" McGarth interrupted. "Damn you, John. How stupid!"

The president glanced at Reza as the terrorist spoke. "I must see Yaqoob this instant!"

McGarth saw a look of fear spread across Reza's face as he repeated his demand. "I must see Yaqoob this instant!" Jabarri exclaimed, visibly shaken.

"I'll deal with you later, John. Just take us to see him right now as Mr. Jabarri wishes!"

No one said anything as Coleman led the group down the hallway to the forensics lab. Not waiting for the president to enter, Coleman walked over to the gurney parked in the middle of the floor. A half-zipped body bag lay atop the portable litter. A man's head was exposed. His neck was chaffed. The position of his head seemed unnatural, as though it had been severely twisted. Dave gave the corpse a cursory glance, then took his position at the foot of the gurney.

Jabarri and Ajmani walked into the room behind the president, speaking excitedly in Arabic. The only word McGarth recognized was "Allah," though he had little trouble imagining the rest. News of Yaqoob's death was having a major impact on the terrorist leader.

As he stole another look at Jabarri's face, Mason realized, for the first time that Reza had never intended to detonate the bomb. The threat was just that. But now, with Yaqoob's death, he had no recourse.

McGarth knew from the anguish on Reza's face that he'd lost that option. Jabarri and his Fundamentalist Coalition were now along for the ride as much as anyone. It was a cruel irony, he thought, as he watched Jabarri labor over the Arab's death.

"Coleman!" McGarth barked. "How is it your men allowed that assassin to get to this man before you did?"

"Sir, we were not aware that Mr. Shah would be on his sailboat. We had two men covering the docks, but our emphasis was on his office and the approaches to it."

McGarth lowered his head slightly, stroking the sides of his forehead with his fingers and thumb. "It's a damn shame we didn't know to tell you to look there," he said, hesitantly.

Dave saw Jabarri look up at the president and wondered what it meant. "Yes. I'm sorry we didn't do it. It was my fault."

McGarth shot Sinclair a disgusted look as he said, "Forget it, Coleman. What's done is done." Dave nodded, but said nothing. Sinclair and the others watched as McGarth waited for Jabarri to speak.

Finally, stepping back from the gurney, Reza said, "Yaqoob's death is a great disappointment to me. And in time, it will come to be so for you, as well, Mr. President. Perhaps you will tell me of Tariq Saif and Jared Hakim. Were they also killed by the woman?"

McGarth turned and looked at Reza, then Sinclair. "John, what did the forensics lab decide about the two men you found murdered in Middleburg? Did she do those, too?"

"We think so, Mr. President, but we have no proof. They did conclude the job was done by a professional. There were no spent casings, no fingerprints. Nothing was left at the site to give us a clue of who had done it or why."

McGarth shook his head and looked at Reza for some sign of what he was thinking. Jabarri gave the president a piercing look and said, "Nsar and I will leave now. I have nothing further to discuss with you, Mr. President. I trust you will continue to comply with our mandate. It remains the only way by which we will remove the bomb."

"Mr. Jabarri, my government is doing everything possible to meet the conditions the coalition has set forth. Can you give me some indication of when a decision might be reached regarding the bomb's removal?"

Glaring at McGarth, Reza said, "It is much too soon to be speaking on this matter. You will be told of our decision when we are ready and not before. Do I make myself clear?"

Infuriated by Reza's reply, McGarth struggled to conceal his anger even as he answered cordially: "As you wish, Mr. Jabarri."

Neither spoke as they rode the elevator to the ground floor. Accompanying Reza and Nsar to their limousine, McGarth watched as the terrorist leader and his associate departed.

Returning to the foyer, the president apologized for the verbal abuse he'd heaped on Sinclair and complimented Coleman on his ingenious plan. After speculating on Jabarri's next move, the president, joined by Lindsey and Elliot, climbed into his limousine and left for the White House. Jacobson left next, returning to the Pentagon. Sinclair and Williamson went to the FBI director's office to discuss the implications of Reza's visit and to await his call to Geneva. Having learned of Yaqoob's death, they were certain he would not wait until sixteen hundred hours. Dave returned to Alexandra's room to wait for her to regain consciousness.

* * *

Ahmed and Mohammed were seated in the cockpit when Reza entered with Ajmani. Seeing that Yaqoob was not with them, Ahmed knew something was wrong. The distraught look on Jabarri's face confirmed his suspicion. Mohammed was silent as usual.

"Where is Yaqoob?" Ahmed asked.

"He is dead, murdered by the same one who killed Abdulla and Rashid," said Reza, grabbing the mobile phone pack.

Paling, Ahmed asked, "How? Was he not in protective custody?"

Reza gave Ahmed a disgusted look as he answered, "The stupid Americans never got to him in time. His neck was broken when they found him."

"That means .....," sputtered Ahmed.

"Yes. It means there's no way to defuse the bomb. I must talk with Geneva now," answered Reza.

"But where will I take the jet?" Ahmed whined.

"Geneva will decide. It is not for you to worry about. You and Mohammed go to the hotel and sleep," Reza ordered.

Mohammed calmly slid the captain's seat aft and left the cockpit without speaking. Visibly shaken, Ahmed followed. Nsar greeted them as they deplaned, then returned to the cockpit.

"Ahmed is not a true believer," Reza said. "He does not have faith."

"He is young, Reza. In time he will come to know the truth." Jabarri glanced at Ajmani. "I fear there will be no more time. We have come too far to back down now."

Nsar stared into Reza's cold, black eyes and wondered about Jabarri's conviction. Was he really prepared to accept a martyr's death, or was he only echoing what was expected, hoping his life would be spared?

Ajmani watched as Reza activated the portable telephone and auto-dialed a preset number to Geneva. Seconds later, he heard the phone ringing through the small built-in speaker.

"Geneva. Go ahead," the voice said in perfect English.

"Andrea, this is Reza. I must speak with Saeed immediately. Yaqoob is dead."

"Yaqoob...dead....?" she asked in disbelief.

"Yes. It was the assassin, The Spider of Baghdad."

"The Spider? You are sure?"

"No, but the assassin, a young Arab woman, fits her description."

"You have seen her?"

"Yes. She is paralyzed and near death. She was shot while attempting to escape from FBI custody this morning."

"And Yaqoob, you are certain of his death?"

"Yes. I have seen him also. His neck was broken. Andrea, I must speak with Saeed.

"I'm here, Reza," Saeed answered. "I've listened to what you told Andrea."

"Then you know we have no way to stop the timer. The bomb will explode now, no matter what we do."

"Yes, Reza. What you say is true. It is unfortunate coalition members insisted that no one except their own representatives have the code material."

"Do we allow Baghdad to have its revenge and destroy Washington, or do I try to negotiate with the president to remove the bomb while there is still time?" Reza asked.

Andrea intervened. "Impossible! We cannot back down now, no matter the cost. If we do, every Arab nation in the Middle East will suffer the world's humiliation."

"But if Washington is destroyed, the Americans will not rest until every Arab nation is laid to waste, Andrea. They, too, could do no less and still save face," Reza argued. "The American president does not want a war, but he will have no choice if we do this thing."

"Even if Washington falls and he learns of our sponsors, he could not attack all the Arab nations, Reza," Saeed interjected.

"How can you think that, Saeed? He would have to act to preserve America's reputation in the eyes of the world."

"I understand what you say, Reza, but he cannot confront the coalition without attacking every Arab nation. That is the only way he could reach our fundamentalist movement. His problem is that we are interspersed throughout all the Arab world. Do you think he would wage war on Egypt to get at the movement there? And what of the Christians in Egypt? Can he afford to let them be slaughtered? He will be limited to covert operations, regardless of the humiliation America suffers. He cannot fight what he cannot see, Reza."

Pausing, Jabarri realized Saeed's reasoning made sense, yet he was certain America's reaction would be stronger than he'd surmised. Saddam had already made a near-fatal mistake by underestimating U.S. resolve. Qadhafi had too. Was the coalition about to do the same thing now, Reza asked himself?

"What am I to do, Saeed?" Reza asked. "Wait while you canvass the members?"

"That is impossible, Reza. I cannot do that. The secret charter we agreed to specifically precludes our making any contact with the sponsor states once we received their contribution. If we were to try now, they would disavow any knowledge of us. That is the agreement we made with them, Reza. We have no recourse."

"Yes, I know what we agreed to in the charter, but no one considered the situation we're facing now," Reza argued. "Do you not think they should be given the option to decide for themselves? If you are wrong in your assessment and the U.S. retaliates with force, they will have no choice but to bear the consequences."

"The Arab world can wait no longer, Reza," Andrea said. "Every Muslim in the Middle East will rejoice in knowing that America has been made to pay for its meddling. Only then will we be able to drive the Zionists from our lands and regain the world's respect for our people. To go now and ask the American president's help in removing the bomb would be an embarrassment of unimaginable proportions for us all.

We have not been given this opportunity to have it squandered by Saddam and our own weakness. We must prevail in this mission, Reza. We can do no less!"

Jabarri knew Andrea spoke the truth. The struggle, no matter its consequences, had to end in victory for the Arabs. How else would the cause be advanced? What better way could the fundamentalists have to dominate Arab thinking, if not by restoring respect for Arabs throughout the world?

"If this must be, then what of my men?" Reza asked. "Are they to prepare for a martyr's death?"

"True believers need not fear. Only infidels need fear death, for they will know unending torment," Andrea said.

"And what of Nsar, Mohammed and me? Is our work done?"

"No, Reza. You must use the remaining time to plan your escape," Saeed ordered. "The Chunnel operation must go as planned. Andrea's reinvestment of our funds will provide us the means to acquire another bomb."

"How much time do I have?" Reza asked.

"The timer was set for sixty hours and was activated as the jet began to decelerate on landing," explained Saeed. "You should be able to figure the exact time by checking the jet's logbook."

"That would make it ten hundred thirty hours GMT or six thirty Eastern Daylight Time tomorrow morning."

"Then you must do whatever is possible to leave before then. We will maintain a listening watch until you advise us of your new location. You have the necessary numbers to reach us."

A moment later, Jabarri slipped the handset back into its cradle and pressed the END button as he glanced over at Nsar. "It is done," he said. "Washington will fall."

Nsar smiled to himself. Saddam would have his revenge.

*   *   *

Ten minutes after Jabarri finished his call to Geneva, an FBI communications specialist delivered a cassette to the director's office. Sinclair and Burt Williamson, the CIA director, reviewed the conversation immediately.

"At least we have a timetable to work with," Burt said.

"If Jabarri's calculation is right, we'll have just enough time for the SEALS to take the jet and get Beacham airborne and into the Atlantic before the sonofabitch goes off."

Flipping open the EMPRESS OPLAN folder, Sinclair scanned the chronological summary page for the planned takeoff time. "The planned liftoff is set for zero four hundred hours Eastern Daylight Time tomorrow. That gives us a two and a half hour window, if everything goes on schedule," Sinclair reasoned.

"Knowing that, I'm sure McGarth will want to move up the time of the assault just to play it safe. In a situation like this, anything could happen."

"I don't doubt that for a minute, Burt. But from what Chris and Clayton said earlier, I'm not sure they're going to be able to move the assault up too much. It will depend on how fast they can get the EMPRESS ready and into position. McGarth may have to live with the time he's got," said Sinclair.

"We should be glad we've got the time we have."

"Yes. It could be a lot worse for us all," Sinclair added.

"What about Jabarri?" Burt asked.

"I don't think the president will allow us to touch him until we've got the jet and the remote control detonator."

"I figured as much."

"Of course, there's always the chance he'll be on the aircraft when the SEALS take the jet," John replied.

"If that happens, we can forget the interrogation option. There won't be enough of him to look at, let alone talk to. The SEALS will see to that," Burt said.

"Our best chance of getting at their leadership will come from the task force," John said. "Emerson Beamer is the best I've got when it comes to hard-core investigative work. He'll keep at it until he's found something. Let's hope he can pin down the coalition's location from Jabarri's call."

* * *

"No, Nelson. I am not going to do any such thing," McGarth shouted into the phone at Senator Garrett. "If you guys on the Intelligence Oversight Committee had done a decent job of supervising our intelligence-gathering, we wouldn't be in this damned mess. So don't give me this crap about not taking decisive action. It was your party who pushed like hell to shift the emphasis toward electronic intelligence to keep your industrial friends in lucrative government contracts.

"I don't give a damn that I can receive photos of Jabarri briefing his terrorists from twenty thousand miles in space. What I need, Nelson, is just one spy in the group who can tell me what in the hell he told them! Do you get my message?"

"Yes, Mr. President, I understand your point," replied Garrett, overlooking McGarth's anger. "Maybe we have gone too far in relying on electronics for our information. Nevertheless, the consensus in the Senate is that you've got to get this thing over quickly, one way or the other. The economy is paralyzed. Nobody is willing to make any decision about anything until this crisis is over. You don't have much time, Mr. President. Some people here in the Senate are already calling for a declaration of war against those responsible."

"And who would they declare war on, Nelson? The entire Middle East? You tell them to spend a little more time studying the problem and let me handle the crisis. We're further along on this thing than you might imagine!"

"How much time are you talking about, Mr. President?"

Mason realized he'd said more than he'd intended. "I don't have an exact timetable, but we have reason to believe the coalition is satisfied with the progress we've made in complying with their demands. We expect to begin substantive talks with them on removing the weapon as early as tomorrow. That's not for publication, you understand."

"In other words, Mr. President, your plans for resolving this crisis, up to this point, are founded on hope and little else?"

McGarth felt the blood surge through his veins as he fought the urge to lash out at Garrett again, but he held his tongue. "There's a great deal more to our plans than that, Nelson, but I'm not going into it over the phone."

Forest stood silently beside the president's desk, looking concerned. The corners of his usually optimistic lips were turned down. He'd learned the hard way not to answer the president's anger. He knew it would pass quickly.

"Garrett and his flock of hawks in the Senate want me to threaten military retaliation against Iran, Iraq, Libya, the PLO and damn near anyone else in the Middle East who might have sided with those countries at one time or another, as if that's going to persuade the coalition to take their bomb home."

"They're feeling the heat, sir. They're just frustrated like everyone else who's had to deal with this mess."

"I know you're right, Forest, but you'd think those guys would have enough confidence in me to ......" McGarth stopped in mid-sentence as Sinclair and Williamson walked into the Oval Office.

"Jabarri's made the call to Geneva?" McGarth asked.

"Yes," Sinclair answered.

"So, what have we learned?"

"In a nutshell, we've found out that the bomb cannot be defused, nor will they agree to negotiate with you to move it. More importantly, we learned that the time of detonation is at six twenty-seven tomorrow morning," Sinclair explained.

A sense of relief spread across the President's face as he recalled the start time of OPERATION EMPRESS. "How did you pin down the time, John?"

"The timer is set to detonate sixty hours after touchdown at National. We had the tower chief reconfirm the landing time with his log. The jet's on-board computer automatically transmitted the touchdown time at National to the airline. They were both the same."

Stroking his forehead, McGarth paced about the room assimilating the information.

"Forest, get Chris and Clayton over here. Then tell Gaylord to join us. It's time we review where we're at with the EMPRESS."

35

AGAINST THE TIDE

Charlie Cartwright pulled up the front part of his pants under his protruding belly and swore again at the jammed winch. It was the third time he'd tried to raise the EMPRESS's modified antenna assembly without success. Spray blowing over the bow of the blunt-nosed barge hadn't helped matters, either. Shoving the stump of his cigar back into his mouth, he slammed the lever into reverse and lowered the array back to the deck. He knew the antenna's weight was to blame. It needed a counter-balance. Muttering, Charlie studied where to add the weight. He didn't see Commander Higgins walk up behind him.

"How's it coming, Charlie?" Higgins asked.

"It ain't. The sonofabitch jams about halfway up every time I try to raise her! Too much tension on the winch. It needs a counter-weight."

Higgins nodded as Charlie computed the weight needed. "Anything you can't fix?" Higgins hollered.

"Naw! It's just one more thing to add to my list of shit to go wrong on this tub. But don't you worry none about it, skipper. I've seen worse. I'll have this antenna running up and down slicker than the one on your car by the time we get to the Wilson Bridge. You just keep this shitbox moving, and I'll have her ready to go whenever you get there, sir!"

Higgins grinned at the veteran seaman engineer and walked back toward the generator cabin. If Charlie said not to worry, he wouldn't.

Anyone who had met and worked with Charlie Cartwright knew he could fix anything. His name was legend in the Norfolk shipyard where, time after time, he'd been called on to solve problems for the Navy and its contractors. It hadn't surprised Higgins that Admiral Sheerer had asked Charlie to honcho the EMPRESS modifications. There was none better suited for the task, if you could overlook his untidy appearance, vile tongue, and his god-awful cigar-chewing.

Stepping inside the makeshift cabin, Higgins cross-checked the chart against their schedule. Assuming they encountered no delays, the EMPRESS would make the Wilson Bridge three nautical miles south of National Airport by 0200 hours tomorrow morning with an hour to spare. Studying the course that lay ahead, he noted the tick marks adjacent to the course line. Each represented an hour. So far, they were on schedule.

In the corner of the shack, a team of electricians worked feverishly, making changes to the powerful generator. Higgins watched them as he finished the last of his coffee. Finding the acrid smell of the bundles of electrical wiring especially irritating to his sinuses, he left the room for fresh air.

Outside, he saw several of the escort vessels flanking the EMPRESS as it lumbered up the muddy Potomac. He could hear the steel towing cable whip the water's surface occasionally as the barge heaved under the choppy surf. The wind from the northwest was unusually strong for summer. A cold front out of Canada had drifted south during the night. He watched the tug churn up the water several hundred yards ahead. Then it happened.

Higgins knew the instant he heard the crack that the towing cable had snapped. Up on the forward deck he saw some of it coiled around the antenna mast. Charlie was nowhere to be seen. Higgins rushed forward. The old seaman's unmistakable foul mouth was in full rage as he staggered to his feet and swore at the wind, the water, and the Navy.

Relieved to know Charlie and his crew had survived decapitation by the steel cable, Higgins turned his attention to his boat, the wallowing barge. It had already fallen off to leeward and was drifting toward the shore. To the stern, he could see the spare tug rushing to intercept the loose barge. Judging its closure, Higgins knew they would be aground before the tug could intercept them.

Pulling the "brick" from his hip pocket, he listened helplessly as the two tugboat captains discussed the situation. The shore seemed to be drawing closer to the barge as they talked. Higgins sensed they would soon be aground. The race for time would begin. He wanted to ask for an estimate, but knew the request would be premature.

Three minutes later and sooner than he'd expected, Higgins heard the screeching and scraping of the hull as it made contact with the river bottom. As the EMPRESS jerked to a standstill, he knew from the sharpness of the sound that it had impacted a rock or sunken debris. Looking at the distance to shore, Higgins suspected the latter, but he would need his chart to tell.

The two tugs, now within fifty yards of the barge, cut their engines, using only enough power to maintain their position against the swift current. Suddenly Higgin's radio crackled.

"FAT LADY! THIS IS BULLDOG ONE. WHAT IS YOUR STATUS?" Higgins raised the small radio to his mouth to answer. He noticed that BULLDOG ONE lay off to his port.

"BULLDOG ONE! "WE'VE MADE CONTACT WITH DEBRIS, JUDGING BY THE WAY THE BOW PIVOTED AFTER IMPACT," Higgins hollered.

"RIGHT YOU ARE, MATE. I WAS AFRAID OF THAT. YOUR POSITION APPEARS TO BE ATOP SOME OLD CONCRETE PILINGS. THEY'VE BEEN THERE FOR YEARS, CAPT'N. YOU'RE NOT THE FIRST TO CRAWL UP ON THEM."

Higgins grimaced at the tugboat captain's effort at humor. Didn't he understand that if the EMPRESS wasn't in position by 0500 at the latest, Washington would become a smoking hole?

"WHAT'S YOUR PLAN, BULLDOG?" Higgins snapped. "WE DON'T HAVE A SECOND TO SPARE."

"Ya damn right we don't!" clamored Charlie, as he rumbled up alongside. "That sonofabitch'in cable like to have taken my friggin' head off before it wrapped its ass around my antenna mast! I got one helluva mess up there now, Commander!"

Higgins gave Cartright a nasty look and shook his head as the brick spit out another message from the BULLDOG.

"FAT LADY. WE'LL MOVE IN AS CLOSE AS WE CAN, THEN LAUNCH A TENDER WITH CREW AND CABLE. MEANWHILE, CHECK ALL YOUR COMPARTMENTS AND LET ME KNOW THEIR STATUS AS SOON AS YOU CAN. I'LL HAVE BULLDOG TWO STAND OFF UNTIL WE GIVE IT A TRY."

Higgins thought for a minute. What if it didn't break loose the first time? How much time would it take to get the second tug's cable attached to the barge? Checking his watch, Higgins keyed his radio. "BULLDOG ONE FROM THE FAT LADY. I WANT YOU AND YOUR BROTHER WIRED TO THIS HEAP WHEN YOU PULL. WE'VE GOT TO MAKE IT OFF THE FIRST TIME."

"AYE, AYE, MATE. WE'LL DO IT YOUR WAY, BUT IT WILL TAKE A LITTLE MORE TIME TO SET IT UP," replied the BULL-DOG.

"I CAN LIVE WITH IT," countered Higgins, stuffing the radio back into his hip pocket. "How bad is it, Charlie?"

"It ain't a pretty sight, boss, but I'll get it up somehow. You just get us off this friggin' rock and back to sea, or we'll all be surfing down the Potomac about daybreak tomorrow!"

The comment struck Higgins as funny and he laughed. For a second, he imagined the two of them riding the EMPRESS back down the Potomac under the thrust of a tidal wave. Charlie must have envisioned the same scene and laughed with him. "I'll bet this tub would be hauling ass," Charlie said. Higgins grinned and walked off to check the compartments for damage. Charlie headed to the bow to check on his men. They both knew the incident had cost them at least one hour, if not two.

* * *

"Agent Coleman? Your prisoner is awake," said the officer.

Walking into the room, Dave noticed that the tubes, bandages, and support equipment had been removed from Alexandra's body. She looked normal, except for the steel handcuffs that pinned her ankles and wrists to the bed frame. He looked into her groggy eyes. Her face still looked puffy from the injections, but the bruises had disappeared.

Seeing him, she asked, "Is it over?" Dave nodded, as he held up the video cassette. "Would you like to see your performance?" A look of surprise flashed in Alexandra's dark eyes as she spoke. "You filmed it?"

"All of it," Dave answered.

"I want to see it!"

Walking to a portable TV/VCR cart, Dave inserted the cassette. "Who should I call you now?" he asked. "Isabel, Alexandra, or The Spider?"

"I am Alexandra," she said. "I have no need for the others."

Smiling at her answer, Dave pressed the PLAY button and sat in the chair next to her bed. The pair watched the short tape in silence.

"Play it again. I want to see it," she pleaded.

"Pretty awesome, wouldn't you say? And you don't remember a thing about it, do you?"

"No. The shots they gave me knocked me out immediately," Alexandra replied. "I still can't believe it. It looks so real! You can see in Reza's eyes that he has no doubt that I am near death. He would have killed me to be certain."

"For a moment, I thought he might," Dave added, rewinding the tape. "Alexandra, I need information about the coalition headquarters in Geneva and about your contact there. It's very important that we....."

"It is Hassan. Hassan Kahlil. He was my contact."

Her directness surprised him. "And where are they?"

Alexandra shook her head. "I don't know where they went after the explosion. He said it was better that I not know."

Dave pulled a photograph from his pocket and held it in front of Alexandra's face. "Which one is Hassan?"

Her eyes widened. "Where did you get that?"

"It was taken by a member of the German State Department during a visit to the coalition's office soon after they established a cultural exchange."

"He's the one on the left."

"Have you met him before?"

"No, but there were only three... Saeed, Andrea, and Hassan. I saw their pictures when I was briefed on the mission."

"Do you know where they live or where they might be found?"

Alexandra thought for a moment. "No."

"Can you remember during any of your conversations with Hassan if he hinted at what he did besides work for the coalition, what he did with his spare time, or where he lived?"

"Hassan spoke once of being in a hurry to return to his flat for something. I think it was for a class. Yes! It was for a class he was taking at the Université. He said he lived across the street from the Université."

"Did he say anything else about the school or his class?"

"No. That was all."

Staring into Alexandra's beautiful dark eyes, Dave smiled. Seeing her now, submissive and dependent on him, made it hard to imagine her so embittered that she would turn to murder. She was not yet thirty. A part of him pitied her — a tragic waste of talent and beauty.

"Your information will help, Alexandra. Try to get some rest. I'll come back and see you later," he said.

"What about my family? You will keep your promise?"

"They should be safe for now. Saddam will learn from Hassan that you have succeeded in your mission, but have been killed. He won't bother them."

"But you promised.... I want them out of there now, please!"

"Alexandra, we will get your family out of Iraq, but it will take time. You must be patient. No one here is going to deceive you. We will do as we promised."

In the hallway, Coleman's only thought was to contact Beamer in Geneva immediately.

*   *   *

Jill leaned back in her chair as she proofread the last page of her article on the small laptop computer. It was a short piece with little real information, but there was enough to carry the story until something more substantive surfaced. Glancing about the Press Corps office, Jill realized it was empty. Her contemporaries had left hours ago, some for good, she'd been told.

As she began to pack up her computer, Jill heard her name called. "Yes!" she said, turning to face her caller. She recognized Gaylord Elliot's face.

"Miss Simmons. May I please have a word with you?"

"Certainly, Mr. Elliot."

Grabbing her computer, Jill rushed down the hallway to join him. After a short walk, they entered a small office.

"Miss Simmons, I'll come right to the point. The president wants to solicit the help of your associate, Bud Waterman, in seeking a solution to the terrorist crisis. I must tell you the task he has in mind carries some risk. Would you be willing to convey the president's request to Mr. Waterman and provide him the exact instructions?"

Jill gave Gaylord a hard look. He wasn't kidding. His silence heightened the tension. It was a reasonable request and deserved an honest answer.

"Mr. Elliot, I'm not sure how to answer. I understand that you and the president would like assurance of Bud's participation before you reveal what's needed, but surely you can see that I'm in no position to sign a blank check for Bud."

"I see your point, Miss Simmons. I should be more specific. Neither the president nor I have any doubt as to your loyalty or integrity. Your promise to keep quiet about this is sufficient."

"You have it, Mr. Elliot."

"We need to get critical information to Sybil DeVires, the flight service manager. Mr. Waterman is in the best position to convey our message. He's the only American Jabarri seems to trust."

Jill took her eyes off Elliot for a minute to think. She could imagine only one reason why it would be necessary to make contact with Sybil. Staring directly into his eyes, Jill asked, "You're planning to take the aircraft, aren't you?"

Elliot paused for a second to weigh his answer. "That is our intention. Do you think he'll help us?"

"When?" she persisted.

"Early tomorrow morning," he answered.

How could Bud turn down the president? How would he live with himself if he didn't and their plan failed? He had to help. He had no choice. No one did.

"Yes, I'm sure he will. What is it he and I must do?"

The tension eased in Gaylord's face as he reviewed the role they would play. Jill listened, apprehensive, but pleased with her decision. It was Bud's duty as an American. To do less would be to live in shame for the rest of his life. Bud would understand. He had to.

36

AGROUND

Forest checked his watch, then scanned McGarth's appointment schedule. It was one-thirty in the afternoon. In another fifteen minutes, members of the NSC would begin arriving for the two o'clock meeting. The president sat at his desk putting the finishing touches on the address he would make to the American people at seven. Forest could tell from his expression that he was having difficulty. Ordinarily, he would have suggested that the president let Frances work on it, but there would be nothing ordinary about this address.

By closing all non-essential government offices and furloughing most government workers, the president hoped to discreetly urge everyone in danger to leave Washington while there was time. He would explain the action as a move to preserve the financial integrity of the Union. Federal troops called to restore order to the District would be reassigned to outlying regions to assist local authorities. The verbage itself presented a daunting challenge. Being too explicit could alert Jabarri. But, if he were too vague, his message could be misconstrued.

Forest decided to let him work a while longer. Frances could always clean it up at the last minute. Reviewing the president's schedule, Forest realized McGarth would not sleep again until after the attack. Stepping into the hallway, he wondered how the president would manage what lay ahead.

* * *

Jill let Bud's mobile phone ring. She knew he was at the aircraft. She couldn't get her mind off the coming assault. She tried to imagine how it would be carried out, and when. How would it begin? Elliot hadn't said when, only that Bud needed to get the information to Sybil before midnight. Jill reckoned the attack would occur before daybreak.

"Waterman."

"Bud, it's Jill. Where have you been? I've been trying to reach you...."

"Hey. Slow down a minute with the twenty questions, kid. I've answered the phone," he said defensively. "I was sitting in the grass under the wing trying to take advantage of what little shade there is in this outpost of misery."

"I'm sorry, Bud. It's just that...."

"What's on your mind? Why the call? It's still another three hours before my piece is due to the news desk."

Jill saw her chance. "That's what I wanted to talk to you about. The staff wants another interview with Jabarri. Do you think you could set one up?"

Bud paused. The question surprised him. "I don't know," he replied. "Perhaps, but why? What could he tell me that he hasn't already?"

Jill could see she wasn't making much headway. She was a novice at beating around the bush. "Bud, we need a follow-up interview. Is it possible you could get him to agree to it?"

"Probably. But I wouldn't want to make any promises."

Jill didn't respond.

Bud knew she did it intentionally. "Look, if it means this much to you, I'll try, okay.?"

Jill swallowed hard. She hated to be deceitful, especially to Bud, but Gaylord Elliot had been adamant about not compromising his message. Was the FC monitoring their call?

"When you talk with Reza, get permission for the chopper to land briefly to drop off extra film, Bud."

"That won't be necessary. I've got more than enough."

"Maybe, but what about your video camera battery? We don't want to lose the piece. Just get his permission and quit arguing with me, will you?"

"All right, Jill. We'll do it your way. I'll call you when it's set up. You really sound irritated. What's bugging you?"

"It's the tension. I'm on edge. Call me on my mobile phone when you know something."

"I'll get back to you within the hour."

* * *

"BULLDOG ONE FROM THE FAT LADY."
"GO AHEAD, FAT LADY."
"SHE'S READY FOR THE PULL. WE'RE STANDING BY," answered Commander Higgins aboard the EMPRESS.

Charlie took a half-chewed piece of cigar out of his pants pocket and bit off the end of it. He and Higgins watched as the two tugs slowly motored out toward the channel of the Potomac.

"They'd better put some tension on those friggin' cables before they start the pull, Capt'n or they'll snap 'em again."

"Let's hope not, Charlie. Let's hope not."

Higgins had the binoculars on the cables as they began to rise out of the water. Returning the glasses to his chest, he keyed the megaphone trigger. "Stand by on deck for the heave."

Five seconds later, both men grabbed on to a nearby stanchion as the barge absorbed the initial jolt and started to scrape itself off the concrete pilings. Higgins gave Cartwright a bewildered look as reverberations from the hull against the concrete intensified. Charlie was expressionless. The pace of his jaws quickened as they bore down on the remains of his cigar. Then suddenly the sounds ceased as the EMPRESS floated free.

Higgins's smile broadened as he transmitted the news to the two tugs. "BULLDOGS! SHE'S UNDERWAY!"

"ROGER, FAT LADY. GIVE US A HULL REPORT ASAP," replied Bulldog One. Acknowledging the request, Higgins looked around for Charlie. Cartwright was already inspecting the first compartment. Higgins joined him.

Peering into the darkness he asked, "Any damage?"

"Nah, none so far," Charlie growled, as he swung the four-celled torch methodically about, looking for water. "But we ain't out of the woods yet! This ole' tub took some real abuse getting off those pilings, skipper." Higgins nodded. He knew Charlie was right. "I'll have them all checked out for you in a jiffy, sir."

Reading between the lines, Higgins knew Charlie didn't need him looking over his shoulder. He'd go forward and oversee the rest of the crew. Pleased to be underway again, he glanced at his watch and calculated the delay. They'd lost an hour and twenty minutes sitting on the pilings. Assuming no further problems, the EMPRESS would make the Wilson bridge by 0320 hours.

Stopping at the generator shack, Higgins called a special DOD number. The call was brief and filled with misleading conversation, but the critical information was received and confirmed by the monitor on the other end.

Stepping outside, he found Charlie at the door. "Skipper, you better come take a look at this! We got water!"

Higgins frowned, but said nothing. The corners of his mouth turned down as he followed Cartwright. He knew what to expect.

Reaching the compartment, Charlie raised the access panel. The sound of rushing water told the story. Leaning over, Higgins stared down into the dark abyss. "How bad is it, Charlie?"

"Judging by the sound and the depth of the water, I'd say the sonofabitch will fill up in another couple of hours, if we don't do something to stop it!"

"What do you suggest?"

"For starters, we can put the pumps on it. That will slow the process a bit!"

Deep wrinkles formed on Higgins's forehead as he fretted. He knew that compartment was the largest. If it flooded completely, the barge would settle deeper into the water and, with the added drag, slow their progress even more. Thank God for high tide, he thought.

"How much displacement are you going to need to keep that hole empty, Charlie?"

Cartwright stood up and leaned into Higgins's face as he answered, "More than we can produce with the pumps you've got on board this ole' tub. They'd crap out just trying to suck the last drop of foam out of a beer can, skipper. We need some heavy duty diesel-driven pumps, if we're going to keep this water from completely flooding this hole."

"You set up what we've got, and I'll get on the phone to Norfolk. They ought be able to fly in what we need by chopper."

"Aye, aye, skipper! I'll see to her right now."

* * *

Wes thanked the motor pool driver for the lift from the VOQ (visitor officer quarters) and walked into the Special Operations building. Marino met him in the corridor. "Sorry I disturbed you, Colonel, but I thought you'd want to look over the final draft DOD just delivered to see if there's anything you can't live with."

"No problem, Doug. I'd been up quite a while when you called."

Wes followed the SEAL commander down the hall to the intelligence office. Entering the classified vault, Wes noted it looked the same as the one he'd spent many hours in some twenty-five years ago while assigned to USAFE (USAF-Europe). Then, it was target study for the big war he never had to fight.

Classified documents lined the opened file safes. Wes recalled the excitement he felt the first time he signed for a classified folder. The whole process had a certain mystique in the beginning. You felt you might be forever tainted by the information in the folder you'd read. Later, after hundreds of hours of study, the same facility felt like the worst library you could imagine — full of shit you hoped you'd never have to look at again.

Doug handed Wes copy number twelve of DOD OPLAN EM-PRESS marked TOP SECRET and endorsed by a host of initiating, approving and controlling authorities.

Plans were all that way, Wes remembered — full of cover sheets, tables of contents, pages of definitions, and scores of numbered appendices and amendments. Seeing the massive single-source document, he recalled how frequently it had taken only a few pages to actually describe the operation. The rest had been devoted to coordination, scheduling, task organizations and details necessary to execute the operation. The whole scene was still a bit of a mystery to him.

Opening the document, Wes scanned the contents page, then thought of Walker. This wasn't the DOD's plan. It was his and Walker's. He wished his son could see the end result of their combined creative effort.

Thumbing to the Sequence of Events section, Wes read through the chronology of events. The item marked Detonation Hour caught his eye. The time beside it read:

1027:00 ZULU (0627 Eastern Daylight Time) 26 August - Time calculated on basis of touchdown of TIA Flight 899 at Washington

National Airport plus sixty hours of mechanical timer countdown. Timer setting obtained from monitoring of call to FC from Jabarri.

That was less than fifteen hours away. His pulse quickened as he imagined what might go wrong to delay the assault. The possibilities were endless; the consequences, appalling.

The assault would begin at 0400 hours local. Twenty-four SEALS in eight rafts using electric motors would launch from the U.S. Naval Station for the short trip across the Potomac. They would make landfall at Roaches Run, a point due north of Runway 36, allowing the team to initiate the attack from the tail of the Boeing jet. Four sharpshooters, using long-barreled rifles fitted with suppressors and infrared telescopic sights, would take out all terrorists outside the aircraft. Advancing toward the jet, the assault team, equipped with specially constructed wing root boarding ladders, would assume positions underneath the aircraft adjacent to the main landing gear trucks. A portion of the team would then move forward and take up positions beside the mobile stairs. A coordinated command signal would be given by Commander Marino. Five seconds later, the aircraft's auxiliary power unit (APU) would be shut down using the external emergency shutdown push button on the aft side of the nose gear strut. Simultaneous entry into the aircraft cabin would occur from the left main cabin entrance door and the two mid-cabin over-wing emergency doors. The command EARLY VACATION would be shouted by team members entering the cabin. The electronic evacuation (EVAC) alarm would also be activated by the first team member reaching the flight attendant service panel.

Wes noticed the Maltese cross beside the EVAC item. Adjacent to the mark at the bottom of the page he read:

The cabin team will have armed the doors in preparation for the emergency evacuation or will attempt to do so upon hearing either the verbal or electronic command.

The reference worried him, even though he'd been the one responsible for writing the task into the plan. How would they know to arm the doors? Had Elliot succeeded in getting word to them?

He tried to visualize the assault. Would any of the crew be hurt or killed? Wes knew the fire fight, though brief, would be intense and result in some loss of life. The thought of another crew member being wounded or killed turned his stomach. Only the element of surprise would spare their lives. Wes knew that if Sybil were able, she would have the crew ready.

Reading further, he saw that four members were assigned to secure the cockpit. Firepower would be minimized to preserve the essential flight systems. Hand-to-hand combat would be used to the maximum extent possible commensurate with the hostilities encountered, the statement said.

Wes found it impossible to imagine how the cockpit assault would happen. How badly might the flight deck be damaged? It could make a difference in the mission's success and on whether he would be rescued in time.

Wes tried not to think of dying, though he considered his rescue a long shot. A kind of numbness had replaced his fear. The sensation was not unique. He'd experienced the feeling long ago in Vietnam.

"What do you think of it, Colonel?" Marino asked. "Pretty much the way you outlined it?"

"Doug, I don't see how you guys do this kind of thing. The tension would drive me up a tree."

Marino smiled. "It can get a little tense at times. You must have forgotten what it was like when you flew those fighters into Hanoi. Having to deal with SAMS and triple A during every mission and ejecting into the Gulf of Tonkin couldn't have been any less hectic."

"Yeah, but I was young and stupid then," Wes replied.

"I guess some of us just enjoy being stupid," Marino joked. "Most of us would rather do this for a living and have the excitement than have to go out and get a real job."

"There's something to be said for that," Wes said.

Returning to the OPLAN, Wes saw that the hostages and cabin team would escape from the aircraft via the two aft slides. SEALS entering the cabin from the mid-over-wing exits would subdue any terrorists in the main cabin at the time of the assault. From their initial entry position, the SEALS would provide a human shield against any terrorists trying to fire at the hostages or cabin team from the forward cabin.

The assault plan looked so simple and straightforward on paper, thought Wes. But he knew better. A jammed door, a collapsed slide, or a crowded aisle would turn the situation into chaos and result in multiple casualties. Still, it was the best they could hope for. Darkness, the element of surprise, and Sybil's team would make the difference. SEALS positioned outside the jet would provide cover and marshall the fleeing hostages to the plane's rear.

There was no mention of how a terrorist grenade attack would be dealt with. That worried Wes. One well-placed grenade could destroy all chances of getting the 767 off the ground. He knew Jabarri's men had them. Reza had insisted on them, along with the automatic weapons.

Reading farther down the sequence, Wes began reviewing the tasks dealing with the launch. Two fuel trucks would provide the servicing. Three pneumatic power carts would provide backup for the engine start in the event the jet's APU would not restart. Two external electrical power carts also would be positioned to provide electrical power for ground-servicing and alignment of the jet's three laser inertial reference systems (IRS). The plan allocated twenty minutes total from the cessation of hostilities to accomplish all ground-servicing and engine-starting. Wes knew that was cutting it close. Alignment would require a minimum of fifteen minutes. The fueling operation would take about the same time.

Spence Riker, TIA's chief pilot, would handle the exterior pre-flight, then come to the cockpit to help with the loading of the two flight management computers (FMCs). He recalled Spence's objection that there would be no copilot. A team of TIA mechanics would be in place to accomplish the launch and handle any last-minute maintenance. A note in the margin indicated all support personnel and equipment would be moved into their pre-assault staging positions inside a maintenance hangar on the south end of the field two hours prior to the assault.

Wes thought through each step of his part of the plan. He was to wait with two SEALS outside the jet until it was secured. Then Marino would give him a visual signal to board the 767. They would transfer the parachutes and life-support equipment to the 767, then conduct a thorough search of the jet for hidden bombs and booby traps.

Referring to the flight plan profile attachment, Wes checked the map for accuracy against the North Atlantic Plotting Chart he'd used to develop the original route. The coordinates checked. Only three waypoints would be loaded. The first, a point considered the minimum distance acceptable from the shore; the second, fifty miles short of the intended crash where he would parachute at five thousand feet above the sea; and the third, a point twelve minutes farther east, at thirty-six degrees North, sixty degrees West — the point of impact. Wes noted the flight would take an hour and forty-seven minutes from brake release to splashdown, some seven hundred nautical miles downrange. Assuming the flight got airborne as scheduled, that would give him a ten-minute window. One way or the other, he would have to put her in the drink before six twenty-seven in the morning.

Looking at the small racetrack symbol on the chart depicting the Navy rescue holding orbit, Wes wondered about the rescue helicopter's showing up. It was asking a lot of them to fly into the face of a nuclear explosion to pick up one man. He wouldn't blame them if they didn't.

He didn't waste any time reading the section entitled "ALTERNATE EMPRESS." Wes knew what it said. It spelled out the terms under which the 767 would be bombed on the ground if the assault failed, or shot down while in flight, if contingencies precluded reaching the impact point. Wes knew either meant instant death for him.

Air support tasking called for F-16's from the 192nd Tactical Fighter Group at Byrd Field in Richmond and F-117 Stealth fighters staging out of Langley AFB to handle the bombing at National, if needed. F-14 Tomcats and F-18 Hornets launched off the carrier Roosevelt would provide escort and shoot down coverage once the 767 was airborne. An Airborne Warning and Control (AWAC) Boeing 707 would monitor the flight from takeoff to impact and coordinate instructions received from Air Force One.

Closing the OPLAN, Wes leaned back in the leather chair and thought for a minute. There were so many places in the plan where a seemingly small obstacle could scuttle the entire operation. He questioned whether they could really pull it off. Was it too much to expect?

Signing over copy twelve of OPLAN EMPRESS to the intelligence specialist on duty, Wes left the intell shop in search of Doug. There were still minor details he needed to clear up. Then he'd call Meredith.

37

THE MESSAGE

Emerson Beamer crawled out of the taxi and walked a short distance to the temporary observation post. There, he met two of the task force agents. Hassan had been found. Although he wanted to rush the flat and seize the terrorist, experience told him to enlist the support of the Geneva police first, especially since there might be bloodshed.

"Donovon, get the police commissioner on the phone for me."

The senior FBI agent nodded and dialed the number. Donovon's French was excellent. A few seconds later, he gave the phone to Beamer with his hand cupped over the microphone. "His English is very broken, but I think you'll be able to make him out. His name is Jacques Deloren."

"Commissioner! Emerson Beamer with the US Joint Task Force.

Donovon listened to Beamer's side of the conversation. He appeared to be getting what he wanted from the expression on his boss's face.

Abruptly hanging up, Beamer announced, "Deloren is sending his senior inspector and a small squad of officers to help us make the arrest. He's willing to let us handle it, but insisted his men be present in case of an inquiry." Donovon smiled. He'd spent most of the day pounding the pavement in search of Hassan.

"Assemble your men and be prepared to move as soon as they arrive. We need to get started with his interrogation ASAP," Beamer said.

Twenty minutes later, the Swiss police assault team arrived. Introducing himself to their squad leader, Donovon explained his plan.

The Swiss police would take up positions in the hallways, staircase, and front and rear entrances only after the Task Force agents were in position to confront Hassan.

With their plan thoroughly rehearsed, Donovon and four armed agents climbed the stairs to the fourth floor of Hassan's apartment building and surrounded the entrance to his flat. Moments later, Swiss assault team members took up their posts.

Donovon banged on the door. A voice called out in English, "Who is it?" In French, Donovon told him a fire had been reported in the building and that he, the fire marshal, was inspecting every flat. Several seconds later, Donovon heard the chain fall from the lock as the dead bolt was retracted from its slot. The door opened.

"What the...!" shrieked Hassan as Donovon stormed the entrance and shoved his snub-nosed thirty-eight into the startled Arab's gut. Fellow agents burst into the apartment behind him in search of companions, but found none.

No one spoke as agents slapped cuffs on Hassan's wrists and ankles, stuffed a sock into his mouth and shoved him down into a straightback chair. Only then did Donovon motion for one of his men to signal the Swiss and Beamer that the arrest was complete. Beamer started the interrogation. He wanted straight answers fast, and he knew how to get them. Rights of the accused and rules of protocol would not be an issue. He and the police commissioner had an understanding.

Motioning Donovon to clear out his men, Beamer walked over to the figure slumped in the chair and removed the wad of cloth from his mouth.

"Hassan Kahlil, my name is Emerson Beamer. I represent a joint task force sent here to apprehend those responsible for the nuclear threat against the United States."

The Arab sat motionless.

"I should also tell you that I have the total cooperation of Swiss government authorities in dealing with you, Andrea Zahar, and Saeed Keshef. It is important for you to understand that the normal rules governing treatment of people sought by the United States government will not apply in your case. There'll be no record of your arrest, interrogation and disposition. You'll have no representation, nor will you be allowed to speak with anyone regarding your status unless you choose to cooperate fully with our investigation now. Otherwise, you are a liability, and you will be disposed of accordingly. Do I make myself clear?"

Pausing, Beamer watched Hassan for some indication of his reaction, but saw none. Walking around to his side, he said, "Isabel, the one Saddam calls The Spider, is dead."

Hearing that, Hassan struggled against the cuffs in anger.

"She is dead?" he asked in dismay.

"Yes, she was killed last night during an attempted escape."

"I do not believe you!" Hassan scoffed.

"It might also interest you to know that before she died, she gave us your name, a description of your duties in the organization and a list of the nations sponsoring the coalition."

"Impossible! She would die first!"

"Shall I spell it out for you? Or perhaps you would have me give you a computer printout of every investment account Andrea has opened since the beginning of the month. We have it all, Hassan. She hid a backup disk under her desk. The fire you started didn't touch it."

Kahlil hung his head. He knew Emerson was telling the truth.

Throwing his head back, Hassan looked directly into Beamer's face. "It matters not what you infidels know. Washington will be destroyed anyway!" he replied, defiantly.

"Perhaps. But, you, my friend, will not live to know the outcome," Beamer countered.

Kahlil looked puzzled. Then his expression turned to fear as Beamer pulled a pistol from his coat and casually began to screw a suppressor to the end of the barrel.

Seeing the anxiety on Hassan's face, Emerson said, "Does it surprise you that certain agencies within our democracy are accorded special discretion in conducting the covert affairs of the U.S. government? Or do you think such acts belong exclusively to the likes of Saddam?"

Hassan stared at the gun, speechless.

"I'm surprised you don't at least have an opinion. After all, you were educated in our country, schooled in our ways, and enjoyed our freedom. Surely you have something to say, Mr. Kahlil?"

Perspiring heavily, Hassan answered in a quivering voice, "I ..."

Emerson took a loaded clip from his pocket and shoved it into the pistol grip. "Yes?"

"I ... I don't want to die — not now, not here, like this."

"That decision is up to you, my friend. Frankly, I don't have the time to mess with you. Either you give me the information I need now, in which case you will be spared, or I'll dispose of you, then go after your two associates. The choice is yours."

Kahlil's eyes darted about the room as he wrestled with Beamer's ultimatum. Emerson looked down at the whimpering young man bound to the chair as he raised the pistol to his forehead. Beads of sweat poured from Kahlil's flesh and rushed down the sides of his neck as he felt the steel barrel's cold tip press against his skull. His body shook uncontrollably as the color drained from his face. Then he heard Beamer cock the weapon.

"I ... They'll kill me if I talk!"

Beamer pressed the barrel firmly against Hassan's forehead. "That's no longer a problem for you, is it? You won't have to worry about them anymore. You've decided."

Kahlil thought for a split second, then cried out, "No, No! Don't shoot! Please!"

"Then talk. Answer my question! Where is the new office, and where can I find Andrea and Saeed?"

"On the third floor of an office building near the intersection of Rue Ancienne and Jacques Dalphin!"

"What's the number?"

"The number?"

"Yes, the number of the building," Beamer snapped.

"Eight. Number eight."

Emerson eased the pistol from Kahlil's head. "I need more. Which door on the third floor?"

"The second door on the right at the top of the stairs."

Beamer fired more questions at the terrorist as Donovon scribbled the information on his note pad. Regaining his composure, Hassan blurted out the answers to Emerson's questions. Then Beamer was finished with the interrogation.

"Have your men take him downstairs and put him in the car. We may need him to pinpoint the locations. We'll visit their office first."

Donovon nodded and left the room to speak with his officers waiting outside the door.

Andrea parked Saeed's Mercedes on Rue de Candolle, a block from Hassan's flat. Not wanting him to recognize the car, she decided to cover the rest of the distance on foot. As she stepped into the street, Andrea saw that two vehicles were double-parked ahead. Both seemed in front of his building. She paused, but saw no one and continued walking.

Would Hassan be asleep? It would make the job easier. She didn't like the idea of having to kill him. He'd been more than an associate to her — a friend and a companion. Yet Saeed was right. Hassan knew too much. He was a threat to their security and to the coalition. His betrayal could not be tolerated.

Barely a hundred feet from the entrance to his flat, Andrea stopped cold in her tracks as she saw two men come out of the building with Hassan. She was too late. Afraid of being noticed, she stepped into the shadow of a tree and waited. Shortly, two other men exited the building and got in the car with Hassan.

A chill came over Andrea as she recalled the information Hassan could trade for his life. He was a coward. She'd always known it. He would never choose a martyr's death. Exposure to the Western world had left its mark. Saeed had to be warned.

Turning around slowly, Andrea walked back toward the car, staying close to the buildings. At a safe distance, she picked up her pace, stopping once to look back. The two cars were still parked in the middle of the street.

Reaching the Mercedes, Andrea opened the door and slipped inside. She sat there for a second and debated what to do. There was no way she could get to Hassan now. Besides, there was a good chance he'd already revealed much of what he knew. Grabbing the car phone, Andrea dialed the covert office number. She let it ring six times and was about to hang up when Saeed lifted the receiver.

"The police have Hassan! I saw two men put him in a car. He was in handcuffs!"

Cursing in Arabic, Saeed asked, "Did they see you?"

"No. I'm certain they did not."

"Good. Then stay in your car and tail them. You should be able to tell what he has told them by where they lead you. I'll get the files, set the explosive timer, and go to my car. I'll need at least ten minutes. Call here only if you are certain they're approaching the office. Let the phone ring only twice and then hang up. Once I'm in my car, we'll decide where to rendezvous."

* * *

Jill stared at Bud's Cessna from the right seat of the WBSU traffic chopper as the pilot descended vertically toward a point just aft of his plane. Looking out to the side, she could see the huge 767 on the end of Runway 36. Jill tried to imagine the assault taking place. She was glad the *Examiner* had decided to relocate its offices to Fredericksburg, though she wondered if that was far enough from Washington.

Clutching two spare camera battery packs, Jill watched as Bud moved toward their intended landing spot. She hadn't seen him since last week. How would he act? She worried about having deceived him. She would explain it all to him now.

Less than fifty feet from touchdown, Jill waved to him. Startled at seeing her on board, Bud returned the salute as the pilot broke their rapid descent rate and gently kissed the parched grass beneath the chopper's rails.

"I didn't expect you to personally deliver the batteries!"

"I had to see you, Bud. We have to talk right now!"

"About what?"

"It's about the interview, Bud. I'm really here because the president needs your help."

A puzzled look replaced the excitement on Bud's face. "What do you mean? What does the president want of me?"

Hesitating for a second, she blurted, "They're going to make an assault on the aircraft sometime in the morning, before daybreak. He wants you to get word to Sybil to have the flight attendants arm all the evacuation slides and stand by for the attack. The password is 'EARLY VACATION.'"

"You're kidding!" Then Bud saw the expression on Jill's face. "You're not kidding, are you?"

"No, Bud. It's for real. They're going to take the aircraft before daylight," Jill said slowly. "That's why I had to invent a reason to come see you. You don't have to do it, you know. No one will blame you if you don't."

Bud turned his back to her and looked at the 767. How could he refuse? He'd met those people. He'd talked with them, filmed them, and prayed for their safety. Their peril had given his career a rebirth. How could he leave them there to die? "Tell the president I'll do it. I'll pass the message."

"Now get out of here, kid. We've both got work to do. Jill touched his unshaved face briefly. "Deliver the message, then fly out," Jill pleaded as he closed the canopy door.

Bud kept his eye on Jill as the helicopter broke free of gravity and rose straight into the sky. He waved and saw her wave back, then she was gone. Following the chopper's path southwest until it was a speck against the hot August sky, Bud relived their brief meeting as he walked back toward his Cessna.

Bud tossed the two batteries on the seat of his Cessna, then gathered his gear for the short hike over to the 767. Jabarri was waiting.

Stopping at the foot of the boarding steps, Bud put his hands on his head and waited. He knew the routine. Neither guard seemed threatened by his presence and gave him a cursory inspection before waving him on.

Approaching the top of the stairs, he saw Jabarri step from the cabin. "Please enter, Mr. Waterman. It is good that we meet again. There is much I have to tell you and the American people." Bud did his best to appear enthusiastic, but his mind was on the message he'd come to deliver. Sybil was nowhere in sight as he entered the cabin.

"You seem...how do you say, 'preoccupied,' Mr. Waterman."

The statement caught Bud off-guard. "No, no. I'm just deciding how to film the interview — mostly technical stuff the studio likes to see," he replied. Reza didn't respond, but didn't interfere either.

Bud started toward the rear of the cabin, but stopped as Reza called out, "You will not go back there. We will talk here."

As Bud turned around, he caught a glimpse of Sybil. "Ah, yes, of course," Bud answered loudly, hoping his voice would draw her attention. He was in luck. Their eyes met briefly. He mouthed, "EARLY VACATION."

"Come, Mr. Waterman, we do not have a moment to waste," Reza commanded. Bud walked back up the aisle and set up the tripod at an angle facing the two seats he and Reza would sit in. Getting to Sybil wasn't going to be as easy.

Switching on the camera and floodlights, he turned toward Reza and asked, "What would you like to tell the American people at this time, Mr. Jabarri?" Reza paused, then launched into a ten-minute tirade filled with fundamentalist fanaticism. Bud didn't interrupt, but used the time to collect his thoughts.

"And are you and the Fundamentalist Coalition satisfied with the progress the United States is making in its withdrawal from the Middle East?"

"Generally, yes, but there are still a number of ships within striking distance of our brother's borders in the Mediterranean. The Americans must exit those waters before we will seriously consider removing the threat. We also note that several European governments seem to be dragging their feet in responding to your government's request that they release all of our political prisoners. The president would be wise to use his influence to expedite their release. The coalition will not wait endlessly for those governments to act."

Bud was about to pose a third question when Sybil passed by his seat and walked to the galley. He struggled to keep his mind on the interview.

"Mr. Jabarri, do you feel that enough progress has been made by our government to warrant your giving consideration to freeing the rest of the hostages?"

Reza gave Bud a sharp glance before turning to face the camera. "In due time it is possible we may decide to release some additional passengers, but for now they stay!"

Cursing under his breath, Bud knew he'd failed in his attempt to have them freed. Some would die in the assault. Continuing the interview seemed pointless.

Bud switched off the camera. "You've given me quite a lot to show to the American people, Mr. Jabarri."

Reza seemed uninterested in his comment. Pulling the cassette from the camera, Bud looked at Reza. "Could you spare a cup of water? I used the last of mine this morning."

"There is water in the galley. Have as much as you like."

"Thanks. I'll get it on my way out," Bud replied. "I've got to get this film to the studio in time for the evening news. Will you allow the TV helicopter to return to pick up the film?"

"Of course."

"And would you instruct the tower to recall the chopper now? It will save time."

"I will give the order," Jabarri asserted. "Then I will walk you back to your aircraft."

Bud watched Reza enter the cockpit, then made his move toward the galley. Sybil appeared busy soaking pillowcases in a sinkful of ice. He guessed she would say they were for her suffering passengers.

"I need a cup of water, please," he said.

"Could you reach them for me? They're on the top shelf."

Bud looked at her, then moved closer to the counter.

"What did you try to tell me back there?"

Stuffing his hand into the upper shelf, Bud whispered from under his arm, "Early Vacation. Get ready for an Early Vacation near dawn, tomorrow."

"Early Vacation?"

"Yes. Arm the doors. It will come before dawn."

"Can I have that drink now?" he asked loudly. "My throat's killing me."

Giving him a nasty look, Sybil filled the Styrofoam cup with ice water. Bud chugged the first cup and motioned for another as Reza appeared. "It is done. The helicopter is returning here now. It is time that you go."

Bud gave Sybil a parting glance. "Thanks for the water. I'll buy you a drink the next time I see you." Sybil fought the temptation to smile. It was his way of wishing her good luck.

Reaching for his equipment and the cassette, Bud made his way down the mobile stairs. Reza followed, but said nothing until they were a safe distance from the aircraft.

"Tell me, Mr. Waterman, what is the range of your Cessna?" The question caught Bud by surprise.

"Maybe three hundred miles on a full tank."

"Can it be flown at night?" Reza asked.

"Sure, if you know what you're doing."

"Do you often fly at night?"

"No. It's a pain in the ass."

"Flying has always appealed to me, but I can never find the time to maintain my proficiency," said Reza. "Did you know that Nsar and I are pilots?" Bud shook his head.

Reza watched as Bud lay the gear on the seat and wiped the sweat from his face. Without thinking, Bud picked up the cooler sitting by the nose gear and held it to his mouth as he pressed the petcock. Water gushed from the spout onto his face. Then it hit him. The water!

"Do you lie often, Mr. Waterman, or only when it suits your purposes?"

"Pardon?" Bud asked, setting the cooler down.

Jabarri was silent.

"Oh, you're asking about the water. I guess you're right. I do have some after all. The truth is, I had wanted to find out about the passengers, but I failed. You've frightened that flight attendant to death."

Reza grinned at the connotation, but said nothing.

Walking under the wing, Jabarri stuck his head into the tiny cockpit. "How is your airplane started?" he asked.

Bud leaned into the cockpit from the other side and showed him the ignition key. "About the same way you start a car."

Reza studied the instrument panel then switched on the ignition. He watched as the fuel tank indicators came to life. Seeing both tanks registered more than half full, Reza switched off the ignition and took out the key. Bud noticed him slip the key into his pocket.

"Mr. Waterman, I want you to personally deliver that cassette to the studio. You must go and write your piece for tomorrow's edition. Your work here is finished for now. I will send for you when I have more to say to your government and its people. You will go with the helicopter when it comes for your video. Is that understood?"

Bud nodded. He knew he had no choice.

Satisfied his instructions would be obeyed, Reza smiled and retreated for his short walk back to the waiting 767. Bud felt a lump in his throat as he cursed Jabarri for denying him the chance to witness the assault, firsthand. He wondered how many of the hostages would make it out alive.

* * *

Andrea eased her car through the busy intersection while keeping her distance behind the unmarked police car. They were heading west on Route de Meyrin. The Geneva police station was in the opposite direction, back across the river.

Glancing at the console, Andrea saw it was nearly midnight. Why hadn't Saeed called? He'd had more than enough time to clean out the office and leave.

The car she was following slowed abruptly and signaled for a right turn. Hitting her brakes, Andrea pulled off to the side of the road and waited. Suddenly, she realized where Hassan was being taken. The road they'd turned onto led directly to the corporate entrance of Cointrin Airport. He wasn't going to be detained in Geneva, but flown to the United States.

From her vantage point, Andrea could see activity around a 707 parked on the ramp. The aircraft was being readied for flight. She watched as a fuel truck drove from beneath its right wing. As his head-lights flashed against the ship's hull, she recognized the U.S. mark-ings. It was Secretary of State Halston's jet, the one they'd had dam-aged earlier in the week. Seconds later, the car Andrea had followed pulled up and stopped at the foot of the boarding stairs. She saw two men escort a third man up the steps.

It was Hassan. He'd made a deal with the Americans. She cursed herself for not allowing Saeed to kill him when they'd had the chance. It was her fault. Hassan knew everything about the FC — their organi-zation, the state sponsors, even their future operations. He had to be stopped now, but how?

Jerking the car phone from its cradle, Andrea punched in the co-vert office number. It rang four times and stopped. The line was dead. Horrified, Andrea realized what she'd done.

Startled by the unexpected blast, Saeed stared in disbelief as the office building collapsed under its own weight, taking with it the five men he'd watched enter about two minutes ago. Flames erupted from the debris as people poured into the darkened street, frightened and confused. He heard sirens in the distance. The police would be there any second.

Leaping from the curb, Saeed whipped the BMW's steering wheel to the left to avoid the rubble in his path. Had Andrea dialed the num-ber or had Hassan already given the police the information? How could she have known he'd planned to use the telephone ringer to detonate the plastic explosives?

As he turned the corner, two fire trucks sped by Saeed. A police car in pursuit ignored him. Two blocks later, he slowed and reached for the mobile phone. Andrea answered.

"Saeed?" she cried. "The line went dead after four rings. I thought you'd been taken!" she exclaimed. "Where are you?"

"I'm headed for The Vineyards. "Meet me there."

"No, wait. They've taken Hassan on board Halston's jet here at the airport. We've got to stop them. He knows too much!"

Saeed remembered the two stolen SA-7 missiles. Although bought to be used against the Israeli prime minister, he could use them now. They were in the trunk of the Mercedes Andrea was driving.

"In which direction are the planes taking off?"

"To the southwest," she answered.

That meant the jet would be taking off on Runway 23 and passing over Route de Meyrin and then the Rue de Champs-Prévost. Launching the two heat seekers from the roadside would be extremely risky, but they would have to try. Otherwise, the coalition's future would be doomed. It was a chance they had to take.

"Where are you now?"

"On Route de Meyrin near the corporate entrance."

"Stay there. I'm about three or four minutes from you."

"Hurry, they're starting the engines now!"

Keshef didn't bother to answer. They'd already said too much, but that couldn't be helped. Hassan had to be stopped.

Two minutes later, he passed over the Autoroute leading from the Vernier tunnel at Pont de Val Ombre. Saeed was near Andrea's position. Two hundred meters ahead, he saw the black Mercedes parked by the roadway. Flashing his lights twice, he pulled off and stopped behind her.

From his BMW, Saeed could see what looked to be the 707 taxiing up the ramp toward the far end of the runway. It would be taking off shortly. Andrea had chosen an excellent position for the shot.

They met at the rear of her car. "We haven't much time!" Saeed said. "We'll have to use the two heat seekers. Do you still remember how to fire the missile?"

Andrea wasn't sure. It had been almost six months since she, Hassan, and Saeed had been to Libya for the training. "I think so," she said, as he raised the trunk lid, illuminating the two missiles and their launchers. He assembled them both and handed one to Andrea. "We'll meet at The Vineyards."

Andrea took the weapon and walked to the right front fender of the Mercedes. Handling the small rocket suddenly felt familiar. Recalling her training, she checked the sight and examined the firing mechanism as the firing procedures came back to her.

"You try for the right engines. I'll take those on the left," he said.

In the distance, they heard the unmistakable sound of the 707's engines spooling up to full power. Andrea looked over at Saeed. He stood ready, facing the sound. Seconds later, they saw the jet rolling toward them, full of fuel. Andrea wondered if it would get airborne.

Then she saw the nose of the four-engine jet lift off, carrying the bright lights with it.

Raising the launcher, Andrea began to track the 707's motion through the optical sight as it passed directly overhead. The sound was deafening. The smell of kerosene filled her nostrils. Through the sight, she saw the main landing gear begin its ascent into the aircraft's belly. Andrea fired the missile directly at the jet's two right engines. The hiss of the missile igniting frightened her as it zoomed off the launcher in pursuit of its target.

She tried to follow its path, but lost it in the scope. A split-second later, she heard the familiar hiss a second time as Saeed's missile left its launcher in search of the same prey.

Time stood still as Andrea searched the darkness for the two missiles, but saw only the fleeting position lights of the 707. Had they fired duds? Had the infrared guidance systems failed? They waited impatiently.

Suddenly, Andrea saw a violent flash of fire followed by an even greater explosion. The jet, now visible, started rolling to the right and coming apart as flames enveloped the wings and fuselage. She watched, spellbound, as burning pieces of the 707 fell back toward the ground.

"Go now!" Saeed screamed, tossing his launcher into the ditch and running to his car.

At first, his words didn't register. Still stunned by what she'd done, Andrea couldn't take her eyes off the sight.

Saeed yelled, "Get in the car, now, Andrea!" This time, she heard him and dropped the launcher. He could already see car lights approaching as he pleaded with her to get into the car. Was she in shock? It was her first time. Then he saw Andrea pull onto the highway abruptly and gun the Mercedes. She switched on her headlights and disappeared over the horizon as he raced close behind.

*   *   *

John Sinclair's secretary transferred Beamer's call from Geneva to his desk. "Emerson, Sinclair here. What have you got?" Beamer didn't reply. John suspected trouble.

"Sir, five of my men were killed thirty minutes ago. We'd captured Hassan Kahlil and succeeded in locating the coalition's new office. I sent Donovon and his men in to secure the place. From what Hassan had told me, I had reason to think Saeed and Andrea might still be there.

"Right after they entered the building, an explosion ripped the place apart. I feel like shit for letting it happen. It was my fault. I should have expected something like this, especially after what they'd done to their first office."

"Don't blame yourself, Emerson. These are the same people who've put a nuke on our doorstep. They'll stop at nothing."

"Yes, sir, I know you're right, but it's tough to accept."

"What about Hassan? You said you'd talked with him."

He's aboard Secretary Halston's aircraft. The flight was supposed to have left fifteen minutes ago for Washington."

"Did you get anything out of him?"

"Only the location of their new office and I'm beginning to wonder if that wasn't a setup," Beamer answered.

"I doubt it. That's giving them too much credit. What about the other two?"

"We'll have to start from scratch now that they've fled and their office has been destroyed. Hassan is still our best chance of getting the information we need to find those two. Now that this has happened, I wish I hadn't sent him back," Beamer complained.

"You made the right call. We'll work on him with everything we've got. Besides, he may be useful to us against Jabarri."

"I hope so," Beamer grumbled.

Looking up from his desk, Sinclair saw his secretary frantically waving at him. "I'll talk with you later, Emerson. I've got another pressing situation to handle."

"Sir, Secretary Jacobson's on the phone. He say's it's urgent he talk with you now. There's been a plane crash!"

38

EARLY VACATION

Sybil peered out of the first class window at the Potomac. From her vantage point, she had an excellent view of the water. She could even make out the more prominent points along the opposite bank. Seat 1-1 had become the closest place she could find to a mental safe haven for the last couple of days. It was her private refuge. There, she had literally relived every important moment in her life, from her earliest memory to the horrible present. With nothing left to do, remembering came naturally.

Sybil thought mostly of opportunities wasted or lost and blamed herself for choosing poorly. Had she been naive, selfish, or just hardheaded? Being honest, Sybil felt she could make a good case for any of the three. She vowed to live differently if fate spared her from what lay ahead.

Knowing a rescue attempt was imminent renewed her hope for a future. Staring out the window again, Sybil tried to imagine where the assault team would come from. How many would die? Who would live? Would she?

Keeping secrets had always been difficult for her. But should she burden the others with the news and have them worry all night or should she keep the secret for a while longer? Implementing EARLY VACATION would not pose a problem for any of her team, but worrying about it might.

Looking up, Sybil saw the Ugly One pass and thought of the nightmare Cynthia had shared with her. What if she were confronted by one of the terrorists and raped, or worse, separated from her companions with her secret untold? What impact might that have on the outcome of the assault? Was it fair to deny them the hope that her message would bring? The secret was about their lives and the chance to reclaim them. She had to tell them.

Turning once more toward the Potomac, Sybil closed her eyes to think. Ahmed would know something was afoot the instant he heard the words, EARLY VACATION. Yet, by trying to further disguise the plan, the message could be misconstrued. She would go with the covert signal and hope Ahmed would remain in the dark.

Sybil saw Chad, his hands tied behind him, lying on his side dozing. She was glad to see him resting. He'd taken the brunt of the terrorists' physical abuse. She noticed the heavy growth on his face. She also saw the bruises on Chad's cheeks and arms where the terrorists had struck him repeatedly for sport while jeering at him and his military background. She would tell Chad first. He deserved to know his torment would end soon.

Sybil walked slowly to the forward lav. Mohammed gave her a disinterested look and waved her on. Inside, she locked the door and took a ballpoint pen from the cloth sheath she wore around her neck. In the palm of her left hand, Sybil wrote EARLY VACATION, NEAR DAWN. As a precaution, she removed the small bottle of moisturizer she had taken from the hotel and poured a dab into her right palm. She pressed the lav flush motor handle, paused, then unlocked the door.

Exiting, her eyes met Mohammed's cold stare. His look unnerved her. She tried to hide her fear with a disapproving glance as she walked toward the cabin. Sybil thought he might suspect her of something, but dismissed the feeling as she approached Chad. He was awake, but still groggy. The lav flushing must have awakened him. Their eyes met. Raising her left hand, Sybil opened her left palm and laid it inside her right one, exposing the message.

Chad looked at her palm, then face. Wrinkles formed on his forehead as he tried to verify what he'd read. Nodding deliberately, Sybil saw a gleam in his eyes. He understood. The color returned to his bruised face. She'd given him a much-needed shot of adrenalin.

Managing a smile, Chad returned the deliberate nod. His excitement gave her courage. One by one, she would spread the secret. They would be ready.

* * *

Gaylord watched from the president's helicopter as McGarth dashed across the lawn and up the waiting stairs. It was unusual to see him alone, but he'd insisted it be done that way. Worried that the press might discover him leaving the White House and make the matter public, Mason had insisted on a discreet departure.

McGarth peered outside as the chopper began its liftoff for the flight to Camp Peary. Elliot opened his brief case and took out a folder containing a summary of the EMPRESS plan and handed him the top secret document. The president scanned the list of sequential events, paying special attention to the chronology. "Is the EMPRESS still on schedule?"

"No, it's running close to an hour behind because of a tow cable breaking."

McGarth looked at Elliot sternly. "When did that happen?"

"Late this afternoon, while you were asleep."

"What time is it now due to be at National?"

"By three, assuming no more delays."

"Isn't that cutting it pretty close?"

Elliot continued. "There's no question that we're facing a dicey situation, but I'm convinced the plan is sound. We still have a good chance of getting that nuke out of Washington."

"And what about Colonel Beacham?" Mason asked. "Aren't we putting one hell of a burden on his shoulders?"

"No doubt about it," Gaylord snapped. "He stands a good chance of not making it back alive, but he'll carry through with it anyway. He's too proud to let anyone down. He'll do everything he can to get that 767 into the Atlantic. I'm sure of it."

"What about the coordination involved here? It looks awful critical to me. I mean all of it has got to happen precisely as planned, or the whole thing could go off in our faces."

Elliot could see Mason was having second thoughts about the plan. "That's true, but the plan is designed for that not to happen. There will still be time to let the fighters bomb the jet if the plan runs into a snag."

"Not if Jabarri discovers what we're up to before the EMPRESS gets into place."

Gaylord didn't reply. It could happen that way.

"How is the coordination sequence being handled?" Mason asked. Gaylord glanced at his notes to refresh his understanding. Then he explained, "Once the EMPRESS is in position, its jamming system will be activated long enough for its signal strength to be measured at six different positions surrounding the airport. Assuming the tests are successful, the system will be shut down to allow all units to receive a precise time hack and to verify that every microwave antenna in the area is shutdown. At that same time, jamming of all communication satellites will commence. As soon as all those tasks are completed, the EMPRESS will be switched back on and the assault will be launched from across the Potomac."

The president looked at the assault map and then back at Elliot. "What's the chance the SEALS will be discovered before they're in position to launch their attack? I recall that both shores are fairly flat and very exposed."

"That's true, except for an area called Roaches Run, the small peninsula extending into the river to the northeast of the airport. Commander Marino has planned to attack from there to take advantage of the foliage."

McGarth studied the chart briefly, then put it away. "I guess what I'm really after is a guarantee this operation is going to work. If it doesn't, I shudder to think of what we'll have to face."

* * *

Wes Beacham and Doug Marino climbed aboard the Navy chopper for the twenty-five minute flight from Little Creek to Camp Peary. Neither had much to say. It had all been said. The plans, coordination, and contingencies had been reviewed and discussed dozens of times. All that remained was the execution.

Wes glanced around the inside of the bird as it rose from the ground and headed west across Hampton Roads toward the mouth of the York River. The scene was familiar. A knot started to form in the pit of his stomach as his mind raced over the myriad tasks that lay ahead. He recalled climbing into the cockpit of the F-105D at Korat Air Force Base, Thailand, and dumping the breakfast he'd been prodded to eat over the side before heading north to Route Pack Six, the Hanoi proving grounds for fighter pilots. He had the same feeling now.

Doug fell asleep as soon as they became airborne. Wes studied him for a while. Young for such command; barely over thirty, but in superb physical shape, extremely intelligent and supremely confident in his ability. Yet, Doug possessed a certain naiveté that belonged exclusively to youth. Though willing to confront any obstacle, he lacked the wisdom to see beyond the conflict to reconciliation. That was the difference between youth and experience. One saw confrontation as a challenge to be conquered at any price. For the other, negotiation held the long-term answer to vital differences or, at the least, to peaceful coexistence.

Spending the last twenty-four hours with Doug and his men had renewed Wes's sense of purpose. Seeing the spit and vinegar with which they'd prepared for their mission had its effect on him, too. Sitting alone in silence, Wes felt responsible for their welfare, knowing they would answer the call unselfishly to undo the mess he'd made.

Having dozed for ten minutes or so, Wes strained to see out the porthole window as the chopper skimmed the York several hundred feet off the water. The Coleman Bridge lay behind them. They would be landing at Camp Peary in about six minutes. His mind turned to the briefing he and Doug would give the president. What would he ask? Would they be convincing?

There, just ahead, lay the unmarked runway of the airport that didn't exist in the minds of the public. Camp Peary, "The Farm," as it was known to the CIA, had always been a mystery to the community and to Wes for the sixteen years he'd lived in Williamsburg. It was rumored that President Jimmy Carter had gone there to approve the plan for DESERT ONE, the rescue of American hostages in Iran.

On the surface, DESERT ONE had made sense. In retrospect, it had been doomed from the start. Bad weather and poor luck had only made matters worse. Would EMPRESS suffer a similar fate? Wes cringed at the thought.

Marino came to as the helicopter touched down and cut its engine. "That didn't take long," mumbled Doug, wiping the sleep from his eyes.

Wes smiled. "You slept like you didn't have a care in the world."

"I didn't until she said it was too soon for us to make it."

Wes laughed. "At least you still have those kind of dreams. They don't last forever, my friend. Enjoy them while you can."

"Good evening, Colonel Beacham, Commander Marino," said the plainclothes man. "The president and Mr. Elliot will be arriving here shortly. You may wait for him with me, or I can have you taken to the briefing area. It's your choice."

Wes and Marino exchanged glances. "We'll wait here," Marino said.

Minutes later, Wes spied the president's chopper as it turned over the river and switched on its landing lights for the final approach to the landing pad. The scene seemed so clandestine. It was difficult to accept that the high school, where Meredith taught, was barely a mile away on the other side of I-64 and their home just four miles beyond this place of such high intrigue.

Seeing the president emerge, they both came to attention. "Colonel Beacham. Commander Marino," acknowledged McGarth as he stepped to the ground and extended his hand. "Good evening, Mr. President," Wes said, shaking McGarth's hand.

"Gentlemen, you both know Mr. Elliot, my national security adviser?" he added. "Yes, sir," they replied as Gaylord greeted them with a handshake.

"Shall we go talk about this for a few minutes?" asked McGarth, as the four climbed into the waiting staff car. McGarth entered first, then Elliot. Wes motioned for Marino to take the front seat before following Elliot into the back.

The ride to the building where the briefing would take place was quick. Stepping from the car, Wes was struck by the facility's austere appearance and the absence of people. A lone sentry stood watch as they stepped from the car. Wes saw that McGarth didn't seem to notice, as though he'd been there before. Marino's eyes swept the landscape, like a cougar. Wes figured it was his first visit.

Inside, plush carpeting lined the foyer and hallway. The corridors appeared to be soundproof, judging by the acoustical tile fastened to the walls as part of the decor. A solid mahogany conference table occupied the center of the room. High-back leather armchairs surrounded it. Indirect lighting controlled by a rheostat illuminated the ceiling's perimeter. A series of floor-length sliding panels facing the table's lone head chair gave focus to the room. A pitcher of water and six glasses sat on the table amid the classified folders in front of each chair.

"Gentlemen, let's get started. Chris and General Griffith will be joining us momentarily," said the president, motioning for them to take their seats.

"I'll come right to the point. This meeting is not about whether I'm going to approve this plan. I frankly don't have a better choice. It's about satisfying ourselves that we're all ready for what lies ahead in the next eight hours. Wes, you and Doug forget that you're talking to the president, if that's possible, and concentrate on telling it like it is. I want to hear your honest assessment of the situation and how you plan to handle the contingencies. Doug, suppose you lead off. Begin with the pre-assault coordination that will take place, if you will."

Wes settled in his chair as Marino led the president through the scenario, pausing only to answer his few questions. The brevity of Doug's presentation surprised Wes until he realized from the president's questions how much detail McGarth already knew. The president had obviously found the time to do his homework.

Then the president looked at him. "Wes, you take it from the cessation of the assault." Wes glanced at his notes and rattled off the activities that would occur in preparation for the launch. McGarth seemed taken by the coordination required, but withheld comment. Wes was finished in five minutes.

No one said anything. Each knew instinctively that the floor belonged to the president. It was his show, his decision.

"Doug, you're accustomed to this sort of thing. What could go wrong?"

"Sir, my biggest concern is over whether they've rigged the jet with explosives. I don't have any information that would make me think they have, but you can never rule that out completely."

"Elliot's assured me that the only explosives they have are grenades. How big a problem will those be for you?"

"Well, sir, I'd like to tell you no problem, but that's not entirely the case. The truth is we can probably handle them, provided we maintain the element of surprise." Looking over at Wes, Doug added, "My main concern is in leaving Colonel Beacham something he can fly."

McGarth glanced at Wes and smiled. "Anything else, Doug?"

"No, sir, Mr. President. My men are ready."

Wes put down his water. He was next. "What about your concerns, Wes?"

"Sir, Doug and I have talked this thing over quite a bit. Preserving the integrity of the jet is a paramount consideration for both of us. If the jet's at all flyable, I'll get it into the Atlantic, sir."

"Except possibly during the period of jamming, I will be in direct contact with each of you from Air Force One. I'm depending on both of you to keep me abreast of any problems that develop before or during the assault and launch. Wes, I'll withhold bombing the jet until the last possible moment if there is the slightest chance you can get it off and away from Washington in time. One other thing, Wes. I insist that you have a copilot. Spence Riker has volunteered to fly with you.

The president's decision didn't surprise Wes. He just hated the fact that another pilot, a personal friend in this case, would also have to suffer the consequences for his mistake.

Then it was over, and the president stood up. Wes noticed that the president's hand trembled slightly as he shook their hands again. "Good luck, men. Our prayers go with you," he said, clutching their shoulders. "Thank you, sir," Wes said.

Before leaving Camp Peary, Wes placed a call to his family in Duck. It would be his last contact with them before the assault. Trying to sound reassuring, he spoke with each of his children first. It was obvious from their comments they understood the danger he faced. In turn, each expressed his and her profound love for him and their hope for his safe return. Listening to them, Wes realized the magic his children had given his life and refused to pity his plight.

As he waited for Meredith, Wes wondered what he could say to her that he hadn't already said. And what could she say to him? Neither had ever been good at good-byes. Both found it too painful and had stopped saying them long ago. It was understood that he would return.

This time was different. The odds were stacked against his making it back alive. Too many critical events had to fall into place for him to survive. Timing would mean everything. But hadn't it always been that way? Nearly every good or bad thing that had ever happened to him had been influenced more by timing than anything. Why should it be different now?

"Wes. How are you doing?" Meredith asked. The softness in her voice told him she'd been crying. She'd already figured out the odds.

"All right, except for missing you."

"I've done nothing but think about you and what you're about to do, Wes. We have to talk about it now, while there's still time. Do you understand? It's just not right for you to go off like this without us saying our good-byes."

"I know, honey. But words can't begin to describe how much you mean to me and the joy I've had living with you for all these years."

"I know. I... I love you so much I can't imagine my life without you in it..."

"Meredith, the best we can ask of life is to have shared it with someone we love. We've only to look into the faces of our children to see what our life together has meant. Each of them is strong, bright, loving, and eager to take on the world as we once did. We must travel into their world now. I must do what I can to preserve the name we gave them, and you must help them understand its importance."

"I suppose I've always known something like this would happen to us, Wes. That's why I hate saying good-byes."

"Then let's don't start now. Don't you worry about me. I'm ready for whatever lies ahead. I'll be okay."

"Then don't you worry about me, either. Use your time to get back here in one piece, Wes Beacham. Do you understand?"

"It's a deal. I'll get home as soon as I can."

"And I'll be waiting for you on the porch with a cold one," Meredith sighed. "I love you, Wes."

"I love you, too," he replied as he hung up the phone.

39

DESTINY CALLS

Waterman tossed the pliers back into his small canvas tool bag and backed out from under the nose gear of his Cessna as gasoline squirted out on the ground. After wiping off his soaked hands, Bud gathered up his camera gear, flare pistol, and portable telephone and walked toward the grassy area behind his aircraft as two of Jabarri's men watched. He was sure they had him in view. The 767's bright runway turnoff light flooded the area ahead of his position. Reaching the spot where the WBSU chopper would land, Bud dropped his gear and waited as the aircraft came into view.

Minutes later the chopper settled to the ground. Motioning to the pilot first for clearance, Bud walked under the rotating blades and opened the cockpit door.

"Had enough of this place?" the pilot called.

"Plenty! But my work isn't finished here yet," Bud said, impatiently. "I need your help. Jabarri has ordered me out of here and has taken the keys to my Cessna. I need this video cassette delivered to Forest Lindsey at the White House. Tell him I'm going to stay here. I'll keep them abreast of whatever takes place, at least until morning."

"Bud, are you out of your damned mind? Those idiots will shoot your ass off just for the hell of it!" the pilot hollered.

"Only if they know I'm here," Bud replied. "That's where your help comes in."

"What do you want me to do?"

Looking over at the two guards underneath the 767, Bud said,

"Let me climb in with you for a couple of seconds while you pivot the chopper around so that it is between me and the guards over there. Then I'll jump out just before you lift off. Your lights should blind them long enough for me to get down on the ground and out of sight."

"You're crazy. If they catch your ass, you're dead meat!"

"Yeah, I know, but that's the price you have to pay for a good story these days," Bud shouted back. "Just get this crate turned around and I'll be on my way," Bud said, eagerly.

"Okay, man. It's your ass. Climb in."

Bud climbed aboard, but left the door open. Switching on all the lights he had to blind the guards, the pilot lifted off the ground two or three feet before swinging the chopper's nose around perpendicular to the 767.

"Now!" he shouted at Bud, banking the chopper.

Diving onto the ground, Waterman buried his face in the grass as the chopper leaped abruptly into the sky. Dust and dirt whipped about Bud's head as the helicopter pivoted, throwing its spotlight on the 767 as it zoomed upward. Hurled by the cyclonic action of the chopper's blades, bits and pieces of dirt and grass found their way into every crevice of Bud's body.

Lying motionless in the grass, his face covered in dirt and sweat, Bud waited, afraid to breathe. The next few minutes would be critical. He knew the terrorists' habits from having watched them for hours at a time. Once the excitement had passed, they would relax their surveillance and go back to their conversation. Eventually, they would nod off while resting against one of the main gear tires. Bud would make his move then.

*　*　*

Higgins lowered the field glasses to his chest. Up ahead, he could see the lights spanning the Potomac. The EMPRESS was within sight of the Wilson Bridge. Checking his watch, he saw they were nearly an hour behind schedule. He wondered what the delay would do to the operation as he walked aft in search of Charlie.

"How's she holding up?" he asked Cartwright.

"Just barely, skipper, just barely," Charlie answered. "It's a good thing you got Norfolk to drop those diesel pumps in to us or we'd be sitting on the bottom of the Potomac with water up to our asses, going nowhere," he added.

Higgins peered into the flooded compartment and shook his head. "It's a wonder we've made it this far, Charlie."

"You got that right, skipper. But if it gets the job done, she'll be worth her weight in gold."

"Speaking of gold, is the jammer ready?" Higgins asked.

"Yeah, she's ready; all but hoisting up her antenna and running the signal strength test. But we can't do that until we've cleared the Wilson Bridge yonder. They finished her up an hour ago. Those poor guys were so exhausted that I told them to try to catch up on their sleep while they could."

Charlie pulled half a cigar from his pocket and chewed off a little more of its tip. "Reckon we'll make it in time?" Higgins looked at his watch. "Yeah. We'll make it, Charlie. Just make certain that jammer is operational when we get there."

Cartwright turned his back to Higgins and spit over the side. "Aye, sir! She'll melt down any crap they want to turn on, sir. You'll see," he answered.

Higgins smiled at Charlie. That was what he wanted to hear. If Charlie said it was ready, it was ready. No need to worry.

The crackle of his portable FM radio interrupted their conversation.

"BULLDOG ONE CALLING THE FAT LADY."

Jerking the transceiver from his hip pocket, Higgins answered, "THIS IS THE FAT LADY. GO AHEAD."

"FAT LADY, WE'VE GOT A PROBLEM WITH THE BRIDGE. I'LL LET YOU KNOW HOW SERIOUS IT IS SHORTLY," replied the tugboat skipper.

"ROGER, BULLDOG ONE. The FAT LADY IS STANDING BY."

"For Christ's sake, skipper! You'd think they'd know how to raise the friggin' bridge by now!" Cartwright howled. "I mean, what in the hell have they had to do but sit on their asses and wait for us to get here!"

"Beats me, Charlie. We'll just have to wait and see."

"We'll never make it under there without it being raised," Charlie snapped. "There's only sixty feet of vertical clearance with it down. We need the goddam bridge full up, skipper!"

Higgins didn't bother to answer. Rubbing the sweat from the back of his neck, Higgins stared at the bridge, wondering silently what the trouble was. He knew it was out of his hands, like everything else in his life.

Being assigned command of a U.S. naval vessel with no means of self-propulsion fell short of what he'd expected as an Annapolis graduate. Where had he gone wrong? Who had he pissed off? Or was it just a matter of being at the wrong place at the wrong time — like being there on a corroding steel bucket commanding a mission he knew nothing about?

* * *

Wes watched from the cockpit of the SEAL helicopter as Marine One banked right over the York River and disappeared into the black night. Wes figured McGarth's trip to Langley Air Force Base would take twenty-five minutes at the most. He, Elliot, Jacobson, and, General Griffith would be airborne in Air Force One within the hour.

Wes peered down at the homes in Queens Lake as the chopper leveled off at six hundred feet and began its flight to Washington. Recalling the many times he'd been to the subdivision to visit friends or to car pool kids, Wes wondered if this would be his last look at a part of the community he'd called home for the last sixteen years.

For an instant, he had the urge to speak with his friends, to thank them for the good times, to bid them farewell. And yet, looking into their yards, Wes knew it was but a wish. They had their lives to live, governed by their own problems, and he had his. He hoped they wouldn't blame Meredith and the children for his mistake.

"Care to fly her for a while, Colonel?" the pilot asked.

"No, but thanks for the offer," Wes replied.

"I guess you're going to have to do a bit of flying yourself before this night's over."

"Let's hope so," answered Wes. "Let's hope so."

Seeing a streak of sharp lightning off to the east reminded Wes he hadn't reviewed the weather. Pulling an envelope from one of the many zippered-pockets of his green flight suit, he tore it open and removed the documents.

The surface analysis chart depicted a low centered several hundred miles to the north of his flight profile. It was expected to remain stationary for the next twenty-four hours, with no increase in intensity. A bit more troubling was a trough extending from the center of the low off to the southwest. Behind it lay a mass of cold air dropping from Canada across the Great Lakes. Checking the winds aloft charts, he noted the jet stream patterns on the chart. A shift in the jet stream could make a lot of difference in what he would encounter en route.

He skimmed over the pages of airfield and alternate weather observations and forecasts. They were irrelevant. His flight wouldn't land. No alternate airfield would be required. Nor would the weather matter — he was going anyway. Releasing the bayonet clip holding the oxygen mask to his face, Wes laid his head against the headrest and closed his eyes.

Thirty-five minutes later, startled from sleep by the skipper's announcement, Wes's eyes flew open. "The Wilson Bridge is just ahead and to the right, Colonel. You should be able to get a good look at the EMPRESS as we cross it!"

Sitting up, Wes rubbed his eyes and stared into the darkness, acclimating himself to the reduced light as the chopper dropped another two hundred feet. Off to the left, Wes saw the EMPRESS under tow, just north of the Wilson Bridge. He grinned at the sight of the large wake trailing its path. "Well, I'll be damned! She did make it through the bridge!" Wes boasted, pulling his mask to his face.

"Yeah, I'd say she'll be in position within the next thirty minutes at that rate," the skipper added.

Feeling a hand on his shoulder, Wes turned around to see Marino gazing down at the EMPRESS and pointing. "She's through the bridge, is she?"

"With inches to spare," Wes added.

"Then it's a go for us," said Doug, brandishing a grin.

Wes gave Marino a thumbs-up as the chopper sped along, hugging the nap of the hillside. They were within striking distance of the coalition and its treachery.

*   *   *

"FURY ONE ONE FLIGHT, CHECK IN," called Colonel Martin.

"TOOP! THREEP! FOURP!" came the snappy replies.

"GIANT KILLER. FURY ONE ONE FLIGHT'S WITH YOU."

"ROGER, FURY ONE ONE. YOU'RE CLEARED INTO WHIS-KEY THREE EIGHTY SIX TO RENDEZVOUS WITH WATERCAN SIX ONE. SQUAWK TWO THOUSAND. YOUR PLAYMATE'S BEARING IS ZERO SIX ZERO DEGREES FOR SEVENTY TWO MILES. HE'S TRACKING TWO THREE ZERO DEGREES AT FLIGHT LEVEL TWO SIX ZERO. UNDERSTAND REQUESTING SELF SETUP. CALL TALLY-HO."

"FURY ONE ONE, ROGER," answered Martin, as he ruddered the other three F-16 fighters into spread formation.

Checking the radar, Martin saw Watercan's paint on the F-16's radar screen at ten degrees port and seventy miles. The blip appeared normal, but he knew Shadow Two One, the second flight of F-117 Stealth fighters was in close trail with the tanker. Martin would call the tanker's turn at eighteen miles range, then close for the rejoin. The mission allocated twenty minutes for the refueling, then another twenty-five minutes to reach the IP (Initial Point). A check of his elapsed time clock showed the mission was right on schedule.

Closing at sixteen miles per minute, Martin's thoughts drifted to the video he'd seen last night of the passengers and flight attendants still aboard the 767. He knew firsthand the anxiety they were experiencing. Having been a POW in the Hanoi Hilton for three years, seven months, and eight days couldn't have been much different, Martin imagined. Launched now to put them out of their misery, he prayed his flight would not be called upon to deliver the killing blow. How many times had he laid on the floor of his cell and begged for the friendlies to rain snake eyes (high drag bombs) down on him and his tormentors? Had they reached that level of hopelessness yet? Did they suspect their lives would end this way? Had they given up hope of being rescued? Were they, too, ready for death's mercy?

With fewer than ninety minutes to go, was there really a chance their lives would be spared? General Hathaway, the strike commander, was right in calling it the most onerous task he could imagine — the bombing of one's own countrymen.

Martin glanced at the radar screen again. "WATERCAN SIX ONE, FROM FURY ONE ONE, START YOUR LEFT TURN AND PUSH IT UP."

"ROGER, ONE ONE. WATERCAN IS COMING LEFT TO ZERO SIX ZERO DEGREES."

Out the left side of his windscreen Martin watched as the rotating beacons of Shadow Two One flight dropped below Watercan Six One. They'd have first shot at the 767. It would be over in seconds. Nothing would escape the rain of carnage that would be unleashed from the Stealths. Even now the special weapons planners were split over whether there would be a secondary explosion, a nuclear detonation. Too much depended on what modifications had been made to the weapon to be certain of either possibility. Either way, Martin knew every person within a hundred meters of the 767 would perish instantly.

Gazing through the darkness at the KC-10 tanker, he saw once more the TV images of those chosen by fate to die so that others might be spared. He offered a short prayer for their souls.

"FURY ONE ONE, YOU ARE CLEARED TO THE PRE-CON-TACT POSITION. CHECK NOSE COLD." Martin glanced down at the armament panel. The master arm switch was in the SAFE position. "ROGER, FURY ONE ONE NOSE COLD, CLEARED TO PRE-CONTACT POSITION."

Focusing on the two rows of flashing lights on the belly of the KC-10, he guided his F-16 effortlessly into the contact position. "STA-BILIZE, ONE ONE," called the boom operator. Two steady green hash marks on the director lights confirmed the refueler's command. "YOU'RE TAKING FUEL, ONE ONE."

* * *

Cynthia watched from her adjoining seat as Sybil's head gradu-ally slumped forward. Her eyelids fluttered for a few moments longer, then closed. How was it possible that she could sleep, knowing their rescue was imminent?

Checking her watch, Cynthia saw it was three thirty a.m. Barely a half-hour to go, she thought. She remembered Sybil's instructions were to be ready at four. Cynthia would let Sybil sleep for twenty minutes.

Glancing about the first class cabin, Cynthia saw that Chad was awake. Studying the muscle tension in his arms, she decided he was struggling to free his hands. Chad looked up. Their eyes met. She saw his boyish grin and smiled back. Cynthia wished there was something she could do to help free him, but feared Jabarri would carry out his threat of death if she were caught.

Her fingers rubbed the scissors buried in the pocket of her smock. A few more passes across the threads of the tiny bolt were all Cynthia needed to separate the scissor blades. She wanted only the sharp-pointed one. She would leave Chad the other half to cut the rope that bound his hands. Looking at him again, Cynthia knew she had to try, or he'd be helpless during the assault.

Rising from her seat, Cynthia walked to the forward lav entrance, pausing long enough to notice that Reza, Ahmed, Mohammed, and Nsar, in the cockpit, were speaking in Arabic. They ignored her as she went into the lav and locked the door.

Cynthia removed the nail file and scissors from her pocket and began filing the last burr off the threaded bolt. Minutes later, she felt excitement build as she spun the locking nut off the end of the small threaded bolt and pulled the two scissor blades apart. It had taken count-less stolen moments to file away the threads of the tiny bolt. Clutching the pointed blade with both hands, Cynthia stabbed the air repeatedly until she was convinced her muscles knew instinctively the path they would take to repay the Ugly One. He would pay with his life. Slip-ping the blades inside her skirt pocket, Cynthia pressed the lav flush handle.

As she left the lav, she recognized Jabarri's voice. He seemed to be giving instructions in Arabic. Cynthia paused only long enough to make sure they wouldn't follow her. Then she walked back toward her seat. Approaching Chad, she pulled the blunted blade from her pocket. His eyes flew wide open. Without speaking, Cynthia slid the blade down his back until she found his opened hand. He seized the weapon. She smiled and withdrew, returning to her seat to wake Sybil.

Cynthia nudged her partner. Startled, Sybil peered into Cynthia's face and whispered, "How long have I been asleep?"

"Not long," whispered Cynthia, "But it's getting close to four a.m.. I must go back to my position," Cynthia added. "Good luck," Sybil replied under her breath as she clutched her companion's hand for a second. Cynthia smiled at her, stood up and pulled back the curtain dividing the two compartments. The Ugly One was nowhere in sight.

Cynthia felt a sense of relief, but knew it would be short-lived.

At her seat, Cynthia stretched out across the two seats and waited. Tension mounted as she tried to imagine how the assault might unfold. Would she survive or be caught in a crossfire? Would she live long enough to see her attacker die? Gritting her teeth, Cynthia felt her carotid arteries bulge as her neck flexed. She pictured herself racing to open her door. Nothing would stop her from reaching freedom, not even a bullet.

40

SHARK ATTACK

Wes watched as the SEALS, their faces blackened with grease, walked their rubber boats into the still waters of the Anacostia River behind the Naval Station boathouse, former berth of the presidential yacht, *Sequoia,* and waited for Marino's visual signal to board. There would be four men per boat and two with one man each transporting the boarding ladders. He would cross with Marino and his communications specialist, a tall, lanky Swede, called "The Blade."

Standing motionless at the water's edge, Marino monitored the UHF/FM transceiver laced into the back of his flak vest. Tiny wires routed to earphones embedded in his safety helmet would carry the message Doug waited to hear. Beside him, Wes listened to the coordination taking place through his own radio.

"FAT LADY. SAY YOUR STATUS."

"THE FAT LADY'S IN POSITION, RAINBOW."

"ROGER. FAT LADY. RAINBOW COPIES. STAND BY."

"RAINBOW. SHADOW AND FURY ARE HOLDING HANDS."

"ROGER, SHADOW. RAINBOW UNDERSTANDS."

Wes knew from listening that the EMPRESS II jammer barge was lying just south of National Airport waiting for an okay from the EC-135 AWAC aircraft to initiate the test signal. That would come next. Hearing Shadow and Fury check in, he knew for certain the F-117 Stealth and F-16 Falcon fighters were holding at their orbit points ready to bomb the 767 if the assault failed. The thought of dying from such carnage sent a chill through his body.

Doug turned his chin to the left, automatically keying a spring-mounted mike beside his jaw. "SHARKS UP," he called out, using the assault team's code name.

"ROGER, SHARKS. RAINBOW'S CUTTING BAIT NOW. STAND BY. WE'LL HAVE SOMETHING FOR YOU SHORTLY."

Eager to begin the assault, Doug grimaced at RAINBOW'S reply.

Wes knew the control center's hands were tied until McGarth gave the okay. Only then could the FAT LADY *sing* and the SHARKS be sent to *hunt*.

"RAINBOW. FROM NEPTUNE. THE FAT LADY IS CLEARED TO SING."

"ROGER, NEPTUNE. RAINBOW COPIES."

"THE FAT LADY COPIES NEPTUNE, RAINBOW. COMMENCING WARM-UP IN TEN SECONDS!"

Wes hacked the elapsed timer on his watch. Looking at Wes, Doug said, "Let's pray the bitch has a strong voice. Otherwise, we're all going to have one hell of a headache for a long time."

Wes nodded his head. Doug's point was well-made. Nothing either of them could say now would make a difference. The EMPRESS jammer had to saturate the 72-76MHZ band with noise and suppress any transmission signal on that frequency or there would be NO assault, NO rescue, and possibly — NO Washington. Wes felt his heart pounding as he listened. He calculated the jammer was thirty seconds into the test. No news was good news, Wes told himself.

Six test signal transceivers positioned on the perimeter of the airport were actively trying to penetrate the EMPRESS's jamming signal to evaluate its ability to block their transmissions. A negative reply from any one of the six would force McGarth to choose Plan B. Suddenly, the tiny earphones hidden in Wes's helmet crackled:

"RAINBOW, THE FAT LADY'S TERMINATED WARM-UP."

"ROGER, FAT LADY. RAINBOW COPIES TERMINATION."

"ROBINS, FROM RAINBOW. CHECK IN."

Wes peered at Doug. The two exchanged pensive looks. This is it, Wes thought, the fork in the road, a confrontation with destiny. He strained to hear, but found the silence deafening. Then they began:

"ROBIN ONE, CODE ONE. TWO, CODE ONE. THREE, CODE ONE. FOUR, CODE ONE. FIVE, CODE ONE. SIX, CODE ONE."

Doug and Wes grinned at each another as they heard the final code one check-in. The EMPRESS tested positive. The assault was a

GO. Anxious to get underway, Doug signaled his men to board their rafts.

"RAINBOW COPIES SIX STRONG ROBINS, NEPTUNE."

"ROGER, RAINBOW. EXECUTE EMPRESS!" Wes heard the FAT LADY and SHADOW acknowledge NEPTUNE's command as he climbed into the rubber boat. Acknowledging the order, Doug answered, "SHARKS COPY."

Seconds later, the eight rubber boats, propelled by small electric motors, moved through the dark waters of the Anacostia toward Gravelly Point, the land on which National Airport had been founded.

Marino's second in command, Striker, led the flotilla first toward the west bank of the Anacostia River, then southwest in the direction of Hains Point, the southern tip of East Potomac Park. The route, though longer, offered greater concealment during the crossings. Reaching Hains Point and the Potomac sixteen minutes later, the flotilla turned right toward the Fourteenth Street Bridge, skirting the park's southern bank until abeam Roach's Run, the tiny gut spilling water under the Washington Memorial Parkway at the airport's northern perimeter. Turning south, Marino aimed for the run, partially concealed by foliage along the southern bank of the Potomac.

Glancing at Doug, Wes smiled to hide his nervousness. It was then that he noticed Marino had lost all expression as though he were meditating. His catlike pupils, fully dilated, were focused elsewhere as he gazed into the unknown, perhaps into the heat of battle.

Approaching the run, Doug signaled The Blade to switch off the motor as he slipped over the side into the knee-deep water. Taking hold of the towline, Doug pulled the rubber boat onto the muddy shore, then reached in and retrieved his Uzi. Wes and The Blade scrambled out and dragged the dinghy farther ashore as the other boats made landfall in rapid succession.

Wes watched the sharpshooters in the raft beside him as they removed their long-barreled rifles from specially sealed bags and loaded them. On closer inspection, he could see each rifle had a suppressor attached. A folding bipod was mounted beneath the barrel. The telescopic sight fastened to the top of the barrel appeared to have infrared laser-ranging capability, though he wasn't certain. He wondered if it were an M-21 sniper rifle. With little to do but stay out of the way,

Wes felt like an amateur as he waited for the SEALS to complete their last-minute preparations. Realizing he, too, might see action, Wes used a few moments to ensure that his Beretta was loaded and ready. Then he waited as Doug deployed his men.

They were impressively armed as they moved out. In addition to their thirty-two clip Uzis, some carried the water-proof version of the Smith & Wesson M39 pistol, the Hush-Puppy. Equipped with a silencer, it fired 9mm Parabellum subsonic ammunition, designed to avoid the sound associated with the projectile's obtaining supersonic velocity prior to impact. Each SEAL carried a knife for hand-to-hand combat.

Knowing that Uzi would be pitched against Uzi, Wes had expressed concern over damage to the jet from the intensity of the possible firefight. Doug hadn't thought it would be a problem, but had discussed it with his men and cautioned them not to use excessive fire power.

Insisting every effort be made to preserve the element of surprise, Doug had assigned the three men carrying the sniper rifles the task of taking out the three guards outside the 767 first. Wes watched as they disappeared into the darkness to take up positions behind the north runway visual range transmissometer, the culvert adjacent to taxiway Juliette, and, from behind the Distance To Go marker sign on the right edge of Runway One Eight.

Crouched in the foliage, Wes and Marino waited with the rest of his team for a fox-mike (FM) call over the assault net radio confirming the shooters were in position. Sweat dripped from Wes's chin as his nostrils picked up the scent of the 767 APU's exhaust fumes blowing over their position.

Suddenly his radio was alive:

"RANGE UP." "CULVERT UP." "MARKER UP."

The sharpshooters were in position. Wes saw Doug check his watch. Thirty seconds later, he would make his call and the FAT LADY would begin barrage-jamming the remote control frequency band as all microwave antennas within the area ceased operating. Three minutes later, the shooters would cut down the terrorist guards outside the aircraft. The remainder of the team would approach the 767 from behind, taking up their positions for the assault's final phase.

Four specially fabricated boarding ladders would be placed against the fore and aft roots of the two wings to allow elements of the attack force to move into position just outside the two over-wing emergency

exits. With the SEALS in their final assault positions, the sharpshooters would move forward to cover the exits.

From his position behind the nose gear, Wes would press the APU
EMERGENCY FIRE SHUTOFF button on the servicing panel aft of
the nose gear strut, killing all normal electrical power and causing a
blackout on board the aircraft. Doug would lead the raid up the mobile
steps and activate the EVAC alarm. Wes was to remain beneath the
plane until it was secured. Gripping the penlight instinctively, Wes
reviewed his assignment and waited for Marino's command.

"RAINBOW. THE SHARKS ARE CIRCLED," Doug transmitted.

"ROGER, SHARKS, STAND BY FOR YOUR FIVE-SECOND
HACK."

Shoving the cuff of his flight suit up his sweaty left arm, exposing
the luminous face of his Seiko, Wes paused. The assault operation would
run on elapsed time.

Hearing the command, "Hack," each SEAL would start the elapsed
timer of his watch. All remaining actions would be conducted at specific intervals.

"SHARKS. RAINBOW WITH A HACK. FIVE, FOUR, THREE,
TWO, ONE, HACK! RAINBOW out."

Activating the elapsed timer on his watch, Wes followed Marino
as he led the assault team out of the tall grasses of Roach's Run toward
the 767, mimicking Doug's every move. They'd been under way little
more than a minute when the FAT LADY broke radio silence:

"RAINBOW. THE FAT LADY IS OPERATIONAL."

"ROGER, FAT LADY. RAINBOW COPIES."

"NEPTUNE COPIES THE FAT LADY. FEED THE SHARKS!"

Barely able to make out anything but Marino's eyes behind the
black grease smeared across his face, Wes grinned at Doug as they
savored the message. They had the president's approval. The rest lay in
their hands.

Striker peered through his scope at the terrorist propped against
the forward wheel of the left main gear. He hadn't budged since Striker
spied him napping minutes ago. Aligning the cross-hairs of his sight
on top of the terrorist's drooped head, he told himself the shot would be
a piece of cake. Then he realized that if he missed, the shot would
pierce the tire, exploding it. "SHARKS. KEEP YOUR HITS OFF THE
WHEELS," he blurted into the spring-mounted mike beside his jaw as

he scrambled to the right to acquire a different angle for the shot. Dropping to his knees, Striker extended the bipod from under the barrel of the rifle again and set it on the ground. Raising the stock, he looked through the scope as the laser range finder recomputed the new distance to his victim. His terrorist was still sleeping. Taking his eye off the scope for a moment, Striker checked his watch, then looked around for his partner. Roper was nowhere to be seen. It didn't matter. He had to have heard the warning. Checking his watch again, Striker's eye returned to the scope as his finger came to rest gently against the trigger. The two-second audible warning beep from his watch chimed twice as Striker squeezed the trigger of his rifle. A muffled sound marked the departure of the 7.62 mm projectile as it began its quiet, but swift journey toward the skull of the napping terrorist.

The dull flash of muzzle fire from the other side of the aircraft startled Bud Waterman. Seeing other flashes in rapid succession accompanied by strange, shrouded sounds to his left, confirmed the assault's unfolding. Reaching for his video camera, he tried to make use of the magnifying power of the camera's lenses, but found it useless against the black night. Looking to his left again, Bud saw images, maybe a dozen or so, charging the rear of the 767. The assault was on; the SEALS were advancing. Searching under the aircraft, Bud no longer saw the three terrorist guards. He assumed they were the unknowing recipients of the devastating sniper fire he'd just witnessed.

Passing under the empennage (tail) of the 767 and the constant drone of the APU's tiny jet engine, Doug directed three of his men to check on the downed guards while the others took up their final assault positions at the boarding ladders and underneath the mobile stairs. Trailing the SEALS, Wes reached the nose gear ten seconds later and located the APU Fire Shutdown button on the aft panel of the strut. Barely able to make out the panel, Wes recalled an exterior lights test switch was also on that panel. Activating the switch would turn on all the jet's exterior lights for twenty seconds. He cursed himself for not having remembered to mention it to Doug.

Cynthia clutched the scissor blade in her right hand as her heart pounded mercilessly inside her chest. Staring aimlessly into the darkness, she'd seen two quick flashes from the small oval window of the

767 and knew the assault was imminent. Unable to sit any longer, Cynthia rose from her seat and walked quietly forward to warn Chad and Sybil. Drawing closer, she heard voices speaking in Arabic coming from the cockpit. Nsar and Mohammed were dozing on opposite sides of the first row of first class. Cynthia knew the voices belonged to Reza and Ahmed.

Chad watched her shadow move cautiously up the aisle floor. Reaching his side, she stopped and peered down into his face. Their eyes met again. Nodding deliberately, Cynthia continued toward Sybil. Chad knew why she had come.

Sybil shrieked as Cynthia's hand touched her arm. Her eyes opened as she leaped to her feet. Cynthia tried to muzzle her, but it was too late. The damage was done. Sybil's cry startled Nsar and Mohammed from their sleep. Awake, Mohammed leered at Cynthia as he brandished his automatic pistol and motioned her to the rear of the cabin.

Hearing the cry, Reza left the cockpit to investigate. Reaching the forward cabin area, he found Sybil standing with her hands pressed tightly over her ears crying profusely. Angry over her disturbance, Jabarri knocked Sybil to the floor and kicked her twice in the ribs before returning to the cockpit.

Cynthia heard Sybil cry out in pain as the blows took their toll, but she couldn't look back. She had her own troubles — the Ugly One had also heard the cry and stood three feet away, directly in her path. Grabbing her left wrist, he twisted it up behind her back and lifted her off the cabin floor with it. Cynthia screamed in pain as he laughed. Then shouting something in Arabic, he threw her to the floor.

Knowing she was safer, Cynthia stayed there. The pain in her left arm and shoulder was horrendous. Her shoulder felt like it was dislocated. Reaching into her smock pocket with her right hand, Cynthia clutched the scissor blade and swore at the Ugly One under her breath. She would kill him, no matter the cost. She didn't care.

There was nothing Chad could do but wait. If he tried to defend either one of the attendants, they would kill him. Was Cynthia mistaken? Why hadn't the assault begun? Chad watched Sybil pull herself into a seat. She was holding her left side in obvious pain. That bastard, Reza, has broken several of her ribs, he thought, fighting to control his anger. What's keeping them? What the...? The APU has quit! No! No! It's the assault. It's started!

"The lights! What is wrong, Ahmed?" clamored Reza, in the cock-pit.

Ahmed knew what had happened. Reaching for the auxiliary power start switch he said, "The APU has tripped off the......"

"No! Wait! What is that noise?" Reza demanded.

Looking up at the overhead panel, both saw the red EVAC Alarm light flashing and heard the loud piercing beeper. It's the EVAC Alarm!" Ahmed answered.

Reza broke in. "No! No! There is no reason...! It is a trick, Ahmed!...The Americans! Ahmed! ...The controller! Get the controller!"

Fumbling for the remote controller in his kit bag, Ahmed tried desperately to locate the device in the darkness as Reza reached for the Uzi submachine gun lying in the jumpseat behind him. But both were too late.

Ahmed screamed in pain as the initial round from Marino's Uzi hit him in his left shoulder, shattering his socket. Doug's second and third rounds tore through Ahmed's left forearm and lodged in the thigh of his right leg. The remote controller fell from Ahmed's hands as he slumped over the yoke.

Reza, his hand on the trigger of his Uzi, fired wildly, missing Marino. Pivoting to the left, Doug returned the fire, striking the coalition leader twice in the chest. Jabarri died instantly.

Chad, his hands now free of the rope bindings, leaped to his feet and ran to the right forward entry door. Mohammed fired at him, but missed. "Marine at the door!" yelled Chad, jerking the door handle outward. A SEAL saw the muzzle flash from Mohammed's automatic and fired a short burst in that direction. Chad bent over and grabbed the bottom lip of the big mechanical door to open it as the Ugly One swept the curtain separating first class and raised his weapon at Chad.

Diving to the floor, Chad threw himself on top of Sybil as Cynthia plunged the scissor blade into the left side of the Ugly One's back.

"Oh, God!" she screamed in disbelief! I've killed him!"

Hearing the hissing of the evacuation slide inflating, Chad hollered, "Early Vacation! Early Vacation! Get out now!" Taking hold of Sybil, Chad carried her toward the right forward exit door as Cynthia, still in shock, rushed forward to help. Reaching the door, Chad yelled for Cynthia to jump into the inflated slide first. Hesitating for a moment, Cynthia leaped as Chad followed with Sybil in his arms.

Wes saw the right forward slide deploy and hit the exterior light switch. Seven lights along each side of the 767 instantly lit up the ground around the aircraft as Cynthia reached the bottom. Rushing out of the darkness, a SEAL took Sybil from Chad's arms as he and Cynthia ran behind him.

Suddenly, Wes saw Mohammed jump from the slide and toss something into the intake of the right engine. "Christ! A grenade!" yelled Wes, as he ran toward the intake.

Standing in the right entrance doorway, Doug had seen it, too. Jumping into the slide, Marino careened through the air toward the intake as Mohammed turned and fired at him, but missed.

Seeing Doug was closer to the engine, Wes drew his Beretta and fired at the Arab. His first two rounds ricocheted off the runway, but a third found its mark. Mohammed, struck in the chest, collapsed, mortally wounded, as Marino dived out of the intake, shielding the grenade with his body. Seeing Doug in mid-air, Wes knew instinctively too much time had passed. The blast ripped the SEAL leader's abdomen apart, killing him instantly.

Rushing over to Marino, hoping by some miracle he might still be alive, Wes rolled his dismembered body over. It was not to be. Doug's lower torso was missing. Bloody tissue was everywhere. There was no respiration; his pupils were fixed. Marino was dead.

Wes wheeled around to see passengers spilling down the aft slides. Sharpshooters stationed outside were providing cover for their escape, firing as necessary, to keep the terrorists pinned down. Wes rushed to the mobile stairs and bounded up the steps.

Reaching the main cabin entrance, he paused to listen as the firing ceased. Not wanting to be mistaken for a terrorist, Wes grabbed the PA handset off the flight attendant service panel and shouted, "SEALS! THIS IS COLONEL BEACHAM! THE FORWARD CABIN IS SECURE!! WHAT IS THE SITUATION IN THE REAR?"

"It's secure back here, Colonel!" yelled a SEAL. "All the passengers and crew are out," he added.

Dropping the phone, Wes headed for the cockpit to restart the APU when he heard the sound of gunfire. Raising his Beretta, Wes eased forward. Peering around the corner, he saw the right cockpit windscreen was covered in blood. A portion of Ahmed's head was missing, blown away from the self-inflicted gunshot.

Wes tried not to look at the carnage as he started the APU, switched the radio to Guard channel and keyed the mike.

"TOWER! THIS IS COLONEL BEACHAM! THE AIRCRAFT IS SECURE. GET THE SUPPORT UNITS OVER HERE NOW! THE TEAM HAS TAKEN A MAJOR HIT! SEND THE MEDICS ASAP!"

"ROGER, COLONEL. THE UNITS ARE ON THEIR WAY."

Keying the mike for a second time:

"RAINBOW! THIS IS SHARK TWO! THE JET IS SECURE! I SAY AGAIN. THE JET IS SECURE! PROCEEDING WITH PHASE TWO!"

"RAINBOW COPIES SHARK TWO. IMPLEMENTING PHASE TWO."

"ROGER, RAINBOW! I'LL HAVE AN ALBATROSS REPORT SHORTLY!"

Tossing the mike down on the center pedestal, Wes bolted from the cockpit as Striker charged up the aisle from the rear of the cabin. "Where's Doug?" Wes motioned to the R-1 door. "He's out there. Dead. He ate a grenade Mohammed tossed into the engine."

"No way," Striker snapped, his eyes burning. Wes saw pain in the young SEAL's eyes. "If he hadn't done it, that grenade would have destroyed any chance of getting this bomb out of here. Doug knew what he was doing. He bought and paid for the Capital with his life."

"Yes, but...Jesus! Why did it have to be him?" cried Striker.

Wes shook his head in despair. It was a question for which Wes had no rational answer.

"How many casualties did you suffer in the rear?" Wes asked.

"None, except for the terrorists," Striker replied. The two flight attendants, Frederick and Arron, took out two of the terrorists with some cord and their bare hands. How about here?"

"Doug took care of Reza and tore up Ahmed pretty bad. From the looks of it, Ahmed finished the job on himself. I got Mohammed, but not soon enough," Wes added.

"What about Nsar?" Striker asked. A look of surprise spread across Wes's face.

"He wasn't in the back with the others?" Wes asked.

"If he was, he went out with the passengers!"

"Damn! You've got to find him. For all we know, that sonofabitch might have one of those remote controllers."

"We'll find him, Colonel. Doug didn't bring us this far to have that asshole fuck things up for us now," Striker growled as he bounded to the door and leaped into the slide.

Wes rushed back to the cockpit and grabbed the mike.

"RAINBOW FROM SHARK TWO?"

"GO AHEAD, SHARK TWO. RAINBOW'S WITH YOU."

"WE'VE GOT A PROBLEM HERE, RAINBOW. ONE PIECE OF BAIT IS MISSING. WE'RE TRACKING IT DOWN RIGHT NOW. KEEP THE EMPRESS AT FULL POWER UNTIL ADVISED."

"ROGER, SHARK TWO. COPY BAIT MISSING. CAN YOU ID THE MISSING BAIT FOR US AT THIS TIME?"

"SHARK TWO CONFIRMS CHEVY CHASE BAIT, RAIN-BOW."

"ROGER, SHARK TWO. KEEP US ADVISED."

McGarth looked over at Elliot from his seat aboard Air Force One. "What do you think, Gaylord? How long should we give them to track down Nsar?" Elliot glanced at Chris Jacobson and Clayton Griffith before he answered. Neither seemed eager to intercede. "At least another ten minutes, I would think, Mr. President."

"That's a long time, Gaylord. You're that confident of the jammer?"

"It's worked so far. I'd suggest we give the SEALS the time they need to mop this thing up," Elliot said.

McGarth turned to General Griffith. "Clayton, how quickly can you have the fighters bomb that jet once I give the okay?"

"Within three minutes, sir. They're orbiting over Andrews Air Force Base at this very moment."

"Good. We're not out of the woods yet, gentlemen. I don't think we can rule out their use until I've received confirmation that Nsar has been accounted for and that 767 is off the Atlantic coast. Until then, every minute is a gamble against fate."

Elliot gave McGarth a concerned look out of the corner of his eye and nodded. Mason was having second thoughts about using the fighters. Having the passengers and crew off the plane made the bombing scenario more acceptable, but no less dangerous. The next ten minutes would be difficult for the president.

Bud watched as a lone figure broke from the crowd of fleeing passengers and raced toward his Cessna. Busy watching the assault from his vantage point, he couldn't tell from which part of the aircraft the figure had escaped. His instinct told him it was one of the terrorists. Was it Reza? For a second, Bud debated trying to surprise and subdue the figure, but grabbed his portable phone and punched in the familiar number to the control tower. Raising the handset to his ear, he found there was no dial tone. The circuit was dead. Tossing the phone aside, Bud peered through the telescopic camera lens. He could see the figure climbing into the cockpit of his Cessna. It was either Reza or Nsar. Besides Ahmed, they were the only two who could fly.

Looking back at the crowd as they fled toward the terminal, Bud saw the oncoming procession of vehicles. Glancing again at the 767, he saw that no one seemed to be paying any attention to his Cessna. Having drained the tanks nearly dry, Bud knew whoever was in his Cessna would crash on takeoff. Then it hit him. Suppose the terrorist didn't intend to take off, but crash his Cessna into the 767 on the ground. Bud's blood ran cold as he imagined the damage that could be done. There was no time. He had to act.

Jumping to his feet, Bud charged the Cessna as its small engine sputtered to life. The lone figure hadn't noticed him yet. Barely sixty feet from the plane, Bud stopped abruptly and crouched, firing his flare pistol directly at the left side of the engine's cowling. Suddenly, a white phosphorus flash lit up the dark sky as the white hot wad streaked toward the Cessna, striking it and spewing liquid fire onto the gas-soaked grass beneath.

Watching in awe, Bud marveled at the flames leaping upward, rapidly enveloping the tiny fuselage as the lone figure frantically struggled to escape the inferno.

"Drop it!" called out a voice as Bud turned to face two SEALS pointing their Uzis at him. Letting the flare gun fall to the ground he said, "I'm Bud Waterman, the reporter with the *Examiner*! That's my airplane I just fired on!" he shouted. "The guy inside is one of the terrorists!" he added. "Yeah! Who?" demanded the same voice. "Either Reza Jabarri or Nsar Ajmani," replied Bud, as curdling screams came from the Cessna's half-open cockpit door.

Lowering their weapons, the SEALS gazed at the flailing figure. No one spoke until the screams subsided.

Seconds later, one of the fire trucks responding to the assault rumbled over from the 767 and quickly suppressed the flames as one of the two SEALS rushed forward to examine the dead man. Bud, still in shock over killing a human being, felt sick and vomited on the ground as the other SEAL stood by.

"First time for you?" he asked sympathetically.

Bud nodded.

"The first time's always a bitch," the SEAL added. "It gets all of us like that."

"Raven!" called his buddy. "Waterman was right. The man's definitely an Arab. He fits the description of the one Striker said was missing. He's still holding one of those remote controllers, but it's pretty well-cooked! Better haul ass over there and give Beacham the news. I'll stay here for the mop-up."

"Right," shouted the Raven. "Waterman, you come with me. Striker and Colonel Beacham will want to personally shake your hand." Wiping his mouth, Bud hustled to catch up to the Raven.

"Feeling a little better now?" asked the Raven as they jogged toward the 767.

"Yeah. I'll manage," Bud replied between breaths.

"Good. Glad to hear it. You did us all one hell of a favor stopping him like you did. No telling what he might have done with that plane. Some of those guys just love to blow the ever-loving shit out of themselves while taking the rest of the world with them. I don't understand it myself."

"Colonel Beacham!" hollered the Raven. "The last one's been accounted for." Wes rushed out from underneath the belly of the 767 to meet them. "Where did you find him?"

"Waterman here caught him trying to steal his airplane and hosed him down with a flare gun." Wes glanced at the smoldering Cessna. Looking back at the SEAL, he asked, "You're sure it was Nsar?"

"Yes, sir! I'd bet my ass on it! My partner checked him out. No doubt. He was definitely an Arab. Spanner found him clutching one of those remote controllers Marino told us to watch out for."

Wes thought a moment. Unless Sybil had miscounted, the man in the Cessna had to have been Nsar Ajmani. Having been found with one of the two remote controllers made it a near-certainty.

"Find Striker and tell him to call off the search," Wes said. "I'll advise RAINBOW."

"Aye, sir!" the Raven answered. Wes and Bud exchanged looks.

"Are you going to fly the bomb into the Atlantic?" Bud asked.

"I'm going to give it my best shot," said Wes, retreating toward the left side of the aircraft amid myriad vehicles.

"Mind if I come aboard for a few minutes before you take off?" shouted Bud, chasing Wes around the jet.

"Be my guest! Just don't get caught on board. I don't have an extra 'chute'." Bud smiled, following Wes up the stairs.

Returning to the cockpit, Wes saw that Reza's and Ahmed's bodies had been removed. Two fleet service men were busy cleaning the blood and tissue splattered across the instrument panel. Wes made a quick check of the cockpit.

"RAINBOW FROM SHARK TWO," said Wes.

"RAINBOW'S LISTENING, SHARK TWO."

"SHARK TWO, REPORTING ALL BAIT ACCOUNTED FOR. I SAY AGAIN, ALL BAIT HAS BEEN ACCOUNTED FOR. BE ADVISED, THE ALBATROSS IS A CODE ONE!"

Bud listened intently over the cockpit speaker as the AWAC controller confirmed Wes's report. He figured a Code One meant the jet was okay for flight.

"EXPECT A LAUNCH WITHIN THE NEXT FIFTEEN MINUTES," replied Wes as a familiar voice barked at him from behind.

"You weren't thinking about leaving without me, were you, Wes?" growled Chad, as he crawled over into the right seat.

Wes looked at his first officer as Chad adjusted his chair and began cranking the rudder pedals forward to accommodate his long legs. A broad grin crossed Wes's face.

"Where in the hell have you been for the last three days? Are you going to load the FMCs for me, or just sit there and gawk?" joked Wes, glancing at the IRS control panels above his head.

"I'm going to do more than that for you, my friend. It's my leg, remember?" Chad said.

"Not required," Wes snapped. "I can handle this leg alone."

"Won't happen, Wes. DOD won't allow it," Chad countered. "Or have you forgotten that handling nuclear weapons still requires two-man control?"

"This situation is different," Wes argued. "Yeah, well that may be, but I just talked to Spence. He volunteered to fly as your 'co-jock' after he got a call from The Joint Special Operations Agency (JOSA) over at the pentagon saying the president had insisted on it. That's how Riker got into the act. I didn't know it, but he's still active in some "trash-hauling" squadron somewhere out West flying C-141s. The Special Ops guy from OSG-TIWG handling the ground operation here okayed my taking his place after he got confirmation of my clearance."

Wes shook his head as he punched in the present-position coordinates for National Airport. "Well, if you're coming, we'll need another parachute, helmet, and survival kit," snarled Wes. "They've already been put aboard, skipper. I checked them over myself, then had them buckled in the seats near the R-4 and L-4 doors. That's where you've planned for us to take our flying leap?"

Wes looked at Chad with a serious expression, "Yeah, I figured we'd have a better chance of making it from there, even if we do get smacked by the slab on the way out."

"Makes sense. Hope it works that way," mumbled Chad as he typed in the three sets of coordinates Wes handed him.

Wes tried not to think about the flight's final phase. There was no data on whether you could successfully dive out the doors and miss the horizontal stabilizer. No one had ever tried it.

"Not much of a flight plan," Chad said.

"What did you expect? It's your leg!" answered Wes, trying to get his mind off what really lay ahead.

It troubled him that Chad had chosen to go. He was young and full of life, with so much to offer. It seemed a terrible waste to send him along for the ride just to appease the military bureaucrats. Yet, if he had to have one, Chad was the best. A fighter pilot's fighter pilot.

Glancing at the instrument panel clock, Wes compared the time with the ACARS digital readout. They were exact. Then he removed a small plasticized schedule card from the chest pocket of his flight suit and scanned the events while checking the time again. "Shit! We're four minutes behind schedule," he announced, turning in his seat.

Out the left side panel Wes could barely see the lights of the fuel truck. Looking up at the center overhead panel, he watched as the digits in the left and right tank columns quickly changed numbers. The totalizer showed 6000 pounds in each tank. The profile called for 21,000 pounds. At roughly 3000 pounds per minute, fueling would take another three minutes.

Looking down at the left flight management computer, Wes called up the LEGS page and switched the mode selector to the MAP mode. Then he cross-checked Chad's three Lat/Long entries. As expected, there were no errors. The FMC showed the distance from brake release to impact at thirty-six degrees North, sixty degrees West to be 831 miles. It calculated the flight time to be exactly two hours using standard power settings. He could shave the time a little by using a higher cruise mach, but not by much. Favorable tail winds would make a greater difference.

"Want me to load the winds for you?" Chad offered, knowing what he was thinking. "If you don't mind. I want to coordinate the start sequence, just in case there's a problem," Wes answered.

Stepping from the main cabin entrance, Wes saw the flurry of activity outside as maintenance crews worked furiously reinstalling the over-wing doors and removing the inflated slides. Two external pneumatic power carts were being wheeled into place in case the APU failed during engine start. Numerous security trucks circled the big wide body, their flashing lights casting eerie, moving shadows off the jet's fuselage. Riker and a man he didn't recognize met him at the bottom of the mobile stairs. Wes figured he was the Special Ops guy Chad had mentioned.

"We'll have you buttoned up within three minutes, Wes. Another thousand pounds and you'll have the twenty-one you need. Chad put the parachutes and kits in the rear," Riker said. "Anything else we can do for you?"

"Yeah. Make sure my wife and family don't get screwed by the company and the government if I don't make it back. They've already put up with enough, Spence."

"I'll see to it, Wes. You've got my word."

"Captain Beacham, you've got your fuel. I'll have this hose off her in thirty seconds," the fueler hollered from atop the pumping tower on the truck.

"Thanks! I'll catch the paperwork later," shouted Wes, rushing up the stairs.

"Good luck!" shouted Spence as he tossed Wes a thumbs-up for good measure.

Reaching the main entrance doorway, Wes signaled for the mobile stairs to be removed as he closed the huge door electrically and armed it. Force of habit caused him to bend down and check the two arming flag indicators after the door closed. Not that it mattered, but it was the only entrance that still had its emergency slide available in the event of a ground abort. He swore it wouldn't happen.

Before returning to the cockpit, Wes hustled through the cabin to see that all the doors and emergency exits were secure. While aft, he paused for a few moments to inspect the parachutes and survival gear. Everything appeared in order for the egress.

Chad was already on the interphone with the crew chief and had pressurized the hydraulic systems in preparation for start.

"Read the checklist!" shouted Chad as Wes hopped into the left seat. Seeing the time, Wes looked over at Chad and asked, "Are you satisfied you covered all the items?"

"Yeah!"

"Then let's skip the responsive reading and get this show on the road. We should already be airborne now."

"Suits me," said Chad as he keyed the interphone mike. "Ground, we're turning the right engine!"

"Hold your start! They're still trying to get the mobile stairs truck away from the side of the aircraft," Ground answered.

Wes whipped his head around to the left. The stairs were still right where they'd been for the last three days. "Sonofabitch!" Wes shouted. "Ground, is there a tow tractor nearby?"

"No, sir. They didn't figure we'd need one," came the reply.

"What else could we use to pull it away. Time is critical."

"There's a fire truck standing by, but he hasn't got a tow cable and there's no way he could maneuver close enough to move the stairs without damaging the left engine," explained the crew chief.

"I've got an idea," Chad said.

"Let's hear it."

"Suppose we start the engines and use reverse thrust to back away from the stairs. That should give the fire truck all the room he needs to ram the stairs truck and push it off into the grass."

"That's a hell of an idea, Chad. Let's do it."

Chad briefed the crew chief and started the engines while Wes coordinated with tower and the fire truck. Minutes later, the Boeing 767, its reversers operating, slowly began backing away from the mobile stairs. After moving sixty feet aft, Chad closed the thrust reversers and parked the brakes. Within seconds, the powerful fire truck rammed the mobile stairs truck, driving it off the runway, into the grass. Chad extended the flaps, set the stabilizer trim, and cycled the flight controls as Wes called for the clearance. Tower responded immediately.

"ATC CLEARS THE ALBATROSS TO DESTINATION AS FILED VIA UNRESTRICTED CLIMB TO FLIGHT LEVEL THREE SEVEN ZERO. TURN LEFT IMMEDIATELY AFTER TAKEOFF TO A HEADING OF ONE ZERO NINE DEGREES. HIGH SPEED APPROVED. SQUAWK TWO FIVE ZERO ZERO AND GODSPEED, GENTLEMEN!"

Acknowledging the clearance, Wes dialed in the transponder code.

"Read 'm and let's get out of here," Chad said. "I need a bath real bad!"

"It's all done. What are you waiting for?" Wes grunted. It was 0817 ZULU; four seventeen in the morning local Washington time. They were seventeen minutes late.

The sun was nowhere in sight as Chad released the brakes and advanced the throttles to takeoff thrust. Weighing only 215,000 pounds, the 767 leaped forward, bounding down the seven-thousand foot asphalt runway and into the air in barely a minute. Rotating to twelve degrees, Chad called for gear retraction as he rolled the accelerating 767 to a heading of 109 degrees. Retracting the flaps on schedule, the widebodied jet continued to build speed. Reaching three hundred fifty knots, Chad engaged the autopilot, punched the L NAV and SPEED mode buttons as Wes keyed his mike.

"RAINBOW! THE ALBATROSS WAS AIRBORNE AT ZERO EIGHT ONE SEVEN ZULU. ESTIMATING T.O.T. AT ONE ZERO TWO FIVE ZULU. WE EXPECT TO MAKE UP FIVE MINUTES IN FLIGHT."

"ROGER, ALBATROSS. RAINBOW COPIES. WE HAVE YOU IN SIGHT AND ON RADAR. YOUR ESCORT IS BEARING ONE EIGHT ZERO FOR TWENTY MILES. CALL TALLY."

Chad peered into the dark, southern skies for the flight of FA-18 Hornets. "I've got their beacons!" Chad announced, pointing upward. Wes acknowledged the tally.

"RAINBOW. WE'RE VISUAL WITH THE HAWKS."

"COPY THAT, ALBATROSS. THE HAWKS WILL BE ON 'FREQ' MOMENTARILY. STAND BY."

Wes rogered the AWAC controller's transmission as the 767's autopilot captured thirty-seven thousand feet. Checking the FMC computer, he saw they were eighty-one nautical miles east south east of the airport, already over the Atlantic.

A sense of relief swept over Wes as he realized the threat to Washington and the government of the United States was finally over. No matter his own life, the seat of American power was intact. Staring at the ocean below, Wes offered the Almighty a prayer of thanks. His greatest wish had been answered.

41

FLIGHT OF THE ALBATROSS

Wes stared at the red and yellow mass obscuring the upper portion of the radar screen as he slowly raised the radar antenna. Outside, he could see the line of towering thunderstorms stretching endlessly to his left and right. Active cells gave no warning as they randomly illuminated the horizon. Glancing back at the radar scope, he searched again for a break in the line.

"We're not going to top them, are we?" Chad asked.

"No. We'll have to deviate to the south."

"We don't have that much time to spare, Wes."

"Yeah, I know, but there's no way we can penetrate that front without getting the shit kicked out of us," Wes argued, scanning the plotting chart for a new set of coordinates south of the weather.

Chad watched him enter a new waypoint into the flight management computer. Checking the FMC, Wes saw the deviation would cost them sixty-three nautical miles and eight minutes. "For Christ's sake, Wes, the computer shows us getting to the impact point with only a minute to spare," whined Chad, as the 767's autopilot started a gentle turn toward the southern end of the squall line.

"We'll make it up in the descent," Wes countered.

"RAINBOW! THE ALBATROSS IS DEVIATING SOUTH TO THREE FIVE NORTH SIX THREE WEST BECAUSE OF THUNDERSTORMS. ADVISE SEA HORSE TO ADJUST THE RENDEZVOUS FOR PICKUP."

"ROGER, ALBATROSS, RAINBOW CONCURS. WE SHOW

THUNDERSTORMS ASSOCIATED WITH THE SQUALL LINE ARE TOPPING FIFTY THOUSAND FEET. WILL ADVISE THE SEA HORSE."

"I hope Sea Horse gets the change," Chad growled, "or we'll both be shark bait."

Wes frowned. "Rainbow will make sure they copy the change. My concern is whether they can make it there in time to grab us before this bomb goes off," Wes said. "That squall line is apt to be a problem for them, too."

"We'll know soon enough," Chad said gravely.

Now flying parallel to the line of thunder cells, Wes worked the radar feverishly, searching for a hole in the storm's ominous wall, but there was none. The waypoint he'd given Rainbow was also embedded in the storm. They would have to deviate even farther south than he'd estimated — at least another thirty miles. Checking the time to go to impact, Wes knew it was impossible. They would have to penetrate the storm's wall.

Looking to his left, he saw the angry flashes of lightning leap from cell to cell, then explode inside the dark billowing cumulus-nimbus clouds. A small knot started to form in the pit of his stomach as he imagined the violence they might encounter. The vertical wind shear associated with the core of a cell could rip the wings off. Glancing again into the radar, he searched frantically for an opening — anything. To the right, twenty-one miles ahead, appeared to be an area of less intensity. Chad saw it, too, and nodded in agreement.

"I guess that's the best opening we're going to find."

"I'm afraid so," Wes said, cinching his seat belt and shoulder harness. "Better go ahead and rig for rough running while we still have the time."

"Yeah, from the looks of those cells, I'd say we're going to get slapped around pretty hard in the descent," Chad remarked, as he switched on the engine anti-ice and selected the Flight Start ignition mode.

Wes turned on all the lights inside the cockpit, then donned his sunglasses. They would help attenuate some of the flash blindness from the lightning strikes he was certain they'd encounter.

Approaching the turn point, Chad took control of the aircraft's heading from the computer and manually turned the 767 into the storm as he retarded the throttles. Wes set "2000" feet in the altitude alert window as he keyed his mike:

"RAINBOW, THIS IS ALBATROSS. WE'RE UNABLE TO CLEAR THE STORM. WE'RE PROCEEDING FROM PRESENT POSITION TO TARGET. DO YOU COPY?"

"ALBATROSS FROM RAINBOW! YOU'RE UNREADABLE! SAY AGAIN!"

Wes realized he'd waited too long to make the call. Now within seconds of entering the storm, he heard the familiar crackle of electrical interference in his earphones, a forewarning of heavy precipitation.

Suddenly, the nose of the 767 pitched up and shuddered as it absorbed the initial impact of the violent updrafts. Its airspeed began bleeding off rapidly as though the knots were being poured out of a pitcher.

"Oh shit!" yelled Chad, fighting to decrease the pitch attitude as the auto-throttles, sensing the loss of airspeed, raced forward, developing more thrust. Without warning, the nose pitched down ten degrees below the artificial horizon as the airspeed rapidly increased. Seeing that the autopilot could not manage the rapid oscillations, Chad clicked off the autopilot and auto-throttles as he pulled the throttles to idle.

"Come right twenty degrees!" shouted Wes as the roar of precipitation against the outside of the fuselage drowned out all but his loudest commands. Chad rolled the jet to the right while checking the radar. Seeing the solid line of crimson red blanketing the upper third of the scope, he tightened the turn.

Shocked by the deafening sound of thunder, Wes ducked instinctively as a lightning strike exploded on the jet's radome in front of his face. Glancing back at the scope, Wes saw it was black. Switching to the other radar made no difference. "That one fried the antenna!" Wes yelled. "You're on your own now!"

"Then let's get the hell out of here fast!" said Chad, reaching for the spoiler handle.

Wes checked his altimeter as the jet was buffeted by the shearing winds.

Passing through twenty-three thousand feet, they took another lightning hit. This one struck close to the plane's nose temporarily blinding both pilots.

"Sonofabitch! Chad hollered. "Is this the best route down you could find?"

"You'd rather we turn back now?" shouted Wes over the roar of the screaming wind.

"No way! We've come this far. We may as well catch the whole bloody show!" Chad bellowed.

"Sure glad it's not my leg!" joked Wes, trying to make light of the situation.

Chad managed a tight grin for a second before another lightning bolt clobbered them.

Approaching seventeen thousand feet the oscillations became more violent. Wes watched the gauges intently as Chad struggled to keep pace with the jet's wild gyrations. Checking the SAT [static(outside) air temperature] indicator, Wes saw it read two degrees Celsius and dropping. The most savage part of their descent would be encountered as they passed through the freezing level.

Suddenly the 767's nose, struck by a brutal wind shear more devastating than the first, pitched uncontrollably upward for several moments. Chad shoved the yoke forward to avoid a stall.

"Airspeed!" screamed Wes as they both watched the jet lose sixty knots instantly. Suddenly, the left wing dropped.

"Let her go!" shouted Wes. "Stay with the pitch until you get your speed back. We'll lose her if you don't!"

Holding the ailerons neutral, Chad forced the yoke forward as both men stared in horror. There was nothing more they could do until the airspeed bleed-off reversed its course.

Seconds later, Wes called out, "Your speed's increasing! It's building rapidly now — you can pick up the wing!" Rolling the wings level, Chad hauled the yoke aft as the jet's speed continued to build.

Watching the airspeed indicator, Wes shouted over the pounding rain, "Speed's no problem now. Shoot for a target speed of two hundred, eighty knots!"

"I'm getting there!"

As they passed through twelve thousand feet, the turbulence began to subside. Peering out the windscreen, Wes saw that the sky ahead was brighter. Another minute and they would be clear of the cells. "We're through the worst of it."

"Let's hope so," snapped Chad, breathing a little easier. "I don't know how much more this crate can handle."

Wes grinned. "Speaking of crates, it's a wonder that nuke didn't decide to go off back there."

"Thank God for small favors," replied Chad. "I'm not ready to check out of the game just yet."

Wes understood. For them, life had always been a game of chance with every crisis an inning to be won or lost, depending on skill and luck. He wondered how fate would decide this final inning. Wes noticed a broad grin spreading across Chad's face as the sun's vivid rays poured into the disheveled cockpit.

"We made it!"

"So far, so good," echoed Wes, reaching for his sunglasses before remembering they were already on his face.

The deviation turning point was seven miles dead ahead. Wes read their latitude and longitude position off the FMC screen and cross-checked it against his plotting chart. Switching computer screens, he noted the ETA to the impact point read 1028 Zulu. "Damn!" Wes exclaimed.

"What's the problem?"

"The computer shows we lost three minutes deviating for weather," complained Wes. "On top of that our ground speed is thirty knots less than we'd planned. There's no way we're going to get to the impact point before that nuke goes off unless we increase the speed to at least three hundred sixty knots."

"What's our fuel? Do we have enough to do that?"

"I don't know. Just a minute, I'm figuring," Wes muttered.

Watching the computer change active waypoints, Chad read the new distance. "One hundred fifty four miles to impact."

Wes looked over at him. "We can barely make it." Nodding, Chad set "360" in the airspeed window. Out of the corner of his eye, Chad saw the auto-throttles move forward and felt the big fan engines respond. Wes was on the VHF radio.

"SEA HORSE. THIS IS THE ALBATROSS. DO YOU READ?"

"I SAY AGAIN, SEA HORSE. THIS IS THE ALBATROSS. DO YOU READ?"

Hearing no reply, Chad looked at Wes. "We're too low."

"Yeah, I'll give Rainbow a call. They can relay," said Wes, switching over to the number two VHF radio:

"RAINBOW, DO YOU READ THE ALBATROSS?"

"TWO BY" ALBATROSS. YOU ARE BARELY READABLE. GO AHEAD."

"ROGER, RAINBOW. ADVISE SEA HORSE OUR NEW PICKUP POINT IS THREE FIVE DEGREES, FOUR ZERO MIN-

UTES NORTH AND SIX ONE DEGREES, ZERO MINUTES WEST, COPY?"

"ROGER, ALBATROSS. COPY NEW POINT AS THREE FIVE DEGREES NORTH, SIX ONE DEGREES, ZERO MINUTES WEST! CONFIRM?"

"NEGATIVE, RAINBOW!! LATITUDE IS THREE FIVE DEGREES FOUR ZERO MINUTES NORTH! OVER!

"ALBATROSS! YOU'RE COMPLETELY UNREADABLE! SAY AGAIN PLEASE!"

"Shit! hollered Wes. "We're too friggin' low! Take her up a bit!" he shouted as Chad dialed "10000" in the altitude window. As he punched the Flight Level Change button, the 767's autopilot increased its pitch smoothly and began a climb toward ten thousand feet.

"RAINBOW! HOW DO YOU READ THE ALBATROSS NOW?"

"ALBA... YOU... STI... UNREAD....WE .... MESSAGE... SEA."

"It's that damn squall line. He's on the other side of it and we're running away from him like shit through a goose!" hollered Wes.

"What about the Sea Horse?"

"Same thing. He's probably trying to pick his way through that line at low altitude and he can't read us either," Wes shouted. "I'll keep trying. You better go get your wet gear on. I'll depressurize the cabin, set up the autopilot for V NAV (Vertical Navigation), then join you."

Chad was hesitating.

"Chad, this bomb is less than a hundred miles from the splashdown. We've got about seven minutes left until feet wet. Get a move on it."

"What about the pickup point?"

"We've both got ELT's (emergency locator transmitters)! They'll find us."

"Not in eight minutes, Wes!" Chad shouted. "We're screwed!"

Wes knew he was right. Without the exact coordinates, neither had a prayer of being found before the nuke exploded. Who was he kidding?

Wes looked over at his friend. A wild-eyed look of fear covered Chad's rugged face. The veins in his neck were throbbing. Nothing Wes could say would change their fate now. Time was about to run out for both of them and he sensed it.

"Better get ready to hit the silk, good buddy. We've got one last ass to kick!" said Wes.

"Whose? The grim reaper's?"

"Who else?" Wes grunted.

Crawling out of his seat, Chad stuck out his hand. His grip said what time would not allow.

Wes watched Chad leave the cockpit, then reached up and spun the cabin altitude selector so that it matched the jet's altitude. Then he shut off both air-conditioning packs, robbing the cabin of pressure. Slowly, the cabin began its climb to match the altitude outside the 767 as Wes made a final check of the vertical profile in the flight management computer. Dialing "00000" in the altitude alert window, he observed the 767's nose drop slightly below as the autopilot captured the descent profile. It would guide the jet into the ocean at a speed of 250 knots, impacting the water at the exact coordinates he'd assigned.

Satisfied with the profile, Wes tried several more times to reach Rainbow on the assigned frequencies and Guard channel before he gave up. "Shit happens!" he groaned, pondering the thought of being swallowed up by the Atlantic.

Seconds later, Wes felt the pressure change in his ears. Looking up, he saw that the cabin door light was on. Checking the computer, he watched the digits begin to align on the pickup point. Scrambling out of his cockpit chair, Wes hustled through the cool, moisture-laden air toward the right rear emergency door. Drawing closer, he heard a shrill whistling sound. The opening in the hull was disturbing the laminar flow of air along the fuselage.

Reaching the cabin's aft end, Wes saw that Chad and his gear were gone. Had he cleared the horizontal stabilizer successfully? No one had been willing to assure him it was possible, no matter how they exited the doorway. Wes wished they could have dived out together.

For a second, Wes had an urge to go to the door and look out, as if he expected to see Chad being hoisted upward toward the belly of the hovering Navy rescue chopper. Stopping abeam the row of seats that held his own gear, he knew it was sheer fantasy.

Donning his parachute, Wes attached the survival kit containing his life raft and rucksack to the chute's harness. Slipping on his helmet, he waddled over to the open doorway, not sure of how best to exit.

Two thousand feet below him the Atlantic churned restlessly, beckoning him to taste its power. Winds swept over its foaming water, stripping the waves of their peaks. Wes tried to swallow. His throat, already dry, said no. Fear enveloped him as he peered into the threatening abyss. Raising his blood-shot eyes, Wes scanned what he could see of the horizon for the rescue chopper, but saw only a continuous line dividing the Earth from its atmosphere. There was nothing else to see, save the sun's rays skipping across the rolling sea.

Wes knew he must fight to live. Stripped of everything but his gear and his soul, he studied the angry water below, then stepped into the opening. Outside and just aft of the small doorway, he saw for the first time, the knife-like edge of the horizontal stabilizer challenging his successful passage. It appeared closer to his pathway than ever before, its blade ready to slice his body in half, should gravity not seize him instantly.

Stooping into a crouched position, Wes lay on his left side with his head level with the floor and his legs drawn up against his abdomen. Pivoting his body slightly, his boots found the door jam. It would do. Coiling his body into a human spring, Wes tucked his head close to his chest while pausing to catch his breath.

With one mighty effort, Wes thrust himself out the doorway and into gravity's arms.

Clutching his body instantly, an invisible force drew him downward toward safety as the knife-edged blade of the horizontal empennage slashed through the air inches above his head.

He was free of the ship.

Euphoric, he extended his limbs, stabilizing his falling body. Gasping, his chest expanded as his heart, starved for oxygen, snatched all the precious fluid his lungs could provide. Seeing the ocean rushing up to meet him, Wes closed the palms of his hands around the D ring, and flung them outward as far as his arms would go.

Without warning, the opening canopy seized his crotch violently, causing him instant pain. The pain disappeared as quickly as it had come, leaving only the firm grip of the harness tugging at his loins and buttocks.

Looking upward at the orange-colored panels of his parachute, Wes saw only one blown panel. He was safe for the moment. Reaching down alongside his left leg, Wes released the handle to his survival kit, deploying his life raft. Looking down, he watched as the CO_2 cartridge inflated it. Then, summoning both hands to his chest, Wes searched for the lanyards to inflate his water wings. Finding them, he jerked them simultaneously. Gas rushed into the two banana-shaped bladders, filling them rapidly.

Using the little remaining height to his advantage, Wes pulled on one of the risers, turning himself as he scanned the horizon for a final time. He saw nothing — no ships, no planes, no rescue choppers, only angry water. Pulling harder on the riser, Wes swung around to face the wind and removed his helmet. An excruciating pain in his left leg begged attention, but there wasn't time. A second later, Wes plunged into the salty froth of the Atlantic.

The water's coldness shocked him, but eased the pain in his leg. Bobbing to the surface, buoyed by his water wings, Wes felt his body being dragged by the wind-filled canopy across the open water. Rolling over on his back as though it were a giant slalom ski, he flailed about in search of the two quick release clips pinning him to the now-dangerous parasail. He reached behind his head for the two risers and traced their paths down to the clips on his harness, jerking them open. Freed of his dead weight, the orange canopy sailed up into the sky briefly, collapsed and then fell back into the sea.

Spitting the salt water from his mouth, Wes coughed the rest of it out of his lungs. Seeing the dinghy nearby, he found the lanyard it was tethered to and pulled it to him. The surging waves made the task difficult, not wanting to yield its prey. Though weakening fast from exertion, Wes tugged relentlessly at the dinghy until it was beside his face.

Fatigued, his body aching, Wes rested in the water as he closed the two release clips. Pleased that he had remembered to secure them, he grabbed the tiny yellow raft, plunged it under his chest and mounted it, dragging his wet belly and legs behind. Exhausted, he lay on the raft, his cheeks chafing against the abrasive wet rubber as the wind swept across his exposed body, robbing it of precious heat.

Able to move again, Wes rolled himself over without flipping the dinghy. Sitting upright, he cupped his hands and bailed out his home at sea. Realizing his trembling had intensified, he sought warmth inside the tiny boat. Zipping the panels over his body and pulling the hood over his head, Wes felt the heat return. He'd made it this far, but what of the 767 and the nuclear bomb — and his rescue?

He searched the sky once more, but saw nothing. Unzipping the cocoonlike panels, Wes stuck his arm out into the brisk air and checked his Seiko. The digital readout showed ten twenty-five Zulu — six twenty-five Eastern Daylight Time. He had two minutes left to live — he would not be rescued. Alone and afraid, Wes bowed his head in prayer and waited for death.

42

COVERT DECISION

Stepping into her worn leather sandals, Meredith grabbed the portable radio off the credenza and stole out of the house into the early morning darkness. Sleep had abandoned her at four a.m. She had awakened thinking of Wes. Certain the assault would take place before dawn, she feared for his safety.

The cool night air was still and wet. Lights left on by renters unaccustomed to the neighborhood pierced the darkness, casting strange shadows on the road as she walked. Beach towels draped over deck rails confirmed the number of lodgers. Cicadas, rubbing their legs together, gave life to the night as Meredith made her way along Tuckahoe Drive but their sounds did not register. Nor did she notice the clutter of overstuffed garbage containers that usually annoyed her. The assault and Wes's flight into the Atlantic monopolized her thinking.

Reaching the end of the boardwalk, Meredith slipped off her sandals and sat down on the salt-treated bench. She switched on the tiny radio and scanned the band for conversation. She found one immediately. Listening for a few seconds, Meredith learned the 767 had been observed flying eastward. The announcer put the takeoff at four seventeen a.m. There was no word of the jet's destination nor would the White House be commenting for at least the next several hours. Remembering his wish of wanting to rid Washington of the scourge he'd unknowingly planted there, Meredith smiled. Wes got what he wanted most. At least he was back in control of the situation, she thought, as she picked up the radio and stepped onto the beach.

The damp sand felt refreshing to her feet as she walked alone by the surf. Stopping often to gaze eastward, Meredith fantasized catching a glimpse of him. He was there, somewhere in the Atlantic. Searching toward the northeast, she tried to imagine her bearing to him. She would focus there, channel her feelings in that direction. Intuition told her he was listening, that he would know what she wanted to say to him. Facing the ocean, she closed her eyes and telegraphed her thoughts to him:

I love you, Wes, wherever you are. Though our bodies are separated by this water, our souls are not. Think of me now and remember that I've always loved you and will forever. Even death will not dissolve our love. Let it comfort you now. Use it to overcome despair and find hope. Let it be your peace.

Standing motionless, Meredith listened. Had he heard her? Was her message in his mind? Did he sense her presence? Was he trying now to answer, to reassure her? Hearing nothing, Meredith suddenly felt foolish trying to communicate with Wes by telepathy.

Climbing the small dune separating vegetation from beach, Meredith collapsed onto the sand, burying her face in her hands. She wept uncontrollably as sorrow replaced hope. Inwardly, Meredith knew Wes was gone. She would never see or touch him again. Lying on the sand, she realized life with him was over, their parting permanent. There would be changes, many changes.

Sitting up, Meredith took a tissue from her pocket and wiped her eyes. As she stared again at the sea, she saw the first vestiges of dawn. Rays of sunlight beamed high into the sky above her, waiting for the Earth's turn to lower their aim. How many times had she and Wes risen early as the children slept and made their way to the beach to mark the beginning of another day of happiness together? Without him, those celestial sunrises would become painful reminders of the love she'd lost. It was but one of the many wonderful experiences they'd shared together, but one she must now learn to do without.

The walk back to the cottage was a lonely one. She felt as though she were leaving Wes behind. The sun's glare was blinding without her sunglasses.

Rounding the crooked road, she saw Walker and Tucker on the porch. Seeing her, they waved. Meredith continued plodding up the hill toward the driveway. As she reached the bottom of the stair tower, Walker leaned over the rail. "They've rescued the jet, Mom. According to the news reports, Dad took off over two hours ago!"

"I know," she answered, holding up the small radio.

"The president is going to address the nation in a couple of minutes," he added.

Climbing the staircase, Meredith stopped at the first landing to pick the dead geranium stalks off one of her plants. Looking at the flowers, she remembered badgering Wes into going with her to buy them. He'd been good-natured, she recalled, even becoming fussy over finding the properly shaped plants. His concern had amused her. It was so like him.

"Where have you been, Mom?" Jacqueline asked.

"I couldn't sleep, so I walked down to the beach."

"They've rescued the hostages. Dad flew the jet out of National Airport about two hours ago!" said Caroline as Meredith settled onto the sofa. "The president is going to be on in a minute to talk about it," she added.

Meredith brushed her hair from her face. She felt uneasy. The news would carry a bittersweet message to her and the Beacham family.

Jacqueline interrupted, "He's coming on now."

Conversation died as the newscaster announced that President McGarth would be speaking momentarily from aboard Air Force One.

Good morning, my fellow Americans! Shortly before four this morning under the cover of darkness, Navy SEALS conducted an assault of the Trans International Airways 767 held hostage by the now-familiar group known as the Fundamentalist Coalition or FC. In a dramatic and highly successful attack, the assault team overpowered the terrorists and freed all hostages aboard, though the SEAL team did sustain a casualty.

At four seventeen a.m., some twenty minutes after the assault ended, Captain Weston Beacham and First Officer Chadwick Sanderlin took off from National Airport bound for a destination in the Atlantic Ocean with the nuclear bomb on board the jet.

On the basis of intelligence information gathered during the last several days, I learned that the weapon was set to detonate at exactly six twenty-seven this morning, roughly thirty minutes ago. National Reconnaissance Satellite Command assets maintained constant surveillance of the jet's flight path into the Atlantic and has provided positive confirmation that the jet did, in fact, crash into the ocean. I can also confirm that detonation of the nuclear weapon did not occur.

First Officer Chadwick Sanderlin has been rescued and is in satisfactory condition aboard the USS Roosevelt. An extended search for Captain Beacham will resume as soon as authorities have determined it is safe to proceed into the area. Recovery of the two pilots was hampered by severe weather adjacent to the impact zone.

Preparations are being made to restore all governmental operations. I have directed all military units, including all those who withdrew from the Middle East, to return to their pre-crisis assignments immediately. Key personnel previously deployed to alternate agency locations have been directed to return to Washington. The Eighty Second Airborne Division is moving into position to assist Virginia and Maryland State Police, District of Columbia Police and other local law enforcement agencies in controlling re-entry into Washington and the surrounding areas. Sloan Kilgore, director of the Federal Emergency Management Administration (FEMA) will follow this broadcast with specific instructions you will be asked to follow.

Citizens, as your president, I must apologize for necessarily deceiving you and the media during this ordeal. No doubt, you found my answers vague and indecisive at times. Demands placed on me by the terrorists accounted for some of my misleading statements. Others were made to conceal your government's response. I can assure you now that both I and the National Security Council were in constant communication with those agencies critical to our plan's success at all times. And, at no time did this administration waver in its determination to remove those hoodlums and their bomb from our soil. I trust you will accept this explanation pending a full congressional hearing, which I anticipate will begin shortly.

As your president and commander in chief, I found it particularly burdensome to have to submit to the will of these terrorists. I know and can appreciate firsthand the anger and humiliation that you as Americans have had to endure over the last three days. I commend you for your perseverance and support and I pledge that this administration will not rest until every participant is held accountable and brought to justice.

Americans, this must never again happen on our shores. Thank you for your attention, and may you enjoy once more the freedom of your heritage. Good day.

Caroline brushed her tears aside and asked, "Why do you think they didn't find Dad, Walker?"

"You know Dad. He probably stayed with the jet until the last minute. They should search the impact area."

"Maybe we should try to contact the Navy and tell them to look there first," Jacqueline said.

"If he's alive, they'll find him," Walker answered.

"Don't you even say that, Walker," Caroline cried.

"Caroline, I'm not saying Dad's dead. I just think we have to be practical. Dad's plan was extremely dangerous and he knew it. I don't think we should get our hopes up too high until we know something more definite."

"Walker's right," Meredith said. "Your father, in his roundabout way, left no doubt in my mind that he felt he might not make it back. I think that was what he was trying to prepare us all for during his visit. The best we can do for him now is pray and hope that they can find him quickly. In the meantime, we need to ......"

"I'll answer it!" cried Jacqueline, scrambling to her feet. Suddenly, the room fell silent as she picked up the phone. No one wanted to breathe.

"Walker, it's for you. It's Mr. Elliot. He said Dad told him to ask for you," she said, handing him the phone. Meredith looked on in horror as her son raised the phone to his ear. "This is Walker, Mr. Elliot."

"Yes, sir, I expect he would have done that."

"You say no signals have been received from his ELT?"

"How long before the search will resume?"

"Well, that's cause for some hope."

"I appreciate your calling us, sir. It really has helped."

"Yes, sir. I have the number. He left it with me."

"Thank you. We'll wait to hear from you, sir. Good-bye."

"What did he have to say?" Meredith asked anxiously. "They haven't found Dad yet. Mr. Elliot thinks Dad may have stayed with the ship until the last minute. He said the Navy will begin its search there and work outward. They haven't picked up any signals from his emergency locator transmitter. They expect to begin the search within the next several hours once the area is deemed safe to operate in. The president wants us to know that they are doing everything possible to find him and will keep us informed of any changes."

"So what are we supposed to do now?" sobbed Jacqueline.

"We wait, hope and pray, honey. That's all we can do," said Meredith, her lips quivering. Fighting the tears, she turned toward the window and gazed out into the Atlantic — in the direction she thought Wes must be — and silently prayed. Sensing their mother's pain, Caroline and Jacqueline moved closer to console her as Walker and Tucker offered words of encouragement.

*   *   *

Wes rubbed the last bit of sunscreen on his forehead and under his burning eyes as he baked in the blistering sun of a second dawn. Shocked at being alive, he searched the horizon once more for some sign of help — a ship, a plane, — anything, but saw nothing. As he scanned the barren skies, he promised himself he would make the most of his second chance, God's gift to him.

His parched throat cried for water. The pain in his left leg had become worse, aggravated by the constant flexing of the rubber dinghy, and yet he refused to complain. He was certain he'd suffered a hairline fracture during his egress from the jet.

Nine hours had passed since the bomb was to have detonated and ended his life. Exhausted, Wes fought to hold his head up. He had to stay alert. With no radio or ELT, he had little chance of being spotted unless he stayed awake, ready to use the signaling mirror he'd looped around his neck.

Losing most of the contents from his survival kit was a cruel stroke of luck, but one over which he'd had no control. Violently thrown from his dinghy by a renegade wave as he struggled to close the zipper of his rucksack, the opened bag had followed him into the sea, spilling its contents into the ocean. Climbing back into the raft a minute later, Wes had found the lanyard and pulled the water-logged bag up from below. Missing was his emergency radio, flares, dye marker, a desalting kit and a can of water — all dumped in an instant. Wes counted himself lucky for having tied the signal mirror to his flight suit earlier. He wished he'd done the same for the radio.

Positive he'd seen the ELT secured to his parachute harness inside the jet, he could only imagine how it had separated from him. Wes decided it had sheared off as he'd maneuvered himself into position for the jump, though he refused to accept the blame.

Lulled into restful sleep by the undulating motion of the waves, Wes drifted aimlessly for several more hours, oblivious of the band of clouds approaching.

Startled from sleep by the familiar sound of the HC-130 Hercules's turboprop engines, Wes searched the skies for the rescue aircraft. Then he saw it — low on the horizon, maybe five hundred to a thousand feet above the ocean. The four-engine aircraft appeared to be angling slightly to his right. Reaching for his mirror, Wes realized the sun was totally obscured by clouds. His mirror was useless.

Seeing the HC-130 approaching, Wes waved his hands frantically, hoping to see a wing dip, but it was not to be. His eyes followed the bird until it was a speck against the clouds. Then he saw it turn, rolling out on a parallel course. He'd won a second chance. Wes studied his track as the Hercules approached again. His course would pass to the left of his raft. Plunging his hands into the chilly water, Wes fought to pivot the raft around to offer the greatest frontal exposure. Anxiously, he waited as the big transport grew larger by the second. Sensing it was time, he threw his arms into the air again, madly fanning them about. His aim — to portray motion, develop contrast, draw attention. Yet, as the plane plowed straightly by, Wes knew he'd failed again.

Forced to watch helplessly as the mighty Hercules methodically criss-crossed the ocean in front of him, Wes sat silently in his raft, knowing these waters would not be swept again. His fate was sealed. Again, he was doomed to die. The only question, was when?

Twenty minutes later, the plane was gone. And so too were the clouds whose cruel cover had robbed him of the chance to be rescued.

Determined not to squander what time he had left, Wes decided to relive the special moments of his life. It was the best he could do, short of capitulation. That would come soon enough, he imagined, rezipping the panels around his body to ward off the chilling breeze.

Looking west, Wes gazed at the sun sinking low in the crimson sky as he maneuvered his body into the fetal position to ease the cramping in his stomach. Resting his head on the inflated rim of the small dinghy, he allowed his eyelids to settle over his burning eyes. Reasonably comfortable, he would focus on his life and what it had all meant, trusting in sleep to come and take him to meet death painlessly.

DAY SEVEN - 27 August   *WILLIAMSBURG, VIRGINIA*

Taking her mind off Wes for a moment, Meredith took inventory of what needed to be done to the yard. The once-lush green lawn he'd toiled over each day last spring lay in ruin, scorched by the summer's unrelenting heat and deprived of moisture for days on end. People would be coming to pay their respects and offer condolences. Something would have to be done immediately, Meredith decided, turning into the driveway. Stopping in front of the garage door, she switched off the engine and looked around. The driveway was empty. His car was missing, the little Honda he loved so much. Suddenly, Meredith's eyes filled with tears as she thought of the countless times she'd watched him through the kitchen window, laboring over the family cars and fussing over the messes she and the kids made of them. Pulling a tissue from her purse, Meredith wiped her eyes and scolded herself for crying. She realized it wasn't going to be easy learning to live without him, but knew she must — if not for herself, for the children.

Stepping into the oppressive afternoon heat from her air-conditioned Jag, Meredith immediately wished she could return to Kilduck Station. Perspiration wasted no time in seeping from her pores. Meredith hated summer in Williamsburg. She didn't want to be there, especially now. Leaving the beach was a mistake, but one over which she had no choice. There would be relatives and friends to greet and arrangements to be made. Smiling briefly, Meredith recalled how angry Wes had become when she'd refused to discuss his possible death. "The day the grim reaper gets hold of my ass and I buy the farm will be too damn late for any more planning!" he'd said.

Meredith studied the entrance to her house as though it were a place she'd never been before. Loneliness hovered over her as she swept the cobwebs from the door and shoved the key into the slot, giving it a familiar turn. The musty smell of stale air greeted her as she bore through the doorway, eager to restore the home to life. After switching on the ceiling fan, she threw open the doors and windows. It didn't matter that the outside air was warm and moist. Anything would be an improvement for the time being.

Returning to the car, Meredith began dragging the clothes she never wore back into the house when Bailey, her Himalayan cat, registered his disgust at the heat and demanded to be removed. As she lifted his kennel from the car, Meredith heard the phone ring. Her blood turned to ice, hoping the call would signal Wes's recovery, but knowing it would confirm his loss.

Setting Bailey free, Meredith raced into the house and seized the phone from its hook. "Hello!"

"Mrs. Beacham?"

"Yes, this is Meredith Beacham."

"Mrs. Beacham, this is Gaylord Elliot, President McGarth's security adviser. I spoke with your son, Walker, early yesterday morning."

"Yes, Mr. Elliot, I recall. Have you found my husband yet?"

"No, Mrs. Beacham, I'm afraid we haven't. That's why I wanted to call, to let you know."

Meredith's lips began to quiver as she fought back the tears and cleared her throat.

"You will continue the search, won't you?" she begged in desperation.

"I....we have decided to call off the ...."

Interrupting, "You mean that's it? Just like that? You search for two days and give up? Please! Don't you think my husband deserves better?" she cried, her heart pounding mercilessly.

"Yes, Mrs. Beacham, he does and we have flown more than two hundred sorties devoted entirely to trying to locate your husband, but he is nowhere to be found. If he were alive, we would have him home now... I'm... sorry."

"No. Please forgive me, Mr. Elliot. It's just very difficult for me to accept what you are telling me."

"I understand how you feel, Mrs. Beacham. I'm just sorry the news couldn't have been better. The country owes your husband a debt of gratitude for what he has done."

"Thank you for saying that. It means a lot to me, as I'm sure it will to our family, Mr. Elliot. Please tell the president thank you for us."

"Yes, I will, Mrs. Beacham, and would you please keep me informed of your plans? The president has said he would like to personally pay his respects as it becomes appropriate."

"Thank him again, Mr. Elliot. I will call when our plans are definite... Goodbye."

Placing the phone back on its hook, Meredith wandered into the guest bedroom, and fell across the bed in which she and Wes had shared so many special nights, her heart crushed by the news she'd known would find her. Wes was dead.

Seeing Meredith's car in the driveway and the side door to the Beacham house open, Claire Adams, Walker's fiancée, walked inside and switched on the lights. "Mrs. Beacham, are you here? It's Claire!"

Claire listened, but heard no reply. Walking through the great room and into the kitchen, she heard sobbing. It was Mrs. Beacham. She hesitated for a moment, debating whether to interrupt. Knowing the search for Captain Beacham had ended, Claire could guess the reason for her crying.

Reaching the bedroom door, she paused. "Mrs. Beacham, I'm here with you, if you need me." Meredith rolled over and sat up on the edge of the bed, surprised to see her. "Oh Claire, they've stopped searching for Wes. They're certain he's dead," she cried out helplessly.

"I know. I heard it on the radio as I was driving here. I'm sorry," Claire said softly. "I've been praying they'd find him." Meredith pulled a handkerchief from her pocket and wiped her eyes. "Wes thought this might happen," she said, trying to regain her composure. "We spent what little time we had together preparing for it, but since he left, I haven't allowed myself to even think about it. I was so sure he would make it back alive."

Claire wondered if she should risk telling Meredith of the strange dream she'd had last night. It had been so vivid and full of detail, like the others she'd had since a young child — more like a vision. It had frightened her. She knew it was the truth — Wes was still alive, but should she say anything about it now? The pain it would cause, of wanting to believe him alive, yet knowing the search was over. "I think we must pray for his safety and trust they are wrong," Claire said. "God will watch over him," she suggested, afraid to say more.

Meredith stared into Claire's large brown eyes, sensing there was more she wanted to say. Claire was like that. Walker had mentioned once that she seemed to know things from dreams she had. "What is it, Claire? Tell me if you know something."

Claire looked toward the window at a passing car before she replied, "I...I just don't want you to be hurt any more than you already are by what I feel."

Meredith took Claire's hands and held them. "Nothing could be worse than losing Wes, Claire. You can tell me."

Claire paused to be sure. "Wes is alive. I know from the dream I had. He is alive," she half-whispered.

"...But the call said they didn't find him, Claire. They've given up the search," Meredith said.

"I know," Claire answered, "But it won't matter. I know he will be found."

Meredith said nothing, stunned by Claire's revelation, her heart longing to believe what her mind said was impossible. Could Claire's dream be true? Was the government wrong? Had they just given up too quickly?

But what reason could she give — a dream, a hunch, her intuition? The government would want proof, something tangible. They wouldn't reopen the search unless there was cause to suspect a mistake had been made.

"Claire, how strongly do you believe in the dream you had about Wes? I want to believe it, but I wasn't there. I can't begin to imagine what you experienced. You have to help me," Meredith implored.

"It's difficult to explain. I feel so foolish...."

"No, you mustn't feel that way," Meredith cautioned. "It's a gift. Wes believed in mental telepathy. He didn't think it was mysterious or supernatural, but merely part of man's evolutionary process. There have been times in our marriage when he simply knew things, things he couldn't have known otherwise."

Claire gave Meredith a penetrating look. "I know. We talked about it several times at the beach last summer."

"You think Wes is alive, don't you?"

"Yes, I do," Claire answered firmly.

"Then I must act, no matter what," Meredith said, still trying to convince herself that she believed Claire's dream. "The least they can do is go search the area where Chad was found one more time. It can't cost that much or take that much time," she said, heading for the phone.

"I presume that was Colonel Beacham's wife pleading with you to reopen the search?" Elliot nodded. McGarth removed his glasses and rubbed his eyes. "I suppose it's the least we can do for her, don't you think?"

"That's the way I see it. I'll call Chris and have him draft the order to get the rescue team back into the air at first light tomorrow."

"Have him let me know the minute he finds out anything one way or the other. I don't want to put off meeting with those who were involved any longer than I have to," said the president.

Staring back at the paper on his desk with a look of concern, he said, "Before you go, Gaylord, I want your opinion on this Black Program directive Sinclair and Williamson have drawn up.

"What do you want me to tell you, Mason, that it's legal if you reinterpret Saddam's position as that of a military commander and not the head of the government of Iraq? Or that it's justified on the basis of a threat he made against our country, regardless of the law?

"You and I both know it's an illegal act and one that could cause you a lot of problems if the wrong people find out. Yet, we both agree that bastard should have been done away with long before now. As I see it, the question you have to answer is whether you want to take the risk of its becoming public knowledge. And that has to be your decision," said Elliot. "For what it's worth, I'll back you all the way if the issue ever comes to light."

"I appreciate that," said the president, scribbling his signature on the document. "Let's hope word of this will never be traced to this office."

"I'll take care of it," Gaylord answered.

43

REFLECTIONS AT SEA

Wiping the sweat from her forehead, Pamela eased the destroyer wheel slightly to port and paused. Invisible spinning wind currents, eddies, lapped at the luff of the mainsail as the thirty-eight foot sloop slowed. "Steady her right there and I'll have her fixed in a jiffy," her husband called out from below. "We'll be in irons in another twenty seconds," she shouted back.

Noting the sun's position, Pamela estimated it was close to noon, not that it really mattered. They still had another two and a half days of hard sailing before they made Bermuda, and that was assuming they didn't run into any more bad weather.

"Bring her back to starboard now," Jim shouted. "It's done."

Pamela shoved the wheel to the right and watched the Genoa billow as the laminar flow of wind returned to the sail. "It's much better," she said, noting how smoothly the stainless steel wheel handled. "What was it?" she hollered.

Crawling out from the sail locker Jim said, "A piece of line was caught in one of the steering blocks. It probably happened during the storm."

"You made a bloody good job of it, love. Can I put her on the autopilot now?" Pamela asked in her decidedly British accent.

"Give her a go at it. I'll go down and check our position and pass you the new course."

Pamela smiled, recalling that only two days ago both had thought their lives together were over for good. Caught asleep at the helm, both had been awakened by the howling winds of an advancing gust front. Fighting winds in excess of sixty knots in darkness, Pamela had instinctively released the autopilot and tried to turn the vessel into the intensifying gusts as Jim had gone forward to struggle with the mainsheet.

The knockdown had come without warning. She had clung to the destroyer wheel and screamed in horror as the boat heeled violently before slamming the tip of its mainmast into the ocean and tossing Jim into the center of its mainsail. Wearing no safety line, he'd scrambled over to the mast and using the mainsail's halyard had climbed back into the overturned sloop as she'd searched frantically for their life jackets.

Without warning, the vessel was righted by another violent surge of wind, this time nearly throwing Jim overboard again. Seeing the boat had righted itself, he'd released the tension on the mainsail's halyard, allowing the sail to collapse as Pamela had turned the floundering boat into the wind.

Frequently interrupted by the deafening sound of lightning striking the water around them, both had spent the next ten minutes reefing the mainsail and setting the storm jib.

Numbed by the knockdown they'd just survived and their storm preparations complete, Jim and Pamela had retreated down the companionway ladder, stopping only long enough to install the batter boards and slide the hatch cover closed.

"Set a course of two hundred degrees, Pam," Jim called out.

"Two hundred degrees, you say?" she asked, her mind still occupied with the events of several nights ago.

"Right," he replied. Looking down at the ship's steering compass, Pamela made a slight adjustment to the heading and re-engaged the autopilot.

Brushing the crumbs from the morning's breakfast off the cockpit seat cushion, Pamela sat down, bracing her shapely legs against the opposite seat. Lowering her head, she removed her sunglasses and wiped the lenses, using her T-shirt as a towel. Slipping them back on, Pamela gazed across the gently rolling seas from the cockpit of *Astor's Lady*. It was then that she noticed a blinding sparkle of light flashing at her.

Shielding her eyes, Pamela stared back in the same direction, but saw nothing. Then a second later, it flashed at her again. What could it be? Pamela asked herself, her curiosity building. "There it is again!" she said aloud, fascinated by the brilliant, shimmering light. "Love, hand me the glasses. I want to have a closer look at something," Pamela shouted.

"What is it?" Jim asked, handing her the binoculars.

"A flashing light. It's quite bright actually, a reflection of some sort," she explained, raising the glasses to her eyes.

"What do you see?" Jim asked, curiously.

"Can't tell. The rolling sea's making it hard to focus."

"I see it now!" he announced. "By Jove, it is bright. Shall we have a closer look?"

"Could we?" she exclaimed. "It's got my interest up."

Jim swung the destroyer wheel hard to starboard in the direction of the glittering light as Pamela reset the sheets. Peering through the binoculars again, she saw that the flashing light appeared to be resting on a platform — no, a raft. "It's a raft, I think, Jim," Pamela said, undecided.

Jim said nothing, but steered toward the flickering light, his own inquisitiveness aroused. "It is a raft, Jim! The light's coming from a mirror. Wait — there's someone in the raft! A man. Yes, there's a man lying in the raft! The mirror is on his chest," Pamela exclaimed.

"Is he moving?"

"No. He's either dead or asleep. I can't tell for certain." A bit leery of the situation, Jim steered *Astor's Lady* to pass the raft to starboard.

"What are we going to do, Jim?" Pamela shrieked.

"We'll stand clear and try to arouse him," said Jim, turning up into the wind twenty feet away. "Give him a toot with the air horn. That will bring him to his senses if he's alive."

Pam pulled the canister from its caddie and gave the trigger a good squeeze, holding it for a second. The piercing wail of the horn approached the threshold of pain as it echoed across the open water toward the motionless body.

"He's dead. That blast would have awakened anyone else."

"What do we do now?" Pam asked.

Satisfied they were in no danger, Jim said, "We may as well have a look. At least we can notify the authorities when we reach Bermuda." Pam nodded, continuing to watch for some sign of life.

Opening the diesel's fuel line, Jim switched on the ignition and started the sloop's iron sail. Next, he roller-furled the jib and lowered the mainsail. "You take the helm, Pam," he ordered. "I'll check him out."

Pam took the wheel, put the engine in gear, and opened the throttle slightly to overcome inertia as Jim tossed a warp over the stern in case he fell overboard.

With the raft fewer than four feet abeam the sloop's cockpit, Jim motioned for Pamela to cut the engine as he reached out with an extension pole and snared a line dangling in the water. Pulling it to him, Jim fished the raft alongside their boat and leaned over the side to examine the body.

Peering into the man's scorched, unshaven face, Jim pushed the mirror aside and touched his hand. He found warmth, not the hand of a dead man. Raising the eyelids with his thumbs, he saw the man's pupils try to constrict. They were not fixed — no bilateral dilation. Taking his left arm, Jim loosened the man's sleeve and measured his pulse. It was weak, but present. "He's alive, Pam, but just barely. Get me the boatswain's chair and fasten it to the mainsail halyard. I'll winch him into the boat."

Pamela opened the port sail locker and removed the canvas harness and handed it to her husband, then fetched the halyard and stood by. "What do you make of him, love?" she asked, watching Jim thread the man's arms through the loop. "He looks to be an American fighter pilot of some sort judging by his insignia, but he seems rather old to be playing at that, you'd think."

Jim looked around for a second. "Loop the end of the mainsail sheet and tie it in a slip knot. I'll put it around his arms and draw it tight to keep his arms by his side." Pamela grabbed the loose end of the sheet and did as he asked. "Splendid," remarked Jim, pulling the loop tight around the stranger's arms. Handing her the shackle, he said, "Fasten this to the halyard and I'll man the winch."

Cranking the handle slowly at first, Jim checked to see that the rig was holding. Seeing the stranger's slumped-over head rise above the rub rail, Jim quickened the pace, eager to revive him. "Pull him into the cockpit, if you can," he told Pam. Reaching for his legs, Pam pulled.

Suddenly, the stranger moaned.

"He is alive, Jim!" she shrieked.

"Never mind the chatter," Jim remarked, annoyed she would doubt his earlier observations. "Just help me get him into the cockpit, so I can go to work on him."

Pamela overlooked her husband's snide comment and pulled the stranger into the cockpit. Jim climbed down from the mast step and disconnected the halyard from the boatswain's chair, handing it to her to secure. Then he unzipped the man's flight suit down to his waist and listened to his heart. Examining him more thoroughly this time, Jim saw that his lips were parched. Opening his mouth, he smelled his breath. Jim detected a faint odor of ammonia. His kidneys were obviously suffering dehydration. "Pam, get a water bottle and some smelling salts. This bloke needs water."

Pam disappeared down the companionway, returning a few seconds later. Jim held the salts under his patient's nose. The stranger moaned again. "Do you hear me?" Jim said loudly, shaking the stranger firmly. "You need water. You must drink this water now! Do you understand?" he commanded. "Nod your head if you understand me."

Seeing a slight movement, Jim motioned for the water bottle. He began by pouring it around the man's face, then around his neck. "Get me a towel or a sponge, Pam."

Soaking the towel with water, Jim pulled the man's mouth open and mopped the inside of his mouth. A second later, the man's jaw closed on the towel. "Give a tug on that leg you pulled a moment ago." Pam reached down and gave his left leg a strong pull.

The stranger cried out as Jim flung water into his eyes.

"Where...What tha...."

"Shut up and drink this water. You can talk later," Jim snapped as he elevated the stranger's neck and poured a small stream of water into his mouth. Seeing him swallow, Jim poured a bit more, then even more as Pam watched in surprise.

"Better fetch me another pitcher. This chap's going to have this one done with shortly," Jim said, smiling at his success.

The next twenty minutes passed quickly as Jim continued to feed the stranger water, and small quantities of broth Pam had warmed in the galley. Content to quench the stranger's thirst, Jim withheld his questions. There would be ample time for those later. "Want to take over for me for a while, Pam?" he asked. "We need to get underway."

Pam gave her husband a hug and knelt beside the stranger. "What's your name?" she asked.

"W..e..s," he mumbled.

"Did you say Wes?" she asked. He tried to nod.

"His name is Wes!"

As Jim finished pulling the dinghy aboard, he glanced back at the stranger. "See what else you can get out of him."

Pam studied Wes's eyes as she fed him more broth. They were friendly, caring. She noticed the worn gold band on his ring finger. "What's your wife's name?"

"Mere..dith,"

"Meredith?" she repeated, wiping the broth from his lips.

"Yes," he said in a slightly stronger voice. "I need to reach her, tell her I'm okay. Tell the government to call off the search. Can you do that?"

Looking into his troubled face Pamela answered, "I'd like to Wes, but we lost our radio antenna in a storm two days ago. We won't be able to communicate with anyone until we reach Bermuda."

"Oh, oh," he moaned as his head slumped into her arms. "I didn't know. I'm sorry."

Pamela smiled. "Of course you couldn't have known. From the looks of it, I'd say you must have been in a terrible storm yourself!"

Wes tried to grin. "How long will it take to reach Bermuda?"

"My husband thinks we'll make it in another two and a-half days," she replied. "That will give you enough time to gain your strength back." Mustering a weak smile, his eyes closed.

Seeing he had fallen asleep, Pamela placed his head on a life jacket then helped Jim erect the canopy over the cockpit to block the sun's rays. Then she went aft to have a look at the small dinghy lying on the stern of the boat.

"Jim! Come look at this! He's written a message here on the raft! It's a letter to his wife, Meredith, and their family."

"Thank goodness we found him," Pam exclaimed. "I wouldn't want to have to read a message from you like that, love."

Hearing Wes cry out in his sleep, they both stole back to the cockpit anxious to do whatever they could for him. Neither one saw the wind blow the tiny dinghy off the boat minutes later.

*   *   *

Ross Straton opened the lid to his laptop computer and turned on the power. As he waited for the word processor software to boot up, he thought of how to break the news to his father. Seeing the blank screen appear, he began to type:

Dear Father,

Where do I begin? An hour ago I learned from a State Department intelligence brief addressed to Riggs that my friend, Hassan Khalil, was killed on takeoff from Geneva several days ago.

I also learned that he was one of the leaders of the Fundamentalist Coalition that planned the nuclear terrorist attack against us. The news of his involvement and death has left me devastated.

Hassan and I met while at Georgetown as students and became lovers—yes, I am a homosexual. Though I tried to hide it and become straight for your sake, I found it impossible. I've known since I was a child that I was different, that I desired the companionship and affection of other men. I cannot apologize. I am, like it or not, what nature bestowed upon me. It was not my choice that I was condemned at birth to suffer the embarrassment and humiliation of my genetic difference. I cannot begin to tell you of the torment I have experienced, nor will it matter any longer. Until I found Hassan, I felt I would have to live my life devoid of all sexual expression.

You'll recall that I was adamant about wanting to work in Europe following graduation from Georgetown. It was so I could be close to him. Your help and influence with Riggs was the most I could have hoped for. Being appointed his special assistant has afforded me the cover and means by which Hassan and I have been able to be together these last few years.

Learning that he used me to plan and carry out the terrorist attack is more than I can cope with. His betrayal of my love and trust is more than I can stand.

I realize it is only a matter of time before the FBI learns of my unknowing complicity in perpetrating the crisis.

It was I who betrayed your confidence and told him about Caroline Beacham and her father, the captain. It was I who took him to her branch office and pointed her out. It was I who accompanied him to Dulles and used my position to introduce him to Captain Beacham some months ago.

Please understand, I never thought my helping him open an account at NOVA Bank would lead to Miss Beacham being kidnapped. Or that introducing him to Captain Beacham to allay his fears of flying back to Geneva would result in her father's death.

I cannot live with myself knowing I have caused this much pain to others, nor do I want to bear the shame of dishonoring you further. Being a homosexual and spending the remainder of my life in prison is not something I want to endure either.

Father, I am sorry I have not lived up to your expectations. If I could have, life for both of us might have been more fulfilling. Please try to understand what I feel I must do. I love you.

Your son

Satisfied with what he'd written, Ross printed his letter and signed it. A moment later, he picked up a loaded thirty-eight special, stuck it into his mouth and squeezed the trigger.

DAY NINE - 29 August   *IN THE ATLANTIC OCEAN*

Awakened by the smell of fresh coffee, Wes kicked the quilted blanket off and stretched his arms into the air, rubbing them. His body ached from having slept on the Fiberglass cockpit floor, but the pain in his left leg was gone, replaced by a dull soreness. Hearing voices, he sat up and looked around, but saw no one. Deciding the sounds were coming from the bow, Wes rolled over and pulled himself to his feet. He felt faint. Holding on to the hatch cover, he waited a few seconds for his head to clear before he called out, "Good morning!"

Jim and Pamela popped up instantly from behind the front of the cabin. "Good morning yourself," she answered. "How do you feel?" she asked with excitement.

"Better than yesterday," Wes replied, wiping his hand along his unshaved jaw. "Could I have some of that coffee I smell?"

"Of course. Let me get it for you," Pamela offered, jumping to her feet and picking her way aft with Jim in tow. Reaching the cockpit, she stuck out her hand and said proudly, "My name's Pamela Astor, and this is my husband, Jim. We found you adrift yesterday afternoon and hauled you aboard."

A broad smile spread across Wes's face as he shook their hands warmly. "You both saved my life. How can I ever thank you enough?" he asked earnestly.

"Not necessary, mate. The privilege was ours. Pamela and I are just glad our courses crossed when they did. From the look of your dinghy, provisions seemed to have dwindled dangerously low."

Wes laughed as Pamela disappeared into the cabin. He liked the Englishman's humor and especially his British accent. "My galley was grossly understocked," Wes joked.

Jim reached around to the inside of the companionway and produced a baseball cap. "Take it," he said a bit more seriously. "You've had enough bloody sun for this voyage," he teased.

Wes slipped the hat on, tilting the visor just below his sight line.

Pamela reappeared with a cup of hot coffee and a bottle of water. "You can have your coffee after you drink this water," she insisted. "I don't want you dehydrated again."

Wes nodded obediently and chugged the bottle of water.

"That's a good boy," she said as he finished. "Now I'll go and cook us breakfast. You and Jim sit and talk. He's dying to know how you ended up in that little life raft."

"I guess I do owe you and your wife an explanation," Wes said apologetically.

"Only if you feel like talking about it, mate," said Jim.

"How long have you and your wife been at sea?" asked Wes.

"We left Stephenville, Newfoundland, six days ago. Why?"

Sensing the Englishman had no idea of what he was leading up to, Wes asked, "Are you aware that a group of Middle East terrorists threatened to detonate a nuclear weapon in Washington nearly a week ago?"

"No bloody way! I don't believe it!" shouted Jim, leaping to his feet. Jerking the pipe from his mouth, Jim hollered down to Pamela. "You better come up topside, love. Wes has a dandy of a story to tell!"

Pausing, Wes waited to see if Pam would join them.

"So what's it all about, Wes?" sang Pam as she emerged from the cabin. Jim interrupted. "He asked me if we knew about some Arabs trying to blow up Washington with a nuclear bomb, love!"

"Oh my God!" Pam exclaimed in horror. "When? We don't know a thing about it."

The account of what had happened left the English couple flabbergasted. "And you actually dived out of the jet less than fifty miles from where the bomb should have exploded?" Jim asked in amazement.

"Yes, except that because of the weather, we had to fly farther to the south than we'd planned, and that fouled up the Navy's rescue plan."

"So you'd spent nearly two days in the raft when we spotted you?" Pam summarized. Wes nodded silently, not wanting to recall the two most horrifying days of his life.

Shaking his head in astonishment, Jim said, "Well I'm glad we didn't learn of it until now, mate. If that bloody nuke had gone off, we all would have been vaporized."

Wes cringed. Jim continued, "Come to think of it, we're not that far away from it, even now. I guess that explains the aircraft I saw flying around here early this morning."

"There were planes out this morning?" asked Wes.

"Yes, actually quite a few, as I recall. They seemed to be in some sort of search pattern, but paid no attention to us. Of course they may have been looking for you, ole' boy." Wes cursed himself for not having heard them. With the sun shining, he could have attracted their attention.

"It's a pity we have no way to contact them," said Jim, still in shock over the news. Remembering breakfast, Pam excused herself and returned to the cabin, stunned by the disclosure. Looking more concerned, Jim said, "I'll fetch my charts and the GPS (Global Positioning System) Receiver from below. Then you can show me where your jet crashed with that nuke. I'd like to know just how far away from that wretched bomb we are."

Left alone, Wes thought again about Meredith and the children and their anguish. Frustrated, he could do nothing but wait.

44

HOMECOMING

Thank you for seeing me on such short notice, Mr. President," Halston said in a subdued voice. "I'm afraid I bear much of the responsibility for what has happened."

"What do you mean, Riggs?"

"It's all here, Mr. President...in Ross's letter."

McGarth took the letter and read it.

"When was this written?"

"Sometime yesterday Ross wrote the letter to his father, Blake Straton, a friend of mind and president of NOVA Bank & Trust, then he shot and killed himself. Blake went to his son's home this morning and found him and the note and called me. Apparently, Ross left a message on Blake's answering machine urgently requesting his help. Blake brought the letter to me. "He asked me to tell you of his extreme sorrow for what his son has done and to offer his personal apology."

"Did you know Ross was a homosexual?"

"Not really, although at times, I suspected it."

"How often do you suppose they met in Geneva, not that it really matters?" the president asked.

"That's the part that troubles me, sir. I sent him there frequently to coordinate arrangements for meetings with other governments and had him accompany me on all my trips. He's been in Geneva at least two or three times a month for the last several years with the arms talks."

McGarth thought for a moment. "Sinclair will want a thorough investigation into everything Ross did. With Hassan dead and Saeed and Andrea missing, our chances of finding the evidence we need to confront the state sponsors is dwindling rapidly."

"Mr. President, there is something else. It's my letter of resignation," Halston said as he handed him a letter.

His comment brought a look of surprise to McGarth's face.

"Why, Riggs?"

"Sir, we're at opposite ends of the political spectrum in our thinking...I hired Ross over your office's objections...I'm part to blame for...."

"Riggs, I haven't asked for your resignation and I don't intend to. From what I've read, Ross had no idea he was aiding and abetting the coalition. So how could you? Besides, I'm going to need your hard-driving approach to our foreign policy if we're going to overcome the embarrassment we've suffered internationally."

"But, I thought you..."

"Take this letter and tear it up. We've both got too much work ahead of us to be dealing with this."

McGarth offered his hand and Halston took it.

*   *   *

Startled from her nap by the ringing telephone, Meredith struggled to her feet and made her way to the kitchen to answer, her heart pounding with each footstep. Glancing at the clock on the microwave, she saw it was after four p.m.. She'd been asleep longer than she'd planned. Fearful of what the caller might have to say, she paused to reassure herself that she could handle it. Lifting the receiver, she answered faintly, "Meredith Beacham."

"Mrs. Beacham, this is Gaylord Elliot." Meredith recognized his voice immediately. His tone frightened her. Hope left as quickly as it had come. Her apprehension heightened as she forced herself to respond. "Yes?"

"Mrs. Beacham, I'm afraid the news is not good. We searched the area you requested for a second time this morning and found only the raft. Wes had written a short message to you and your children on it. I'm having it delivered to you now... I'm sorry." Clutching the edge of the small phone desk, Meredith labored to steady herself, her heart unwilling to accept what her mind knew was true. Her lips trembling, she said, "Thank you, Mr. Elliot. At least now we know his fate. It will help our healing."

"Mrs. Beacham, please accept my heartfelt condolences. The president and I both had the greatest admiration for your husband. Colonel Beacham was an outstanding leader."

"Thank you for saying that, Mr. Elliot. It meant everything to him to be given the chance to fly that mission. He could not have lived with himself otherwise," Meredith said, brushing the tears from her cheeks.

"Yes, the president and I were aware that he blamed himself for much of what happened, even though we had felt from the start his feelings were never justified. I'm just sorry we didn't find him, Mrs. Beacham."

"I understand. Thank you, Mr. Elliot, for all of your help."

Hanging up the phone, Meredith walked over to the kitchen window. It was her favorite place from which to view the birds feeding and to await Wes's frequent returns. It would now become a place to avoid. It harbored too many fond memories to be of any comfort. Perhaps later, after the pain is gone, she told herself. Nothing would ever be the same. If she were to survive, she would have to begin her life anew, as others had before her. She would have to find new friends and new interests, learn to live differently, but with the memories of what they'd both shared indelibly planted in her heart. It was what he'd tried desperately to tell me she thought. He knew this was going to happen.

The knock at the front door surprised her. Stopping off in the guest bathroom, Meredith brushed her hair and wiped her face with a moist cloth. In the mirror she saw her anguish. Her eyes reflected the despair she felt in her heart. It was an expression that would be difficult to overcome, no matter how hard she would try.

Opening the door, Meredith recognized the Air Force uniform. It was the second time in as many days a stranger in Air Force blue had visited her. She noticed the package in his left hand. He was a young African-American. He seemed ill-at-ease, but well aware of the purpose for his visit.

"Excuse me, ma'am, but are you Mrs. Meredith Beacham?"

"Yes, Sergeant, I'm Meredith Beacham."

"Well, ma'am, I was told to deliver this package to you personally. It's from the White House."

Meredith took the package. It was heavy. "Won't you please come in, Sergeant? It's too hot to stand in this heat for long."

"No, ma'am. I have to get back to D.C., but thank you...I'm real sorry about your husband. He was an okay guy."

Meredith nodded. "Did you know him?"

"No, not exactly. Except that I met him the night he stayed at the White House. We talked for twenty minutes, I guess."

"Are you certain you won't come in for a moment, Sergeant?"

"No, ma'am, I best be on my way. I'm on the midnight shift."

Meredith thought for a second. "Are you on duty now?"

"Not exactly. I volunteered to bring you the package," he answered modestly. Meredith smiled.

"Tell me your name, Sergeant. I want to remember it."

"Jonas Worthington, ma'am," he replied.

"Thank you, Jonas. I'm most grateful. This package means a great deal to our family."

Stepping back, Jonas smiled and retreated to the blue sedan in the driveway. Meredith watched him back out and waved as he pulled away. She would remember his kindness long after the hurt had passed and her grief spent.

In the living room, she tore off the wrapping and opened the box. The smell of salt water rose to meet her as she lifted the sheared piece of raft. There in the center she saw Wes's message to her. The lettering, though faint, was familiar. It was Wes's writing. Moving it closer to the light she read:

MEREDITH, I WILL LOVE YOU FOREVER. FIND HAPPINESS. I WILL WAIT FOR YOU. ALWAYS, WES. JACQUELINE, CAROLINE, WALKER, YOU HAVE BEEN MY GREATEST JOYS IN LIFE. I PRAY LIFE WILL RETURN TO YOU THE LOVE AND HAPPINESS YOU'VE GIVEN ME. STAY IN TOUCH WITH EACH OTHER AND LIVE YOUR LIVES TO THE FULLEST.
LOVE ALWAYS, DAD.
CLAIRE, TUCKER, I LOVE YOU AS MY CHILDREN AND WANT FOR YOU THE SAME. I ONLY REGRET THE YEARS I WILL MISS WITH YOU ALL. LOVE ALWAYS, WES.

Meredith read it again before putting it on the antique drop-leaf table, in the same spot that so many happy announcements had occupied in days gone by. Her eyes wandered about the room as she began to think of what should be done next. There would be ample time for grieving. For now, she had think of the children and of how to bring closure to her most intimate companion's life. It would be her final act of love to the man she'd adored since childhood. That would be enough to see her through.

DAY TEN - 30 August   *IN THE ATLANTIC OCEAN*

Up since first light, Wes scanned the horizon continually searching for signs of land. According to Jim's calculations, they should make Saint George's Harbor around zero eight hundred. Checking his watch, Wes saw it read zero seven twenty. They were close. Restless and eager to reach Meredith, he picked up the glasses and resumed his search pattern.

Jim watched Wes with amusement, knowing that once he sighted land, he would become even more impatient to reach the shore.

"Sighted land yet, mate?" Jim called out.

"No. I guess we're still out too far," Wes answered, easing the glasses back to his chest. "Still think your estimate of O eight hundred is going to hold?" Wes asked, anxiously.

Jim pulled the pipe from his mouth and began scaling out the bowl with his pocketknife. "Yes, give or take five minutes."

Satisfied with Jim's confirmation, Wes abandoned the search and pulled his coffee cup from the drink caddie. Pamela's strong brew tasted especially good to him.

Emptying the unfinished coffee over the side, Wes scanned the horizon once more. To his surprise, there, off in the distance, lay Bermuda. Judging from Jim's nautical chart, they would enter Saint George's Harbor from the northeast. Bermuda Naval Air Station lay to the south end of the harbor and was only a fifteen-minute cab ride from the town. With luck, he could make Williamsburg by early afternoon.

"Have room for breakfast, Wes?" called Pamela.

"You bet. I've learned you never pass up a meal at sea."

"Then you best join us," she replied with a broad smile.

Crouching low, Wes worked his way down the windward side of the sloop to the cockpit. The fresh wind against the one twenty Genoa sail kept the boat's leeward rail close to sea and made moving topside a challenge, but Wes didn't mind. Jim had been doing everything possible to expedite their arrival in Bermuda.

Pamela looked up. "Your plate is in the oven. There is tea and scones and more coffee."

Wes's eyes lit up. "You made scones?"

"Do you like them?" she asked, surprised by his outburst.

"I love them," he replied, hustling down the companionway steps.

A minute later, Wes returned with his plate. It bore two scones.

"You do like them, don't you?" Pamela remarked. His mouth already full, Wes nodded his approval. She gave him a smile and went below. Returning, she handed him a crumpled package. "It's for your trip home," Pamela said. "Sorry about the wrapping," she added. Wes set his plate aside and opened the parcel. It was his freshly washed and mended flight suit, three photographs and a letter.

"I want you to look sharp when you arrive home," Pamela said proudly.

Grinning broadly, Wes studied the Polaroid photographs they'd taken the day they found him. "I'm surprised you let me aboard looking this bad," he said playfully. "We did debate the issue before deciding to haul you in," Jim laughed.

"We did no such thing, Jim, and you know it," she snapped. "The letter's to your wife," Pam continued. "It's just a short note to tell her what a good boy you've been for the last two days and all that stuff, you know."

"Is it a good report?"

"Of course. Otherwise we would have simply tossed you back into the sea," joked Pamela.

A serious expression returned to Wes's face as he gazed at the two of them seated together. They both sensed he had something to say and waited. "I owe my life to you," he said. "It is a debt that I will never be able to repay, but one which I will gladly remember. Thank you."

"You have no debt with us unless it's one of a lasting friendship," Jim replied. "Finding you has made this voyage exceedingly worthwhile and a memorable one for us. Pamela and I wish you and your family the best and hope our paths will cross again someday."

Unable to reply for the lump building in his throat, Wes smiled, then looked away. Pam stood up and scanned the harbor entrance quickly. "The first channel buoy is over there, Jim. It's to your starboard," she chimed. Wes excused himself and went below to put on his clean flight suit.

Watching his new friends guide *Astor's Lady* into the harbor while furling her sails, made Wes long to return to the sport he and his family had enjoyed so much in years past. He loved the excitement the sea offered those who ventured there. He envied them and their freedom to sail anywhere. He admired their independence and graciousness. They were wonderful people — the kind you could enjoy being with in any situation — like those he and Meredith had known when they'd sailed before. Adjusting the fenders as Jim brought the sloop alongside the pier, Wes decided he and Meredith would become sailors again soon.

Unfamiliar with nautical debarkation procedures, Wes followed Jim and Pamela to the customs office. After reciting the essentials of his rescue and presenting his military ID, Wes was granted entry and offered the use of a phone. He dialed the number to his beach home in Duck, but got no answer until the tape came on advising him to call his house in Williamsburg. Realizing he had been given up for dead, Wes debated calling Meredith, thinking the shock might prove a mistake. Reneging on his better judgement, he placed the call anyway. After three rings, an automated voice explained that the phone service was experiencing local difficulties because of extensive storm damage to the lines and would be unable to complete his call for several hours. Grimacing, Wes hung up.

Remembering the private number to the White House, the number Elliot had given him, Wes thought of calling Gaylord. Having his help would expedite his return. Wrestling his water-logged billfold from his left pocket, Wes found Elliot's business card. Flipping it over, he read the blurred number. He could still make it out.

"Forest Lindsey speaking."

"Mr. Lindsey, this is Wes Beacham."

"Beacham?...Wes Beacham?...Colonel Beacham?"

"Yes," Wes replied.

"Good Lord, man, you're supposed to be dead...I mean...Christ! This is unbelievable...how? Where?"

"I'm in Bermuda at the customs office, in a town called Saint George just across from the airport and Naval Air Station. I'm okay, but I need some help with orders and transportation..."

Forest broke in. "Just hold for a minute, Wes. I want to tell the president...I don't believe..."

Wes waited, not knowing what to expect. The news of his survival was more of a shock to Lindsey than he could have imagined. How would Meredith and the children react?

"Colonel Beacham?" Wes recognized the voice immediately.

"Good morning, Mr. President," Wes replied, cheerfully.

"Colonel, hearing your voice is the best piece of news I've had since we fished your ornery copilot out of the sea four days ago. Welcome back."

"Thank you, sir."

"Forest says you're in Bermuda. Is that right?"

"Yes, sir, I'm near the Naval Air Station."

"You feel like traveling now?" the president asked.

"Yes, sir. The sooner the better."

"Have you contacted your family yet?"

"No, sir. I can't get through. There's a problem with the phone lines, according to the operator."

"Yes, I recall hearing something about that on the morning news...nothing serious you understand. Would you like me to give her a call or send someone?" Wes thought for a minute.

"Sir, I'd feel better doing it in person. I'm still not home and ...you know."

"I understand completely," said the president. "Besides, your surprise arrival there will make the meeting I've planned a real homecoming."

Confused, Wes said, "I don't quite understand..."

"Of course you wouldn't. No one had planned on your being there. Forest, my chief of staff, has arranged a private reception at Providence Hall in Williamsburg at two o'clock this afternoon to honor those of you who were directly involved in the Gravelly Point Affair, as it's now being called. I felt making it private would be less painful and would offer me the chance to express my condolences more sincerely to the families of those who did not survive. There was also the question of exposing the identities of certain civilians assigned to the SEAL's assault force. Your family is planning to come, so you will have to be there, too."

Wes checked the time.

"I certainly want to, Mr. President, but I don't know whether its possible. I don't know what the..."

McGarth interrupted. "I'll give you back to Forest, Wes. He can handle it. I look forward to seeing you at two p.m., Colonel. Welcome home."

"Thank you, sir."

Forest picked up the phone a few seconds later. "Colonel, grab a cab and head for the base. By the time you get there, I'll have a flight set up for you. What are you wearing right now?"

"My flight suit."

"An escort will meet you at the gate. He'll handle it from there. See you in Williamsburg," Forest said.

As Wes turned around, Jim handed him a newspaper. "It's not often we meet someone on a first-name basis with the president of the United States," exclaimed Pam.

Wes blushed. "Thanks for the paper. I'll read it on the plane. I've got a lot of catching up to do," he said. "I've got to make Williamsburg by two p.m. I'd better be going."

Extending his hand to Jim, they shook hands firmly. Waiting her turn, Pamela leaned forward and embraced him with a kiss as Jim looked on approvingly.

Backing away, Pamela brushed away a tear and gave him a lusty smile. "Take care of yourself and stay in touch."

"I promise!" echoed Wes, heading for the door.

"See ya, mate!" Jim called out as he gave Wes a thumbs-up.

Pausing in the doorway, Wes glanced back at the two of them and waved good-bye.

Two hours later, Wes climbed aboard a C-9 Med-Evac jet, the military equivalent of the commercial DC9. It was ten-fifty a.m. The flight was running late. Poking his head into the cramped cockpit, Wes said, "Good morning, gentlemen. I'm Wes Beacham."

"You can't be!" growled the major in the left seat. "He's out in the Atlantic chasing mermaids!"

Wes roared with laughter, knowing the voice belonged to Hank Cummins, a first officer at TIA. "Dreaming you'd moved up another number on the seniority list were you, Hank," snapped Wes.

Hank spun around and grinned at Wes. "Naw, I was just pulling your chain 'cause you took Chad and not me with you on that 'ditching exercise' the other day."

"You better talk to Chad about that. He might have a different opinion, now that he's been there."

"I have. Talked to him yesterday. He said it scared the ever-loving shit out of him, diving out that door into that boiling sea. He's worried his ass off about your not being found. Riker grounded him for the week. Ordered him to take some time off on the company," Hank said, completing his cockpit check.

"Did he get picked up okay?"

"Yeah, except for a big bruise on his right leg. Said he pissed in his pants when he looked around and didn't see the chopper. Figured his ass was going to be grass when that nuke exploded. Then he said he heard the chopper and looked up to see it pop out of a rain shower. He said he couldn't have been in the water for more than six minutes. He and the chopper pilot got into it, big time, when he saw they were withdrawing. The pilot told Chad he could get the fuck out and look for you then if he wanted too. You know Chad. He was ready to kick the guy's ass right there on the spot."

"Tact never has been his strong suit," Wes joked.

"You got that right," said Hank, switching on the rotating beacon. "You want to ride up here and keep us company?"

"Thanks for the offer, but I need the sleep."

"Suit yourself, Wes. I'll hang her on the 'barber pole.' I'll have you there in no time," Hank boasted.

The cabin was nearly empty except for a few patients on stretchers being shuttled to military hospitals on the mainland. One, a young boy, suffering a severe concussion was said to be in serious condition, struck by a motorist while riding a moped. A few dependents on emergency personal leave made up the rest. Wes stopped and chatted with the lad briefly, then found an empty row of seats and strapped himself in. Tucking a pillow against the bulkhead, Wes closed his eyes in search of rest. The impending excitement of seeing Meredith and the children held his consciousness for several minutes before letting him go.

The roar of the C9's two engines going into reverse startled Wes from sleep. For a second, he thought they'd aborted the takeoff. Peering out the window, he saw an assortment of FA-18 Hornets, F-14 Tomcats, and A-6 Intruders parked on the ramp near the hangars to the north of the field. As the jet turned off the runway, Wes got a better glimpse of the field. They were exiting the runway at Naval Air Station Norfolk. He was nearly home.

Sticking his head into the cockpit, Wes thanked Hank for the fast ride home and complimented him on his "greaser."

"You're welcome," said Hank in his Texas drawl. "I'm just happy to see you made it back alive, man! Take better care of yourself next time, will you?" he added.

Grinning, Wes countered, "I promise I'll work on it."

Stepping out into the glaring sunshine atop the mobile stairs, Wes fumbled for his sunglasses. Looking down, he saw a Navy commander waiting at the foot of the stairs. Reaching the ground, he returned the officer's salute and extended his hand.

"Wes Beacham, Commander!"

"Arnold Webber, Colonel. Sir, the chopper is standing by."

Surveying the flight ramp, Wes saw a Navy CH-53 settle onto the apron not far away. Wes stepped into the staff car quietly, disappointed that he'd have to forgo the call to Meredith. He couldn't keep the president waiting.

* * *

Alone and sitting quietly in her sunroom, Meredith gazed out at the massive green canopy covering the yard. Rays of sunshine splashed the ground through gaps in the mantle, changing patterns as a gentle breeze rustled the leaves about. She stared at the empty love seat nestled inside the white picket fence Wes had built for her years ago and recalled the happiness they had shared there, surrounded by azaleas and daffodils. She would miss the meaningful discussions they'd had about life and their children. Glancing at the miniature English boxwoods that circled the birdbath, Meredith relived the joy they'd had planting them together.

She longed to live her life with Wes over again. Yet even as she wished it, Meredith knew it was not possible. Life, unlike history, could never be repeated. For her, the love seat was now but a reminder of the life and love they had shared, a symbol of their past. Gone was the growing season of their love, replaced by a harvest of the memories. A cloak of sadness passed over Meredith as she turned from the window.

"I'm ready to go now, Mom," said Jacqueline as she took her mother's hand and pressed it to her cheek.

Meredith stood up and embraced her daughter for a moment before they walked to the door.

"Are we waiting for Caroline and Walker?"

"No," Meredith answered. "They've gone ahead, honey."

Outside, Meredith glanced at the hospitality banner suspended above the garage, fluttering gently in the warm summer breeze. Its resemblance to a flag pained her. Receiving the American flag honoring her husband's service to his country would be the most difficult part of meeting with the president.

How many times had she and Wes stood by and observed the same event, seen the young widow clutch the coarse cloth as her tears buried themselves into the cushion of grief? It was her turn now.

*   *   *

Seated in the cockpit of the CH-53 helicopter, Wes listened to the exchange of information between Marine One and his flight. Over the James River at five hundred feet, Wes could see Busch Gardens and the brewery straight ahead. Off to his right, he could see Fort Eustis and the airfield, to the left the Surry nuclear power plant. Banking the chopper slightly to the right, the pilot asked for vectors to Providence Hall. His instructions were interrupted by a call from Marine One.

"CREEK TWO ONE FROM MARINE ONE. REQUEST YOU HOLD SOUTHEAST OF RENDEZVOUS POINT UNTIL FURTHER ADVISED."

"ROGER," replied the skipper. "SAY YOUR POSITION?"

"MARINE ONE'S LANDING AT THIS TIME. EXPECT A THREE MINUTE DELAY."

"I've got a tally-ho on him at your right one o'clock for two miles," Wes called out as he watched it start to disappear into dense green foliage surrounding Colonial Williamsburg's Golden Horseshoe Golf Course. Scanning the treetops, the skipper said, "I don't have him."

Coming closer, Wes picked up the roof of Providence Hall. Just short of the building and separated by a large hedge, he spied the president's chopper sitting on the golf course, its rotors barely turning. "Check this side of the rooftop at your twelve o'clock," Wes directed.

"Got it," snapped the pilot.

"CREEK TWO ONE, YOU'RE CLEARED TO LAND. MAKE YOUR TOUCHDOWN ONE HUNDRED METERS SOUTH OF MY POSITION."

His heart pounding, Wes watched impatiently as the big chopper eased toward the golf course below. In the distance, he could see the president's party standing at the break in the hedgerow. As he watched, others appeared to join his party, then all but a few vanished behind the tall green hedge. Wes would be on the ground in seconds.

* * *

Having viewed the president and his entourage land from their vantage point at the hedgerow entrance, Meredith and her family retreated to the patio to await his arrival. A man emerged from the group and walked directly toward her.

"Mrs. Beacham?"

"Yes."

"And this is your family, I presume?" he asked cordially.

"Yes," Meredith replied curiously.

"Mrs. Beacham, I'm Forest Lindsey, the president's chief of staff. The president wishes to meet with you and your family privately for a moment. If you would, please follow me."

Surprised at the request, Meredith hesitated, unsure of herself.

"Mom, don't keep the president waiting," Jacqueline urged. "Mr. Lindsey asked us to follow him."

Satisfied Meredith understood his meaning, they walked quickly back through the hedgerow entrance. There, less than ten feet away stood the president. Another man stood beside him. Meredith and her family stopped and waited as Mr. Lindsey approached the president and spoke to him. The president stopped his conversation and walked to where Meredith and the children were standing.

"Mrs. Beacham, I'm Mason McGarth. It is a pleasure to finally meet you and your wonderful family. I feel like I already know most of them."

"Thank you, Mr. President. It is an honor to meet you, sir. My husband had the highest regard for your leadership," Meredith said, shaking his hand.

"I would also like for you to meet Gaylord Elliot, my adviser for National Security," the president added.

"Mr. Elliot, I must apologize for my rudeness to you. I ..."

"Nonsense," he said warmly. "I would have felt the same way."

Stepping back, Meredith proudly watched as the president greeted each member of her family. His kind words were comforting and sincere. The gleam in their eyes told her the president's greeting meant a great deal to them. If only Wes could be here to see this, Meredith thought, as she listened to Walker modestly explain his role in helping his father come up with the EMPRESS plan. It was then that Meredith realized she was straining to hear their conversation over a loud noise.

At first, the helicopter's sound had been but a nuisance, pounding the air as it settled lower on the horizon. Meredith was used to having them darting across her housetop at all hours of the day. Paying it little mind, she mover closer.

From nearby Fort Eustis, the choppers were always training — climbing, diving, and auto-rotating, whatever that was; "yanking and banking," Wes would call it. There was something different about this one. Its path appeared to be more purposeful, as though it intended to land on the course, not merely hover over it and leave. Meredith noticed the president was eyeing it even as he continued to speak with Caroline and Jacqueline. Was he expecting someone else?

The president abruptly ended his conversation and turned to face the craft as it landed. Meredith and her family stood watching, bewildered over the importance the president was ascribing to the event.

A lone figure emerged from the helicopter and started moving toward them. Drawing closer, Meredith saw it was a man, a man wearing a flight suit. No, it can't be — impossible...

"Dad!" screamed Jacqueline. "It's Dad! He's alive!" she cried out as she ran toward him.

Astonished, Meredith froze. Unable to speak; wanting, hoping, and praying that it was Wes, but afraid to believe it. Then Caroline and Walker saw it was their father and raced after Jacqueline to greet him. Holding her breath, Meredith saw Jacqueline leap into her father's open arms and knew it was him. Seconds later, his arms opened once more and closed around Caroline and Walker. Trembling, Meredith began moving toward them, walking slowly at first, then quickening her pace as she closed the distance between them. Claire and Tucker looked on, waiting their turn.

A breath away from him, Meredith paused and waited. His eyes caught hers amid the children's embraces and he smiled. Knowing the pain they had suffered and the love they had for their father, she nodded her approval and smiled back at him.

A moment later, the circle opened once more as Wes reached out for Meredith, taking her in his arms. They caressed each other passionately as their children watched with tearful delight.

No one saw the president and Mr. Elliot slip back through the hedgerow, as Tucker and Claire eagerly joined the Beachams' homecoming.

45

A FLAG REMAINS

Spontaneous applause erupted as Wes and his family entered the garden patio of Providence Hall. Learning just minutes earlier that Wes had been rescued and was alive came as a shock to everyone there, especially Chad. Blushing at the attention he was receiving, Wes smiled at his well-wishers and then turned toward the president to await his comments.

White House Chief of Staff Forest Lindsey, the president's Adviser for National Security Gaylord Elliot, Secretary of Defense Christopher Jacobson, and Chairman of the Joint Chiefs of Staff General Clayton Griffith flanked President McGarth on the podium as he prepared to speak.

"Ladies and gentlemen, families and friends. I have asked you here this afternoon so that I might have the opportunity to personally thank each one of you for your courage and determination in helping defeat what could have been this nation's worst disaster. I also came here to pay tribute to those families who suffered the loss of a loved one...."

As the president spoke, Wes's eyes strayed to the young boy standing beside the elderly man. They appeared to be alone. A look of sadness stretched across the old man's face as he listened to the president's speech with interest. Wes saw the child bury his face in the old man's side to hide his tears as the president called Leigh's name.

Feelings of guilt gnawed at him as he turned away. He was to blame for the pain Jason felt and it crushed him. If only he hadn't told

Leigh she could come to the cockpit.

Meredith, still in shock over finding Wes alive, watched his every move. She immediately noticed the young boy Wes was watching. Seeing the anxiety in her husband's eyes as he turned away from the child, Meredith understood the reason for his pain and the helplessness he felt. The anguish in his face confirmed the affair she had suspected for several months. Curious, Meredith wondered about the relationship. How long had it gone on? How serious had it been? Had he loved her?

A list of questions entered Meredith's mind as she tried to imagine the extent of her husband's infidelity. Did she want to know about the affair? Would he speak to her of it or remain silent and hope it passed unnoticed? And if he didn't, should she confront him or pretend she suspected nothing? Could she forgive him?

Looking again at the child and then at her husband, Meredith saw the tragedy of it all and the mistake he had made. A part of her wanted to reach out and say, "I understand. I forgive you, Wes." Yet, the other cautioned her against it, pleading silence as the best course. Was it not enough that the affair was ended, that Wes would suffer for it for the rest of his life? Would his knowing that she knew of the relationship serve any purpose, make his grieving any less painful, or her acceptance of it any easier?

Troubled by the truth of her intuition and uncertain of her feelings, Meredith suppressed the issue and tried to focus on the president's comments.

"... and so in closing, I want you to know that the nation owes each one of you a sincere debt of gratitude for the contribution your family has made to end the horror that besieged us. On behalf of the American people, I thank you."

Moments later, the president began presenting citations and commemorative flags to the families of Doug Marino, the SEAL commander; the FBI/CIA Task Force members and flight crew killed in Geneva; Ray Outland, the secretary of state's bodyguard; the four men slain aboard the jet; and finally to Jason, the young son of Leigh Simpson.

Looking at Wes as the young boy received his flag, Meredith saw once more the torment in his eyes. Taking his hand, she squeezed it reassuringly as they watched the widows tearfully accept their flags from the president.

Then the president presented Wes and each member of his crew a Presidential Citation for their heroic efforts at combating the terrorist crisis. As Meredith looked on, she saw that one flag remained on the table—the one meant for her. Glancing at Wes, Meredith remembered Claire's prophecy and offered a silent prayer of thanks for his safe return.

Expressing their sympathy first to Mrs. Marino and then to Mrs. Outland, Wes and Meredith made their way over to where the young boy and his grandfather were standing. Wes bent down and offered his hand. "Jason, I'm Wes Beacham."

"Yes, sir, I know," he said sorrowfully. "My mother showed me a picture she took of you. She told me she loved you," he added, his voice trembling.

Squatting down so that they faced one another evenly, Wes said, "Your mother was a wonderful and kind person, Jason. She meant a lot to everyone who knew her and especially to me, son. I'm truly sorry for what has happened... I don't know what else to say."

Fighting to hide his tears, Jason nodded his understanding as his grandfather spoke. "Thank you, Captain Beacham. No one blames you for what happened to Leigh. It was God's will and we must trust in Him."

Wes looked into the old man's penetrating eyes and saw that he knew of the affair. For a second, he felt the need to explain himself, but thought better of it. It would make no difference. There was nothing more to be said.

"I'm sorry..."

"We all are," replied the old man, "but time will heal us."

Meredith looked on Jason with compassion as Wes nodded his understanding and stood up.

"Good-bye, Jason," said Wes, fighting back his tears.

"Good-bye," uttered Jason, clutching his folded flag.

Wes spent the rest of his time paying his respects to the other families whose husbands had made the supreme sacrifice and answering questions about his rescue at sea. And then it was over.

Walking to the car with Meredith, Wes noticed her quietness. She was distressed by what she had witnessed.

"Meredith, I owe you an explanation, I ..."

"No, Wes. Please. Spare me the details. I don't want to know what was between you and Jason's mother. Whatever it was, it's over and I will try to forgive you. But please, let it be." Stopping, Wes gazed into Meredith's troubled face as she continued. He saw the concern in her sparkling blue eyes.

"It's Jason that I worry about, Wes," she said in her caring way. "He's alone except for his aging grandfather... You owe that child something."

"I know...I'll have to find a way," Wes sighed, agonizing over what Meredith had said. He knew she was right.

"In time, you will," Meredith said as she leaned over and kissed him gently on his cheek. "Let's go home now," she whispered.

POSTSCRIPT

Though this book is fiction, events in the world today suggest that such a situation could happen. One has only to recall the bombing of the New York Trade Center Buildings to imagine the scope of the next threat, given the hate some fundamentalist organizations harbor against the United States.

Can we be certain that all nuclear weapons of the former Soviet Union will remain under the control of responsible people and their governments? Can we assume, with any degree of confidence, that all fissionable material has been accounted for by those entrusted to monitor the dismantling of the USSR's nuclear arsenal? Is it possible that one or more weapons could have been stolen and gone undetected? Even in the United States, presumably under the watchful eye of dedicated government agencies and the media, small amounts of weapon-grade uranium and plutonium have disappeared. Can we be sure the same thing hasn't occurred in the Soviet Union? I think not.

Is it possible that a coalition of Muslim extremists — fundamentalists — might realize the advantage of joining to press their cause to greater heights? Traditional thinking suggests they are incapable of exercising the discipline to form such a cohesive organization. Infighting among factions is often cited as a primary cause of their divisiveness and supports the argument against their mounting such an effort. Yet, if we consider the increasing number of Western educations provided contemporary Muslim youths, we can begin to see how their understanding of organization and structure could support their cause.

Americans must understand that the fundamentalist movement is not one devoted exclusively to the poor and the oppressed. Successful Muslims — businessmen, educators, government employees, as well as the mullahs — support and actively participate in the "movement." Such talent, over time, will rise to the level of sophistication needed to effect such a coalition.

Nor should we depend entirely on technology, the basis of much of the Western world's success to date, to ensure America's safety. As the Muslim world gains experience in using our inventions, it will acquire the finesse needed to work our technology to our disadvantage.

We need to question our foreign policy with respect to the Middle East and its exportation of terrorism. Policies of appeasement and accommodation are ineffective and reveal the naivety of our policy makers in dealing with the fundamentalists. The term "moderate fundamentalist" is an oxymoron. Rationalization is not a concept easily embraced by the fundamentalist, especially when its application goes against the teachings of Islam. Contrary to Western beliefs, compromise is not always available as a means of settling differences in the Muslim world. As Americans, we find it difficult to understand why the fundamentalist isn't willing to negotiate. His religion is often an obstacle; for us, it seldom is.

If we are to effectively confront the fundamentalist, we must know him, learn his values, and understand his society. We must educate ourselves to his culture and religion. Stereotyping all Muslims as radicals and all Islamists as extremists must give way to more thoughtful reasoning.

In America, we judge a man by his deeds. We must apply the same standard to our Middle East neighbors. To do less is to encourage racism and spawn more hatred. The essence of a lasting peace lies in finding similarities to build on, not in highlighting our differences.

America must continue to actively seek dialogue with the Muslim world while keeping a watchful eye on extremists groups who perpetrate mischief. To do nothing about our current relationship with the Arab world is to disenfranchise an entire culture and ultimately risk Armageddon.

A man is no greater than that for which he is willing to give his life.
Trust in God, that you may choose wisely.

Author